The D[illegible] Splend[illegible] an Unknown World

FIRST EDITION

Visible Love Publications, LLC
BOULDER, COLORADO, USA

ISBN: 978-0-61546-892-1
Printed in the United States of America

Cover Painting by nina
David's Out of Phase Moon
Deep Into Artlife West Blog & Gallery
deepintoartlifewest.blogspot.com

Book Design by Jessica Xavier
Planet X Graphic Design
www.planetxdesign.net

THIS BOOK IS DEDICATED TO:

Billy Rodenberg

Through Hell and high-water,
through every dark and dangerous place,
of which there were many and in every moment
of desperate need,
You were there, my truest friend.

Introduction

THIS BOOK HAS HAD A MIND of its own and in many respects wrote itself. I was available for the grunt work and I did the best I knew how to. Any errors that may exist are the result of gaps in my understanding of how certain esoteric forces work. Where there is clarity you may be sure it was provided from another source.

There seems such a dearth of good occult fiction that I felt compelled to finally contribute to the larder myself. Whether this is a legitimate addition is for you to decide. I tried to write the kind of book that I have enjoyed reading from authors like Dennis Wheatley, Frank Lauria, Clive Barker and Dion Fortune.

Certain of my readers may be expecting something other than what they will find in this book. What they are looking for is there, to be sure, but this is also a thriller, constructed to read like a movie and to cater to the tastes of those who like crime dramas, supernatural horror and thrillers. There's gore and gruesome mischief. There's violence and pure psychopathy. There are more deranged characters than those who are sublime, just like it is in this place some call the "real world". I don't call it that. This world is a perversion upon something of a greater and more enduring beauty. That is not to say that this world does not have its charm and wonders but… they are all designed to break your heart.

In any case you have been warned. This isn't a philosophical or mystical text in the pure sense. Those modalities are expressed through a particular template. Those elements are here but they're sharing the space with the world, where the things contained in this book happen every day.

Along the way I have had some help and assistance in my labors and it is only fair that I thank those individuals who made my labors less arduous than they might have been. My consort Susanne and her wonderful mother Liselotte Kramer have blessed me with a wonderful environment of love and support. I cannot thank them enough but I will spend my life trying. Bud "The Birdman" Clifton saved my ass several times when my world collapsed. His generosity is unrivaled in my experience. He is also a gifted martial artist and we have spent many an hour knocking each other about, much to the consternation of whoever might have been standing nearby.

Let me convey my overdue gratitude (in no particular order) to Paul Dumont, Beate Dumont, Peter Blum, Svargo Bernard, Michael Perkins, Gary Irving, Gerald Stewart, Isaac Shapiro, Bruce Metz, Howard Coon and Douglas Hume, Franklin Russell, Bob and Denise Lowe.

A very special thanks is due to Karyn Weese who is largely responsible for you possessing this book and whose assistance has been beyond the call.

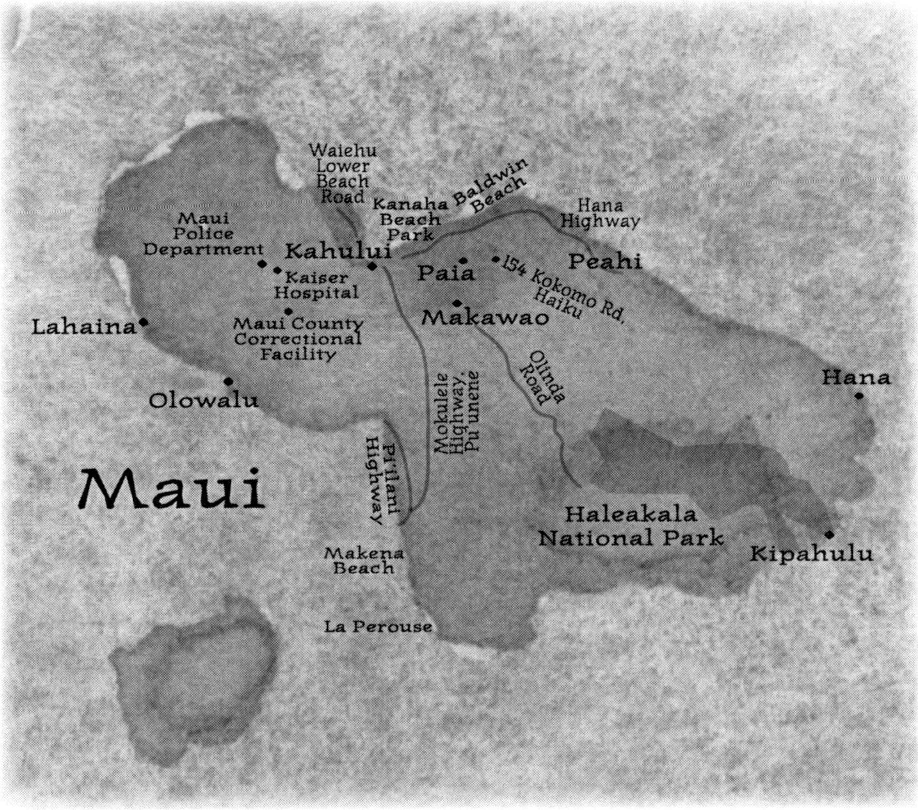

Cave! Cave!, Deus Videt.

Prologue

SUMMER 1542, FLORENCE, ITALY

Two men dressed in the garb of Catholic monks were sitting at a roughhewn table, carefully studying a richly-illustrated parchment book. There was an oil lamp burning dimly between them on the table and the two men were arguing in low voices. One of the men was talking about a magical process that was outlined in the book. The other was shaking his head and repeating, *"Il pericolo è estremo, pericoloso!"* before getting up and leaving the room…

Several hours later, in the courtyard of a medieval castle, the same monk was sitting on a stone bench beside two other men. One of them was a Bishop and the other a wealthy gentleman dressed in outrageous finery, with a huge head of black curls falling down around his shoulders, a large hooked nose and coal-black eyes. The monk was carefully listening to instructions being given to him by the Bishop, a haughty-appearing man with the visage of a Roman Emperor. He had a cruel slit of a mouth and narrow animal eyes. *The Bishop and the monk were discussing performance of a magical ritual…*

As dusk approached, several coaches and men on horseback were passing down a narrow country lane. The lead carriage abruptly turned into a road that opened up on the right, the wheels sliding and sending a cloud of dust into the air. Ahead, on a low sloping hill, was an immense stone building that appeared to have been partly destroyed by fire. Inside the building, a small crowd of people gathered around an altar upon which burned red and black candles. There was a fetid stink in the air of burning excrement and rubber. Behind the altar was the Bishop, wearing a large inverted crucifix around his neck. He was arranging objects on the surface of the altar. Standing in front of the altar, the congregation was chanting ominously in Latin. All were dressed in hooded black robes and wore masks with fearsomely exaggerated features of wild animals.

From the burned out doorway of the building, several hooded figures approached the altar. One of them was having trouble walking and had to be assisted by the others. They proceeded to the altar and stopped before the Bishop. He came around the altar and drew back the hood from the head of the one who had been led. It was a young girl. The Bishop untied her smock at the neck and it dropped to the floor. Underneath she was naked.

The Bishop gestured and two figures came out of the crowd and lifted the girl upon the altar where she moved uncomfortably, reacting to the hard surface and the chill of the cold stone beneath her. She made no effort to get up. The Bishop began painting symbols and words upon her body with colored paints. The chanting increased in volume and another procession entered, six more forms walked toward the altar, four of them hooded. In the front was one dressed in a crimson robe with a crown of thorns on his head. *It was the monk.*

A crown of thorns had cut into his scalp and small rivulets of blood flowed down his face. Alongside him walked the wealthy gentleman from the courtyard, who was naked except for an amulet and a sword buckled about his waist. His partial erection swung from side to side as he moved. The monk's eyes were vacant and he stared emptily into space. The naked man brought him to the side of the altar as their escorts quietly faded back into the congregation.

The Bishop finished his ministrations and then stepped back from the altar. He raised his hands high and the chanting abruptly ceased. There was complete silence. He gestured toward the monk, who slowly came around the altar to stand next to him. The Bishop opened a drawstring purse and poured a measure of its contents into his palm. He sprinkled them over the girl's body. The symbols painted upon her body began to glow a fiery red and there was an iridescent shimmer in the air above her. He raised his left hand and the chanting resumed. The girl started to writhe upon the altar, her pelvis lurching spasmodically into the air.

Above her an image formed in the air, the translucent outline of a horned demon. There was a reckless thrilling energy filling the room as the chanters began to sway and wave their arms in the air. The Bishop reached into the folds of his robe and extracted a silver dagger, which he presented ceremonially in the air to the wraith. Then he turned to the monk and handed him the dagger. *The chanting became frenzied, robes were falling from the bodies of the congregation, their naked bodies jerking and twisting as if they were being electrocuted…*

Chapter One

SEPTEMBER 21, 1995 • NEW YORK CITY, NY

Early mornings were the worst time of the day. Alan could never sleep past 5:00 a.m. and it didn't matter how late he had gone to bed the night before. The grief gave him no peace, even in his dreams. The alcohol amplified it, made it terrible to bear, but he knew that without the alcohol he could not bear it at all. His life had become a pattern of such ironies. He drank from the moment he awoke until he passed out at whatever moment oblivion finally arrived. It never lasted for very long, a few hours to drain the cortex and then back on the train, a gone dead train, sooner or later it would run out of track. The sooner the better as far as Alan was concerned.

For as long as he could remember Alan had led a life of discipline. It was the glue that held his life together. Now it was in the toilet along with his career and all that he loved, six months of grayscale existence edged in black, three of those months while he was still on the force and three since he'd gone his way. One night he'd have enough of it, swallow his gun and say good-bye.

Two things still stood between him and the void, the mystery of Elizabeth's death and his faith in a supreme being. No matter how bad it was, he had been unable to let go of either one. As he lay in the darkness his heart reached out for comfort from the one that had guided him all of his life. Earnestly he reached for understanding, but the darkness of his room mocked him. There was no one there. Racked with sorrow, his eyes filled with tears that flowed slowly down his face to the pillow beneath his head. He had never imagined that his life would come to this. He had wet himself during the night and now lay on the cold urine soaked bed, still drunk but needing a drink, trembling, stinking and praying for death.

With the back of his hand he brushed angrily at the tears and pushed the blanket from his body. Rising to his feet, he moved unsteadily to the bathroom where he fell to his knees and brutally retched into the toilet. Fury boiled in his gut as he felt the wetness of his clothes and the cold touch of the porcelain base. He cried again in despair, but it was all routine now.

Alan wiped the bile from his mouth and slowly pulled himself to his feet. Unable to both stand and pull his pants off at the same time, he had to sit on the toilet in order to remove them. He climbed into the shower and turned it on.

Ten minutes later, having shaved and dressed, he filled a glass with ice and

Bourbon. Later, there would be no ice and often enough, no glass. He took a long draught and dropped to the couch. Fumbling in the cushions he found the remote and switched on the TV. He lit a cigarette and stared through the smoke at Geraldo Rivera on a stage full of grossly overweight women of various races. Alan heard and saw nothing. His mind was already far away, searching in the past for answers that would not come.

In the first month after he quit the New York City Police there had been phone calls from some associates and the few friends he had made in his years with the department. An intensely private individual, Alan did not make friends easily, nor did he have a lot in common with other police officers. He wasn't one to go out of his way to encourage relationships with others unless they shared his interests and few did. Very soon the calls decreased, and then stopped altogether.

Alan had slain several men in the course of his duties. This was an anomaly in a field where the larger percentage of his colleagues never even fired their guns at anyone. A superior had once commented that the reason he was so good at his job was because he was exactly like the men he pursued, friendly and engaging on the outside, dark and dangerous within. He had been jealous of Alan's accomplishments. Though what he said might not have been true, it was true that Alan saw deeper into the motivations of his prey, deeper into the workings of their demented psyches, than any of his contemporaries.

He'd found and killed the Central Park Ripper in a howling blizzard on Thanksgiving night in 1987. Two years later he ended the insane career of Richard Bolen, moments before he would have killed his thirteenth victim. The inquiry that followed had determined that Alan acted with necessary force when Bolen ignored his command to surrender and then raised the massive butcher knife to kill his seventeen-year-old captive. There were those, rivals in the department, politicians and journalists of a certain liberal bent, who felt that in neither case was Alan justified in his actions.

The shit hit the fan in July of 1994. For six months Alan had been the lead investigator in a series of brutal homosexual murders that were taking place in the meat packing district in and around Fourteenth Street and the docks in Lower Manhattan. The area was host to a number of rough gay bars that came and went on a regular basis. Some were no more than empty basements or lofts with mattresses in dark corners, where projectors screened pornographic films on rough concrete walls. In one place, the bar was made of two sawhorses over which a sheet of plywood had been set. Also in the neighborhood were dozens of abandoned and condemned buildings and open truck trailers, where anonymous sex took place every night of the week. The perpetrator was luring victims to an unknown location where possibly torture, followed by dismemberment took place. Body parts wrapped in brown butcher paper had been discovered in some sections of the city, usually in places with a high daytime concentration of people.

The packages were roughly marked with their contents, weight and a price in black ink. Rumor also had it that someone was distributing unidentifiable cuts of meat to the city's homeless, who were known to barbecue whatever they could get on old refrigerator grills in abandoned lots.

The very politically powerful gay community was inflamed. Large demonstrations had been organized in front of police precincts and the mayor's mansion. Patrols of militant gay activists took to the streets in the areas of disappearance, seeking to accomplish what the police had so far been unable to do. Five days after this was initiated, the paper-wrapped organs of two activists appeared in front of a very chichi gay restaurant in the East Fifties. The meat had been marinated in a variety of herbs, and a recipe for sweetbreads had been attached to one of the parcels with masking tape.

Enormous pressure was brought to bear on the department. Alan had been summoned to the office of the Chief of Detectives on two occasions to be threatened, pressured, cajoled and promised anything if only he would quickly solve the case. Finally, he disappeared into the gray underworld of the City of Night. In the process of the investigation, Alan encountered a depravity he had not previously imagined. Some of the settings he came upon reminded him of a Boschian nightmare, a spiritual wasteland of tormented souls, who wandered the dark landscape of the city's nether regions.

He'd met a number of homosexual men in his travels, cloaking himself as a passive Voyeur, and he had been able to avoid the contact they sought. He trusted in his instincts to reveal the beast he pursued. He continued onward through elaborate torture chambers, razor blade branding bars and defacatoriums, always guided by that rarefied awareness that had made him such a gifted man hunter. One night Alan finally met his nemesis.

He found Arthur Penace in an illegal club called The Mine Shaft. It was a dank cellar with moss growing on the exposed concrete. The toilet was composed of a row of bathtubs in which men lay awaiting some unknown moment of epiphany. There was one large room with a rough-hewn circular bar that served nothing but beer in the can. Smaller rooms led into private worlds without light.

Penace was a hulking bear of a man, over six feet tall and weighing close to three hundred pounds. He sat by Alan at the bar, posturing like a queen and had set off his antenna by pretending to be more intoxicated than he was — and from the looming menace in his eyes. The eyes remained flat and cold, regardless of the face's changing expressions. *There was too much force of will. Here was a man who compelled others to do what he wanted. Here was a man who might be capable of anything.* This is what Alan's instincts told him. Penace invited Alan back to his restaurant in the West Village. A fine dinner would straighten them right up, he leered, hoping Alan would catch the reference.

Alan Douglas was forty-two years old at this time. As tall as Penace, he weighed one hundred and eighty pounds. He was an accomplished martial artist and temperate regarding those practices that cut short the lives of so many of his peers. He wore his dark hair in a military cut, luminous black eyes were framed by regular features, except for the nose that had been badly broken once and had healed in a twist to the left. Elizabeth said that it gave his face character and saved him from looking like every other boring man with a handsome face. He had a deep cleft in his chin and a brilliant smile that would light his face with a childlike enchantment on the occasions he permitted himself to smile. Too often, the nature of his work gave him the serious mien of a Jesuit.

Alan went with Penace back to the place of business that he operated as a chef/owner. Penace told him that it was one of the busiest in the neighborhood. Now it was dark except for a light over the bar. Penace had promised Alan "a fantastic meal" accompanied by a "magnificent Merlot." It would be an intimate meal, to be followed by intimacies of another sort…

Alan stood watching Penace dancing through his kitchen, like a Sumo Wrestler who had studied for the ballet. All appearance of intoxication had fallen away from him. Irrespective of the outward charm and bonhomie, there was no mistaking the aggressive glint in his eyes. Alan's sensibilities had been honed by a lifetime of police work. He felt that he could actually hear warning bells ringing in his mind. There was something very amiss about Penace. He gave off waves of ill-concealed rage as he worked.

Alan knew from forensic reports that the previous victims had all been drugged. Penace didn't appear to mind being observed in his preparations, so Alan assumed that the potion would be contained in the wine.

Penace prepared a table in a rear alcove of the restaurant. Upon it he placed a tablecloth, candles and eating instruments, along with a bouquet of white carnations in a blown glass vase. There would be atmosphere, fine wine and who-knew-what for the main course. Various parts of the victims remained undiscovered, amidst the slaughtered ruins of the dead.

The wine arrived already in the glass. *It was definitely the wine then.* This in itself was a departure from the ritual corking and tasting one would expect under the circumstances — a chef in a trendy eatery seeking to impress his date with the pomp and ceremony of a special night. There was a Caesar salad to begin with, followed by the main course. It was served in the nouvelle tradition that had become fashionable in recent years. There were small medallions of (what appeared to be) beef with a multi-colored *béarnaise* sauce trickling over the edges and surmounted by a teepee of decorative vegetables.

Penace sat down and raised his glass to Alan with a toast, *"Bon appétit!"* He took a sip of his wine and then suggested that Alan do the same. He claimed that his cousin had sent the wine from the Napa area of California. Alan replied that he never drank with his meals and would drink the wine upon the completion of the dinner, which he had no intention of eating. Penace laughed humorlessly and suggested that perhaps this time he should make an exception. There was a palpable force coming at him. Alan could feel the man's will compelling him to drink. He demurred and said he would save the experience to cleanse his palate later. Penace again insisted, all humor gone, and his face now dark and grim.

Alan held his gaze. His spirit remained calm in the midst of this murderous charade. He asked Penace why he wasn't frightened to travel at night in the areas of the murders. Alan could see the red highlights of madness dancing in his eyes. *The beast was rising and the man was gone.* Whatever Penace may have seen in Alan's face, he never said. Suddenly he knew that the game was at an end. Penace's features transformed themselves into a thunderous scowl.

"Won't drink the wine will he, wants to save it for later, later..." Penace was looking down into his plate as he spoke to himself. Alan watched him carefully, the hairs on the back of his neck trembling from an invisible wind.

"Wants to talk about murders but he won't taste the wine. We'll show him murder." Penace's hand suddenly emerged from below the tabletop, gripping a gleaming cleaver. With a speed Alan could not believe, the man launched himself across the table, swinging the cleaver at Alan's head. A lifetime of physical training saved his life. He brought his left hand up, moving Penace's wrist and lifting it. The force of the swing bore the cleaver so close past the top of his head that he felt the edge of it whisper across his scalp. A deadly struggle ensued and in the process, Alan broke Penace's neck. During the fight he received a serious cut to his left shoulder.

The next day from his hospital bed he learned that the meal Penace had prepared for him came from the rump of one of his recent victims. A search of the restaurant revealed other cuts of meat that had been butchered into portions. It later came to light that Penace was well known on the gay scene for rough, violent sex.

With typical irony, certain vocal elements of the gay community began calling for Alan's head. Citing his previous use of deadly force, they charged him with overreaction and some even accused him of "homophobically" inspired murder. Alan did not endear himself to them when he asked a reporter from *The Village Voice* for the etymology of the word...

Representatives of the local press openly speculated about why yet another of Alan's investigative targets had died without the benefit of trial or treatment. More privately, some of Alan's superiors suggested he was exhibiting a strong and undesirable maverick streak. It was against every rule in the book to confront a suspected murderer without the assistance of a partner or a back-up unit. Alan pointed out that the Chief of Detectives had told him to use any means necessary within the law, but no one else in the department had been given any idea of what Alan had been doing. The affair did not blow over quickly. Even several months later, there was the odd article calling for further investigation. Regardless, the average "man in the street" considered Alan a true hero. Perhaps it was the hundreds of calls and letters that came in during the first month that saved him from official charges and more penetrating scrutiny. When the worst of all possible events happened to him twelve months later, these questions would surface again, adding to the unbearable sorrow of a man broken by terrible fate...

Two slim black men slouched low in their chairs, with their hands thrust into their waistbands, had now joined Geraldo's obese guests. Alan rose to his feet and went into the kitchen, where he filled his glass with ice. He returned to his seat, poured bourbon to the top and took a long slow drink. A calm had begun to settle over his features. He even smiled briefly to himself as he thought of how his life could be even worse. He could be Geraldo. Then he would have no choice but to kill himself immediately. It had surprised him for some time that, in this age of homicide, in this city of killers, no one had yet focused on talk show hosts. He had little doubt that sooner or later it would happen. Then the problem would be to find someone to investigate and prosecute what was less a crime than an act of public good.

His momentary ebullience soon crumbled as the mind was drawn inexorably back to the well of memory. For an instant he could see his wife standing in front of him, her long brown hair falling around her shoulders in soft waves, dark eyes brimming with love and shining with that special wisdom of life upon which he had relied for so long. The image faded and tears formed in the corners of his eyes. Once again it was Memorial Day evening of the previous year…

Alan had been pulling a lot of overtime that month, trying to clear the books of several drug murders. These were the result of a turf war between an entrenched, Jamaican posse and the advance guard of a newly formed Colombian cartel, which was replacing the decimated ranks of the previous cartel.

Alan often worked late, as did Elizabeth, who was a psychiatrist at Bellevue. Evenings were the busiest times for psychotic admissions and this was when Elizabeth chose to work. Alan liked the advantage of the night. It was also the time when those that he hunted were most often afoot.

In the previous weeks, Alan had begun to feel uneasy. He became concerned for Elizabeth and had been asking her to take a cab home. She'd brushed off his fears and told him his job was making him paranoid. She loved the excitement of the subway. It was her curiosity about the human mind that had led her to her profession. What better place was there in the entire world to satisfy it than the New York subway, where the entire spectrum of the human experiment was in evidence? She had pointed out that she had never had a single problem coming or going and that Alan should have more faith. Angels watched over them. Hadn't he always told her so?

Earlier that evening Alan had located Bosco Rawlings. Rawlings had shot gunned the relatives of Emanuel Rodriguez — father, mother and two sisters. Rawlings was an enforcer for the Black Jam Posse. They'd decided to take a page from the Colombian's own book and kill the families too. Under very tense circumstances, Alan, along with several detectives and uniformed police, had managed to separate Rawlings from his associates in a downtown rap club without a shot being fired. A long evening of booking, interrogation and witness I.D. lay ahead of him.

The call came in six hours later. Alan had finished up and was having a cup of coffee with his crew. Elizabeth had been hurt and was in the emergency room at Bellevue, no other details. Alan flew out of the precinct and into his city issue car, red light flashing from the driver's side roof, driving as if all of the demons of Hell were on his tail. He was too late, would have been too late in any case, Elizabeth was DOA. In an apparent act of attempted rape, Elizabeth's neck had been broken and her lifeless body had been thrown on the tracks, where mercifully, the train's motorman had seen it and stopped before it was cut to pieces.

A dark abyss opened at Alan's feet. His heart and his life fell away into nothing. Elizabeth had meant everything to him. Now she was gone and there would be no returning. The immensity of his loss swept all thought from Alan's mind. He was adrift in an alien landscape. There was nothing he could recognize. Rage would follow, but for the moment there was only despair and incomprehension.

The next day he learned that transit authorities were searching for one Calvin Withers. Withers had a long record of assaults against women. He also had two felony drug arrests and was a member of the Black Jam Posse. A man had been seen running from the station at the time of the murder and Withers was later identified by several of the witnesses.

Alan's superior placed him on forced compassionate leave. Alan was never able to remember any of the events of the following week. The combination of alcohol and sedatives blotted out all memory.

Three days later Calvin Withers was found chained to a railing in the same subway station in which the crime had taken place. Someone had poured gasoline over his body and set him on fire. When detectives arrived at Alan's apartment, they found his formerly tidy quarters in a state of chaos. Lamps had been knocked over, the bookcase pulled to the floor and the books strewn everywhere. Liquor bottles lay where they had dropped or been thrown. Alan was filthy, unshaven and incoherent.

On the surface it seemed doubtful that he could have had anything to do with the murder. But one thing could not be resolved. Investigators had found his business card taped to the railing next to the smoking corpse. On the back of it, in a fine copperplate script, someone had written, "Too little... too late."

As the investigation continued, it became clear than Alan could not account for his whereabouts. He had no alibi. His distinguished record and the faith of the department stood in his defense. No one in a position to charge him believed that he had carried out the act himself. But had he arranged it? Then again, who would leave his own business card at the crime scene? The note was not in Alan's handwriting and there was no other evidence, no fingerprints or witnesses to place him at the scene. Alan had been spotted in several bars during the preceding days. He'd been thrown out of one and others had refused to serve him. The investigation continued.

Two weeks later Alan returned to work. He'd trembled in his bathtub for twenty-four hours and except for being very shaky and malnourished, he seemed okay. But he was not okay. He struggled hard to focus on his work and to put distance between himself and the terrible events of Elizabeth's death, but he was only going through the motions. He might have made it, if not for the fear and the terrible nightmares. Each night he was assaulted by horrible visions of Elizabeth's last moments. Only one thing would give him peace and it was not prayer or any spiritual technique which he applied to the pain. It was alcohol.

At certain points in the day he would shudder from a palsy of fear that had no determinable source. It was a wave of fear without attendant images. Once again, nothing would make it retreat except more alcohol. A few drinks would push the visions and the fears into the background — not gone in any sense but muted, like distant music. You could still hear the song that was playing far away in the background. Given enough drinks it could be turned down completely, with nothing remaining but melancholia and despair.

His colleagues, in sympathy for his loss, tried to overlook his condition. His supervisors turned their heads. He practiced maintenance drinking during his shifts and then drank himself blind afterwards...

Alan began to miss important crime scene evidence. He snapped at his associates and embarrassed himself in front of his superiors. Counseling and help were offered but Alan ignored it. Prosecuting Attorneys ceased to call on him for court appearances. He was no longer effective in his work and he didn't care. Alan had become a liability to the department he loved.

One night he ran his car into a fire hydrant and word soon came down from above. A compassionate Chief of Detectives offered six months in an upstate facility with the promise of a return to duty. Alan said that he didn't give a shit, so he was told to put in for retirement. He could either receive his pension and move on or he would be fired. Alan retired. His friends shook their heads and let him go. His enemies smiled and said that the department, after all, would be better for his departure. With none of the fanfare that so often accompanied the retirement of a decorated police officer, Alan turned in his particulars and walked away...

For all of his life, Alan had had a deep and abiding faith in a guiding force. He had probed at the mysteries of creation and seen there a divine symmetry, governed by an invisible hierarchy of beings who shepherded humanity through the ages, always in the direction of good. In former times he would retire to his study and read the works of mystics and philosophers. He had lately begun to read alchemical texts, opening up an entire world of new perspectives. He very soon realized that alchemy had nothing at all to do with "turning lead into gold" and everything to do with transforming one's baser qualities into *spiritual gold.* Having read much of Eastern religious texts over the years, he saw tremendous parallels between alchemy and yoga. Except for the terminology and certain physical applications, they were basically the same. The foundation of all his spiritual studies and endeavors was a faith in the divine rightness of things. He had always felt that he was being guided to a higher understanding that would eventually transform his life in a profound way. Elizabeth had begun to share his interests. So much was coming, but in the end, it seemed angels were not watching over them at all. Alan had failed the test. What test that was he did not even know, but he had failed it and now only desolation and ruin remained…

Elizabeth had a brother fifteen years her junior. When their parents died in an automobile crash, they had taken "Whip" in to live with them. Because of the disparity in their years and Elizabeth's inability to bear children, he had quickly become like a son to them. Alan shared his martial arts experience and coached him at baseball, which soon became the consuming passion of Whip's young life. Under Alan's ministrations, Whip developed into a talented baseball player and won a full scholarship to Stanford. It was Whip's intention to play Major League Baseball and in the two years he'd been at Stanford, he had drawn the attention of several scouts.

Whip returned home for the funeral as devastated as Alan, but where Alan's grief was obvious to anyone who looked at him, Whip had become as cold and remote as a dead planet in space. They hardly spoke during the funeral. When it ended, he was gone. During a rare moment of clarity Alan later called Stanford. Whip's roommate said he had not yet returned. It later occurred to Alan that Whip might be responsible for the death of Calvin Withers. It did not explain the presence of his business card at the scene but the thought would not go away. So the days passed, one following another.

During brief intervals of sobriety, Alan could see that his state had become pathological beyond the ordinary grief of mortals. He would sit back astounded at the wreckage of his life and his lost career. He wondered where his strength had gone. *How had he come to change into such a weak and despised creature?* These moments would not last, soon the spell would overpower him again and he would tumble under the water to be spun around with the sand and the seashells and the sharp coral...

Finally one night, Alan's reawakening arrived. After a week inside his apartment, he decided to take a rare walk to the package store. It was never necessary to leave your apartment in a city where everything could be sent out for. It was nine thirty in the evening when Alan descended unsteadily into the street. He'd been drinking throughout the day with nothing to eat since the night before.

The sidewalk glistened from the intermittent rain that had been falling for the last several hours.

Alan walked up 64th Street toward First Avenue. On his way he would get some takeout from a nearby Indian restaurant. He didn't care if he ate or not but the food would make the drinking easier. He had finally begun to learn that there were certain rules to follow on the path to self-destruction. You had to be practical in the process of drinking yourself to death. As thoughts formed, he pushed them away. He had no interest in the workings of his mind. *Everything was shit.*

He was half a block from the avenue when he heard a woman scream and saw a scuffle taking place across the street. Two men were wrestling with the woman, attempting to separate her from her handbag. As he watched, one of them delivered a blow to her head.

Without thought Alan shouted, "Police Officer!" and ran across the street. The assailants released the woman and turned to flee until one of them got a good look at Alan. Alan didn't look like a police officer. He looked like a bum, a bum with no visible gun and no badge.

Alan jumped the curb, preparing to land in a position for combat. The result was not what he intended. Months of inactivity and alcohol, coupled with the drunkenness of the moment, caused his feet to slide out from under him. He skidded on his ass and slammed into a wrought iron railing. The woman fled while her attackers put the boot to Alan's crumpled form. He was lucky. The woman ran directly in front of a passing police car. At the sound of the siren turning down 64th Street, the men ran away.

Alan was taken to a hospital and treated for his injuries — these included a concussion, contusions, abrasions and three fractured ribs. In the morning he was so sick from withdrawal that they transferred him to the detox ward.

Through the days that Alan remained in the hospital, his eyes were finally opened to the state of his life. Something inside of him gave way and an ocean of grief and loss came pouring out. Life as he had known it was at an end, but he now began to realize that he did not have to die on some nameless street. He did not have to spiral around the rim of the toilet bowl until he was sucked away into oblivion. Something new was stirring inside him. If he had been asked to describe it, he would have said it was like hearing the sound of a friend's laughter, forgotten until that moment, bringing with it an attendant rush of memories that had the power of life in them. A wonderful calm entered his heart from an unknown source and he suddenly knew that he had not been abandoned after all. *Terrible things happened to people every day, and life still continued.* A determination was growing in him to see what lay ahead. There was so much that he could not understand. *Perhaps, somewhere ahead, the answers were waiting.*

Leaving the hospital he returned home and began to make arrangements. As his head cleared, he began to feel a strong conviction that he should proceed with care. He was struck with the seemingly irrational feeling that there might be unknown forces at work. There was an unshakable sense of danger in the air.

Over the course of the following days, he packed the things that he still cared about, his beloved books and mementos of his former life, reminders of Elizabeth and a few pieces of furniture. He reflected on the chain of recent occurrences. It made no sense that the Black Jam Posse could have orchestrated Elizabeth's death in such a short period of time, or at all for that matter. It was an extreme overreaction. Had he not been so grief-stricken and then besotted, he would very quickly have seen through the absurdity of it.

It seemed too much of a coincidence that Calvin Withers perpetrated a crime of opportunity and… *who had killed him?* Who had left Alan's card at the scene? Where was Whip? It was as if some inexplicable forces were manipulating his life. On the face of it, that seemed ridiculous. Alan studied his past, looking for an enemy with the resources, the brainpower and the motivation to do anything approaching what had been happening. In his line of work, it was a given that you made enemies and most of the enemies were bad ones. But criminals rarely went after the cops that put them away. Both sides recognized the nature of the penalties involved in the game they played. Alan could think of no one, no one living, who could have accomplished all that had transpired. He felt like a fool just to be considering it. Distance and time would bring new perspective. There was nothing left for him in New York except memories.

He was going to Maui. They had been married in a small church on the rugged, sparsely inhabited, eastern coast. Since that time they had returned, every other year, for a month long stay. They loved the wild beauty and the natural serenity that permeated the island. Alan often said that if God had a hideaway, this was it. For years they had planned to move there when they retired. If any environment could provide the much needed healing for Alan's broken heart and troubled soul, it was the blissed out shores of this island paradise. Once there he would return to his disciplines and his studies.

Alan listed his apartment with a realtor he had met on a case some years before. The man owed Alan a debt of gratitude for clearing him of a murder charge. He was pleased with the opportunity to return the favor and promised absolute discretion. Alan gave him a price and power of attorney. Finally, he consolidated all of his other assets into a cashier's check.

Alan stood before the large bay window in his kitchen. He rubbed his hands over the dark wood of the eating nook. He looked out at the tree-lined street that had become so familiar over the years. He turned and took in the nearly empty apartment. *A life had been lived here.* Memories welled and tugged at his heart. He felt a catch in his throat. For a moment his eyes swam, as a parade of images flowed across his mind screen. The regret ached, but there was a nervous thrilling in his stomach as he considered the unknown that now waited for him, just beyond the front door. He pushed aside his memories and regrets. This part of his life was over. He walked quickly into the living room, picked up his bag and walked away.

Chapter Two

JUNE 21ST, 1996 2:30 PM • MENDOCINO, CALIFORNIA

Corrina Bettencourt was washing her breakfast dishes when the phone rang, she reached for the phone on the wall and it squirted out of her hands. "Shit!" she exclaimed as she picked it up from the floor. "Hello?"

Although she could hear breathing on the other end, there was no answer. "Hello..." she repeated. She stayed on the line for several seconds more and then slammed the phone down. "Fuck!" she exclaimed. The phone call had made her nervous. She was due at the St. Albans Daytop Motel in an hour and, no two ways about it, she was going to be late. This was not the reason that she was nervous however. She was nervous because she had a date for sex with one of her husband's customers, Bobby Datour.

If her husband found out, Datour would die in one of a number of unpleasant ways, all of them involving the removal of his manhood and Corrina would receive the beating of her young life. She'd been warned once after Royce had seen her getting too friendly with a guest. The memory made her wince. But except for a few cursory blowjobs, Corrina hadn't had any sex for months, and blowjobs didn't count for much satisfaction on her end. Royce had been heavy into the user end of his product lately and either it was affecting his sex drive or he was getting it somewhere else. Most likely he was getting it somewhere else, since he was *Mr. Big Time Gangster-Drug-Kingpin, Royce Bettencourt.*

Royce hadn't been around much lately, acting very mysterious, setting up some big deals that were, "none of your fucking business." She wondered for a moment if the silence on the other end of the phone was a warning, some mind game of his. He wanted her to believe that he had his eyes everywhere. She knew otherwise though and she doubted that it was him calling. He was devious and clever but he was not subtle.

Corrina was twenty-one going on thirty-five. There wasn't much she hadn't done in her short life. Before she met Royce she had been on the arm of one small time operator or another since she was fifteen years old. Action and adventure drew her like a moth to a flame. So far her youth had protected her beauty. She knew it wouldn't always. She was intelligent but she had no spine, no discipline and no patience. She loved the comfort that easy money brought and it didn't matter where it came from. She had no intention of working in the straight life. All she had to do was open her legs or her mouth and the world came.

She was a visual delight, a pocket Venus, barely over five feet and ninety-five pounds. Royce called her "a spinner" and he'd shown her why. She had curly blonde hair that framed a perfect heart shaped face and bow-shaped, bee-stung lips. Her most common expression was one of petulance, followed by mischief or, alternatively, boredom. She knew she was unique. A lot of women looked like the real article but performed no better than a blow-up doll. Corrina fucked like some wild jungle cat. She was to die for. All in all, Corrina could name her price but she could not find her way free to a life of her own.

Royce Bettencourt was the main supplier from Seattle to San Francisco of a variety of illegal comestibles and related felony product. He was a handsome, rich and ruthless sociopath who by the age of thirty-five had broken every law on the books. He was presently in L.A., on his way to Phoenix to purchase twenty-five kilos of 87% pure rock cocaine. Corrina knew nothing about this. Royce knew nothing about the phone call or Bobby Datour but if anything ever happened, he would. He owned a half interest in the St. Albans Daytop Motel and used it for the same purpose that Corrina intended to use it.

The few dishes done, Corrina left the kitchen and went upstairs to the bathroom in the master bedroom suite. The house was a beautiful two-story redwood with a wraparound deck. The western face extended out over a sheer cliff. A hundred feet below it rolled the long combers of the Pacific Ocean.

Corrina stripped in front of a floor to ceiling mirror. Staring at herself she laughed and cupped her breasts, "This is power," she said. In a little while Bobby would concur. She had met him at one of Royce's parties, which were frequent whenever he was in town. Late that night everyone had jumped, naked and stoned, into the pool. Corrina could not forget the sight of Bobby's cock. It was as large and thick as any she had seen and she had seen a few. Bobby had noticed her interest and he had let her know he was interested too. He had called a few times when Royce was away. Corrina, her survival instincts prevailing, had resisted but NOW she was pissed off. *Fuck Royce!*

Corrina pulled at the blonde tuft of hair between her legs and shivered in anticipation, an afternoon and evening of fine cocaine, wine and sex. This was what she needed. Royce might own her but he couldn't be everywhere all the time. She stepped into the shower, set the dials and pulled the curtain closed.

The brown UPS delivery van parked in the driveway. The driver stepped down with a computer pad and package, hurrying up to the door as UPS drivers do. He knocked at the door and waited. A moment later his hand grasped the knob and he entered the unlocked house. He walked through the downstairs until he heard the sound of the shower above him. He smiled to himself and set the computer pad on a coffee table. Whistling softly through his teeth, he climbed the stairs with the package in his hand.

9:37 PM, THE SAME EVENING.

"Look Pritchard, leave me the fuck alone!" Lt. Augustus Boren of the California Highway Patrol loomed over the Channel 7-News reporter like the *Angel of Death.* "I don't give a shit what you want right now and I don't give a shit what you want at any other time either. If you don't get out of my face pronto, Corporal Williams over there is going to haul that fire hydrant ass of yours behind those squad cars and let the police dogs piss on you!" Boren was spitting in the reporter's face with every word as he backed her up over the lawn to the news van. This accomplished, he turned on his heel and walked back to the house.

"You can't threaten me you jerk!" She screamed at his retreating back. Boren took no notice of her. She'd been caught trying to slip through a window at the rear of the house. Emily Pritchard was universally despised and feared by every civil servant that had crossed her path, except for Boren, who simply despised her. He had once kicked her in the ass and sent her head over heels down a highway embankment into a drainage ditch. She had slipped into a crime scene and begun to go through the evidence that was temporarily stored in the back of a police car. Boren had come upon her and in a rage, had spun her around and booted her down the hill. Only two other officers, who both swore that she had tripped, had observed the act. The thin blue line remained intact. The lesson had no effect on Pritchard, who had worked for the tabloids before coming to television.

Two reporters remained near the front of the house along with one cameraman. Boren's face was red from anger and years of drink. The cords on his neck stood out like rebar. "When I know what's happening you will all know what is happening. Is that clear?" No one answered him and he continued, "Until that time, no one will be allowed beyond the yellow tape and anyone that attempts to will go directly to jail, especially you Ms. Pritchard!" This last was delivered over his shoulder as he re-entered the Bettencourt house.

The call had come in three hours before. A friend had dropped by to talk to Corrina and had found the house open. She walked in and eventually discovered the body when she heard the shower running upstairs. Lt. Boren had been nearby in St. Albans on another matter. He came on the scene shortly after. What he found was as gruesome a tableau as he had seen in his career. A witness had placed the UPS truck at the house that afternoon, but UPS had no record of a delivery scheduled for that address. Boren assumed that one or more assailants had hijacked a truck and used it for camouflage. Presently one truck and a driver remained unaccounted for.

"Clifford?" Boren called into the bedroom, where the crime technicians and members of the coroner's office were at work. Moments later a tall thin man in a lab coat appeared in the doorway. "Yeah, Gus, what can I do ya?" Clifford Whelans, the County Coroner, snapped the latex gloves as he removed them from his hands and dropped them into a sanitary basket that stood by the side of the door.

"You ready to talk to me? The vultures are slathering on the lawn and more are coming. I need to tell them something." The murder of a drug lord's wife in an upscale California arts community was big news and would be getting bigger as soon as word got around. These days word spread quickly. "I'll meet you downstairs in a minute." He pushed his glasses back up on the bridge of his nose and disappeared into the bedroom.

Lt. Boren returned downstairs and sat at the kitchen table. He was going over his notes when the coroner came in followed by a short, very fat man in a shiny brown suit. The fat man was detective "Stew" Copely who, after wrestling with his weight for years, had finally given up the struggle and put on nearly fifty pounds in the last year. This was the result of his marriage to a Lebanese woman whose passion was cooking. Copely would not be with the force much longer if he didn't get a grip. Boren figured that it was a toss-up whether the department or a heart attack would get there first. The floor trembled as Copely landed in the chair across from him.

"Jesus, Stew!" Boren grimaced as the chair groaned under Copley's bulk. "If you don't lose some of that weight, you're looking at a custom casket with a lot of unhappy friends who won't be able to lift it." Copely smiled and lit a cigarette, "Lieutenant, if I can't eat, I don't want to live. I denied myself too long. Let me have my heaven before I go into the deep freeze." As if to punctuate this statement Copely unleashed a voluminous fart. Clifford laughed while Boren just shook his head. Turning to Clifford, he asked, "Well?"

"Well what?"

Boren snorted in exasperation, "You know goddamn well what, Clifford, now let me have it!"

"We've got one dead woman," Copley interjected.

"I know she's dead, Stew. I'd like a little more detail from the doctor here."

Clifford slipped around behind Boren and took a seat on the other side of him as far away from Copley as he could get, waving his hand in the air, whether from the fart or the cigarette was indeterminate. He set his clipboard down and pretended to read from it for a few moments. This was a dance that had been going on between Clifford and the Lieutenant for years. Boren knew by now that the quickest way to get what he wanted was to do and say nothing more.

Finally Clifford cleared his throat and began, "Death occurred sometime in the late afternoon. There were a lot of fun and games prior to the event. Subject was raped and sodomized. Ligature marks at the wrists and ankles indicate that she was hog-tied during the recreational period. Whatever implements were used on her are gone, otherwise nothing but some fibers. We won't know about prints for a while but I wouldn't be optimistic, we've got smudges and other evidence that suggests the killer wore latex gloves. The perp may even have worn plastic shoe covers. It looks like whoever did this is more than half careful and all crazy, did a hell of a cleanup job on the bathroom. We'll have to wait on the lab, maybe we'll get lucky..." Clifford paused at this point and began to worry the inside of his left ear with a forefinger. Boren stared in fascination at the abundance of hair that trembled and twisted in all directions away from the rooting finger. Boren had not seen so much hair growing out of an ear since 1974, when he went with his new wife to see the gorillas at the San Diego Zoo.

"Subject was tortured extensively. Tongue was removed, probably early on, this would cut down on the noise factor. The eyelids were removed along with the nipples."

"Ouch!" Boren winced as uninvited images forced their way into his thoughts. Clifford continued without pause, "He used some kind of burning device that left circular marks similar to the coil on a cigarette lighter but it couldn't be that. I can't see him running back out to his vehicle every time the thing got cold. Besides, they don't have cigarette lighters in UPS trucks, do they?"

"I don't think so," Boren replied.

"Anyway, there are twenty-seven such marks on the torso, neck, soles of the feet, behind the knees. That's a bad spot I hear. This guy really knew how to inflict pain. He took his time and must have enjoyed the work. He painted a smiling face on one butt cheek with a lipstick. And, her ears were boxed so hard that both of the eardrums were ruptured. I'm assuming that from the blood and bruising."

Copely laughed, "I can just picture him saying, "Listen up. Can you hear me? Where's the money and the coke?"'

"Put a cork in it, Stew." Boren snapped, "And what makes you think it's got anything to do with drugs?"

"C'mon Gus, that's Mr. Coke's old lady up there. It's academic."

"Nothing is academic, Stew. There were two killings just like this in San Francisco last week and neither of the victims were into drugs. One of them was a priest."

"Priests don't do drugs… in San Francisco?" Copley looked skeptically at Boren. Boren, a Catholic, stared him down until he looked away.

"All right," Boren said. "You nail things down in here and I'll go talk to the honey bucket patrol. Thanks Cliff."

"Don't you want to know about the note?" Clifford said to Boren's departing back.

Boren whirled, "Note, what note? I didn't see any note."

Clifford smiled, "You should have looked in her pussy Lieutenant. It's kinda wet but you can still read it."

Boren winced again. "Just tell me what it says, Clifford. You know, you and Copley should take your act on the road. You could dress up like something out of *The Munsters* and call yourselves 'The Gallows Brothers.' Don't you have any respect for the dead?" In all of his years as a policeman Boren had never become inured to the tragedies of the human estate. He had especially not grown used to the callous commentaries of his fellows.

"Gus, when you've been around as many dead bodies as I have, shit! I see more people dead than I do alive. It gets to be like going home to see the wife." Clifford was slouched in the chair now looking gray and beaten. The humor had vanished.

"You don't respect your wife either?" Boren asked.

"No Gus, I don't." There was a story there. Boren saw the emptiness in Clifford's eyes. He let it pass.

"What does the note say?"

"See you in Hawaii." Clifford replied.

"What the hell is that supposed to mean?"

"I don't know Lieutenant but whoever it was must have meant it. I looked in there myself and the surfboards are gone." Copley interjected.

"You know Stew, you're a real card. Have the flight manifests for every airline in the state that does Hawaii on my desk tomorrow." Boren punctuated this with a big grin when he saw the look on Copley's face.

"Hey," he said. "You never know."

JUNE 22ND, 10:47 AM, 3800 BLOCK WONDERLAND DRIVE, • TOPANGA CANYON, LOS ANGELES

The phone started ringing as Jennifer Gladden came into the house from the pool where she had been sunning herself for the last hour. She opened the connection on the cellular phone in her hand and said, "Hello." She brushed a strand of blonde hair away from her face as she waited for a reply. There was nothing, just the empty hum of an open line.

"Who is this?" The hum continued. Finally she switched off the phone and set it down on top of the television. Jennifer thought no more about it. A lot of unexplainable things happened every day and Jennifer paid no attention to any of them. Jennifer's world was Jennifer. If it didn't directly concern Jennifer, it had no relative importance.

She'd come to L.A. from Wisconsin to be an actress. She had gotten some modeling work. She was a striking woman, tall and slender with hypnotic green eyes. Everyone thought that she was an L.A. native. After six months of on-again, off-again work, with barely enough to live on, she had met John Morales. Morales was a Colombian national, a drug trafficker and Royce Bettencourt's partner and best friend. His house in Topanga was a fortress.

Morales had spotted her one evening at "On the Rox," an exclusive location for Hollywood insiders. It was a private party and she had been invited as the friend of a friend. Morales noticed her and made inquiries, then arranged to have her invited back to his house for an after-party. Morales came up with the idea when he decided that he had to have her that night. He had to fuck her and then he had to own her. Morales was into control, first of himself and then of everyone and everything around him. For the many transplanted women with dream dust in their eyes, Morales had another kind of dust to make them dream of him in their minds. A woman's fortune could change dramatically under the tutelage of Señor Morales, as long as she acceded to his every wish, as long as she realized who was in control. On those occasions when it seemed that this was not understood, Morales had the mind and means to be instructive and no woman, no matter how hard she might try, could avoid the need for such instruction on the occasions when Morales considered it necessary. It was the price of being with John Morales. Only Royce and a few others had any hope of parity with him. The word of John Morales was law.

After that first night it was only a matter of days before Jennifer came to live at the house. She had been living there for six months now, heir to all of the amenities, both abundant and cruel, that such a residence conferred. Other women came and went but so far, Jennifer alone remained. The price she paid was worth the goods received. She enjoyed it. Whether Morales knew of this she was not certain but she would never tell him. She knew the rules of engagement. She knew them intuitively in that place where her soul might once have lived. Her fear made John Morales' cock as hard as an iron bar and Jennifer did not even have to pretend that Morales scared the shit out of her. The fear was so much a part of her sexual being that it thrilled as much as it terrified. The pain that came with it was gravy.

When Morales told her to service Royce, or some other acquaintance, in front of whomever might be there, she did it with all the joy and servility she might have felt having tea with the Queen. On occasion, he would use her as an end table or serve coke from on top of her naked ass. She was a perfect archetype in John Morales' perfectly controlled world — tame and obedient until death on the choke chain of life.

She walked into the living room and removed an ivory case from its niche in the bookshelf. Then she carried it into a sunken sitting area of couches and low tables, setting it down on a lacquered table emblazoned with scarlet and emerald dragons fighting in a sky of lapis. Opening the case she withdrew a tiny golden axe, two-headed, like the ones used by Viking Berserkers when they plundered the Irish coast. With it she removed a golden straw and a small Petri dish upon which glistened a single large rock of cocaine. Slowly and carefully she shaved away at the rock with the axe, occasionally grinding with its flat face upon the crystals. When she had a significant mound of it prepared, she cut away two lines and snorted them with the gold tooter. As she felt the rush of the coke flood to her brain, she fell deeply into the couch and threw one leg up over the back.

Jennifer was on a cloud. She had been on a cloud since Morales took over her life. Sometimes it was a white fluffy cumulus cloud, like last night when she had done the speedball and sailed her couch across the starry seas of the California night. Sometimes it was wind torn cirrus, high and distant in a cold blue sky. Sometimes it was a massive thunderhead, when Morales was angry with her and she was about to be punished. They were all good. *Life was good.* "*Yes!*" she thought. It was like the commercial says, "It doesn't get any better than this."

Jennifer was slowly sliding down the side of a glacier in her imagination when the phone rang a few minutes later. This time it was Roberto, the guard at the gate.

"Ms. Jennifer, there is UPS here with a package."

Jennifer sighed while formulating a reply. "Well just sign for it Roberto and then bring it up to the house."

"Can not do, he say only you or Mr. Morales can sign, is very important package."

Jennifer looked at the mound of coke on the table. There was time for a couple more lines before the delivery arrived. "Okay Roberto, send him up."

Chapter Three

LOS ANGELES, CALIFORNIA

CarryAnn lived in a world of plenty. She had never known it to be any other way. Unlike the many who struggle to survive or work each day to realize their dreams, CarryAnn had never known lack of any kind.

She was generally blind to the conditions of other lifestyles besides her own. It wasn't that she had not seen people suffering or in want. She'd been downtown on occasion. She had seen her share of movies and television. But it wasn't real to her. She had no perspective on suffering. She was like so many who drove the highways in their air-conditioned cars and looked out of their windows at the people for whom the street was their life. When she saw someone hitching by the side of the road, their presence did not register as anything more than an image on a movie screen. When the show was over, everyone went back home. This was America and there was plenty for everyone here, or so it seemed to her. She wasn't selfish. She shared with her friends, who were also rich and shared with her. But there was so much, why not share? In many ways, CarryAnn did not have a clue to what went on in the world.

CarryAnn's mother was a television actress in a long running situation comedy. With residuals what they were these days and the other bonuses and windfalls attendant, it could be said that she was very well fixed indeed. She got the house and even more money when she divorced CarryAnn's father, an Italian film producer. He had discovered the joys of his own sex several years earlier. CarryAnn's mother returned home unexpectedly one afternoon, a day early from a trip to New York, to discover her husband slamming into the butt cheeks of the Filipino houseboy. He hadn't even bothered to stop when she screamed. He calmly asked her to wait downstairs until he was done.

The divorce was speedily accomplished by mutual consent and since that time Anise Camiliano had seen a series of men, none remaining for any length of time, until she met Simon Stein, a literary agent, in front of the avocados at The Ranch Market. Simon moved into the house several weeks later, a move he orchestrated after getting an eyeful of CarryAnn. CarryAnn at fifteen and a half was gorgeous, with olive skin and big blue eyes, framed by an ocean of raven hair that tumbled down her back. Simon had a predilection for teenage girls that hadn't changed from the time he was closer to them in age. Now he was forty-six and if anything, he desired them even more. CarryAnn became a magnificent

Sugar Plum Fairy that danced in his head. Still, this was Hollywood, where you could fuck anyone or anything, no matter what age, provided you were the right person and the wrong people did not catch you. Even then, it might not be much of a big deal depending on *who* you were. In that respect, CarryAnn could be considered ripe for the picking. Girls younger than her were making their living at it every day in Hollywood.

Strangely enough, CarryAnn was still, for the most part, inexperienced. In contemporary Hollywood she was something of an anomaly among her friends, being still a virgin. Unlike her friends, she loved to read and had been through *The Lord of the Rings* six times already. CarryAnn wanted to be in Middle-Earth a lot more than she wanted to be in Hollywood, especially since her mother had started in on the cocaine. As the use increased, Anise became less and less controlled about her behavior. On several occasions she had come upon her mother being serviced by Simon in the living room and once on a stair landing. On one such occasion, Simon had seen her watching and smiled at her.

Because Anise worked long days on the set of her show she was seldom at home, except in the late evenings and on Sundays. Simon, on the other hand, was usually at the house. His office consisted of a telephone and a computer, which he could put anywhere and which for the moment was placed right down the hall from CarryAnn's bedroom.

Simon was a charmer. He'd had years to perfect his craft, which was applied in a variety of ways. He applied it to publishers when he wanted to promote a book. He applied it to Hollywood when he bargained for motion picture rights. He applied it in nightclubs and anywhere else whenever he wanted to get laid. Simon knew the workings of a young girl's mind and he knew how incredibly easy they were to manipulate if you pushed the right buttons. He had often remarked that they were the stupidest creatures on earth.

Simon was the present source of Anise's cocaine. He had access to every other recreational drug as well. He knew the power and effect of various drugs and used them shamelessly in pursuit of his primary ambitions, which were always the same — power, money and pussy. Simon was also an avowed Satanist and belonged to an elite group of Hollywood insiders who shared his tastes and ambitions. Satanism was very big in Hollywood, always had been.

CarryAnn was a piece of cake. The first thing Simon did was to show her a single face, a kind, good, loving face. He spoke in even mellifluous tones. He moved in an avuncular and non-threatening manner. In a couple of weeks they were having a daily afternoon cocktail by the pool. The cocktail, along with alcohol, contained increasing amounts of an Ecstasy-like compound that quickly brought CarryAnn into a sexually awakened mood. Simon began to turn her on. A part of Simon had never grown up and that part of Simon was the same age as CarryAnn. He made her laugh.

One day it happened. Simon had moved from the casual touch, to the occasional kiss. He was a master of terms of endearment. He swam nude. He managed, by indirection, to persuade CarryAnn to begin swimming nude. Effortlessly and slowly he brought her to a willing state. That afternoon he performed oral sex on her in her bed. Following that it became a regular occasion. Two weeks later, Anise came upon them in the pool cabana shower to find half of Simon's cock buried in CarryAnn's mouth. The moment could not have been better timed as Anise had a young writer in tow that she had brought home to meet Simon. Simon was so far gone in the throes of passion that when he pulled free from CarryAnn's mouth, in the surprise of the moment, his cum shot into her hair and onto the concrete floor as his cock jerked up and down in orgasm.

Anise screamed and raced into the house for her handgun. She was going to kill Simon dead. Simon pulled on his pants and fled to his car, the tires smoking as he peeled out of the driveway. CarryAnn quietly dressed, never looking at the young writer who stood there in shock and had not moved an inch.

Later, CarryAnn's tearful explanation revealed the sequence of events. She told her story with such a little girl's sense of confusion that Anise was in tears. Simon had won her confidence, had helped her with schoolwork. As she told her story the picture emerged in Anise's mind of a skilled Lothario overwhelming a curious and impressionable girl with his vast experience of life. From friendly hugs and brotherly kisses, he had moved to acts of arousal. He told her that he would make her so skilled at the intricacies of love that no one could resist her. After he first pleasured her, she no longer had the will to resist him. He then convinced her to pleasure him as well, but he had not penetrated her. CarryAnn did not know why, but the fact was that taking her virginity raised a gray area of legal implication in Simon's mind. He had never expected to be discovered at work but he believed that should anything happen later, the fact that CarryAnn was still intact would protect him. He had promised her that he would consummate the act at a future time, but for now he would be her teacher in all that was arcane in love.

Finally, CarryAnn produced a squeeze bottle of honey that Simon had given her. He had told her to squirt it in her mouth while she sucked him. It would make his cum taste sweet. Anise screamed in rage. She would call the police and

Simon would go to prison. CarryAnn begged her mother not to. She could not stand to be interrogated by the police. She could not bear to testify in court. Her friends would find out and she would look like a whore and a fool. The police would wonder what it was like to do the same things to her that Simon had.

Though Anise burned with rage and a thirst for revenge, she understood her daughter's pain. She knew that all of what she said was true. Quietly she agreed. They would put this behind them. CarryAnn would get counseling. Anise would spend more time with her daughter. She hugged her close as they both wept. Afterwards they went back into the house. CarryAnn went to her room and Anise went in search of some coke and a drink to get her through the rest of the day. Hours later when CarryAnn emerged from her room to get a drink of water, she found her mother screwing the writer on the sun porch, both of them too stoned to notice her as she got her water and went back to her room.

In the following weeks Anise became increasingly more degenerate. A new progression of men through her life was draining her physically and emotionally. It coarsened her nature and left her even more dependent on alcohol and drugs than ever before. Only the discipline of her work kept her from losing it altogether. Because of this, she did not notice CarryAnn. Simon's influence had introduced her to a realm of sensation she had been previously unaware of. Besides the erotic experiences, there was now the supersensual realm of drugs. CarryAnn had really enjoyed the substances that Simon had turned her on to. Now, with the impact of what had occurred weighing heavily in her mind, she began to steal her mother's drugs. Being high meant not having to think about anything you didn't want to think about. *Being high wrapped painful thoughts in a thick gauze that insulated the heart.*

What hurt the most was how quickly her mother had pushed the events with Simon aside. After their initial talk, Anise had not wanted to discuss it again. She enrolled CarryAnn in therapy and told her to "work it out." The truth was that Anise could not deal with the terrible guilt of what had happened and the certain knowledge that she was in some way responsible. So she ran away. For all her success and power, there was a great emptiness in her life, a dark void bereft of meaning. Combined with the chemicals, it made for an unfulfilled state of being. It was an all too common reality for those who lived in the never-never land of… *movies equal life, life equals movies.* It was a place where nothing ever satisfied the deeper necessities of the heart. Gibran had spoken of her kind when he said, "…pass out of love's threshing floor, into the seasonless world where you shall laugh, but not all of your laughter, and weep, but not all of your tears." Anise was slowly, inexorably, going the way of so many of her peers. It seemed to her that she had been happy once, but she could not really remember when. In any case, her happiness had been based on ignorance. What she didn't know hadn't hurt her until she knew about it. Bereft of love, real love, real purpose and a real life, she relied more and more on the dream enhancing chemicals that fueled her day-to-day passage through celluloid zombie-land.

In a parallel dimension, CarryAnn was waking up to the realities of life. There was no other adult figure in whom she could confide, since she did not trust the therapist and she could not talk to her mother. She certainly could not have discussed any of it with her friends. Far away on the East Coast she had grandparents that she seldom saw. She began to see how really alone she was, but nothing had changed except her perceptions. *She had always been alone.*

A few weeks later, Anise met Royce Bettencourt. With the amount of coke that Anise was going through and the company she kept, it was only a matter of time before she came into the realm of Mama DeCoca's darker acolytes. Throughout this time CarryAnn had been closely watching her mother. She had watched her mother get drunk. She had watched her snort cocaine. She had watched her fuck her boyfriends. Her mother had no idea that CarryAnn was watching her. CarryAnn loved her mother, yet on a deeper level she was in competition with her. Part of her wanted to be just like her mother. She wanted to have the things that her mother had, so she would drink her mother's liquor, she would smoke her mother's cigarettes. She would smoke her pot and snort her coke and she would dream herself into the erotic dreams of her mother. She was her mother, as she lay in her bed and imagined Simon or another, thrusting into her as he had thrust into her mother.

Anise never knew. Her image of her daughter was an earlier image of herself. It was an image of stuffed animals and crushes on boys who didn't know, of long phone calls with girlfriends and all the awkward poses of development into maturity, which was such a far, far distance away. She did not see the blooming Venus that sat at her table every day. She saw a little girl who played with make-up and wrote in her diary and talked relentlessly about Elves and Ents. She did not see the confusion, the resentment and the fear that was now emerging and threatening everything that was once safe in CarryAnn's mind. Anise got through her days by force of habit and will, doing by rote those things she had long ago become skilled enough to do with half her mind, doing the things that only took half a mind to begin with…

Tommy White was a sometime screenwriter and full time cocaine dealer, a mid-level purveyor to the stars and their satellites. The totality of his screen writing opportunities had come about through connections he had made while selling cocaine. He was not an inspired talent but he'd often done work on rewrites, when the original ideas did not have to be his own. Too often his work resembled some recent major success where the comparison was too close for comfort. This sort of thing was fine for television because television was shit. All the shows resembled each other. The characters might be different but the plots were always drawn from the common events of the day and were the same on every network. The dialogues and plots were a perpetual rehashing of the same tired themes that involved doctors, or lawyers, or powerful executives in an exchange of endless banalities.

Anise's television show centered on a single mother raising two children in a ubiquitous urban setting. It was an updated version of *One Day at a Time.* It featured a black family next door, a Jew who owned a deli and two Homosexuals, who employed Anise in their furniture store and were always working to bring the ideal man into her life.

Anise had purchased coke from Tommy in the past. As her use increased, she arranged for Tommy to be a writer on the show so that he was always around. It worked out well for both of them. Tommy got the appearance of a legitimate job and Anise got her coke whenever she needed it.

Tommy got his coke from John Morales. Every week he drove to Topanga Canyon for a quarter of a pound that he turned into six ounces. A few weeks following the event with Simon, Tommy was invited to a party at Morales' house and he invited Anise to come along. Morales was big on entertaining celebrities and Tommy knew that he would score points if he brought a famous television actress along. With the way Anise was doing cocaine lately, she would be glad to be in a place where it flowed like the proverbial milk and honey of the Promised Land.

From the moment that Anise saw Royce, it was as if no one else was in the room. Royce had that effect on women, handsome, magnetic and elegant, with an undercurrent of mystery and evil that drew them like the dove to the cobra. He was dressed in a white on white suit, tall and slender as a knife with the *de rigueur* ponytail that no music promoter or drug dealer was ever without. He was the tall dark stranger that the gypsy fortuneteller said was "going to come into your life." He was a younger, better looking Steven Seagal and easily as dangerous. Royce often personally administered the violence that was sometimes necessary in his line of work. He felt this inspired the fear and respect that was bottom line necessary for his survival in the business. When Royce came to call, you didn't know for which of two reasons he had come. He had, by his own accounts, killed half a dozen men and two women. Not all of the deaths were quick or painless.

Cool under all circumstances, emotionless and devoted to the pursuit of personal ends beyond all else, of course the women loved him. Evil men fascinate women. Whether it was the greasy punk in the black leather jacket, cigarette hanging from the lips, the imitation James Dean slouched against the school yard fence, waiting for the kids to be let out for the day, or a millionaire coke dealer like Royce Bettencourt, it was just a matter of degree. The reasons for this lay obscured somewhere back in the primitive origins of life.

Anise had done two large rails in the car before coming to the party. She felt electric and in love with the night. She sipped her wine and watched Royce work the room. She knew that he would find his way to her at some point. It was in the nature of things. She had never had any problem attracting men. It was part of the aura that she brought to acting. She'd had men in her hip pocket since puberty. It was second nature to her now. This arrogant self-assurance left her blind to the intentions of one to whom her superficial posturing was like that of a child learning to dance.

Royce had seen her across the room. Like her, his vanity assumed that no woman would be able to withstand him. But Royce was not limited in his actions by the benefit of conscience. He didn't care what happened to people after he was done with them. For him, the destruction of another person's sense of self had the same sense of exhilaration as winning at tennis. It made him high. They met twenty minutes later when Tommy went to the bar for new drinks. Royce walked up to her and said, "Hello. I've seen you somewhere before. I can't remember where and it is driving me crazy." He said this last with a rueful smile on his face, showcasing his brilliant white teeth, as if it implied a lack of courtesy on his part.

Anise smiled and ran her fingers through her long black hair, "I'm Anise Camiliano," she replied, extending her hand. Royce took it and said, "Call me Royce. I am a friend of John Morales and this is his home." Royce swept his hand in an expansive gesture that seemed to say that everything, the house, the people in it, everything, was the property of John Morales. "Where is this John Morales?" Anise asked.

"Regrettably he was unable to attend. An urgent matter causes him to be away. Are you a friend of Tommy's?" Royce's black eyes had a luminescence and a depth to them that reminded Anise of ambergris and whirlpools.

"Tommy works for me," Anise replied. She was studying Royce's features and she liked what she saw, the cruel mouth that suggested a possibly violent sexuality, the high cheekbones and almost oriental eye orbits.

"That still doesn't tell me who you are... what you do..." Royce trailed off as his eyes watched her. "You are very beautiful," he continued. "Of course you are in pictures?"

"Television actually, I'm in a show called 'Ramona.'" Anise felt slightly uncomfortable saying this, as if what she did was a lot less important to Royce than it might be to anyone else. He confirmed this with his reply.

"I seldom watch television. But had I known, I would have made the time."

"You are very gracious," Anise replied.

They stood there quietly studying each other until Tommy reappeared with the drinks. "Hi Royce," he said as he handed Anise her wine. "I see the two of you have met."

"How's it going Tommy?" Royce inquired as he turned to him and looked down into Tommy's eyes from his superior height. Tommy backed up a step. Royce had this effect on people, always standing too close, intimidating, making people feel uncomfortable, seeking the balance that had suddenly gone missing. It had one effect on men and another on women, but the result was the same. You felt compelled to do what he asked, to please him, to return into his good graces, which for some reason it appeared that you had lost. No one ever pleased Royce, so the effort never ended. It was the best of all techniques in this age of guilt and personal uncertainty.

"I'm doing good, Royce." Tommy moved from foot to foot as he said this, uncertain of how to play the situation. He had slept with Anise on one occasion when they were both stoned out of their minds. It was not likely to happen again. It was nothing to him if she went off with Royce. Yet he felt he might not want to relinquish the illusion of his position just yet, before he saw what it might be worth to him.

"I'm surprised you didn't inform me that you were bringing such a beautiful guest." Royce turned his attention back to Anise. He had noticed the dilated pupils. Her voluptuous body was encased in a shimmering body sheath of iridescent blue, perfectly matching her deep blue eyes that swam in their wide sockets. She had flared nostrils and full rich lips, all framed by a dark countenance. Royce could feel the heat in her and knew she would be worth the effort. He had fucked actresses and they'd all been good. For them the bedroom was just another place to put on a show.

Anise reminded Royce of someone from another time. Over the years he had seen a change in the female climate and his instincts had begun to steer him away from certain women, women that Morales found so much of a challenge. Women who were no longer women but some hybrid, part machine, part Rottweiler bitch, part Medusa. In certain cases and imbued with enough cocaine, Royce would swear that he had seen their hair writhing like snakes. For Morales, it was all the more fun to break and humiliate them. Royce could be cruel with women but it wasn't a necessary part of his game plan. He much preferred to be charming. He wished rather for women to admire than to fear him. Of course, if they did not admire him, fear would do.

Royce took Anise's arm above the elbow and said, "Please, why don't you both join me privately for a moment." He steered them through the crowd into a long hallway. Near the end, Royce opened a door and gestured them in. It was a library, the walls composed of dark wood paneling, filled with matching tables, burgundy leather couches and overstuffed chairs. They sat around a low inlaid table. Royce reached into his jacket pocket and extracted a slim gold case that proved to be a cocaine traveler's kit. There were items of paraphernalia and a glass enclosed section that held a considerable portion of shimmering flakes. Royce used a pair of tiny golden tongs to remove the substance. It looked like white mica with opalescent pink striations.

As Royce prepared it for them he said, "I doubt that you have ever had anything like this. It is called *Madre de Christos* and it is very rare, the very finest of Bolivian flake."

Their eyes were riveted to the product as Royce prepared it.

"I've never seen anything like it!" Anise exclaimed.

Royce nodded and answered, "I think not." His eyes twinkled with animal delight as he looked at her, "Ladies first."

Anise took the tooter from Royce's extended hand and bent to inhale two moderate lines. "Oh my God," she gasped.

Royce smiled widely, revealing two rows of perfectly capped teeth. "Exquisite isn't it? …and as with all things of this nature, very hard to come by."

After he had taken his lines, Tommy got to his feet and said he thought he would get himself another drink. Royce got up and pressed a small glass vial into his hand. Tommy thanked him profusely and then left. After some conversation and more lines, they made their way back to the party. Anise was floating on a velvet cloud. She was sure she had never been this high before. The party lights cast a surrealistic sheen over everyone and everything. Anise felt as if she had somehow crossed over into another land of wonder and enchantment.

Tommy had attached himself to one of the many bimbettes who were scattered through the room like party favors. The next several hours passed like a dream for Anise. She toured the party on Royce's arm, laughing and talking, drinking, snorting coke and remembering nothing. When the time came to leave, Royce offered to drive her home. Tommy had long since disappeared. Invited in by Anise, they left a trail of clothes on their way to the bedroom. They spent what remained of the night, snorting coke off of one another's bodies and making love until the sun came up. They were still at it when CarryAnn peered through the space at the door hinges. She had watched her mother make love before. Previous acts of voyeurism had helped Simon in his initial seduction of her.

He was better looking than Simon was and if her mother's cries were any indication, just as accomplished a lover. He had her ankles pinned at her ears and was slowly rotating himself in and out. CarryAnn watched them for a while. Her interest was more on the mirror of cocaine on the dresser than on the sex that was taking place. She hoped they would leave it there when they went downstairs. Her mother's eyes were half-shut and staring into emptiness. Her right hand gripped a handful of sheet and she was using this purchase to lever herself up into the hips of her lover.

Feeling arousal beginning to build in her body, CarryAnn turned away and slipped down the stairs and outside to the pool. When she returned an hour later, she found them having breakfast in the kitchen. Her mother was buttering a bagel and her friend had the morning paper on his lap and a cellular phone in his ear. The other hand held a cup of coffee from which he took intermittent sips.

"Good morning, darling. Would you like some breakfast?" Her mother's voice was full of cheer but CarryAnn could see how stoned she was. The bottle of brandy on the table was not there for display.

CarryAnn shrugged and said, "No thanks, I had something earlier. I'm going to go upstairs and change. I think I'll catch a movie this afternoon. Isn't it a little early?" She nodded her head at the brandy on the table.

Anise shot her a warning look and then glanced over at Royce to see if he had been following the exchange. He was scanning the newspaper and appeared oblivious of them. Occasionally he would speak "yes" or "no" into the phone. All of the conversation was taking place on the other end.

"Hell, Carry, it's the weekend," her mother replied, fixing her with a "don't mess with my good time" look. "I'm taking a little quality time for myself. I work so hard all week and I've got to relax when there's a chance."

CarryAnn nodded and smiled, "I'm sorry Mom, you do good, and you deserve it." They stared at each other for a while, wishing words across the distance between them, words that would not be the same once they had been spoken and therefore would never be spoken. She was turning to leave when Royce abruptly hung up the phone and set it on the table. He turned his attention to CarryAnn and said, "Good morning, I'm Royce."

His eyes pinned her and probed. She felt an involuntary shudder pass through her body.

"This is my daughter, CarryAnn," Anise said.

"Hi," CarryAnn replied. The terry cloth robe effectively concealed the lines of her body, but Royce's imagination artfully sketched in what he could not see. "Nice to meet you, got to go." Saying this, she turned and quickly left the kitchen.

Royce grinned at Anise, "Teenagers are always in a hurry."

"Yes, they are," Anise replied as she watched her daughter disappear.

CarryAnn took a quick peek into her mother's bedroom and when she saw the mirror still in the same place, still heaped with coke, she hurried to her bedroom and grabbed a magazine and a pack of matches. Returning, she cut away an amount of powder she did not think would be noticed and then retreated to her room. Once there she locked the door and then poured the majority of the coke into a film canister that she secreted in her daypack. She inhaled what remained on the magazine and then launched herself upon her bed. She rolled onto her back and gazed into the space between her and the ceiling. Slowly the pleasure began to rush through her system as the exceptional cocaine followed the blood into the brain. "Wow," she mouthed, "Wow, wow, wow." Then she laughed thinking she sounded like a dog with a speech impediment. "Wow... This is great!"

Downstairs, Anise poured more coffee into their cups and then added a shot of brandy into each. "She's been through a lot, growing up in Hollywood. I'm proud of the way she handles her life, especially since I can't be around all of the time."

"She seems very poised and self-possessed. I guess she'll be off to college soon."

"Not so soon," Anise said. "She's not sixteen for a few more months."

"Really," Royce answered, "I would have never guessed. I thought eighteen.

She's gorgeous but there is no question in my mind where she gets it." Royce gave her a look of desire that Anise immediately returned.

"She is beautiful," Anise answered. "She doesn't have any boyfriends yet. She doesn't encourage them. She's had some bad experiences and spends most of her time with a couple of girlfriends or with her nose stuck in a book. That will change eventually, I'm sure."

"Everything changes," Royce replied.

Anise nodded. There was a brief flash of sorrow across her face as she said this. Just as quickly, it was gone as she watched Royce pull the silver bullet snorter from his pocket and dangle it by its chain in the air. "Would you like some?" Anise reached out and touched his hand. "She'll be leaving soon and then will be gone for hours. Maybe we should go back to my bedroom, just in case?"

A smile tugged at the corners of Royce's mouth as he looked at Anise, then it broke on his face and his teeth gleamed against the dark contrast of his skin. "There's no problem there."

While Anise practiced her fellatio, Royce mused over his discovery. He'd noticed the missing cocaine immediately. Royce never missed something like that. His strength was built upon recognizing the weaknesses in others and then exploiting them. He took advantage wherever he could find it. From the moment he had met Anise, his mind had gone to work on ways to exploit their relationship. Now his thoughts encompassed CarryAnn as well. There was no question that John Morales would instantly want to possess her. CarryAnn could have many uses for a man like Royce. Certainly he would fuck her and instruct her in every act that might entertain him, but this was only one facet of the thing. Royce had beautiful women all the time. CarryAnn would have far more value to him as coin of the realm.

He could not hide his surprise when Anise had told him she was only fifteen years old. The combination of such youth and mature beauty could name its own price among the men with whom Royce did business. Surely Morales would appreciate her, but Eduardo, head of the Colombian cartel, would be considerably in his debt for such a fine gift. There was no telling what benefits Royce might reap from the girl. That she was the daughter of a famous American television actress would only increase her value.

It would not be long before Anise would do anything to maintain her supply of Royce's coke. Where else could she obtain it except from Royce? How could she snort the shit she had been snorting after tasting the real thing?

Royce laughed and then thought to himself, "*How ya gonna keep 'em down on the farm, after they've seen Paree?"* Probably she would not give him her daughter, not directly, not consciously, but there were a lot of ways to make something happen. It was only the results that counted. Royce would provide Anise with coke and Anise would provide Royce with CarryAnn. She was "liquid smoke" as Morales liked to say. She was something to inhale and absorb, to suck the nectar from until the petals darkened and curled and then fell away. He wondered how extensive her sexual experience was, probably extensive considering her poise and her background, regardless of what her mother had told him. Then again, if not, so very, very much the better. Royce gripped Anise's hair in his hands and moved her head to and fro. Maybe he would get the mother and daughter together, who knew? He closed his eyes and dreamed of things to come, and eventually he did.

Chapter Four

ISLAND OF MAUI, HAWAII

Alan opened the sliding glass doors and walked out on the deck. He set his mango shake on the railing and stared out into where the blue Pacific disappeared below the horizon. Except for some high cirrus tracings scattered to the West, there were no clouds. It seemed a lot longer than eight months since he'd left New York behind, but not for the grief that tugged at the edges of every day, and not for the scars that he would carry forever. Time had dulled the pain and there were days now when he was almost free of the memories until something, a song, a smell, someone's voice, would trigger it again.

He hadn't had anything to drink since New York. Several times he had ordered a beer without thinking and then left it on the bar. It wasn't that he was afraid of what might happen. He didn't think he was an alcoholic, he hadn't been one before Elizabeth's murder. But there were places he didn't need to ever go again. There were emotions that did not need to be stirred up and it was no loss to him to be without alcohol. *There was no good or noble purpose served by alcohol.* One could live a complete and successful life, without ever having recourse to it. He found all of his other disciplines much easier to maintain with a clear mind and they were providing him with the power to carry on. Since the age of sixteen he had been a practitioner of the martial arts, ever since his father had relocated the family to Hong Kong in the early seventies. Now, at the age of forty-three, he was a master of several forms, including Kenpō Karate, Wah Lum Kung Fu and Hapkido. Each morning found him in his garden working through a routine of complicated katas and calisthenics, from which he had woven his own synthesis.

At times, Alan was beginning to feel that he finally had himself in hand and was ready to get on with his life. But he never knew when, out of the blue, a giant relentless hand would squeeze his heart like a wine press and force the tears from his eyes. It was then he realized he was still fooling himself.

He had spent the first few months making extensive renovations to the house and land he had purchased in Haiku. It was a pleasant, rustic neighborhood, set back on the southeastern slope of the dormant volcano Haleakalā, which rose to ten thousand feet and dominated the island. Finally he saw that he'd made all the changes to the house that he could make, without tearing down what he had built to start all over again. Work on the grounds would continue for some time, but that was in the hands of the gardener.

He'd made a new friend in Ben Kamamoto, a lieutenant with the Maui Police Criminal Investigative Division and his sparring partner at the gym. It was through Ben that Alan had first met Wendy Carlson, a deputy prosecutor with the District Attorney's Office. Alan had been on half a dozen dates with her. It was apparent that she was attracted to him, but the one evening of fumbling uncertainty, followed by regret, served to put that aspect of their relationship on hold. There had been a misunderstanding followed by harsh words. She later told Alan there was all the time in the world, for everything, whenever he was ready. Alan wasn't sure that was the truth.

He sipped his mango shake and thought about Wendy and her similarities to Elizabeth. He wondered if something like that could ever work, when every time he saw her he was reminded of the past.

Alan had arrived in Maui with a luxury denied to many — money. He'd never paid much attention to money and was amazed when he found out how much of it there was in their accounts. A large sum left to Elizabeth upon her parent's death had been wisely invested and the principal balance never touched. Their collective salaries had been more than enough to meet their needs. Over the years, good management and high returns had swollen the original principal to several times what it had been initially. Elizabeth had always done the bookkeeping and their savings had never even been discussed. It was always for their retirement in Maui and for their children, but they never had any children.

Alan had been surprised to find he was a millionaire several times over. One of the millions went for the purchase and improvement of his new home. The price of real estate in Maui rivaled that of the most expensive mainland communities. Alan acquired a custom cedar home on ten acres of partially landscaped rain forest. A good portion of it had been shaped in the oriental fashion of working with nature rather than attempting to dominate her. There was a koi pond surrounded by decorative rocks, sitting cloisters and an abundance of flowers and fruit trees. The only clear and open place was the lawn around the pool where Alan worked out every day. Alan had laid out the paths so that they doubled back upon themselves or ended in cul-de-sacs. Ben had once said that Alan's property was the smallest place he had ever gotten lost in. It was possible to go places in the garden and not be found if that were the intention.

He'd just finished the last of his shake when the telephone rang. It was Wendy. "Good morning soldier. Are we still on for lunch this afternoon?" Wendy had spent four years in the army after graduating from college. She still liked to draw from the lingo.

"At ease rookie, nice to hear your voice. I was just this moment thinking about what I would wear."

"And?" she teased.

"Right now I'm leaning toward shorts and a T-shirt," Alan said, a smile moving over his face.

"You do that and I'll bust a cap in your ass mister. My boss and the mayor are going to be there!"

"Jeans and a T-shirt?" he asked hopefully.

"Gray slacks and a blinding white shirt to go with that beautiful island tan of yours."

"What... no tie?" Alan was just teasing. There was no way he was going to wear a tie. Even dead he would not wear a tie.

Wendy laughed, "Only lawyers, Mormons and timeshare salesmen wear ties in the tropics."

"Umm," Alan exhaled as if he had just confirmed a dental appointment. "I don't know how I let you talk me into this. I'm not very good around important people that I don't know. Hell, I'm not very good around important people I do know."

"You'll do fine," Wendy said, her voice slightly anxious as if Alan might still back out. This was the first social event that she had gotten him to agree to attend. Several times already he had procrastinated until it was too late or flat out refused to come. Wendy wasn't taking any chances. "Anyway," she continued, "You know Aaron, and Ben will be there too." Aaron Wilson was the Maui County District Attorney and Wendy's boss. "Besides, you agreed to come because deep down inside you are terribly fond of me."

Wendy had a brash, up front personality that was beautifully balanced by a rich femininity. This attracted the alpha males like bees to the flower. She was 5'9" with waves of auburn hair that fell about her shoulders. She had piercing green eyes and a strong thin nose that was dotted by hundreds of tiny freckles. Her face was one that was filled more with character than beauty, and an inner light seemed to illuminate her features. It was a face that would become more beautiful as it aged. She had a scathing wit that was not apparent in a face that appeared guileless. Many a would-be suitor and courtroom adversary had underestimated her and lived to regret it.

"Maybe I am," Alan replied.

"Only maybe?"

There was silence for a moment and then Alan said, "Maybe."

"Well, I guess I can live with the possibility. I'll see you at The Charthouse at 11:30. And don't be late, we need to go in together." She didn't offer any explanation for this. Alan assumed it had something to do with seating arrangements, or the awkward searching for one another under the eyes of others in a public place. Everyone knew Wendy, hardly anyone knew Alan. He searched his mind for an appropriate closing.

"See you then, I guess," is what he came up with.

He placed the phone back in the cradle and then flopped down onto a futon couch, one of several that were placed around an enormous redwood coffee table nearly seven feet in diameter. Alan ran his hand over his chin as he wondered why he had so much trouble getting outside of himself. Somewhere between his mind and his mouth was a jammed valve. He thought it might not be that as much as a deeper uncertainty about life itself. *Nothing was what it used to be anymore and it wasn't just the loss of Elizabeth. There was an ominous undercurrent to things.* What Alan had first felt in the hospital and then in his apartment had somehow followed him to Hawaii. There were the dreams too.

Many nights his sleep turned into an Armageddon of images from some battle being fought on the playing fields of his subconscious. When the forces of light would prevail it was wonderful, Alan would awaken with a sense of peace and innocence he had not known since childhood. When the outcome was less clear, the darker images were a long time fading and would trouble his day for hours. Despite all of this, there was an assurance growing in his heart that often made all of his concerns fade to nothing. Regardless of the paranoid uncertainties, there was a clear purpose emerging in his life. No matter what happened he would never be overcome by personal weaknesses again.

Alan crossed Kamehameha Avenue and followed Pu'unene Avenue to The Charthouse parking lot. It was 11:15 when he parked the Jeep. Even though the luncheon was scheduled for noon, the parking lot was already half full. Wendy had told him the affair was a fund-raiser for the battered woman's shelter. Hawaii had a very high incidence of spousal abuse. What was surprising was that it also had the highest incidence of battered husbands and boyfriends. There were some really big women in the islands. Alan had asked her when they would have a fund-raiser for the guys. Wendy informed him that there was little sympathy for that, but she had acknowledged the irony.

Alan was standing in the lot when he saw Ben Kamamoto climbing out of his county issue sedan. Alan smiled and gestured. Ben waved and pulled a red paisley bandanna from his hip pocket. He was mopping his brow as he walked up to Alan. "Fucking, non-working air-conditioned piece of county shit!" he exclaimed. Indeed, Ben had sweat pouring off of his brow as he extended his palm for a high five from Alan. Ben Kamamoto was a solidly built man, a shade under 5'10." Certainly not short, but still several inches shorter than Alan, even though Ben outweighed him by twenty pounds. This served him well when the two of them sparred. He had an open moon shaped face that carried a look of perpetual surprise. His mouth always looked like it was about to say "wow!" and the eyes accented this affect.

When you were around Ben you often had the feeling that something exciting had just happened or was about to. His appearance and demeanor were very effective during interrogations. A suspect had once said, "I thought I already confessed. I didn't know I was doing it for the first time." He had thick, wavy black hair and large, luminous brown eyes. He was nearly always smiling. This trait was made all the more strange considering his line of work.

Ben's most defining characteristic was his scatological and sacrilegious sense of humor. Ben would literally say *anything.* No politics, no religion, no race or color was safe from his barbed wire tongue. He was also several years older than Alan but looked ten years younger. Alan said it was all part of the inscrutable oriental mystique, "You never know what they are thinking, you never know how old they are and you never know what they are going to do." After hearing this, Ben had replied, "So now you know, don't turn your back."

Ben was dancing around on the balls of his feet and Alan said, "What? Are you about to sing something from *The Sound of Music* or do you just have to go to the bathroom?"

"Neither, *compadre,* I've got a pretty bad semen backup and I have to keep moving so it doesn't blow the top of my head off."

"Cute, Ben, that's very cute."

Ben shoved his bandanna back into his pocket and said, "Thank you. Where's Wendy?"

Alan looked at his watch, "Well, its 11:28. Somewhere in the next two minutes she'll be pulling into the lot. She asked me to wait out here for her."

Alan was glad to see Ben. They had fallen into an easy camaraderie that consisted of putting each other down or in Ben's case, anyone else that came to mind. There was nothing intentionally malicious. They were both students of human nature and found great amusement in the comedy of life. Both of them especially hated sham and hypocrisy. Where Alan would observe it and often withhold comment, Ben would share his opinion with anyone in reach, especially those he thought might not share his particular view of the subject or event.

"Actually, I do have to take a leak." Ben said, "C'mon."

Alan laughed, "People will talk Ben, especially with that red bandanna of yours. Do you remember which side you put it on? You giving or taking this afternoon?"

Ben snorted, "Yeah, a guy like you, from New York. You'd know all about that kind of thing. Anyway, let's go. I don't care what people think." Ben turned and headed into the restaurant.

"I've got to wait for Wendy," Alan called.

"I'll be at the bar then," Ben replied and walked inside.

Alan checked his watch again, which now read 11:35. He would tease Wendy when he saw her. Wendy was *never* late.

Fifteen minutes later Ben came out and found Alan sitting on the restaurant steps. "Not yet, eh?"

Alan looked up and shrugged, "Something must have come up."

Ben nodded and sat down next to him, "There's some funny shit going on."

Alan looked up at him, "You mean with Wendy?"

"No, like funny, weird shit."

"Funny shit is always going on Ben. I assume you don't mean funny 'hah-hah'."

"No, more like funny strange, but when you are only seeing a small part of the picture, it's hard to know what the whole thing looks like."

"You going to tell me about it, or is this one of the things you can't talk about?"

Ben cleared his throat. "I've wanted to talk to you for a while, you having all that big city experience and that Wyatt Earp reputation."

Alan looked at his watch again. Now it was nearly noon. Foot traffic into the restaurant was increasing and Alan got to his feet. "I'm going to call her service. She got hung up, probably tried to reach me here and I've been outside the whole time." Alan headed into the restaurant.

"She told you to wait outside. She would have known to send someone out here for you," Ben replied.

"I'm going to make the call anyway."

Ben nodded, "I'm going to my table." At the entrance they parted and went their separate ways.

Chapter Five

LOS ANGELES INTERNATIONAL AIRPORT, SIX WEEKS EARLIER

Balfire Tweeds and Malcolm "The Great" Kahn, emerged from the Jaguar XJ6 and opened the trunk. Balfire pulled two large suitcases from the interior and Malcolm extracted one more along with a slim attaché case. Behind them a skycap was trying to get between them and at the luggage. Malcolm bumped him roughly with his shoulder sending the man lurching back up on the sidewalk.

"We'll take care of them," he said with a malicious smile and brushed past the man into the terminal. Balfire slammed the trunk and tossed the keys at a homeless man who was panhandling the stream of people flowing in and out of the building's entrance. The keys bounced off his forehead and fell to the ground. Balfire followed in Malcolm's wake. The homeless man, who was broke and an alcoholic, was not stupid. He picked up the keys, got in the car and drove away.

They waited in line at the United ticket window and ten minutes later headed for the airport lounge with first class tickets in their hands. Malcolm had insisted they buy the proper attire before taking off. They sported loud Hawaiian shirts, khaki shorts and sandals. Balfire even had a straw hat. Malcolm had said it was who people thought you were, not who you really were that mattered. So now they looked like thugs dressed up as tourists.

It didn't matter what they wore and their parameters of action and behavior were tightly circumscribed in any case. They worked for The Doctor now, there wouldn't be any more problems. In the weeks prior, they'd been in business for themselves, two classic representations of a burgeoning American phenomenon. Balfire and Malcolm were serial murderers, bright-eyed, merciless psychopaths on a whirlwind tour of the West.

They had met three years earlier at San Quentin. Balfire was doing a straight eight for armed robbery. Malcolm had preceded him by nine years, in for the rape and murder of a ten-year-old girl and a suspect in the deaths of several others. It was more than that of course.

Malcolm hated children and in his time had visited upon them every indignity his twisted psyche could imagine. His own childhood had been a horror show and perhaps this was the reason for his behavior. Malcolm figured he was just bad to the bone. He never had a moment's regret about any of the things he'd done. He enjoyed all of it and lived for the day when he could do it again.

He was 5'9" and 165 pounds of hard muscle with hair the color and texture of corn silk, pitiless blue eyes that showed no human emotion other than rage, set in a round, ordinary face with a pugged nose. His ears stuck out from his head and to mask this he wore his hair long enough to partly cover them. He would have been indistinguishable in a crowd except for the long jagged scar that cut down across his right cheekbone and ended in the corner of his mouth. This gave the appearance of a permanent sneer that was greatly amplified on those rare occasions when he smiled.

Balfire had asked him once how he had managed to lure away all of the little girls he killed, looking the way he did. "Fear," Malcolm had replied. "It's the ancient magic of fear and fascination." Balfire had understood this, he was a little afraid of Malcolm himself, no small compliment considering Balfire's size and reputation.

Before he went to prison Balfire had murdered too. For this he had never been caught. He had raped and burned and pillaged. He had sodomized men, women and animals. He had beaten and betrayed, sold women, drugs, guns and anything stolen that could be sold. He was thirty years old and a ranking member of the Aryan Brotherhood. He stood six and a half feet tall and weighed nearly three hundred pounds. An observer would be hard put to notice any of it creeping over his belt. He had been a dedicated iron freak since he was a teenager. Balfire had flaming red hair, worn long over his shoulders with a prominent beard. He had deep set green eyes that at all times were filled with menace. He looked like some post-apocalyptic hellhound when gotten up in his biker gear with his head stompers on.

Where Balfire was all size and primitive fury, Malcolm was more the serpent — far more skilled in the fighting arts that his companion, a master of the knife and a black belt in *Taekwondo.* In an open space he was probably Balfire's equal in a fight. He possessed the adrenaline intensity of a tiger coupled with tremendous physical speed. He had gotten his nickname, "The Great Khan" from an incident that had taken place in San Quentin. Malcolm was also a member of the Aryan Brotherhood and the collector (along with Balfire) for all sports betting which the Brotherhood, for the most part, controlled. During the 1989 NBA Playoffs some extra heavy action was going down. The two teams, Detroit and Los Angeles, were very well represented on the inside. A lot of Detroit felons on the run wound up in California, where they committed new crimes and then wound up guests of the state at the "Q" as its residents knew it.

Sports betting was one of the few areas of interaction between the races, that and homosexual rape. A couple of black iron freaks had lost two grand to Malcolm over the series. Because it was a personal debt and not a debt to the Brotherhood, the debt would be erased if Malcolm were not able to collect it. It was a lot easier to kill him than to pay him. And as long as no one witnessed the actual deed or told anyone that mattered, retribution would not occur.

After so many years in prison, Malcolm had become a creature of habit. Rockhead and Motormouth figured they had a big edge two-to-one. Then there was their size, surprise and weapons. Malcolm could well be carrying too, but it was their intention to see that he never got a chance to reach his piece. They were waiting for him when Malcolm came through the laundry on his way to settle some accounts with the guards at the East gate. Malcolm did this three times a week, no exceptions. For the consideration of forty dollars and the promise of a blowjob from a newly "turned out" fish, a guard had left a tool room in the hallway unlocked for them.

Rockhead had jumped out of the shadows, hooked Malcolm around the neck and thrown him into the room toward Motormouth. Malcolm danced just out of reach as Motormouth lunged for him with an ice pick. Motormouth laughed and said, "You gonna die boy, be easy or slow, that part's up to you."

Malcolm studied Motormouth, while glancing continuously over at Rockhead, who was moving in from the side. "You don't want to pay your bill, that's what this is all about?"

Rockhead slipped closer toward him, "Like they say in that wop movie, this isn't nothing personal, you just ain't worth the money."

Motormouth jumped at Malcolm just as Rockhead leapt in from the side. When the pick was inches from Malcolm's stomach, he grasped Motormouth's right wrist with his left hand. Turning to his side, he guided the pick hand past his body, stepped inside and delivered an elbow to Motormouth's nose. He continued pulling so Motormouth's body now shielded him from Rockhead, who held a sharpened butter knife. Malcolm twisted Motormouth's wrist down and out, slamming him under the jaw with a backhanded fist. As he let go, Malcolm side kicked him into Rockhead.

"Ow, muthafucka...muthafucka," Motormouth groaned as he tangled with Rockhead, who was scrambling to get around him and at Malcolm. Malcolm snatched the ice pick from the ground and danced away from the confusion. Now he laughed, lightly tossing the pick from one hand to the other. Motormouth lay on the floor, dazed and still. Rockhead stood before him crouched low, all of his attention riveted on Malcolm. Rockhead no longer wanted to be where he was but he also knew there was only one way out and that was through Malcolm.

"You one dead motherfucker now," Rockhead said as he closed in on Malcolm.

"Let's see, why don't we," Malcolm replied. Rockhead swiped with his knife at Malcolm who took this opportunity to smash him in the knee with the heel of his foot. Rockhead screamed as he felt the knee dislocate. As Rockhead stumbled, Malcolm hopped quickly forward and drove the pick into his throat.

Rockhead gurgled as blood began to seep from the wound. He still held the knife clumsily in front of him, swiping it from side to side, with one hand holding his neck, his injured leg no longer able to bear any weight. Behind them, Motormouth was up on his hands and knees, trying to get back on his feet. Malcolm saw this and went into a reverse back kick, putting the side of his foot against the man's jaw. Motormouth went back down, face flat on the floor. Malcolm quickly turned and smashed the heel of his foot into Rockhead's knife hand, reaching down to pick it up as it skidded away. He squatted down in front of Rockhead and said, "This just isn't your day, is it hoss?" Rockhead looked up at Malcolm. Malcolm smiled and then stabbed the knife into Rockhead's eye, burying it deep into his brain.

He then turned his attention back to Motormouth, who was again rising unsteadily to his feet. Malcolm stepped in toward him and slammed his palm into the base of his nose, driving splinters of cartilage into his brain. Motormouth fell back to the floor, dead. Malcolm quickly wiped his prints from the ice pick and knife, then placed the weapons into his two assailant's hands. Checking himself for blood, he opened the door and walked away. No one was ever able to pin the killings on Malcolm but word circulated through the prison quickly, as it always did.

Two weeks later, a bunch of inmates were sitting in the TV room watching a bad movie about Genghis Khan. He had just finished killing a group of enemies and was leaning on his sword, surveying the carnage. Dustman, a lifer who thought everything was funny and made references to things that no one ever got, rose up out of his seat and turned to Malcolm, pointing his finger and saying, "You the Great Kahn, man, you The Great Khan."

Balfire was released from prison five months before Malcolm. He spent that time getting things ready for the day Malcolm got out. Malcolm was due for mandatory release, so there was no question but that he was going free. Balfire's efforts on their behalf involved one death, eleven robberies and two rapes. The rapes were crimes of opportunity that coincided with the robberies.

On the day Malcolm walked out of Q, Balfire was parked down the road in an eighty-seven Dodge panel van covered with airbrushed surf scenes. There was a pad waiting, a farmhouse he'd rented right outside of Fresno. The boys rode off into the sunset to do bad things once the sun had gone down. By the time they met Doctor Faustus, they were doing them in the daytime too.

Malcolm and Balfire were made for each other, like hell and high water, or death and dismemberment. Their time in prison together had made them into something like friends. They got on well enough not to get on each other's nerves and both of them had many tales to tell about the dark and labyrinthine ways that had led them to one another. If there was ever a point of contention between them, it was that Malcolm liked to fuck and kill little girls, but after a while Balfire figured, "What the hell, different strokes for different folks." Still, it gave Balfire a chill to watch Malcolm as he talked about the things he'd done, his eyelids drooping over his cold blue eyes, his empty face reminiscent of a Halloween jack-o-lantern. It was terrifying to think of what might have passed through a little girl's mind when she saw him, when she realized what he was, finally, in a place where there was no one else around.

Doctor Faustus had changed everything. It was like destiny and it was right on time. In their brief month of freedom the pair had left many a clue and the heat was on. It was time to head south, or north, or somewhere. On that night they had been driving aimlessly for some miles when Malcolm said he was hungry. Balfire pulled into an all-night Denny's. They took a table near the door.

"Not much is happening in here," Balfire said as the lone waitress approached their table. They ordered some food and drink. Malcolm surveyed the room while Balfire talked about what he thought they should do. Malcolm's eyes landed on a customer sitting at the counter with a cup of coffee. He did not look like he belonged there. He was dressed in an expensive blue suit. There was gold on his hands and a flash of gold at his wrist. He was a slender man who held himself erect, his face looking forward, not even turning down when he lifted the coffee to his lips.

An easy mark, Malcolm thought, not that they needed money, they were flush but opportunity was not a thing to deny. Both Malcolm and Balfire would do a crime simply because the potential was there. It was in their nature to take advantage wherever they found it.

Balfire looked at Malcolm and saw his attention was fixed on something behind him. They had the telepathy of wolves. "See something good?" he asked.

"Maybe," Malcolm replied. "Man at the counter, expensive threads and lots of jingly shit on his hands, might be worth a look." At that moment, the stranger reached into his pocket and drew forth a bulging money clip to pay for his coffee.

"Let's get it," Malcolm said. They slid out of the booth and Malcolm, catching the waitress's eye, threw some bills on the table. Once outside, they stood by the car and waited for the man to exit. Soon he emerged and walked to his car, which was conveniently parked right beside their van. It was a brand new Lincoln Town Car. As the man bent down to put his key in the lock, Malcolm came around the car with a .45 Colt revolver in his hand.

"Don't say a…" he began to speak and stopped — the man had vanished. Balfire, who was coming around the other side, was greeted with the look of astonishment on Malcolm's face.

"What the fuck!" he exclaimed.

"The guy did a Houdini," Malcolm said, and then got down on his knees to look under the car.

"Are you gentlemen looking for me?"

There he was, standing by the side of his car directly behind Balfire. Balfire whirled and felt an electric shock pass through his body as he stared into the man's eyes. Malcolm jumped to his feet and pointed the gun at him.

"Don't worry," the man said. "You won't need that. I'm not going to hurt you."

"No... but we're going to hurt you if you don't stand still." Malcolm replied with a sneer, cocky again now that the man was standing there and he had his gun trained on him. Balfire started to laugh but it froze in his throat. Suddenly he was very much afraid. Malcolm was quiet and motionless. The man's eyes began to glow, and from the pale light shining on his face his features emerged.

It was a face straight from hell. The flesh was moving as if hundreds of worms were crawling beneath its surface. The hair on his head was also moving and there was a sound of dry rattles shaking in the air. Balfire pissed himself but could not move. He was rooted to the spot. The stranger's mouth opened to reveal a row of brilliant white teeth, each as sharp as a tiny dagger. Then the face increased in size until it took up all of their vision. Malcolm's knees were trembling and his hand went to the car's hood to support himself. They stood there for a long time, each immersed in their own private vision of alien worlds. Malcolm saw darkness and evil that he had never imagined. Balfire was adrift in a terrible sea filled with vengeance and hatred. For what seemed a lifetime, the vision held.

When it passed, they saw a tall slender man with gold-rimmed bifocals standing in front of them. He looked like everyone and no one.

"Get in the car," he said. "We're going to have a talk."

They got into the back seat of the Lincoln Town Car and sat quietly. No one spoke. The car rolled silently out of the parking lot and onto the highway. They drove quietly for a while and then the man said, "I'm Doctor William Joseph Fausten, but you two," here he grinned into the rear view mirror where both of their eyes were instantly fixed, "can call me Billy Joe. It was my name once. That little demonstration back there was so that we completely understand each other."

Billy Joe turned around in his seat now, taking his eyes completely off the road but he continued to steer the car just as well as if it had his full attention. Balfire and Malcolm looked at each other, a sick smile on both of their faces as if to say, *"well we've gone and done it this time, we tried to rob the devil and now we're fucked."* Billy Joe laughed, reading their thoughts.

"Not quite, but close enough. Now you know that there is nothing you can do to me but I can do plenty to you, things a lot worse than physical pain, things you can't imagine until I make it possible for you to imagine them right before I do them to you. Though, like I said, I'm not going to hurt you. I need you and you need me." All the while he was talking to them his eyes searched their faces and never once returned to the road. Balfire, frozen in his seat and unable to move, was afraid he might shit himself next. Billy Joe laughed again, a harsh laugh like dry leaves scraping against a curb, "Not in my car, you won't. Don't worry, my control can extend right down to the curling of the hairs on your toes."

Suddenly able to speak, Balfire asked, "How come I pissed myself then?"

"Sometimes the best thing is to let people feel what they're feeling, to really get in touch with their feelings. It's about time your inner child went to school Balfire, yours too, Malcolm." They both winced at the sound of their names in the man's mouth.

Billy Joe continued, "I will give you both the power to do what you do without the fear of getting caught. No one will stop you. You will live better than you have ever lived before." Billy Joe had been gradually letting up on his absolute control over their minds. The sight of his red-glazed eyes, like the pinpoints of distant fires glowing in the darkness as the car sped down the highway with no one at the wheel, chilled them to the marrow. Billy Joe had abandoned all pretense of driving and was leaning over into the back seat with his arms crossed under his chin, making Balfire squirm like a frightened rabbit.

Malcolm sat motionless, far wiser about the situation than his companion, though equally ignorant of the means by which these events were occurring.

Billy Joe's eyes flamed briefly as he noted Balfire's discomfort. "It's nice to know the impact that fear can have on another, yes?" Another evil grin split Billy Joe's face. "As I was saying, because of me your lives will change in ways you've always wished for. I will give you real power. You will do as you like, when it does not go contrary to my purposes, and no one will stop you." At this point Billy Joe ceased to use the spoken word and switched to a telepathic format. Part of this was revealed to the conscious minds of his listeners and part of it bypassed their attention altogether and went straight into the subconscious where he programmed them to the requirements of his will. A much greater determination than theirs had now taken over. There was no question of opposition. It just was... and it had never been different.

Sometime later the Lincoln pulled back into the Denny's parking lot. Billy Joe steered it to the farthest reaches of the lot and then exited the car. His new acolytes joined him by the trunk. Billy Joe opened it and then stood with his hand on the lid as he turned to face them.

"You've both been very bad boys lately, not that there's anything wrong with that, but you have been sloppy and that is unacceptable." Billy Joe made a clicking sound with his tongue against his teeth. "You are going to have to develop some proper table manners." The street lamp's glow shone upon Billy Joe's razor sharp teeth. The image sent a shiver up Malcolm's spine. He wondered how the man could move through the world looking as horrifying as he did. Then into his mind came the thought that Billy Joe looked different to everyone who saw him. Billy Joe paused in his speech and winked at Malcolm.

"As I was saying, your methods and technique leave a great deal to be desired. In a few days the police would have had you in hand once again and, as generous as the courts can be, I think it would have been many, many a day until either of you saw the street again." As he spoke his hand was pressing up and down on the trunk's lid. This punctuated his words with a continuous squeaking sound. "You'll go from here to Arizona. There's some business I need you to take care of. There is a packet containing directions to a house and everything you need to know in the glove compartment. You'll leave the Lincoln there and take the car that's waiting for the rest of the way. I expect you'll be tired when you get there so I've provided a little wake-up, a little surprise and a token of my appreciation." This said Billy Joe pulled up the trunk lid. Both Malcolm and Balfire laughed when they saw its contents. There on the floor were two forms tied back to back, their mouths sealed with duct tape.

One was a beautiful teenage girl with dark hair framing a face out of which stared two very frightened eyes, the other was a young girl, no more than eight or nine years old. They could have been sisters.

"From Arizona you'll go to the airport in L.A. As I said, all the details, everything you need to know, money, identity papers, everything you need is in the packet."

Billy Joe slammed the trunk shut and said, "I'll be going now." He placed a hand on the outside shoulders of each of the men and swept his gaze across them. "We've got some beautiful moments to come. Have a safe trip. See you in Hawaii." Having said this, he turned on his heel and walked out of the lot and down the shoulder of the highway. They watched the darkness swallow him up.

Balfire said, "I guess he don't need a ride."

"Let's get it done," Malcolm replied, and then a snicker escaped his lips. "Nice gifts, huh? Just what the doctor ordered." Their laughter streamed out of the car's windows as they turned onto the highway and sped south into the wide empty American night, each one's mind filled with the riffling images of the good doctor's promises to come.

The poor souls in the trunk struggled fruitlessly, their hearts crying out for a rescue that would not come, as the car's taillights winked out of sight…

Chapter Six

MAUI, HAWAII

Alan waited another half an hour and made several more calls before driving to Wendy's apartment. He found the key that she hid in a planter and after knocking several times, unlocked the door and let himself in.

There was the usual clutter that Wendy lived in. The apartment itself was neat, the kitchen spotless, but paperwork and half-read books were everywhere. The only things that stood out and caught Alan's attention were two wineglasses on the coffee table before the couch. One was half full and the other had about a tablespoon remaining. There was also an ashtray with several cigarette butts of a brand Alan did not immediately recognize. He picked one up. It had a gold filter with a black barrel. Alan had never seen one like it before.

Wendy did not smoke and it would be unusual for her to let anyone do so in her apartment. This small evidence disturbed Alan. He could feel wrongness in the air. There was a metallic flavor in his mouth that he recognized from other crime scenes in the past, usually where blood had been spilled, but there was no sign of it here. He let his mind flow out into the apartment but could get no sense of anything. The one place he had not checked was the bathroom and he went there next.

The shock that hit his system made his skin feel clammy under his clothes. Someone had written in pink lipstick on the mirror, "Too late again lover boy?" On the sink was balanced another of his old business cards from New York. There was one spot of what seemed to be blood covering the letters of his first name. Its shape looked like sealing wax. There were no other signs of anything out of the ordinary.

Alan backed out of the bathroom and paged Ben. The call back was swift. Alan picked up the phone and said, "Ben?"

"Yeah, Alan, what's up?"

Alan sighed, a wave of black depression spreading across his mind, "I think you'd better come over here right now. I'm at Wendy's apartment."

Two hours later, after the uniformed police and several technicians had left, Alan, Ben and Assistant D.A. Richard Finch remained behind in the foyer. Alan wished they had sent anyone but Finch along. Before Alan had shown up in Wendy's life, she'd had an on-again-off-again relationship with Finch. Finch had been a lot more serious about Wendy than she had been about him. When her interest in Alan began, Finch had been unceremoniously deleted from the equation. He bore Alan no small amount of ill will. During the immediate investigation, this feeling had not been concealed from anyone present. Finch was playing his power cards, making Alan as uncomfortable as possible, with Ben working to ameliorate the effects of Finch's probes as best he could.

Richard Finch had come to the Maui District Attorney's Office as something of a fair-haired boy. As a Harvard graduate and valedictorian of his class, he'd had his pick of job offers. He came from a wealthy Massachusetts family with a strong political base. It was expected that he would do a few customary years of public service in his home state and then join his father's law firm as a stepping-stone to higher office. But there had been bad blood between him and his father. Finch hated him, or so Alan had heard from Wendy, and had picked the furthest location he could find in order to practice his profession and to live his life.

Wendy had told him that Finch's father was the head of the Democratic Party in Boston, an old school politician given to arm-twisting, favors and anything handy to advance his own interests and the interests of the party. Finch had told her his father was corrupt down to his shoe bottoms and that he wanted nothing to do with him.

Richard Finch was a manifestation of that newest of cultural mutations, a politically correct lawyer. Wendy had told Alan that in another century Finch could have been Robespierre's right hand man. She'd told him that it was this quality in Finch that had made the idea of a deeper relationship between them impossible. He had a draconian slant to him that was noticeable even in a profession that harbored such personality types. Finch's dream was to sit on the Supreme Court, "The" Supreme Court, and barring that, any Supreme Court. Finch wanted power to interpret the law.

At the moment he was interrogating Alan as if Alan were an actual suspect and Ben was hard pressed keeping the two of them apart. Alan was becoming more and more irritated at Finch's innuendoes.

"Look Richard, there's no evidence Alan had anything to do with this and we have no idea whether Wendy is missing or not. There are a lot of possible explanations for where Wendy might be." Ben said this with confidence he did not feel. He too was afraid something bad had happened to Wendy. He felt sure however, that whatever it was Alan had nothing to do with it.

"I'm not actually accusing Alan of anything."

"Right," Alan hissed, the heat evident in his face, hesitating as he struggled for control.

Ben laid a restraining hand on his friend and said, “Chill out, Alan. You may not like Richard’s manner but he’s doing his job the way he sees it. You’ve got to cooperate.”

“As I was saying,” Finch added, “I’m not accusing him of anything but there are a lot of strange things going on here and whatever Mr. Douglas’s role in all of it may be, some of these things appear to link him to whatever events may have taken place here today.”

Finch played with his tie as his eyes bored into Alan’s. Richard Finch was 5’9” tall and rapier thin. Alan figured he didn’t go over a hundred and forty five pounds with all of his clothes on. Whatever disadvantage he may have felt having to look up at Alan’s greater height, he more than made up for in attitude.

Finch was as much of a dandy as his grandfather’s trust fund allowed for in his blue pinstriped Armani suit, Eton school tie and Phi Beta Kappa pin. He had thick curling black hair, worn full over his ears and horn-rimmed glasses neatly framed his most prominent feature, coal black eyes. From his straight patrician nose to his thin lips and narrow, nearly pointed jaw, everything spoke of one “to the manor born.” His carriage was almost ridiculously erect and when he used his hands to illustrate his speech, there was an arrogant certitude to his actions that told Alan this man was a lawyer to his soul, regardless of law degrees to that effect.

Finch had paused in his delivery, searching for a way to continue. Finally he said, “Then there’s the matter of the door-to-door inquiries. Two different neighboring tenants overheard what appeared to be sharp exchanges between Wendy and Mr. Douglas here.” Finch slashed with his hand, palm up, in Alan’s direction. “That certainly bears looking into and it certainly demands an explanation.”

“Look, Dick.” Finch bristled as Alan used the undesirable nickname, but held himself in check. This would not be forgotten though, no one called Richard Finch, Esq., “*Dick.*” “I can’t really go into what Wendy and I were talking about the other night. Your prior relationship with her makes it impossible for me to share any intimate details about my conversation with her. But I will say this. We weren’t fighting and if I could tell my story to someone else it would be a lot easier.” Here Alan shrugged and smiled. He suddenly realized anger and confrontation were not the answer. “I want to cooperate and I’m really sorry for the personal shit we have. Neither of us picked things to be the way they are...” Alan’s voice trailed off as he observed the venom in Finch’s eyes. *No*, he thought to himself, *there isn’t anything I can say or do to get along with this guy.*

“Whatever we may think, we need to follow procedure right now and wait for that blood sample, if that’s what it is,” Ben said, trying to mollify the animosity between the two. “Why don’t we leave things as they are for right now? Tomorrow’s another day.”

“There might not be a tomorrow for Wendy,” Finch said, a note of sincere anxiety creeping into his voice. He turned back to Alan. “If you know anything I want you to tell me right now!”

Alan just shook his head and looked at him sadly. “I don’t know any more than you do Richard.”

Alan and Finch held each other’s eyes for a time, nothing passed except anger and frustration. Finally Finch broke off the contact. “I guess I don’t have to tell you not to leave town, do I?” Then he turned around and left.

“Whew,” Ben said. “I’m glad that’s over. I’m afraid you made yourself a bad enemy though.”

Alan put his hand on Ben’s shoulder. “I’m less worried about anything Finch can do to me than I am about Wendy. Something is very, very wrong. What the hell is going on, Ben?” Alan looked at his friend with disbelief in his eyes. “First New York, and now here, I don’t even have any of those business cards left. Whoever put it in there today didn’t get it from me *here.*”

“I don’t know, Alan. On the outside it looks very strange. I get the chills thinking about it. But I’ve seen a lot of mysteries in my line of work. One thing you always find out in the end, after all the facts are in and you’re looking at the whole thing from the other side, is that the answers were right there all along. You just hadn’t known where to look. Hang in there and we’ll get this thing set right.”

Ordinarily Alan would have been amused at Ben’s vernacular, it always made him laugh to hear such perfect American speech proceeding from that Oriental countenance. This time there was no amusement. This time there was nothing but foreboding. Deep in the core of his being there was a thick rising tendril of fear.

Chapter Seven

LOS ANGELES, CALIFORNIA

Royce watched her go into the mall's main entrance at 12:30. He'd been at the house while Anise was speaking with her on the phone earlier and learned that CarryAnn was going shopping at the mall near her house.

John Morales was part friend and part mentor to Royce Bettencourt. Fifteen years Royce's senior, Morales had built an empire from the drug trade. Years before he had funneled the majority of his profits into fine art and antiquities. His home in Topanga Canyon was a museum and in most of the circles in which he traveled, he was known as a respected dealer in fine collectibles. Very few people knew about Morales' other life. On certain occasions in the past, individuals had paid with their life for that knowledge. For all the appearance of urbanity, charm and seeming *bonhomie,* John Morales was a ruthless killer, a man who enjoyed the opportunity to do harm even when there was no real requirement to do so.

Morales was built like a tank at 5'10" and two hundred and ten pounds. His shaved head and thick neck made him look like a wrestler. He had narrow brown eyes and a flat Indian nose. The mouth was a thin compressed line. He looked like what he was, a dangerous amoral gangster.

At the moment, Royce was talking to him, sitting in his Porsche Turbo Carrera with his cellular phone to his ear. They were talking about their former supplier, a man who was known as "Mr. Poole." Mr. Poole had been their main provider of quality snortables for the last three years. Millions of dollars had changed hands over that time. They had always received first class merchandise for a fair price, with the explicit understanding that they would not purchase cocaine from anyone else. But a recent change in the power structure of a Colombian cartel had put an old friend of Morales at the top of the pyramid. Morales had decided to change suppliers and would soon be taking their first shipment in Phoenix, Arizona. When Mr. Poole had contacted Morales several days earlier about his standing order, Morales had told him they no longer wanted it.

Mr. Poole had responded with a cryptic, "I see."

Morales had told him to look for new partners, that he and Royce were through working with him. Mr. Poole had answered, "Indeed you are," and then broke the connection. It was about this situation that he and Royce were now talking. Morales had just finished telling Royce that Mr. Poole would have to be taken care of before he caused trouble of his own. The problem was that they did not know how to find him and were discussing precautions that might have to be taken until they did find him. There had been tales about Mr. Poole in the L.A. area for years. Bad things had happened to people who crossed him.

Royce asked Morales how the weather was in Phoenix. Morales responded with, "Hotter than sixteen year old Mexican pussy."

"I'll be down in a couple of days," Royce answered, "And I'll bring you a surprise."

"Really, what might that be?"

"That's why they call it a surprise, John. You don't find out ahead of time."

"Okay... Good... Get here as soon as you can. We'll unwind for a couple of days. Thomas will be here on the weekend."

Royce lit a cigarette and expelled twin streams of smoke from his nostrils. "The day after tomorrow John, it's the best I can do."

"All right, *hombre,* I'll see you then. *Ciao."* Royce put the phone back in the console and got out of the car, set the alarm and headed into the mall after CarryAnn.

He soon located her browsing in a clothing store. After a few minutes CarryAnn exited with a small shopping bag and Royce called out her name. "What you got in the bag, babe?" CarryAnn knotted her brow, not sure how to respond to this familiarity. Royce gave her an engaging smile and patted the bench. "Have a seat. I want to talk to you."

CarryAnn remained standing. "What is this about?" she asked.

Royce continued smiling, he held her eyes and replied, "Something you took from me. Have a seat."

CarryAnn felt a prickly embarrassment flush her face. She was unable to reply and just stood there. Her eyes were now sweeping the ground. She didn't want to look at Royce anymore.

"Look," he said, "I'm not angry, so you shouldn't feel bad. We all do impulsive things. C'mon and sit down." She pushed several strands of hair out of her eyes and slumped down beside Royce, her eyes straight ahead staring back into the store from which she had come, the bag at her feet.

"How did you know?" she asked.

"It's my business to know. Did you like it? Look at me and tell me if you liked it." Royce tapped her on the shoulder and she turned around and met his eyes. There was still a high flush on her cheekbones and her eyes were wary, wondering what Royce was up to.

"Yeah… I liked it a lot," she replied.

"Of course you did. It's the best money can buy." The smile never left Royce's face as his eyes stared into hers. "Even if you had the money you probably couldn't get it. It's very rare. Would you like some more?"

CarryAnn hesitated, she was confused by the speed of events but inside her mind there was an excitement that answered for her and Royce read this.

"I'm headed over to your house now, why don't you let me give you a ride and I'll lay some on you."

"I'm not sure my mom would like that, my getting a ride from you. There was a problem a little while ago with one of her boyfriends and she might get uptight if she saw us together."

CarryAnn was trying to work out in her thoughts how to get some of the cocaine, without creating a compromising situation with her mother when Royce said, "Not a problem, I'll drop you a couple of blocks away and you can walk the rest of the way."

"Why do you want to give me coke, especially if it's so valuable?"

"I'll explain that in the car," Royce answered.

"Okay." CarryAnn picked up her bag and the two of them left the mall.

Royce drove them to a small park a mile from her house and prepared some cocaine. He handed her a gold straw, holding the mirror with his hand while she snorted two lines of the shimmering powder. When she was done he took the mirror from her and did some himself. They sat in the car in silence, waiting for the rush that was only moments away.

"This is one of the good things about tinted windows, no one can see what you're doing." Royce set the mirror on the dash and then leaned back into his seat. CarryAnn had inhaled a larger amount than she was used to and prismatic colors were dancing in front of her eyes. She could feel the undulation of sensual waves of pleasure coursing through her body. Everything was tingling. Some of the cocaine had run down the back of her throat and numbed it. She could taste it in her mouth.

Royce turned his head toward her and opened his eyes. "How do you feel?" he asked.

"Incredible," she replied.

"Every time I look at you, I can't believe how beautiful you are." Royce said as he streamed his fingers through a lock of her hair.

"Thank you," CarryAnn replied. She could feel the sexual energy in the car. It exerted a powerful pull on her, but the thought of her mother never left her mind. She didn't know where this was going or how to handle it.

"Tell me about it," Royce said.

"About what?"

"About what happened with your mother's boyfriend?" Royce continued to play with her hair, occasionally brushing her ear with his knuckles.

The coke had put her in another world. Her inhibitions receded. CarryAnn gave Royce an account of her adventures with Simon, haltingly at first, embarrassed by the details. Royce urged her and eventually got most of the story from her.

"So, he never fucked you though?" CarryAnn looked out the windshield at several children who were chasing each other around a Jungle Jim.

"No, he never did."

"But you wanted him to?" Royce caught her chin with his hand and turned her face toward him. When she didn't reply, he continued, "You wanted him to fuck you?"

"Yes," CarryAnn replied.

"I want to fuck you too," Royce said, maintaining his light grasp on her chin. "But I won't get you in trouble with your mother. I will take really good care of you." Royce's eyes were twinkling as he retained her gaze. CarryAnn was good and stoned now and he was a master at all the little steps necessary toward the end result. His eyes radiated power. There was a power in his will that overwhelmed her, coupled with the coke she felt paralyzed and detached from a familiar center of being. She didn't know what to say and she didn't know what to do. She had suddenly been moved from one point to another without seeing it occur.

He separated two more lines and extended the mirror to her. CarryAnn sucked them up and then wiped her nose with the back of her hand. Royce slid the back of his hand across her neck and then down over her breast. This slight contact caused her nipple to harden and extend through the fabric of her T-shirt. She shuddered and involuntarily moved back. Royce leaned across the seat and kissed her. Then he abruptly broke contact and opened the glove compartment removing a small oval silver case. He opened it and showed CarryAnn the contents.

"There's a quarter of an ounce in here. It's probably worth a couple thousand dollars, that is, if you could put a price on it. I'm going to give this to you, but I want you to do something for me. I'd like to see your breasts." Without waiting for a reply he reached to her waist and gripped her t-shirt. The action was so direct and commanding that CarryAnn just let him take it off.

It was as if another person inhabited her body. He removed her bra and then pressed her back into her seat. For some time, he only looked at her. Prickly heat danced across the surface of her skin. Royce reached a hand forward and began to stroke her breasts. Then he leaned closer and took one into his mouth. "You give me what I want," he said, "and I'll give you what you want."

CarryAnn moaned, unable to answer. Cocaine accelerated desire was coursing through her body.

"Let's start with you doing for me what you did for Simon." His eyes searched hers as his will encompassed her thoughts.

Later, when it was over, Royce asked her if she would like to take a trip with him.

"My mother would never let me." CarryAnn replied through her T-shirt as she was pulling it back down over her head.

"Your mother is not going to be home."

"What do you mean?"

"I mean she's going to South America for me this weekend and she won't be back until Monday. She's done shooting until Wednesday and she's offered to take care of some business for me."

"You're not going to get my mother to smuggle coke for you!" CarryAnn exclaimed, fear widening her eyes.

Royce gave her a reassuring smile. "No, of course not, it's more of a social thing. I've spoken with some friends of mine and they like the idea of a television star coming to visit them in their homeland. I have a friend who is an important media figure that I want her to meet. It's good public relations for me and your mother won't be anywhere near cocaine," Royce lied. In fact, some of what he said was true, but Anise was going so that she could snort her brains out and with the promise that she might get her hands on a large quantity of blow for her personal use for nothing more than taking a meeting. Anise had been snorting coke full time recently and was strung out enough to believe anything Royce told her. He had invented the whole affair to make it possible to take CarryAnn away with him. Of course, Anise would be getting stoned and she would be getting coke, but it was really all about CarryAnn.

"It sounds okay, I guess," CarryAnn murmured, adrift on a cotton candy cloud. With her eyes closed she beheld a kaleidoscopic vision of colors and shapes, turning and merging.

"It will be good," Royce responded. "It will be very, very good."

He let her out of the car a few blocks from her house and said, "I'll be in touch." He watched as she walked away down the street. *"Shit,"* he thought to himself, *"Wait until John gets a taste of that,"* because that was his intention. To get all the sweetness out of her that he could and then to pass her around as a party favor among his associates. Later he would give her away as a favor not to be forgotten. Royce couldn't care less what happened to her after he was done with her. She was just another commodity like the other commodities in which he dealt. Perhaps he would fly her to Bogotá after it was all over and give her to Eduardo Corona. Eduardo liked young girls and boys, preferably both together.

MAUI, HAWAII

Kimo Nakamura was a very angry young man. The focus of his anger was not the reason for his anger, but no one could have convinced him of this. Kimo was angry because he was only five feet tall and had been continually picked on while he was growing up. He was angry because his father ridiculed him and laughed at his obsession with the *haoles.*

His father would say, "Betta you work hard and not tink so hard. What you gone do anyway?" He was angry because his mother told him it was wrong to hate anyone and that Jesus would punish him for it. Kimo didn't give a shit whether Jesus liked it or not. Jesus was a *haole* too. He had read plenty about what the Jesus people had done to the land and the Hawaiians. Now their descendants owned huge tracts of land across the islands and threw large exclusive parties upcountry where they got drunk and fucked each other's wives. He'd made deliveries to their houses and he'd seen how they'd looked down at him, an ignorant local. He was angry because he was only a truck driver for a meat wholesaler instead of the boss. He knew that his supervisor disliked him and had passed him over for promotion because he was too short. Kimo had short man's disease. Many people had died over the centuries because men like Kimo had this same disease. What Kimo's boss really thought was that he was too angry to work with the customers.

Even though Kimo was only five feet tall, he weighed one hundred and eighty pounds. This was because Kimo spent a great deal of time pumping iron, otherwise he was usually at the library. He was in the library now. It had been raining all morning and the Wailuku Library was crowded. Libraries and Laundromats were always crowded when it rained. Kimo didn't go to work until one in the afternoon today. Because of the smaller chairs, he'd been sitting in the children's section since the library opened. On the table in front of him were half a dozen books dealing with Hawaiian history. Kimo was seething. He was always angry but today more so than usual. He'd found an account of yet one more instance of rapacious genocide performed on the Hawaiian people.

It was hard for Kimo to have a conversation without the inclusion of "fucking *haoles*" liberally interspersed throughout. *Haole* was a word that translated as "foreigner" and was basically used as a negative. The irony was that Kimo himself was the offspring of foreigners. His father was Portuguese and his mother Japanese. This was not uncommon in the Hawaiian Islands, where there were very few native Hawaiians left.

Another thing that was not uncommon in the islands was racism. All the races disliked each other and the only thing upon which most of them agreed was their hatred of the white race. So it was not unusual to hear "fucking *haoles*" from a Portuguese whose people had distinguished themselves in their kindness to the residents of many lands they were not native to. It was not unusual to hear it from a Japanese whose people had bombed the shit out of Oahu not so very long ago. One could hear it from a Filipino, or a Tongan, or a Samoan but almost never from a native Hawaiian who, for the most part, lived on islands less traveled and kept to themselves.

Finally he closed up the books and left. He got to his workplace, Island Style Meats, at a quarter to one. It used to be that the other workers would make an effort to engage Kimo in conversation, asking about his health or how his day had been going. Nowadays there was nothing more than automatic pleasantries, because it was possible that anything one said, any question asked, would set Kimo off on a rant.

Kimo slammed the gearshift into third as he hit the straightaway. Three more stops before his break but he could forget his break today. He had daggers in his gut. He was sure that he was going to die. He couldn't understand why he wasn't coughing up blood yet. In the movies when people had a pain like this in their guts they were always coughing up blood. He was going to have to see a doctor soon. The pain had become unbearable. He was afraid of what the doctor would tell him but he couldn't put it off any longer.

The only bright spot so far was that the pain wasn't constant. It might be with him for two minutes or ten minutes. It could go away for several days or it could happen six times in one day. There was no telling. Sometimes his anger became so great that it almost replaced the pain, a red-hot, seething anger. Sometimes he would scream curses at the top of his lungs, his face contorted and drawn as he tried to stay focused on his driving.

Kimo pulled the truck into the parking lot of The Green Papaya Restaurant. Jumping out, he went to the back and ripped open the double doors. He switched on the hydraulics and brought the lifting floor to the ground. As he grabbed the hand truck, it felt like a giant fist punched him in the stomach and knocked him to his knees. Tears came to his eyes. He couldn't breathe. There was an inferno in his belly and he would have cried out, would have screamed and screamed but he could not draw a breath. Then, as quickly as it came, the pain went away and relief flooded his body. He wiped the tears from his eyes as he got back to his feet. He finished the delivery and then the next two without another attack. Then he drove to the warehouse and told the dispatcher that he had to see a doctor, right away.

He sat in the waiting area, thumbing through a *TIME* magazine. Images of violence swirled through his head as he read about the adventures and lifestyles of "rich *haole* fuckheads." Except for a dull ache in his stomach, caused by the clenching strain on the abdominals when the pain came, he felt okay. But he wasn't fooled. He knew the monster was lurking in there, waiting to knock the living shit out of him with no warning. Something was very wrong.

He was only twenty-one years old. He had hardly lived at all! It enraged him to think that his life might be ending before it even began. He wanted to smash something, smash it into tiny little bits. He wanted to smash someone, maybe one of these fucking *haoles,* who were over-running his island like giant cockroaches.

Everywhere he looked there was nothing but *haole* shit! Every beach he went to was full of fat sunburned *haoles.* Inside his mind he was screaming, "Death to the *haoles*! Death to the *haoles*!" He knew that if it weren't for the *haoles* he wouldn't be sick. It was worrying about them that had made him sick in his stomach.

"Kimo Nakamura?" He snapped back into present time. Somebody was calling him, he looked up and there was a *haole* woman calling his name. It was the nurse.

"Yeah," he replied, getting up and walking toward her. She smiled at him and handed him a folder.

"Take this and go to Section B, see Dr. Bentley." Kimo took the folder and glanced at the nurse as she walked back into the office compound. One pretty *wahine,* he thought. A *haole* though and so was the doctor he was going to see.

Kimo was wondering to himself just how many *haoles* he could kill before anyone stopped him. He figured plenty if he had the proper firepower. He'd always felt that the body count was small compared to what was possible in all those post office and fast food restaurant murder sprees. It seemed to Kimo that with the proper planning, training and concentration, a man with the right instincts ought to be able to take out at least a hundred people before they stopped him.

He handed the folder to the nurse in Section B. She looked inside and then told him to follow her. She opened a door to an examination room and put him through the preliminaries of blood pressure, temperature, height and weight.

"Just have a seat, Mr. Nakamura, and the doctor will see you shortly." Kimo sat on the examination table and pulled the *TIME* magazine from his back pocket. He'd been to the Kaiser clinic before. It was anyone's guess how long he would be sitting there. To his surprise the doctor arrived in less than five minutes.

Dr. Bentley was a tall, stoop shouldered man in his early sixties. He was nearly bald, which made his prominent features all the more conspicuous. He smiled at Kimo, revealing a row of yellowing teeth as he pulled his reading glasses from the chest pocket of his hospital jacket and read from Kimo's folder. Setting it aside after a few moments, he turned his attention to Kimo.

"I'm Doctor Bentley. What seems to be troubling you, Mr. Nakamura?"

"I got one bad pain in my stomach."

"How long has that been happening?"

"Mebe one month?"

Doctor Bentley nodded to himself and asked, "When does the pain usually come?"

Kimo fixed the physician with a cold look, his *haole* hating consciousness reawakening. "It comes when it wants, anytime."

"I want you to take off your shirt and lay down on the table." The doctor waited until Kimo had done so and then palpated his abdominal area. He got no reaction from this and then queried Kimo about the type of pain, its location and duration.

"Okay, you can get up and put your shirt back on. I'm going to send you to the lab for some tests. We'll know more about what's happening with you when we get the results back. Do you worry a lot, Mr. Nakamura?"

"No, Doc. What I got to worry about?"

Doctor Bentley smiled and said, "These days it seems everybody has something to worry about. I was just asking because worry can sometimes create conditions that bring on a lot of physical pain." He wrote out a prescription and handed it to Kimo. "I want you to take one of these pills next time you feel the pain. But remember, if it gets really bad you should go right to the hospital. Don't take any chances. Come back in on Friday afternoon. The nurse outside will give you an appointment, we'll have the test results by then."

Kimo left the clinic two hours later after a battery of tests. Some of them were uncomfortable. Kimo didn't care, whatever it took to get rid of the pain.

That was all that was important. It had become more than he could bear. Kimo was very afraid of death. He did not want to die.

Chapter Eight

Dawn had finally broken in Alan's mind. He had no idea who and he had no idea why, but there was no doubt in his mind that someone was out to get him.

Someone was trying to inflict as much personal pain on Alan Douglas as could be managed and though, so far, it had been focused on hurting the ones he cared about, sooner or later, like Mercury, it was going to go direct.

It took an incredible discipline of mind for Alan not to allow his thoughts to contemplate what he had no doubt was now true. There was a growing presence of anger. Alan supposed that he should be afraid too, but there was no fear.

He couldn't tell Finch what had taken place the other night, Finch of all people. Wendy had kissed him, nuzzled his ear and then slipped her hand inside his shirt. Alan had let the moment take him away. Soon Wendy was astride him, or attempting to be. Alan wanted to make love to her, but he could not. Involuntarily, he had called out Elizabeth's name. Earlier, Wendy had made a large pitcher of margaritas, most of which she had already consumed by this time. The alcohol brought out a reaction in her that might not have been so severe if she hadn't been drunk.

There had been words. Alan tried to leave as quickly and diplomatically as possible but Wendy was having none of it. As he'd gone out the door she had continued to call in a loud voice, "What's wrong with me?" Then, she was yelling at him from the railing of the walkway, wanting to know if he planned to "sleep with the dead for the rest of his life." The words had stung Alan to the core. He'd shouted back, "Leave Elizabeth out of it!" and then, realizing where he was, he'd stormed off to his Jeep and left without another word.

When he got home there were several messages from Wendy, apologizing and begging him to call or she would be unable to sleep. They'd talked it out for over an hour and all was well again when they had finished. He'd forgotten about the incident completely and it surprised him when Finch had mentioned what her neighbors said.

There was a sense of orchestration that baffled Alan. Someone, or several someone's, was directing a lot of effort and malice in his direction. Moreover, whatever mind was behind it was highly sophisticated. A bullet in the dark was more to be expected from the men Alan had put away. This was a far more oblique effort.

He racked his mind but could come up with no direction in which to work. The men he might have considered even remotely capable of anything like this were all either dead or still in prison. But he knew he would eventually get to the bottom of whatever was happening and he would clear the decks once he got there. He tried not to think of what he might do if he came across the man responsible for Elizabeth's death.

Ben had called to tell him that the District Attorney wanted to see him in his office at 9:00 a.m. He told Alan there was nothing new about Wendy. They'd know about the results of the blood tests tomorrow. He said he wouldn't be coming by today after all. Something had come up but he went into no detail. They'd talk in the morning.

After Alan hung up the phone, a resignation began to settle over him. He felt the creeping lassitude that he knew would soon give way to a terrible indifference. It was a dangerous place for him to be, so he walked into the living room and removed a key from beneath a book. Tossing and catching it, he walked out of the house and onto the deck. At the far end of the deck was a Japanese-style wooden door. He inserted the key and opened it. Walking inside, he turned on the light and closed the door behind him.

The room, which was really two rooms, was one of the additions Alan had made to the existing structure. The first was a study. Entrance to the succeeding room was through a bamboo curtain. That room was bare of furniture, except for a plush oriental rug and an altar with a bookcase next to it that Alan had built into the eastern wall. For years he had been fascinated with the Tarot and regularly received lessons from a group near Los Angeles, who were stewards of what was known as "ageless wisdom." In the small bookcase were selected volumes on the Kabbalah, Esoteric Astrology, the Tarot and related subjects. In the study was an even larger library of similar volumes.

The altar itself was formed of a slab of mango wood. On the wall behind it was a color poster of The Tree of Life, a pictorial representation of the *Ten Sephiroth,* the stations of consciousness leading to union with the supreme. On the altar was a wooden incense holder, a square of black velvet and a deck of Tarot cards that Alan had colored in himself. Every morning and evening he repaired here for study and meditation.

Alan's knowledge of the Tarot was extensive and he knew that although they did indeed predict the future to one who was able to read their meaning, this was the least part of them. The twenty-two Major Arcana cards were in fact graphic images of various attributes or archetypes of the human psyche such as

Reason, Memory, Concentration and the like. People who meditated upon the images would create a sympathetic vibration within themselves, awakening the qualities of the archetype. The qualities of humanity were also the qualities of God, only differing by degree. In his bedroom, Alan had a picture entitled *The Macroprosopus* that showed an ancient bearded man looking down into a mirror from which his image looked back. With his arms crossed in front of him, the image created the six-pointed Star of David, a symbol of the Greater and Lesser Countenance of divinity reflected in humanity. Through his studies, Alan had found a continuing explanation for the questions of human existence.

Very few people were aware of his interest in arcane things. Alan usually kept it to himself. The word "Occult" was often associated with things Satanic or dark. In fact, "Occult" simply meant "Hidden," things hidden from the eyes of those who were not permitted to see. The force that kept people from being able to see into the mysteries was their own blindness. One's vision was profaned by the nature of one's desires. *Only the pure could part the veils of the High Priestess.* Early on, Alan had learned the folly of trying to discuss the things that he had learned with individuals who were not prepared to understand them. Many dabblers in occult matters actually were motivated by material interests and those who thought they were motivated by powers of light were often deceived as well.

In the years that Alan had been working on this path of ancient wisdom, he had seen a great deal. The outrageous, the dangerous and stupid, as well as those who professed to knowledge they did not have, bound by imaginary oaths of silence, pretending to secrets that could not be revealed until the searcher had passed the right tests... and given over enough of their assets to be deserving of some deeper entry.

Alan sat before the altar and lit a stick of incense. From the pack of cards he chose The Moon, one of whose definitions was "hidden enemies," and another was "deception." He knew that meditation might stir his subconscious to provide a following insight into the nature of whomever it was that meant him such terrible harm. After a period of silence, Alan focused his attention on the card and let his eyes take a continuous photograph of it. This would trigger an area within him that might send back indications to him of events in his past relating to his present condition. It might initiate an illumination to take place while he slept, as the majority of Alan's spiritual experiences took place while he was sleeping. Then again, nothing at all could happen. Generally there was always a result, except when the question concerned Elizabeth. In that regard he had learned nothing.

Years before, he had told Elizabeth that focusing on the cards had a similar result to the ingestion of food. Just as the mouth and stomach digested the food and turned it into energy that made physical action possible, the same cycle occurred in the mind when one concentrated on an image from the Tarot.

After a time Alan closed his eyes and brought the likeness of The Moon before his mind's eye. He sat in silence but received no insights. Soon he dismissed the image and began to meditate, but there was a heaviness on his heart that he was unable to escape. He felt blocked and cut off from the divine. Finally he ended his efforts and left the room. Unable to find any answers or to achieve any peace in himself, he had a glass of water and went to bed.

His alarm went off the next morning at six o'clock. Alan lay in his bed for a few moments trying to remember the dream he had just awakened from. He was trembling but whether from fear or excitement, he could not tell. Try as he might, he could not remember where he had been. He got up and dressed in loose cotton pants and a t-shirt and then went out into his back yard. For the next hour he went through a series of intricate Kung Fu movements ending with a furious series of *katas* from the Kenpō Karate discipline. At the finish he was exhilarated, the blood was pumping furiously through his body and he was drenched in sweat. He went back into the house to shower and get ready to drive downtown.

Driving on the island of Maui was a joy seldom equaled on the mainland. Beauty abounded in all directions. The varieties of color and the clarity of the air were dazzling. Tourists who had forgotten to pay attention to the road caused any number of fender benders. It never seemed to take any time to get anywhere because your attention was always on some extraordinary feature. And there was always the ocean, the graceful waves rolling toward the shore where they exploded into shimmering foam and then disappeared into the sand or were sucked back into the sea to repeat the process all over again. Living on Maui naturally led the mind to the contemplation of beauty. The lifestyle was easy, the climate was perfect and the majesty of nature was always in evidence.

Before he'd even had time to think about the morning's meeting, Alan found himself in Kahului driving up Kamehameha Avenue toward the town of Wailuku and the seat of government. Ben was waiting in the parking lot when he arrived.

"On time as usual," he said.

"One discipline I've never been able to shake. What's this all about, Ben? I figure you didn't come by last night because you were afraid you were going to have to talk to me about it." Alan was half-serious when he said this and was surprised to find out that he was right when he saw the look on Ben's face.

"I'm sorry Alan, Aaron asked me to keep my mouth shut until he spoke with you."

"Aaron? I thought I was here for more of Richard Finch's famous bedside manner." Alan looked closely at his friend.

"I said the District Attorney's Office. Aaron is the District Attorney, not Richard, however that may pain him at the moment."

"I don't understand. What does Aaron Wilson want to see me about?" Alan knew there was a different equation at work now, and he searched Ben's eyes for an answer.

Ben held his hands up in front of him and said, "Please, Alan. I can't tell you anything. But trust me, everything's going to be okay, all right?" Ben reached out and took Alan's arm and they walked into the building.

The elevator opened on the seventh floor, they turned left and walked down the hallway. When they reached the frosted glass door with "Maui County District Attorney's Office" emblazoned upon it, they went inside. The receptionist looked up and nodded to Ben, "He said to go right in."

Ben nodded and said, "Thanks, Lehua." Ben turned the handle on the heavy oak door and they stepped inside. Aaron Wilson was sitting behind his desk, his chair turned toward the floor to ceiling window that looked out over Kahului Harbor. He was slouched down with his legs extended straight out and crossed at the ankles, his elbows resting on the chair's arms, hands clasped across his middle. When they came in, he turned his head to the side to watch them. "Take a seat." He gestured toward a row of chairs that were arranged in a semicircle around his desk.

Ben counted five chairs. "You expecting somebody else?" he asked. Aaron, who had moved nothing but his head until that point, slowly swung his chair around to face them.

"As a matter of fact, yes," he said. Then he pulled himself upright in the chair and leaned onto the desk to hit the intercom. "Lehua, call downstairs and have them come up." This done, he leaned back in his chair and studied Alan and Ben for a moment.

Aaron Wilson had several of the characteristics of big men. At 6'4" and around 250 pounds he moved slowly, as if in deference to bearing a greater pressure from gravity. He used only the amount of words necessary to say what he wanted to say and he exuded the confidence that all big men seem to have. In reality, he was not slow at all and had run the hundred-yard dash in 10.5 when he played middle linebacker for Georgia Tech in the early sixties. He didn't waste his words because he'd grown up that way. In the South, people who talked too much were not trusted. He was always telling his staff that you learned a lot more with your mouth shut. Most people were not comfortable around him because of his disconcerting habit of staring at you without speaking for a long period of time. He did not do this to make people feel uncomfortable, although he considered it a positive side effect in his work. He did it because people fascinated him and he found silence as instructive as speech. He would have become a film director if he had not gone into the law but his daddy had been a lawyer and his daddy before him. Aaron figured it was as close to movies as you could get in real life. In the movies there was the appearance of justice done. In Aaron's line of work, there was sometimes the reality of justice done.

Aaron Wilson hated bad guys and it made his day, his week and his month, every time he had a hand in putting one of them away. He was very good at his job and still took the odd case when he felt it required his attention. Naturally suspicious, he trusted no one. Right now neither Alan nor Ben felt very comfortable in the silence between them.

Alan had met him exactly twice, both times in Wendy's company. Both times they'd had extended conversation about Alan's New York cases. Aaron seemed to want to know all of the details, and Alan had opened up to him on a subject that was usually closed to most inquiries. It was hard to deny Aaron Wilson information if that was what he wanted. He had seemed to Alan both friendly and remote at the same time. At the moment, the friendly aspect was not in evidence. Alan had retreated within himself and although he was aware of Aaron's scrutiny, it did not affect him. He knew the truth concerning himself and his actions. It was all he needed to know.

Aaron must have seen something, because a smile flickered across his face before he turned around and stared out of the window again. Almost immediately Lehua's voice came over the intercom, "They're here, Sir."

"Send them in," Aaron replied.

The door opened and in walked Richard Finch, a police officer Alan recognized as Captain Millard Rusk and an officer from the Sheriff's department

"Gentlemen, most of you know each other and them that don't will soon. Sit down." Nods were exchanged but no handshakes. All eyes were on the District Attorney, who continued to speak while the fingers of his left hand toyed with the edge of a manila folder that lay on his desk. "Before we get into anything, do

I have a general consensus that I am in charge here?" He looked intently at the group. Some nodded, no one spoke.

"I take your silence to indicate full agreement." He waited for a response, when there was none he continued, "Some of you have an idea of the problem we're facing. Mr. Douglas may or may not know, according to some of you."

"Why is he here?" Captain Rusk asked. Rusk was a man almost as large as the District Attorney and though he'd kept quiet, he didn't like anyone who talked about being *in charge* unless it was himself. He had a great shock of white hair and the florid complexion of an Irishman who was fond of his whiskey, which he was. Like Aaron, he was running towards fat around the middle and his features were suggestive of Senator Patrick Monahan. Ben had once pointed this out to Alan and then gone on to say, "Less fat faced and more fat headed."

"Because I asked him to be," Aaron replied. "As I said, Mr. Douglas may or may not know what we will be presently talking about, but with his permission we'll soon find out. This man from the Sheriff's office is Sergeant Louis Bednar, did I get the name right?" The officer nodded his head, his face expressionless.

"I'm not going into any details here, except some that concern Mr. Douglas. We can all find out about what little we know on our own time. I take it that no one knows the nature of this meeting except Lieutenant Kamamoto and me?" No one answered him.

"Let's get to that," he said. "Bear with me while I share some details of Mr. Douglas's life with the rest of you. That okay with you?" He looked pointedly at Alan.

"I'm not sure where this is going, but I've got nothing to hide," Alan responded.

"Okay, here's the record book. Attended John Jay College in New York City, majored in criminology, joined the police academy and served twenty-one years with the New York City Police Department, thirteen of those in Homicide. There are many commendations, responsible for the arrest of numerous outlaws and the permanent retirement of several serial murderers."

Here Aaron paused and, picking up the folder, turned around toward the window again, the folder on his lap. No one spoke, although Rusk had begun to fidget in his chair. After about thirty seconds, Aaron continued. "Wife Elizabeth murdered in a New York subway attack year before last. Alleged assailant murdered shortly thereafter. No one was apprehended, case is still open. After his wife's murder, Mr. Douglas went to pieces. Is that how you would put it?"

Alan pushed aside the annoyance that was about to shape his answer. He didn't know what Wilson's game was. He'd wait and see.

"Pretty much," Alan replied.

Wilson spun his chair around again and tossed the folder on his desk. "Mr. Douglas remained on the force for another six months. There were numerous complaints about his performance. He was finally forced to retire. He became a drunk and eventually got beaten up and put in the hospital, even though Mr. Douglas is something of a martial arts expert. After discharge from the hospital, Mr. Douglas disappeared and resurfaced in Maui. Shortly after his arrival he made the acquaintance of a member of the District Attorney's staff. There were rumors of a romance. Yesterday that staff member disappeared."

Wilson rose slowly to his feet and put his hands in his pockets. Once again he looked out of his window. Alan repressed a smile. *There was a whole lot of actor in Aaron Wilson.*

Wilson must have caught Alan's reflection in the window. Perhaps this explained what seemed on the surface to be nothing more than theatrics, because he turned around and said, "You seem amused, Alan."

"I'm feeling a lot of things right now, Mr. District Attorney. I don't think I could explain them really, but guilty of any crimes, other than a period of weakness after the loss of my wife, I am not feeling. I'll smile if I want to. I've had precious little to smile about for a long time now." Alan said this without anger, but there was resolution and strength in his voice.

Now, surprisingly, Aaron smiled too, but it was more a combination of ruefulness and irony than merriment. Aaron did not respond to Alan's reply but went on with his discourse. "There is one very disturbing element in all of this and no one has any satisfactory answers yet. At the scene of one crime in New York, Mr. Douglas's business card was found. At the scene of what, for the moment, is the disappearance of yet another lady involved with Mr. Douglas, his business card has shown up again. Certain individuals feel that this is enough to cast the shadow of suspicion on Mr. Douglas. I have my own feelings, feelings I believe strongly enough in to act upon. First, we've got to clear the air."

"Alan," Aaron said, "Sergeant Bednar here is a truth seeker and, as much of the truth as we can get at, we need to get at now. Would you be willing to submit to a lie detector test, right here, right now, to help us clear the air?"

Alan looked at Ben and then looked back at Aaron. "Certainly, whenever you're ready Sir."

"Sergeant?" Aaron gestured to his desk. At this point Finch interjected, "I don't get the point here, Aaron. Lie detector results are not admissible in court and whatever we do find out could severely compromise any case that may later be developed against Douglas."

"Richard, I don't plan on prosecuting Alan for anything and if you could see beyond your wounded pride, you would agree with me." Aaron waved a hand to cut off his protestations. "This procedure is not to satisfy me, but hopefully will satisfy certain others as to the question of Alan's culpability in recent events."

Captain Rusk shifted in his seat and raised his hand, "Now Aaron, I have to agree with Richard, you know the fact that lie detectors don't prove a damn thing is the reason they are inadmissible in court. They are especially ineffective when dealing with psychopaths. There are numerous episodes where the technology has been fooled."

Aaron nodded at Rusk and then looked back at Alan. "I'm a bit more sanguine about the process than you are Millard. What lie detectors do not prove in court they do prove quite effectively in a situation like this, especially when administered by an expert such as Sergeant Bednar here. We're not going to be satisfied with uncertainty here. We have a truth machine, in a room full of truth seekers. I think we will do very well. We are also looking for a complete indication of truthfulness, anything less, any ambiguity — except where appropriate, taints it all."

"That may be all well and good," said Captain Rusk, now beginning to sound contentious, "But I don't know what I'm doing here. I'm less interested in the results of any lie detector test than I am in what the evidence has to say. And just because Douglas's business cards are found at the scene of a crime does not automatically exonerate him and point the finger elsewhere. Anyone familiar with criminal procedure, as Douglas surely is," Rusk waved his hand in Alan's direction, "knows the value of misdirection."

"Millard, these are all good arguments. This is what we have available. We'll get to the reason for all of this in good time."

Finch could no longer restrain himself. "Aaron, I have to register a very strong objection to this plan. It will compromise any hope of a future case against Douglas. It just isn't done! He doesn't have a lawyer here! Has anyone read him his rights? What happens if the results are incriminating?"

Aaron turned to Finch with a casual ease. "These are all points I've taken under consideration. I've given a great deal of thought to this whole thing. In the end, I bear any responsibility for whatever problems, legal or otherwise, that may arise. You'll just have to be content with that assurance for the moment. It will all be clear soon enough."

By now Sgt. Bednar had set up his apparatus and made the necessary attachments to Alan. He looked to the District Attorney, who nodded. "You comfortable?" he asked Alan.

Alan shrugged, "As much as I can be."

Aaron nodded to Sgt. Bednar who asked Alan some routine questions, how old he was, what day it was, what town they were in, switching back and forth from the general to the personal. Then he asked Alan if he knew who Wendy was. He asked him if he knew who killed Calvin Withers. He mentioned names that Alan had not heard before and if he had written or knew about any notes sent to the police. He asked him when he had seen Wendy last and if he had harmed her, if he knew who had harmed her. Finally he shut off the machine and disengaged Alan. He left the room for a few minutes, while Ben told a funny story about a Japanese policeman and two Portuguese who had stolen a pig and put it in a dress.

Sgt. Bednar returned and handed Aaron a sheet of paper. Aaron studied the paper and then handed it to Rusk who was nearest on his right. Aaron turned to Bednar and shook his hand, "Thanks for coming down Sergeant, appreciate your help."

Sgt. Bednar nodded his head and said, "A pleasure Mr. District Attorney, Gentlemen." Then he picked up his case and left the room.

As soon as the door had closed behind him, Aaron said, "A lot of times with these tests the results can be inconclusive. This is what Captain Rusk was referring to earlier and why they're not admissible in court. In other words, we're not certain if the person is lying or not. Other times they very definitely indicate one way or the other. My greatest concern was that the test might prove inconclusive, for whatever reason. Although it would not have altered my personal opinion, it might have been a great deal more difficult getting the support I hope to obtain from the men in this room. I'm happy to say that there is absolutely no indication that Alan was lying in any way and every indication that he was telling the truth." He looked at Alan and then said, "Congratulations."

Captain Rusk snorted loudly and passed the test results to Finch. He was put off by what he was sure was some kind of elaborate charade. He knew something was coming and he knew he wasn't going to like it. Richard Finch looked indifferent as he glanced over the paper. Finch was smart enough to keep the further appearance of personal enmity from his superior's attention, knowing that Aaron considered that kind of behavior unprofessional.

"Well, now," Aaron Wilson leaned his elbows on his desk and clasped his hands together, "To the point. Yesterday evening I met with Lieutenant Kamamoto. We discussed the recent disappearances of which Wendy is now one and we also discussed possible actions that might be taken to get to the bottom of them. In the process an idea surfaced that, we felt, had considerable merit." Here Aaron abruptly stopped his speech and his eyes drifted over to the bookcase on his right and there they remained during a long pause.

"I know that what I am about to do is not going to sit well with everyone here," he said, his attention still on the bookcase over which his eyes moved as if he were searching for something in particular. "It's a decision to which I've given a lot of thought. I've made the decision and here it is. I plan on asking Alan Douglas to join my staff as a Special Investigator into these disappearances, and I'm asking for full cooperation from the police in any requests he may make, for information, or assistance of any kind."

"What the... you're way out of line here, Aaron! Even if the man is not culpable about anything concerning Wendy, he's still a cowboy and a drunk and was forced to retire from his last job!" Rusk was apoplectic, his face a mean crimson and both hands had whitened knuckles from the pressure of his grip on the chair's armrests.

"Cool your jets, Millard." Aaron turned to Alan and asked him, "You got any western wear at home, Alan?"

"Not really," Alan said with a laugh, "Unless you count blue jeans."

"Are you a drunk?"

"I don't think so. I don't drink anymore."

"Not at all?"

"Not a drop."

"Look, Aaron, this is bullshit and I don't work for you anyway. We've got a full team at work on this thing and that's all I've got to say on the matter." Alan looked at Rusk. It was difficult to understand what Rusk had against him that had caused such a strong reaction. Finch, who had far more reason to dislike Alan, wasn't even speaking to the matter.

"Let me put it this way, Captain Rusk. Are you sure you don't work for me?"

"What! What!" Rusk was up out of his chair now. "Of course I don't work for you! I work for the county and the people of it, just like you do!"

"So if I were to make a phone call, just one mind you, and the result of that one phone call was an order for you to cooperate with me to the fullest, wouldn't that sort of mean you work for me?"

Captain Rusk ran the possibilities of Aaron's question through his mind. As a matter of fact, he realized, there were several people Aaron could call to achieve the very result he had mentioned. Rusk bit off whatever reply he'd intended and stared stonily at Aaron. "So, it's like that is it?"

"It's like that if you want it to be Millard. What exactly is your beef with Douglas?"

Rusk turned toward Alan and scowled. "When Ben introduced us, when I started seeing him around, I called some people back east. Mr. Douglas here is a glory boy, he's also trigger happy and unreliable. There are a number of questions too, still unanswered, about what really went down back there. Some of the people I spoke to had nothing good to say about him. We're talking career officers and representatives of the New York City Police Department."

"Well," Aaron sighed, "You're welcome to other people's opinions. I like to form mine first hand. But you're a professional Captain, this situation and its resolution is a hell of a lot more important than any personality conflicts. I need your help and I'd like to get it willingly. I'd also like you to donate the services of Lieutenant Kamamoto in the interest of creating a joint effort, we…"

Rusk cut him off. "Spare me the rest of the routine, Aaron. I'm not going to argue about it. Do what you want." Rusk picked his cap up from where it had fallen on the floor and stormed out of the office.

Alan held back his immediate reaction. Aaron's announcement had startled the hell out of him. His primary instinct had been to stop the confrontation by saying he hadn't been asked and wasn't interested. Then, something seemed to say to him, *wait and see, give it some thought before you make up your mind.* It was almost as if, for a moment, someone else was in his thoughts and looking through his eyes. One thing he realized was that more than anything else, he needed to unravel this mystery or it would torment him for the rest of his life.

"Aaron, I'm going to need some time to think this over." To Alan, this seemed like the best answer that he could give until he'd had some time to collect his thoughts. "I'm more than a little overwhelmed. This is completely out of left field. Let me have a couple of days?"

"We don't have a couple of days, Alan. I'd really appreciate it if you went with Ben and listened to what he has to say. Will you at least do that?"

"Sure, Aaron." Alan wanted to say more, he wanted to thank Aaron for his confidence, but he found his mind to be utterly blank of anything more to say.

"Let's get on it then," Aaron said and turned his chair toward the window again. Alan and Ben left, leaving Richard Finch behind with Aaron.

"I'm sorry everything was so hush-hush Alan. Aaron wanted it all on the table at the same time."

"I'll remember this, Ben. One fine day when your back is turned and your butt's exposed and three points wins," Alan said.

Ben clapped him on the back. "Remember when we were talking at the restaurant? I told you something weird was going on?" Alan stared at Ben, waiting for him to continue. "Over the last three weeks a total of five people have disappeared, plus now Wendy. We can't pinpoint where or how they disappeared, they're just gone, all with strong ties to the community. There's a woman in her seventies, a local papaya farmer of the same general age vanished while making his deliveries, a postman out making his rounds, something other than, *'snow, rain, heat, or gloom of night'* seems to have gotten its hands on him. A Mormon housewife in her thirties went to the grocery store and never came back. Last week, a nine-year-old Oriental girl, Nikko Hasuko, was last seen on her way home from school. She's a latchkey kid, unusual for an Asian. Her father's a lawyer, mother's an accountant. They work together in a Kahului tax office. Nikko was their only child." Ben handed Alan a large brown envelope. "Everything's in there."

Alan took the envelope. "That's it?"

"No, that's not it. I wish it was," Ben said sadly. "Five days ago, some *pakalolo* growers were on their way to their patch over in Olowalu. They heard a vehicle and jumped into the brush. A dark van went by and stopped up ahead of them. They saw a big dude with red hair get out and observed him messing around on a hillside. Then the van left."

"They get a license number?" Alan asked.

"No, but they did go up to check it out. Here's where it gets kind of grim. They found five crosses hammered into the side of the hill with a heart impaled on each one. After the growers saw this they hotfooted it down the hill and gave us a call, which was pretty decent on their part considering the business they're in. After what we found out, no one's going to be bothering about them."

"Which is…?" Alan spoke with his back turned. He was refilling his coffee cup. He knew the answer, but he asked anyway.

"What we found were human remains. We've run tests on blood typing and we found one AB Negative. You know how rare that is?"

"Pretty rare," Alan responded.

"One of our missing has that type and the other types matched the rest. It gets worse, Alan." Ben stabbed his cigarette out in the ashtray. "Early this morning another package of entrails showed up, taped to the front door of that restaurant by the Olowalu store. There was a sausage making recipe included."

"Wendy?" Alan asked, as an involuntary shiver ran through him.

"We don't know that yet. In the envelope were copies of five handwritten notes that had also shown up at the station in the last couple weeks. They arrived one day after each disappearance."

"There's something you need to know," Alan said. "I was up hiking in the Olowalu Valley a few days ago. As a matter of fact I camped there overnight."

"I'll be damned," Ben said.

Alan reached up and adjusted the gooseneck lamp. The paperwork he had received from Ben earlier was spread out over the desk. He studied the note that had arrived after the disappearance of the young girl.

"Young and supple-
Sweet and clean,
What I have planned is quite obscene.
Her torment short,
My pleasure great.
Preserved forever-
At one and eight."

He reflected on the words. He assumed "one" and "eight" meant nine, her age at the time of her death. He'd decided right then to take Aaron up on his offer. *Destiny was a funny thing*. He had spent years tracking killers like this, often by feeling alone. Now here he was, six thousand miles away, having put as much of the past as he could behind him, about to do the very same thing once again.

He was having trouble concentrating. Maybe he'd been away from this kind of work too long. His mind kept fogging up. In the past, possibilities and alternatives were always leaping into his mind as he pursued an investigation. Now he was finding himself fighting a heavy lassitude. He felt as if he was swimming through cotton candy. He got up and walked out of his study to the deck. Rising up before him were the massive broken teeth of Haleakalā. It was sunset and the sky was a fury of colors ranging from orange to purple. Alan felt his heart soar and his mind cleared instantly. He could hear Beethoven thundering in the air almost as if it were coming from his stereo, the image before him conjuring up the power of that great composer. What had been happening to him lately?

He'd be going along just fine until some alien presence intruded itself into his thoughts and turned the whole world gray. Ben had said this was a common condition for alcoholics, something about serotonin flow. Alan had doubted that was the answer. The phone rang. He walked back inside and picked up the receiver.

"Hello," he said.

"Is that you, Alan?" The voice on the other end was familiar to him but he couldn't immediately identify it.

"Who's this?" Alan asked.

"It's Whip, Alan."

"Whip, what…!" Alan's voice was filled with astonishment and delight. "Where are you?"

"I'm in a Sizzler restaurant and I'm about to do the salad bar."

"I mean, *where* are you?"

"Well, I can't pronounce the name of the town. Hang on a minute." There were several seconds of telephone noise and restaurant chatter in the background when another man's voice came on the phone and said, "He's in Kahului."

"You're here?" Alan asked, stunned by the news.

"Yeah, Alan, I am, you hungry or what? I guess I could wait."

"Jesus, Whip, I'll be right there." Alan set down the receiver, his mind in turmoil. *What the hell is happening?* He grabbed his keys and ran out of his front door into the night.

Chapter Nine

More than a year had passed since he'd last seen Whip. As Alan drove down the highway, his mind scanned back over the years they had known each other.

Whip had been eight years old when Alan and Elizabeth were first married. After their parents died in an automobile accident, he'd come to live with them. Alan had put a great deal of himself into Whip, schooling him in the martial arts and helping him train for baseball season. Whip's dream had been to pitch in the Major Leagues. Alan wondered how baseball figured in his life now.

Whip had been like a son to him and Alan had worked hard to smooth the rough edges of his personality. He had been darkly sardonic even as a teenager. He bore a striking resemblance to the actor James Dean and Alan wondered if he had not been subconsciously playing out the role of *Rebel without a Cause* in his efforts to combat the "forces of intellectual repression" as Whip had labeled the campus representatives of political correctness.

Whip had a great deal of contempt for what had once been fringe elements, now gone mainstream. In many cases Alan agreed with Whip's logic concerning the contemporary madness of Western Civilization. Alan though, was a master at keeping his thoughts private and censoring his speech. Whip was not. Whip could and did say anything if he felt like it. There was a lot of righteousness in Whip. Alan feared he might wind up like Savonarola and often cautioned him against voicing everything that was on his mind. He had tried to teach him tolerance and went to great pains to explain that tolerance was not acceptance. "Things came and went," he'd once told him, "cultures, governments, lifestyles." Alan laughed to himself when he thought about Ben meeting Whip. *Two loose cannons in one room.*

It was important for Alan that Whip knew the folly of thinking you could change the world. The only thing you had any power over was yourself. He'd begun introducing him to the writings of various arcane philosophers. After Whip went away to college, every month there would be a new book in the mail. It seemed to have had a positive effect in removing his focus from transitory externals to a more permanent, less pedestrian point of view. Still, Whip had been waging a constant battle with the forces of political correctness and administration policies. It seemed to Alan that Whip an unhealthy interest in adjusting the scales of fair play. *The world was not fair and only a fool expected it to be.*

It was great that Whip had arrived at this time. Alan really needed the proximity of a close friend with whom to share his thoughts, someone who knew him before all the recent troubles had come.

He'd gotten the nickname Whip for two reasons. First, Elizabeth had been fond of saying, "you're smart as a whip," then later, because he was so physically fast and threw the ball so well, Alan often called him the "Whippet." Whip had stuck.

Alan walked into the restaurant and carefully scanned the room. It was a big place and Alan could not see Whip from the position he was in. He was about to walk through and check the tables when he felt a tap on his shoulder. He turned, and there stood Whip.

"So, still sneaking up on people, I see," Alan said as they embraced.

"I'm the invisible man, Alan, you know that." They both laughed. Alan held him off at arm's length and studied him. Whip was dressed in a light white cotton outfit, the sort of thing that is ubiquitous in the Far East. His hair was cropped close about his scalp. This was not the Whip he knew. There was a serious look in his eyes and none of the amusement Alan remembered.

"It's great to see you Whip, but, uh… you haven't gone and joined a cult or something?"

Whip laughed and a genuine humor lit his eyes. "Geez Alan, no, the clothes are a concession to the climate where I've been. As for the hair, I caught a parasite, it'll grow back. I see you're in shape," he said, lightly tapping Alan on the stomach. "Still working out a lot?"

"That'll never change. Let's get some food. I know how you like to eat."

Whip's appetite was legendary. Growing up, he had always been hungry. No matter how much he ate, he always remained slender. They had attributed it to a high metabolism. There was an urgent energy to him even when he was sitting still.

Soon they were seated at a table. Alan watched him eat for a while without touching his own plate. Whip looked up and said, "Aren't you hungry?"

"At this point, I'm more curious than hungry."

"There's a lot to talk about, Alan. We'd better wait until we get home though."

That was all he would say about it for the rest of the meal. After they were done eating, Whip asked him what he was up to. He didn't even seem surprised when Alan filled him in on recent doings. Later, when they were driving back, Alan brought up the question of his previous whereabouts, but once again Whip begged off and told him it would have to wait. Alan didn't argue.

When they got to Paia, Alan pulled into a gas station and Whip followed him inside. They were standing at the counter with some items when Alan felt a tingling in the small hairs at the nape of his neck. He turned and saw two men approaching the counter from the cold drinks section of the store. One of them was carrying a cold pack of Budweiser. Alan studied them. The big one had dirty red hair that snaked out of a knitted Rasta cap. He was clean shaven except for a bushy handlebar mustache. His mouth was in a perpetual snarl from which Alan could see broken, badly cared for teeth. Aside from a broken nose that had a slash of scar across the bridge, as if it had been hit by a length of chain at one time, his most arresting features were the deep set eyes that resembled a feral pig's. Alan almost stepped back from the menace in them.

The companion was shorter and slimmer, though well-muscled. His arms bulged where they emerged from his Hawaiian shirt. Where the big man looked like the kind of demented biker scum common to the American Southwest, this one reminded Alan of a type he had often dealt with before. Empty flat eyes, a cold blue without expression — they revealed nothing. There was a mean slash of mouth above which sat an incongruous button nose. On a girl it would have been considered cute. On the man in front of him it set off an alarm. He'd seen a face like that before on a killer from California, who with a companion, had traveled the freeways of southern California abducting teenage girls. After they had bound their wrists with coat hangers, they raped and tortured and finally killed them. They also tape recorded each event and then played the recordings back for their amusement.

The men were sizing Alan up as they came up to the counter. Their eyes said, "Cop." The big one smiled and said, "Evening, it's a fine night for a beer, eh?"

Alan could feel the violence openly radiating from him. This fellow liked to hurt people, probably kill them too, if there was the opportunity. The other one was a deep water snake, no telling what he was capable of, given the chance. The air stank of ozone, as electricity crackled in the air between them. Whip had finished paying for his items and was waiting for Alan, tuned in to the message in the air.

"Yeah, sure is a good night for a beer," the big man said again.

Alan didn't move, holding his place for several heartbeats. Everyone knew the game being played. Finally he said, "Enjoy those brews." Then he turned with Whip and headed for the door.

"You fellas have a nice evening now, you hear?" The voice followed them out the door. They could hear laughing and indistinguishable words as it closed behind them.

"Twenty-four carat felons," Alan said, as they pulled onto the Hana Highway.

"Definite bad vibrations," Whip answered. "I thought the big one was getting ready to fire on you."

"No, that was just an intimidation thing. It's something you refine in prison where, I'll bet you anything, those two have spent some serious time. I kept getting the feeling that I recognized the smaller one, but I know I've never seen him before. I wish I could place it."

"It's just a fact of life, Alan."

"What's that?"

"Everywhere you go there are lowlifes."

The dark blue Ford van sat with its nose facing the ocean on the soft sand of Baldwin Beach. Though the moon was nearly full, it would have been impossible to tell whether the van was occupied due to the heavily tinted windows.

Now the window of the passenger's side rolled slowly down and an arm extended through the opening. The hand held an empty beer can which was pitched out on to the sand with a flick of the wrist. It hit one of its predecessors, sending a tinkling sound across the still air.

"Damn!" Balfire exclaimed. "The only thing better than a cold beer, is another cold beer."

Malcolm belched from the driver's seat. "I know something even better and that's the feel of a warm pussy growing cold underneath you, preferably with very little hair on it."

"Fuck, Malcolm," Balfire looked at his companion in disbelief. "You've got to be the sickest dude I ever met in my life."

"Ain't it the truth?" Malcolm belched again and then reached into the cooler for another beer. They'd already gone through one twelve pack and were now at work on the last one they had just bought. "I'm a beautiful human being, Balfire, and you're one hell of an environmentalist, recycling them beer cans on the beach."

"Son of a bitch, Malcolm, I don't want them rattling around in the van. There's a lot more room outside than inside." To punctuate his message, Balfire hurled yet another can through the window.

"He don't look like much," Balfire said. Malcolm gave him a confused look, though he was very familiar with his partner's tendency to jump subjects without warning.

"Who don't look like much?"

"The cop in the store, the one Doc sent us to scope out. Who was that skinny little fuck with him?" Malcolm looked at Balfire with annoyance when he remembered that Whip was actually taller than he was.

"How the fuck should I know? Maybe it was his boyfriend, all the bad luck he's been having with women, maybe he switched." They both snickered at the idea of Alan having to switch his sexual preference because all his women kept dying on him.

A young couple came walking down the beach. The two men watched them approach. When they were about twenty yards from the van, Balfire pitched another beer can. It clinked on one of the growing collection of empties strewn in front of the van. This was followed by his cigarette that tumbled like a firefly until it landed among the cans. The two were hippies from the look of them. The guy had long hair and a poncho, the chick was in a long flowing granny dress.

"Hey," the male yelled at them. "This is a beach, they've got garbage cans right over there!" He pointed behind him at a large cabana.

"You talking to me?" Balfire asked.

"He means we have to keep the beach clean for everybody. Children play here in the daytime." Now the bitch was throwing in her two bits.

Balfire climbed out of the van and stood like a towering basilisk in the shadows.

"Look, sweethearts, I hear one more word out of either one of you and I'm going to walk over there and shove a beer can down both of your throats so you don't scream so loud when I fuck you in the ass."

They hesitated there on the beach for several seconds, digesting the totality of Balfire's statement. Then the boy grabbed his companion's hand and ran with her back the way they had come.

"What d'ya say bro, wanna have some fun? I haven't seen anyone else around here for over half an hour." Balfire had terrible teeth and as he grinned at Malcolm in the moonlight, he looked like a gargoyle.

"Nothing I'd like better," Malcolm replied. "But you know what the Doc said. We don't kill nobody unless he says we can."

"Yeah, Khan, I remember. I'm not so sure I like somebody telling us what we can do all the time. We're freebooters man, wild and free. I didn't do so well in the military." Malcolm knew that Balfire was just about drunk now. He always started calling him "Khan" about that time.

"It's like this, bubba. The Doc says one more month, maybe two, and we're rich and out of here with a pot load of money, passports and on to other countries. He's going to show us how to do some of that shit he does. Show us things that keep us from getting caught. We do like he says, we got it made. We fuck up, he's going to turn us into female dogs or sewer rats. I don't think I could handle that. He's like the devil or something." Malcolm's mind was very clear about everything that concerned his relationship to Billy Joe.

"Yeah," Balfire shivered when he thought about it, the memory cutting briefly through the alcohol. "Or something worse."

Chapter Ten

ONE MONTH AND THREE DAYS EARLIER • LOS ANGELES, CALIFORNIA

Anise looked at her daughter with a mixture of concern and excitement. "You sure you'll be all right? You've got food and money. Tommy said he'd check on you every day." She'd never been to South America before. Royce had assured her there was no danger. She would meet powerful individuals, stay at a fabulous home and be wined and dined in a manner exceptional, even to one who always got the star treatment in L.A.

Royce had also told her it was customary for Eduardo to make a special gift to those who visited him in his retreat outside Bogotá. Usually it was a large amount of cocaine sent via diplomatic pouch. She would be Royce's emissary, bringing a certified check for his recent purchase. Royce had promised to meet her at the airport upon her return.

"Mom, I'm here all the time without you, I'll be fine. I'll probably just hang around the house and entertain myself. Is Royce going with you?" CarryAnn was wearing a white strapless sundress and with her hair brushed and shining as it fell over her shoulders, she looked like she was on her way to communion. It was a calculated effort to look prim and proper for her mother's peace of mind. Her dark sunglasses hid her eyes which were dilated from the two lines she'd done just fifteen minutes earlier. Anise's mind, however, was already on the plane. She probably wouldn't have even noticed if she'd seen them. She was every bit as stoned as her daughter.

"No, he had to go to the East Coast on business. He caught a flight this morning."

"Well, have fun then." CarryAnn hugged her mother then walked her out to the limousine with her arm around her waist.

"I'll make it up to you when I get home, darling. We can go to Palm Springs or something." Anise kissed her on the forehead. The driver opened her door and she got inside.

"Really, Mom, I'll be fine."

"I know you will. I'll call if I can." The driver shut the door and moments later the car disappeared around a bend in the driveway.

CarryAnn watched it disappear. She waved once before it was gone.

Royce arrived two hours later. The first thing he said was, "I spoke with Tommy and told him I'd do the checking up. He knows the score." He sat down

pussy was sore but the sensation was far away in her mind. A part of her, a darker, unknown part, enjoyed the rough handling of John Morales. In combination with the cocaine, Quaaludes and wine, rough was the only way to feel what was happening. CarryAnn was in a borderland of pain and pleasure, no longer sure which was which.

It had been easy to talk her into it. Once the superficial aspects of her personality had been bypassed, there was nothing familiar that remained for her to measure herself against or to define what was happening to her. Lost in a cloud of altered perception, there was no way for reality to rear its head. Sensation on all sides was in a controlled format. CarryAnn no longer knew who she was or where she was and it didn't matter. She didn't care who fucked her now. Mostly she had no thought of who was doing it. She only wanted to be high and dancing through the dizzy unknown territories of new sensation and to keep away from the fear that trembled and scuttered like nervous leaves in the background of her mind.

Last night John Morales had fixed them all up with a combination of cocaine and other things that had sent her outside of her body so that at times she was able to stand apart and watch herself independent of the actions of her body. She'd felt like she was in an airplane that had stalled and was rushing to the ground but never hit.

When she'd seen streaks of blood on the sheets where she had been with Morales the night before, she had laughed. That was how fucked up she was.

Royce and John had laughed too. They laughed because they were invincible princes in the kingdom of Satan, despoilers of all that was good, exulting in the joy of evil for its own sake. CarryAnn was nothing but a pastry, crafted by a master chef, of which in the end all that would remain were the crumbs.

Royce went to the hotel room door when the buzzer sounded. He looked through the peephole and then opened the door. Two short swarthy men entered the foyer, one of them carrying two suitcases. He continued on into the living room area. His empty handed companion remained to embrace Royce.

"Thomas, what a pleasure it is to see you again!" Royce said with affection.

Thomas stepped back, his hands gripping Royce's arms. "As it is for me."

He was short and wide, like many of his countrymen. Regardless of any effort to control it, one's attention always found its way to his face. Years ago Thomas had received a severe beating from two enemies that left him hovering near death for several weeks. He'd never had the damage repaired, leaving his nose smashed to one side. The broken jaw and occipital cavity on the right side made him look like he had two different faces. The nerves there were dead and any animation in his face came only from the left. Ugly scar tissue was everywhere, as he had been worked over with a knife as well as beaten. He vowed that his face would always remain so, as a reminder to him of what can happen when you trust another. It remained also to remind all others of what had happened to his assailants.

Once he had recovered from his injuries, Thomas had the two men hunted down and brought to him at a coca processing plant in the Amazon. It had taken them over a month to die. Thomas carried photos of the process in his wallet and would sometimes show them to men who sought to do business with him.

His companion was handsome and unmarked, in his twenties. He was a soldier who accompanied Thomas on his journeys, who picked up the cocaine at whatever mainland site it was delivered to and whose only other duties were to guard it with his life. Thomas ignored him except when instruction was necessary.

Royce gestured towards the suite's kitchen area and said, "I have a wonderful Burgundy decanted and breathing on the bar. Perhaps it would help to wash the dust of your travels from your mouth?"

"That would be nice, Royce. Where is John?"

"He is preparing a gift for you and will be with us shortly," Royce said as he handed Thomas the wine. "How is Eduardo?" Royce was as courtly as he could possibly be. Thomas and his reputation made him uneasy. One never knew what might offend him. Thomas had reputedly killed men for no other reason than the impression that they had been impolite to him, men with whom he had done business of a far greater value than this present deal, and men he had done business with for considerably longer. He had no friends except possibly John Morales, who was a native of his country and had known him even before his accident.

"Eduardo is fine and sends you both his regards for your health and happiness. He is much pleased to be doing business with you again."

"Please thank Eduardo for us. Tell him that fortune has never smiled greater and that we have him alone to thank for this."

The door to the bedroom opened and John Morales entered the room. He walked quickly toward Thomas who rose to embrace him. They remained this way for half a minute as if the length of time given over to such a thing might somehow give credence to a friendship that in reality did not exist. Both men were long past caring about anyone or anything but whatever matter was at hand. The impression of friendship would remain as long as the bottom line was respected. As with everything in the cocaine business, the bottom line was money. Because Morales had always been good with the money, the illusion of a close friendship was maintained.

Finally they separated and Morales said, "You look well, Thomas."

"And you John, remain unchanged," he replied.

The bedroom door opened again and CarryAnn walked in, freshly scrubbed, coked and dressed to kill. A body hugging white dress set off her curves and worked a beautiful contrast against her olive skin and lustrous black hair. The deranged look in her eyes only accentuated the complete picture of utter desirability.

For the first time there was a real flash of animation in Thomas's left eye. She walked over to Royce and said quietly, "I've got to eat something. I'm going out."

Royce bent his lips to her ear, his hand on her arm applied a pressure that was more than a suggestion of control, "But CarryAnn, we have guests."

"I'll do anything you want when I get back, just please let me go and eat. I'm sore all over and I'm starving, please?" She breathed into Royce's neck.

"Of course," he replied. "We have business to discuss anyway and will be busy for a while." He pulled her toward the others and said, "Thomas, this is CarryAnn."

"I am most charmed to make your acquaintance. I have heard wonderful things about you," he lied. "But I see now that their poor words have done you no justice at all."

CarryAnn kept her face as controlled as possible and her attention on Thomas's eyes. It was a no-win situation whether to focus on his twisted features or the cold malevolence of his one good eye.

"It is a pleasure to meet you," CarryAnn replied.

She turned and headed for the door, followed by Royce. He handed her a hundred dollar bill and said, "Why don't you catch a movie while you're at it. Come back in a few hours when everyone's in a lighter mood." He leaned down and kissed her cheek, brushing her ass with his hand as she went out the door.

CarryAnn exited the elevator and walked out through the hotel lobby into the fierce noon heat of downtown Phoenix. Her mind was filled with a thousand conflicting images. Half an hour ago she had finished with Morales, kneeling before him on the bed as he slammed his way to orgasm while standing behind her. She had felt clear in her mind about fucking anyone who wanted to fuck her. She could have sucked a thousand cocks. It seemed to be what she was made for. Now, all of a sudden, she didn't care if she ever had sex again.

She was high from the coke she had just snorted in the bathroom, but it was not the same high as before. She felt completely blue, even cold, in the heat that pressed down upon her. She felt used and dirty and would have given anything to feel like a little girl again. She missed her mommy but her mommy was far, far away and just as fucked up as she was. There didn't seem to be a positive opening anywhere in the road that extended before her. She wished she were dead and was very much afraid that she might soon be.

Now here she was on the streets of this large southwestern city, looking for somewhere to eat and maybe a movie or a place to sit, where she could forget for a little while what she had become and what waited for her when she returned to the hotel. She would probably have to fuck the Colombians and maybe Royce and John again, too. She shuddered at the thought of Thomas and his disfigured face. The coke would help her through it, but she would wish she was dead again afterwards, even more so than she did now. As bad as some of the things she had done seemed to her right now, she knew that she could feel worse, that worse things could happen. The downward spiral led to far greater darkness where finally she would be left a soulless husk.

For all her lack of experience concerning the outside world and the privileged surface existence she had led until now, CarryAnn was an intelligent girl. She was seeing the future that lay in front of her. She did not want to go forward. She did not know how to go back. She was very much afraid…

"Give us a couple more!" Balfire yelled down the bar at the fat Chicano bartender. "Damn, that is the slowest greaser I've ever seen in my life." He turned to Malcolm who was picking the dirt from under a fingernail and said, "I'll bet you that fat fuck could set out to swim the Rio Grande and wind up back in Mexico before he got to the other side."

Malcolm laughed. Balfire's comment was funny. It didn't have to make any sense. They were in a biker bar on the south side of Phoenix. It was empty except for a couple of worn out whores that the bartender was talking to and one lone wolf at the pool table. They'd been there for an hour waiting for the phone call.

Balfire slammed his hand down on the bar top and got up from his stool. He made his way down to the end of the bar. "You!" he snarled at the bartender.

"Yes. Yes, *hombre,* I have heard you. I was just this moment to get your beers." He smiled, exposing four gold teeth in the front.

Balfire fixed him with his look of death. "I don't like to have to get up to get somebody's attention. Usually when I have to do that somebody gets hurt. Because you may not have known this I am going to overlook your born Mexican laziness. But if it happens again..." Balfire reached into his hip pocket and withdrew a pair of needle nose pliers that he used as a roach clip. "I'm going to pull out those gold teeth just like I was a death camp guard and then I'm going to sing you a little SS lullaby. You got it?"

The bartender was flying down the bar with their beers halfway through Balfire's speech. "I am so sorry *Señor*," He looked imploringly to Malcolm, hoping for sympathy from another quarter.

"Leave the beers and get the fuck out of here!" No mercy.

Ten minutes later the phone rang. Malcolm was already standing behind the bartender when he turned around to call him. He lifted the receiver out of his hand. "Yeah, uh-huh, uh-huh, hey you!" Malcolm gestured to the bartender. "Bring me a pen and paper."

The bartender was now moving fast despite his weight. Malcolm continued to talk, writing down instructions. Finally he hung up and went back to where Balfire was sitting and drained off the last of his beer.

"Showtime, bro, let's roll."

Once they were in the van, Malcolm pulled a bindle of crystal meth from his pocket. Taking two snorts from a rolled up twenty-dollar bill, he passed it to Balfire. "Bang it back big guy. We need the power of the Force with us now."

Balfire chuckled and snorted twice what Malcolm had taken, a guaranteed overdose for some. For Balfire, it was all in a day's work.

Six miles down the road, Malcolm turned right towards downtown. Neither man had spoken in a while. They had both become internalized into the imploding Methedrine Bomb Syndrome, ripe and ready for the deep uglies. They were running their own film clips of events to come.

"That's it up there, Ballowire." Malcolm pointed to the Marriott Hotel that loomed ahead on their right.

"I told you not to call me that, Khan." Balfire's eyes were bulging out of his head. Little drops of clear fluid glistened on his mustache. He was primed.

"Stay cool, bro. It was a slip of the tongue." Though his features did not register it, Malcolm was both pleased and amused. The angrier and more fucked up Balfire was the better. Mean as he was, he sometimes hesitated in the face of real evil. This was the reason Malcolm had scored the crank.

"Yeah," Balfire growled. He was already another ten miles down the road. His big ham sized fists were beating a wicked tattoo on the tops of his thighs.

Gonna be some serious black and blue tomorrow, Malcolm thought. But not as serious as the folks they were going to visit. Major grief was coming down. Malcolm glanced at his watch as he made the turn into the hotel parking lot. "The Doc said any time after noon, looks like we can head right in."

Balfire grunted in reply and squinted into the sun shining directly through the windshield. He was raging from the speed heat that was lighting up his nervous system like a Christmas tree. He had been reduced to animal noises. There was no way that the immolation of thousands of brain cells could be communicated through speech.

Malcolm guided the service van into a parking place at the far end of the lot. He shut off the vehicle and then climbed into the back. Pulling up the rug, he exposed a trap door in the van's floor. He opened it and began removing items from the compartment and placing them in a large toolbox that lay open beside his knee. He screwed silencers on two machine pistols and said to Balfire, "Sweet little lullaby makers the Doc got us."

Balfire only grunted again, he was filled with an ice white Methedrine rage and becoming all the more angry as he tried to put on the brown jumpsuit within the confines of the van. The rapidly rising temperature inside the van further compounded the situation, now that the air conditioning had been turned off. Balfire had begun to bang his head against a panel as the juice rocketed through his system.

"Yo, Balfire, that's going to sound real strange to anyone who's walking by the van right now. We got to be cool, even if the Doc has got mojo on the scene."

"Right," Balfire gasped, finally able to articulate a single word. Malcolm knew the routine. He'd timed it out. He knew that in about ten minutes Balfire would be in another phase, cold, focused, and ready to deal.

Malcolm checked off the contents from a clipboard list. Duct tape, mat knives, a linoleum knife, metal shish-kabob skewers, a propane torch and a hi-8 video camera. Into his pocket went a master passkey. He was humming "A Few of My Favorite Things" as he went down the list.

Balfire was chuckling at this. "You're one stone killer, Kahn, a livin' nightmare. Doc said there'd be a girl in there for us, hey?"

"That's what he said, immobilize her and put her away until we're done with the others." He slipped into his jumpsuit. "Need to put the air on high when we get there. It's gonna be mighty warm with the plastic rain gear on over this shit.

You carry the toolbox. I'll take the bag." Malcolm pulled a leather and canvas bag from the rear of the van. From the clipboard he detached two plastic covered nametags and tossed one to Balfire.

"Shit! How come I got to be Ernie and you get to be Bert?"

"Nobody is going to look at the goddamn name tags Balfire. No one is even going to notice us. That's what the Doc said. Give me a break!" The heat was getting to Malcolm and his temper was rising with it as he tried to stay on track with everything. There was no coming back to the van if they forgot anything.

"If it doesn't matter, then how come I can't be Bert?" Balfire persisted.

"Goddamn you," Malcolm hissed. "Here's the fucking tag. Now give me the other one and shut up!" Malcolm threw the nametag at him and grabbed the other one back.

"Thanks," Balfire said, grinning as he attached the ID to his shirt pocket.

Malcolm glared at him and said, "Okay now, tell me how it's going to go down."

"I follow you up to the room. We don't look at anybody. We don't talk to anybody. After you open the door I jump past you and level my piece at whoever's there." Balfire paused, adding up the information Malcolm had made him memorize on the long drive down to Phoenix. "If anyone moves or goes for a weapon, I blast them at the knees. I don't kill anyone unless I have to. I make sure I don't shoot through a window."

"Good, good," Malcolm interjected.

"I cover them while you check the other rooms. If you find anyone you bring them back. Then I keep them covered while you search them for weapons. Then I duct tape and gag everybody except the California dealers, them, I just tape. You set up the video camera. Then after you talk to them for a while, we go to work. We save the girl for last, then we can do anything we want to her and then we crucify her to the bathroom door. Everybody's dead, no witnesses, we pack up and go."

"What about the dope?" Malcolm was pleased. If Balfire remembered everything the way he'd just said it, there would be no problems.

"Yeah, I remembered that. I was just going to say it."

"Then say it, and don't leave out the last part."

"We take most of the dope with us, except for a couple of bags that we cut open and spread some around. We toss those bags on the table. When we get back to the van we put the tools inside and change out of the uniforms and leave."

“Mostly right,” Malcolm replied. “The Doc just told me over the phone that he’d be parked here in the lot when we come out. After we stash everything and change, we’re supposed to give him the dope. He’ll signal when it’s time.”

“How’s he going to signal?”

“How the fuck do I know? That’s what he said.”

“I got one question, Malcolm, usually when there’s a big dope deal going down there’s a lot of money around too. How come nobody said anything about the money?”

“There isn’t any money, Balfire. Everything’s been paid in advance.”

“How come you didn’t tell me that before?” Balfire looked at Malcolm with suspicion in his eyes.

“Look, Balfire, it wasn’t important. Just keep your goddamn mind on the job or what happens to those guys is going to look like nothing compared to what will happen to you after Billy Joe gets done.” The sound of the doctor’s name silenced Balfire.

“Let’s get the fuck out of here before we melt.” Malcolm opened the van and they exited into the parking lot.

Nobody saw them go in the rear entrance. They passed several people on the way to the elevator who were intent on their own business. The elevator was empty when they got on and stayed that way. Malcolm felt invisible and invulnerable. He pulled out the passkey in front of Room #528. He turned to Malcolm and pumped his fist. In went the key and quickly they were through the door. Balfire leveled his gun at the four men sitting around a large coffee table.

Malcolm whisked through the rest of the suite, checking every room, in the closets, under the beds, bathrooms and shower compartments, smooth as silk with one tiny hitch.

“Where’s the girl?” Malcolm asked when he returned into the living room.

“The fuck are you?” asked John Morales. No one else had said a word. All eyes were on the silenced machine pistols and the large clips that hung beneath them. On the table, one of the suitcases lay open, rows of sealed plastic bags full of white powder inside. One bag had been removed and lay open on the table. Malcolm searched the men while Balfire covered him. Thomas’s bodyguard made a grab for him while he frisked his boss and Malcolm broke his nose with a quick backhand. Except for the guard, no one was carrying a gun. Malcolm then stepped back and covered them with his weapon while Balfire removed duct tape from the toolbox and bound their hands behind their backs. Finally he taped their ankles and then retrieved his weapon.

"I'm going to ask you one more time, where's the girl? You don't answer then, I'm putting a round in your kneecap." Malcolm addressed the question to Morales.

"She went out to get something to eat," Royce said.

"When's she coming back?"

"Whenever she's done, maybe an hour."

"She got a key?"

"No," Royce answered. His mind had become completely still. He had no doubt these men intended to kill them when the time came. In his back pants pocket was a straight razor that Malcolm had missed in his cursory search for handguns. Malcolm had also missed a .45 automatic that was sitting on the side of the couch that Royce was up against. If he could cut the tape with the razor, he had a chance to grab the gun and use it. It was a long shot but for Royce there was no question about it.

Malcolm digested the information. This was something he had not anticipated. He stood there watching the men. Then he went to a dresser that was set against the wall behind him and set his weapon down. He said to Balfire, "Bert, I want you to stand over by the door and when she knocks, you open it and let her in. Chances are she won't know whether you're supposed to be here or not. If she shows any hesitation, you snatch her in quick and muffle her. I'll take care of things here myself. You can leave off the rain gear."

Balfire was so pleased that Malcolm had called him "Bert" that he didn't mind being left out of the fun. He knew someone had to watch for the girl anyway and Malcolm was a lot better at the crazy shit than he was.

Thomas's eyes had opened wide when he heard the word "rain gear." He'd used plastic before for particular reasons and he was afraid now that the reasons were exactly the same.

"Well," Malcolm said with a tight smile on his face. "Let's get down to business. First, Mr. Poole sends his regards." Royce and Morales turned and looked in alarm at each other. Any hope they had that this was a simple rip-off was now gone. Royce shifted his position. Now he had better access to the razor. Two of his fingers touched it and he began to slowly withdraw it from his pocket.

Malcolm was concentrating on Morales. "I see the name means something to you. Mr. Poole was unhappy that you chose to break an agreement. He feels that if you do not respect him, then no one else has reason to either. Therefore a message has to be sent."

"You gentlemen are in a great deal of trouble," Morales said. "Eduardo Corona will make you beg for death. It would be better for you if you released us now and went your way."

Malcolm laughed. "Now there's an interesting choice of words, considering the situation. Mr. Poole doesn't care about you or that big grease job Corona back there in the sticks." Then he turned away and removed the video camera and began setting it up. He'd been around some very bad people in his life. Malcolm was curious about how they would respond to torture.

Royce had opened the razor and was nearly through the tape around his wrists. He could smell the nervous sweat on himself and his companions. Never before had he been in a situation like this. He could feel fear tugging at his mind. It took all the steel that was in him to concentrate on the task at hand and not let it overtake him.

Malcolm finished with the camera and then walked over and lifted the toolbox on to the table. He removed an X-Acto knife and picked up the bag of coke from the table and scooped a portion into each nostril. Then he handed the bag to Balfire, who took the bag and applied several large pinches to his nostrils.

"Tastes like a fine product you've got here," Malcolm said. "That may be why you felt the need to switch distributors." He squatted down in front of Morales. Then, quick as a rattlesnake's strike, Malcolm slit open one of his nostrils with the knife. A high squeal escaped Morales' lips before he could cut it off. A stream of blood ran down his face and began to drop from his chin. "First thing I've got to tell you is not to write checks that your ass can't cash."

Morales glared at him with a venomous hatred in his eyes. He wanted to speak but was restrained by the possible result.

Royce's mind raced. He knew now that there was little time left. He could no longer hope for CarryAnn's arrival to provide an opportunity to react. His hands were free and the razor open. His right hand flashed from behind his back and whipped toward Malcolm's throat. If he had not been turning his attention in that moment over to Royce, it would have been a killing stroke. As it was, Malcolm's head had dropped with the movement and the razor slashed across his cheek.

Royce was turning and frantically searching with his left hand to connect with the automatic. Malcolm grabbed the hand that held the razor at the wrist and drove his fist into Royce's neck. Grabbing his collar, he pulled him forward before Royce could locate the gun. Royce landed across the table, breaking it under his weight.

Royce began to convulse and strangle from the crushing blow that Malcolm had dealt to his throat.

"Wait!" Malcolm screamed as Balfire leveled his weapon at Royce. With blood streaming from his face, he grabbed the X-Acto knife and performed a rough tracheotomy on Royce saying, "You ain't gonna die on me boy, not yet you're not. Hell can wait."

There was the sound of air, sucking and shuddering into Royce's throat through the air hole. Malcolm ran to the bathroom, grabbed a towel and tore away a strip. He wiped the blood from his face and then pressed the strip tight against the wound. Returning to the living room, he tore off pieces of duct tape and affixed it to his face as a crude compress. Escaping blood was already turning it red.

"Tape him up again Balfire and set him back." Morales and the bodyguard were wrestling frantically with their bonds but to no avail. Thomas just sat there staring implacably at Malcolm.

Malcolm was enraged. His cheek was throbbing with pain. "It's time to go to work," he said. He pulled on the rainwear and then plucked a propane torch from the toolbox. He lit it and then stood there, a vicious smile on his face. "Hell's not going to seem half bad by the time you boys get there."

CarryAnn took another sip of her iced tea and looked out of the diner window. Her face was filled with despair. The remains of lunch sat on the table in front of her. In the distance, she could hear the bustle of the crowd, unintelligible voices mingled with the clatter of plates and silverware. It all seemed very far away from CarryAnn. Her experimentation with being an adult had snowballed into something out of control.

She lit a cigarette. Smoke floated out of her mouth and wove its way up over her head. It was a wonder she could eat anything after all the coke she had done, but somehow she had managed to consume most of a large tuna salad. She could feel her body slowly trying to come back into balance. With it came the growing certainty that she had to get away from Royce and the others. But she was going to have to go back there. Her money was in her bag at the hotel. She could probably get a bus ticket home with the change from Royce's hundred, but she didn't want to leave her things and she needed some more coke. She just needed a little more coke until she could get back home and quit doing coke. The saddest part of the whole business was that this did not even sound absurd to her.

Lost in thought, she stubbed out her cigarette, paid her bill and left. She turned in the opposite direction from the hotel. She was going to walk for a while, think things out.

Fifteen minutes later she came to a shabby multiplex that was showing several out of date films. She checked the times above the ticket window and saw that one of the films was just beginning.

"Can I help you?" asked the attendant.

"*What's Love Got To Do With It*," she said with a smile. She took the ticket and walked into the theater. The decision saved her life…

Malcolm pulled off his gloves and dumped them in a garbage bag. "Hey Balfire, did you see their reaction when I explained what I'd done to their old ladies?" Balfire was snorting some more coke. His mustache looked like he'd been eating Frosted Flakes and he was grinning like a maniac. The place was a slaughterhouse. Balfire was standing well away from the torn and smoking forms that lay twisted at odd angles all about the couch, which was stained and spattered with blood and other fluids. There was a heavy smell of excrement in the air and there were patches of flesh and clumps of hair and scalp on the coffee table and the floor.

"Yeah," Balfire replied, "but I don't think it penetrated past the pain. Besides, they probably treat the bitches almost as bad as you did. I think they were a lot more impressed when you burned that guy's dick off."

Malcolm was in a fugue state, intoxicated with the violence he had wrought. He felt cleansed and purified by his savagery, a condition of psychopathic rapture that always followed a bout of torture and murder. He felt saint-like, mystically washed in the blood of his victims. Much had gotten on to the rain gear, but his uniform was clean beneath as he stripped the plastic away.

"Where is the girl?" he muttered to himself and then he laughed, "Always room for dessert."

"I don't think she's coming, Malcolm. If she walks in right now we've barely got the time to kill her and nail her to the door."

"Let's flush this toilet," he growled. "We did what we were supposed to do. It's time to get out." He touched his face. There was a neater bandage now. He'd rubbed a considerable amount of coke into it and was barely aware of the pain. He grabbed the suitcases full of cocaine. Balfire picked up the toolbox and they walked out into the empty hallway.

"We're living a charmed life since we met the Doc," Malcolm said as they approached the van. He stopped by the side of it and scanned the parking lot. Suddenly he saw a figure pop up several cars away. It was Billy Joe. He waved them over and opened the trunk of a large blue Mercedes. They deposited the suitcases inside and Billy Joe shut the trunk.

"Get in the car," he said. Malcolm jumped in the front and Balfire into the back. Once the door was closed he turned to Malcolm and asked, "How did it go?"

Malcolm paused for a moment, noting the peculiar smell that accompanied Billy Joe on each occasion that they had seen him. It was a heavy smell with a soporific quality to it, something like cloves but it wasn't cloves. It seemed to Malcolm that there was something else on the other side of the smell, but so far he had not been able to get to it. He thought of it as Billy Joe's magical after-shave. It made him drowsy to be around it very long. He told Billy Joe about what had taken place in the hotel room. Billy Joe laughed darkly at several points along the way, as Malcolm spared no gruesome detail.

"I don't understand about the girl," he said after Malcolm had finished.

"She just wasn't there, Doc."

"I know she wasn't there but there was no reason for her not to be there. She was supposed to be there." Billy Joe fell back against the car seat and closed his eyes. Someone, something was fucking with him. Something had been fucking with him ever since he'd gone to work on that little matter with Alan Douglas, but actually not such a little matter, not to Billy Joe. In the main, things had moved perfectly, except where Douglas was concerned. Now this and he did not see how this was even connected with Douglas. In his mind the girl had been in the room.

Billy Joe suddenly sat bolt upright and said, "She's on her way. Let's go."

They left the car and went back into the hotel, walking purposely but without apparent speed. Billy Joe led them through the lobby and to the elevators. Malcolm marveled once again as he looked around him. It was as if they were invisible. People seemed to look right through them. Not once did he catch anyone's eye.

CarryAnn walked out of the movie theater mulling over the events she had seen on the screen. She was disturbed by the events of the life of the woman in the film. The bright image of romance had a dark underside. She couldn't understand why something that felt so exciting to begin with left her afterwards filled with self-loathing. Her body wanted the cocaine and the sex. Her mind had no idea what it wanted. With few reference points, it was lost in a sea of exotic imagery. Her heart felt so very heavy.

She walked with dogged steps back to the hotel. She was going to be passed around like candy when she got back. She had done more cocaine in the theater bathroom before leaving and could feel the sensuous thrilling of it rushing through her. Her nerve ends tingled as she tried to push aside her despair. She had been surprised to find the small container of coke in her pocket when she'd gone to the bathroom. She'd forgotten it was there. Confidence in her ability to endure rose up inside her. She would do whatever. She would not fold and break and lose what there was left of herself in this madness, this madness that had arrived out of nowhere and threatened to swallow her whole. She felt a sudden strength within her. She would make it through. Tears came to her eyes as she received a clear vision of herself in the times before Simon had come to live in the house.

She tried to understand where the darkness had come from. It was as if another person had come into her body and carried out the actions that followed. Before that, she had avoided sex. She had rebuffed a multitude of boys from anything heavier than make-out scenes. She'd been told she was frigid. *How did it get to this?*

Tears came to her eyes as she remembered her dreams of the future. Now she was a slut, sleeping with anyone who got her high. She wrestled with the despairing images in her mind. Like Little Red Riding Hood, she felt she could make it to grandmother's house if she just kept her eyes in front of her and kept walking. *Whatever it took*, she thought. She'd do whatever it took and start all over… somehow.

She was several feet from the door of the hotel suite when she first sensed something wrong. The hairs on the nape of her neck began to shiver from an invisible breeze. There was a smell in the air like roasting meat, underlying this was another smell that she remembered from when she had once burned her hair with a cigarette. She knocked at the door. There was no response. Her bad feeling increased. She extracted the key from her pocket and inserted it into the lock. Just before she turned it, she felt a flood of relief. They would have had to test the cocaine. That explained the strange smells and why no one had come to the door. Royce knew that she had a key. *The smell was from chemicals, which often had an unpleasant odor.* This comforting thought remained with her until she swung the door open.

The carnage that seared its image into her mind was like a nightmare from Hell. A hideous stinking abattoir, filled with the smells of burnt hair and flesh, vomit and shit with the coppery under-taste of blood. It overpowered her and she fell to her knees retching forth the half-digested contents of her meal. It was hard to stop, her eyes kept being drawn back to the massacre in front of her.

She had seen horror films, violent crime thrillers, but nothing, nothing had prepared her for this. Eyes had been burned from their sockets. Ears and lips were missing. Morales' crotch area was a black ruin. They had been beaten, slashed and burned beyond recognition. Royce's penis hung out of his mouth onto his chin. Except for their clothing, CarryAnn would not have even known who they were.

The feeling of lightness that she'd had earlier suddenly turned to something very strong and concentrated. Her mind was removed from its inability to deal with what it saw. It was replaced with another awareness and in the middle of it, CarryAnn felt a terrible urgency. *Danger was imminent.* She jumped to her feet and ran in to the bedroom. She jammed her clothes and her purse into her overnight bag. As she was racing through the living room, she noticed one of the remaining kilos of coke. She slid it into a paper food sack and this too went into the bag. Then she was out the door.

They got into the elevator, which was again empty. Malcolm and Balfire stood to one side, giving Billy Joe his own half of the elevator. Neither of them liked to be too close to him. He gave off waves of evil that made even hardened criminals like themselves cringe. Malcolm studied him as they rode up. He looked very different from the first time they had seen him. His features seemed to rearrange themselves, but it was always him. There was a haze surrounding his form that made him seem blurred. He was wearing jeans and a western shirt with a ten-gallon hat on his head. He looked like a cowboy from Arizona. He smiled to himself as he toyed with the bolo tie around his neck.

CarryAnn ran out the door. She looked down the hallway and, seeing no one, ran toward the exit stairs. As she passed the elevator she slowed her pace, continuing at a hurried walk toward the fire door at the end of the long hallway.

Behind her she heard the elevator door opening. She looked back and saw three men emerge, moving quickly in the direction of the room. She felt a cold knife of fear dig into her bowels.

Suddenly one of them turned and called out to her. She felt her limbs become dead as she struggled to keep walking. It was like being under water. She stopped and turned. The man who called out was walking toward her.

There was thirty yards between them but she could hear with a supernatural clarity everything the man was saying. CarryAnn was trembling but unable to move.

"Where are you going little girl?" Billy Joe asked. He was gliding toward her and there was a dark corona glowing around his body. CarryAnn could see lights that burst like camera flashes and then disappeared. The corona swelled until it seemed to be touching the walls on either side of the hallway. She felt a terrible chill pervading her body, coupled with a drowsiness that threatened to put her to sleep on her feet. She found herself walking toward him.

"I'm going to die," she thought. "I'm going to die just like those men did."

As Billy Joe came to the elevator, it suddenly opened and a house-cleaning cart was pushed out in front of him, followed by two uniformed cleaning women. His way was blocked and the spell abruptly broken.

CarryAnn's mind was immediately freed from Billy Joe's control. She turned and ran with all her strength to the exit, went through it and flew down the stairs, through the lobby and into the street where she jumped into a waiting cab.

"Where to?" the driver asked.

"Just go. Go now!" she cried.

Back on the fifth floor, Billy Joe probed the minds of the cleaning ladies and emptied their memories. Then they went down on the elevator and Billy Joe sent his companions back to the van. Later he rejoined them in the parking lot. "Head for L.A. now." He handed Malcolm a cell phone. "I'll call you tomorrow. We'll finish up our business. You've got a flight out the day after."

"What about the girl?" asked Malcolm.

"She'll be taken care of." Billy Joe's wicked smile remained with them for most of their ride across the desert. Not even a great many beers were sufficient to erase it.

Chapter Eleven

Forty-five minutes later, Detective Bill Swanson walked past a weeping chambermaid and shouldered his way into the room. The first policeman on the scene had mercifully opened the windows, but the charnel house smell was still strong. There was fresh vomit on the floor, joining CarryAnn's. Swanson had also stepped over it in several places on his way down the hall.

"Who found the bodies?" Swanson asked no one in particular.

"Kieler, sir," answered a patrol sergeant. "He's not feeling too well right now."

Swanson grunted and looked at the display in front of him, slowly shaking his head. "This is about as bad as I've seen. What are you doing here?" He turned to face the officer.

"Kieler called for backup. We were the closest unit." He gestured to his partner, a large black man who was leaning against the wall by the front door.

Swanson looked at the technicians milling around. "This scene virgin?"

"Other than the upchuck, first thing we did was close everything off. Only person actually inside was Kieler and he didn't stay long before he got into trouble." The patrol sergeant nodded with his head in the direction of the bathroom. "Maids found the bodies when they came to clean. They didn't even go in, just stood in the hallway screaming until the manager came. They were outside when we arrived. I talked to them all. The manager doesn't know anything except what's in the computer. I've got that info here. We've just been waiting for you." He handed Swanson his notebook. "The maids are disoriented and I haven't gotten anything out of them."

Swanson looked at the officer's nametag, "Good work, Officer Cuso. Maybe you and your partner could get Kieler squared away. I'll talk to him later. I want him down by the elevator. Keep away the curious and the press. You two make the rounds, interview the guests and talk with the staff. I'll send you some help when they get here."

"Right." Cuso waved to his partner and they left.

"Swannee." He turned to find "Mr. Rogers" standing behind him, so called because of his resemblance to the kiddy TV show personality. Despite his benign manner, Lt. Vernon Butler was one of the most decorated police officers on the Phoenix police force and Swanson's superior in the department.

"Afternoon, Lieutenant." Swanson stepped back to give him access to the room.

“Jesus Christ! What happened here?” Butler surveyed the bodies. “You know anything yet?”

“I just got here. So far nobody saw or knows anything.”

“Why am I not surprised to hear that? I hate to sound like somebody from the Psychic Friends Network but it looks to me like we’ve got a few drug-related homicides here.”

Swanson arched his eyebrow at the lieutenant. “Well, there’s white powder scattered everywhere, three of the dead have a south of the border look. I’d say you’re demonstrating that uncanny cop sense you’re noted for, Lieutenant.”

Butler chuckled and winked at Swanson. “*Touché*,” he replied.

“We meet again I see.” Another man had now entered the room. Around 5’2”, he might have weighed a hundred pounds and looked like an undernourished sixteen year old boy, except that he was losing his hair. A transplanted Mexican national, Dr. Alfonso Fuentes was the assistant medical examiner. He was actually the head of the department in everything except name because no one ever saw Dr. Postern, who had not worked a case in ten years and retained his post through long standing political connections.

“Well, let me by,” he said testily, “I’ve got work to do.”

Neither detective was offended as he pushed past them. It was a long-standing game with them. Fuentes set his case down and went toward the bodies.

Butler said, “May I suggest the Johannesburg Riesling ‘72 as an accompaniment, followed by the Helter Skelter ‘69?”

“Very funny,” Fuentes said over his shoulder but they heard him snickering as he investigated the bodies.

“See anybody you recognize from the old country, Doc?” Swanson asked.

No one in the room cared about the men that were sprawled about. Without anyone having said so, it was already decided that they were scum. For most of the officials on the scene, especially those with a few years on the force, this was as close as they ever came to seeing justice done. They’d long ago given up on the court system.

Fuentes pulled at the cuffs of his surgical gloves, getting a crisp snap from each one of them. He turned and said, “What we have here, Sergeant Swanson, is something rather less than ethnically identifiable. What we have here is ALPO.”

Laughter filled the room as Fuentes went back to work. By this time the room had become crowded and flashbulbs were going off as evidence was being gathered. Lieutenant Butler grabbed Swanson by the elbow and guided him from the room. “Doesn’t that one near the wall look like that skell Bettencourt that we pulled in for a double homicide last year, those black dealers from Scottsdale?”

“You can find anything remotely identifiable from that?” Swanson gestured at the gruesome tableau.

“The ponytail… I don’t know… just a vibe I guess.”

“Would be too bad if it was, wouldn’t it?”

“Yeah, it really would.”

They came on a still white-faced Officer Kieler near the elevator. Swanson put his hand on his shoulder and asked, “You feeling better now, son?”

Kieler was a slender young man in his mid-twenties, blond and tanned. He looked like a thousand other young men in the Phoenix metro area. Swanson wondered how long he would last. “Yes, Sir,” he replied. “I’m sorry I got sick. I’ve never seen anything like it. I can’t believe you ever get used to something like that.”

“You don’t really,” Swanson said with a smile. “You just tell yourself that you do.”

After Swanson and Butler had made their way to the elevators, Butler turned to him and said, “That was a nice touch, Swannee. I didn’t know you had all that sensitivity in there with those tire irons and busted door jambs.”

“I don’t Lieutenant, but he doesn’t need to know everything right away.”

ISLAND OF MAUI, HAWAII

As they came out of the small strip town of Kuau, Ho’okipa Park began to emerge on their left. It was a week shy of the full moon and moonbeams danced like thousands of shattered spotlights on the thundering waves that rolled in huge combers to the beach. Ho’okipa had become world famous in recent years as a wind surfing beach and now devotees flew in from all over the world to take advantage of its perfect conditions.

“Wow,” Whip exclaimed as he leaned toward the window and looked out over the majestic vista. “It’s something...” his voice trailed off as he realized the futility of words.

Alan smiled, “Beautiful isn’t it? This is one of those rare nights when the waves are really up. There are probably a lot of board surfers out there right now. You want to pull in for a bit, or are you too tired?”

“No, I mean yeah, let’s stop and no, I’m not tired. I won’t be able to think about sleep anyway until we’ve talked a little.”

Alan looked at his brother-in-law as he hit the turn signal. There was weariness about his features that belied his words. He felt an awful fear that Whip was going to confess to the murder of Calvin Withers. But if that was the case, Alan knew he would take no action. What he feared was the discovery of some darkness in Whip that, motivated by blind rage, had made it possible for him to burn a man alive.

He steered the Jeep to the edge of a bluff. Whip followed Alan as he climbed over a railing and found a seat on the grass. They sat for a while, each lost in his thoughts.

Alan turned to Whip and put his hand on the back of his neck and began to gently knead the muscles. His touch told him that Whip was tense. "So, what is it?"

Whip turned from the water and caught Alan's eyes. "It's hard to know where to start, Alan. I've been looking for a way to explain and I still haven't come up with a method I like. It's all so unbelievable. I can't imagine what you're going to think when I'm done."

Alan removed his hand and leaned back on his elbows, watching the moon move in and out of the clouds. "Whip, whatever you have to tell me might be strange, but sooner or later you're going to have to tell me and it's not like I'm a stranger, or unaware of how strange things can be."

Whip lit a cigarette and blew out a long stream of smoke. "First I have to apologize for running out without a word. That was a rotten thing to do to you."

"Go on," Alan said.

"I don't know how to explain what Elizabeth's death did to me. I left the funeral early. I couldn't take it anymore. I was angry, really angry. I hated my life at that moment. Maybe I was angry with you too, for not protecting her. I rented a car and drove to Florida, some vague idea connected with playing baseball, I guess, but I just drove around for weeks. I stayed in Key West for a while and then one day I just got on a plane for India."

"India!" Alan sat up. "I've got to ask you Whip, before we go any further. Did you kill Calvin Withers?"

"Who is he?" There was confusion and curiosity in Whip's face and Alan did not doubt he was telling the truth.

"It's not important now, go on."

Whip looked at Alan as if he wanted some further explanation but then continued. "Well, I traveled around India for a while. I went to Egypt and Cyprus, a lot of places. They're not important. Then I went back to India again. Something kept calling me back there and one day I wound up in the foothills of the Himalayas. I'd been walking all morning, mostly up hill and I hadn't eaten for the better part of a week. I'd been fasting. I'd taken some psychedelics a few days before, so I was still tripping. Let me tell you, tripping in India is not like anywhere else."

Alan interrupted him. "I've never known you to experiment with drugs, Whip."

"I did a lot of them for a while and a lot of good things happened as a result. I just don't want you tying in what I'm going to tell you with a drug experience. This was way past that. Anyway, I got really tired at one point so I climbed some rocks and stretched out in the sun, closed my eyes and just drifted away. The next thing I knew I was floating through the air."

Whip saw the look in Alan's eyes and said, "Just listen to the story all the way through, make up your mind then. It's not going to make any difference if you believe me, except to maybe put you on guard and save you some real trouble, because this is all about you."

"Me!" Alan looked incredulous.

"Just let me tell you what happened. I was floating over the same path I had been walking on. After a while I turned onto another path and then another and then another. Finally I came to the top of a ridge and I could see below me a huge bowl, an amphitheater of forest and meadows. There was a cabin off to the side hidden among some trees. Smoke was coming from a chimney. I floated down to the cabin and there, sitting on the steps out in front, was this ancient man. He had a colored hat on, like a skullcap. It was mostly a deep red but it had many other colors woven through it. He looked Chinese, like one of those carved ivory figurines you see in antique shops. He even had the long mustache. He looked up and saw me floating in the air and he raised a hand and waved. Then he smiled. God, Alan, when he smiled it was like the power of the sun was inside him. At that exact moment, the images faded and I woke up back on the rock."

"So you weren't actually flying then?" Alan was teasing him.

"Jesus, Alan. You want to poke fun? You're not making this easy on me. I haven't even gotten to the hard part yet."

Alan's face grew serious. "I'm sorry. I didn't mean anything by that. Go on." Alan urged.

Whip couldn't hide his smile. "It's ironic really, if you were the one telling the story, you know that I would be ten times worse."

Alan laughed, "That's a conservative figure!"

"So, I woke up. I was filled with this burning urgency to be up the road. I remembered every detail of the way to the cabin from the dream and I was filled with energy. I could have climbed Mt. Everest right then. I took off, and after many a winding and turning, I saw the cabin ahead of me as dusk was falling. I can tell you no one ever finds their way there by accident.

"As I made my way to the cabin, I saw the old man sitting on the steps, just as he was in the dream. He had the hat on and he was smoking his pipe. He was blowing smoke rings and grinning at me. 'Hah!' he said, and then got up and went inside. He came back out with two cups of tea. He gave me one and patted the space next to him on the steps. I sat down. I sat down and drank the tea and neither of us said a word for a long time. But Alan, that time was as filled with things, things I'd never thought nor dreamed, but more real than anywhere I have been in this life." Whip paused here, unable to go on for a while.

Alan stared off at the waves crashing on the reef. He felt very different than he had when Whip had started. He was feeling something he could not define, but within that feeling was a trace of poignant regret and an uneasiness that gave him a brief shudder.

"Finally, he spoke." Whip stood up and stared away into the darkness that crouched over the ocean. "He said I should call him Ming. 'That will do,' he said. He'd come from Tibet a long time ago. I asked him if it had something to do with the Chinese occupation and he laughed, 'Oh, long before that.'

"I felt this immensity of time afterwards. It's almost impossible to explain what was happening to me. I kept getting flashes of places, towers shrouded in mist, Mongol warriors on horseback and a man in bright brocaded green and yellow robes standing in a courtyard in the sun, a spider crawling across a flagstone. For the moment I beheld them, they were as real as the moment we're in right now." Whip paused, his mind searching for words that would not come. They sat there in the night, watching stars twinkle in and out of the clouds.

"I asked him any number of questions. He kept saying, 'I don't know' and after a while, I was saying it too and it was like I really didn't know. My identity, my sense of self, had been sucked away. I asked him what his purpose was, what he did... He said he was a pilgrim, a seeker after the higher order of things. He said there was something called 'ageless wisdom' that had been known by certain individuals since before recorded history. It was always the same no matter through what tradition one might discover it. He said there were, are, gateways to it through every religion and culture, but religion and culture were blinds.

"You know Alan, when he was talking to me it was like he wasn't using words. I didn't realize this until afterwards. It was more like food than anything else. It changed me. It's still changing me, and I can still see his face as clearly as if he were still standing there."

Alan tossed a pebble at the ocean, his mind still drinking in Whip's reflections. "There are a lot of strange things in the world, Whip. Looks like you ran across one of them."

"More than strange, Alan. This happened at the end of my trip. I'd seen plenty strange before that. This man was different from all of the rest. I don't know how else to put it. It wasn't just the power of his presence. I'd met some powerful beings before that, 'gurus' they called them. I'd seen magicians, fakirs and other things. This man had a goodness about him that just washed over you. He was so small and meek, yet at the same time, you felt like he could lift his hand and move a mountain if he wanted to. There's a lot more, too."

"A lot more what?" Alan asked.

"A lot more that has to do with you."

"You going to tell me about it?" He was anxious for Whip to go on but he was very much afraid of what Whip was going to say.

"I want very much to tell you, it's not easy though. It's important that you believe me but I'm afraid you won't or that you'll get angry."

Alan's discomfort increased. "Whip, I promise to keep my mind open and my emotions in check. There have been a lot of things going down that don't make sense. Maybe this is the part that is missing."

"It is, Alan. Just let me get through it. Then we can talk. I spent the night there. He put me up in a little room in the back. I never slept so well in my life. The next morning, while we were having more tea and some cakes he mentioned your name."

"My name?" Alan felt goose bumps rising on the surface of his skin.

"He said, 'Alan Douglas is your friend.'"

"Jesus!" Alan exclaimed.

"He mentioned Elizabeth, that she was dead and nothing we knew concerning her death was real. You can imagine my reaction. He raised his hand and said, 'Sit, sit.' I sat. You okay to hear the rest of this? It's going to be outrageous. I was right there and I couldn't believe it."

Alan could feel the nerve currents humming in his body. The air around him was charged with energy. Maybe now he would find the answers to the questions that had eluded him for so long. "Tell me your story Whip."

"There's a man out there somewhere, Alan. Ming didn't tell me where and he didn't tell me who. This man is committed to your destruction, not just your physical destruction, not just the ruin of your life and everything you love but the eternal torment and enslavement of your soul. He killed Elizabeth, or had her killed and there is someone named Wendy who is going to die soon."

"Wendy is already dead." Alan said softly.

"I see," Whip replied quietly. "Wendy and others, many others, are dead because of this man. This man, if you can call him that, is a devoted practitioner of evil. He has considerable power and he is dedicated to your ruin."

"Why me?" Alan questioned with a nervous laugh. From anyone else the things he was hearing would have seemed absurd. But Whip's words rang with truth in the place inside him where he judged such things.

"Ming says that in your past life, you were a student of the occult arts in the city of New Orleans. You had a deep understanding of the practice of Magic and you used it for the betterment of those around you."

Whip continued, "During this time, there were a series of disappearances, mostly prostitutes but other women as well. Several bodies were found and there was evidence of torture. The local police were powerless to discover the perpetrator. The daughter of a powerful industrialist disappeared and finally her father came to you. You had a reputation for finding things that were lost, even people on occasion.

"At this point you began to investigate, using certain supersensory powers that you possessed. After a series of events that nearly cost you your life, you were able to bring to justice one William Joseph Fausten."

"Jesus!" Alan exclaimed, "Billy Joe Fausten. I've heard of him. I studied those murders!"

"Then you've also heard of Axel Touissant."

"Incredible," Alan murmured.

"Ming says you were him. With the help of the police you were able to rescue the missing daughter. Fausten was caught in the act of sacrificing her. Based on physical evidence and your testimony, Fausten was sentenced to death in the electric chair. He died there cursing your name and swearing eternal vengeance. The ceremony you interrupted was for the purpose of raising Fausten to an exempt state in the infernal order. He would have been forever beyond the reach of the justice of man, if the ceremony had been completed. Several of his lifetimes had been dedicated to that moment. Very few ever reach it. He would have had tremendous power if he had achieved it. Because of you, it didn't happen."

"Well I guess he's got a reason to be pissed off," Alan said with lightheartedness that he did not feel. "So he's back now?"

"He's back Alan, and he's behind everything that has happened. He had Elizabeth killed. He was responsible for the conditions that cost you your job but, except for Elizabeth, nothing has gone exactly the way he intended, because of Ming."

"How's that?"

"When Elizabeth was murdered, you were supposed to go mad from grief and alcohol. That didn't happen. Fausten does not understand who or what is thwarting his efforts. He is probing everywhere to find the cause, but he can't see Ming. Besides all of this, he is now very much involved in again completing the same ritual that you stopped. This will give him the exempt status he wants more than anything, even more than your destruction. The conditions are right every forty-nine years. Those conditions will exist again in three weeks."

"Jesus!" Alan exclaimed again. "This is like something out of a Dennis Wheatley novel."

"As fantastic as it sounds Alan, yes. But you are not alone, Ming will help you."

Alan tossed more pebbles towards the sea. The moon had gone behind a heavy bank of clouds and their features fell into shadow. "Why is Ming helping me?" he asked.

"Apparently you did him a great service once. At the time you were both members of a monastic order in Italy. Ming was in grave spiritual danger. You saved him and brought him to safety. Ming says the entirety of existence is woven on a web. Everything is connected to and affects everything else. Our manifest world exists in a place known as the sub-creation, or sub-matrix, the world of Karma. It is here that Fausten and others like him operate. It is composed of all the thoughts and actions of humanity. It is not the real world. The real world is heaven. The job of people like Ming is to free the human soul from its bondage to the sub-creation. The intentions of people like Fausten are to keep them there. But there is a system of checks and balances in this world. Ming and his kind are only allowed certain latitude. Events must be allowed to run their course. Painful trials must be endured. However, Ming owes you and because he owes you, he is free to help you."

"One thing, Whip, how come if I was an Italian monk in one life and a powerful white magician in another, I'm a homicide cop in this one?"

"Ming says things don't run in a straight line, logic must be discarded. You are what you are in response to the way everything else is and to the needs of your personal growth. The scene is always set for the most perfect resolution of the outstanding needs of Karma. In the end everything works out. But that might be tomorrow, or it might be ten thousand years from now. This is where personal initiative comes in. He says you have everything you need at your disposal, it just has to be accessed. He's going to help you do this. He also said that no matter what, you still wouldn't be able to defeat Billy Joe."

"What!" Alan cried. "Then what the hell is the point?"

"Relax, Alan, Ming is going to explain everything."

Alan sighed and got to his feet. "When's that going to be?" The moon had just emerged from the clouds and now all of the landscape was bathed in its light. Alan looked at Whip, once again able to see him clearly.

Whip grinned and put his arm on Alan's shoulder. "Whenever it happens," he said softly.

Billy Joe had been sitting motionless for hours, but no matter how intensely he concentrated, he had no success. He could see the girl. He could touch her with his mind, feel her fear and confusion. He could smell it. It wreathed through his mind like a fine perfume but he could not pin her down as he had others in the past. She moved like a blob of mercury on a vibrating glass. When he tried to fix her, hold her, she was no longer there. Anger was welling in him, throwing off his concentration. This had never happened before. *Someone, something, was fucking with the equation.* He looked everywhere around her for its source but he could find nothing.

Earlier he had probed for Douglas and had similar difficulties. One moment he could see him clearly, read his thoughts, see all that he saw through his eyes and then he was gone, the connection was broken. He found that he could travel with Douglas for hours, then all of a sudden he would be there no more and all his arts would avail him nothing until the door was opened again.

What was he missing? The hearts and thoughts of others were generally available to him. This power he'd carried with him into this life, he had achieved it centuries ago. Now he was having difficulty with the girl as well. Who was blocking him? *Douglas didn't have the juice for it.* He hadn't thought much about it the first time their paths crossed. Douglas had power then himself but now he did not know about it and therefore he did not really have it. *Douglas had no idea about what he had been in the past.*

He rose up from the woven mat on which he had been sitting. His satin robe made a hissing sound as it slid across the hardwood floor. The room was in shadows except for the long table towards which he was walking. A direct beam shone down from an overhead track light. Below it hung an elaborate complexity of tubes and variously shaped containers. There was a haze of heat vibrating just above one beaker under which a small metal coil glowed.

The scream would go on until it died from the lack of breath to propel it. Then the small form that lay beneath the twisted apparatus would shudder and suck for air until it had taken in enough to scream again. Billy Joe needed, or felt that he needed this operation to tune his consciousness to a specific state. He admitted to himself that it might not be strictly necessary. He could have played the tape of one of his previous sessions and put it out over the sound system. *But where was the fun in that?* And there was a particular school of thought which said that authenticity was required in every act that sought to produce accurate results. One would hardly use a fake hand, however artfully crafted, when a "hand of glory" was called for. You could scarcely sacrifice the same victim twice in two separate ceremonies. Some members of the infernal kingdom could take a deadly offense at that sort of economy. Besides, why should he? There were more warm bodies about than he would ever need and he was a purist.

The truth was that he loved his work. He loved every detail of it and he knew that if it produced no other results than the intense enjoyment he received from its practice, that was surely enough. Many of his breed had no finesse at all, no control of the wonderful passions that such artistry provoked. The ecstasy that he obtained was every bit as transcendental, as much of a transfiguration as the rapture of the saints. Truly it was much, much more... or he would have gone that route a long time ago. He'd looked into it. He'd gone a ways with it but compared with this there was no contest and no satisfaction. That road was a lie and they deserved the results they got. *What did you expect from a God that crucified his own son?* This was proof that God hated weakness. Jesus had embarrassed God and God had then humiliated him for all eternity. The reality of the true God, the reality of nature, was blood and destruction. What fool would see it otherwise? What did history show? *Did the tiger spare the deer from some higher altruistic motivation?* That would surely be the end of the tiger.

He looked down at the small form that was bound by strong leather cuffs on all four limbs, in two places across the torso and one thick band across the forehead. The eyes stared upward at him. He drank in the absolute terror that he saw there. It made him as high as if he had just taken a shot of pure coke. The mixture of unbearable pain and horror was a heady brew indeed. He ran one white manicured hand through the damp hair that lay limp against the scalp. "Hot enough for you?" he asked. Another scream pierced the air and continued until it ended in a bout of asthmatic gasping.

Above the buckled form, two glass spouts rotated at opposite ends in a figure eight. Their paths moved from the feet, inside to the hips and across the stomach to the shoulder, across the neck and then back to the feet in an opposite curve. One of the tubes ran directly from the heated beaker. The other extended out from a similar beaker, but this one sat in a bed of dry ice. The naked body of the young boy was stitched with red blisters of a woven infinity. The tubes that moved in the air above him varied in their speed so that the drops fell in places that could not be anticipated. The timer controlling the flow of liquid was set to release the drops at odd moments. Sometimes nothing would fall for a minute or more. Then, six drops might fall in one minute. There was no way to anticipate whether the drops would be hot or cold.

He had cleaned out the boy's system prior to strapping him to the table. The idea of the smell of shit mingling with his meditations, under the present circumstances, was not useful to the proceedings. It was not that he was opposed to the smell of shit. It was a part of life and certainly had its place in his rituals. This was just not one of them. The boy had wet himself several times and he could taste the acid tang of it in his nostrils, but this was okay.

He had appropriated the boy from a park near his house earlier in the day. That part of things was always easy. He would just reach into the mind and place whatever image was suitable there. Very shortly his victims would present themselves to him.

"Please, please, let me go. I'll do anything!" the boy cried. Billy Joe cocked his head to one side and looked at him. He knew what the boy meant. The boy was around eleven years old, still pre-pubescent, but street wise.

"You would in any case," he replied. "Do you think I would go through all this trouble just for that? If that were what I wanted, you would run across broken glass to give it to me. A nice image, don't you think?" He smiled as he said this, drinking deeply again from the boy's fear. He had done things of a certain kind with children of either sex in the past, when he had wanted to, had done them because they swelled the sense of evil within him and as an insult hurled at the heavens. Sexual desire, manifested out of a driven need, was not in him. His sexual desire had long been transformed into something else. He saw himself as the power behind that drive and would often encourage perverted acts in the minds of those who might be even slightly so disposed. He chuckled at the memory of some of the lives he had ruined in this way.

"No, I do not think that is what we have in store for you tonight." He walked to a computer bank against one wall and tapped a button. The machinery above the boy stopped turning. Two final drips hit his body producing another scream. He started unbuckling the restraints. "I've been remiss in my duties as a host. There's another part of the house I want to show you, someone I want you to meet. His table manners are bad, so I'm afraid the room is not as nice as this." Horror shook the boy's frame as the import of some greater torture went through his mind and he began to struggle violently. The man made a pass with one hand over his head and spoke a brief series of words. The boy's trembling stopped and he lay quite still.

The room was quiet except for the barely perceptible whisking of a fan high overhead. It was time now to try another tack. He stared down benevolently at the boy who, eyes wide, stared back at him. "I hope you don't think this is all I had planned for you. That was just a warm-up. As they say in show business, 'you ain't seen nothing yet.'"

"Please, please, God, let me go," the boy whimpered.

Billy Joe bent low to his ear and said, "I'll tell you a little secret. I hope it will make you feel better." He brought his lips very close to the boy's ear and inhaled the stink of his fear. Then he whispered, "There is no God."

There is nothing like being thrashed on coke, lack of sleep and in fear for your life to make an airline flight memorable. An extra edge is added when you are not yet sixteen, don't know where your mother is, just walked in on a massacre and are in fear that an unknown stranger with magical powers is pursuing you. CarryAnn would have lost it, would have gone screaming down the aisle and become *The National Enquirer* cannon fodder, if not for the large bottle of Grand Marnier that Royce had bought for her days ago which, by fortune or fate, had materialized during a search of her daypack. She was further aided by the fact that several days of round-the-clock partying had added adult shadows under her eyes and various temporary lines to her face. No one paid too much attention to her, and the plane being just half full had made it possible for her to sit alone.

The first half-hour found her teetering on the edge of an all-out panic attack. Finally, the alcohol, adrenaline poisoning and lack of sleep caused her to drift off into a trance state of dark dreams. Very shortly the plane landed at LAX. She went through the motions of negotiating her way to the front gates, passing as just one more travel wearied stranger among thousands headed in every direction. She jumped into the first cab she could find and went directly home.

Home did not look the same anymore. She felt chilled as she walked toward the large empty house. Evening was soon to fall and already little shadows had gathered in the corners. Night was coming. Fear surged in her as she fought the rising panic. They would come for her. She knew this. She had seen them, not very well but they would not know that. She ran to her room and packed a suitcase with everything she thought she might need in her flight to safety, to a place she had not yet discovered.

Going into her mother's room she rummaged everywhere. Luck was with her. Along with a good sum of cash, she found a bank card and hidden away in the far reaches of her mother's clothes closet, wrapped in a red evening dress, a large zip lock bag filled with cocaine. Royce had mentioned in passing that he'd left a stash at the house. She sat there on the floor of the closet, the bag in her hand, tears running down her face. Here was the source of much trouble and she should leave it and go. At the same time, her mind told her this was coin of the realm, negotiable for cash and services everywhere. Her mother was gone in South America. *Maybe she would return that evening. Maybe she would never return at all. Royce and all of his associates were dead. Who knew how far the violence extended?* In the meantime, she was in certain peril. She could not stay in the house. She shoved the cocaine and money into her bag and carried it downstairs with her suitcase, which also contained cocaine.

Half an hour later she was trudging up the long driveway to Tommy White's Topanga Canyon home. The terror continued to tear at her insides. Bad men were looking for her and Tommy White had been a friend of the men they had killed. No one was at the house when she arrived. Setting down her suitcase she searched and found a front door key stashed in a potted plant, just where she had once heard Tommy tell her mother it would be. She let herself in and locked the door. She secreted her suitcase behind a couch and went in search of a place to sleep. There was peculiar smell like food gone bad. She had heard her mother comment on what a terrible housekeeper Tommy was. *He had left something out and it had spoiled during his New York trip.* She had no idea when he was supposed to return. She hoped she might be gone before she saw him or anyone she knew. She would have left already but she needed sleep and she needed a plan. Perhaps her mother would be back soon. She would know what to do.

On the back porch she found a day bed with half a dozen pillows propped up on it. She grabbed several and arranged them underneath it. Then she crawled in and made herself comfortable. The comforter fell nearly to the floor. Anything less than a concentrated search would not discover her. Feeling as secure as she thought possible, she closed her eyes and was soon fast asleep.

Alan rose from his bed as the sun was rising. He went out to the lawn area by the pool and began his morning ritual with a yoga routine known as "The Sun Worship." It was a series of twelve positions that flowed into one another and whose principal benefit was that of stretching. Then he moved into a combination of warm-ups. Some of them were torturous and designed to develop the strength necessary to move quickly from position to position. By the time he had finished these, his body was dripping with sweat. He was toweling off when Whip came out on the deck that encircled the house on the second floor.

"Glad to see you haven't let that part of your life go," he said.

Alan tossed the towel to the grass. "How about you Whip, you still practice anymore? Still remember anything?"

"You looking to find out?" Whip began to roll his shoulders like a prizefighter getting loose in the ring. Then he thumbed his nose twice. Alan laughed.

"Well?" he asked again.

Whip grabbed the railing of the deck and vaulted over it. He plummeted ten feet to the ground, rolled and came up into a crouch.

"Shit, Whip! You could have hurt yourself!" Alan looked at him with alarm.

"You were wondering if I had been staying in shape. I figured you needed an object lesson."

Alan horse-stepped quickly into striking range and threw two quick hand feints at Whip. Whip moved to parry the blows. When he did this, Alan dropped to the ground and caught him behind the ankles with a leg sweep, dropping him quickly.

"Nice, Alan, caught me off guard."

"Don't let it happen again," he said. They sparred vigorously for the next fifteen minutes. Alan dominated the conflict initially, with Whip more or less holding his own toward the end. Though Alan was certainly the superior fighter,

Whip had the advantage of youth and greater speed.

They finished up with a brief *Jujitsu* primer. Alan was anxious to show Whip some of the techniques that the police and professional bouncers used to subdue violent aggressors. Finally they fell to the ground and lay still in the bright sunlight.

"It seems kind of faraway right now. Hard to imagine," Alan said.

"What does?"

"The things we were talking about last night."

"Yeah," Whip scratched his chest, his eyes looking off into the empty blue sky. "Ming says our biggest influence is the power of the day to day, the endless progression of the familiar. It runs on a track from the cradle to the grave and only great souls can break free of its power."

"What does that mean?"

"It means that a man with two heads can say good morning to you, twice. That evening it will have become two men sitting close together. It doesn't mean that a man with two heads did not say hello. I saw things in India that were miraculous. They defied the laws of physics. But the truth is that we just don't know all of the laws of physics. The mind prefers familiar ground. You don't expect to be hit by a car when you cross an empty street, but you still look both ways when you cross. I'm trying to say something but I'm doing it badly. This kind of thing does not lend itself readily to the spoken word."

"You've changed, Whip. You were never interested in anything but women and sports before."

"Well, I'm still interested in women," Whip laughed. "Be careful. Ming didn't tell me everything and he said he'd help but that doesn't mean a whole lot can't go wrong."

"Point taken," Alan pulled himself to his feet. "Let's get cleaned up and have some breakfast."

While they ate, Alan filled Whip in on what he knew concerning the disappearances and the events at the District Attorney's Office. He'd be leaving soon to start his investigation.

"I'm not going to be much good as a tour guide, Whip. You'll have to find the island by yourself," Alan said as he put together the things that he would take with him, including the Glock 9 that he had brought with him from New York.

"I'll catch a ride with you to the car rental place then, if that's okay?" Whip popped a last papaya wedge into his mouth and got up from the table. He started clearing away the table when Alan stopped him.

"Don't worry about those. I've got someone who comes by to put the place in order. As for a car, I can do you one better. Come with me." Alan led him out the front door into the parking area and around the side of the house to the garage. He pressed a button in a concealed recess and the garage door lifted up. "The ultimate island car," Alan said and gestured toward the interior at a shiny, red dune buggy. "You're free to use it while you're here, Whip. There's a lockbox by the shift, it contains the CD player and a bunch of discs. I don't know what you listen to but there's a lot of Springsteen, Neville Brothers, Stevie Wonder and of course, Tom Waits."

"Yeah, I remember you used to drive Elizabeth nuts playing Tom Waits so much. This is great!" Whip walked around the car and jumped in. The keys were in the ignition. He turned the key and the car started with a throaty roar. "Wow! Quite the power plant."

"She's supercharged. Be careful, this baby can really move." Whip pulled it out into the sunlight and then turned it off. He got out and walked around, inspecting it closely. His eyes lit up as he studied the chromed engine extending from the rear.

"You must have spent some money on this!"

"Ten grand, but you can hardly get an economy car for that." Alan flipped the front catches and pulled the top back into the trunk. "I haven't used it much, but it will go anywhere. There's a lot to see on this island, excellent maps in the glove compartment, an anti-theft switch under the dash. No one can steal it. Even the battery needs a special key to come off. We get a lot of vehicle crime here. Look, I've got to go downtown now. I'm late as it is." Alan pulled a card from his wallet and wrote a number on the back. He handed it to Whip. "Call me and we'll make plans for dinner later. There's a house key on the car ring. Lock up when you go, okay?"

Alan's cheeks crinkled in a smile. "It's really good to see you again, Whip." He raised his hand in a wave and walked off toward the Jeep.

Whip watched him go, his heart warming with the flood of memories that came as Alan climbed into the vehicle. Seconds later he was gone. A multitude of birds was singing in the trees that surrounded the house. The scent of many different flowers was in the air. Whip thought how close to heaven it was here. *So hard to imagine that the darkness which pursued them could ever make its presence known in a place like this.*

He walked to the edge of the driveway that ran for fifty yards before it met the road. He looked back at the house and thought how much it resembled the house Alan had always told him he would build here. It was a two-story pentagon built principally of cedar, with some redwood and other woods he didn't recognize. The house was set on metal pylons that raised it up into the air. A large deck encircled the second floor. On the near side, the ground rose up so that the first floor was just a few feet above the ground. Large flagstones ran to a wooden staircase. On the further side, the ground fell steeply into a gully where pieces of rebar jutted up from the bottom in preparation for a cement pour. There was a profusion of flowers everywhere. Whip had seen many of them in his travels, hibiscus, oleander and bougainvillea. The garage was set apart from the house and ten feet further along there was a large outbuilding he assumed was a workshop and storage area. Between it and the garage ran another flagstone walkway that led to the back of the house. Flowering vines ran up the side of the garage.

Whip followed a set of steps around to the rear of the house. Besides the pool and cabana, there was a redwood hot tub set at the edge of a ravine that fell away into jungle. Directly behind the pool, a path ran by the side of a massive banyan tree whose double trunk and dropped roots encompassed an area of over one thousand square feet. Whip walked under it and came into an orchard. Because the land fell away in a gradual descent he could see that Alan had inherited a maze of fruit trees that covered several acres of land. There were bananas, papayas, avocados, macadamia and several mango trees. Many of the plants had obviously been there for some time. The mango trees were enormous and ran in a line down the gentle slope. Whip followed a wide path into the orchard and found that it met with other paths that ran in every direction. There were several little cloistered areas he passed. One was a grape arbor with a table and chairs. Others held stone benches and cast figures of the Buddha. Whip whistled softly through his teeth.

He sat down on a bench by a small koi pond and drank in the serenity of his surroundings. Alan had finally built the dream home of which he had so often spoken, but he'd built it after the death of his dreams. Whip hoped he would be able to enjoy it and perhaps find someone to replace Elizabeth in his life. This would never happen though, until Billy Joe, or whatever he was calling himself now, had been dealt with, if that were possible. When he had asked Ming if it would turn out all right in the end, he had just shaken his head and said, *"I don't know."*

Chapter Twelve

Alan drove through the glistening Haiku morning. It had rained the night before and the sun danced on the moisture-laden foliage. The road received only the minimum of attention necessary to negotiate it. Most of his thought was focused on the struggle to digest the bizarre twist of circumstance that had found its way to his door. He was overjoyed at Whip's return, as for the news he had brought with him, that was another thing. He was shaken to the core, a condition he did not reveal to Whip.

A part of him fought desperately to reject what he had heard. This would mean having to accept the fact that Whip had gone insane. *But what about the information, some of which he could not have received through any normal avenues? How could he know these things?*

If Whip were not insane, then everything else was. It was terrifying to face the reality of things he had long pursued and believed true — that there were other realms of existence every bit as real as the one he dwelt in — now finding he had not *really* believed. Just as before, when he had thought his faith so strong, only to find himself crushed by the loss of his wife.

Suddenly he laughed out loud as he realized he had been saying, "*I don't know*" in his mind. In that instant a face flashed before him, capturing his entire field of vision, and a voice boomed into the car as loud as if it had been emitted from stadium speakers at a rock concert, *"FUCK YOU, DOUGLAS!"* His entire body trembled as if he had received an electric shock. Shaking uncontrollably, he pulled quickly to the side of the road and stopped.

"What the hell!" he exclaimed, still trembling. He did not trust himself to continue driving for a moment. He'd seen something, a momentary flash of features, gone too quickly to recall. There had been an awesome malevolence that chilled him to the bone. He looked at his hands. The knuckles were white where he was gripping the wheel. Slowly he released them. As he held them in front of him, another bolt of electricity went up his spine, less intense than the first.

Alan slowed his breathing and focused on letting the tension ease from his body. Gradually the tremors faded and his calm returned.

"Ming," he voiced in his mind, "if you're real, I could use some help. I don't know what's going on. If you can hear me please...?" For some minutes he remained motionless. He was not strong, outward appearances to the contrary.

Something had been taken out of him during his fall into purgatory and the climb back out. He was less trusting of his own abilities, less clear about who he was. It left him with a dangerous uncertainty that had not been there before. It was the worst kind of liability for a law enforcement officer. Alan had seen it before in members of the force who had been shot or had shot someone else. There was a small hesitation that compromised one's training and it could get you or someone else killed.

It had been some kind of astral attack. Was his adversary coming out of the shadows? Did he know what Whip had told him? These things happened in books and movies. They happened to other people but they did not happen to Alan Douglas. What was he going to do? His usual weapons were clearly no good against someone like Billy Joe. *You can't shoot or handcuff a ghost.* Alan felt a great rage burning inside him at the thought of this vile creature that had so far killed his wife, Wendy and nearly destroyed him as well.

Alan drove the rest of the way to the police station in a state of apprehension, fearful that another attack might be on its way. Nothing like this had ever happened to him before. He'd had positive spiritual experiences and many instances of telepathy and precognition in his work, but there had never been something as cold and alien as this. Alan could feel the taste of iron on his tongue and a cold sweat on his forehead. Slowly, the after-effect receded. By the time he parked his car and was on his way to Ben's office, the painful sting of the memory had faded.

Alan knocked on Ben's door and walked in. Ben was sitting at his desk. The sleeves of his blue shirt were rolled up to the elbows. A fan ruffled his hair as he studied some paperwork before him on the desk. He looked up as Alan walked in. "Nice of you to drop in," he said sarcastically. "Have a seat."

Alan smiled, "Thanks for the warm reception there, Ben. I left you a message saying I'd be a little late. My brother-in-law came in, totally unexpectedly, last night."

Ben laughed, "You're too easy, Alan. I got the message but it is my nature to fuck with everybody as often as I can. It helps me keep my edge."

"You're a truly beautiful human being, Ben, please don't ever change." As he said this, Alan moved to the coffee machine and prepared himself a cup.

"Well, thank you for noticing, Alan, speaking of which, you okay? You look several shades lighter than the last time I saw you."

"I'm fine, Ben, just missed a fender bender on the avenue." Alan lied without thinking about it. There was no way he was going to share the preceding events with Ben. Ben would make lunch meat out of him. Alan fully realized now that, except for Whip, he was all alone. There was no one he could talk to. He saw now how much relationships were built on familiar things, the common ground. Alan wondered how many inhabitants of insane asylums were not actually crazy but victims of situations similar to his own. *How many people talking to themselves, as they walked down a city street, actually had a companion that others could not see?*

Ben stared at Alan for a moment, probing. "Glad you're all right then. Where was this brother-in-law of yours?"

Alan sipped at his coffee and regarded Ben's narrowed eyes. He was going to have to be careful. Ben would quickly notice anything out of the ordinary. Sooner or later an explanation was going to be necessary and no matter when it came, it was not going to be easy. Alan was not comfortable with deceit, but sometimes the truth was even more uncomfortable.

Alan set the coffee down on the desk. "He's been doing a little world traveling, trying to get his mind clear. It surprised the hell out of me, him showing up."

"He set your mind at rest any?" Ben's eyes watched Alan's. Alan had shared his concern about Whip's possible role in the slaying of Calvin Withers.

Alan's face broke up into a broad grin. "As a matter of fact, he did, didn't even know anything about it. A relief for me but it just raises the question again of who did do it."

Ben nodded. "We just need to pull out the right block and all the rest of them are going to come tumbling down." He tapped the paperwork in front of him. "Our disappearances have been upgraded to suspected homicides, blood types all match up. I'm saddened to say that includes Wendy's as well. The remains in the package have her blood type."

Alan's face went grim at the news. He had been prepared for this eventuality but there was always hope. He shook his head as his eyes searched the corners of the room. There was nothing for him to say.

Ben continued, "We sent officers and a forensics team into the homes and neighborhoods of the missing persons and the locations where they were last seen. We might have found something."

"What?" Alan sat forward in his chair.

Ben picked up the phone. "I'll have Manu tell you himself." He spoke into the phone and hung up. Almost immediately the door opened and a Samoan detective entered the room. Alan stared at him in open wonder. He could not believe the man was as big as he was, close to seven feet tall and almost a yard wide. The man smiled and extended his hand to Alan as the introductions were made. Sgt. Manu's hand was as big as a baseball mitt.

Ben watched the exchange and laughed. "Manu is in big demand on narcotics busts when the suspects refuse to open the door. He's also really good during interrogations, just standing around." Ben gestured at a chair and told Manu to sit down.

Manu shrugged. "No can sit dere, chair too small," he said. "I just go stay standing." Manu crossed his arms and faced Ben.

"All right, Manu." Ben grinned at Alan. "Tell us what happened."

Manu's eyes shifted from Ben to Alan and then back to Ben again. "So, Kealoha and me was working da neighborhood where da little *wahine* stay. We talkin to the da neighbor when dis old Filipino come cross da street waving his hands, talking loud but can no tink what he saying."

Alan and Ben were grinning as Sgt. Manu slowly made his way through the story in the pidgin medium that was the *lingua franca* of the islands. What was more amusing was the way Manu was acting out the exchange with body language. Alan was surprised that there was enough space in the room for him to accomplish this.

"So he grabs Kealoha, try pulling him cross da street. Kealoha no wanna to go, look like maybe goin beef him upside da hed." At this point Manu stopped to pull at his crotch. Alan wondered where the man got his suits. They had to be specially made.

Having made an agreeable adjustment, Manu continued, "Anyways, I tell Kealoha wait one minute. I tell de lady we talking to wait one minute, we coming back. Mebee someting happen. Maybe some upcountry cowboy goin trace his dog to da man's house and there gone be trouble." Everybody laughed at this reference to Filipino dog eating, especially black dogs. There were always messages on bulletin boards around the islands for owners looking for their missing "black" dogs.

"So, we go to de guy's hous, all time him talkin, talkin and no can understand a ting. Tank God his daughter at de hous, she gone translate. She say on da day de girl go missing, de ole man on de side house messing wi his flowers. He see little *wahine* come home an go da hous. Ten minutes, one dark van comin up. Two men in jumpsuits, some kine company coverall - can't tell who — no van logo — dey go up and knock den go right in."

Ben and Alan sat quietly drinking in the tableau being painted by Manu, both of them thinking about the van seen in Olowalu, the one that had delivered the crucified hearts.

It took what seemed to Alan a very long time for Manu to complete his tale. "Talking Story" was an art in the islands that had been honed for generations. It was considered very bad form to rush anyone in the process of their tale. Manu went on to say that one of the men had emerged from the house and pulled a footlocker from the van, which he then carried inside. A few minutes later they came back out with it, loaded it into the van and drove away. The reason they were only hearing about it now was that the old man had left that evening on a plane for the homeland and had only just returned. When he'd asked his daughter about the two detectives across the street at the neighbor's house, she had told him about the missing girl. Then Manu delivered the bombshell. *The old man had gotten a very good look at both of the men.* Good enough that he was at that very moment in another part of the station with a police artist working on likenesses.

Alan leaped from his seat and shook his fist in the air. "Alright!" he cried.

"You know it!" Ben exclaimed as they high-fived. Both of them calmed down very quickly when it looked like Manu might want to celebrate too…

They entered the room and lined up behind the artist. The little Filipino man, who looked like he might be as much as ninety years old, was talking a mile a minute. His daughter, an elderly woman with white hair, was calmly translating and using far fewer words in the process. The artist was sitting in front of a computer sketch machine.

"How are we doing, John?" Ben addressed the artist, who was busy working the controls at the direction of the woman. The artist stopped what he was doing and held up his hand to silence the old man.

"We've got one done, there are copies in the print hopper and this one is just about *pau*. Nice looking dude, eh?" They were looking at a drawing of Balfire, large protruding forehead, eyebrows that joined at the center of the forehead, broken nose, thick brutal lips, two weeks growth of beard and a wild mane of red hair. "The old man says this one could be as much as six and a half feet tall and go maybe two hundred and eighty pounds and he's not fat."

Alan felt an eerie sensation crawling up his spinal column. There were alarm bells going off in his mind. "I've seen this man," he said.

"What!" Ben exclaimed.

"I have definitely seen this guy, but I don't know where or when."

"*It seems we stood and talked like this before*," John the artist started singing in a low bluesy growl.

"Save it for the shower," Ben said. Turning to Alan, he said, "Maybe if you see the other guy, maybe that will do it." They waited several minutes for John to put the finishing touches on the composite. It was not as good a likeness as Balfire's. They hadn't gotten the eyes and the chin was wrong.

Alan studied it for a long time, finally he said, "I've seen him too, I think, but this is not the way he looks."

"Let me see if I have this right, you've seen him but this is not the way he looks?" Ben said, "Is that right?"

"You're good, Ben, time has not dulled those razor sharp instincts. It's there for anyone to see, why they pay you the big bucks." Alan looked at the drawing of Balfire again. After a moment he said, "I have definitely seen this guy before and it was not very long ago."

Ben turned to the artist and said, "John, once you're done see that I get a dozen copies of each and extend the thanks of the department to these fine people."

"You got it, Lieutenant."

As they made their way back to Ben's office, Alan said, "Why don't you join Whip and me for dinner this evening?"

Ben stopped outside his door and regarded Alan for a moment. "You know, sooner or later, hopefully sooner, you and I are going to be spending most of our time together. You want to start doing that before we even have to?"

"I'd like you to meet Whip, Ben."

"All right," Ben rolled his shoulders. "I've got no plans for the evening, where do we meet?"

"Charthouse at 7:00. I've got to get over to the DA's now and see what the budget says about hiring a forensic shrink. I want somebody to look over the notes and other evidence, see if we can come up with some profiles."

"Okay." Ben walked into the office and sat down in his chair. "How soon will you be back?" Ben paused and looked at Alan for a few seconds without saying anything more and then he said, "Why do I get the feeling that something is going on… something you're not telling me? If so, I need to know why. Is it a matter of trust or something?"

Alan was momentarily stunned and then shook his head vigorously, "I haven't known you long Ben, but I'd trust you with my life in a moment. If there is something I know, it may be that I feel it's too fantastic to share with anyone else. I can't afford to lose any more credibility."

Ben cocked his head to one side and drummed on the desk with his fingertips. "Now we're getting somewhere," he said. "From the moment you walked in this morning, I could see there was something up. The only thing I know that is different in your life is that your brother-in-law showed up. Whip told you something, told you something fantastic."

"Jesus, Ben, you are scary." Alan's face was plastered with a rueful grin that said it all. "But I'm not talking a little fantastic. I'm talking over-the-river-and-through-the-woods-to-grandmother's-house fantastic."

Ben gave a weary sigh. "Alan, if it's true, whatever it is, no matter how fantastic, then it's true. If it's not — and I'm sure you would have no problem accepting that — then it's not, and we move on to what is. In the meantime, anyone in a position to help can help all the more by knowing what the fuck you know, or think you know."

Alan laughed, a deep down laugh that released a river of stored tension. For a moment he felt dizzy from the change in pressure. "Tonight Ben, I promise. I'll let Whip tell you what he told me. Now I've got to go." And without waiting for a reply, he strode off down the hallway.

Aaron Wilson sat back as far in his chair as he could go without actually tipping it over and crashing to the floor, or so it seemed to Alan. He had remained in that position the entire time that Alan was bringing him up to speed on recent events. Copies of the sketches lay on Aaron's desk. As Alan finished up with his request for forensic help, Aaron slowly brought himself back to an upright position. "I'm not getting the sleep I should be getting at this time in my life," he said.

Alan nodded. Aaron didn't expect a reply and Alan didn't give him one.

"You're in luck, Alan. First of all, we've got one of the best forensic psychiatrists in the country right here on Maui. Secondly, he's free." Aaron held up his hand to cut off Alan's questions. "For years we've had to send away long distance whenever we needed this kind of help, which, thank God, hasn't been all that often. Name of Philip Abadon ring a bell?"

"Oh yeah!" Alan replied. "He worked that L.A. serial strangler case. He wrote the definitive book on behavioral profiling, *The Second Self.* He's a legend, Aaron. He's here?" Alan stared at him in disbelief.

"Well, your timing couldn't be better, a few months ago he dissolved his practice and moved here, said he was tired of the rat race. I met him at one of the mayor's functions when he first arrived, seems like a nice guy. We had a long talk about law enforcement concerns and in the process he offered his services, free of charge, anytime we needed them. Well, we had a big murder case last month, he stepped in and on the basis of his testimony we put a real shithouse rat away for the count.

"When I asked him why he walked away from the limelight and a celebrated career he threw that Nietzsche quote at me about 'looking overlong into the abyss.' He's been focusing his attention in the areas of right and left-brain studies, neurolinguistic programming. He said there is an as yet undiscovered technology in there that could revolutionize the way we handle criminal rehabilitation, which is something both you and I and every rational member of the law enforcement community know is presently a joke.

"I don't know if this makes me prescient or what, but I just got off the phone with him minutes before you walked in. I thought I'd call him, now that we know we're dealing with murder. He wants to talk to you at your convenience. Take your sketches out there. He's supposed to be the best in the world at drawing up profiles based on physical appearance." Aaron was openly grinning now. "Makes you feel good when things start to fall in line, doesn't it? Kinda like help from above. I have a feeling we're gonna nail this scum to the wall soon. I just hope we get there before any more body parts show up." Here he paused and concern flowed into his features. Then he said, "I'm really sorry about Wendy, Alan. It's not definite of course but the numbers, blood type…" He trailed off, unable to continue.

Alan blew air out between pursed lips. "We were getting there. I'll never know now. I do know that I miss her. She made me laugh a lot."

"She made us all laugh. You didn't want to take yourself seriously when she was around. You can cut the atmosphere around this office with a knife. We want these fuckers bad."

Alan got to his feet and extended his hand across the desk to Aaron, "Nobody wants them more than me, Aaron."

"I'm sure you're right, Alan," Aaron replied as he shook his hand. "All the power and assets of this department are behind you and woe befalls any official on this island who impedes your efforts."

Aaron pulled a business card from a leather folder on his desk and passed it to Alan. "That's got the good doctor's particulars. Good hunting."

Alan touched his nose with his left forefinger and said, "Hi ho, Silver" over his shoulder on his way out the door.

As the door closed, Aaron leaned back in his chair, once again indifferent to the possibilities of the law of gravity.

Chapter Thirteen

Billy Joe's rage was like a force of nature. He had been hovering there in Alan's mind, probing for an answer. He had masked his presence, lying in wait like a moray eel for whatever might be swimming by, very still, motionless, holding to a state of non-being, absent, waiting to pounce. He was determined to identify whomever it was blocking his access, impeding his way and then he was going to destroy him. There were ways and Billy Joe knew almost all of them. It was while he was in this place of quiet cloistered observation that someone, something, had slipped inside his mind and given him the psychic equivalence of a tap on the shoulder, a pinch on the ass. Billy Joe's entire being had become inflamed with dark red anger, embarrassed, outraged, violated. He had lost control and betrayed his presence to Douglas, something he had not wanted to do.

The swimmer turned towards the open sea, suddenly possessed of a tremendous vitality coupled with reckless abandon. Somewhere in the back of his mind, warning bells were going off. This was the Pacific Ocean and you did not mess around with the Pacific Ocean, but he had never felt like this in his life. He was unstoppable. The air and water had combined to create a physical ecstasy that flowed across the entire surface of his body. He didn't know why it was happening and he didn't care. His cock was throbbing inside his swimsuit and felt like it was going to explode. Any moment now and it really would explode. He closed his eyes and felt the thick luxurious syrup engulfing his being. An unbearable tickle was coursing up his urethra.

The fifteen-foot tiger shark hit him simultaneously with the first spasm of orgasm and tore out a large chunk of his waist. The rapture was instantly gone, the vitality and confidence gone. Raw cold fear swept through him as he saw the blood swirling in the water. He screamed as the shark hit him again, tearing away a portion of his left calf and shredding his foot. Now another shark hit him in the right shoulder. The water became a thrashing bloody madness as the man died.

High on a bluff overlooking the water stood Billy Joe. No longer enraged, it could not be said he was no longer angry. Anger was always a part of Billy Joe. In fact, if any normal person were to feel the anger that Billy Joe carried with him on a regular basis it would burn them to a cinder.

"Sex and death," he murmured to himself. "What a unique relationship. How splendidly they complement one another." Billy Joe had been in the swimmer's mind throughout the experience, had used it to bring himself back to center. He drank in the fear, bewilderment and pain the way an epicure would sip a rare cognac. Now he was wonderfully fine. And it would last until the scales began to shift once more. For a while he could plot and orchestrate like a surgeon, clearer in mind than any mortal, until the oil of evil and dark sacrifice was required again. Without it, the wheels would seize and Billy Joe would crystallize into something resembling a lump of coal. This never happened, however, because there was always evil to be done.

Billy Joe thought of himself as beyond the restrictions of the common herd. He was free to do his own will as no other was, above limits and laws, past apprehension, unreachable, untouchable, an entity unto himself alone. This is what he thought. But this is not what he was. Everything he did served the will and the interests of a force far older and deeper than he would ever reach. In comparison, he was like a child playing with blocks. Billy Joe served a master who was loyal to no one, just as he was loyal to no one. There were many men like Billy Joe in the world, some less accomplished in their evil, but all moving deliberately down that ancient staircase into the dark splendor. From the ranks of the military and the priesthood, the worlds of politics, commerce and art, from every walk of life they came, again and again, following the image of the false self, into the false light, through countless lifetimes of sorrow, for as long as it might take until their eyes were finally opened…

Kimo pulled his truck into his parent's driveway, turned off the engine and sat where he was. He'd had a full and exhausting day but now the pain was coming back. It had been sneaking around at the edges of sensation for the last ten minutes. He was familiar with the pain by now. He knew its ways, its peculiarities and its temperament. It was sometimes like a spear of fire from out of nowhere, sometimes like a train coming down a long grade, closer by increments. It was a relationship much like a bad love affair. You could see the argument coming. From far down the highway, you could see it coming. The argument that you would not win, that you could never win, that would end the way it always ended — with you, the loser, bleeding on the floor.

It had come before the same way, so many times. Early on you tried to head it off, tried to distract it, change it into something else but it was smarter than you were. *It knew all of the tricks.* It knew what you were up to. It humored you. It could be affectionate even, backing off for a time and letting you breathe, knowing how much greater the shock would be when the facade was ripped away and its real face emerged, the face of pain, devouring pain.

Finally, you didn't try to outsmart it. You knew no matter what you did, it would get you. You could walk around the bear in the clearing. You could wait in the woods for the bear to go away. You could walk boldly out of the woods, right by the bear. No matter what you did, the bear was going to get you. And when the bear got you, it was going to hurt. It was going to hurt a lot. The pain in Kimo's stomach was an argument. It was like a violent argument between your parents when you were six years old and laying in the darkness of your room.

You want them to stop. You pray that they will stop but they don't stop and neither does the pain. The pain came smoking down that long ten percent grade, running for miles and miles, a freight train with a hundred and fifty cars, pulled by three engines and pushed by two. It is a nightmare with red eyes, roaring through the darkness, filled with unbearable sound, filling all space with its presence — demanding and getting your absolute full attention. *It was coming now, coming like the whirlwind in the Bible.* This time though, something else was coming with it.

Kimo lunged across the seat and opened the glove compartment. He fumbled around until he found the amber prescription bottle that he had gotten at Kaiser. He opened it and shook out three Percocet, washing them down with the last of his grape Snapple. The pain was flying down the grade now. The engineer had a big grinning devil's face with razor sharp teeth and it came rending and tearing its way home, home to the center of Kimo's guts.

He climbed from the truck with one hand on his stomach, the one with the pills. In agony he made his way through the garage and from there to his room. Kimo fell on his bed and curled into a fetal position waiting, waiting for Freddy Krueger's hand to play the piano on his stomach. Sweat was breaking out on his brow. His feet were arching in his shoes. Yes, all of the preliminaries were making themselves known. Tiny little *haoles* with red hot metal skewers were lining up in disciplined ranks to begin marching under Kimo's skin for the grand finale.

But what was this? The pills had started to work. There was a distance happening now in Kimo's mind between him and the pain. The pain was still there, it was still coming, but it had switched tracks. It might go on by Kimo this time instead of through him. Gossamer layers of angel hair gauze were wrapping themselves around his nerve endings, divorcing him from the pain. But the pain was still there. *Will the pills be stronger than the pain? Will the pain be stronger than the pills?*

Kimo lay there waiting, experiencing the wonder of modern pharmaceuticals at war with one of the great curses of mortal existence, pain. Now, as Kimo lay there, something new introduced itself into the equation, something besides the Percocet. Along with the pain, riding it like a surfboard across angry waves, dancing in and out of the Percocet rush, came The Voice. Perhaps the voice had been there before but Kimo had not heard it. Perhaps the all-encompassing howl of the pain had drowned out the voice. Maybe the Percocet had quieted Kimo's thoughts enough that the voice could now be heard. Kimo could hear it as clearly as he had ever heard anything. This is what the voice said:

"Kimo? Hey there, Kimo-Sabe. How you feeling? Would you like the pain to go away?" Kimo nodded, not answering aloud. He understood that there was no reason to answer aloud. The voice was inside his mind. The most unusual thing was that Kimo did not find this to be strange. It was as if Kimo had always known that the voice was going to come.

He pulled his knees tighter to his chest as the voice continued, *"Kimo, I can make the pain stop, or I can make the pain far worse than it was before and the pills will not help, nothing will help. Check this out."*

A thunderbolt discharged in Kimo's stomach. A wildfire sprang up and began to devour him, to eat him alive. Kimo opened his mouth to scream but no sound came out. The pain had paralyzed his vocal chords. Where was the sweet distance of the pills? Nothing had prepared him for this. The earlier pain had just been fooling around. "God! God! Oh, please, God!" Kimo screamed.

"There is no God but me," the voice answered, *"and that will do for you, watch."* Magically the pain receded. It went away like it had never been. Tears of joy sprang into Kimo's eyes. Not only was the pain gone but the anticipation of pain as well. The exquisite floating peace of the Percocet was doing rock-a-bye baby in Kimo's mind.

The voice returned, *"Kimo, do you believe me?"*

"Yes," Kimo responded in his thoughts.

"I wonder," the voice continued, *"maybe I should bring the pain back, just for a moment. I'm not entirely sure that you believe yet."*

"No!" Kimo cried out, having found his voice. "I believe you!"

"Yes!" shouted the voice. And there it was again, just like it had never been anywhere else but right there in the pit of Kimo's stomach, its home, the place where it lived. Kimo's legs were jack-knifed forward, his fists buried in his abdomen. Wild colors flashed across the backs of his closed eyelids.

"Please, please, make it go away! I believe you, I believe!"

"Okay," the voice said. Instantly, it was gone. *"You see now, do you not? You see that I can send it away and I can bring it back, can't I?"*

"Yes, oh, yes. Don't bring it back! I'll do anything!" The relief that was flooding Kimo's body with the retreat of the pain was almost painful in itself. *How could anything feel this good?*

"You will do anything I ask, won't you?" The voice now had a wheedling insinuating tone, the sort of voice that on the street would have made Kimo angry just to hear it. It was like the voice of an angel to Kimo now. The pain was gone and everything had a heavenly patina. *"I have something I want you to do Kimo,"* the voice said.

"Anything." Kimo replied.

"It will not be hard for you to do what I ask, Kimo. It is something you have wanted to do for a long time. I am going to help you accomplish what you would not have actually done on your own. Because you would not have done this on your own, the pain in your stomach would have come eventually. The stress of not doing this thing would have brought you the pain. Now you will not have to worry about the pain because you will do this thing. You are going to kill and it will make you happy. Once you have done this for me I will need you for a little while longer and then I will go away and you will be free."

Kimo considered what the voice had told him and asked, "If I kill, won't I have to go to prison?"

"You may be locked up temporarily," the voice said, *"But then you will be released. I promise you this. But you would do it for me anyway, wouldn't you Kimo?"*

Kimo felt the pain begin to coil once more in his stomach, a slowly growing awareness that said, *"I can keep right on coming. Oh, yes. Here I come."*

"I'll do anything you say!" Kimo screamed and it was gone again. He straightened his body out on the bed and began to weep. The full import of what was taking place was beginning to come through. He was being possessed by the devil. He was going insane. Was he going insane? Was he really going to kill someone soon? With all of the times he had fantasized about killing, he now saw that what the voice said was true. It had only been a fantasy. A part of Kimo was realizing that this was a critical revelation. He would never have actually killed anyone. He saw that it was his thinking about it, his anger and his frustration that had brought him to where he was now.

"Why do you concern yourself with the devil?" the voice asked. *"Do you know who the devil is? You do not know."* The voice had such authority that Kimo could not reply. He only listened and absorbed. *"You only know what you have been told by people, who were told by others, who themselves did not know. You are not going insane. Hearing voices does not mean you are insane, not if the voice is really there. And my voice is really here, isn't it, Kimo?"*

"Yes," Kimo replied.

"I want you to trust me, Kimo. No harm is going to come to you and you are going to get to kill the people you want to kill and get away scot-free. Trust me, Kimo. You don't have a choice anyway. Do you?"

"No," Kimo answered. "No I don't." Then the voice released him and he fell into a deep and dreamless sleep.

Alan was gazing out upon Kahului Harbor with a fruit drink in his hand when Whip arrived at the table right at six thirty. "Well, Sir Douglas," he said, "well ensconced before the appointed hour I see."

Alan turned to face Whip. A brief smile flashed across his face and he gestured to a chair across from him. "So, you got my message. Good, sit down. What are you drinking?"

"I'll have a beer," Whip replied.

Alan arranged for Whip's beer and then turned to him with a serious look on his face. "I wanted you to get here early, Whip, because we're having dinner with Ben, my partner. A lot has happened today and I wanted to talk to you about it before he gets here."

Whip's beer arrived. He took a long pull and set it down on the table. "Fire away," he said.

Alan told Whip some of the things that had happened since he'd last seen him, the psychic attack, the witness ID and his upcoming appointment with Dr. Abadon. He finished with his promise that Whip would tell Ben what he had told him.

When Whip heard this, he raised his eyebrows and said, "You sure about this? I mean, I don't care if people think I'm crazy or not, but you have to work with this guy, right?"

Alan laughed, "Yes, I do and he will assuredly ridicule me for some time after he hears what you have to say. But Whip, he won't let up until he hears something and if he's not hearing everything, he'll know and he'll be relentless. Bottom line, he's my friend. I can't say how he'll take it all but what you told me is true, right?"

Whip nodded. "It's all true."

"Since it is true, we're going to be seeing the effects of it sooner or later. At some point we're going to be dealing with flesh and blood representations of all this and sooner or later it's got to come out. I mean I can only hope..."

"So I tell him everything I told you?"

"Everything."

Whip took another long sip at his beer and said, "You got it."

"Now then," Alan signaled to the waitress and proceeded to tell him in more detail about his experience in the car earlier. "What do you make of it?" he asked.

"Alan, I have the benefit of some time with Ming. The most important feature of that is the way the contact has altered my thinking. So, maybe I have some insight here, but you've been studying things like this your whole life and I think you probably know more than you think you know. What Ming would probably say is that Billy Joe is becoming increasingly frustrated with his efforts to find out who is blocking him. Right now he may or may not be trying to overhear our conversation. If he is hearing it, he is not hearing what we are actually saying, or he may be getting fuzzy images like you see on the Playboy Channel if you're not a subscriber. He is not in control and this is as infuriating to him as anything could be because he is all about personal will and control."

"So you think he just flipped out for a minute?"

"Maybe."

"Okay for me to join you?" They turned to find Ben standing at the table, the waitress reaching around him to place an iced tea on the table.

Whip got to his feet as Alan made the introductions. After shaking hands they sat down. For a few moments no one said anything. Ben looked from Alan to Whip, his eyes full of curiosity. Then he said, "So, Whip, Alan tells me you've been doing some traveling?"

"Yeah," Whip replied. "Mostly in the East." Whip played with his watchband and glanced over at Alan. "I've got to say though, driving around this island today, Maui is as beautiful as anywhere I've ever been. I came here a few times with Alan and my sister, but I guess I wasn't paying much attention. I just remembered the beaches."

Ben turned to Alan and said, "Is that enough?"

"Enough?" Whip asked, confusion washing over his features.

"He means have we made enough small talk to be polite so now we can get down to business."

"Jeez Ben, are you from New York or what?"

"He's like you Whip, a total smart ass. Don't take it personally. I'm sure he was joking, partially anyway."

"Sorry, Whip, I haven't yet understood that there is a difference between the understanding you can expect to get from someone you know and someone you just met." That said, Ben stroked his chin with his left hand and leaned back into his chair. "Why don't you let me in on what's going on?"

Whip laughed and said, "Too much. Well... Alan has asked me to tell you what I know about what's happened. I don't know if that's a good idea. It places too much strain on credibility. Even if you wanted to believe, it would be hard."

"Try me," Ben interjected.

"We'll see how you feel when I'm done. I just don't want this to compromise your relationship with Alan."

"Nothing you say, Whip, will ever change that."

Whip looked at Alan and let out a deep breath. "All right, here goes." For the next fifteen minutes Whip outlined in detail his experiences with Ming. Alan heard once again the whole story that Whip had told him the night before. It sounded just as incredible the second time around. Alan kept his eyes on Ben throughout the narration. Once again he was made aware of Ben's Oriental roots. It was impossible to tell what was passing through his mind.

Alan and Whip both watched Ben closely, waiting for whatever comment would first emerge from his lips.

"Would you please excuse me?" he asked. Then he got up from the table and walked out of the restaurant.

"Shit!" Alan exclaimed. "I should have known better. No one, no one sane, would believe a story like that."

"It's not the reaction I would have expected," Whip replied. "Ridicule, disbelief, yes, but not this." They both sat staring glumly at one another. That was how Ben found them when he returned a few minutes later. He sat back down at the table and wiped at his eyes with the red handkerchief in his hand. It looked like he had been crying.

"I'm sorry," he said. "I had to go outside right away. Maybe it was a nervous reaction, I don't know. I ran over to the park next door."

"And...?" Alan asked when the silence lengthened.

"And I had to laugh really hard for a little while, but I'm all better now," he said, a chuckle escaping his lips.

"So you don't believe a word?" Alan asked.

"*Au contraire, mon ami.* It is one of the few scenarios that makes sense out of all that has happened to you. But it is not something the logical mind wants to hear. It's certainly not something I would mention to anyone else. True or not, it doesn't really change our game plan, Alan. It just adds some extra features.

"I think you know that I am not a Christian, I am a Buddhist. We view the world visible and invisible a little differently than you Christians. Some things are very much an accepted part of reality for us." Ben sipped at his iced tea, pausing in his speech. No one else was saying anything. Ben set the tea down on the table and continued thoughtfully. "It has always amused me that Christians have this religion... It's filled with devils and angels, a virgin birth, a savior that rose from the dead, eternal life and on and on — no pun intended. Why should it be so hard to believe in a story like Whip's?"

"I don't believe I'm hearing this!" Alan exclaimed.

"Believe it," Ben replied. "Now, what are we going to do about it? It would help if you could remember where you saw those two thugs."

"Nothing yet," Alan replied.

"Well, now that we know what we know, maybe they're from New York?"

"No, that doesn't ring a bell either," Alan added. "Have you got the sketches with you?" he asked Ben.

"Sure," Ben replied. Reaching down at his feet he pulled his briefcase onto his lap, opened it and extracted the two composites. Alan reached across the table and took them from Ben.

"It's the strangest thing," he said, after studying the sketches again. "I know I've seen these guys and what's even stranger is that I've always had great recall. It's not like me to be so blank."

Whip reached out and took the drawings from Alan's hand. As he studied them his eyebrows arched in amazement, then he laughed. "Well gentlemen, I have also seen these two before but I do remember where and when."

"No shit!" Ben cried as he leaned forward waiting for Whip's answer.

Whip had a big grin plastered across his face when he said, "Isn't the suspense wonderful? Perhaps we should have another beer and savor this moment, knowing that all too soon it will end."

"Whip," Alan warned.

"Sorry Alan, but opportunities like this don't present themselves every day. We saw them together. You were with me." Alan still had not put it together, so Whip continued, "Last night, in the store, on the way home?"

"Right! Right! What the hell's wrong with me?" Alan snatched the drawings from Whip's hand and looked at them again. This time he remembered everything. He could even smell the beer and cigarettes on the big guy. "We saw these two in the Paia Convenience Mart last night around 11:00 p.m., probably just before. They were buying beer, a couple of serious skells. It makes no sense that I couldn't remember them. Both Whip and I got a bad hit off of them. No doubt in my mind these creeps could be part of this."

As soon as Ben got the details of the encounter he was on his cell phone.

Alan said, "He's blocking me, isn't he? But he can't block everybody all of the time and that's why you were able to remember."

Whip nodded his head, "Yeah, that's clear but he could have blocked me too. I think this is another case of Ming poking holes in his envelope. He said he would help whenever he could."

"What's that mean, whenever he could?" asked Alan.

"Sometimes you're just on your own Alan," replied Whip.

Ben returned to the table and sat down. "Well, I've put out the word. Now I think we should mosey on over and talk to the employees at that mini-mart."

"Dinner?" Whip looked crestfallen.

Alan looked at Whip, "You don't mind do you?"

"Yeah, I mind, this looks like a great place to eat. Shit! Let's go."

They pulled into the store parking lot, one after the other. Alan looked at his watch. It was 8:15 p.m. Ben walked up to the cashier and showed her his badge. Alan briefly flashed his own and then returned it to his pocket.

"Were you working here last night?" Ben asked the lady behind the counter. She was about fifty years old, of Hawaiian-Asian extraction, slender, with dark intelligent eyes framed in tortoise shell glasses.

"No," she said, "but Tamayo was here. She in de back taking one break." She reached under the counter and pressed a button. A few moments later a door in the rear of the store opened and Alan recognized the woman who had waited on them the previous evening.

"That's her," He said to Ben.

Whip was prowling through the store, watching the action but staying out of the way. Ever since his experience with Ming he had felt like he was in a movie. There was a sense of exaggeration and unreality to everything that was happening. He felt like he had been deprived of sleep and had entered a state of consciousness where hallucination was as normal as breathing.

When the lady arrived at the front, Ben showed her his badge. Her eyes opened wide. She was about twenty years younger than her co-worker and also of Asian mix. "Yes, officer?" She looked up at Ben from her barely five feet of height.

"You were working here last night?"

"Yes."

"Well then, Tamayo," Ben handed her the pictures of Malcolm and Balfire. "Have you ever seen these men?"

Tamayo looked at the pictures for about two seconds and then quickly nodded her head. "Yes, I have seen them. These are bad mens. I no like see them come in here. They scare me. They look at me like they want do bad tings to me. You know what I say?" Alan and Ben nodded their heads affirmatively. They did indeed know.

"So," continued Ben, "they've been in here before?"

"Yes. Tree times already I see dem. They always get same tings, Budweiser cold packs and Pall Mall cigarettes."

"Did you see what kind of vehicle they were driving?" Alan asked.

"Yes, they have dark panel van. I see when they getting gas."

"Bingo," said Ben.

"They didn't happen to pay with a credit card, did they?"

"No, pay with cash, I no see license plate."

Ben asked her if there was a particular time when they usually came in and was told, "Night time." They walked outside. "This looks like a righteous stakeout," Ben said. "How do you want to play it?"

"I'm going to leave all of the strategy calls in your court, Ben. This is your island. What I do know is that you're right about the stakeout."

Ben called Vice and arranged for a couple of hippies in an old car to be posted a short distance away from the store, then he said goodnight to them and left for home.

Alan and Whip were having breakfast and talking about baseball when the phone rang. Alan picked up the receiver and said, "Hello."

"Hi, Alan." It was Ben. "We've got a meeting in the Captain's office in forty-five minutes. You need to be there."

"Absolutely, anything I should know?"

"We're not sure. A twelve-year-old boy didn't come home from the video parlor last night. He's in the middle of a custody dispute between mom and dad, so that's likely it. We can't find the dad but that's not unusual apparently. On the negative side, a couple of his buddies saw him talking to two hard cases in the parking lot. They were busy trying to impress some girls so they weren't paying a lot of attention. Missing kid's name is Paco Rodriguez. The Captain's all antsy about it. He's wondering whether we should publish the sketches in the newspaper and release them to TV, even though it could well spook our prey and they could bail off the island. He's going to talk to us first. I think Aaron told him he had to and that all major decisions were in our hands. This did not improve *Der Führer's* temper."

"Hmmm," Alan replied. "I don't like the idea of releasing the sketches at all. We're so close, I think we might have them soon. Okay, I'll see you in about forty minutes."

Alan hung up the phone and turned to Whip who had been watching him throughout the call. "Bad news?" he queried as Alan set the receiver down. Alan told him what had transpired as he was setting his shoulder holster in place.

"I've got to run, Whip. Call me and we'll get together later." Alan's brow was furrowed and his eyes narrowed with concern. "Look out for yourself, Whip. I don't know what else to say."

"I'll be okay, Alan. You remember what you used to tell me? You said, 'Learn how to fight and pray you don't ever have to.'"

Alan laughed as he grabbed his briefcase from the kitchen counter. "How come we never take our own advice? That's got to be one of life's biggest mysteries."

"One of them," Whip replied as Alan went out the door.

Whip took the dishes to the sink and washed them. When he finished, he walked out into the back yard and followed a path until he came to a little cloister in which there rested a stone bench. Sitting down, he closed his eyes and relaxed his body. His breathing became deep and rhythmic as his awareness of the outer world diminished. He sat there for some time. This is how Ming found him.

"Well little brother, how are you?" Ming's voice resonated through Whip's being.

"I am well, Ming," he replied.

"Danger is moving toward you but it only has the power of your belief in it. It is through this that our enemies can reach us. It is only in our surrender to something higher that we are made safe. We come under the protection of that which we surrender to."

As Ming was talking, Whip's third eye gradually opened. Light had flickered and faded until it became stable and Whip could clearly see through it. Before him was the form of the Tibetan. Great age and timeless youth moved across Ming's features. The eyes were deep pools of magnetic light filled with a wisdom and love beyond the ken of Whip's mortal state. There were other things in Ming's face that set his appearance apart from that of ordinary humanity. There were no lines except when his features formed an expression. There was a visible corona of light around his head. The virtue that was in him cast an illumination similar to that seen in the icons of Christian saints. One way that Whip might have described Ming was to say that his presence made you feel safe, made you feel there was nothing that could harm you so long as Ming was about. It was like being in your mother's arms. A mother, who if needed could become the greater mother, could become bad to the bone if she had to, and nothing would harm the child.

"I have looked into Alan's thoughts and I see that he believes what you have told him could be true. He badly wants it to be true, but the rational part of his mind cannot entirely accept it. He will continue to use those tools that are familiar to him and have proven their worth. This is good. If his focus is upon what he knows, that which knows him can lead." Ming smiled and Whip felt the power of the sun flow through his heart.

"Little brother, there are no boundaries or barriers where faith is strong. Nothing is concealed from the open heart. Tell Alan I will speak with him soon. Badges and guns and fighting arts will be of no use against what is coming. Billy Joe has a thousand weapons, Alan only a few.

"The one thing that Billy Joe does not know about is me. This he will not find out until it can no longer be hidden and not until the end will he know. He cannot penetrate to where I am, yet I can see where he is at all times. I am bound by laws and may not directly interfere, most of the time." Once again, Ming smiled. This time he looked like an eight-year-old boy who had stolen a cookie and consumed the evidence.

"I am like a baseball coach, Whip. I can teach the skills of pitching and hitting. I can show you how to steal bases and I can transmit the savvy of the game that separates a great player from the run of the mill, but I cannot play the game for you." While he was speaking, his face had slowly morphed until Whip was looking at the outrageous head and features of Don Zimmer, a famous baseball coach. He had a big wad of tobacco in his cheek. He spit a long stream to the ground below and Whip erupted with laughter.

"I know a few parlor tricks as well," Ming continued. "If you listen to the coach and combine his wisdom with your natural skills, you have a great opportunity to win the game. If you don't, well, you might get lucky and you might not. Lady Luck is fickle and cannot be depended on. She'll come into the room on the arm of one man and go out on the arm of another. It's like playing chess with death. It doesn't matter what game you play with death, death always wins. And death wins precisely because one believes there is a contest. Death cannot come for one who has no death to die. The only one who beats death is the one who sees through death. When you understand the nature of death, death no longer exists."

Whip formed a question in his mind and before it was completely imaged Ming began to reply. "If you heard me as I was actually speaking you would not understand me. What I am saying is being translated into terms that your mind can understand. The baseball metaphors are ones that you are familiar with. This will always be the case. The secret of all inspired music, great art and poetry relies on this. And it doesn't matter how it is said as long as it is understood." Ming's eyes crinkled and Whip could feel them reach into the very essence of his being. He laughed when he thought what it would be like to attempt to conceal something from Ming.

Ming nodded his head as he read this thought. "I'll be going now. Keep your eyes open. Things are going to be expected of you. You are a critical part of the movie. Remember." Ming paused and cocked his head to one side. Whip was reminded of Nipper the RCA dog listening to His Master's Voice.

"Precisely," Ming continued. "Listen... listening is a great art. Very few people practice it these days." As he said this, Ming's image faded. It flickered for a moment and then shrank to a pinpoint of blue white light and disappeared.

Whip slowly returned to the physical world. He opened his eyes to colors more rich than the ones he had left. It was always this way after a session with Ming. Every sense was more alive than it had been, gradually integrating back to ordinary perception.

He got to his feet and went into the house. There he changed into a pair of black cotton drawstring pants, a black T-shirt and black Kung Fu slippers. Spinning and turning, he danced his way up to the deck where he began working through the short form of the Southern Praying Mantis style. Most of the moves in this system were close to the body. Whip looked like he was wrestling with a snake. Alan had taught him a number of defenses to counter the many possibilities of assault that might come from any corner. Alan himself had become almost entirely defensive. He'd told Whip that a good defensive fighter had the greater advantage of winning the conflict regardless of the old adage about a great offense beating a good defense. It was why Alan was more and more gravitating toward *Aikido*. He loved Kung Fu for the aerobics and the pure ballet of the movements but was now incorporating the two. Alan had shown him *Aikido* wristlocks that were instantly effective and disabling.

Until he had begun to study *Aikido*, Alan had been fond of more linear forms. He had taught Whip well, especially the quick reaction moves so lethal during street confrontations. Alan had told him there were two kinds of martial arts, the kind you use in the gym and at tournaments and the kind you used on the street in defense of your life. Many martial artists had wound up seriously hurt or dead from getting them confused or from not having learned what they really needed to know.

They had both laughed while watching the *Ultimate Fighting Challenge* on TV. The combatants were constantly putting themselves out of action by breaking their hands or other parts of their bodies and, even though they had won a contest, they could not return for the next fight.

Whip was sweating profusely as he finished off his efforts with a series of complex *katas*. Finally he lay panting on the deck, exhausted but feeling purged. Endorphins roared through his blood stream. His pulse was thundering in his head as the warm sun poured its honey down upon him. There was a trace of breeze washing over his flesh. With his eyes closed he could still see the bright blue sky above him and the soft white clouds passing by.

As his breathing slowed and his heart rate returned to normal, Whip felt a sense of well-being so keen and complete that tears formed in his eyes and flowed down his cheeks.

"What a riddle," he said aloud, "that there can be such peace and beauty available in the world and still so many negatives predominate over them." Then he laughed, thinking, "*So many versions of peace and beauty in the world, many of them not peaceful or beautiful but all of them worth fighting for by somebody*." He had a momentary vision of the pope with a big unwieldy staff sparring with a Hassid who carried an enormous club. Neither could really hit the other and both of them kept falling down. He laughed when he saw a Muslim come into the picture dragging a scimitar that he could not even lift.

Whip wondered if there would ever come a time when a common truth would be understood and shared by humanity. He played with the thought, musing about how it might come to pass. It occurred to him that life on Earth was not about universal brotherhood and understanding. *It was about the fight to achieve these things. Life was not about good always winning out over evil. That was for books and movies. Life was about the struggle of good against evil.* There did appear to be an evolution of sorts. The quality of life had improved for the general public, at least for the general Western public. Civilization was the result of humanities reaction to pain. The comfort margin for some had certainly increased. At the same time it could not be said that the hearts and minds of the people were very radically transformed. In some ways it seemed that people were worse off, more confused about their course of action.

Television and bad music had lobotomized them, up sometimes seemed to be down. Bad behavior was often no longer considered bad but amusing. Good behavior was ridiculed. There were far more sophisticated weapons now. Warfare had become managed conflict, carried out in locations where there were no great business interests, or where great business interests wanted to go. *Fifty thousand Africans did not have the same currency as fifty thousand Americans.* Corporations ran the governments. Jefferson and Lincoln were long gone. When a man or woman of character did emerge they were generally shot. People listened to rap music and pornography was the Internet's biggest and most profitable commodity. One could argue that this was what people chose and they should have the freedoms of their choice. Whip was not sure that this was what people chose at all. Whip thought that the need was first manufactured and then the product created to fill the need.

So, was life about an ongoing evolution into a golden age? There had been times that had been labeled golden. Whip did not know if they were in fact. But the golden ages had not lasted. The most part of history was filled with bloodshed and tyranny, with oppression and appalling ignorance. There seemed to be a dancing creature that appeared before the eyes of the world, a sort of kaleidoscopic monster that manifested as the object of desire. Humanity marched blindly forward into what was in fact a wide mouth filled with rows of flashing, bloodstained teeth.

"*No,*" he thought, "*it's not about peace on earth and good will to men. It's about individual struggle and the hope of resolution in some place beyond. Earth is a battle-*

ground and one needs to be a courageous and honorable warrior. One needs most of all to know and be certain of the truth of what they are battling for."

Whip got to his feet and leaned over the rail, staring at the rising mountain before him. The rim looked like broken teeth, like the lower mandible of some giant, fallen away from the skull, fallen from some great height and buried into the earth. "*Yea, life is all about war, about war and hunger. What one hungers for is the impetus of their war. One needs to have a righteous hunger.*"

Chapter Fourteen

Alan and Ben emerged from the Captain's office, exchanging grins that had certainly not been on their faces when they had entered it earlier. "Way to go there, Ben, I was sweating bullets for a minute."

"Hey, I'm with you, Alan. I don't want these creeps spooked any more than you do. At least we've got twenty-four hours. It could have gone either way."

They strode purposefully through the long corridor to the elevator. Passing policemen would nod or shout hello to Ben, while casting curious and sometimes hostile looks at Alan in the manner of policemen the world over.

They reached the canteen and once they had their coffee and rolls, looked around until they found a table to themselves.

"You think there's anything to the cliché about cops and coffee and donuts?" Alan asked.

Ben took a sip of his coffee and looked at Alan, "Ask me if I give a fuck."

Alan looked at him in confusion.

Ben laughed, "Aw, hey man, I didn't hurt your inner child or something, did I?"

Alan shook his head. "It never ends, huh?"

"Oh, it ends alright," Ben replied, "You just don't know when. Anyway…" Ben blew into his coffee. "You were going to get into something about the case earlier, something going on that you didn't understand?"

Alan thought for a moment and then his eyes lit with recognition. "Right. I just can't figure out what these kidnappings and murders have to do with me. I don't know any of these people and except for Wendy, hurting them doesn't hurt me. They're bringing down all kinds of heat on themselves that they don't need if the object is to fuck me over. It doesn't compute. It doesn't compute at all."

Ben nodded. "You've got a point, but we've seen these things before. You can't look for rational behavior from irrational people. Besides, this Billy Joe, according to Whip and Ming, is a man of powers. He's got an agenda we can't see. We know he's out to get you but we don't know what the methodology is. If he's all he's made out to be, he can do a lot, probably is doing a lot, to keep us off the trail of his wolves."

"Then there's the Ming factor."

"You have to accept things that work Alan, whether or not you understand the how or the why. At the moment we don't know jack shit but there could well be a Jack Shit. It comes back to that quote about more things being in Heaven and Hell than we know anything about."

Ben sipped at his coffee and continued, "Most of the time the evidence follows in a logical sequence. The perps are usually what you expect or they slip up so bad it's not hard for you to track them down. Every now and then though, you get something outside the spectrum. It's kind of what happens occasionally to a chess master playing an amateur with a good sense of the game. The master gets beaten sometimes because he's used to playing people who perform along traditional lines. He's used to seeing certain openings, certain defenses. His subconscious is set up to see the game going in a certain direction. The conscious mind might not be doing its job. This amateur knows how all of the pieces move. He knows the object of the game. He's played enough times that he's developed a few strategies that don't conform to what the master expects."

"What are you saying, Ben?"

Ben rubbed his jaw and looked down into his coffee that he was stirring with a wooden ice cream spoon. "I'm saying something very different than what we're used to could be going on here. Hell!" Ben exclaimed, "We already know that something different — something flat out fucking weird — is going on. We need to look for this hidden agenda. Think about what there is that could be used to hurt you. Except for the obvious, Wendy, you're right. None of it makes any sense."

"You really believe what Whip told us?" Alan looked bemused.

Ben grinned back at him. "Well, I'm not planning on attending any séances and I'm not trading in my gun for a Ouija board, but to paraphrase the great Sherlock, 'after you have investigated the obvious and not found it, whatever remains, no matter how improbable, must be the answer.' I'm not ruling anything out. Stranger things have happened. You ever read the big book of *Ripley's Believe It or Not* or *Stranger than Fiction*? Most things do follow a logical progression, but every now and then you have to throw out all of the rules and approach the situation the way you do a hole in a rock. It might have a bag of gold and then again, it might have a rattlesnake's nest. You have to poke a stick in there first."

"I can go along with that. The one thing I'm sure of is that there's no rattlesnake in this hole." A grim look came over his face, "It's something far worse." Alan swallowed the last bite of his cruller and brushed at his shirtfront to free it of any stray crumbs. "I've heard of a lot of fantastic occurrences in my life. History is full of them. I never had any trouble believing them, even the most outrageous ones. I wanted them to be true, I needed them to be true, because I never wanted to believe that what you see is what you get. I had to believe in a higher power that dispenses justice and drives us toward goodness, and now such forces, both good and bad, have entered my life for real. It's a lot harder when it happens to you." Alan looked off into some middle point in the air, his forefinger clicking back and forth on the table as he stared into nothing.

"You're going to see the Doctor this afternoon?" Ben asked after a few moments had passed.

"That's the plan," Alan replied as he got up from the table. "He's over in Maui Meadows. I'm supposed to get there any time after one o'clock." Alan looked at his watch. "That means I should be heading back to your office and picking up the rest of the paperwork right about now. This should be interesting. I had this one doctor in New York actually describe the suspect's appearance, right down to the brand of tennis shoes he wore. We've got a lot more to work with here than we did there."

Balfire and Malcolm sat around the kitchen table in the house Billy Joe had rented for them in Olinda. It sat hidden from the road at the end of a long driveway, nestled in a copse of surrounding evergreens, the perfect hideaway.

There was a wrought iron gate at the entrance that was set into large stone pillars and opened by remote control. The property was six acres in size and beautifully landscaped. Billy Joe had told the realtor that he had his own gardeners so that there wouldn't be anybody dropping by, same thing with the pool. For the time they needed to be there they wouldn't even need to cut the lawn.

The house rented for $4,500 a month plus utilities. It was a large custom barn home with four bedrooms and three and a half baths. There was a huge living room that took up the bottom front half of the house. The other half was composed of an eat-in kitchen with attached arboretum (Balfire liked to go in there and piss on the plants), a pantry with washer dryer, a dining room and what would have been called a study by more refined tenants. There was a hot tub out by the pool and a screened in gazebo where one might eat lunch, or just enjoy the sights and sounds of nature. Balfire had, as he put it, "fucked the living shit" out of a local girl in there and in the throes of passion, accidentally snapped her neck. Malcolm had just shaken his head from where he sat in the hot tub.

Balfire had been trippin' on crank and Budweiser at the time. He preferred crank to the fine cocaine that was always available to them.

He'd had the foresight to tape the woman's mouth shut before he brought her out of the house, but even so he caught unholy hell from Billy Joe over it when he showed up later. Billy Joe knew everything that happened whether he was there or not and though he had laid a veil over the property and was not expecting scrutiny, obedience from his minions was everything. He tore Balfire a new asshole for disregarding his direct order never to mess with the victims outside of the garage. The garage had been soundproofed for that very reason.

As a sign of his displeasure and the need to instill a greater awareness in him, Billy Joe demonstrated to Balfire the excruciating terror of primal fear. It was an easy feat. He simply opened that part of Balfire's mind where the things that scared him lived. Then after Billy Joe added a few touches of his own, he animated them and brought them to life. Balfire had spent that evening alternatively throwing up and trembling in a corner and then had wet his bed when he did finally manage to fall asleep, after Billy Joe lifted the fear.

It was difficult to speculate on whether this would have any lasting effect on Balfire's behavior. Balfire was not very smart, though he had a lot of low level cunning, so most lessons, no matter how frightening, passed away with time.

The garage had been turned into a medical laboratory under the direction of Billy Joe. Malcolm was skilled in most of the building arts and Balfire was an adequate helper. To the informed observer it would have appeared to be a place for the preparation of the dead, something you might find in a funeral parlor. There was lots of stainless steel and rubber hosing. They'd hooked up a drainage system that ran into the septic tank. The *pièce de résistance* was a real post-mortem table that Billy Joe had picked up somewhere. A delivery van had brought it in the first days they were there. They'd since used it for the dead and the living. Billy Joe said that the atmosphere it created aided in his research on the effect of fear upon the human mind. Malcolm had sniggered when he said this. Though Billy Joe needed bodies for the coming presentation, he was always about the business of harvesting etheric energy that he used for various purposes. He said it was like "money in the bank." They were also a kind of fuel. Billy Joe had told Malcolm, "Gasoline burns and so do they. The only difference is that gasoline doesn't scream."

There was the garage for the wet work and the converted study for the finish work. They'd moved all of the furniture into the living room where it rested against one wall. Neither Malcolm's nor Balfire's sense of aesthetics was unduly affected by this haphazard placement. Malcolm was nominally cleaner that Balfire but this was something he had learned by default as a result of living for years in a six-foot by eight-foot cell with another person.

Whenever Billy Joe came by, which was fairly often, he would tell them to "clean up the fucking place" because he couldn't think in the middle of a landfill. This usually meant sweeping the beer cans and bottles off the kitchen table and other surfaces throughout the house, emptying the ashtrays and washing the dishes. This was a job that Balfire loathed and which, because of this, Billy Joe made him do every time. Billy Joe often toyed with the idea of turning Balfire into a "bitch."

He chuckled at the thought of this huge red-bearded Reaver dressed up and made up as some deranged Valkyrie, mincing through the house with a big feather duster, every once in a while backing up toward Malcolm in estrus or dragging himself across the floor on his hands, just like a real female dog. So far Billy Joe had only toyed with various ugly ideas concerning his henchmen. It wouldn't affect the work he needed them to do and it would make them even more frightening, but so far he'd left them as they were. There had been years and years in which Billy Joe had indulged himself in all manner of things. This kind of dalliance was not important in the face of larger issues.

Billy Joe's hatred extended to every living thing. Humanity had no guidelines for understanding Billy Joe. They did not understand the minds or motivations of even the garden-variety psychopaths that prowled through their world. Billy Joe was a cloth of a different cut. Comparing him to others was like comparing an eight-year-old boy with a baseball to Greg Maddux, a gecko to a dinosaur. Yet Billy Joe was not omnipotent. There were boundaries he could not cross, people he could not hurt. Things he could not and did not know.

Fear was his greatest power. If he could make you afraid, he could hurt you. There were other levers too. Billy Joe had no power as great as virtue, but virtue was not a common attribute in the present day and age. Everything was breaking down, morality and character, a clear idea of right and wrong. These were all fading or obscured. In such a climate, creatures like Billy Joe flourished. The present culture was a hothouse for a virus like Billy Joe. Society was becoming a flyblown carcass, ripe for the bloom of thousands of maggots, all waiting in ravenous need for the command of Billy Joe. It was in the music, it was in the magazines and it was on all the moving screens on which so many, many eyes were locked.

Billy Joe reached out in his thoughts to bend the will of those whose services he required. It was such a simple thing, to influence those who had given their sense of self over to network TV and McDonald's. His voice had a soothing hypnotic quality that lulled the unwary into actions they would have never considered on their own. With all of his victims, acolytes and slaves, Billy Joe started out with little corruptions, corruptions of thought and feeling. He would incite anger or resentments at imagined slights and then feed them as a woodsman might feed a small flame in the wilderness. He would encourage them through their unconscious to speak things they would not have said under normal conditions. The corruptions would grow from little dishonesties and minor hurts into a conflagration of actions that would open the gates of Hell.

It has been said that you cannot cheat an honest man. Then again, it might not be all that easy to find one. This was one of the great contributors to Billy Joe's power, the pervasive decadence, the epidemic of lawyers, the sexual ambiguity and media infestation akin to a plague of flies, the erasure of childhood and intelligence in the MTV classroom, the buggery of innocence. Like Quasimodo as maestro, Billy Joe conducted the mutant orchestra in Hell's unfinished symphony.

Malcolm dropped a Pall Mall butt into an empty Budweiser can and then farted. "I just blew you a little kiss there Balfire, don't be bashful now, just go ahead and enjoy it."

"You goddamned asshole!" Balfire yelled as he jumped out of his chair, waving his hands in the air to dispense the noxious fumes.

"That's the ticket Bailiwick, mix it up until you got it just the way you like it, add some of your breath and a little bit of oxygen." Malcolm was grinning that evil grin of his, a fair warning that he was becoming dangerous. He was bored and Malcolm was at his worst when he was bored. He'd killed several people for no other reason than boredom. For the last half hour he had been picking at Balfire, zoning in on him for lack of any other target. Earlier he had slowly strangled a stray cat that he had managed to entice into a noose with a piece of roast beef.

This had finally pissed off Balfire so much that he had jumped to his feet and stomped the cat into the kitchen floor. Balfire knew where Malcolm was headed and he was trying to avoid it. That is, if he could keep his temper. He was having a hard time of it. In a confined space like this he could surely kick Malcolm's ass. Out in an open space it would be a lot harder with Malcolm's speed and martial arts dexterity. But Balfire was in no mood for a confrontation right now. He was still raw and bleeding in his mind from his encounter with Billy Joe. Now and then he would be hit by an electric shudder and his tongue would snake out of his mouth and wash nervously across his lips. God forbid he should have any flashbacks of the creatures he had seen yesterday. He had gone to Hell. There could be no worse place. Balfire's imagination did not permit for such a possibility. Billy Joe had smiled when he read this thought in Balfire's mind.

Malcolm laughed, "You know, Balfuck, when someone farts they're making their stink a part of your body."

"How's that?" Balfire looked warily at Malcolm.

"Well now, there's this thing called the blood oxygen exchange. It takes place in the lungs. This means that when someone farts it goes into your bloodstream. Then it goes to your brain, maybe, or some other part of your body where it becomes part of your cellular structure."

"I wish you wouldn't fuck with me Malcolm. You forget I'm your friend. I'm the one who waited for you outside the gates of Q, waited with wheels and money and drugs and took you to a nice crib." Balfire spoke with real injury.

Though he was a bad man, he was not evil in the same way as Malcolm. Balfire had a lot of normal human feelings. Under different circumstances, Balfire might not have turned out the way he did.

Malcolm looked at Balfire with pitiless eyes, eyes that would never know remorse or kindness, burned out and buried long ago. The evils that Malcolm had done had shut the door on his humanity. It would not emerge again, not in this lifetime. "Now ain't that sweet," he said. "You're talking like you want to be my punk or something. That true?" Malcolm was radiating malevolence now. Nothing pissed him off more than when Balfire tried to relate to him on a human level.

Balfire went to the icebox and pulled out a couple of Budweisers. Opening one, he took a magnificent draught and nearly drained it. Then he wiped his mouth with the back of his hand and said, "Well, there's no use talking to you, you get like this. Sooner or later you'll remember who's who and what's what. I'm going outside. You can enjoy your own company. You can't enjoy nobody else's."

He walked out of the kitchen and through the living room. He was at the front door when he heard the alarm bell that signaled the opening of the front gate. Someone was coming in. Balfire peered through the peephole and watched. When he saw that it was a black Mercedes, he stepped out on to the porch. The long car with smoked windows came up the drive and pulled to a stop in front of the garage. The driver side door opened and Billy Joe stepped out of the car.

He'd recently taken to wearing different outfits every time they saw him. Once he'd shown up in a black silk jumpsuit. Another time he came by in a Century 21 gold blazer and on yet another occasion in maroon motorcycle leathers. Today he was wearing a red aloha shirt with tigers and boa constrictors along with Levi's and cowboy boots.

"Into the house Balfire, we're going to have a little chat." Billy Joe took Balfire by the elbow and walked him around the house to the kitchen door. When Balfire entered, Malcolm had his mouth open to deliver a nasty crack but he shut it when he saw who was with him. Immediately he got up and went to the icebox for a beer. Billy Joe made him nervous. When he was nervous he got very thirsty. Being a conscienceless person who would do anything to anyone at any time, whether there was a reason or not, Malcolm recognized in Billy Joe someone to watch, to learn from, and to fear. Billy Joe was just like Malcolm only much, much more so. This meant to Malcolm that he was in a whole hell of a lot of danger.

"That's right, Malcolm, you want to remember that." Malcolm choked on his beer when he realized that Billy Joe was replying to his most recent thoughts. Neither he nor Balfire had gotten used to Billy Joe being in their minds. Each time it happened it came as a surprise to them. They were just unable to accept it.

"Both of you sit down," Billy Joe commanded. Once they had done so he went and leaned against the kitchen wall and studied them for a time. Balfire was thinking how he looked like the dude in that Warlock movie, very grim and alien, his black hair streaked with silver. His mouth was a continuous mystery when he smiled. *Was he smiling? Were his expressions ever an indication of the man within, if man it was?*

Billy Joe said, "Something has come up. You were both spotted when you picked up little sister, and when I say spotted I mean identified as well."

"No way!"

"Shut up, Balfire, you were seen by an old man who shouldn't have been able to see across the street, much less make you out on the other side of it. Plus I had a shroud on the area. There's something strange going on here. You two have any idea of what I'm talking about?" Billy Joe scanned their minds as he said this, found nothing as he suspected, and listened to their protestations in silence. It was stupid to ask them in the first place. It was a rhetorical question. They could no more hide something from him that a baby could hide a load in its diapers. He silently raged at the interference. He could not be everywhere at all times and during the times when he was not in one place, someone else was.

Billy Joe cut off their clamor. "The important thing now is that they have good sketches of you. Right now the police have them, soon the media will have them. I'm going to have to make some adjustments to ward off any possible harm to our plans. In the meantime, you boys go nowhere."

"Shitfire and fuck!" Malcolm cried. "I'm going crazy in here."

"You know, Malcolm, you're showing a real lack of discipline for someone who spent all that time in the joint under much more extreme conditions than this. It appears that you don't respect me as much as you did the screws that controlled your every movement. Is that true Malcolm? Do I command less discipline and respect than the screws in the joint?" As Billy Joe was saying this he brought a little of his will to bear on Malcolm. Malcolm felt his bowels turning to water. Suddenly he felt lucky to be breathing at all, much less ensconced in a beautiful home in Hawaii with all of his needs covered and the promise of a ticket anywhere in the world once his work was done. He struggled to speak but no words would come out of his throat.

Billy Joe could have exercised a more severe control over the both of them at any time. He could have emptied their minds and glued them both to the ceiling with the force of his will. But where was the fun in that?

"No comment, Malcolm? Maybe that's better. Maybe you have less to say than you think. Isn't that true Malcolm?"

Malcolm's Adam's apple bobbed as he struggled to swallow. It was painful. The fear was so acute. He had no idea why he was frightened. It didn't matter.

Billy Joe spoke in a sonorous voice, his eyes holding Malcolm's with the force of his will. "I know what's wrong with you, Malcolm. You need to kill again, don't you? What's it like Malcolm? Is it like constipation, heroin withdrawal, a woman's period? It's its own kind of thing but it's like all of the others a little bit. It's like the way it is for an alcoholic when he can't get a drink, he starts to get real nervous. All his senses are heightened while his perceptions are fucked up. He bumps into more things now than he did when he was in the bag. He can feel insects crawling under his clothes. He starts to see things out of the corner of his eye but they're not really there. Don't tell him that though, because he won't believe you. And please, don't turn out the lights!"

Malcolm screamed in pain and fell forward holding his head in his hands. Billy Joe walked over to him and put his hand on his head. "There, there, son, Daddy knows what you need. He knows you can't help yourself. Sometimes it's so hard to be patient. But you've got to remember you went a good long time without killing anyone before. So, if your Daddy tells you you've got to wait a little bit, then that's the way it's going to be. Isn't it?"

Malcolm nodded his head, not speaking, not able to speak. Billy Joe continued to run his hands through the killer's fine, corn silk hair, as if he were stroking his own wild animal, in his own private jungle, to leash or unleash upon an unsuspecting world. "Malcolm, you know you are under my protection. You are my own dear boy."

Billy Joe was kneading Malcolm's shoulders now. His fine porcelain features seemed waxen and bathed in an eerie glow. His dark full hair was combed straight back and gleamed like wet asphalt under a street lamp. Billy Joe had a feline grace about him but it was not entirely that. He was more a combination, half serpent and half cat. You saw the feline quality when he smiled, he looked exactly like a cat and even licked his lips the way a cat would. He was dainty as a cat, yet his movements also reminded you of a snake in sinuous flow. He was a hybrid being from some parallel world. He was what we all eventually become, a physical embodiment of the inner self. After the course of enough lifetimes, Billy Joe had gradually been molded into one of the dark one's multitudinous aspects, a smaller shadow of a larger, deeper darkness.

"Balfire, get us all a beer and then have a seat." Balfire went to the icebox as Billy Joe sat down. They drank their beers in silence. Billy Joe wasn't speaking right then and no one else wanted to until he did. Balfire lit a cigarette and then caught himself as he was about to lift his legs on to the table. He let them fall back to the floor.

"You're both going to stay here until further notice. The trunk of the Mercedes is full of beer and food. There's liquor and cigarettes and," Billy Joe paused as the corners of his mouth tugged up into a brief grin, "drugs. There's a red toolbox on the passenger seat. Bring it in when you unload the rest of the shit. I estimate that you're only going to have to spend a few more days here, maybe a week at the outside, until certain business has been concluded. After that, we'll go back to the way things were before, except for certain cosmetic changes."

"What's that mean?" asked Malcolm.

"It means you'll dress differently. Balfire will shave and get a different hair color. Certain other props will be added."

Balfire shifted uncomfortably in his seat when he heard this news and began stroking his beard in a proprietary way.

"What *certain business*?" Malcolm asked.

"That's on a need to know basis and you don't need to know yet. No one knows where you are but if they ever got to you, you could only reveal what you knew."

"We're not snitches!" Malcolm exclaimed with as much outrage as he thought he could get away with.

"I know that son, but there are other ways to find out what someone knows. Someone who knows how could find out everything that was in your mind without you ever being aware of it. I've got reasons to be concerned about that. Pretty soon though, it's not going to matter." Billy Joe rubbed his hands together, an awful gleam in his eye as he rose up out of his seat. "How's the kid?" he asked.

Malcolm answered. "He's all right, immobilized. He was banging his head and feet against the wall in there for a while until Balfire went in and showed him his dick, said he was going to fuck him in the ass if he didn't stop. He stopped."

Billy Joe laughed and the sound of it made them both stiffen. There were bad dreams hidden in that laugh. "That's sweet, Balfire, I may just have you do that."

Balfire shrugged and said, "You're the boss."

Billy Joe got up and walked into the dining room where young Paco Rodriguez lay on a slim futon. There were handcuffs on his wrists and ankles and the flesh was rubbed raw on all of them. No compassionate heart had wrapped cloth around the bitter metal. The creature comforts of the hostage did not factor into the equation at all. There was a wide slash of duct-tape across the mouth.

In a motion almost too quick to see, Billy Joe reached down and ripped the tape from the boy's mouth. Paco howled with pain and surprise. Fear and anger warred in his eyes as he watched Billy Joe. Earlier he had been full of arrogance with Balfire and Malcolm. He had seen kids on TV in similar situations and had tried to "Hollywood" his captors. Balfire finally got up and gave him a tremendous backhand across the mouth and then duct-taped it shut. The left side of his jaw was now purple from Balfire's blow. Balfire had taken most of the fight out of him with this and his hints at things to come.

Originally he thought friends of his father had kidnapped him. They looked like the kind of losers he hung out with. This had pleased Paco because it made him think his father cared for him. Now he was not sure what was going on. He thought maybe this was about a drug deal. His father had burned someone in a *Batu* deal and they were holding him until things were set right. *Batu*, also known as Ice, was a smokeable speed that made you crazy and dangerous.

"So," Billy Joe lisped, "how are we doing today?"

Paco looked at him warily. "Okay, 'cept the cuffs hurt. Who you?"

"My name is Billy Joe. I am the one who decides what will happen to you."

"What's going happen to me?" Paco cried. He was fighting a losing battle with his self-control. Fear was swarming the ramparts and the dike was close to breaking. After all, he was only twelve years old.

Billy Joe's face creased into a grin and his eyes twinkled with false warmth. "I'm afraid it's not going to be very pleasant but you must bear it. You have no choice. You don't have to worry about being good though, because it won't make any difference."

Paco screamed and his back arched as he struggled to push himself free of his restraints. Trails of blood ran from his wrists and ankles where he had torn the skin.

Billy Joe kneeled down so that he was about a foot away from Paco. He radiated fear and an awesome finality that filled Paco with crushing despair. "You should be excited," he said. "You are going to solve one of life's oldest mysteries. You are going to experience it personally. You are going to find out what happens after you die." Billy Joe chuckled after he said this. His eyes were gimlet hard.

"No!" The boy screamed again and again. Billy Joe remained where he was, very still and watching. He remained that way for a long time and he never moved at all.

Chapter Fifteen

LOS ANGELES, CALIFORNIA • SOME WEEKS EARLIER

It was hours later when CarryAnn woke up in total darkness. At first she had no idea where she was, she had never been in darkness so complete before. In the hours that she had slept the cocaine had worn off. Now she was wide awake and filled with terror.

Very quickly the past came flooding back and she remembered everything. Now the fear had a face and it was much worse than not knowing. She could see the face of the man at the hotel as clearly before her mind's eye as if he was standing in front of her. She pushed in her mind to rid it of his image but it would not go away. From deep within came an even greater fear, because she suddenly realized that she had not just woken up on her own, but something had awakened her.

There was a presence moving through the front part of the house. She could hear footsteps. Her heart leaped at the thought that it might be Tommy returning from New York and then it froze when she felt the probing.

Something was pressing in her mind, calling to her, telling her to come out. Her body began to shake with fear as she fought to hold still against the urging to expose herself. The pressure grew and she knew that she would not be able to resist for much longer. The force was stronger than she was. She felt her will melting and a terrible lassitude overtaking her. The voice wove a tapestry of images filled with security and warmth, if she would only trust the voice...

CarryAnn ached with the need to expose herself and was in the process of moving from beneath the bed when the voice stopped. She could still hear movement at the further end of the house but the voice and its influence had gone. In its place, CarryAnn could feel another sensation now pervading her mind. This new influence drove her further under the day bed until her back was flush against the wall. It had only been a sensation at first, a sensation filled with an intelligence that CarryAnn instinctively understood. Then the sensation transformed itself into words.

"*You must trust me and I will protect you,*" the voice said. "*If you will let your mind accept me I will surround you and hide you. You will not be found.*"

"Motherfucker!" Billy Joe screamed, filling the air with enough force that Balfire jumped six inches in the air and peed in his Levi's. "I had her locked! I had her locked on, now she's gone!" Billy Joe's forehead looked like a thundercloud. He spun around in the living room, his thought pressing in every direction for his lost contact with CarryAnn.

"She's here, she's in the house, got to be," Billy Joe snarled. "I could smell her. The fuck is going on!" Billy Joe had started to morph into something that Balfire could not look at. The rage was shaping his form into some human-reptilian hybrid from the Island of Dr. Moreau. He couldn't look. He wasn't going to look.

"Balfire," he said, voice filled with menace, "go out to the car and get Malcolm. I want this house systematically searched, every square foot until that bitch is found and then we clean her clock so it never tells time again."

CarryAnn let herself fall back into the consciousness that enveloped her. Desperate fear and helplessness tore at her, told her to run this minute, run as fast and as long as she had ever done, run until her heart burst if it had to, but run, run! She fell back into the trust and closed her mind off to the terror that was flooding the house like a poisonous gas. She fell back into the trust and waited.

The men moved through the house. Items shattered as they were periodically thrown against the wall, furniture was overturned. There were curses and terrible descriptions of the fates that awaited her. There was the voice of Billy Joe and the thought of Billy Joe pressing, but CarryAnn lay very still, even when Malcolm came in and the light went on and he began to search the room, even when Billy Joe came in behind him and stood in the doorway, singing snips from the Hollies' song, *Carrie Ann*, she lay very still.

Into her mind came the voice again. CarryAnn felt something happening to her body. She felt herself falling into a vortex. It was like being sucked backwards into a funnel. The voice said, *"I have to make you very small, too small to see."*

Malcolm grabbed the comforter on the daybed and jerked it up, kneeling down to take a look underneath. An evil smile lit his features, "Well, well, what do we have here?" Billy Joe dropped to his knees as Malcolm tore away the comforter and ripped the pillows away.

CarryAnn saw the features of both men clearly. Under any other circumstances, she would have been terrified. Now she felt as if she were watching them from a great distance, a distance too vast for them to cross, though she knew that was not the case. She saw the looks on their faces, as the pillows were removed and she lay there, curled up in a ball. Fear screamed at her for recognition but she was removed from it, contained in a protected space by another will.

"Fuckin' shit!" Malcolm exclaimed, as he and Billy Joe stared into the emptiness beneath the bed. There was no one there.

Billy Joe's eyes narrowed. There was something wrong here. He knew there was something wrong but he did not know what it was. He passed his hand under the bed as if expecting to encounter something not revealed to his eyes, but there was nothing. He began to press with his will and in that moment there was the sound of a slamming door and a cry from Balfire. They both leaped to their feet and ran to the front of the house.

"Someone just ran out of the door!" Balfire yelled. He was standing on the porch pointing into the darkness.

"Why didn't you catch her you moron?" Malcolm yelled at him.

"I didn't even see who it was. It was too fast and then they were gone."

Billy Joe's eyes raked the darkness. Nothing stirred. "Branch out and search the grounds!" he ordered and then leaped from the porch himself in pursuit.

CarryAnn lay unmoving in a crack in the molding, reduced in size to that of an ant. For a time she heard the men crying to each other and then there was silence. Time passed and then finally she heard the voice again. *"They won't be back. You can go now."*

Now the process reversed itself. When she was restored and had climbed from beneath the bed she asked, "Who are you?"

"A friend," the voice replied.

"What am I going to do now?" she asked. There was no answer.

"But..." CarryAnn felt the questions bubbling inside her. She shook her head, her mind unable to process the recent events. Still, she was calmer than she had been in a while, the gray depression of past hours had given way to a lightening. A subtle sense of hope was in the air. CarryAnn would take it.

She wandered through the house, not really knowing what she was looking for, peering into rooms. There was that same smell she had noticed before, the smell of something rotting, only it was much worse now. As she began to walk upstairs the smell increased. Suddenly she knew what she would find if she kept looking. She went back down the stairs and retrieved her baggage from under the couch which had been overturned upon it. *"Thank God they hadn't found that!"* she thought.

The voice had rejuvenated her, made her stronger. It was time to go. She could feel the trails of evil that remained in the air after the men had gone. She paused for a moment on the front stairs, looking out into the darkness before her, then resolutely stepped off into the night and disappeared.

Alan gathered together copies of all of the research and police reports and left the station. Soon he was humming along on the crowded Mokulele highway that joined two of Maui's major towns, Kahului and Kihei. It ran for several miles through waving fields of cane and it was too narrow, badly paved, very crowded and unsafe. Even though Hawaii could have been one of the most economically sound states in the union, the powers that be on Maui had paid little attention to infrastructure. It had not kept pace with the rampant development of resorts and condominium complexes. Hawaii had been run by a good ol' boy network for years and was filled with corrupt unions, cronyism and all manner of graft and incompetence. Ben had remarked that sooner or later, real problems were going to surface. The developers, contractors and foreign interests had everything go their way for many years and had paid far more attention to their own profits than to the good of the islands and its peoples.

Alan wondered how things would develop with Rusk. There was no mistaking the antipathy the Captain felt for him. Captain Rusk had been with the department for over twenty years. Ben said that he was "hard but fair." Alan knew that this was not the case and found him to be rigid, unyielding and pompous in the extreme. He was constantly giving you the benefit of his years of experience, regardless of how many more years of experience you might possess.

He interfered in investigations and he disciplined his subordinates in front of other officers, which, to Alan, was one of the worst things any commander of men could do. He clearly held a particular dislike for Alan. Alan had made every effort to find harmony with him but to no avail. Alan's reputation as a man hunter, where the Captain had no reputation except that of a bureaucrat, made him see red.

Ben wasn't comfortable talking about it. The Captain could do him plenty of harm and he was determined to avoid it if possible. Taking Alan's side had already brought him grief. Alan was amused to note this area of self-preservation in Ben's personality. In every other respect, he acted with a reckless disregard for the opinions of others. Alan smiled ruefully as he thought about human frailty. *Everybody had chinks in their armor.* It wasn't too long ago that he had learned just how frail he was himself.

He came to the end of the Mokulele and turned left on to the Pi'ilani Highway. This was a bypass with exits into Kihei proper, Maui's geriatric *haole* corridor. It ran on to Wailea, where the wealthy from many parts of the world lived in opulent seclusion. A series of resorts grew along the beach and beyond them the road led to Makena, a world famous stretch of beach, and then finally to La Perouse, a huge tract of tumbled lava that ran down the mountainside to the sea. It was here that the road ended. Just before Wailea there was a turn up towards the mountain (*mauka* side as the locals called it). Here a community of expensive homes was spread about on some low foothills of the volcano. It was an eclectic community with more than a smattering of Hawaii's large new age community in residence. The climate and Hawaii's easy going lifestyle attracted the spiritually challenged from all over the world. There were also professionals and the independently wealthy for which this was only one of their homes. It was into this winding complexity that Alan was bound.

Dr. Philip Abadon was a noted psychiatrist who specialized in criminal forensics. Alan was familiar with his reputation, had read several of his works and knew that Abadon was considered one of the foremost experts in the pathology of the criminal mind. He was a member of the new school of thought that believed it was impossible to affect a cure in most sociopathic and psychopathic personalities, and that it was a waste of time and money to try. In one of his books, he suggested that modern society was a breeding ground for these types, predicting that a time would come when it would be forced to do something with them as a matter of survival.

Alan remembered another article by the doctor that he had read recently. It dealt with the personalities of O.J. Simpson and the Menendez Brothers, three of the most famous psychopaths of the present era. Abadon said they were prototypes of a new creature that was materializing on the American scene. Not all of them would be murderers, but all of them would bring hurt into the lives of those they met. He also discussed the personalities of famous sports figures, rock and roll performers, artists, television and movie actors who lived in a world of continuous privilege and excess. Many were without conscience or concern for anyone but themselves, and believed in their own positions in the same way that royalty had once believed in *droit de seigneur,* the divine right of kings.

It was an impressive article, very convincing. After he'd read it, Alan found himself looking at the behavior and lifestyles of the rich and famous in an entirely different way than he had ever done before. What amazed him was how nicely all of what the doctor said tied in with what was taught in the holy books and by the teachers of wisdom, concerning the destinies of those who sought fulfillment in the needs of the personal self. He was anxious to meet Philip Abadon. He hoped the doctor would have some answers for him.

Alan wound his way through the serpentine streets of Maui Meadows. It was necessary to follow directions exactly or one could get nicely lost in this randomly appointed warren of exotic side streets that curved and doubled back upon themselves. After a variety of twists and turns, he finally pulled up to the gates of 2865 Keaha Place. As he was getting out of his car to ring the bell, the gates opened up. Alan drove in through beautifully landscaped plants that filled the space on both sides of the concrete driveway for almost a hundred yards. He was amazed at the size of the property. Most of the homes in Maui Meadows were built on lots of less than an acre. This one was much larger.

He came round a bend and there was the house before him, a tall one story Spanish style home of white stucco and a red tile roof. The entrance was a deeply recessed double door of some exotic black wood, with smooth lava rock steps leading up to it. As Alan emerged from his Jeep, one side of the double doors swung open.

Whip was sailing down the highway in Alan's gleaming dune buggy with two hundred watts of Springsteen's "Promised Land" blasting out into the cloudless blue sky.

He looked at the lush bounty of foliage that swept by on both sides of the road, so many things in competition for life. It reminded Whip of a plant version of Hong Kong. He could imagine being here and letting the years roll by unnoticed. It was easy to see why Alan had relocated here after the tragedy. There was a healing power to the landscape. Whip had been feeling it every minute since he had arrived.

Whip's thoughts turned to Alan and the many contradictions that he represented, part hard ass, man hunter, part spiritual mystic. He lived in a world of good guys and bad guys and if you were a bad guy, you wanted to stay away from Alan. Whip had seen that first hand. You didn't run around a city like New York for any length of time and not run into your share of violent intrusion. Whip had been with Alan on one occasion at a Yankees game when thugs in the parking lot accosted them. Alan had sent them both to the hospital when they wouldn't just take his money and leave but instead remained to torment them.

This had created Whip's fascination with the martial arts and from that day on he'd been a devoted student.

He admired Alan in so many ways, emulated him and hoped that the qualities that lived in Alan would also grow inside him. He'd wanted to grab him the other night and shake him, to physically transmit to him his sense of the danger that was making its way inexorably toward him. Alan would deal with it the same way that he dealt with everything, when it materialized in front of him. But this time the danger was not like the other confrontations in Alan's life. A drop kick or a hollow point was not going to stop this one. Whip was reminded of a phrase from the Bible, something to the effect that, "We war not against flesh and blood but against powers and principalities and evil in high places." There was more to it. He remembered that it implied invisible energies of evil, inimical to mankind, something very old and filled with hatred for all living things.

Alan had been fascinated with the invisible worlds for all the years that Whip had known him. Whip remembered when he was a child, seeing Alan studying the Tarot. He'd told Whip they were the keys to the secrets of the universe and that a man who understood them could remake himself in the image of the divine.

He'd looked over Alan's library earlier that morning. It was filled with volumes on the Kabbalah, Astrology and Ceremonial Magic, the last of which Alan had said was one of the most dangerous pursuits of all. It was not just your life that you risked in the pursuit of its promises. An aspirant had to be possessed of unshakable virtue.

He'd told Whip that he did not have what it took to master any one of these complex and mysterious sciences, but that he could not help but continue to study them. He was drawn to the arcane like a lover to the object of desire. He despaired that he would never be more than a collector of these things, a collector of tales and a speculator in the truths that they veiled.

Whip knew that having a good heart was no safeguard against evil. Alan knew this even better than Whip, but Alan also believed that his skills, his instincts, his training in law enforcement techniques, his clarity of mind and his honesty would protect him from the darker intentions of the world that surrounded him. Whip knew that he believed this, even though his loved ones were dying around him. Whip was not so sure that good always triumphed. History did not prove this. *All relative evil did eventually fail but often too late to be of any comfort to its victims.*

Ming had been quite explicit. Even if Alan survived what was coming, he would not be the same at the end. He'd told Whip that he also had a part to play, that Whip should be aware. That was what he was doing, studying the terrain of the battlefield. He didn't know who or what he was looking for, but he was looking. Ming said, "The very act of looking reveals." He also said that if you concentrated on any problem or condition, and did it properly, the solution would be impelled to expose itself by the directive of natural law. He had explained how you could walk into a forest or a meadow, searching for something that could not possibly be found in either place and still find it, if not right there, at some point in the journey that led you out of the forest or meadow. The point was that it did not matter where you started looking for something. What mattered was that you kept on looking. There was a force set in motion at the moment you began to look and this force led you unerringly toward the thing you sought. No matter if it was within you or without. If the only person in the entire world who knew the answer lived in a cave in the Andes Mountains, you would be led there or they would be drawn to you.

What caused so many people not to find that which they sought, was that they did not continue to look. It was not important enough. They became distracted by something else, or became discouraged. This applied to every area of human endeavor. *There was nothing, nothing denied to the one who remained steadfast in his pursuit of the goal.*

Whip thought about all of the bitching and moaning he had heard in his life, on street corners and television shows. *The incredible foolishness of the Rosie's, Oprah's and the Gerry Springer's, who daily encouraged a nation of whiners, who daily embraced every cloying stupidity the world had to offer.* The more moronic, the more celebrated it was, HIV Positive Skinheads who were Sexually Molested by their Sister's Boyfriends, Coprophagial Dog Owners who Killed their Mothers. *Worst of all was the saccharine moralizing of the parasitical hosts, who amassed fortunes pandering to the trivialization of the human experience.* Trivia was a big thing now. It summed up America. The spiritual bedrock upon which America had been built was crumbling. *The lunatic fringe was going mainstream and an evil as potentially destructive as the rise of fascism in Germany was on the loose under the name of Political Correctness.* Whip was sure that the Red Chinese had imported it into the country but Ming had laughed when he told him this.

He had outraged gays, feminists and sundry with his vision of the natural order of things. What Whip could not understand was the violent and emotional reactions these "true believers" had to the dynamics of argument. Whip believed that debate was good for the soul and most of his problems were caused by the nature of the questions that he asked. Alan had once pointed out to him that Socrates got into a lot of trouble that way. He'd gone on to explain that people who were on shaky ground in their attempts to rewrite history, or who felt that any deceit was permissible in righting real or imagined wrongs, became very disturbed when the lack of a foundation for their argument was pointed out to them.

Here was another amazing thing that was taking place these days. Members of the general public, who had little access to real information and not much of a mind to use it even if they did, were being asked what they thought was *true* and then their responses were declared to be "the truth." *Staggering!* Whip had very little respect for a body of people who knowingly poisoned themselves, elected presidents who bankrupted them and then spent hours each day watching network TV until their asses were broader than the chairs built to contain them.

He made a right turn off of the Hana Highway onto Baldwin Avenue in the town of Paia. In moments, he was out of the town and back into the countryside again. This time it was nothing but sugar cane on either side of the road, another contribution from the missionary kings. Alan had told him that American sugar lost big money every year and would fail entirely without price supports, yet stockholders were paid "dividends" every year that were no more than gifts from the American taxpayer. These days, the growing of cane was merely a way of controlling large tracts of valuable land, as agricultural taxes were very low.

Tom Waits' mournful ballad "Foreign Affairs" returned Whip's mind to a time when his sister was alive. He shook away the memory as he entered the town of Makawao. Once a cow town known for its weekend rowdies and horses tied up outside the pubs, it was now home to a plethora of new agers on trust funds, marijuana growers and transients of various purpose from anywhere in the world. It had the trendy panache of a Woodstock, New York only friendlier and on a smaller scale. He removed the CD player and locked it in the onboard safe. He pocketed the key as he jumped from the vehicle and headed down the street, casually looking into the store windows as he went by them. He passed boutiques, a deli, and a naturopathic healer's clinic featuring a chiropractor, a kinesiologist, and a restaurant.

He walked along until he came to a health food store where he entered and bought himself a soda. He stood for a time reading the bulletin board outside the store while he consumed his drink. Continuing on, he came to a spiritual bookstore. The smell of essential oils and incense warred with one another for the superior position in the olfactory lobe. The shelves were full of books on channeling, visitors from outer space and various forms of healing. There was a wailing sound filling the shop that made Whip think of seagulls fucking in Jell-O.

It was amazing how lost people seemed to be these days and in what unusual places they would look to find themselves. That is, as long as it could be accomplished in two weeks, over the weekend was even better. It was better still if it could be accomplished without any pain or struggle or giving up anything that might stand in the way. It was okay if it cost a great deal of money and it didn't matter how stupid or preposterous it sounded, in fact, the more outrageous the claims, the better. *One had only to scan the varieties of techniques and philosophies being hawked from the shelves of this one bookstore, hundreds of which purported to have the answer to those most profound of life's questions: Who am I? Where am I going? What is real? What happens when I die? How do I find God? How do I find Love? How do I become successful? Who are all these people in my head? And, where is the bathroom?* Whip smiled at the thought.

Certain titles kept cracking him up and occasionally he would begin laughing. It was while he was chuckling at one particularly ludicrous sounding book that someone behind him whispered, "Can I help you with something?"

Whip turned to find a Maynard G. Krebs look-alike standing behind him, wearing blue Ben Franklin glasses and a white jump suit.

"You work here?" Whip asked.

"Yes," the man replied very softly.

"No, thanks," answered Whip, "I'm just checking out the books."

"Well, that is perfectly fine," he continued, "but your laughter could disturb the chakra cleansing that is taking place in the meditation room."

Although Whip had not been laughing very loudly, he was standing right next to a curtained off area that he presumed must be the meditation room. The conversation between them had drawn the interest of several other browsers who were watching the exchange with varying degrees of interest. Whip had no doubt annoyed one of them earlier and they had gone and gotten the employee.

"Are you telling me that my low level laughter was causing a negative reaction in a... what did you call it, a chakra cleansing? I didn't realize that laughter was a negative factor. I thought it was life affirming."

"Yes, well, that is true." Krebs was squirming now and trying to guide Whip away from the curtained room. "It's more of a concentration thing you see."

"And it's happening right there?" Whip pointed at the curtained room.

"Yes, yes," Krebs replied, reaching for Whip's elbow.

Whip moved out of his range and said, "Well, I suppose I could move." Whip was studying the man with the trembling lip and trying hard to keep from breaking into a full-blown smile. "Certainly I could move, but have you considered putting a door there? I mean with all the money you are making selling these important works, I'm sure it's affordable. People must talk in here all the time. Or don't they?" Whip looked inquiringly at Krebs.

"Well, most of our customers recognize that efforts are being made... Ah... through the day with clients and healers. We are a healing center here and we like to keep our voices low."

"You're not a bookstore then?" Whip's eyes opened wide. "You're more like a church or a funeral parlor?"

Someone snorted with laughter in the aisle across from them.

"Please," the man pleaded with Whip, not knowing how to contain him and not wanting to let go of his self-control, which was the only weapon he had in a game he was unlikely to win.

"Okay, then, answer me this question and I'll be on my way. Just what does this chakra cleansing cost?" Whip smiled in his most engaging manner, as if to say, "I'm not such a bad fellow, we got off on the wrong foot. I'm just confused."

Krebs' eyes darted to the left and right seeking the rabbit punch that he thought might be hidden somewhere in the request. "It's by donation, of course," he replied.

"And is there a suggested donation?" Whip was without mercy now.

Krebs was shifting from foot to foot, wishing perhaps that someone would ask him for help but no one seemed to want any. "The suggested donation is $100.00."

"Ah," Whip sighed, "Now I understand. It's always better to be quiet when that much money is involved." He reached out and took the man's arm and started walking him toward the front of the store, a direction that Krebs was very willing to go in. There was a sniggering sound coming now from the area in which the snort had emerged earlier.

"I do, however, think that you should install a door there. What if lower chakra energies or demonic entities should slip through the curtain during the session and take control of a client's body while it was in a vulnerable state? You could be legally liable for the results."

"What?" Krebs looked at Whip in shock. He did not know if he was serious or not.

"Yes, in New York, a few months ago, a lady sued for astral invasion which took place during a session where the treatment room was not properly sealed.

She claimed she had been possessed by the soul of a subway alcoholic who had been run over in one of the tunnels. She said she dreamed nightly of the event and at inopportune moments would be forced to scream out obscenities, grab her crotch and spit at people. She received a settlement of $2.5 million dollars."

"What! Is this some kind of a joke?" Now Krebs was raising his voice.

"Absolutely not," Whip replied indignantly. "Why would I make something like that up? I'm an attorney. I knew some of the people who worked on the case. You can't be too careful." Whip was now wearing his most serious face.

This was apparently too much for the person who had been making the noises. She rushed from the store with her hand over her mouth. "How do you know when your chakra needs cleansing?" Whip asked, distracting the clerk from his observation of the woman's sudden exit.

"Lady Ariel recommends every three months. However, if you are going through a stressful period, you should have them more often."

"What do men do?" Whip asked, deadpan.

"Pardon me?" Krebs inquired, feeling himself drifting further and further out to sea with no chance of return.

"Well, men don't have periods," Whip said.

"Sir..." Krebs was getting more and more uneasy. That feeling that he was the target of some private joke was growing. Yet Whip seemed so serious, Krebs had not been faced with this kind of behavior before.

One blue rinsed lady in a purple dress with a large ungainly crystal around her neck was openly staring at Whip as if he had just crawled out from under a rock. She wasn't fooled, oh no. She was hoping her evident disapproval would hasten Whip on his way.

"I wasn't speaking of that kind of a period. I was speaking about a segment of time."

"Oh..." Whip replied, letting the light dawn in his eyes, nodding his head in understanding at the lady in the purple dress, giving her that look of melting compassion he reserved for those who turned the scorn gun on him. He had found from experience that this look drove all things sanctimonious and self-righteous into a ravening frenzy. "Okay, thanks for your insights. I may be interested in a chakra cleansing at some later point. I'll be going now." He patted Krebs on the shoulder, nodded to the purple lady and left the store.

He walked back toward the health food store. He had already forgotten the incident and was thinking about Ming when he was arrested in his steps by a hand firmly gripping his left arm. He leaped forward and spun around to find himself facing the woman who had run laughing from the bookstore.

She retreated in shock and then laughed. "Sorry!"

Whip laughed, too. "No, I'm the one who's sorry. I don't know anyone here and didn't expect it." Whip studied her. She was around 5'8", dressed for Marin County, in a wide-brimmed sun hat, a blue flowered granny dress and a pair of Doc Martens lace-ups. There was an ocean of black hair tumbling out and down over her shoulders. She had the deepest blue eyes Whip had ever seen and a radiant smile framed by full red lips in a face from the Renaissance.

She was so beautiful she made Whip feel short of breath.

"Are you a comedian?" she asked. "That was one of the funniest routines I ever saw."

"Worse," Whip replied. "I'm a psychic terrorist dedicated to overthrowing the Emerald Cities of the mind, a man with no values and no respect for contemporary mores."

"Wow, all that, huh?" Her eyes went wide in the perfect look of a Pollyanna.

Whip laughed again, blushing slightly from the impact of her beauty and the confusion in his hormones. "Some would say," he replied.

"Some, but not everyone, eh?"

Whip stuck his hands in the pockets of his jeans and shifted his weight. "I guess I don't know." They stood there awkwardly for a moment until Whip finally spoke. "My name's Whip," he took her hand.

"Christienne," she replied.

"Uh... look, I'm new here and I'm really hungry. Maybe you could recommend a good place to eat?" Whip was looking everywhere except her face where those twin pools of blue destroyed his reason every time he looked into them.

"Depends on what you want." The atmosphere was definitely heating up.

"Depends on what there is." They both laughed.

"Well..." Christienne trailed off and gestured expansively around her. "There's a Mexican restaurant back at the corner, an Italian deli, take-out from the health food store and a local deli back down Baldwin."

She was so beautiful, Whip was thinking as she recited the litany, pale creamy skin with a smattering of freckles, an appealing gap in the middle of her oh-so-white teeth. That long flawless neck and the hidden promise of whatever danced beneath the blue flowers on her dress. "I wonder," he said.

"You wonder what?" Her eyes crinkled at the corners.

"I wonder if you would join me at your choice of restaurants, being as you are the first stranger to talk to me and I would forever be wondering about you if it ended now."

She brushed a stray strand of hair away from her face and laughed. "So you are a poet too, as well as a comedian. Well, I am hungry too and I was going to eat soon. Let me see your hands."

Bemused, Whip extended his hands to her. She took them, turned them over and released them. "Hmmm," she murmured. "Your hands are clean, you don't look dangerous and you have nice eyes. I think it's a risk I'm prepared to take."

"Great!" Whip answered enthusiastically. "Where do you want to go?"

"The Mexican restaurant I think. It has a nicer atmosphere and the food is pretty good. That is, if you've not from a big city, or you've never been to a border town, or deeper into Mexico. Then it's not so hot, but for Maui it's pretty good."

"Let's do it then," Whip replied and they turned as one and walked toward the corner.

Chapter Sixteen

A tall slender man in a blue suit came out of the house and walked toward Alan with his hand outstretched. He had a beautifully manicured salt and pepper goatee, a scimitar of a nose, hooking over broad sensual lips, deep-set wide apart black eyes, a high unlined forehead topped by thick black hair, parted in the middle and flowing back over his ears and onto the collar of his shirt. He was immaculate.

"Detective Douglas? I am at a loss for how to address you." A wide grin split his face as he said this, revealing small white teeth with flashes of gold. He shook Alan's hand.

"No need to stand on ceremony, Doctor Abadon. Just call me Alan."

"Yes, of course and you must call me Philip." His calm patrician manner immediately put Alan at ease. "But you do have a rank? On the phone you said 'Special Investigator.' What's that all about?"

"I was a homicide detective in New York City. I recently retired. It was the District Attorney who gave me my present title, when he asked for my help on the case."

"I see," Abadon replied as they entered the house. "I believe I've heard of a Detective Alan Douglas from New York, who was instrumental in the apprehension of several infamous killers a few years back. Would that be you?"

"That would be me," Alan answered.

"Indeed!" Abadon's eyebrows arched with surprise and interest. "I have wanted to meet you for some time. I have often wished that I might ask you some questions concerning your adversaries. Could we do that at some time?"

"Sure, I'd be glad to," Alan replied and he meant it. Abadon was a legend in his field and Alan was sure he could learn a great deal from him in exchange.

He followed the doctor through a long wide hallway with closed doors on either side into an enormous living room with a vaulted groined ceiling interlaced with skylights of various subtle hues. The scene laid out in front of him took his breath away. He had never been in any living room like this before. It was part museum, part antique shop and part movie set, an incredible display of different times and cultures. There were African masks and Oriental vases, ebony, teak and bamboo furniture. The living room looked out upon a lava rock pool into which plunged a small waterfall. It was a courtyard of jungle surrounded by what had to be a very large house. To Alan's right were two grand pianos encircled by a custom-made maroon leather couch. The room was hexagonal and had three separate levels. The stuffed form of an Asian rhino dominated the highest point to the right of the pianos.

There were other hunting trophies throughout the room. A twenty-foot anaconda was draped through the limbs of an ancient gnarled tree growing out of the earth, which was exposed in a five foot circle scalloped from the living room floor. One wall was a large bookcase beneath which sat a library reading table. There was Greek statuary and many exotic plants in pots of varying sizes. A polar bear stood in one far corner with his paw resting on a bust.

Abadon saw the direction of Alan's gaze and said, "Plato. I think he would have appreciated it." Then he laughed. Alan joined him, not knowing what to say about this outrageous setting that would clearly take a long time to even casually investigate.

"I deal with the mind," Abadon said, "with the mind and the problems of the mind. Besides the fact that this room has a very calming effect on me, it also takes the focus of my patient's minds off their problems and gives them some perspective. The complexity and shock of the surroundings occupies the conscious mind so much that I have a much easier time getting into the subconscious, where the conditions lie." Abadon laughed, "I feel like a computer programmer most of the time, going into DOS and fixing the software conflicts, cleaning up the registry and system files. I've come to the conclusion that most psychological conflicts are mainly about bad programming, with the original programmers being parents transferring the bad programming they received to their children and *ad infinitum*." Abadon's eyes twinkled as he said this, pulling at his ear with a wry smile on his lips.

"I've never heard it put that way," Alan replied, "But it makes sense."

"Well, now you see what they say is true. We are crazier than our patients."

Alan laughed, "Hardly, considering the types you've dealt with, but the jury is still out on everyone else. Still, this is the most fantastic living room I've ever seen in my life. Did you hunt these animals yourself?"

Abadon gestured for the couch. "Let's sit down, shall we?" Alan followed him over. "I used to hunt, mostly in Canada, moose, elk, bear sometimes with a bow. My wife did not approve, as women rarely do."

"Your wife must be happy with the move to Maui. There's little hunting here unless you like wild pig."

"My wife is dead, Alan."

"I'm sorry. I lost my own wife not long ago." Alan paused and both men sat in silence for a moment.

Finally Abadon said, "You have some things to show me, would you like something to drink? I am going to have a special blend that my houseman Kim prepares. It is a blend of herbs and several teas from other parts of the world. Interested?"

"Sounds great," Alan replied. His attention focused on the ornamental table in front of them. "What an unusual piece. I've never seen anything like it." The table was of some dark wood with dozens of fantastic nightmare creatures carved into its face. A sheet of glass lay over it.

"It's one of a kind, done by a Romanian woodworker for a wealthy patron in the sixteenth century. It was a wedding gift from my wife on our twentieth anniversary. It has a sad history. The woodworker committed suicide shortly after it was finished, the end product of a love gone wrong. The patron was hanged for an excess of political ambition. After that most of its owners lived normal lives. But then, what is normal?"

"There's a line in a song, '*the trouble with normal is it always gets worse*.'"

Dr. Abadon laughed. "Ah, that is very good indeed. Who said that?"

"A Canadian songwriter, Bruce Cockburn."

"I'll remember that."

Into the room came an Asian man. He was taller than any Asian Alan had ever seen. The effect was increased by his skeletal appearance. He was dressed in a maroon, mandarin gown buttoned from groin to neck. He glided to the table and placed the tray between them. With beautiful movements he poured the tea from a beaker into two glasses, setting one of them in front of each of the men. A platter of pastries followed and then he left the room as quietly as he had come.

"What an extraordinary man," Alan commented, "and a martial artist?"

Dr. Abadon gave Alan a startled look. "How did you know that?"

"Not so difficult doctor, I am a practitioner myself. You get a sense of it in others."

"You are a man of many parts, Alan. Please give me what you have and enjoy the comestibles while I read. Feel free to remain or to wander about the house and grounds. I am a man of intense concentration when I work, so I won't be available after I start."

Alan opened his briefcase and removed the file. He handed it to Abadon. Then he sampled one of the small cakes and a sip of the tea. "My God!" he exclaimed. "This is incredible."

There was no response from the doctor who was already immersed in the material. Alan went back to the food. After a while he got up and walked away, afraid that he would consume everything on the table and embarrass himself.

For a while he moved through the living room taking in the various creatures and objects of art. Alan imagined that the doctor must be very rich to afford all that he possessed and Alan had only seen one room of it. He wandered off through the door where Kim had exited, walking through a sunroom full of exotic plants, and on the other side was the kitchen. It was a wide airy room with a central counter over which hung a medley of pots and pans. Everything gleamed from the light that streamed through the French windows that were all along one wall and half of another. A long line of appliances sat under them. In a large eating nook, Kim sat at a round table sipping from a cup of tea.

"How are you?" Alan asked by way of greeting.

Kim watched him, looking through the steam that rose from his cup. It was an eerie sight. Alan felt as if he had walked through a time warp into another century. "I am well," he replied.

Alan shifted his feet. The man's calm was unsettling. "I understand you have studied in the martial arts."

"Yes," Kim replied, not moving, nothing moved except his lips.

Damn, Alan thought. *This was not easy.* "I've studied them myself," he added.

"Yes," was Kim's reply, still no movement. Now, finally, he took a sip of tea.

Alan felt like a ten-year-old kid in the presence of a mysterious adult. His mistake, he realized, was in thinking that verbal conversation was required, a typical western assumption that the air needed to be filled with words and if no one was talking, then something was wrong. Alan wanted to question him on what form he studied but he was not going to do that now. He studied Kim for a while. There was nothing more to say and Kim did not seem the least discomfited by the scrutiny or the silence. His age was indeterminate, except that he had to be at least fifty years old. He was clean-shaven, which surprised Alan. He would have expected some curling beard or a Fu Manchu moustache. His face was compressed, as if invisible lines of force were holding it in place. The top lip curled over the bottom one. The eyes were held in a powerful squint and gleamed like black pearls. The muscles of the forehead were pulled down toward the bridge of the nose.

They held one another's eyes for a moment. Alan could feel the power of the man radiating from his eyes, black eyes with a yellow pupil like a cat's. They were unsettling eyes, full of presence but revealing nothing.

"Would you like to see the house?" Kim asked, using more words in the one sentence than he had spoken before. He was on his feet in a single motion. It was remarkable the way that he moved. The man had a grace about him that Alan rarely saw outside of the animal kingdom. Alan was impressed, believing, especially in the martial arts, that form was function.

Kim took him through the house, opening various doors at random and leaving others closed. Not one room resembled the other. One room looked exactly like a Howard Johnson motel room. The next was a blue cavern with an enormous waterbed in the center. There was a small planetarium and a recreation lounge with pool and ping pong tables, pinball machines, video games and a wet bar from the Roaring Twenties. There was another kitchen, different than the first but just as well appointed, all dark woods with no windows and everything one could desire in the way of amenities, including an eight burner Wolf stove, a salamander and a pizza oven, copper pots hanging on the wall over a ten-foot preparation table and a whole shelf of Braun appliances.

"You must have some dinner parties here," Alan remarked.

"Sometimes," Kim replied.

"Beautiful equipment," he continued.

Kim nodded.

They came to a sauna and steam room, then a large office and study complex where Alan was not allowed to linger. Kim drew him on and they were once again in the first kitchen. Somehow they had made a circle of the house without ever having entered the living room again. Alan tried to figure it out but was unable to.

"Tea?" Kim queried.

"Yeah," Alan answered. "What's in it by the way?"

"Tea and herbs," Kim replied.

"Yes, but what kind?"

"Chinese." And so it went.

Alan could not get a handle on Kim. He was there but he was not there. The energy that came off of him was neutral. Alan could not read the actual thoughts in a person's mind but he could usually, with consistent accuracy, sense a person's intentions and level of humanity. It was one of the gifts that had made him such a successful policeman. Kim was completely unreadable. There was something going on inside of him but Alan had no idea of what it was. There was a sense of antiquity too, as if he were far older than he appeared to be. Alan attributed this to a lifetime of discipline, which had placed Kim in complete control of himself. Maybe like a mountain or a lake, he just was.

Alan had given up on having a conversation, so they sat and quietly sipped at their tea. As the minutes passed, Alan's thoughts drifted back into the past, back to New York and happier times with Elizabeth. He remembered a particular summer they had spent upstate at Lake George. They'd been married nearly five years at the time and after numerous attempts and many doctors, had finally come to understand that Elizabeth would never bear any children. He remembered how painfully beautiful and vulnerable she had been as they discussed the future. She had wondered if he wanted to leave and find someone else. She said she would understand and he remembered the tears that had sprung into her eyes. He had taken her into his arms and told her that he would never want anyone else and he had meant it.

"The doctor will see you now," Kim said. Alan's reminiscence dissolved and he returned to the present. He had heard no summons but it didn't surprise him. Ordinary means of communication were apparently not needed in this house.

Alan excused himself and went back into the living room where the doctor sat exactly as he had before. He looked up as Alan came around the couch and sat back down.

"Did Kim show you around the house?" he asked.

"Yes," Alan replied. "This is some kind of place."

"I designed it myself."

Alan's surprise showed in his eyes. "You're an architect too then?"

"I dabble," the doctor said.

"Some dabbling, it must have cost a couple of million to build."

"Three and a half," Abadon replied, "But it was not my money. My wife was very rich. Esmeralda came from one of the wealthiest families in Spain, descended from Ferdinand and Isabella, the financiers of Christopher Columbus' expedition. She made the house possible and bought many of the works of art. She had very eclectic tastes."

"Who found Kim?"

"Ah, Kim." Abadon took a long drink of tea. "I found him, years ago. He's been with me for a long time but that story must wait until another time for the telling."

Abruptly Abadon reached toward the file and tapped it with a finger. "The world is filled with mysteries and I came into my present occupation because they fascinate me. I think one of the reasons that I have been successful in my work is because I cannot let something rest until I have understood it. In my business they call that an obsession. Some mysteries are easier to solve than others, some we never solve. There are things I can tell you about this case, things that I feel fairly confident of. Other things that I can tell you are more speculative but worth consideration.

"These two men, they've been in prison, probably until just recently before their arrival here. They were in prison for crimes of violence that may have been tied to material gain but that would have been incidental. Of course, you have probably deduced this yourself. Are you familiar with phrenology?"

"You can tell a person's character by reading the bumps on their head?"

"Very good," Abadon replied. "It is an old science, now fallen into disrepute outside of the Orient. It is in fact somewhat more complicated than just the bumps on the head. It includes cranial structure, the lines in the face, the features. All of these elements taken together produce a reading, not only of character but of destiny too."

"I've heard it said that character *is* destiny."

"Hmmm… I often make use of Phrenology. I have the benefit of certain definitive texts and I find them illuminating. Did you see my library?"

"Only briefly, Kim did not seem to want me to linger."

Abadon grinned. "Yes, well he is a bit proprietary. I shall see that you get a better, longer look at another time. I brought up Phrenology to alert you to the fact that my methods are often unorthodox. I am interested in results and I will take from any science that gives them to me. I find Phrenology to have great practical applications, but I am sure few of my colleagues would agree with me. It is important for you to know that my conclusions are not always based on mainstream empirical methodology."

Alan nodded his head. "Doctor Abadon, you can read tea leaves or throw knuckle bones for all I care. I am also after results and I don't care how I get them."

"Good. Good." Abadon lifted a mahogany box from the table and opened the lid. He extracted a cigarette from it and then offered the box to Alan.

Alan shook his head.

"As you wish." As Abadon placed the box on the table, Kim appeared with an onyx ashtray and a lighter.

After he left Alan asked, "Does he always show up like that?"

"Over time Kim and I have become attuned," Abadon replied. He blew smoke through his nostrils and leaned back against the cushions. His eyes moved across the curved ceiling as he spoke. "Both of these fellows have committed multiple acts of violence. They will not stop as long as they live. They are most likely from California or perhaps one of the other Mexican border states. I would send the sketches to law enforcement agencies in these areas, you could get lucky. The smaller one is the brains. He's also a pedophile. He's killed children, enjoys it, and if they are responsible for these disappearances, then there is little hope that any of the kidnap victims are alive.

"It is unusual for them to have come to Hawaii, a small place hemmed in by ocean, much more difficult to escape from than where they left. It is an exposed position they've put themselves in and it contradicts what I know about their nature. Also, these crimes, the notes, this does not resemble the ordinary operational patterns of the type. I'd look for a third party who is in control with an agenda of his own. There is a stage being set for some kind of unveiling. I have a couple of theories but I'll hold off on them for now. You've got plenty to occupy yourself with until I am more certain.

"Contact these same states about prison releases over the last year. Confine your inquiries to those incarcerated for violent crimes. Have them check also for unsolved highway slayings involving torture, check into any torture related deaths, especially multiple torture slayings and most especially rape torture slayings. Both of these boys have serious sexual pathologies. The big one will do almost anything when he's high and that will usually be on some kind of speed mixed with alcohol. He's an impulsive disorganized personality. He might even have real regrets afterwards but they don't last. After enough time has passed he will often wonder whether the event even occurred. He could well be schizophrenic as a result of serious abuse as a child."

Abadon drew twin curls of smoke into his nostrils and looked at Alan. Alan was immersed in the tale. He had badly wanted to interrupt when Abadon had mentioned the third party but had held off. The good doctor dealt with crazy people. Alan didn't want to start telling his own story and lose his trust.

The doctor took another sip of tea and continued. "The smaller one is a piece of work, much more organized, a pure sexual psychopath. I believe that many of them are born, not made. They're like that from the beginning. He has no conscience and most likely relives his acts again and again with the benefit of masturbation, when he can't get a live one. He hates everyone and believes he is above all natural restraints, all conventions and laws. He picks children because of the innocence they possess and the horror, the paralytic terror he can induce. He may talk very soothingly to his victims the whole time he is committing the most unspeakable outrages. He hates every good and decent thing.

"Now, for the third party, and I'm sure there is one. He's got a very detailed plan and he's got good reason to believe he is in no danger of apprehension. At the moment I get no feel for why this might involve you. I refer to your business card being found at the scene. There is research involved. A clever mind is at work. There was the staging of the hearts and the interesting conundrum of the victim's ages. It is almost like he's creating a family. He's got everyone now but 'baby.'"

"Baby?" Alan's brow furrowed as he digested this.

"Yes, look for an infant to be next. That's all I can tell you for now."

Alan rose to his feet followed by Abadon. "One other thing, contact all of the local real estate agencies about the rentals or purchases of secluded properties in the last six months. Because those two were spotted in Paia, I would concentrate on that area as well as the East end and upcountry. They need a secure place to hide and to have kept, or keep, their hostages for whatever period they remain alive. They apparently have money, so they can afford what they need. If you should come up with any new information, I want you to contact me immediately, day or night, I am available."

Alan nodded and assured the doctor he would do just that. He picked up his briefcase and walked with Abadon to the front door. Kim had materialized again and walked in front of them, getting the door as they arrived.

"It's been a real pleasure meeting you, Alan. I hope we'll be able to continue to see each other later on. I'll be sure to invite you to our next affair here. A lot of very interesting people attend."

"Count on it, Philip." They shook hands. Alan thanked Kim for the tea. He smiled but said nothing. Alan turned away and walked to the Jeep.

As he drove out of the complex his thoughts drifted to Wendy. *It was strange how quickly the image of another blurred.* You couldn't remember their features, just a gauzy outline. The sound of their voice was gone. Sometimes a certain smell would trigger a momentarily clear picture. The sense of smell had a way of doing that like no other. Then, it too would fade. *In the end we held on to nothing.* Our memories of everything became increasingly more unreliable as we drew nearer to the void. *Did it happen that way? Did it happen at all?*

Alan thought about all of the lives that moved around his own, billions of them, all of the intricate destinies woven into a vast mosaic of existence. *Where was the meaning?* You came into the manifest realm, an unknown stranger from another place. You became part of a family, part of a blood tie attachment. As you formed and began to identify life in your own unique way, you moved out of the protective coloration of the family unit, out into the world, forming other associations that no one else in your family would ever make. Maybe you began a family of your own. Then one day you were gone. The family you were a part of continues, expands, interweaves with other destinies, laughter and tears, triumphs and defeats. Then one day there is no memory of any of it, no evidence of it, like Atlantis. *Atlantis must have had its own version of men like Shakespeare, Da Vinci, Hitler and Stalin, great artists and dark destroyers. Who could recall a single individual or any provable event now?*

There were the Chaldeans and Plato's Greece, Egypt and Rome, ancient civilizations that in many regards had not been improved upon save for the technology in use. There were so many theories and so few facts and everything was filled with contradictions. *No one really knew how long the pyramids had been there. Scholars still couldn't explain why the pyramidal shape would sharpen a razor blade or what had happened to the Mayans.*

Meanwhile, Alan was in a tiny envelope of time, pursuing villains. *The world never ran out of bad guys.* Lawmen had been hunting criminals since Cain brained Abel. There were no reductions in their relative numbers save for the rare golden age. Justice was sometimes harsher and sometimes swifter. *Sometimes it appeared that there was no justice at all.* Five hundred tons of dust landed on the earth every day. Someone was always going to have to clean it up, or thought they did.

It was a terrible irony that Elizabeth had been murdered. He'd spent his life protecting the public and in the end he could not protect the one he loved the most. *Life seemed like dust in the wind, dust and the wind that whipped it in no set direction.* It followed no discernable pattern, but like the sand on the beaches and all the drops of water that composed the ocean, always falling perfectly together. *Something made sense.* We just didn't know what it was, because only perfection could see perfection. Every human being was blind to some degree, could not see certain connections and could not see the mandala before them. They saw things in fits and starts, short portions of a dream that fell away into a gray haze fore and aft. *Was it any wonder that some grew disturbed in their sleep and flailed about at the other dreamers, gripped in an awful fear of the unknown?*

Alan felt a great thankfulness well up in his heart at the gift of faith, the faith that did not fear the uncertain night. A faith that he believed would lead him finally to understanding. *In all the emptiness of space, the separations of hearts and minds, in the seeming isolation of the soul, no one really walked alone, only thinking made it appear so.* It only seemed that way, a personal blindness surrounded by conscious light. He knew that this must be. *No matter what lay ahead, in every moment, in every day, revelation was at hand if there were faith enough.*

Chapter Seventeen

The restaurant was done in upscale Mexican generic, with bullfighting and tourism posters, strands of Christmas lights, dark booths and tables along with an overkill of hanging ferns. There was a loud bar at one end that looked to be filled with an overflow of regular customers who took their consumption seriously. Looking around, he spotted a side room with a few tables and a window that looked out on the street. Whip steered Christienne in this direction and they took an empty table.

A waitress approached and took their orders. Christienne ordered a large carafe of wine. After the waitress had left Whip asked, "Trying to get me drunk?"

She smiled, "Not at all. I drink. What you do is up to you. Some might say I'm a little too friendly with the wine. I've got my reasons even though they may not be that relevant anymore."

Whip's eyebrows arched, "And they are?"

"Something not for the present," Christienne said, but in such an engaging manner that Whip was not rebuffed.

The wine arrived and Whip filled their glasses. Christienne fumbled in her purse and said, "You mind if I smoke?"

Whip shook his head. "No, in fact you can let me have one too."

Christienne grinned and handed Whip a cigarette. "I didn't take you for a smoker."

Whip lit the cigarette and blew the smoke through his nostrils. "I didn't take you for one either. Your teeth are so white."

"That's technology and personal effort at work." She took a sip of her wine and then set it down. She removed her hat and put it in the seat next to her, shaking out her hair.

"A lot fewer people smoke these days," Whip said.

"Maybe the Surgeon General has a point. I imagine I'll stop sometime but not right now, too much going on."

"In your life?"

"In my mind, there's nothing going on in my life." She said this so matter-of-factly that Whip felt a keen edge of sorrow pass through him.

"Life is strange," Whip said, not sure what else he could add.

Christienne shrugged and said, "What about you? What do you do? Where did you get that name?"

"I don't know what I do yet. I like to travel so whatever I wind up doing will probably include that. I don't really have to work, courtesy of a modest trust fund."

Christienne let out a laugh of pure enjoyment. "Me too!"

"Only in America," Whip replied. "Two people on trust funds meet, they have lunch and..."

"Then they fight over the check." Merriment gleamed in her eyes. Whatever momentary shadows had been there, they were gone now.

"Anyway, I was going to be a baseball player. That's on hold now, but it's how I got my name. Pitchers whip the ball, I am a pitcher, therefore 'Whip.'"

Christienne refilled her glass. "There's no baseball on Maui, not if you're talking professional baseball. Why are you here?"

"I'm visiting my brother-in-law. I've been in the Far East for a while. This stop is on the way back to the Mainland. I don't really know how long I'm here for, a month or so anyway. Certain things have to be resolved. To be truthful, I have no plans at all right now except lunch and maybe getting to see some of the more primitive spots on the island."

"I could help you there."

"Really," Whip stubbed his cigarette out. "How's that?"

"I'm a hiker. I've been on all the marked trails and plenty that aren't. I mean, if you'd like that." She turned away for a brief moment with the thought that she might have offered too much too soon.

Whip smiled, just having imbibed again from her blue eyes that were almost too much to bear. It was like a dream of flying. "What's not to like?"

The food arrived and it turned out to be good. They were both hungry and for a while, conversation was suspended.

Christienne was on her third glass of wine when they finished eating. Whip, his second glass half finished, sat it down on the table. She offered him a cigarette, which he took.

"So what about you?" Whip asked.

There was a moist alcohol sheen on her eyes. Her face was slightly flushed and she looked even more beautiful, if that were possible. She stared out of the window for a moment. Smoke flowed toward the glass and brushed upward against it as she exhaled.

"I'm still looking for myself. I had a boyfriend until a year ago. We'd been together since college. He wanted to come to Maui to surf and get his head together. He'd been having a rough time with certain chemicals. He plays the guitar. Actually he's pretty good in a calculated, antiseptic sort of a way. He doesn't have a message but he knows what sells." She took another sip of wine and smiled thinly.

"He was going to write hit songs, has a rich father with contacts in the industry. We came here and I bought a house in Huelo, and rich daddy wouldn't help with that since it included me. So here we were, he started surfing by day and playing in the clubs at night, and night and day he played me… for a fool. There are a lot of beautiful girls on this island. I got tired of it and finally threw him out. It wasn't easy. I got beaten up a couple times with some violent sex thrown in."

"Hey," Whip said, reaching for her hand.

"Ah, it's all right. I get a little sardonic about it sometimes. Anyways, after the last time, I'd had enough. I hired a couple of locals to beat the living shit out of him and break a few fingers while they were at it. After that he left me alone." She stubbed out her cigarette with an air of finality.

"Shit!" Whip cried. "You did that?"

"Yeah, I did." She grinned like an imp, full of satisfaction.

"That's the greatest thing I ever heard of." Whip was grinning from ear to ear and shaking his head. "Are you usually that pragmatic, that ruthless, or was it a one-time shot?"

She filled her glass again and topped off Whip's. "I try to be honest. I know I'm loyal and I'm worth the time anyone would take to spend with me. One thing I'm not going to be is a victim. It took a lot of soul searching for me to do what I had to do. If he hadn't been such a son-of-a-bitch, if he hadn't laughed about it while he was slapping me around, I might have pursued it in another direction. In the end, it seemed like the only thing I could do. These days the police are next to useless and I would have gotten caught up in a major sequence of extended bullshit and embarrassment. As it was, I caught a little grief from the law but they couldn't prove a thing." There was a cold gleam in her eyes when she said this.

"You see I couldn't resist telling him it was me and that he would be dead the next time. His daddy raised hell."

Whip studied her as she was speaking. She reminded him of a woman from a painting that he seen in a museum in Florence. *The planes and angles of her face recalled a vanished time. Shadows and flashes of light played in the hollows of her neck.* Whip wished he could bury his face in there.

Ming had told him that every event in a person's life, no matter how seemingly insignificant was a particular dealing of God with the soul. He said that grace was happening at all times but that we rarely see it. He had also said that there were no accidents. Since meeting Ming, much had changed in Whip's view of life. His objectivity had increased and he no longer accepted the surface presentation of events. *Things were not as they seemed.* Life emerged from a mysterious source and its appearance on the observable face was supported by and controlled by unseen forces.

"Enjoying yourself?" Whip asked as she poured the rest of the carafe into her glass.

She smiled a slow, lazy smile and lit another cigarette. "Sometimes I have trouble being myself. I haven't been comfortable with myself lately. With a few glasses of wine, I'll have the courage not to second-guess everything I say. I'm less defensive and paranoid around people. I'm less self-conscious. It's a poor excuse probably."

Whip reached across the table and took her hand, gently kneading the top knuckles with the ball of his thumb. "I hope it's not me. I've really enjoyed this. The day's taken a magical turn for me. I don't know you very well, but I like what I've seen so far, a lot."

Christienne's eyes were brimming, whether from the wine or the smoke laden air, or the emotional content of the moment, Whip didn't know.

Her eyes dropped to the table, unable to look at Whip. "Oh hell, I'm a lot more complicated than I used to be and no matter what we say to somebody, we never reveal who we are. Only time and experience will expose that. A lot of the time we're better off not finding out. This is just another day like a lot of them lately, when I've got nothing to do and I think too much. I haven't been around a lot of people lately, maybe that's why I'm baring my soul to a stranger."

"You sound borderline depressed," Whip said. "Usually when I get like that, I push my body. It seems to drive out the mental and emotional toxins."

"What… like running or swimming?"

"Yeah, you might try it, make yourself so tired you can't stand up."

"I keep drinking this wine and I'll achieve the same result."

"So, let's go for a ride. I've got a great little dune buggy with state of the art sound."

"Really!" Placing her empty wineglass on the table, she considered Whip for a moment. "Sure, why not," she replied with a smile.

Alan found Ben behind the desk in his office. He was wrapping up the paperwork on a recent investigation.

"Hey Lone Ranger, how was the dry side?"

"Still dry." Alan said, dropping himself into a chair beside the desk.

Ben closed the folder in front of him and leaned back in his chair. "Well, this slimeball is not going to see the street for a long time. This new witness nails him. You know, it's amazing how many times someone just happens to see us when we're sure there's nobody around."

"Sounds like the three disciples and the chicken."

"How's that?"

Alan looked at the large poster of dawn breaking over Haleakalā that hung on the facing wall. He pulled at his ear and said, "It's a Sufi tale. This Master gives each of his three disciples a chicken. He tells them to take the chicken and kill it where no one can see them. Two come back fairly soon with a dead chicken but the third doesn't come back for some time and when he does, he still has the live chicken. The Master asked him what happened and he said, 'I can't do it. Everywhere I go the chicken sees.'"

Ben laughed and slapped his desk. "Cute. I'll have to adapt it with local players. So, how did it go with the doctor?"

"Ben, you shoulda been there. Philip Abadon lives in his own private Xanadu. He's even got a Chinese manservant that doesn't talk. Well, not much." Alan went on to give a description of his meeting.

"He raises some good points." Ben hit the intercom and asked for a detective to come to his office. When he arrived he gave him detailed instructions to carry out concerning what Abadon had told Alan. "Oh, yeah, Whip called. I told him where you were. He's going to call back later."

Alan nodded. "What about that missing boy, any word yet?"

Ben shook his head, his face grim, "Nothing, the mother's frantic. We haven't reached the father yet. He's *opelu* fishing in Hana. We're hoping the boy is with him."

"Anything new from the Captain?"

"No. He's still basically pissed that the DA didn't bother to ask for his counsel before he appointed you and then set up an investigative unit outside the department. I can understand that. It makes him look incompetent."

"People usually achieve that without any help." Alan said this with no rancor.

"Well," Ben said, not disagreeing with him, "You've got all these decorations for bravery. You've been wounded. You've worked on celebrated cases that we've heard about way out here in the sticks. It makes him feel small. You understand."

"Ben, I've dealt with his type for years in New York. All this politicking and backstabbing is not going to deter me. The captain's a proud man with not a lot of reason to be. I didn't plan the events that got me decorated. As the Hindus say, 'It's Karma.' I didn't plan on being brave. I'm not even sure that I was, it all just happened. The media made it into something that it wasn't. Under fire your instincts take over, you don't have time to think. Many other men would have behaved in the same fashion. The next time was the same, I just happened to be there. Two policemen died. I can't see where I become a hero when I couldn't prevent that."

"I know this, you know this. The captain doesn't and he could cause a lot of trouble as we go along. Hell, I know you'll do your best. I just wish things were otherwise."

"The second time I killed someone, I caught a lot of negative shit, not exercising due restraint, like I had a choice. There were wisecracks behind my back, the newspapers were worse. I even had a couple of near physical altercations, couldn't avoid them really, officers blaming me for their comrade's death. I did what I could, turned down promotions and sweetheart transfers, but if someone is going to dislike you, they're going to dislike you and sometimes there's nothing you can do about it, and the effort you take to do so makes it even worse."

"Life isn't fair, is it, Alan?" Ben's eyes were laughing.

Alan smiled, "Gee, Ben, maybe not."

Ben got up from his chair and stretched, "I thought I might mosey over and see the owner of that arcade where the Rodriguez boy was last seen. Want to come?"

"Assuredly," Alan replied and followed Ben out of the office.

CarryAnn watched the clouds passing under the wing of the jet. She wondered how her mother was doing, and whether she was even still alive. The idea that her mother might be dead, that she might never see her again so unnerved her that she was immediately compelled to go to the bathroom and toot up more coke. It was a difficult feat with her nerves what they were and the vibration of the plane, but soon she was feeling better. Her emotions were nicely sealed in a psychotropic haze. Now she could see things from her window that had not been there before.

There was no way she could remain in California, not when the terror that pursued her there had tracked her down by means that could not be human. She shuddered at the image of that terrible face as it had peered under the daybed. Maui was the only place she could think of. Though she had never been there, friends of hers had and they had all raved about the beaches and the easy lifestyle. She felt good about the decision. She needed a place like that, somewhere to get it together until she could find out about her mother, a place where nature might give her the opportunity and space to clean out her head and her system.

After withdrawing money from the bank, she'd paid cash for her flight and used an assumed name. No tracing her now but then maybe they didn't need physical evidence, maybe they already knew where she was. She forced the thought from her head. *Better not to think about them again.* Maybe thinking about them and what happened sent them a signal and told them where she was.

The drug was doing its thing in her head, making the improbable plausible. However, in this case, for once, the drug was right.

She had a great deal of cocaine and no idea of what to do with it. Hopefully she would find a clientele, lots of people did coke. They didn't need to know it wasn't her coke. She would do what she had to do to survive. She'd use her head. She'd use her body if she had to. She'd already been used. *What difference did it make?* A few small tears formed and ran down her checks but she didn't even notice.

Whip pulled off the highway and ran the buggy down a cane field road. The dust billowed behind them. Soon they emerged out of the field and on to a high bluff overlooking raging surf hammering against the rocks several hundred feet below. "The Price You Pay" was dueling with the wind and winning as Bruce Springsteen's voice rose high and clear above it.

"This is beautiful," he said. "I see why you come here."

Christienne was tying her hair back with a band. "Hardly anyone is ever here. The signs discourage them, I think. If I see another car, I just leave. This place is only a few miles from my house so it's convenient, too. But I didn't plan on driving like we were in the Oklahoma Land Rush. What happened back there?"

"Something told me to get gone."

She looked at him perplexed. "What's that about, is somebody after you?"

Whip felt stupid. He was going to have to tell her something. She had an uneasy look now and he was afraid he might have made her suspicious of him.

"Some very bad people want to hurt my brother-in-law. That means me, too. It's why I'm here. I've got no evidence that they have any idea where we are or that they would do anything if they did, but it's got me acting very jumpy and I'm sorry. I probably ought to keep to myself until it's over. You're probably in danger just being around me."

Some of the uncertainty left her eyes and was replaced with a look of cynical amusement. "This is what you do to get girls hot, take them into the outback and tell them ghost stories? Next you'll be telling me you're with the CIA."

Whip's face had a serious look, "I wish it were only that."

"Damn!" Christienne shouted into the wind. "Why couldn't you just be some normal guy with…?" Then she laughed and the tension evaporated. She turned to Whip and gave him a level gaze. "I guess you better tell me about it." She took his hand and led him to a flat rock that sat a few feet back from the precipice.

Whip told her what he could, leaving out Ming and the fantastic elements. It still wasn't easy, but she made it less difficult when the smile never left her eyes. When he was done, he threw his hands in the air. "There, I've said what I could. Now I'll drive you back if you want."

"Uh huh… and fuck you? Girls can't have adventures too? Like I couldn't use some excitement? This sounds like fun." When she saw the look Whip gave her, she said, "I'm sorry."

"It's not fun, Christienne. I appreciate that you're not intimidated, but there's no fooling around here." Whip had a sudden terrible thought that Christienne might be part of the larger plot. He pushed it aside. Something told him that he would feel it if it was so and he didn't.

"I know it took a lot for you to talk to me. I appreciate the confidence. I really do. You don't even know me."

Whip's heart warmed. There was so much about her that moved him in a way he had never been moved before. His approach to women had always been cavalier. It was something he didn't take seriously, too early in his life for that kind of thing, but maybe not anymore. He raised his hand to touch her face and then let it drop to his knee before it was accomplished. His confidence was shot. *Maybe this was love. All of a sudden you were ten years old.*

She saw the gesture and turned away to look out to sea.

Whip got to his feet and walked to the edge of the precipice. He could feel the power of the ocean surging below him. He felt wonderful. At that moment,

Christienne poked him in the ribs. Whip nearly jumped out of his skin, his body spinning around in the air.

"Sorry!" she cried.

He came down on Christienne and bore her to the ground, but distributing his weight so that she was not hurt. Then he buried his face in her neck growling like a wild animal.

She squealed in mock terror. It had happened very quickly. Whip rose up and got to his feet pulling her after him, exhilarated and trembling from the experience.

"How did you learn to move like that?" she asked, her eyes wide.

"You fool around, you see what happens." Whip said. Doubt was pulling at him again as he realized he could have fallen from the edge. Once again he pushed it away. There was no guile in her face. "You like rough housing?"

"Depends on who it's with," she replied. The air was sexually charged and suddenly they were both looking in other directions again. Whip felt the pressure of a growing tumescence. *She was standing so close.* Whip reached forward and pulled her into his arms. Her face came up to his and he kissed her mouth. Neither of them wanted to break it. Whip pulled back first.

"Couldn't help myself," he said.

"I didn't mind," she replied. "I wanted you to." Then she leaned forward and kissed him again. Her lips were full and soft and tasted of the wine she had been drinking. She held his head in her hands and slowly traced the outline of his mouth with her fingers. "You are a very nice man. I haven't felt this good or this free around anyone in a long time."

Whip drank in the affection from her eyes. Within the blue windows of her eyes, he could see the clouds passing as they reflected down from the sky. He sensed the deeper delights of her being simmering beneath the surface of her physical form. An ache was growing within him to be somewhere in darkness with her where everything was done in Braille. They stood there in the afternoon sun, speechless, watching each other, both of them aware of the possibilities of the other and luxuriating in the timelessness of the moment.

"We're going out to dinner this evening, Alan and I, to a restaurant nearby. I'd love for you to come, meet Alan." He let the invitation hang.

"I'd like that," she answered.

"Then we should get to a phone and let Alan know what's up." They walked back to the car and climbed in. Whip rummaged through the CDs until he found something appropriate.

"Breezing" by George Benson poured out of the vehicle, joined by the sounds of the perpetually rustling sugar cane as they drove back down the dirt road, considerably slower than they had come in.

Just as they reached the highway, a black Mercedes touring car went rocketing by, its occupants invisible behind the smoked glass, going somewhere in a hurry. It was already gone from sight as Whip pulled onto the asphalt, a cold wind trailing in its wake…

Captain Rusk sat behind the wide mahogany desk in his office, the walls lined with dozens of mementos from his past. There were various pictures of him with visiting dignitaries, fishing in his native Seattle, ballroom dancing with his wife and in the act of accepting many civic awards for minimal efforts he had made with exactly that in mind. The Captain was a vain man. His life and career had been devoted toward casting himself in the best of lights. No opportunity for personal gain had ever passed him by. Though he was not corrupt in the respect of ever having directly taken money to circumvent the law, he would do almost anything else if it secured the desired result.

Right now he was turning events around in his mind and trying to find a way to screw up Mr. Bigshot Alan Douglas. What was frustrating him was the District Attorney, Aaron Wilson. Lately Rusk had not been feeling himself. He had been having some very disturbing dreams and he had not been sleeping well. He was sipping from a flask of bourbon that he kept in his desk and feeling mean, feeling especially mean. Someone was going to catch hell today. He planned on it. He'd just called the mayor to protest Wilson's handling of the case. He thought he'd better since Wilson had implied he might call the mayor himself if Rusk made any trouble. He wanted to give his side of things. The mayor had been understanding but firm. Wilson could call the shots as he saw them.

He took another sip of the bourbon. The worst scenario he could imagine was that Douglas would crack the case. He would bide his time. Sooner or later, he would have a little something for Mr. Super Sleuth, Cowboy Hero, motherfucking Douglas, a little something special. He ground his teeth and took another sip.

Whip called Alan and settled on meeting him at six thirty for dinner. They wandered around Paia for a while. Then Christienne had taken Whip part way into a bamboo forest, a place of perpetual dusk. Whip felt a great peace come over him as he walked in the shadows of the waving stalks. He thought how much he would love to have a little cabin right in the middle of such a place. He'd never seen such large bamboo. Some were as big around as a small tree.

They came early to the restaurant. Christienne wanted more wine. Whip wondered if she was an alcoholic but she didn't show any signs of degeneration or radical mood swings. Then again she was still young and it wasn't his place to speak. Certainly not now and certainly not when there had been no incidents of regret. He was no one to talk anyway.

They sat in a beautiful courtyard setting and watched the shadows of evening approach. For both of them the world was a fine and splendid place. There was a magical hue over everything surrounding them, especially when their eyes fell on each other.

"Tell me about Alan," Christienne asked.

Whip stared out at the water that was now darkening at the sun's departure. "That's a hard question for anyone to answer. You describe a person and they always become something different than your description, no matter how accurate you may have been.

"First, Alan is a good person, deep down good. He's also an achiever. Whatever he sets out to do, he accomplishes it. He never complains and he seldom criticizes. I've known Alan since I was about eight years old. He's been like a father to me, a big brother and most of all a mentor. He's been through hell the last few years, losing his wife, my sister, leaving everything that he's known. Then he comes here to start over and just as things are smoothing out, he loses his friend Wendy. He rarely lets you know what he's really thinking, what's going on inside of him. He doesn't talk about himself very much. As much as I like him, I find it difficult to know him as a person sometimes. He's got this very private side and sometimes he's like water, colorless, transparent. He doesn't stand out."

Whip set his drink down and his eyes grew thoughtful. "He likes metaphysics and mysteries. He's a world-class martial artist, so he's very disciplined. I haven't been around him much in a while. He's changed, but not in any obvious way, a little more serious maybe. Did you ever read *The Lord of the Rings*?"

"It's my favorite book of all time!" Christienne exclaimed.

“How about that,” Whip was grinning like a madman, “Me too! You remember Frodo and how the wound he received at Weathertop would trouble him? In the end he had to go to the Grey Havens because of it?”

“Certainly, I’ve read it ten times at least.”

Whip was impressed. “That’s how Alan is now, kinda like Frodo after Weathertop.”

“Wow. What a great image.”

“It’s the only thing I could think of that would fit.”

“Well, is he tall, dark and handsome?” The wine was backlit in her eyes and they seemed incredibly large and luminous in the diminishing light.

Whip knew she was toying with him but he told her the truth anyway, “As a matter of fact, yes.”

“Umm...”

“You aren’t going to cause any problems are you?” Whip asked in jest.

“Right now I think I’ll start with you and work my way up.”

“Up, up — not down? What’s that supposed to mean?” Whip glowered.

“I guess I meant up and down,” she said sweetly.

Whip blushed. This woman was gaining a power over him like no one else ever had. Half of him wanted it and half of him was becoming disturbed at the effect. Even more disturbing was the way it was taking his focus from the things Ming had warned him about. *Ming had never said anything about this kind of love!*

Whip knew that he couldn’t stop looking over his shoulder. The dark and the dangerous were out there and they were looking to deal major injury. It might not come into the restaurant but it could well be waiting outside. When darkness fell, every dark corner was suspect. Whip knew that Billy Joe could hurt in many other ways beyond just the physical. He’d nearly destroyed Alan with alcohol and despair. He flashed again on Christienne’s drinking. She was pouring herself yet another glass. *They were all in danger.*

Billy Joe could be watching them right now, Whip didn’t even know what he looked like. He scanned the restaurant and the bar area. There were several men alone or talking to each other. *It could be any of them.* Maybe he should have a gun, but what good was a gun against Black Magic? Ming had said that Billy Joe was a ranking member of the Dark Brotherhood, with access to many of the powers of his infernal master. He could change his physical appearance to all but the most spiritually discerning. He could enter through locked doors or turn himself into an animal.

"Whip?" Christienne was talking to him.

"Sorry," he said, coming back out of himself.

"What's on your mind, Whip? Your eyes went out of focus and you disappeared."

"Thinking about the danger, the danger we could all be in, wondering what to do with you."

Steel came into Christienne's eyes. "Look Whip, let's get this squared away, then we can get on with it. I accept the risks and I don't accept you making decisions for me concerning the risks. I don't know where any of this is going to lead, but I'm not going to let any assholes run me out of town!"

Whip laughed in merriment. "You are something else," he said.

Christienne regarded him warmly. *This had to be the best of days in some time.* Lately she'd been drinking too much wine and smoking too many cigarettes. It was the loneliness that was doing it to her. She didn't have to be alone. She knew that. Men were not difficult to come by but too often they were users who trashed her self-respect, leaving her feeling violated and cheap. *They fucked you in more than one way.* She knew that she was bitter, that many men did not fit that description, but she also knew that she had run into a lot of them that did. Maui, a land of transients, was especially supplied with them.

The whole game was different for a woman. There was something about having a womb, something about taking someone inside you that left you vulnerable to all things negative. The very positioning of a woman in the act of sex was one of extreme openness to the penetrator. If the energies were low then you were left with them. She thought about certain nights when she had gone home with someone when she was lit, laughing, fooling around, only to wake up after a night of sex with a stranger, certainly stranger than he seemed the night before, feeling like something precious had been stolen from her.

She wouldn't do it anymore. She just couldn't take the sense of loss. She didn't think she'd been loose, just a woman of the times in a time that was so much more permissive of a woman's right to behave as she chose.

She didn't think of herself as a feminist. She hated the constant axe grinding. But she was an individualist. She had a strong sense of herself. She always felt that a woman had command of her life if she wanted it. She didn't need to be part of some larger revolution that was mostly controlled by women who hated their fathers or who didn't even sleep with men in the first place. She liked men. At least she was prepared to like men. She just hadn't been very lucky but she hadn't given up either. *There was no question that many men sought control, were selfish and indifferent to a woman's needs, but not all of them. Whip was nice, easy to be with.*

She looked at Whip who was looking at her. They'd not said much for a while. The moment was too full for words. She reached across the table and took his hand. "Whatever happens, Whip, it's been a good day."

"Yes, it has," he replied.

Lost in one another, they failed to see Alan, who had shown up and was standing behind Whip with an amused look on his face. Finally Christienne looked up and caught his eye. Whip turned round.

"Alan, great, you're here!" Alan placed a hand on Whip's shoulder and pressed him back into his seat when it appeared he was going to get up.

"Sit, sit," he said. Then he came around the table and took a seat.

"How long were you standing there?" Whip asked.

"About fifteen minutes," he replied matter-of-factly.

"Liar," Whip replied. "Christienne, this is Alan."

She extended her hand and they shook. "Hi," was all she could manage. She felt foolish at her monosyllabic greeting but she had been caught off guard and her mind had gone blank. Something about Alan left her with very little to say. His brooding eyes seemed to see right through her, right past all of her defenses, yet it did not make her uncomfortable. She wasn't sure how she felt.

"A pleasure to meet you," he said. Sensing her discomfort, he sought to put her at ease. "Whip said he'd made a friend but he did not prepare me for you. You have a great face."

This peculiar wording was so unexpected that everyone laughed. "What, did I say something?" Alan gave them a gooney look and then signaled the waiter who had been hovering nearby.

"You're right, Whip. They always turn out to be different."

"Talking about me behind my back again I see," Alan quipped as he scanned the menu. "You're in for a real treat if you haven't eaten here before. The fish is out of this world."

Billy Joe and Malcolm sat at the bar. Malcolm had been dressed and coifed by the master himself. He didn't look like Malcolm, wouldn't have anyway with Billy Joe's veil on him. Billy Joe looked like Sting.

"Cute little fuckers with the target," Malcolm said. "Sure would like to rip a piece off the bitch if I got a chance."

"She's a little old for you, but maybe you will," Billy Joe murmured. "Might be just the thing, do the boyfriend too, maybe he'll fall in love with you."

Malcolm snickered and downed his cognac. He couldn't take his eyes off of Christienne. She looked like proper violation material. Dress her up in white and then tear to her pieces. Afterwards he'd display her in a special way, scatter Plumeria flowers over the body and place an eyeball in each open palm. He laughed a laugh of pure evil. The spirit of Billy Joe was upon him and he was badder than he'd ever been. The Master smiled. *Retribution was coming soon.*

Dinner was over and the three of them sat replete and waiting for their after dinner drinks. Christienne excused herself and went to the bathroom.

Alan looked over at Whip, a silly grin lit up on his face, his eyes filled with warmth. "She's a beauty Whip."

"Yes, she is, Alan. What a day, I think I'm in love and this island… powerful."

"Uh huh, be careful. Evil's greatest joy is to strike the thing you love."

"I know, Alan. Ming came to see me this morning, in my meditation. He will see you soon. He said to tell you that."

The waiter placed the digestifs and coffees on the table.

"Good," Alan replied. "But what does that mean? He's here?"

"Alan, he could be anywhere and everywhere. He doesn't have the ordinary limitations."

"Well, I guess I'll burn that bridge when I come to it. What are your plans for the evening?"

"Everything's up in the air right now. She wants me to see her house. It's down in some place called Huelo."

"I know it. Watch yourself down there, bad roads and roads that don't lead anywhere. When it rains, and it does a lot, the dirt roads turn to mud. Good thing you've got the buggy."

Christienne returned to the table biting her lip and giving them both a curious glance. "You know," she said, "It's one of the peculiarities of human behavior that we always talk about the person who's not present and we stop talking about them as soon as they return. And since everyone has been there, everyone knows it's true. However, most people deny it when they're confronted so I always bring it up just to check out the response."

Alan laughed, "Of course, we were talking about you part of the time but we're not going to tell you what it was."

"Okay," she said.

Everyone laughed. Alan waved them off when the waiter brought the check. "It was very nice to meet you Christienne. Have Whip bring you up to the house one of these nights and I'll make dinner, got to go." Alan winked at Whip and went out the door.

Later, outside the restaurant, Christienne said, "I like him, Whip."

"Yeah, he's special." Whip turned out of the parking lot and headed back upcountry to where Christienne had left her car. The night was filled with stars. They listened to the wind rush by them until Whip punched the CD player and Bruce revved his engines down "Thunder Road" and flooded the night with song.

Chapter Eighteen

Balfire was hard at work. He was an artist and like most artists he needed to be alone when he worked. Otherwise he got very testy and prone to violence. Even Malcolm was careful around him during these times. Balfire had learned the trade when he was a teenager, during one of the few quiet periods in his life he'd spent some time with a rancher in the Sierra foothills. Bradley Sessums had taken Balfire into his home on a work arrangement with the California Youth Authority. Fresh from eighteen months inside, for two robberies and an assault charge, Balfire found himself on a cattle ranch in the middle of nowhere. He'd never been anywhere like it before. In his short life he'd never gotten more than ten miles outside of L.A.

Balfire was already over six feet and two hundred pounds though he was only fifteen years old. Bradley Sessums was bigger and stronger. He worked from the time the sun came up until it went back down. For recreation he competed in rodeos. The first time Balfire mouthed off to him Bradley slapped him silly and then he worked Balfire into the ground until he could hardly finish his dinner before falling asleep. But violence had never had any positive impact on Balfire's education. What had worked was the strength of Sessums' will and the fact that Sessums hated religion of any kind, loved to gamble, drink and was fair in everything he did. If Balfire had to work like a dog then Sessums worked even harder and whatever good things Sessums enjoyed, he shared with Balfire.

Two months into his stay Sessums brought two local hookers back to the ranch for the weekend. It wasn't very long before Balfire looked upon the man as the father he never had.

Real change was taking place in Balfire's life and, if the circumstances had continued, things might have turned out differently for him. Such was not to be. Eighteen months after Balfire arrived at the ranch, Bradley Sessums fell dead out of the saddle from a massive heart attack. Things quickly reverted back to their previous course. Balfire had grown to love the man and now the man was gone, but he'd passed a skill on to Balfire, the skill he was taking such pains with now.

Balfire stepped back and studied his work, walked around it, came in close and then stepped back across the room. He nodded his head and smiled. *Pretty fucking good*, he thought.

Whip parked the dune buggy in the lot behind the Italian deli and climbed out into the clear mountain air. Christienne came around from the other side and walked over to a new Land Rover Discovery.

"Very nice," Whip commented, "But I had you figured for something else, a Saab or maybe a little red sports car."

She laughed, "I've had them, but where I live, you drive this or you don't drive back out. You'll see. Most normal cars have to park part way down the road. Follow me." She gave him a quick peck on the cheek and then climbed into the Rover. Whip waved his hand in the air and went back to the buggy.

Soon they were winding around on narrow twisting jungle roads. Here was another side of the island that Whip hadn't seen yet. It was completely dark except for what was caught in his headlights. At one point there was a huge muddy cliff on his right while the road curved so intensely that Whip had to slow down to under ten miles an hour. He was exhilarated. They were coming into wild country, though he could see little of it in the darkness.

After several miles of torturous road, they reached the Hana Highway and turned right. Whip was glad for the change. He thought he might have become seasick if it had continued. After several more miles, Christienne signaled for a left turn. The road now became dirt and a light rain was falling. He soon saw what she had been talking about. Previous rains had caused massive erosions that would have made the road nearly impassable to conventional vehicles. Finally Christienne turned right and drove about a hundred yards, pulling into a cleared area on the right in front of a metal gate. She opened it, drove through and Whip followed her up to the house.

The area was brightly lit. The house was a large geodesic dome with a wrap-around deck sitting in a meadow. The dome looked like a flying saucer to Whip, with the light streaming from the row of windows that ran around the structure.

"This is beautiful," he said.

"You should see it in the daytime," she replied. As they approached the house more lights came on to illuminate the steps that ran up to the second story.

"You've really got your lighting trip together out here," he remarked.

"It's more of a security measure than anything else. Timers turn on the lights when it gets dark. I'm lucky there's electricity down here. A rich rock star bought the piece of property in front of me and brought all of the utilities down. I already owned the land or I could never have afforded it after he made it civilized. I wanted you to see the set up so that you'd know that I'm safer than you may have imagined. There are motion sensors around the house that activate the outside lights and if anyone opens a door or window after I set the alarm, it sounds like World War Three. I'm a single girl living alone in the jungle. There's always the potential for trouble around here. I've got industrial mace secreted in every room and two loaded shotguns where I can get to them quick, one inside, and one outside. I got raped here once."

"Jesus," Whip said. Her matter-of-factness made him sadder than the thought of the violation.

"Don't say anything, Whip. It's over now. It wasn't a particularly brutal experience. He didn't beat the shit out of me or anything and it was mostly my fault."

"Your fault?" Whip didn't know how to take that statement.

"Let's go inside," she said. They were at the top of the stairs, she worked the key and they went inside.

Whip looked around as he removed his shoes. The interior was one big room and looked like a New York loft, at least fifty feet in diameter. Space was obviously a consideration. Everything was set back against the wall in little alcoves. There was a kitchen niche built inside a large bay window, a futon with easy chairs and table set around an entertainment center and past that an office area with a computer. There were colorful rugs scattered everywhere on the hardwood floor and many hanging planters. There was a large loft that extended halfway across the room. Above, in the center of the roof, was a round skylight. Whip could see the moon through it. "What a nice space," Whip said.

"I'm glad you like it. I don't have a lot of stuff. If I don't use something I figure I don't need it. I've got a ping-pong table and a pool table down below but otherwise what you see is what you get. There's a nice rolling lawn outside with a picnic table in a screen house, a hundred feet after that it's jungle. There's a cliff that drops down to a good-sized stream that feeds into a beautiful swimming area. I've got a little over five acres, which is enough to play your music loud and to walk out the front door naked if you want to. The place can't be seen from anywhere, except maybe the top ten feet of the dome. It's private and quiet, the way I like it. You want a drink?"

"What have you got?" Whip asked.

"I've got everything."

"Everything?"

"Trust me," she smiled.

"I'll have a Martel Cordon Bleu then, neat." Whip followed her into the kitchen. "What if I'd asked for a Midori on the rocks, some Laurent-Perrier champagne, or Old Mr. Boston Sloe Gin?" Whip asked as he studied the gleaming fixtures in the kitchen.

She turned and curled her finger, beckoning him to follow. She went to a set of double doors to the right of the kitchen and flung them open. A light went on automatically and Whip found himself staring at an enormous carousel that held hundreds of bottles of every type of liquor. Next to it was a large icebox. When she opened the door, Whip saw it contained only wines and imported beers.

"Good grief!" he exclaimed.

"Like I said… everything. You probably think I'm a world class alkie by now but the truth is I hardly even come in here unless someone has a request and, since I don't have many guests, there are very few requests. The wines I drink are in the regular refrigerator," she said as she searched through the bottles.

"Here we are." She displayed the bottle of Martel the way a sommelier might do in a fancy restaurant. "I inherited all this booze from a rich friend who gave up drinking right around the time the house was being finished. I had this area built to contain it all. At the time I thought Richard and I would do a lot of entertaining with friends, other couples, that kind of thing. Boy was I wrong."

She poured some of the cognac into a snifter and handed it to Whip. Then she poured herself a glass of white wine and led him toward the living area. They sat on the futon in front of a table made from the crosscut of a tree. She reached under the table and pressed a button and the area was illuminated by rose colored light.

"You've got a thing for lights, eh?" Whip said.

"I do. I suffer from depression. Changing the lights often helps change my moods." She took a sip of wine and then lit a cigarette. "Now let me tell you about my big moment of forced passion, the thing all women really want but won't admit to themselves, at least that's what this asshole implied."

Whip was once again without words. He kept quiet, listening seemed the appropriate thing.

Smoke streamed from Christienne's lips. "Brian was a friend of Richard's. After we broke up but before I had Richard fucked up, Brian called me and asked to come over. He said he'd left some chart music in the game room, which used to be the rehearsal space for Richard's band. It was a reasonable request. Richard hadn't gotten all of his shit out of there yet. I said to come on over. That was my first mistake. That's when it started to be my fault."

"You couldn't have known what was going to happen," Whip interjected.

She just looked at him, her eyes unreadable. "He came over and I let him into the game room. He rummaged around for a while. He couldn't find his sheet music, since there wasn't any in the first place, and then said he had to use the telephone, so I let him into the house. He asked if he could have a beer. I gave him one, two more things that were my fault. Then he started coming on to me, telling me what a hot number Richard always said I was, how much it affected him just thinking about it.

"He knew that I wanted to. He told me so and now that Richard was out of the picture it was okay, as he put it, to 'get it on.' I told him to get out of the house but he said he wasn't going anywhere. He said no one could hear us and no one was going to stop him so I had better cooperate if I didn't want to get hurt." Christienne stared off into space as if reliving all that had taken place.

"He's a big guy, a lot stronger than I am. Maybe if I'd clawed at him, kicked him, run into the kitchen for a knife — I didn't have the mace or the guns then — I could have gotten him to leave, maybe not though. Maybe I would have gotten hurt. It felt like if I fought him, that he was going to hurt me. So I took the easy way out and let him fuck me. He laughed at me when it was over. He told me he would be back for more.

"The next day, Richard came over. There was another argument about me taking him back. He said I needed him here to protect me. I told him I would never take him back and then he smacked me around some. At least there wasn't any sex. I got away and locked myself in the Rover. I went into town and ordered the guns, bought some mace. When I got back he was gone. I put two and two together and figured out that he had set up the rape. That's when I decided he needed to pay. I think one of the reasons he didn't try to rape me that day was because he thought I was used goods since his friend had just raped me, ironic huh?"

"You didn't call the police?" Whip asked.

"There were just too many complications. I got Brian to use a condom when he raped me. How would that look in court? I handled it."

There was a cold resignation about her that chilled Whip. He reached over and pulled her to him. "No one and nothing is going to touch you while I'm around," he said.

"Thanks, Whip." She said it so quietly he hardly heard it.

She pulled away from him and took another sip of wine. There were tears in her eyes now, as well as anger. "If any of them ever set foot around here again

I will blow them away with no more feeling than I would if I stepped on a cockroach. I felt so dirty afterwards. I knew it was my fault and I wondered if I hated myself so much that I'd set up the whole thing just to show myself what a worthless piece of shit I really am." Tears were flowing down her face now and she could no longer talk. Whip held her and let her cry herself out.

When she was done, Whip got a towel from the kitchen and dried her face. Then he kissed her cheeks and her forehead. He stroked her hair and brushed it back out of her eyes, then held her face in his hands. "I don't know what to say to you. You're not a piece of shit though and inside yourself, where it really counts, you know that. What happened to you could have happened to anyone. You may feel stupid for not having seen it coming. We all make mistakes in judgment. I think we blame ourselves too much for the mistakes in our lives. A lot of the time we just have to learn our lessons the hard way. We don't understand why things happen. We think it happens because of us, because of something wrong in the way that we're made. I think it's all part of making us who we are coming to be."

Whip kissed her mouth and watched her eyes, smiling into them with all the reassurance he could muster. "I know how trite some of what I've said may sound, but sorrow and misfortune just seem to be a part of life. Gibran once said something about it. I can't remember the exact words but it was something about our sorrow just being the sword that cuts deeper into the cup that holds our joy."

"That's beautiful," Christienne replied. "I've never heard that before."

"Yeah, he was a beautiful guy. I once met this Old Catholic priest who had known him briefly. He said that he was a sweet and compassionate man but that he drank too much wine."

"Like me," Christienne smiled.

"Yeah, like you." Whip kissed her again. Soon they were in a passionate embrace. Whip felt transported. She was so warm and wonderfully pliable. Their hands explored one another and Whip felt as if he would explode. They were both breathing quickly when he broke away. "I want to make love to you, badly," he said.

"What?" Christienne laughed, "You mean like with poor technique?"

Whip grinned. "You are truly something else. No, I mean, I want to but… I don't feel comfortable being that close this soon."

"Whip," She stroked his face, "That is incredibly sweet and incredibly timely too, because I wouldn't have let you anyway." They both laughed now. The passion had been reduced to something more manageable.

Whip got to his feet. "I'm really glad it can be like this. It is the perfect ending to a magical day and it keeps the energy strong between us."

"Amen," she said. "I really, really like you, Whip."

Whip kissed her again. "I really, really like you, too."

They walked arm in arm to the door. "Wait a minute," she said and walked back into the kitchen. She wrote on a piece of paper and then brought it back to him. "How are we ever going to find each other if you don't even have my number?"

Whip took the paper and put it into his wallet. "You will be careful?" he asked.

"Very," she replied. "You just take the road back out and when you hit the highway, turn right. About seven miles down the highway you'll see the sign for Haiku. You should have no problem from there, right?" Her eyes were shining, filled with promise and hope.

"Right," Whip kissed her quickly and then trotted down the stairs. He turned at the bottom and waved. "*Aloha*," he said.

"*Aloha*," she replied.

It was late when Whip arrived back at the house. He'd managed to get lost for a good half an hour before he found a phone booth and called Alan who gave him the blueprint home.

"I'm out here Whip." Alan's voice came in from the deck. When Whip found him, he was leaning against the railing with one of his fruity concoctions in a tall glass. "So, how was your little trip?"

"Great, she's got this dome out in the boondocks, quiet and very private."

"You're doing okay for a guy that just got here Whip, beautiful woman, looks like she likes you too."

Whip smiled, "She's special but it's not a cloudless sky what with Billy Joe running around. I feel like I should be camped out in the bushes around her house."

"We can't be everywhere all of the time. Some things we have to take on faith. Otherwise I'd be in the tower room with a gun."

Whip inhaled the jasmine and plumeria that filled the night air. "How did it go with the shrink today?"

"The good doctor has a very keen insight into human nature. I'm damned if I can figure out how they come up with their profiles. He seems to use a mixture of modern psychiatric technique and more arcane modalities."

Whip laughed. "Remember what you told me that time I was ten years old and got beaten up by those kids on my way to school?"

Alan was thoughtful for a moment. "Actually, no."

"I came home all banged up. They'd kicked me after I hit the ground. I had a chance to use a rock and a piece of wood, but didn't because I didn't think it was fair. You always taught me to be fair. You remember now?"

Alan was nodding his head. "I'm getting some images."

"I came home and you were there. You asked me what happened and I told you. You said, 'Use whatever works.' When I asked about fair, you said 'fair is relative.'"

"You've got a good memory," Alan replied.

"I never forgot that. A couple of weeks later they were laying for me again. I ran into this abandoned lot where we used to play catch and I grabbed a piece of pipe that I knew was there and then I wailed on them, especially the leader. Later the cops came by with the leader's dad. They knew you and after you'd had a few words with them, they told the dad to go home or he'd wind up looking like his kid."

"Yeah, it's lucky that I knew them. In those days, it was easier to see justice done without everything passing through the hands of incompetent social reformers. As I remember though, you never had any trouble with those kids again."

"They were replaced by bigger and faster models."

Alan chuckled. "So you're saying, 'use whatever works,' huh?"

"I'm just quoting the master. If the doctor has to call an astrologer to get results, as long as he gets them, that's what counts."

"I'll keep it in mind. You should see how this guy lives." Alan filled him in on all that had taken place that afternoon.

"You say his houseman is a martial artist?"

"No question, there was big time *chi* just radiating out of him and the way he moved, he didn't walk, he glided. It was like he was on rails."

"What form do you think?"

"I don't know. He's Chinese, so I guess it would have to mean some kind of Kung Fu. He wouldn't talk about it."

"They don't call it the inscrutable Orient for nothing," Whip said.

Alan yawned and covered his face with a hand. "I'm tired, Whip. I think I'm going to have to hit the rack." Alan yawned again and then put his hand on Whip's shoulder. "It's definitely time for me to head back to the bunkhouse, pardner."

"Good night, Alan," Whip said, as he departed down the hallway to his bedroom.

Whip looked up at the stars twinkling high above him in the darkness. He wondered how many people in how many different times had looked up at these same stars, men on the verge of tragedy and triumph, plotters and those plotted against. *How many had cried out to these same stars for help but the stars had never answered them at all. Galileo had perhaps cursed these very stars for the shame they brought upon him. Saint Francis had stood below these same stars, Ted Bundy, too. Neither of them were here now, or were they?*

Ming had said it was all the same Mind. *Those who knew this were capable of feats impossible to those who believed that we all possessed a mind of our own.* He said it was our sense of separateness that doomed us to all of the suffering that we experienced. Whip thought of the peculiar dichotomy that allowed people to profess a belief in the underlying unity of life but permitted them to believe they acted as a thing apart.

In Whip's mind, anyone who had questions about whether there really was an unseen world of forces that shaped the visible world, or whether there was a Supreme Being, had only to take a handful of magic mushrooms and walk into the forest for a day. *They would not walk out again the same.* Whip knew this was probably the real reason that drugs were illegal, along with the efforts of the very powerful alcohol and tobacco lobbies and the efforts of all of the alcoholic lawmakers who shaped the nation's legal policies. It astounded him that alcohol was legal and pot was not. He'd never heard of a marijuana-impaired driver who was involved in a highway fatality, but there were probably a handful of exceptions somewhere. He knew that more people died from alcohol related causes in one year than had died from all drugs in the past century. *There was definitely a lot of bad thinking going on.*

Psychedelics were one thing, alcohol was a horse of a different color. You never woke up feeling better the next day as a result of drinking but like everyone else he still did it. *It was there. It was part of the human experience.* You did it without thinking about it most of the time. Christienne was right about that, for a little while it made you feel better about yourself. It could also make you hate yourself more than you had ever thought possible.

Ever since meeting Ming, Whip had less desire for anything. Nothing he ingested seemed to satisfy him anymore. It all went to feed the hunger inside and it just made the hunger more intense. Increasingly, meditation was providing for him all of the things he had formerly sought in other mediums.

Christienne had come at just the right time in his life. He was looking forward to seeing her tomorrow. He laughed silently. *Love really did make the world go round.* Her features filled his mind when he closed his eyes. He could still smell her, could still taste her on his lips. He felt equal to any adversity that might step between them. *Love bestows such incredible confidence*, he thought, *an unshakable belief in the rightness of things. Without it, we are as bereft as one marooned on a deserted island. It made a palace of the most dismal hovel and its absence turned all of life's riches into something as palatable as dust.* He hoped in the rough and tumble of the days to come, that he never forgot this. He could not have been happier.

Chapter Nineteen

Alan was dreaming. High over a turquoise ocean he soared, passing through clouds that blew apart into tendrils of mist. As he looked down upon the waters, he could see cities beneath the surface, a wonderful music moved in the air. It was more feeling than sound, a liquid vibrating water through which he moved. Ahead of him was a massive cloudbank. Suddenly he felt a great excitement. He could see nothing but the clouds, yet he was in an agony of anticipation. Light was streaming all around him. Abruptly the cloudbank parted and there was Elizabeth walking toward him through the light. Behind her was a diminutive man wearing green and yellow robes. They came together a few feet apart in the air and a lifetime of communication passed between them in a heartbeat.

Immediately, Alan knew everything that had happened. A great sorrow engulfed him and he struggled to move toward her, but he could come no closer than he was.

Elizabeth held forth her hand and said, *"Don't grieve, Alan. It is past time for that. My pain is over and a long-standing debt paid. I am freer and more at peace than I have ever been. I love you."*

"Elizabeth." Alan groped for words but could say nothing beyond her name.

For what seemed a very long time they stood there in wordless communion. Between them in the atmosphere their thoughts wreathed and twined. Then Elizabeth said, *"I must go now, Alan."*

For a moment his heart leapt as if it could bridge the gap. Then he felt himself surrender as all his sorrow fled away.

She smiled at him and the sweetness of it broke his heart. *"We will not be apart forever but the living and those who have passed on are of different worlds. No true lovers are ever parted for good. We will meet again."* As she said this, her image began to fade. Soon she was gone completely.

He stared into the space where she had been standing. A great weight was finally lifted from his heart. He had seen her! He'd had the opportunity to tell her all the things that had been left unsaid by her death. *Elizabeth was in a safe and beautiful place.* He knew that now.

"Greetings, Alan."

Alan turned and looked at the man who had been standing behind her. His robes gleamed with a light like that of the sun shining upon water. An ageless

Oriental countenance looked back at him. The man smiled and said, "I am Ming."

Alan felt suffused by the extended warmth of the man's presence. He was remembering now some of the things that Whip had told him, but nothing Whip said had prepared him for the reality of Ming. He knew that he was dreaming, yet he was more awake, more aware than he had ever been in his day-to-day consciousness. He could feel the integrity of his being changing.

"If you are wondering what is happening, Alan, I suppose the simplest way to explain is to say it is like downloading a software program. The universe on every level is composed of letters and numbers. There is a code written into the fabric of existence. It maintains all forms and the space between them. Our vibrations are now harmonizing to assist in later communications. It is not important for you to understand it, what can be explained will be explained. The rest…" His hand moved to indicate that there was that which could not be said.

"I didn't know if you were real or not," Alan said.

"I am as real as anything is. The Divine is sleeping and this life is the dream. Within this dream are all the possibilities of expression, what you call good and evil, working their way toward their final resolution. The most important thing to remember is that the luminous light is everywhere and in everything. Divinity is all. What is called *evil* is a mask. Love is behind this mask, too. The Divine is hidden behind the veil of relative appearance. If you know this, then no seeming appearance can affect you. Fear of appearances is the tool of the enemy. It is fear that must be overcome. Fear is made possible by uncertainty. Uncertainty is made possible by a lack of faith, virtue and the absence of a purified will.

"Even though I have said there is only The Divine and even though good and evil often change places with one another, humankind does indeed have an enemy. It is to be supposed that this enemy serves the cosmic will, as everything must ultimately. The circumstances of the moment require certain things of us. I am bound by the laws of Karma not to interfere in events that do not concern me. In your case, I am free to help because of past debts. You once helped me. In a moment you will relive this, just as you will relive events from yet another lifetime. It is from there that your present troubles have come.

"One thing further I can do and that is to awaken latent abilities in you that have been sleeping in this lifetime until now. I am not talking about psychic or magical abilities. They will not help you now. I am talking about the qualities of divinity that live to some degree in every human being. I have acquired some amount of grace over the previous centuries. It is up to me how I use it or if I wish to transfer some of it to another, just as if I was a man of wealth and I desired to give a portion of my goods away. Since it is my wealth, come by through my own efforts, I can do with it as I wish."

As Ming was speaking, Alan felt veils falling away from his mind. An intense clarity came to him. All weariness departed. He had no idea how tired he had become from living. He had become so accustomed to his world-weariness that he had forgotten it was there. His vision expanded and now he could see, vibrating in the clouds behind Ming, in the sky beyond them and in Ming himself, a fiery alphabet.

"What you are seeing is the flame alphabet that forms the vibrational integrity of all form. Note that the figures are different on me than they appear in the sky. Look at your hand."

Alan brought his hand in front of his face and saw the pattern they made in his hand.

"Patterns of being are maintained by vibration. If you could lower or raise the pitch of an object's vibration, you could change its form. Therein hides the secret of transmuting lead into gold. Everything is made of the same energy vibrating at a different rate. Certain geometric forms have great powers of preservation and destruction." As he spoke, symbols appeared in the air before them, crosses and stars, *yantras* and *mandalas*, circles containing mysterious letters and other forms within them. As each one materialized and then disappeared, Alan received intuitive flashes of their power and their use.

"These are some of the mediums that are to be used in your defense against the enemy. You do not have to concern yourself with their application. That is my job. Your greatest defense is your link to the brotherhood of which I am a member, that and your enemy's ignorance of who I am.

"Your enemy has some weaknesses. One of them is his fixation on revenge. This makes him vulnerable. Another is his arrogance. He does not expect you to be in any position to defend yourself.

"You are fortunate to have this opportunity. This man is one lifetime away from becoming another Hitler or Stalin. Should he be destroyed, all of creation will be grateful. You have the opportunity to reduce him to nothing. The evil efforts of many lifetimes, the terrible identity he has created by the force of personal will, can be annihilated as if it they had never been."

At this point Alan interjected in his thoughts. Through all of the remarkable changes that were taking place he still felt doubt rising in him. *How can I know what to do? How can I overcome an enemy like Billy Joe?*

Ming smiled, "It is not something that you will do. Any attempt by you at direct confrontation will lead to tragedy for yourself. You must focus your thought upon me. You do not know me. How can you trust me that much? Nevertheless, it is what you must eventually come to do." Ming paused to let the import of his words sink in.

Then he said, "You do not remember learning to walk, yet it is one of the greatest achievements of your life. Now when you walk you do not even think about it. Your immune system protects you from the invasion of harmful microbes that seek your destruction, yet you are unaware of its work. It operates without your knowledge or permission. To operate under the protection of the higher power, you have only to put yourself in the way of it. It overshadows you as a mother does her child. A willful child insists on doing things its own way. What can the mother do? All disharmony and suffering is the result of this rebellion. A good child surrenders to the greater wisdom of the mother." All this time, as he spoke, his eyes held Alan's. *The portion that passed between them in words was the smallest part.*

"I will take you now to another time so that you may better understand our relationship. This will serve to make you more comfortable with who you really are. We go now to the *Hall of the Akashic Records.*"

Ming reached forward and took Alan's hand. As they flew, it seemed to Alan as if he were passing through a kaleidoscope with the physical sensations of a lava lamp. It was more like oozing than flying. As their speed increased the forms on either side of the spiraling corridor became smears of phosphorescent color.

"It is amazing," Ming said, reading Alan's thoughts. "You would be surprised to know that there are beauties and ecstasies far beyond these, in fact these beauties are a trap for those who allow themselves to be drawn into seeking them. In the Hermetic Teachings there is a warning given. It has to do with the seductions of the world and the mind, both subtle and gross, as they appear to one who is rising on the path. The potentials for enjoyment are far beyond that of most mortals and the pull is very strong. One is advised to resist this. One is advised not to go down into 'The Dark Splendor' as it is called. There are many illusions along the way to The Kingdom, the more subtle the plane the more subtle the illusions."

Time was altered here, or did not exist at all. Alan was thinking that it surely must be morning by now, so much had happened and yet there was more to come. A point of light appeared in the distance and grew larger by the moment.

Soon he could see the outline of a building that resembled an ancient Grecian temple. They set down gently on the steps before it. Massive columns rose up supporting an ornate triangular roof whose peak was lost in mist. Before them was a large arched opening from which flowed a soft blue light. Ming released his hand and walked between two columns and through the aperture. Alan followed him into a vast domed space that reminded him of Grand Central Station.

"We see things here based on what is familiar to us. One of Christian orientation will see western design, an Oriental might see something based on his own traditions. This is the place where all that has happened may be seen as it actually occurred. This is the Great Hall of Memory."

Ming led them to a scalloped opening. There was a flat oval screen set back against the facing wall. It shimmered like water. Above the screen were flaming letters which read, "*May your life be more compassionate because of what you have learned here. Do not regret.*"

"I suppose there are volumes to be read in those words," Alan observed.

"Indeed," Ming replied. He raised his right hand and made several gestures. The screen became brighter and Alan heard a soft resonating hum that moved over him like wind.

"There's no one else here. Aren't there others who use this place?" Alan asked.

"Others are using it right now, Alan. Everyone has their own temple in which to access the past. This place is inside your own mind."

Faint images began to appear and quickly became crystal clear. Alan saw two men dressed in the garb of Catholic monks sitting at a table studying a book. There was an oil lamp burning on the table. The men were arguing in low voices. The view rotated until Alan could see the faces of the men. He gasped. It was Ming and himself. Even though Ming's features were westernized, it was clearly him.

Ming was talking about a magical process that was outlined in the book. Alan was shaking his head and repeating the word, "Dangerous." Ming continued arguing his point adamantly but Alan got up from his seat and said, "It is on your head," and then he left the room.

The scene suddenly changed to the courtyard of a medieval castle. Ming was sitting on a stone bench with two other men. One of them was a Bishop, the other a gentleman dressed in outrageous finery with a huge head of black curls falling down around his shoulders. With his large hooked nose and black eyes, he looked like a Captain Hook that Alan had once seen on Broadway. The man's face caused a disquieting sensation in Alan but he could not place him. Ming was listening to instructions that were being given to him by the Bishop, a haughty man with the visage of a Roman Emperor. He had a cruel slit of a mouth and narrow animal eyes. *Like Nero*, Alan thought. He and Ming were discussing a magical ritual.

The scene changed again to a narrow country lane. There were several coaches and men on horseback passing by. It was approaching dusk. Alan could feel menace radiating. The lead carriage abruptly turned into a road that opened on the right, the wheels sliding and sending a cloud of dust into the air. Alan could sense the urgency of the moment. Looming ahead on a low sloping hill was an immense stone building that appeared to have been partly destroyed.

Now they were inside the building. A small crowd of people was grouped around an altar upon which burned red and black candles. There was a fetid stink in the air that made Alan think of burning excrement and rubber. Standing behind the altar was the Bishop that Alan had seen earlier. He was arranging objects on the surface of the altar. In front of the altar, the congregation was chanting in Latin. They were dressed in hooded black robes and wore masks.

Alan saw wolves and bears, cat and pig faces. From the burned out doorway of the building there now came several more hooded figures. One of them was having trouble walking and had to be assisted by the others. They proceeded to the altar and then stopped before the Bishop. For the first time Alan noticed the large inverted crucifix hanging from his neck. He came around the altar and drew back the hood from the head of the one who had been led. Alan could see that it was a young girl. The Bishop untied the smock at the neck and it dropped to the floor. She stood there trembling, naked.

The Bishop gestured and two figures came out of the crowd and lifted the girl upon the altar where she moved uncomfortably, reacting to the hard surface and the chill of the cold stone beneath her. She made no effort to get up and Alan could see by her eyes that she had been drugged. The Bishop began painting symbols and words upon her body with colored paints. The chanting increased in volume and from the front of the room another procession entered, six more forms walked toward the altar, four of them hooded. In front was one dressed in a crimson robe with a crown of thorns on his head.

Alan saw that it was Ming. The crown of thorns had cut into his scalp and small rivulets of blood flowed down his face. Alongside him walked the gentleman from the courtyard. He was naked except for an amulet and a sword buckled about his waist. His partial erection swung from side to side as he moved.

Ming's eyes were vacant and he stared emptily into space. The naked man brought Ming to the side of the altar as their escorts faded into the congregation. The Bishop finished his ministrations and then stepped back from the altar. He raised his hands and the chanting abruptly ceased. There was silence. He gestured toward Ming who slowly came around the altar to stand next to him. The Bishop opened a drawstring purse and poured a measure of its contents into his palm. He sprinkled them over the girl's body. The symbols on her body began to glow a fiery red and there was an iridescent shimmer in the air above her. He raised his left hand and the chanting resumed. The girl started to writhe upon the altar, her pelvis lurching spasmodically into the air.

Above her an image formed in the air, the translucent outline of a horned demon. *It looks like a hologram*, Alan thought. Suddenly he knew what was going to happen. *The girl would be sacrificed with a consecrated knife. As her blood flowed out, the wraith would feed on it and then materialize into physical form.*

There was a reckless thrilling energy filling the room as the chanters began to sway and wave their arms in the air. The Bishop reached into the folds of his robe and extracted a silver dagger, which he presented ceremonially in the air to the wraith. Then he turned to Ming and handed him the knife. The chanting became frenzied, robes were falling from the bodies of the congregation, their naked bodies jerking and twisting as if they were being electrocuted.

All at once there was a tremendous howl from the entrance, followed by the crashing of steel on stone. Into the room burst half a dozen men on horseback with whips and clubs who began laying about with them into the crowd. One horseman galloped to the altar and clubbed a man with painted genitals. Then he reached down from his saddle and hauled Ming up and over his pommel. Alan saw that it was himself. There was a wrath and a fury in his face. The air was filled with screams as the congregation was driven about in every direction. Then the horseman called out and they all galloped away out of the church with Ming over one saddle and the girl upon another.

The scene slowly dissolved. Alan was stunned.

"That was in the summer of 1542 outside the city of Florence. You brought the girl and me to a friend's home that night. The friend was a priest familiar with the effects of black magic on the human mind. He treated me for some time and eventually restored me. The young girl was my niece.

"Shortly after that we took a boat for Greece to escape the retribution of the Bishop, a very powerful man with the ear of the pope. The naked gentleman with the sword was Billy Joe."

"My God," Alan exclaimed.

"Gradually, I realized the full extent of my activities and how close I had come to perdition. That night was only the beginning of what they had planned for me. After that, I devoted the rest of my life to the charitable pursuits of my faith. It is because of your intercession that I was saved an enormous and lasting grief, and your efforts on my behalf eventually cost you your life. Some years later, you returned to Italy and the Bishop had you killed."

"We come now to another time, in New Orleans seventy years ago." Ming gestured and new images appeared. Alan saw a section of Bourbon Street in the '20's. A festival was taking place. Strolling musicians played in the crowd and the people were dancing and raising glasses. The view moved to a side street and then through a series of streets until they came to a graveyard. A prostitute was standing by a wrought iron fence smoking a cigarette. Several cars passed, their headlights muted in the fog. A car pulled up to the woman. After a brief conversation she entered the car and it drove away.

The car entered a driveway and then parked before a large antebellum plantation house, surrounded by weeping willows, through which illumination shone from the lights of the house. Inside, a gathering was taking place. Many cultures were represented. There was a woman in a sari with a red caste mark on her forehead, a huge black man in a tiger skin, an Asian man wearing only heavy chain and shackles, along with several men and women in evening dresses. Some of the men were as artfully made up as the women. Two mimes were engaged in a silent duet to which no one was paying any attention.

There was an enormously fat woman who was sitting naked on a velvet cushion. All over her body there were ropelike scars. She had a golden razor blade hanging from a chain about her neck. A full-grown Bengal tiger lay on the floor near her. Someone in a werewolf's mask was playing the piano, a giant cigar protruding from the mouth hole. There were some forty people in all. There were naked men and women with metal piercings serving drinks and food. Alan winced when he saw this. The one thing common to them all was the look of cruelty and dissipation on their faces.

A door opened and a man stepped into the room. The man was tall and slender and dressed in a skintight leather body suit. He was completely bald and had the pink eyes and white eyebrows that bespoke a true albino. The face was like a Byzantine mask, the forehead thrust forward over deep eye sockets. The nose was long and thin, its edge seemed as sharp as a knife. The tip hooked downward like a bird of prey over the full slack lips of a voluptuary. The chin came to a point. His cheeks were hollow as if there were no teeth in the mouth, but this was disproved a moment later when he smiled. There was no humor or friendliness in that smile. It was the smile of a wolf before it bites. Alan had almost expected to see fangs, but no, the teeth were normal and uncommonly white.

He'd seen this man before but he had not looked the same as he did now. Here was the one that the others had come to see. They crowded around him, fawning. The women made it a point to touch him. He spoke briefly to each of them as he made his way to the center of the room, expressing his hopes that they were all having an enjoyable evening. He added that everything was being prepared and that shortly they were all welcome to join him in the music room. This last comment was followed by a cold laugh that sent a shiver up Alan's spine.

The scene shifted and another room appeared. This one had no windows and all of the walls were painted black. It was long and narrow, perhaps it had originally been a formal dining room. At the far end was a terrible sight. Ten human skeletons were hanging from hooks in the ceiling. At the feet of each was a vase filled with black and purple flowers. Incense curled up in the air and wreathed around the bones. There were pictures of horribly mutilated women placed against the bases of the vases and in the center of the room was a wooden table three feet wide by seven feet long. There were buckles and leather restraints attached to it, reminding Alan of the tables used in mental institutions at the turn of the century for shock treatments. The sound of recorder music filled the air in a dissonant snake charmer's dirge and the room's occupants were all naked. The Indian woman was fellating the man with the werewolf's head and the large black man was sodomizing one of the male servants. Others were slowly dancing or leaning upon one another.

The albino came into the room and once again all attention was focused on him. He quickly noticed the two acts of sex that were taking place and clapped his hands together once. Immediately the activity stopped. Several heartbeats passed and then he said, "Those who cannot control their appetites until the appointed time could well become food." Alan could see the Indian woman's complexion turn pale. The aura of fear hung heavy in the air. "Lucky for some, meat has already been provided," he added.

The door through which he had entered opened again and two male servants brought in the prostitute he had seen entering the car earlier. She was screaming and struggling, but to no avail. The servants held and carried her as if she were made of balsa wood. Very quickly she was strapped to the table. There was a profane eagerness in the eyes of the onlookers as they watched her struggle at the restraints. The albino walked to the table and then called the people forward. He scanned the room, searching the faces. Then he addressed them.

"Who am I?" he asked.

The crowd repeated in one voice, "You are the one."

"And what am I?"

"You are the life-taker."

"And what are you to me?"

"We are your children."

"And what am I to you?"

"You are our father."

"And what does a father do for his children?"

"He feeds and protects them."

"And if they disobey?"

"He punishes them."

"And if they obey?"

"He rewards them."

"Is there anywhere on all the planes that they can hide from him?"

"No."

"Is there any way to deceive him?"

"No."

"Shall they be separated from him by distance or death?"

"No."

"Shall the enemies of his children prosper?"

"They shall be destroyed."

"Shall his children prosper?"

"They shall rule on earth and in hell."

"From whence comes the power?"

"It comes from the spilling of blood."

"Whose blood?"

"The blood of those who fear to die."

"How can this power be increased?"

"Increase the fear."

"How can the fear be increased?"

"Increase the pain."

"How can the pain be increased?"

"Increase the fear."

"How?"

"Increase the fear!" They were screaming now. Their faces filled with madness. It sickened Alan to look at them.

"How?"

"Increase the fear!"

They were jumping up and down now like *Watusi* warriors. *They looked like mental patients on pogo sticks*, Alan thought.

The albino man clapped his hands and another naked servant came into the room pushing a metal cart in front of him. On the cart was an array of gleaming surgical instruments and other devices that Alan did not know the purpose of. He picked up a scalpel and bent over the horrified victim.

"Are you afraid?" he asked.

"Yes," she replied in a whisper. She licked her lips, which had become dry and cracked.

"Good," the man replied. "Very good."

"Please let me go," she begged.

"You shall go. By inches and by degrees, you shall go." The man smiled. Alan shuddered.

They had bound her head to the table so that she could not move it to either side. The man held the scalpel in front of her eyes and let the light flash off of its stainless steel surface. She closed her eyes tightly.

"Oh no," he whispered, "You have to see to believe." Then he removed her eyelids. Her screams tore at Alan's heart. He knew it had all taken place a long time ago, but the knowledge didn't help. Alan understood that the albino man was Billy Joe. Mercifully at this point the setting dissolved and another appeared in its place.

It was a library in a private home. Three men were sitting in comfortable armchairs around a coffee table. One of them was him. He looked different. Maybe it was the beard. He also looked about ten years older than he was at present. One of the other men was describing a series of murders and disappearances. Another mentioned torture, and he asked Alan for his help.

The location shifted again, then came a series of events that showed Alan talking with people, wandering through city streets, going in and out of clubs, hotels and restaurants. Finally there was a sequence of Alan watching the albino man eating in a restaurant, traveling to different locations as well as to the house and grounds where the ceremony had taken place.

Then there was a large planning session in a police station, which then moved to a raid on the house where another ritual was taking place. They were just in time.

There was a trial at which Alan gave evidence and the albino man was sentenced to death in the electric chair. Alan was present at the execution. Right before the sentence was carried out, the man gave his final statement. He roared at Alan that he had disturbed the work of lifetimes. Alan would pay. He would come back from the grave and he would make Alan pay. Alan's eyes were riveted to the screen. It was as if he was seeing across time into the moment that it occurred. Then the electrocution took place and the man was dead. The screen went blank.

"And now you have seen what was. He will stop at nothing until he has destroyed you and everything that you love. He is expecting an easy victory. He does not know what you know. He knows that all is not as it should be, but he does not know why. He will be working very hard now to find out who is interfering with him." Ming's eyes were serious as he spoke to Alan.

"I thought there was a higher justice in the universe that punished the wicked, if not in life, certainly after death. How is he allowed to continue?"

"There is indeed justice, Alan, but it is not at all what mortals imagine it to be. Billy Joe's soul is in Hell, regardless of wherever else he may appear to be. Yet there are souls who delight in evil. They are allowed to continue for reasons beyond human understanding. God is compassionate. If there is any chance that a soul might turn from its tragic course, then every effort is made to give it that chance. No one and nothing is discarded. The hope of redemption is held out until there is no possible recourse.

"The heart and mind of the divine is incomprehensible, we can never completely know it. Through the ages we all have our roles to play. We all reap the fruits of our actions and not even the all-powerful can set this aside. There are those exceptions that we call miracles, but even they are subject to the law. Though evil may seem to prosper, so does good. There is an old Taoist saying, 'Though heaven prefers no man, the wise man prefers heaven.' What you need to know, you will know when the time comes." Ming paused and studied Alan then he asked, "Do you accept what help I can give?"

"Yes," Alan replied. "Yes I do."

"Good, then it is now time for you to return. I will always be near. I will advise you when I can. There is more than enough in you to achieve this victory. If one acts toward the highest good, nothing can stand in his way. Have no fear."

Ming raised his hand in the gesture of blessing and said, "Peace." Then he was gone and Alan was standing alone in the hall. He marveled at what he had seen and then he was sucked away out of the building, up into the air and speeding once more through the corridor from which he had come. Somewhere between leaving and arriving, he fell into a sound, dreamless sleep.

Chapter Twenty

CarryAnn climbed into the taxi a nervous wreck. She was barely able to shut the door. Through the entire flight it had never occurred to her that there would be anything like airport security. In her young life the idea had never surfaced, nor had there ever been reason for concern until now. The first things she saw coming through the gate were two policemen and a dog. Instantly fear filled her veins like ice water. Although the bulk of the cocaine was in her checked baggage, she had a vial in her purse. She made it through, but from that point on she lived in terror. Everywhere she looked there were people in uniforms. When a soldier at the baggage claim said hello to her, she wet her pants. In the taxi she stuttered when she gave the driver her destination.

Before leaving California she'd called a travel agent and arranged for a room at a motel near the airport. She had no idea where she was going next and wanted a central location. The cab turned into a large motel complex on the main drag called The Maui Palmetto. She checked in without trouble, blessing the foresight that had inspired her to buy a false identification card through one of her girlfriends. On the surface she was eighteen and legal.

The room was plain but clean. CarryAnn had all the amenities she needed in her purse and she went immediately to it. Very shortly a swell of confidence rushed through her. She had evaded death twice and run the gauntlet at the airport. She took off her clothes and stepped into the shower, washing the road grime and urine from her body. She looked like a dreaming muse standing under an ancient waterfall, eyes closed, with her head lifted upward as the water sluiced through her hair and down her body.

Later, she stood naked looking out her window at the harbor. There was a large cruise ship docked there. She wished she could board it now and sail for months and months to the far horizons of the world, somewhere that she would be safe from the terrible men who had pursued her. Were they still looking for her? Why was she so important? She could barely identify them and she never would. *It seemed far away now.* They must know that she had not gone to the police. *Maybe it was over.* She lay on her bed smoking and sipping from what remained of the Grand Marnier. She'd started smoking cigarettes after she met Royce. There was a bottle of Absolut that she had found at Tommy's. She hoped she could stop soon, but she needed time before she attempted it. The anxiety that came from even the thought of giving it all up was too much to contemplate at the moment. She would pace herself until she was more secure. *There was plenty of time now.* She had money, she had coke and she had the tremendous hope that it would all work out. *It had to.*

It was dawn when Alan awoke to a new consciousness of life. He felt like a child on the most wonderful Christmas of his life. The birds singing outside his window were a super physical sensation. He had never experienced sound like this before. When he opened his eyes, there was a colored outline to every object in the room. He brought his left hand up and could see a green silhouette extending a half an inch outward from the flesh. Peace flowed in his heart like a deep underground river. He felt the energy of a man half his age. *Had it really been like this once?* He was amazed and rolled from the bed, his heart suffused with gratitude. Silently he offered a prayer of thanks. It was as if he had drunk a magical elixir.

He had to get outside. He ran from the room and down the steps leading from the deck. The air, the marvelous air that filled his lungs! Was it air, or some enchanted nectar that flowed like honey? He danced like a child might have in the first morning of the world when all was new and without tarnish. Tears streamed down his face from the sensations in his heart.

"Thank you, Ming," he said. "Thank you, thank you, thank you." He stood with his hands at his sides, inhaling the essence of life through every pore in his body. After a while he opened his eyes and found Whip standing beside him.

"You're turning into quite an Indian, Whip, sneaking up on me without my noticing."

"I'd like to think I'm becoming a stealthier dude but you were obviously preoccupied."

"Is it that apparent?"

"Very," Whip said, a smile creasing his face. "I see Ming paid you a visit."

Alan sighed, not having the words to reply. *"Visit" certainly didn't cover it.*

He looked at Whip with his new eyes and saw so many things. He saw the youth and eagerness for the future, the wealth of innocence that remained in him and he saw Elizabeth. Alan reached forth and embraced him. They stood there for a long time, feeling the love that they bore for one another.

Whip stepped back and said, "You must have had quite a session. There is some serious force coming off of you."

"I couldn't even begin to explain. I saw Elizabeth," he said, the remembrance rushing forth into his eyes.

Whip arched an eyebrow, "Do tell. That must have been… something." His throat grew tight as he remembered his sister. "How was she?"

"Wonderful and at peace. I owe Ming a tremendous debt of gratitude for that alone." Alan wiped at the tears that had formed in his eyes. "He gave me a gift… I couldn't put a value on it… Priceless." Alan struggled for words and then fell silent.

Whip rolled his shoulders and looked away. "I am really, really glad for you. Just for a moment I felt cheated that you got to see her, achieved closure and I didn't. Still, I wish I could have seen her too."

Alan placed his hand on Whip's shoulder. "She asked me to look after you. She said, 'Tell Whip that I love him.'"

The moment passed in silence, the sun shining down upon the two from out of a perfect blue sky. The dew glistened on the grass and a soft wind slipped around them. There they stood, each lost in their memories of someone who had meant so much to both of them. Whip brushed aside the anger that rose for an instant at the thought of the one who had stolen her from them. A sweet regret filled his heart.

Alan broke the silence. "What are you doing today, or do I have to ask?"

"I'll probably call her soon. I know we'll be getting together." Whip rubbed his hand across his eyebrows and turned away from facing the sun.

"Well, I don't know where I'll be or what I'll be doing. I've got some things in mind but we both know how that goes. In case I get free, what about you two having dinner here tonight, or would that be too confining… just having met her and all?"

Whip grinned, "Ordinarily, situation like this, we'd probably do something on our own. Things aren't *normal* though. I'm more inclined to want to be around other people when I'm with her, safety in numbers and all that. I guess I can find you later…"

Alan turned toward the house. "I'll just pick up food, whatever, we'll leave it loose. Kind of food I make is just as good the second time around."

Whip laughed, "Yea, you should have those little white boxes for when you store it in the icebox, just like real Chinese takeout."

"You don't find it strange, I'm not talking about what happened and you're not asking me questions? It's like I said a couple of things, you said a couple of things and we're right back into the day-to-day."

Whip's eyes grew serious for a moment. "What I find strange is that people think there is such a thing as the *day-to-day*. Some things you can't talk about anyway. You know that. It just diminishes them. I don't know what I'm holding on to any more, what's holding me, what's real and what isn't. It seems to make the most sense just to keep moving and stay focused on the moment."

Alan nodded. "Yea, people go through all the things they go through and they don't even know who it's happening to. They don't know what it means and it isn't too long before they can't remember it. When they do remember it, it has become a different event. What I seem to be noticing is that there is something that holds everything together. It's like gravity. We're in it and it's in us all... all around us. You might know that it's there but you can't see it. You can't measure it. You can't define it. You can only accept it, or not accept it and it's not affected at all by either relationship."

Whip put his hand on Alan's shoulder as they walked into the house. "Remember the first thing you said about slipping back into the day-to-day?

"Sure."

"You just answered it."

Twenty minutes later, Whip waited with Alan at the door.

"I'll try to be back around six. Oh yeah, if you do come, you'll probably want to pick up some wine. I don't know what you guys like. From what I could see, Christienne seems to enjoy the stuff."

"Yeah, she does at that."

Alan was scanning the overnight teletypes when Captain Rusk came up behind him. "What are you doing Douglas?"

Alan turned around. "Good morning, Captain, I was just checking to see what's new."

Rusk frowned and shook his head. "That's probably something you should leave to officers working for the department. I can't see where anything there would concern you."

Alan nodded, keeping the smile on his face. "Captain, I'm working a case and any avenue that might provide me with possible information interests me."

"Just the same, I would prefer you use Lieutenant Kamamoto for things like this. We've had a lot of information leaks around here lately and it's going to stop."

Alan stared at him for a moment, surprised that he would focus on something as petty as the teletype, certainly not a secure information source by any stretch. "As you wish, Captain, but the information on the teletype is available through a variety of mediums to a lot of people who are not even *in* law enforcement."

"I've made myself clear, haven't I?" Rusk's aura had several dark patches vibrating in it. Alan could see them quite clearly. He was waiting for any sign of resistance from Alan so that he could make a scene. Several officers had stopped all pretense of being about their duties and were watching the exchange with interest.

"Perfectly," Alan replied and walked away down the hall toward Ben's office. Rusk stood watching him, the fingers of his left hand twitching like those of a man on the verge of a stroke.

There was a message to call a Lt. Boren of the California Highway Patrol. Alan picked up the phone and called Wilson's office. After a wait of a few minutes, Aaron Wilson came on line. "Sorry for making you wait. I was in a meeting. How are you doing?"

"Good Aaron and you?"

"Trying to keep from putting on weight, trying to keep the streets safe, the usual war of attrition. By the way, Captain Rusk came over to see me yesterday. I don't know the details or if there are any, but he feels you're not cooperating in your investigation, sharing information and so forth. Before you say anything in your defense, I told him you were not exactly required to share with him directly, that it didn't work that way, and the only information you had to share was what in your judgment, you felt he needed to know. I can tell you he didn't like that."

"I guess not," Alan replied. "Well that explains his little psychodrama this morning."

"What's that?" Aaron asked. Alan related the details of their earlier encounter.

"Hmmm," Aaron murmured. "He was mostly steamed about your contacting out-of-state police organizations with the suspect's descriptions after 'browbeating him,' his words, into holding off their release on Maui for twenty-four hours."

"Out-of-state police and local press are two different things," Alan countered.

"You're telling me. Anyway, he's suffering from several of humanity's ancient curses, too much pride, too much vanity and, as ever, with too little reason. He thinks your only motivation is the attention the case will generate and on a darker level, a possible distraction from your involvement in it and I can't disabuse him of that. I just need to let you know that he's a bad enemy. He's ruined a few men who've crossed him. You're not in the same position they were, but you've got to know he'll do anything to put you in a bad light."

"Well, what more can I do? I'm as civil and non-confrontational as I can be."

"Probably nothing, once he's decided he doesn't like you, there isn't much anyone can do. I just want you to keep your eyes open and stay out of his way. I've never seen anyone win him over if he doesn't want them too. He'll be gone in a year or so, that much I know. You know, in Rusk's mind you're an MTV version of Kojak. Rusk can't stand the idea that a celebrity gunslinger is tossing down shots in his saloon. Bottom line, he's going to be a pain in the ass. However, I'm calling the shots and I can shut him down anytime. Right now though, I'd like to hold off on the heavyweight shit if we can — just go along, put up with it — as long as it doesn't compromise the operation. Let him hang himself if it comes to that. If I had my way, he'd be buried out in front of the station with nothing but his big butt sticking out of the ground and the motorcycle cops could use it for parking their bikes. Whatever happens, I'm behind you one hundred percent. You report to me, just dance around him. You can do that?"

"I'll do my best, Aaron."

"Good. Keep me posted."

"Roger," Alan replied and then signed off. He scratched the side of his face as he mused over the irony of it all. A line from one of Dylan's songs ran through his head, *"If my thought-dreams could be seen, they'd probably put my head in a guillotine."* If Rusk or even Aaron knew what was really happening, if he had to explain it, how much support could he count on after that? Would anyone believe him? *Not likely.*

Today he was in far too good a mood to worry about Captain Rusk. He dialed Ben's number.

"Lieutenant Kamamoto."

"Ben, this is Alan."

"Hey, how you doing?"

"Great," Alan replied. "You know anything about this Lieutenant Boren? I got a note on the desk to call."

"Didn't see it, must have come in after I left."

Alan closed the connection and began to dial the number in California. After talking with a secretary and being put on hold for a few minutes a man's voice came on the phone. "This is Lieutenant Boren."

"Lieutenant Boren, this is Alan Douglas in Maui."

“Oh yeah, how’s the weather over there in paradise?”

“Beautiful.”

“It’s raining hard here. Look, we got your composites and I think we may have what you’re looking for.”

“Really!” Alan felt the hairs on his arm rise.

“Well, it may be them and it may not. You know how it goes. We’ve had a series of murders here in the Golden State, some in my venue, and some in other areas. I’m not going to go into the details now. You’ll be getting a packet. We got prints from several of the scenes. What’s interesting is that we’ve got two different kinds of murders going on here.

“On the one hand, we got some rape murders. Men fitting their description were seen in the area of two of the abductions, hard evidence, prints, semen, plus strong circumstantial. On the other hand, there were three separate homicide incidents, seemingly drug-connected. The scenes were very clean. They killed two UPS drivers and their trucks were stolen to gain admittance in two of the hits. There was a partial on the steering wheel of one of the trucks. They were wearing latex gloves but apparently the thumb on one of them tore away and we got a nice fat print. The print matches one of them with the rape murders. Two of the murder victims were the love interests of a couple of major cocaine dealers. Then, there was an awful massacre in Phoenix that featured these same two snowbirds and their Latin supplier, zero evidence at the scene. Phoenix police canvassed the town and placed our boys that same day in a little cantina a few miles away. Owner was very happy to cooperate, said they were real bad *hombres* and threatened to do his laundry while he was still in it.” At this point he began coughing and Alan had to wait for him to get back on line.

“Sorry, caught this damn flu.”

“Take your time Lieutenant, I’m impressed.” And Alan was. Somebody was doing some fine police work. *But maybe there was Ming’s hand again — the torn glove — the lucky hit at the cantina?*

“What I don’t get is how these boys could be so sloppy and then suddenly upgrade their performance just like that. We were just about to grab them in L.A. and they were gone. Had their house surrounded, found a beer on the table that wasn’t warm yet. Then they pull all of this off in Phoenix and disappear. Well, it appears that way.”

“It does sound strange,” he replied, knowing full well that this was Billy Joe’s hand in the mix. What would Boren say if Alan started talking about black magic? He shook his head.

"Anyway," Boren continued, "I've sent you all of the particulars via Federal Express, your name, care of Wailuku Station. Is that how you say it?" Alan pronounced the name properly for him.

"Very nice people these two, Malcolm Kahn, forty-eight years old, pages of priors. ADWs, attempted murders, armed robbery, homicide and rape-torture of prepubescents."

"Jesus," Alan said.

"Yeah," Boren continued, "He was convicted in the rape-murder of a ten year old girl, just finished doing seventeen years at San Quentin."

"He actually served seventeen years?" Alan asked.

"Surprising, huh, considering the way they turn them loose these days? He had a lot of priors plus the court must have known he did other little girls.

"Asshole number two is one Balfire Tweeds, how about that first name? It's like his parents, if he was really conceived in a normal fashion, already knew what was coming. Member of Satan's Slaves, priors for dealing crank, numerous assaults, enforcer, suspected in several murders, no convictions. Some rape arrests, one conviction, did a year. He walked on a lot of shit. He's thirty-two years old and just did time on an eight-year bit for a rape and armed robbery of a topless bar. I guess the court took into consideration that she was asking for it. Both of them were members of the Aryan Brotherhood on the inside. What I don't understand is what they're doing in Hawaii. They've got to be a lot more vulnerable in your locale than here on the mainland."

"It's as strange to us as it is to you. We've got these disappearances with suspected mutilation and murder with no motive we can figure." Alan went on to give him what details he could.

Boren sighed. "Well, you should know that they've got plenty in the way of finances now, it looks like a whole lot of money and a lot of cocaine. That's what Phoenix indicates anyway. You keep me posted, okay?"

"I'll do everything I can."

"One more thing, Alan, there's a Sergeant Swanson with the Phoenix Police. He's the OIC on that case. You might want to give him a call."

"I'll do that and thanks a million for your help. We're way ahead of where we were before. We'll get them."

"I hope so. *Aloha*," and the phone went dead.

Alan sat lost in thought. It was the most unusual scenario he could imagine. He knew what was going on and he didn't know what was going on. He couldn't tell anyone. If he tried, he'd be off the case regardless of Aaron's support.

The first priority, of course, was to catch the two front men. Billy Joe would at least have his present plans brought to a close if that happened. Did Billy Joe know what they knew? *Probably.* Alan twirled a pencil between the fingers of his right hand, his mind drifting back to the events of the night before, remembering Elizabeth. Her image sprang full and radiant in his mind, his heart filled with love. There was no more of the complexity of emotions that had always appeared whenever he had thought of her. Now he felt only the fullness of her presence and the knowledge of her peace, except for the sense of loss. There would always be a sense of loss.

Kimo sat at the kitchen table reading the newspaper and having a cup of coffee. His mother, who had been fixing breakfast, brought the food to the table and sat down, looking closely at Kimo. "What? You going to eat?"

"I'm not hungry, Ma," he said, not taking his eyes from the paper.

"What the matter boy? You no eat. You no talk. You sick… stomach hurt?"

Kimo looked at his mother. He saw the concern in her eyes. It tore at him. "My stomach okay, I go see the doctor, can find out about my tests today."

"But you got to eat," she declared. Like mothers everywhere, she knew there was something wrong with her son. Kimo had not been acting normal for several days. Though he was usually surly and hostile, he always talked to his mother, especially if something bothered him. He would talk to her if only to complain about the injustices in his life.

She knew he was worried about his test results. She thought it was caused by stress, the result of all the anger he kept, often unsuccessfully, bottled up inside of him. She wished that he would find a girlfriend. Her son was awkward around women. She'd tried to interest him in various girls around the neighborhood and from her church, to no avail. He spent all of his time in his room or out on the *lanai* pumping weights. He didn't even have any real friends.

"No bother with my stomach, Ma. I eat one big lunch later." He smiled at her reassuringly. He wasn't going to work today. He'd told his boss two days previously that his visit to Kaiser would take all day. He'd told his mom he would be right back afterwards. She could cook him a big lunch. That would get her out of the house and down to the store so he could be alone.

"We got mangoes?" he asked his mother, knowing that he had finished up all of the mangoes the night before. "I need mango for my power shake."

"I go to store soon," she replied.

"Okay, Ma, I stay lifting till I go." Kimo put down the paper and got up from the table, heading out to the *lanai* where the weights were. He went through the motions of working out until he saw his mother go out the front door. He waited a few minutes and then went into the garage that had been converted into a game room for Kimo's dad and his cronies.

Kimo's dad was an avid gun collector and possessed a large assortment of weapons. He went to the massive gun case and opened it. From the rack he removed an M-16 and four clips of ammunition. He taped them together in pairs so that they could be easily reversed. Next he picked up a 9mm Beretta and inserted a clip. He grabbed two spares and walked back into the house to his room. The firearms, ammo and clips went into a laundry bag, which he then tossed on to the bed. Then he showered and put on a pair of black jeans and a black T-shirt.

Trembling, he sat down on the bed and pulled on his black engineer's boots. Tears that had been welling in his eyes began to run down his cheeks. He thought about his life, what little there had been of it, his family and the love that he felt for them that he had never been able to express. All the rage that coiled about his heart like a poisonous snake that had crawled up out of he knew not where, but mostly he thought about the voice that had come into his mind, the voice that made his stomach hurt as if burning coals had been deposited there. He did not know what was going to happen, but he knew that it was going to be bad, very bad. In his heart he cried out for help from somewhere, anywhere. He cried to God but he had never bothered with God before and didn't really believe in God. He was not surprised that there was no answer, just a driving compulsion to get on with the day's events.

He grabbed a blue windbreaker from his closet and as he was putting it on, he looked down at his closet floor and saw his baseball mitt and boxing gloves, a football, a basketball, the evidence of his athletic youth. Kimo's heart was tearing in his chest as a rush of memories shot through him. There was nothing he could do. No matter what lay ahead, it could not be any more terrible than what would come if he didn't do what he was told.

He picked up the laundry bag and took one last look around his room, the place where he had spent a great portion of his life since the day he was born. He searched for some clue to his identity. He had no idea who he was and now he would probably never know. The door closed behind him.

Kimo parked his truck outside the clinic and sat watching the people going in and out. There was a brisk wind that tugged at their clothes and cut the sun's heat. He could hear birds singing in the nearby trees. He waited in his truck as if for some signal to proceed. Kimo felt detached from everything around him. It was like watching a movie. Then a door opened in his mind and in came the voice.

"Good morning, Kimo. Are you ready?"

"I'm ready," Kimo replied.

"Good, I know that you are concerned about what is going to happen to you. I assure you Kimo, no matter what happens to anyone else today, nothing is going to happen to you. I will protect you. Let my will be your will and there will be no trouble carrying out what needs to be done. They deserve this Kimo. They have offended you and they have offended me. These are the people who have kept you down. They are the ones who caused your stomach to hurt. Your stomach hurt before I came along, didn't it?"

"Yes," Kimo answered.

"And I made the pain go away, didn't I? Of course, I was able to bring it back, just to show you but I didn't create it, Kimo. They did." As the voice was talking, Kimo felt cold rage. He felt hate for all living things, especially the *haole* motherfuckers who were the cause of all of his troubles. He could see clearly now that they were the ones who were responsible for all of his difficulties. Nothing would satisfy him now but revenge, and he would have his revenge, and no one would be able to stop or hurt him.

He slipped the spare Beretta clips and the Beretta into the opposite pockets of the windbreaker. Then he sat staring out of the windshield into the parking lot. Into Kimo's mind crept a reptile intelligence, an intelligence filled with hideous intent and the memory of countless evils. Kimo's awareness of himself was erased, replaced by a stronger will that now reached down and opened the door. He crossed the parking lot to the doors of the clinic. Behind a van he reached into the bag and extracted the M-16, slipping the spare clips into his waistband. He came around the van and immediately spotted a security guard standing by an outdoor food kiosk. Kimo raised the gun and began firing. The guard danced across the entrance like a marionette on invisible strings.

"Get down Michael Jackson!" Kimo howled.

As he came inside the screams of panic and terror began. Mothers reached for their children and people began running in any direction that permitted escape from the madman with the gun. He walked deliberately down the hall firing short bursts into anyone who caught his attention. Here and there bodies fell to the floor twitching. One woman crawled toward the exit, pain etched in her features. Kimo sighted along the barrel and her head exploded like a watermelon being hit by a sledgehammer. Pieces of skull and brain splattered a young woman and her son who had been crouching nearby.

"It's two for one night at Little Caesars!" Kimo cried, laughing maniacally. He walked deliberately in the direction of Section B and Dr. Bentley's office. With perfect calm he killed two white men dressed in business suits. Jumping through the pharmacy window, he killed the pharmacist and badly wounded several other workers. Hopping back over, he sprayed twenty yards of floor to ceiling windows, the heavy panes of glass shattering and the bullets continuing and doing the same to the windows on the other side of the atrium. Bodies flew from the impact of bullets and exploding glass. Carnage walked the halls with a hard-on. *Chaos ruled.*

He reversed the clip and walked on, spraying the contents of the entire clip in every direction. Ricochets whined like angry hornets, soloing through the chorus of screaming wounded. He only hit 2 people, but it had been something he'd always wanted to do, blow the fuck out of *haole*-land. He switched to the backup clip and began to run. He hit Section B just as Dr. Bentley and two nurses were attempting to flee through a back exit. He shot one of the nurses through the left calf and said, "Stop or you die." They stopped. "I've come for my test results." Kimo said with a smile. The doctor's face was ashen.

Suddenly Kimo's face went through a series of paroxysms. His eyes seemed to spin in their sockets and then went up into his head until nothing but the whites remained. It was a terrible sight as he stood there before them. Another voice, deep and muffled as if from a cavern said, *"I can still see you, so don't even think about it."*

"Let me help the nurse, she's bleeding badly," Doctor Bentley asked, speaking in a calm sonorous tone, his years of discipline mastering the panic that filled the moment.

"Fuck the nurse, heh...heh...not a bad idea actually," he said in a perfect upper class British accent. *"Here's what you do, doctor, do it and you live. Don't do it, and you all die. No questions, understand?"*

"Yes," the doctor replied, quietly exhaling the pent-up air in his lungs at the prospect that he might actually survive this encounter.

"Grab the nurse and drag her into your office. You..." He pointed with his rifle at the other nurse, a pretty Japanese woman in her twenties. *"You follow along, quickly now!"*

Impossibly fast, he whipped around on one knee and shot two police officers who had been sneaking quietly along the wall so they might fire on him without hitting the doctor and his nurses.

Sirens were in the air now as the killer marched his captives toward the office, one of them leaving a smear of blood as the doctor dragged her by the arms after him.

The doctor's office was a windowless room, twelve by twelve and furnished with a large glassed in medical cabinet, a bookcase, two large wooden filing cabinets and a large plain desk fronted by two gray upholstered chairs.

The killer looked around and said, *"Kinda plain for a doctor. You one of those altruistic fucks who's in the business to help people?"* The voice had a mid-western twang to it now. He smirked when the doctor did not reply. The killer locked the door they had entered through and then went quickly through another door into the adjoining examination room, where he locked the other entrance. He then wedged a chair under the handle and came back into the doctor's office.

Dr. Bentley was applying pressure to the nurse's wound. He looked up as the killer entered and asked, "Can I attend her now?"

"*Sure, sure, it'll keep you occupied won't it?*"

"I need to move her into the treatment room."

"No, you don't," the voice said. "*You do it on the desk. You ever bend either of these ladies over that desk?*"

"No," the doctor replied.

"Maybe we'll give you the chance with Little Miss Sukiyaki here." He gestured at the other nurse whose eyes were wide with confusion and shock. He grinned knowingly at her. "*Take off that dress.*"

"Please," the doctor pleaded.

The killer whirled, *"You...shut...the...fuck...up!"* He snarled in a voice of pure menace, now it was Dennis Hopper. *"I will fuck you up. Now..."* He turned back to the nurse. *"Take off that dress or I will remove your kneecaps without anesthetic."* The nurse unbuttoned her uniform, her eyes riveted on the gun whose ugly snout pointed unwaveringly at her legs. The uniform fell to the floor. She stood there in her panties and bra, unable to move.

"Now, take off the rest," the killer said softly in the voice of Dr. Hannibal Lecter. *"And do not hesitate."* She quickly removed the two items. *"Nice tits,"* the killer said. *"But you need to shave that bush. If the doctor went hunting down there he'd have to take a machete to hack his way through. That's pretty impressive for a slant, eh, doc?"* He turned back to the doctor who was making do with items from the cabinet. The doctor kept his eyes on his work.

"When I ask you something, you answer."

"I don't know," the doctor replied.

"Well, then look, shithead!"

The doctor looked.

"See." The voice had now shifted into a Mexican accent. *"The reason I asked you to look, is seence you a doctor, you confirm that it doesn't go sideways. I always hear that kinna pussy goes sideways so it sounds like a motorcycle when they slide down the banister."* The voice let out a phlegmy chortle. Then Dr. Lecter returned, *"You can come and go in this room and the next, while you help the good doctor,"* the voice said to the naked nurse, *"Remember though, if I hear that chair move, I will shoot you through the lower spine or in the stomach. I'm not decided yet. If you should die, it will be after a period of great, protracted pain. Also keep in mind that I am faster than you can imagine."* The killer then grabbed a chair and set it in the far corner of the room, catty-corner to the doctor's desk and facing the treatment room door, which was directly in front of it.

The doctor and the nurse lifted the injured woman on to the desk. A sheet had been placed under her. The doctor talked in a calm steady voice to the nurse assisting him. He had no idea of her mental state and he needed her help.

The killer said, *"Pretend you're on a battlefield. It will be good practice. Now, don't you want to tell me about my test results?"*

"There is nothing wrong with your stomach, Mr. Nakamura. I was going to send you to a neurologist." The doctor kept his head bent over his work.

The voice was now that of a woman, atonal, as if reading from a sheet of paper. "*You're wondering what I am about. You're afraid to say much because you're not sure what I might do. You're wondering if I suffer from a multiple personality disorder."* As he said this, the doctor's head jerked upward and his eyes locked with those of the killer. He could not pull away, held there by the force of a superior will.

"Kimo Nakamura is not here anymore, Dr. Bentley. He has gone aloha. The one who is here can read your mind. The one who is here is a transmitting unit for a superior intelligence that you would not believe in even if it were proved to you, and it will be."

The doctor's body was suddenly picked up and slammed into the wall behind him. The nurse screamed and nearly dropped the syringe that she had just been extending to the doctor. Dr. Bentley grimaced in pain from his collision. He was still pinned against the wall. He could not even open his mouth to speak.

"Okay," the killer said and the doctor's body slid slowly to the floor. *"That's*

just a little demonstration with no explanation. Keep it in mind." Dr. Bentley went back to work. He winced as he took the syringe of morphine from the nurse. Something had happened to his back but he had no time for it now.

The phone rang and the killer went to it. *"Dr. Bentley's office,"* he said in the crisp efficient voice of a receptionist. *"How can I help you?"*

"This is Sgt. Kelani of the Maui Police Department. What's going on it there? Is anyone hurt?"

"Well," the voice said seductively, *"I was just sucking the doctor's cock and boy is it tasty."*

"Who is this?" the police officer demanded.

"This is The Dragonsmouth," the killer replied, now sounding like Bela Lugosi as Dracula. *"Vhat can I do for your vine gentlemen in blue today?"*

"We'd like to know who's in there with you, how many, if anyone is hurt and what it is that you want."

"Well now, Sergeant. I've got me a few guests in here with me. One of 'em got a little hole in her but the doc's gonna fix her right up. Fact is he's doing that right now." There was an unmistakable Texas drawl in his voice this time.

"What are your plans?"

"Before I tell you was' up, Holmes, I'm gonna give you a lil' demon…stration, way you can dig this sirius bidness. Teach yo ass to respect me. Let you know this dude is stupid fresh."

"What's that? Whatever you need, we can work something out. You don't have to hurt anyone else."

The killer cut him off. *"Jus watch Homey."* He pulled the Beretta from his jacket, went into the examination room and put four shots through the door. A man screamed on the other side. Almost too quick to see, he was back in the office where he fired two more times into the sheet-rock next to the other door. There were more screams. The nurse working with Dr. Bentley was openly sobbing now.

The killer walked over to her and began running his hands over her breasts. *"You keep crying like that I'm going to come around behind you and do you while you help the doctor. Then what's going to happen is you're going to be more turned on than you have ever been in your life. You won't be able to help yourself. You'll be calling out all kinds of dirty things but you won't care."* She'd turned a bright red as she felt the force of arousal building in her body. He rolled her nipples between his thumb and forefinger while he bent down and looked into her eyes. She stopped crying.

He picked up the phone again. *"Hi, I'm baaack,"* in a perfect mimicking of the little girl in *Poltergeist*. *"Shut up and listen,"* now in a flat cold serious voice. *"You don't need to be asking any questions, by now you know to keep your men away from the door. The three men I hit are hurt but they're not going to die. You're probably wondering how I know all this. That's okay, it's good to wonder, but there's one thing you don't have to wonder about and that's if I'm serious or not.*

"Here's what you're going to do. You're going to get that sack of shit Captain Rusk over here so's we can have a dialogue. You're also going to get Detective Douglas, recently of Manhattan's finest over here as well. Once you've accomplished that, we'll take it from there. Meanwhile, I've got to get Kimo laid just once in his short life. I owe him that much." The killer winked at the nurse and then hung up the phone.

Chapter Twenty-One

Shouts and the sounds of running feet brought them out into the hallway. Ben collared a young patrolman and asked him what was happening.

"There's a maniac with an automatic weapon over at Kaiser! A lot of people down, hostage situation," he said before pulling free and racing off. The two men looked at each other, shock etched in their features. Together they ran after the departing officer.

"Lieutenant Kamamoto!" A woman's voice rang out over the din. They stopped and turned to the reception desk. A female officer was waving them over. When they came to the desk, she said, "I just called your office." At that moment his beeper went off. "And paged you, too. Captain Rusk said to tell you and Mr. Douglas to stay away from Kaiser. He's dispatched Detectives Klein and Santos over to cover for Homicide. He said you should just continue with your own investigation."

Ben nodded, "Okay, thanks." They walked away and left the building. Standing on the front steps, they could see across the street to the Kaiser Building. A dozen patrol cars and other vehicles were drawn up at the entrance, lights flashing. There was a frantic milling of police and civilians as they worked to clear the area. A flatbed truck filled with sawhorses pulled into the lot. "Let's head over to the Ford dealership," Ben said suddenly. "Nothing we can do here."

When Captain Rusk got the news, blood rushed into his face and for a moment, he could not get a breath. "What the fuck did you say?" His features were compressed, his eyes reduced to narrow slits.

"He said he isn't talking to anyone until Alan Douglas gets here," the officer told him again. Rusk stood still for a moment, digesting the information. *What did this mean?* He turned it over in his mind, a mass murderer with connection to Douglas. *Maybe things would turn out somehow.* A brief smile flickered across his face. "Get him, now!" Rusk ordered.

Two minutes later, the officer returned and informed Rusk that Alan and Ben had left the station. "Then find them and get them here!" he screamed.

"That's being done," the harassed officer replied.

The radio call came in as they were turning off of Pu'unene Avenue into the car lot. "What the hell?" Ben muttered, as he listened to the dispatcher order them to Kaiser immediately. "Say why," he replied.

"No details," the dispatcher continued. "Proceed at once."

"Roger," Ben replied, as he turned the car around and headed back the way that they had come.

"Strange news," Alan remarked.

"I couldn't even begin to guess," Ben answered.

There was a scene of mass confusion at the clinic entrance. Already two TV trucks were in the lot. Bodies on stretchers were coming out into the ambulances and there was a horde of onlookers, some shoving for the entrance with anguish on their faces. The police had them contained but here and there, force was being used to keep distraught relatives at bay.

Ben ran through the police cordon to the clinic entrance with Alan in his wake, the blue line opening for a moment and then slamming shut behind them. At the entrance a police sergeant signaled for them to approach. Alan looked at the carnage in front of him. Smears of blood were everywhere and to one side was a row of bodies covered by white sheets. There was a dark haze in the center of the large main room that rose to the ceiling. At first Alan thought that it was gun smoke. As he looked more closely he could see human-like forms twisting inside of it. He felt goose bumps rising on his arms and quickly looked away. Looking again, he saw it was still there. He wondered if this was the result of his encounter with Ming.

"You're to wait right here until Detective Santos arrives," the uniformed sergeant said. He was a small trim Filipino man who was shifting around on the balls of his feet, chewing impossibly fast on his gum. Alan felt the adrenaline coursing through him.

He looked to his right and saw a man in a suit trotting toward them. Alan recognized him as someone he had seen at the station. The man was slender and tall with a thick shock of unruly brown hair, tinted sunglasses and the old scars of a bad acne problem. There were grim lines set in his face as he nodded quickly at Ben and then turned to address Alan. "You're to come with me at once," he said.

"What about Ben?" Alan asked.

"Just you," the man replied.

Alan turned to Ben and said, "Who's this?"

"Herman Santos," Ben replied with a smile. "He's okay, Alan. You go with him, I'll wait here."

Alan shook his head. "Where I go, Ben goes, or I don't go."

Santos face split into a smile. "Captain Rusk is really going to like that. I appreciate the opportunity to give him the news." Having said this, Santos pulled a cell phone from his pocket and punched in a series of numbers. When he made connection he repeated Alan's comment and then listened for a time. Then he broke the connection and returned the phone to his pocket. "I guess you're at Burger King," he said to Alan.

"What's that supposed to mean?" he asked.

"Have it your way," Santos replied with a laugh. Then he added, "But that's not quite how the Captain put it." They followed him back the way he had come.

Santos led them through the path of destruction the killer had created. About a hundred feet down the corridor from the doctor's office was a make-shift command post. There were twenty men and women grouped about the Captain, several of them in full SWAT regalia. Chairs were scattered around a large table but no one was sitting in any of them.

"Any idea of who did this?" Alan asked Santos as they approached the group.

"We're not sure exactly," Santos said. "But from the description and checking the doctor's appointments it could be a Kimo Nakamura. We did a quick check. He's a local boy, no priors and a steady job. It's a very weird scene."

Santo's voice trailed off as they came close to the group of police officers, bodies parted and Alan found himself standing a few feet from Captain Rusk, who was bent over some papers on the table in front of him.

Rusk looked up at him after a few seconds and said, "Well now." There was malevolence in the look that Rusk gave him, but Alan ignored it.

"What can I do for you Captain?" he asked.

"It seems that our boy knows you and made a special request for your presence."

Alan was taken aback by this and searched the Captain's face for some message. Finding nothing, he said, "I'm afraid I don't understand."

"Neither do I but I imagine we'll find out." The venom on Rusk's face made Alan step back. He looked deranged. "Get him on the phone," Rusk snapped at an officer standing beside him. The patrolman immediately picked up the hand-set to a speakerphone and dialed. Alan could see that a sophisticated recording device was already attached to the telephone. He could hear the ringing loud and clear as he watched the tape machine click on, red light flashing. It rang twice and then was picked up.

"*This is Doctor Bentley's office. With whom would you like to speak?*" asked a voice in a clipped British accent. Alan wondered how weird this was going to get.

"This is Captain Rusk. I am here with Douglas. You wanted to talk to us?"

"Puleeze, Detective Douglas, I'm sure. Honey, I don't know. I'm soooo tired and confused. I just don't know what I want." The voice was now that of a Deep South homosexual. There was a sibilant huskiness in it.

Rusk looked at Alan and arched an eyebrow. It was his way of asking him if he had anything to say without actually having to ask him. Into this silence the killer spoke once again.

"Yes Captain, the good detective doesn't know what to say any more than you do. Why are you looking at him?" Alan felt an electric current run up his spine at this new voice, cultivated southern, a clearly modulated bass. *This has got to be Billy Joe*, Alan thought.

"What do you want?" Rusk asked sharply.

"What makes you think I want anything?" the voice continued. *"Maybe I got the urge to kill a few folks. Maybe I'm going to kill these folks in here too and then just surrender into your good graces."*

"There won't be any good graces if you hurt those people in there," Rusk replied.

Alan held off on any commentary of his own. He didn't know what the madman wanted and he was only going to respond to a direct question. He'd already decided that. No amount of understanding or negotiation technique would have any effect here. He knew what the others could not know and there was no way to tell them. He would keep his thoughts to himself and play it out as the moment required.

"You mean you'd kill me if I surrendered after killing these people?" Now the voice was a flat uninflected California accent. *"I think that's against the law,"* the voice continued. *"Anyway, now you've pissed me off."* There was the sound of a gunshot and a scream followed by shouts and cries. "*Don't you do anything stupid Doctor,*" the voice said, *"especially now that you've got more work to do."*

"What's going on in there?" Rusk screamed.

"I shot the other nurse in the leg," the voice replied. *"The good Doctor finished up the other one. I'm just keeping him busy."*

"Is there anything we can do that is going to help those people in there?" Alan said. He was surprised that he had spoken. It happened without him registering the act.

"You're a funny one to want to save people, Detective, with all of the blood you've got on your hands." The voice had just done a perfect imitation of John Wayne. Various officers were looking around uneasily at each other. This was nothing that they had ever been prepared for.

"What do you mean?" Alan asked.

"You know what I'm talking about, Detective. Nobody else does yet, but they will."

Rusk looked up sharply when he heard this. This was interesting. "What are you referring to?" Rusk asked. There was naked anticipation on his face.

"Not now you short-dicked, potbellied, alcoholic candy-ass!" Now the voice was that of a Marine drill sergeant.

Rusk's face turned crimson but he said nothing.

"Look," Alan said, realizing he had nothing but platitudes to offer. "Whatever you think I may have done, whatever you've done, those people with you have done nothing to deserve this."

"There are no innocent bystanders." The voice said in a terrible cold voice. *"Terrible things happen to innocent people all of the time. Fortunes of war you know."* The voice was mocking them now. *"Every day in every part of the world this shit goes on. Get used to it. In this vale of tears we should expect tragedy. It's in the natural order of things."*

"Look," Alan interjected. "You know our names, but we don't know yours. Who are you?"

"You can call me The Dragonsmouth. I already told that first cop who called. I am just a mouth, an orifice of communication for The Dragon, an oracle of disclosure for someone who, at this time, will remain anonymous."

Once again Alan felt a shiver at the return of that southern voice. The voice gripped him, stirring memories, but no image came.

Captain Rusk was now making the crazy sign at the side of his head. "Look Mr. Mouth, we've got people you can talk to, specialists. Maybe they can help you with your problem."

"I haven't got a problem fat ass. You've got the problem and I've already got a Doctor in here to talk to. He doesn't like me right now. He's thinking it would be nice if I got wasted in the process here. Maybe I should shoot myself in the leg, make him feel better, or shoot him in the leg, give him something to work on when he finishes with the nurse. How'd you like that Doctor?"

"I have no control over what you do," they heard the Doctor reply.

"That's right, Doctor, that's what you need to concentrate on now. The others need

to concentrate, too." With this said The Dragonsmouth pulled the Beretta from his waistband and fired three shots through the door. The bullets ricocheted off a tiled wall, screaming like bees as they fled down the corridor where the police were stationed. A fragment of tile clipped the bridge of the Captain's nose.

"Son of a bitch!" he screamed as he hit the floor. The rest of the officers either fell to the ground or ran around the immediate corner. Ben had instinctively gone into a crouch, his weapon pointed in front of him. Alan had not moved. He stood where he had been.

"Get down you asshole!" Rusk yelled at him.

"Nah, he's not going to get down, Captain. He's not a coward like you are," The Dragonsmouth said.

"What do you want?" Alan asked again. "Why do you want me here?"

"All of life's a stage and we are merely players, each having his exits and entrances." The Dragonsmouth replied, *"This is just one of the entrances and a few of the exits. We're not done yet."* Now it was the voice of a British actor. *"What kind of a director would I be, love, if I gave away the plot in the second act? I doubt I would hold the audience's attention for long afterwards, would I?"*

"You've got our attention," Alan replied.

"Yes, I do, don't I? Okay, let's speed it up or everyone is going to miss lunch. I want you to bring in a newspaper reporter and a television cameraman, or is it camera-person now? Bring what I have asked for and we'll set about ending this little charade. Oh and Captain, do get up off your knees. Someone might want a blowjob from you and that's an awfully hard position to refuse them from. Try to manifest the appearance of a little dignity, even though you don't possess any."

There was some snickering from the officers and Rusk looked around angrily trying to catch one of them in the act.

"Your fear of bodily injury and death is not making you look good in the eyes of your subordinates. You're certainly not making the impression that Detective Fearless Fosdick is. No wonder you hate him so much."

Rusk turned beet red. He was on the verge of apoplexy when he finally got to his feet. No amount of danger was worth further ignominy. He was gasping with rage, ready to order the house brought down around him.

"Don't let him get to you, Captain. He's playing you like a violin," Alan said.

"Fuck you, Douglas," he replied. Turning to an officer near him on the floor, he said, "Get on your feet, Murakami, and get this maniac what he wants."

"Yes, sir," the officer replied and ran down the corridor toward the entrance.

"That's right, get me what I asked for, Captain Chickenshit." One of the officers snorted as he struggled to keep from laughing. Even members of the tactical force had turned their faces away so as not to betray their features.

With an effort of will, Captain Rusk gained control of his breathing and consoled himself with the thought that at some point in the near future he would avenge himself for this day's indignities.

The Dragonsmouth spoke again. *"So Detective, how's your wife and girlfriend? You think maybe they're swapping tales, maybe even some spit, in the afterlife?"* The voice now had a wheedling tone like many a New York junkie Alan had listened to in the past.

He detached his mind and emotions from the content of Dragonsmouth's words. He'd seen and heard enough cat and mouse games in his lifetime. This evil entity held all of the cards. If Alan said the wrong thing, he could shoot one of the hostages, or all of them and Captain Rusk would take little time before blaming him.

Even now, Rusk was watching him closely. This new information that the killer knew about Alan's life and the case he was working on made him very curious. Somewhere here there was a lever into the truth and he would find it.

"What do you know about them?" Alan asked.

"I know a great deal, Alan. I know as much as you do, which is more than anyone else here does."

"What does that mean?"

"All things in time, Detective, we don't want to give away the store just now."

Alan felt all eyes focused on him but he was far away, calm and unmoved.

The reporter and the cameraman had arrived, a Mutt and Jeff team. The reporter was an Asian woman who could not have weighed more than seventy-five pounds. The cameraman was a burly local who stood over six feet and easily weighed three hundred pounds. *Samoan*, Alan thought.

"So," Dragonsmouth's voice boomed out, *"The flies have arrived. Won't someone offer them a plate of shit? Watch out they don't land in a pool of blood. I know they're hungry."*

"He's going to kill the hostages," Alan said quietly to the Captain.

"Shut up, Douglas!" Rusk snapped. "Nobody needs your input anymore."

The reporter heard this exchange and asked, "What's going on Captain?"

"No questions are being taken from the press," Dragonsmouth said. *"You are here to witness my surrender and that is all. Otherwise I will start talking about your*

private life." The reporter must have known something about what had been taking place, probably from the officer who had gone to get her, because she never said another word.

"I'm coming out now." It was the little girl from *Poltergeist* again. The Dragonsmouth whipped around and brought the gun barrel viciously across the doctor's temple, fracturing his skull. Then he quickly broke the necks of both nurses, twisting their heads around so that they faced behind them. He placed them side-by-side on the floor. *"I'll bet you look good in a swimsuit, Captain. You should put up a photo in your office where all of your admirers can see it."* The door opened and Dragonsmouth stepped out into view, his hands above his head in surrender. Alan could hear the tape turning in the camera. He did not recognize the man, had never seen him before. He was a short, powerfully built local male. As he walked directly toward them, members of the tactical force immediately swarmed over him and brought him down to the floor, cuffing his hands and feet.

"All right, get the press out of here," Rusk shouted to his officers.

"I'm not going anywhere," the reporter shouted back at Rusk.

"Oh, yes, you are," he said. An officer, bigger even than the cameraman, picked her up off her feet and walked toward the entrance with her. The cameraman followed recording the scene for posterity. He secretly hated working for the woman.

A number of officers had raced into the doctor's office. A moment later one of them emerged and said, "They're all dead."

"Son of a bitch!" Rusk exclaimed. He turned his murderous eyes on Alan. "You're responsible somehow and when I get proof, you'll never see daylight again."

"Captain," Ben said his first words since they had arrived on the scene.

"Shut up!" Rusk screamed at him, a feral light in his eyes and then he ran to the doctor's office.

Alan looked over at Ben and nodded silently, giving him a crooked smile. There was nothing he could have said. What had been unreal for him personally was now unreal publicly. It was more than he could digest. Ben put his arm around Alan's shoulder and they walked away.

Kimo was hustled over to a police van while the lobby and the entrance boiled with activity. Forensics crews and photographers were busy throughout the interior. Outside was bedlam, as the man once known as Kimo Nakamura passed through the crowd of relatives, reporters, TV cameras and rubberneckers.

Fifty feet short of the entrance, Ben said, “Alan, we don’t want to go that way. There’s another way out.” Alan turned without a word and followed Ben back the way they had come. “Jesus,” Ben said, “Rusk looked like Nixon in the final days.”

Ten minutes later they were sitting in a small Mexican restaurant on Dairy Road. Alan pushed his taco salad around on his plate.

Ben looked at him with a worried expression on his face. “What’s up, pardner? You haven’t said a word except to order your food and now you’re not eating it.”

Alan looked in his friend’s eyes and said, “There is nothing I can say, absolutely nothing. This is all about me. None of those people would have died except for my involvement. Dozens… I don’t know how many dead and more to come I’m sure and I can’t do anything. Not a thing.” Alan looked out into the parking lot, seeing nothing.

Ben looked at his friend and said. “You know the situation Alan. You can’t go back, there is no back. You can’t stand still, you’ll get run over. Whatever the uncertainty or the consequences, there’s only forward. Comfort yourself with doing your best. You may think this is all about you, but evil is less specific than just opportunistic anyway. If it wasn’t you it would be somebody else. If someone steals your car and runs over a kid, it doesn’t put you at the wheel.”

Alan looked at Ben. “You put it like that, it makes a lot of sense.” He shook his head. “Something in what you said, for a minute it didn’t sound like you at all.”

Ben rotated his eyes around and then crossed them. “Maybe it wasn’t.”

Chapter Twenty-Two

Billy Joe turned the scenario over in his mind while enjoying one of his special cocktails. There were a number of different ingredients in it, Chinese herbs, cognac, various extracts and tinctures — the power of which were unknown except to a small group of informed individuals. It included several cc's of a rare cocaine solution once imbibed by popes and heads of state and a quarter teaspoon of dried blood and fluid from the hypothalamus of a young child. He'd received the recipe from a powerful demon that possessed many an arcane secret. Billy Joe enjoyed dealing with him. The personal danger was an intoxicating event, for in every transaction, his life and a long term of unspeakable torment were on the line. One misstep and it was all over. Challenges like this were required on occasion. They helped to maintain the courage and power of will that were an absolute necessity in his line of work.

He was pleased, very pleased, with himself. He had accomplished all of what he wanted. The only fly in the ointment was the ongoing knowledge that someone, somewhere, knew more about him than he wanted. He shook his head, toying with the thought, probing, as he so often did now. It was a tremendous annoyance, but he knew better than to let it disturb his balance. Whatever they knew, they did not know it all and when the final moment came it would be too late.

Many times he had searched for the source of the interference in labyrinthine ways. He had found nothing. Soon the time would come for him to access other mediums of revelation. He needed to know. As confident as he was of success, it was essential that he take all care. He hadn't gotten where he was by being careless.

He held the crystal goblet up to the sun's light and watched the colors dance. After a moment, he could see Douglas's face in front of him. The hatred swelled inside him. It was a malevolent fire burning at his core. Part of him was immersed in it, part of him detached and dispassionate. He saw the binding of the trails into the cohesive moment that was to come. Laughter burbled out from between his lips as he thought of the delicious irony of it all. *Douglas would beg, would plead and cry to die, to do anything, but there would be no release and there would be no end...*

Alan and Ben wandered around the new Ford showroom. "Look at this, Alan, a Ford Windstar van only $34,999.00. Maybe we should forget the killers out working on population control and start putting these guys in jail."

"I know what you mean. Car dealers are different than the rest of us. They have to be to do what they do. Just think if that was you." He pointed at a strange character making his way toward them.

"I'd have to kill myself."

"See what I mean? They're different."

"Can I help you with something?" the man asked. He was a surfer dude in shades, wearing a loud Hawaiian shirt with flamingoes and penguins sitting in lawn chairs and drinking Mai Tais.

"Yeah," Ben replied, "You can tell me where you got that shirt."

"You like it?" the salesman asked. He flashed a big wide grin and turned around. On the back were dolphins and polar bears doing the same thing.

"Not exactly," Ben replied. He flashed his badge and said, "We're looking for the manufacturer. He's in a lot of trouble."

The salesman stepped back when he saw the badge and his smile disappeared. "What? Hey, my mother got me this shirt."

Ben looked at Alan and then said, "We're going to need your mother's name and address."

"What is this?" asked the salesman. Unsure what was going on, there was confusion on his face. A muscle in his left jaw was spasming.

Ben laughed and said, '"We're actually here to check on the sale or lease of a Ford panel van, dark color, sometime in the last couple months. I'm Lieutenant Kamamoto and this is Special Investigator Douglas of the District Attorney's Office."

The salesman, an irrepressible sort was already getting over being had. "Wow, I'm glad you're not going after my mother. I don't think she could handle it."

Alan patted him on the shoulder. "Not to worry," he said.

"Uh huh, well, my name's Chuck. I'll be glad to help."

Ben snorted, "We'd like to take a look at your records."

Chuck shrugged his shoulders and said, "Alrighty then, let's go into my office and see what we can come up with. Everybody important is out having lunch with the governor's economic aide. They're working on tax break legislation for new car sales."

"How does it look?"

"I don't know, but everybody will eat a lot of good food and get drunk and have to be driven home in the house ExtendoVan." Alan and Ben laughed dutifully at the image.

They walked through the showroom until Chuck turned to his left and motioned them into a small cubicle office. Chuck sat behind the desk and tapped on the keyboard. Then he reached into his shirt pocket and removed some business cards and handed one each to Ben and Alan. "I hope you'll remember me when it comes time to get a new car. We've got some great deals going on right now." He removed his sunglasses and gave his most earnestly sincere look.

"We'll certainly keep it in mind," Ben replied. "We want to catch some bad guys and you want to sell some cars. We're not so far apart really."

Chuck got no part of Ben's sarcasm and sat waiting with a look of confusion on his face.

Ben pulled his notepad from his back pocket and thumbed through it. "What we have is a panel van. Could be new, looks new, or it could be used. It's dark blue or black. We know it's a Ford, witness saw the logo. Oh yeah, what windows it has might be smoked."

"Three months you say?" Chuck was looking very competent and serious now.

"Uh huh," Ben replied.

Alan was standing apart. His thoughts were caught up in Chuck's aura. He was seeing people as he had never seen them before. There was a sense of empathy now that modified all of his perceptions. It seemed that everyone was doing the best they could with the information that they had. Chuck did what Chuck knew. He didn't know what Alan knew. He shouldn't be judged according to Alan's personal standards. For a moment he had a vision of humanity climbing on a spiral staircase. Its beginning could not be seen and its end disappeared into a cone of light. He was reminded of paintings he had seen by the artist Albrecht Durer. *Each step on the stairway was at a different station of consciousness. The important thing was not to piss over the railing.*

"Okay, let's see what we have," Chuck said. "You're in luck in one respect. August thru early September is our quietest time. The new cars are on their way and we start the closeouts this Monday. There's a possible problem for you though," Chuck added, looking up at them.

"How's that?" Alan asked.

"Well, they could have bought the van anywhere. Not just from a car dealer but from any private person too."

"We appreciate that," Ben replied. "We've got the computers at the DMV going. We just want whatever you've got. We're not expecting miracles, Chuck."

Chuck replied, "I guess it's hard not to leave a trail right?"

"That depends on whether you lie or not in the first place," Alan added, "Use phony identification so legitimate appearing, it fools everyone for a while. There are ways."

Chuck nodded, his attention focused on the monitor. "Here we are, vans, all vans sold over the last ninety days. Eliminate what doesn't fit and… Hey," Chuck said, "What if they painted the van afterwards?"

"You'd make a hell of a cop," Ben stated, "Just give us what you have."

"Here we go, one dark green van, nope. One black but it's got a picture window on one side. Hmmm. Dark blue Econoline, big engine, tinted glass, lots of features for this model. It was sold on July 5th to a Howard Beldano. It's a 1995. We got it on a trade in March. It probably didn't move for a while because of the price tag. Man paid for it in cash, Bank of Hawaii cashier's check. You might get something from the bank. The price was twenty-five thousand dollars."

"What's his address?" Ben asked.

"The mainland address is 4545 Tanglewoods Avenue, Bel Air, California. Local address, Maui Sands Hotel, 1456 Kamehameha. That's a budget hotel right down the street. It says Room 142. ID used was a California driver's license and a gold American Express card that he used to give a thousand dollar deposit until the check cleared. I guess even cashier's checks are questionable around here," Chuck added with a smile.

"Can you print that out for us?" Alan asked.

"Coming right up," Chuck replied. "Can I ride around with you sometime? See how you work?"

"My number's on the card," Ben said. "Give me a call."

"That would really be great," Chuck replied. "Here you go," he said, handing Ben the sheet of paper. "Do I get my Junior G-Man badge now?"

Ben replied, "We'll put it in the mail to you this afternoon. But, we don't want you making any arrests until you have it in your possession. Is that clear?"

"Absolutely, Lieutenant."

In the car, Ben asked, "So, what do you think?"

"The van? Maybe. Then again, could be someone up to something else. But even if it is the van, ten to one the paper trail leads nowhere. I want to get back to the ranch and check out this Dragonsmouth character. I think the path starts there. I don't know that Rusk is going to let me anywhere near him, however."

"I'll look into that Alan. Maybe you could follow up on the van while I check the waters, nose around. How's that feel?"

"Sounds like a plan," Alan replied.

BACK IN HIS OFFICE.

Alan hung up the phone and riffled the pad on which he had been making his notes. His heightened perceptions were confusing the hell out of him. One moment he was focused on the task at hand, the next, he was in La-La Land talking to invisible beings and seeing the external world in an acid fugue state. It was like riding a bicycle for the first time and he felt about as competent.

He knew who some of the players were, their names, their descriptions, but that was a long way from apprehending anyone. The van now seemed a strong possibility. There was no Howard Beldano on Tanglewood Avenue. There was no Tanglewood Avenue in Bel Air. The Bank of Hawaii account had around six hundred dollars still in it but the address of record was the same non-address as the other and the phone number didn't exist. The DMV was also fraudulently processed. They had a license number but Alan was sure it had been switched by now. The motel records revealed nothing. It was all tantalizing but it danced just out of reach, for now.

There were five recent home rentals that looked promising and he was going to visit all of them tomorrow. They were all secluded. Two had been rented six weeks ago, one a month before that, one a week after and one just four days after that. Four of them had been rented by men and the most recent by a woman. It wouldn't be the first time someone used an intermediary.

Twenty people were dead at the Kaiser clinic, twenty-seven were wounded, three of them critically and one was not expected to live. Kimo Nakamura was being held without bail across the street.

Ben had phoned to tell him that the kid's parents were at the station. They did not recognize their son, his features were so changed. He'd finished high school and was well read in Hawaiian history. He was an introvert (no surprise there) with few friends and a lot of rage for what he called the "foreign despoilers" of the island.

Not much had changed from the initial communications that had taken place in the clinic. The Dragonsmouth entity continued to reveal intimate details of the lives of his interrogators to the extreme amusement of onlookers. It had been awhile now since Ben had contacted him, so either something good was going on, or he had managed to make himself part of the interrogation. He knew that Rusk was now gone, no longer able to accept Dragonsmouth's commentary on his manhood, his sex life and his hang-ups in the workplace.

Alan smiled as he thought of some of the scathing comments the killer had made about Rusk. Rusk had been in orbit. It reminded him of a quote by Lao Tzu, "He who feels punctured must once have been a bubble."

He picked up the phone and dialed his home number. A woman's voice came on the line.

"Hello?"

"I'm sorry. I appear to have disturbed a female intruder in my home. I hope I haven't inconvenienced you," Alan quipped.

Christienne laughed. "Hi, Alan, Whip just ran down to the store for a minute. I stayed to explore your house. It's beautiful."

"Thanks, Christienne. I'm just checking in. It looks like there'll be some other guests, people from work." Suddenly Alan could think of no more to say. "Tell Whip I called?"

"Will do." She replied.

"Later." Alan hung up the phone. He'd invited Ben for dinner. Then, an hour earlier, he'd gotten a call from Aaron Wilson. On impulse he had invited him too. Aaron, whose wife was out of town, had immediately agreed.

Alan couldn't shake the undercurrent of anxiety that coiled in his stomach. He felt like some kind of Typhoid Mary. Anyone who came around him was potentially in danger. He knew though, that to give in to the fear was to increase its power. He had to conduct his life in a normal fashion, had to act like he was the boy in Rudyard Kipling's poem *If—*. There was no other option. *Better to die on your feet than to live on your knees,* he thought. If what Ming said was true, then no matter where you were, you were exactly where you were supposed to be. *In that case, Aaron, Ben, or anyone else for that matter, would be in no greater or lesser danger anywhere else.*

Later that afternoon, Alan was shocked to notice that the Kaiser Clinic looked relatively normal as he drove by it. It never failed to amaze him how quickly scenes of horror could appear and disappear. Life cleaned itself up and moved on. It reminded him of what happened when you stepped on an anthill. Ants would scurry everywhere in panic. Five minutes later you came by and it was as if nothing had ever happened. You could do it again and five minutes later it would have once again returned to normal. *Life went on. And they didn't move! No matter what happened. Life went on.*

Soon he was out of the downtown area and into the countryside. "All this beauty," he said softly. The great crater loomed on his right. The setting sun made it appear as if a river of gold was flowing down the Haleakalā Highway. Near its top, the mountain had a purple cast and the multitudes of valleys that ran down from the top made it appear as if a great hand had reached down and squeezed it together like a paper bag. The mountain had a seductive and mysterious magnetism. There was no doubting the sensuous impact of it on the human mind. The primary effect of the island was the overpowering influence of Mother Nature. Life grew with wild abandon nearly everywhere and where it was stark, it was still beautiful.

It remained beautiful despite the fact that the same things happened in Hawaii as nearly everywhere else. The rapacious, vampiristic greed of the sugar companies, endemic corruptions in business, the blatant pandering of television to an over-commercialized world, robberies, assaults, murders — still, it seemed to Alan that it was possible to find a peace here that did not exist anywhere else he had ever been. He could sit by the ocean for hours listening to the sounds of the waves pounding again and again upon the shore. The lines of another Dylan song came into his mind and he sang softly to himself, *"...to dance beneath the diamond sky with one hand waving free... Silhouetted by the sea, circled by the circus sands... With all memory and fate, driven deep beneath the waves, let me forget about today until tomorrow."* Joy coursed through his heart as he sang the words. They came as close to describing how life could be in the islands as anything he could think of. At least that was how it had been for him before the shadow had come once again into his life.

Great art always had the same effect of erasing the anxiety and depression from his mind. He was immensely grateful to the powerful thought forms of those who ennobled the human experience with the promise of a cleaner, brighter world.

Thoughts of Elizabeth passed through his mind. She'd always loved Dylan. She called him the "Poet Philosopher King of our time." Whenever something terrible happened in the world, she would play his music. If it wasn't Dylan, then it was The Beatles. She had told Alan that she believed angels had passed through them and left their heavenly message for the healing of the world. For her, it hadn't been just music. Conversely, she had been just as critical of following trends. *Here,* she'd said, *you had individuals possessed by entities of a different order, with a message of confusion, inspiring chaos and violence.* When MTV first appeared, she was quick to note that they stayed away from the life-affirming entertainers and concentrated almost exclusively on the negativists. As time passed it had become exclusively that way. Rap had really dismayed her. She said it raped the mind. Some of their acquaintances thought her eccentric, but Alan knew she saw things that they did not.

There were primal evils in the world and an individual could overcome them, if he could overcome them within himself. The world in general could not. *A lot of horrors that occurred were spawned from just causes. Terrible deeds were done in the name of family, in the name of God, in the name of country.* These allegiances sometimes required the spilling of blood, either directly, or indirectly.

There were things that Alan knew to be true that you could not say. He thought about the great Indian saint Meher Baba who had taken a vow of silence. He had said that the next time he spoke he would reveal the secret of the universe. Years went by. Decades went by and one day, Meher Baba, at least in the corporal sense, was gone. He had never spoken another word. Alan could understand that.

He thought about the programming and brainwashing in the schools, the heroes that were not heroes and the role models that were not role models. Still, he didn't resent the world's injustices because he suspected that it was all a game of musical chairs. *The beggar would fall asleep one night and wake up the next morning a king. The king would awaken as a beggar. The sugar baron would wake up in chains in the dark hold of a slave ship. The movie actress would awaken to find herself a hooker with bad teeth and the hooker would awaken to be a queen…* There was no injustice anywhere. In the long run, things always evened out.

Whatever waited for him, he felt he could handle it. *Death wasn't final. The pain of living beat the terror of death, hands down. It all worked out as the distance of time granted a greater perspective.* Death was just another unknown, another bend in the road that he hadn't taken, or couldn't remember. *Whoever had said that the fear of death was worse than death itself, had been right.* He was far more concerned about preventing the suffering of others than he was about avoiding his own. God help him to see it coming.

"Greetings!" Alan called as he entered his house. "I come in peace."

Whip raised his wineglass. Christienne smiled beside him.

"I see you started the party without me."

"We had no choice, Alan. The intensity of the pressure to groove was more than we could bear. It overwhelmed us." Christienne replied as she got up. "Can I get you something to drink?"

"There's some mango tea in the icebox. I'd love a glass right now."

When Christienne returned with Alan's tea, he told them of the day's events.

Christienne shuddered when he was done. "It's not safe anywhere anymore is it?"

"There's a lot of confusion and stress in the world these days. Some people just are not equipped to handle it," Alan replied. "Well," he rose to his feet and turned to the kitchen. "I'd better get started if dinner's going to come out on time."

"I'll help." Christienne got to her feet.

"No," Whip said as he touched her arm, "Alan likes to do it alone."

"Can we watch?" she asked.

"That would be okay," Alan replied. "So what did you guys do today?"

"We didn't do much of anything except sit around and talk," Whip said as he kneaded Christienne's shoulders. "Nothing exciting like your day."

Alan nodded. "You know the Chinese have a curse. It's hard to understand it as a curse unless you get its import, 'May you live in interesting times.' Meaning it's preferable to have nothing happening. Adventures are a lot more fun to read about or watch on TV than they are experienced in your life."

The conversation flowed easily and Alan felt some of his earlier anxiety melting away. He loved to cook. It was an art form as intricate and as satisfying as anything he had ever done. There was a subtle chemistry that separated the work of any two people, even if they prepared the food exactly the same way. *Vibes*, Alan thought. *There was a great deal to the theory of vibrations. Vibrations affected everything.*

Soon, the coconut milk soup was simmering nicely. The rice was done and all of the fish and vegetables were ready for the stir-fry when the doorbell rang.

"I'll get it," Christienne said and went out to answer the door. Moments later, Aaron Wilson came into the kitchen followed a few minutes later by Ben and Christienne. Alan made the introductions and Whip made drinks. Alan sent everyone out to the deck while he finished with dinner. Ben returned a few minutes later.

"You want to hear about today?"

Alan smiled and said, "I thought maybe later. I can suppress my curiosity that long and the food has to go out when the food wants to."

"Your call," Ben replied. "Anyway, when it wasn't downright scary it was full on hilarious. Rusk got ripped a new asshole. Whoever possesses that boy has got a knife blade for a tongue. He had Rusk dancing on strings. Every time he couldn't take any more and was headed for the door, your name would get mentioned. It was like watching a crack head trying to put down his pipe and leave."

Alan turned and asked, "My name came up again?"

Ben nodded, "A lot. And there was plenty of innuendo and suggestions that you knew a deal more about what had been happening. He never said what though. It was classic cat and mouse. I think Aaron got wind of it through the day, probably one of the reasons he decided to come."

"You think?" Alan asked.

"Everything's connected, buddy. You tell me that all the time."

"Uh-huh, well, dinner's ready." Alan began to bring the food to the table on the deck. The soft glow of evening danced in the candlelight. Aaron and Whip were talking about baseball.

Dinner was a huge success and for a time it was as if all of the recent troubles did not exist. No one mentioned the tragedy at the clinic. Whip had chosen some excellent wines and they made the conversation light and animated.

Aaron told some very funny tales about his first year as a prosecutor in Michigan. Then Whip described some of the wonders he had seen on his travels in the East. Alan watched from an abstracted distance, bemused. It was as if nothing outside of them was taking place.

Finally, Whip and Christienne began clearing away the table and the others got up and drifted away to a corner of the deck. Aaron lit his pipe and Ben gave Alan one of his Player's Navy Cuts. "One of the great smokes of our time," he said. "It has more tar and nicotine in one cigarette than there is in an entire pack of those low tar jobbies."

"Probably why they have so much flavor," Alan remarked.

"You know why I smoke unfiltered cigarettes?" Ben asked.

"Because you're stupid?" Aaron replied with a sardonic smile.

"Thanks, Aaron. I guess I should have said, do you know why I don't smoke filtered cigarettes?" He paused, holding the moment, waiting for Alan to parrot what Aaron had just said. When this didn't happen he continued, "Because it's like sucking a tit through a sweater."

Aaron swallowed smoke upon hearing this and started hacking. Alan pounded him on the back. When he recovered, he had tears in his eyes. "You have a lovely way of putting things Kamamoto."

"I haven't tried that thing with the sweater, Ben. Is it any good?" Alan asked, still laughing from the joke.

"Obviously not," he replied.

"In a more serious vein," Aaron began, pausing momentarily to puff at his pipe. "Do you have somewhere we can talk a bit more privately?"

Alan got up and said, "Follow me."

When they entered the study, Aaron looked around him. He went to the bookcase and scanned the titles. "Interesting collection of books, I used to dabble in less traditional inquiries when I was in college. I guess the law exorcised that bent. It doesn't permit much of anything outside its own rigid parameters."

"Well, I don't spend as much time with it myself as I used to." Alan couldn't think of anything to add for a moment and then said, "Most of what I get now comes in an intuitive way. What I mean is that I've built up a base of evidence for a certain viewpoint of life. When I find myself being contemplative, the mind kind of sorts through what I've learned and then throws out some answers..." Here he just trailed off, fearing that he might be confusing his guest.

"I get you, Alan. It's not that abstruse. After all, you might say that I do the same with the law, certainly when I need to make it work for me, when the 'by the book' reflex is not enough, I have to go hunting too."

Ben made no comment. He was watching for some clue as to where Aaron might be going, trying to put it together with some of the things he had heard The Dragonsmouth say earlier, comments he'd been privy to but that he'd had no chance to share with Alan yet.

"You want to sit down?" Alan gestured toward a couch and easy chairs.

Aaron sat down on the couch and gazed around the room, puffing occasionally at his pipe. It was as if he was in his own office again, working the silence for the effect it might provide. Finally he asked, "Ben tell you anything about what took place during the interrogation?"

"Nothing except in a very general way," Alan replied.

"Well, maybe I should be a little more specific. You know, like they say, 'my momma didn't raise no stupid children.' I was down there for periods of time, when I could get away and Finch filled me in afterwards."

"This Dragonsmouth, I guess that's what we're calling him now, didn't ask for you like he did at the scene. I was wondering whether there was some benefit to be had for your not being there. I'm a 'read between the lines' kind of a guy. There's the smell of something bad, something phony, in the air. He's certainly playing to Rusk's apprehensions about you and to Finch's as well. He worked Finch over pretty good about Wendy. There is no way he came out of that interview with any warm fuzzy feelings about you. We didn't learn a damn thing about motivation. When we showed him the composites of the California killers, he said we were to ask you. 'Douglas knows them better that I do,' he said.

"By the way, I have my office getting in touch with your former employers. They're back tracking over all your old cases, looking to see who's been released in the last few years, looking for any associates they can come up with, looking for something that might relate to this situation. Dragonsmouth knows a lot about your past. He claims that Spencer Cippolino, the Central Park Ripper was a personal friend of his. Now, the strangest thing in all of this…" Once again he played with the pipe and the lighter, slow draughts and short staccato exhales through pursed lips. Aaron's eyes were now fixed on Alan. "The strangest thing is that this rough local boy, barely old enough to drink, with a very basic education, who's never been further away than the Big Island..."

Aaron paused as if to formulate his words, "I guess we could understand his talents as a mimic, although his parents say he never practiced it. No one else ever saw it. This rough local boy knows all about your private life here, a great deal about your public and private life on the mainland, knows the names of the men you shot, shares anecdotes about one of the killers you shot. No one has ever heard him mention you or your cases before. It's possible he read about, or researched them. But how come no one saw him interested in anything but Hawaiian history and weightlifting, sports, recreational fishing and as he so eloquently puts it, 'Da fuckin' *haoles*'? Still, when you take it all in its totality, it's just too implausible, too improbable." Aaron's eyes had never left Alan's through all of this dialogue.

He fooled with his pipe some more and reminded Alan suddenly of Lee Van Cleef playing "Angel Eyes" in *The Good, The Bad and The Ugly*. It bore an uncanny resemblance to the moment when he interrogates Clint Eastwood and Eli Wallach about the gold. Alan had to shake his head briefly because he really did look like Van Cleef at that moment. Aaron's eyebrows rose slightly and then his attention went to the ceiling at which he released several more bursts of smoke and then said, "Appreciate your letting us smoke in here, Alan. The wife always sends me out on the *lanai*."

"No problem, Aaron. The fumigators are coming tomorrow."

No one laughed. There was a grim atmosphere that denied any attempt at levity.

"And now I see these books of yours and I think about your interest in the supernatural. I certainly heard a lot about it from Wendy. Regardless of my profession, I'm not welded into a materialistic vision of existence. I've had plenty of experiences that tell me there is more to the processing of human events than are reported to us by the physical senses. I do think that when the jury comes in on everything, that it — and all attendant facts — will prove just as logical and understandable as watching a man crossing the street." Aaron was digressing here and both Alan and Ben were waiting to see where he was heading. Neither of them felt comfortable about the terrain over which he was passing.

"So," Aaron looked around the study again, "You got anything to drink in here Alan?"

"A bottle of Wild Turkey," Alan offered. Aaron's unpredictable musings were having an unsettling effect on him. It was as if he were circling closer and closer to something without ever revealing where he was going or what he was thinking.

"I'd like some of the bourbon, neat," he replied. Aaron slowly took a sip of the glass of bourbon Alan had delivered, and continued, "Then again, here is this brother-in-law of yours. He just shows up out of the blue, Alan?"

"Yes," Alan replied.

"Interesting. You know, Alan, we're not so far apart, you and I, in some respects. I think it's a tenet of Eastern thought that everything is related. That's true isn't it?"

"Related how?" Alan asked.

"You know, cosmically…events…people, all the seemingly unrelated things, coincidences not actually being coincidences, like that."

"Poets, philosophers, and mystics have all spoken of the underlying unity of things."

"Emerson, Whitman, people like that," Aaron added, "You know I'm a Mason. I've been a Mason since college and I've come some way up through the ranks, as it were. You're familiar with the Masons?"

"Very," Alan replied. "That is, as familiar as I can be without actually being one. I've studied the tale of Hiram Abiff and its connection with Egyptian Mythology, the story of Osiris, Isis and Horus. I know that Masons built this country and for the most part still control it."

"Exactly. Ben's a Mason too. You knew that right?"

"Yes," Alan replied. Now he really didn't know where Aaron was going. *Was this all about getting him to join the Masons?*

"Anyway," Aaron paused yet again to fool with his pipe. "Masons believe in the underlying unity of things, too. We also believe in things that some might consider fanciful and certainly a departure from the day-to-day beliefs of the common man, struggling with forces he does not comprehend, most of which he may feel comes his way by chance or fate. I'm not going to discuss fate here, but I just want to say I don't believe in chance. I especially don't believe in chance when there are a whole lot of other coincidences in the immediate neighborhood. I hope that makes sense." Aaron was waiting for some kind of reply from Alan.

"I guess I get what you're saying, but I don't know where you're going with this. If I did maybe we could cut to the chase."

"I don't think I'd get anywhere cutting to the chase. Attempting to do that would also spoil the effects of this fine bourbon. You don't mind if I refill my glass, do you?" he asked as he got up from his seat, not needing or waiting for a reply.

Neither Ben nor Alan looked at one another as they could both feel Aaron's eyes on them.

Aaron continued, "I guess I've got a lot of questions and no answers, gentlemen. I have the feeling that both of you know a lot more than I do. I look at everything that I've seen so far and it seems to me that this is not at all what it appears to be. I think I've laid out a lot of conjecture and evidence that makes a strong case for that. It may be that what is taking place is too fantastic to share. Certainly what we know already is pretty fantastic." Aaron returned to his seat and took a sip from his glass. Then his eyes grew dark and lines of tension appeared around his jaw.

"Goddamn it!" he suddenly shouted. He leaned forward with his forearms on his knees. His eyebrows beetled over the intensity of his stare. "I'm not going to let you keep me in the dark and feed me shit like I am some kind of a mushroom. If there's a theory here or some relevant facts, then I want a piece of it. You…are…working…for…me!" he hissed through clenched teeth. "Do either of you understand the position you've put me in if something happens and I don't know a damn thing about it? I have placed enormous confidence in you, Alan. Are you showing any confidence in me?" Aaron sat back in his chair and glowered at them.

Alan and Ben both shifted in their seats. They looked at each other and Ben shrugged, clearly letting Alan know that it was his call. Alan called out to Ming for help. He could not tell Aaron what he knew because of his fear of the information falling into the wrong hands. *Please, Ming, give me some direction here*, he called inwardly. Immediately, he felt a presence and the sense of someone telling him that he could always trust his instincts to reveal as little or as much as he felt comfortable doing. There was an intuition that if he were ever about to say or do the wrong thing there would be an intercession. *A warning would come.* He could be comfortable speaking because the direction of his thoughts was always under guidance.

"This is going to sound really crazy," Alan said at last. "Really, really crazy."

"No shit," Aaron replied, "Why am I not surprised? Out with it, I'm on your side, remember?"

So, Alan told him what he could, not including his trip to the Hall of Records with Ming but rather about Whip's story and how it became probable in light of what Aaron already knew. When he was done, it was silent in the room for several minutes. Aaron did not seem changed by the story he had just heard. He went on messing with his pipe, nodding his head occasionally and then briefly looking at Alan and Ben with an unreadable expression.

Finally, Aaron opened his mouth to speak, and then promptly closed it again. Then he got up from his chair and walked around the room. "Son of a bitch," he finally managed to say, "I guess all my talking up until now has come back to haunt me with a vengeance. Shit! Son of a bitch! I just went ninety degrees into Steven King Land. Now, what the fuck am I supposed to do with this?"

"How do you think we feel?" Ben remarked.

"All right, all right," Aaron held up his hand. "Understood, whatever this may mean and however much of it may be true… Look at the goddamn situation. Well," he waved his hand in the air, "Ordinary police work is not going to help us much here. What am I supposed to do? Deputize this Ming? Issue amulets and holy water?"

Finally, there was a round of laughter in the room, nervous laughter but laughter nonetheless. Sharing their knowledge of events with Aaron brought an immediate relief to both Alan and Ben. They were even more relieved by his reactions.

"I think… I think we're supposed to just follow it out to its conclusion," Alan said. "Even if it's all smoke and mirrors, we've got to use the talents and resources that we have available to get the job done and if help comes from above, we gratefully accept it. But in the meantime we follow acceptable police procedure."

"What about all these bystanders? What about Whip and Christienne? This puts them in big time danger, Alan." Aaron's eyes were filled with concern.

"Whip's fully cognizant of the danger. Christienne worries me, too. I haven't thought my way around that yet."

"Well, you'd better start. Nobody should be alone again until this is over. Christienne ought to be close by. Whip, too. You got weapons in the house?"

"Some," Alan replied.

"I've got guns to lend." Ben added.

Aaron nodded. "Although I don't know what good they'll do against supernatural forces. Still, if you're holding your own against him so far, that's something. If you've got protection from another dimension, Jesus! I can't believe I just said that. Bullets should certainly have an effect on the Bobbsey Twins," Aaron concluded, referring to Balfire and Malcolm.

"We should be getting back," Alan said.

"Right," Aaron concurred. "Keep me directly posted on everything, and I mean everything. It's the least you can do for me if I'm crazy enough to try and believe any of this."

"You've got it," Alan agreed.

When they returned to the living room, they found Whip and Christienne dancing to an Otis Redding song. It was a beautiful scene and Aaron caught Alan's eye with a look of silent admonishment. When Whip saw them, he went to the stereo and turned it down.

He said, "We didn't think you were coming back." Alan looked at the youthful vulnerability in both of their faces and it tore at his heart. *What might actually transpire before it was all over?* Aaron was dead right. They would all have to be a lot more careful.

"Alan," Christienne asked, "Maybe you can help us out with something. Whip says Michael Jackson had his face tailored to look like Diana Ross. I guess there's an argument for that, but here, look." She brought a couple of magazines that had been lying on a table and thrust one of them at him. "Here's a picture of Michael and here," she pointed at a picture in the one that remained in her hand, "is a picture of the woman I think he was really trying to look like. Check it out, it's uncanny." She was pointing to a picture of Joan Rivers, queen of the QVC shopping channel.

The men laughed. It was a great segue from the dark moment just behind them. Alan ruffled her hair and said, "You might just be right, Christienne."

"I mean, she could be his mom if she like, had an affair with Bill Cosby years ago." This caused another round of laughter.

On that note Aaron and Ben took their leave. Alan walked them to the door and discussed some final details for the morning. When he returned, Whip and Christienne were once again dancing. Redding's poignant tale of wounded love, "*That's How Strong My Love Is*" was flooding the air. Christienne's head lay nestled against Whip's shoulder. Alan watched for a moment and then quietly left.

Chapter Twenty-Three

THE HIDEAWAY, MAUI, HAWAII

It was 9:00 a.m. when Balfire crushed the beer can and hit the garbage container for three-point land. He'd had the foresight to bring several to the table on which his feet were nicely propped. He expelled a prodigious belch as he popped the top on another Budweiser, the Official Beer of Olympic Serial Killers. He was watching the Giants play the Braves. It had his attention. He wasn't the werewolf that Malcolm was. He had ordinary human qualities that came out in an unconscious way when he was around normal people.

Unfortunately, Balfire hadn't been around any normal people in a long, long time. What he was basically was brutal and instead of this brutality being channeled into a state-of-the-art linebacker, it had been turned loose on a society that did not wear helmets and shoulder pads. Beavis and Butthead would have said that Balfire was cool.

Billy Joe and Malcolm were snorting coke in the dining room. Neither of them gave a shit about The Giants and The Braves. Coke was a good drug for Malcolm. It was good for blocking out the last dim light of any humanity that might be left inside him. It made the taste of evil very much sweeter. You could really get behind hurting someone on coke. It was better if you gave them some too, like Malcolm had done when he took care of the boy. Billy Joe had watched, coaching Malcolm from inside his mind. He loved being a part of the acts of others, influencing and shaping them. Right now, he was enjoying the taste inside Malcolm's mind. *It was like a fine sherry after an elegant dinner.*

It had lasted a long time, and only the fact that the body had to remain intact kept Billy Joe from unleashing Malcolm into a tearing rending climax, turning the entire room into a Jackson Pollock painting. Only Malcolm was a lot better than Jackson Pollock, who wasn't a "real artist" but a violent drunk and a con artist. Malcolm was the real thing.

Tonight they were going to get the final member of the Holy Family. Billy Joe had devised a lot of things to do on his way to Alan Douglas. There had been other scores to settle, a fortune to be maintained and increased, evils to be done by whose outrage he had become even stronger. As in the corporate realm, in the realm of evil you had to pass through a great many portals. You might, at the time, think that you were bringing yourself to a state of being. In fact, a being that had preceded you along the way was actually absorbing you. All that you did were things that he in actuality had inspired in you on your way to him, so that you could join with him in the unending torture that was his nature. No rational mind could consider such a thing. The mind had to be made irrational long before. It took an extraordinary kind, the same kind that in its own way, made a man into a saint.

To become a man like Billy Joe, you must have a disregard for all constraints. But one power holds the reins, not two. There is only one power and no matter how far gone down the dark highway, this is what everyone finds eventually. This is the law by which Truth and Justice triumph. For everything that Billy Joe knew, he did not know this.

Billy Joe studied Balfire, mindlessly caught up in the ball game. He looked at Malcolm leaning over two more lines of coke. How very far away they seemed on the road he had once taken. He had no inclination to believe that either of them would ever come to the place where he was now. They were mere children, not that much beyond the state of the higher animals. *Let them shit where they liked and sleep where they liked, as long as they killed on command.*

Billy Joe got up from his chair and gestured for Malcolm to follow him. As he walked into the kitchen, he said to Balfire, "Make sure you stay on top of that body. We're on a deadline. Tomorrow you get the last one." Billy Joe flicked a tendril of fear into his mind and Balfire came instantly alert, the ball game forgotten.

"I'll be on top of it, Billy Joe. There's a few hours to go before I can get back to it. You can't rush the process." Fear was in Balfire's eyes as he looked up at Billy Joe.

Billy Joe laid his palm across Balfire's cheek. "I'm sure that's true, just remember the time."

As Billy Joe and Malcolm headed for the door, Balfire got to his feet and said, "I almost forgot. You wanted to see some pictures. I took them this afternoon."

Billy Joe turned and came back to Balfire. He took the pictures from his hand and studied them. "Oh, aren't these nice. Yes." He winked at Balfire and slipped the photos into a pocket of his suit coat and followed Malcolm out of the door.

They left Balfire in front of the TV, the encounter already forgotten. Their footsteps crunched on the gravel as they walked to the garage. Malcolm watched Billy Joe from behind, fascinated by the way he moved. You could almost see the snake in him. It was hypnotic. Every once in a while, Malcolm would shake himself as if to awaken from a dream but he was never able to wake up. New smells had begun to appear in Malcolm's nostrils as he had more and more contact with Billy Joe. The smells were so intense that they would provoke images in Malcolm's mind and he would see things that he had never imagined before. Places would open before his eyes that he could not identify, so foreign was the landscape. Here, terrible horrors cavorted and danced before him. Sometimes he would begin to shake as if he were breaking up inside and being remolded into something else, something that burned with a raging fire, a consuming thing that became hungrier with each thing it devoured. At night in his dreams, he would see a great wheel of fire turning endlessly. Something horrible was waiting, somewhere on the other side of the fiery circle, and Malcolm was headed there by-the-by. At certain times, Malcolm would become aware that he knew nothing about himself, had never known who he was and never would, except as whatever he became under the power of Billy Joe's hand.

They walked into the garage. Here, as in the study, it was perfectly appointed for the work being done. No expense had been spared. Except for this talent, Billy Joe would not have needed Balfire. But Balfire was an artist. Billy Joe was his patron and soon the world would see and marvel at his work.

"Get the bag and take it to the car," he said to Malcolm. "How about that smell? I was in a war zone hospital years ago, a few days after one of the major battles of the war. It smelled something like this. And inside of the smell was this sense of what had taken place. It was so real that you could inhale it and I did, over and over again. Can you smell the things that have happened in here? Can you taste them? You'll learn, Malcolm, and you'll discover a new kind of sex that makes whatever you've been doing seem like child's play. Every pore in your body will feel like a vagina. I'm incredibly hard right now just thinking about what it's like. Come here Malcolm and touch it."

Malcolm walked forward a few paces and put his hand on Billy Joe's crotch. He had no choice anyway, so it didn't bother him. He could feel it pulsing and throbbing. A heat came off of it like a pocket warmer. "Take it out and look at it, Malcolm. You've never seen my cock. It's not like other men's."

Malcolm fell down to his knees before Billy Joe. He pulled down the zipper and reached his hand inside. Billy Joe's cock was enormous and he struggled to pull it out of his pants. Finally the head came out and promptly bit Malcolm's hand. He screamed and looked down, horrified to find that there was a human head at the end of it. Malcolm jerked his hand away, feeling the flesh tear as he freed himself. He stared in fascination, as the cock swayed to and fro like a caterpillar on a leaf. The features on the face were contorted in pain and now

Malcolm could hear it crying out for help, screaming that it wanted to die. Billy Joe reached down and put it back in his pants.

"Interesting case, my dear boy, that was once a very powerful man. Quite the ladies' man too. He fucked with me and I made an example out of him. He's gone to a lot of strange places since he's been living there. It's been many years now. When I first put him there I got into anal sex for a while. The funny thing is he strangles every time I put him somewhere but he can't really die. Of course, when I come, that's a whole other thing entirely. Once he tried to bite me but didn't really have the will for it. I gave him the clap for a few weeks just to show him who was boss."

"Anyway, Malcolm, when the smell of something like this," he gestured at the display in front of them, "can make you feel like I was feeling, you have arrived. How'd you like a dick like mine, Malcolm? Boy, you could sure scare some kids with that."

Malcolm liked that idea. It was another reason to stick close to Billy Joe. Billy Joe was full of really nice surprises.

"Maybe I'll give you the head of Douglas's brother-in-law. Does that sound good?"

"That sounds real good Billy Joe and maybe you could make it big and thick like one of them jailhouse nigger's dicks."

Billy Joe smiled and said, "Anything you want, baby. You take care of that little matter for me today, and I'll have it done for you by tonight."

Malcolm felt an ecstatic thrill course through his body as the image of his new cock grew in his mind. They came out of the garage. For Malcolm, the change in the air was profound. The light was a little brighter than he remembered it. It seemed like more and more, the only way he could tolerate it was with his sunglasses on.

Balfire and Malcolm wore them almost all the time now. Balfire's were the mirrored kind, across which the scenery would wash. Malcolm had become mesmerized watching Balfire work and viewing the operations in the tiny lenses of his glasses. Balfire had wanted to know what he was looking at when he caught him staring.

"I'm not looking at you," he'd replied. "I'm watching what you're doing in your sunglasses. It's weird."

"It's not weird. It's a science. My daddy taught me how to do this. You're the one that's weird. If it makes you feel so good, why don't you get a mirror and watch me in there?"

Malcolm had thought this was a great idea. He went immediately into the house and got a mirror off one of the walls and hung it in the garage and then watched Balfire work in it.

When Billy Joe had seen this, it made him smile. He knew what the mirror was all about. *Everyone on the dark side went through it.*

"You going to tell me what we're up to?" Malcolm asked as he slid into the front passenger seat of the Mercedes.

"Not a problem, Malcolm. This evening, I am picking up the last parcel. It's time I did a little of the fieldwork myself. You are going on a mission this afternoon. I'm going to drop you by the girl's house. Remember, the one from the restaurant the other night? The one you wanted to dress up like a bride? We would have gotten her last night but she never came home. She was supposed to come home but then she didn't. I know she'll be coming by today, so you're going to wait around until she does and then you're going to party down. If the kid should come by with her, I want you to wait until he leaves. If he doesn't leave, I want you to spray some of this in his face and when he passes out, I want you to tie him up and let him watch and then I want you to bring him to me." Billy Joe's face had become so positively evil as he said these last words that Malcolm had to turn away. He felt the contents of his morning breakfast about to come back up the way it had gone down.

"Douglas has just a few people that he cares for and we are going to surgically excise each one. It will be like removing the fingers of the hand he is holding on with. When the last finger is gone, he will fall away and I'll be waiting there to catch him."

Malcolm was wearing blue jeans and a John Deere tractor cap. The hair under it had been turned almost white from peroxide. With the sunglasses and the beard he'd grown, he no longer looked like the man in the composite. It shouldn't matter but, with the problems he had been having lately, Billy Joe was taking no chances. As the moon neared its mark in the heavens, he could feel his power growing. Still, he had not yet identified his adversary. This was an ongoing annoyance, an annoyance that would be dearly paid for once the ceremony was complete. After that, so much more would lay open before him.

The Ceremony of the Black Moon was the ultimate ritual of initiation for one of the dark order. His Infernal Highness was present to confer the titles and power that came upon its successful completion. It was the culmination of many lifetimes. It had been in his grasp the last time and it would have been his, except for Douglas. *Soon now and the final gate would open.*

Alan met Ben for breakfast at Charlie's in Paia. An hour later, they were checking out the first of the rental locations on their list. There were only three left now. The next had been rented to Miles Baker, allegedly a history teacher on sabbatical to write a paper on Portuguese influences in the Hawaiian Islands. Ben had commented that the government must have been funding it. It sounded just like something the government would fund.

The house was on a hill set back several hundred feet from the road. The ground swept up sharply so that it was in full view as one drove past. It was a glorified A-frame with a large wrap around deck, perfect for the magnificent sunsets that Kula was famous for. The routine was that they were on a neighborhood canvass related to a series of break-ins in the neighborhood. They were there to do a walk-around, checking for weak spots in the house's security. There had, in fact, not been any robberies but it seemed doubtful that this would be questioned.

Ben studied the house from the road through his binoculars. There was no sign of activity and no van. They drove up to the house and parked. It was soon apparent that no was home. They wandered around the house and looked into the windows. On the kitchen table Alan spotted a laptop computer, a printer and a lot of paper and books. It looked like the tenant was who he said he was. As they walked back down to the car Ben said, "I guess he's out studying Portagees. I hope he knows what he's gotten himself into."

Alan laughed, "You are a man of great equanimity, Ben."

"Whatever that means," Ben replied

The next house was occupied and though everything was not normal, since the occupants were both stoned and drunk at 10:00 in the morning, there did not appear to be any serial killers or black magicians, just a collection of musicians and teenage girls who were greatly relieved at their departure.

"Well, I know where to come next time I run out," Ben remarked. Alan assumed that he was joking even though Ben was known to enjoy the occasional smoke. Alan gave him a look and Ben continued, "One of the perks of the job." Alan just shook his head and smiled. It didn't bother him in the least that Ben got high. There were much worse things a person could do. He never had understood the national paranoia concerning marijuana.

"I appreciate the fact that you showed enough restraint to hold off on the shakedown, Ben. I'd hate to see a murder investigation compromised because you were out of reefer."

"Jesus, Alan, nobody calls it 'reefer' anymore except maybe the people that make the drug education training films. Mostly around these parts they call it 'Buds' or 'Da kine.'"

"Thanks for the update," Alan replied. "Let's take a run by that next house and then we can break for lunch."

Captain Rusk signaled from his booth when he saw Dr. Abadon enter the restaurant. The Doctor saw his motion and walked over.

"Good morning, Captain. Thank you for inviting me to lunch." Abadon shook his hand as he slid in opposite him.

"I appreciate your coming, Doctor, we've got a complex situation here and the Department would really appreciate your help." Rusk was at his charming best. He needed the doctor on his side. He was hoping to solve a lot of his problems with the doctor's help. If Kimo, or The Dragonsmouth, whoever the hell he was, had anything on Alan Douglas, then Doctor Abadon was just the man to get it out of him.

The waitress came and took their order. Rusk steered the conversation to some of the doctor's earlier cases. Abadon gave him some of the more interesting details on several of them. As the doctor talked, Rusk became more and more impressed with his insights into the human mind. It baffled him, just as it had Alan Douglas earlier, how these forensic psychiatrists could arrive at such incredible detail about men they had never seen. *It was like watching a magician at work.* You saw things appear and disappear but you never saw how it happened. He especially appreciated the way that the doctor was able to translate medically involved conditions into layman's terms. Most of the psychiatrists that Rusk had dealt with in the past had left him knowing no more than he had before they began explaining. On many occasions, he was convinced that the doctors were just as baffled as he was. He had never been able to understand how, for every psychiatrist the prosecution brought to the stand to testify to the defendant's sanity, the defense was able to procure another who would present the exact opposite view. He had come to develop a total contempt for most psychiatrists. As far as he was concerned, they were whores who did it for the money. *They got paid an awful lot of money to present a predetermined opinion.* He'd been prepared to put aside his prejudice when dealing with Doctor Abadon. So far, the doctor was more like a cop than a psychiatrist. Rusk was already very much at ease with him.

The matter of a criminal's sanity was much simpler in Rusk's mind anyway. There was the public and then there were the shithouse rats that fucked with them. He didn't much care what their mothers might have done to them when they were six years old. Millard Rusk didn't care if someone was crazy or not. *What did that have to do with taking them off the streets?* He didn't see any evidence of reform coming out mental hospitals or prisons. You broke the law, you went to jail, end of story.

"Yes, Captain, I find it a lot more difficult to judge a man not guilty by reason of insanity than many of my colleagues. As far as I'm concerned, they usually know what they are doing. They like what they do. In some cases, they are tormented by what they do. There is a compulsion to perform a certain act the same as when one becomes hungry and has to eat. They become hungry and are compelled to satisfy that hunger. There's no real difference except that the hunger is for something that we as a society condemn and prohibit. Also, the hunger they feel may be a lot more intense. But that hunger is a creation of the mind of the one who feels it. They know it is wrong. That is why it torments them. Or they know it is wrong but they feel no remorse whatsoever. Those are the psychopaths. This is why, with a few notable exceptions, I have always testified for the prosecution.

"The criminal mind differs from the normal mind in its definition of personal morality. Most criminals are sociopaths. Their interest is in self-gain and there are no inhibitions, no regulating factors that stand between them and the accomplishment of their ends. They are very cunning beings who will do or say anything to satisfy their ends or to protect themselves. Some of them are very well-versed in the psychopathology of the human mind. They can and do, mimic conditions that fool the experts. However, for the discerning practitioner, there are always ways to find them out, besides the tests which catch quite a few of them."

"For example?" Rusk asked.

"It's like anything else, Captain. The best way to understand someone is to become like them, to put yourself in their shoes."

Rusk laughed mirthlessly, "That could become a problem considering who you are dealing with."

Dr. Abadon laughed, "For some, it has been a problem. Psychiatrists have one of the highest rates of suicide. This is true of policemen as well. You need a real objectivity to practice the profession and not become a victim of your own processes. Actually, I was talking about reversing their own game on them. They think you're stupid, so you play stupid. You let them manipulate you and through their manipulations they expose themselves. You let them take you all the way until they have nothing left to tell you. Then, when you know everything there is to know about them, you reverse the situation and start pushing their buttons. Suddenly they realize that they've been had. It's a new experience for them and it is in the first moments of that revelation that they are the most vulnerable."

"You've certainly got an interesting perspective and technique, Doctor. It seems like you start with the idea that they're guilty until proven innocent."

"It doesn't matter, Captain, if you first believe that they are guilty or innocent. It's what you find out in the end that counts."

"You do what you have to do, eh?"

"I'm a realist, Captain. I have to be in my line of work. In my career I have rarely found a man who was innocent according to what the law requires, according to the McNaughton Rules. Temporary Insanity, which manifests itself in a single isolated outburst of uncontrollable action, is a far more defensible situation than that of a man who has killed a dozen people or more, evaded the law, hidden evidence, moved through society and fed and clothed himself while he traveled. In a manner of speaking, of course they are both insane deeds. No sane person would commit the acts they have committed, but according to the law that defines their capacity, they are not both insane.

"What makes one man kill another, Captain, or many men and women for that matter and one man not? What makes one man commit a wrongful act while at the same time another man with the same opportunity chooses to abstain? Whatever it is, a character flaw, an ungovernable impulse, an aberrant gene or pure evil, it is still a free radical that attacks the body of society. I believe in the greatest good for the greatest number of people and it is always my job to protect that greater number. I do not believe in the homily that it is better for a thousand guilty men to go free than for one innocent man to be punished. That is pure Pollyanna."

"Well," Rusk paused, "You certainly are my kind of a psychiatrist. There are some unusual aspects to this case. Did Sergeant Klein fill you in on any of the details?" Rusk ordered another bourbon from the waitress. Abadon didn't seem to be paying any attention to his drinking and that also made him Rusk's kind of a psychiatrist.

"I was told that a homicidal maniac went on a killing spree at the Kaiser Clinic, about the doctor and the nurses, the telephone conversation. Apparently he's been exhibiting several distinctly separate personalities. Presently he is unrecognizable to those who know him. He's given no reason for his actions." Abadon lit a cigarette and blew the smoke out through his nostrils. "So far he's been baiting his interrogators. He's calling himself The Dragonsmouth."

Rusk poured down his bourbon and said, "That's an accurate assessment. We're even calling him Dragonsmouth, although his real name is Kimo Nakamura. But there is a disturbing side to all of this that concerns a Special Investigator with the DA's office, named Alan Douglas."

"I've met Alan. He came by my home about another investigation. How does he figure into this?"

"Well, this Dragonsmouth has implied that he has knowledge of the kidnappings and suspected murders that he's investigating."

"Oh, come now, Captain, you can't believe that? Alan Douglas is a decorated police veteran. Besides, if there were something wrong with Douglas, it would have shown itself a long time ago."

"I understand, Doctor," Rusk said in his most reasonable manner. "It's what anyone would think. But this Dragonsmouth has information that he could not just draw up out of some fantasyland. Also, Douglas was discharged from his position in New York for incompetence and reckless disregard, and, although it doesn't state this on the discharge and I found this out through back channels, for alcoholism."

At this Abadon's eyes grew wide. "I didn't know that," he said.

"We don't know what to make of it either. We are hoping that you could perhaps get the details, find out if what Dragonsmouth is saying is true or a fabrication. We'd all feel a great deal better if we could eliminate Douglas as a suspect. No one wants to find out that a former police officer could be involved in something like this."

"Douglas is a suspect?" Abadon queried.

"Well, not officially, but some of the things this Dragonsmouth is saying are very worrisome." Rusk was choosing his words very carefully. It wouldn't do for Abadon to read anything personal into the mix. "I can't say that I agree with everything that Douglas has been doing in his investigation. He departs from official police procedure far more than I would like but there's no hard evidence yet that he's involved. However the department would be extremely grateful for anything you could do to help. Your insight into the human mind leaves me with little doubt that you could get to the bottom of this."

"Well, Captain Rusk, I'll do my best to find out everything I can from the man. I imagine you'll want to videotape the session. Let me work through the preliminaries and see what works best. I'll see what I can find out about any claims this man is making. I can't say that I expect there's any truth to it though. I've had a chance to speak with Douglas and he didn't strike me as hiding anything. He seemed very sincerely concerned about concluding his investigation as quickly and efficiently as possible. I understand that this killer has singled you out especially for abuse?"

"Where did you hear that?" Rusk quickly caught himself before the rage of exposure could show on his face. "He's been rough on me, but I just assumed it was because I was in charge, an authority figure."

"Sergeant Klein merely said that he'd been particularly abusive toward you. I didn't get any details. I imagine it is because of your position, however. If he can discredit you in the eyes of your subordinates, he has certainly achieved the disruptive effect he is seeking," Abadon said mildly. It would have been apparent to a less inebriated Rusk that Abadon had seen right through him in this regard.

"Is there anyone else saying anything about Douglas? Are there other innuendos?"

"Not so far." Rusk drained the contents of his glass and set it on the table.

"Well, we shall see what we shall see."

"Thank you, Doctor, there's heat coming down on the department from all directions. Maui's not like a lot of other places. People come here to escape the violent crime that is so common everywhere else. A lot of them have money, which turns into influence, which turns into pressure. I don't have to mention the effect it has on tourism, which is the life's-blood of the islands."

Rusk waved for the check. As they were walking out of the restaurant Abadon said, "I'd like you to do me a favor, Captain."

"Certainly."

"Could I observe the interrogation? I'd like to check him out before I involve myself."

"How about right now?" Rusk asked.

"That sounds fine," the doctor replied.

1:00 PM, OLINDA RD., OLINDA, HAWAII

They parked on a cane road about 250 yards from the property but with a good view of the house and grounds, and got out of the vehicle. There was no view of the house from any other perspective. The military binoculars they were using gave them great detail but so far they had seen very little. The house was a large Cedar barn home with a detached garage.

"Nice place," Alan said.

"Yeah, if you like the *Better Homes and Gardens* look."

"It doesn't look so *Better Homes and Gardens* to me. The grass doesn't appear to have been cut for a couple of weeks."

"You noticed that?"

"I noticed because I have my lawn mowed. You don't even have a lawn. What you have is a great big kitty-litter box."

"Fuck you, Alan. I'll bet you've got hospital corners on your sheets."

"As a matter-of-fact..."

"Wait a minute," Ben said.

"What?"

"I think I just saw something move in that back window. Here." Ben handed Alan the glasses and he looked through them for a while, playing with the focus knob.

Finally he said, "I don't know, could be. It's hard to tell. It looks like somebody sitting in a chair with their feet on the table."

"That's what I saw. Let's go check it out."

"Yeah?"

"I'd say it's enough provocation to go down and ring the bell, see what's what."

When they got back to the car, they were being paged by the dispatcher. Ben answered it.

"Lieutenant Kamamoto, your presence is requested at the Wailuku Station soonest."

"What's up, Officer Lee?"

"I have no details, Sir. Only that you and Mr. Douglas are to proceed here immediately."

"Very good, we're on our way."

"The hell is going on now?" Alan queried. "Dragonsmouth must have requested my presence again."

"Probably, but no one knows exactly where we are or how long it takes to get there, so I suggest we rock on."

"Affirmative," Alan replied as they got into the car.

Ben backed slowly out of the cane road so as not to leave a cloud of dust, just in case these were the ones they were looking for. If they could see them, the reverse could be true as well. They parked by the gate and Alan rang the buzzer. A minute passed and there was no response so he pushed it three times more, then again.

Balfire heard the bell the first time but he ignored it. It could be anyone, no matter who it was they had no business here. After it rang the second time, he became confused. *Maybe Billy Joe had lost the remote? Anyway, who knew they were here? If it was the cops they wouldn't be ringing the goddamn doorbell.* He went to the intercom and asked, "Who's there?"

"Good morning, this is the Maui Police Department. We'd like to talk to you please," is what he heard back.

Balfire froze, adrenaline shot into his bloodstream and he felt a hot flush run up his back, up his neck and on to the top of his scalp. His thoughts raced and he could think of no reply. Finally he said, "There's no one here right now. I mean, I'm here but I'm just the gardener. You'll have to come back tomorrow. No one's here until tomorrow."

"I see," Ben replied. "Sir, there have been a lot of break-ins in the neighborhood. We've been talking to the residents to see if they might have seen anything. Also we've been advising people on their security setups."

Balfire started to relax. *It wasn't about them.* Now he just had to close off the conversation. "Haven't been any break-ins here officer, like I said, you'll have to come back tomorrow. There's nobody here until tomorrow."

There was a pause on the other end and Balfire waited.

"Tomorrow, you say?" Ben finally asked.

"Yeah, tomorrow."

"Okay, and could we have your name?"

His name! His fucking name! *What was his fucking name!* Balfire's mind was scrambling. In all fairness to Balfire, though he was not quick on the uptake, at least he knew this and took the time to think out his reply before he blurted out "Ronald McDonald" or some other inanity. His mouth was dry with panic. His fear was not about the cops. He'd just as soon shoot it out with the cops as talk to them. It was Billy Joe that was making his stomach grind. He'd almost said "Bob Jones." That would have been as bad as "John Smith."

Then, very clearly, he had a name. Suddenly his confusion evaporated and he said, "Bill Floyd." Bill for Billy Joe and Floyd for Floyd Gunnersen, his first "rap partner" who was killed by the police after a gas station hold-up in Long Beach.

"Okay, Mr. Floyd. We'll come back tomorrow. Could you give us the phone number so that we can call first?"

Balfire didn't even know the phone number. "Sorry, don't know it, I just started work here."

"Then maybe you could give us the owner's name and we can look it up," Alan countered.

Goddamn them! Goddamn them straight to hell!!!! The owner's name? Balfire almost laughed out loud, almost said, "The owner's name is Billy Joe and he is a demon from Hell and after he's done screwing my head up inside my asshole he's going to burn your eyes out with a soldering iron!" Then he was cool, really cool. *What the fuck was going on?* "Sorry," he replied. "The owner's name is Razzlewurst or some such. I can't spell it. I don't even know how to pronounce it. I hope that helps you. I didn't go that far in school. It's why I'm a gardener."

"No problem, Mr. Floyd, that's perfectly understandable. We're sorry to take up so much of your time. By the way, the grounds look beautiful. *Aloha.*"

"Good-bye."

As they were going down the road, Alan said, "I'll bet anything that's the place. They left one of them there to watch the place, probably the stupidest one. Nice touch there, Ben, about the beautiful grounds, real nice touch."

"Lighten up dude. Like you said, they left the stupid one. I'd have liked to have gone in there right then. That goddamn Captain Rusk." Ben slapped the steering wheel for emphasis. "I'm with you on the vibes. It definitely feels right, Bill Floyd... Razzlewurst. Shit!"

If Alan had turned his head at that exact moment he would have seen through a sudden break in the trees the nose of a dark colored panel van sticking out a few inches from the back of the house, but the timing would have had to have been perfect…

"No question that there's something fishy going on back there," Alan answered. "If he's the gardener, then what is he doing in the house? He wouldn't be the first person to be goofing off though. And if he just started working there, how did he know about the intercom, or how to work it for that matter?"

"I say we get a warrant and head right back." Ben's face was grim with purpose. "And, I say we don't tell Rusk anything."

"Don't have to tell Rusk. Aaron will get us a warrant in a New York minute."

"We're going to nail them, Ben. I can feel it."

Ben snorted. "I'd like to do whatever it takes Alan, but don't forget Billy Joe. We're not dealing with the usual suspects here."

Dr. Abadon had been watching the interrogation for half an hour, occasionally making notes. It was the same as it had been before. Dragonsmouth would listen and then make some scathing personal comment about his interrogators. There were two detectives already who would no longer go into the room with him. One of them had suffered some kind of a breakdown and was now on medical leave as a result of Dragonsmouth going into detail about his sexual practices.

He referred to Captain Rusk several times as "Iron Butt" always looking up at the opaque viewing window as if the Captain were watching, which of course he was. After the first time, Dr. Abadon had asked him if this was how the men referred to him behind his back. The Captain had said he didn't know. Abadon nodded and asked, "Is this an example of the type of information that Dragonsmouth possesses that he shouldn't have?"

Rusk had just nodded his head, embarrassed. He wondered if the Doctor was curious about why he was referred to by such a disparaging nickname.

Just then, without warning, Dragonsmouth went rigid. He looked like a man going into a Grand Mal seizure. This held for about thirty seconds and then he spoke in the voice of James Earl Jones, *"This is CNN. I want to see Lieutenant Douglas right now. You get Douglas here this minute, Iron Butt, and I will tell you everything I know."*

This was said with such intensity that Rusk got up from where he was sitting and walked into the interrogation room before he even knew that he had done so. Then he caught himself and turned around and then walked back into the interrogation room, "What do you mean?" he inquired.

"I mean what I said I mean, you dumb, megalomaniacal, bourbon swilling offspring of diseased Chinese camel-fuckers."

"The Chinese fuck camels? I didn't know they had camels," said Detective Cabebe, one of the men in the room.

"Get out of here!" Rusk screamed at him. "You want Douglas?"

"You heard me, you self-involved tub of shit. Get him now!" What was remarkable about Dragonsmouth's replies to the Captain was that they were now being delivered in his dead mother's voice. It chilled him to the marrow but he was beyond stopping now. He wanted to know what this hideous freak had to say. If Rusk had been a rational individual, he might have asked himself why Douglas

meant so much to him, might have investigated his motivations and wondered if his building animosity might not be a little extreme, but Rusk was not and had not been rational for some time.

"You get Douglas here within the hour, no later, and I'll tell you what you want to know."

"But I'm not sure I can do that. I don't even know where he is right now."

"Get him!" the voice of Rusk's mother screamed.

Rusk whipped around. "Klein, find Kamamoto and Douglas, tell them to get here and use all available speed." Then he walked out of the room as only a man whipped by terrible insecurities might do, walking taller than he was and harder than he had to.

"What do you make of this?" he asked Dr. Abadon once he had returned to the viewing room.

"Captain Rusk, I've only been watching up until this point. I have no direct experience to draw from. I'm not quite sure yet what is taking place. If it were the fifteenth century, we would probably be talking about demonic possession."

Rusk looked back through the window. Dragonsmouth had now slumped forward, his chin on his chest. It looked like someone had turned the power off. His mouth was slack and his eyes were vacant. The remaining detective was asking him questions but there was no reply. Klein returned a few minutes later.

"Douglas and Kamamoto were up in Olinda. They're on their way back now, should be here inside of an hour."

"Call them back and tell them to put the siren on."

Klein went back out the way he'd come.

"Surely you've got some kind of a profile, Doctor?" Rusk asked.

"I've noted a multiple personality factor but that is evident to anyone. What I don't get is the intelligence factor compared to the background of the individual you arrested. I honestly can't tell you anything yet. What I've been doing is analyzing my approach based on my preliminary observations. There are some tests I want to run, too."

"Whatever we can do," Rusk answered and then got up and went back into the interrogation room. As soon as he entered, there was a transfiguration in the suspect. It was as if some hidden puppet master had picked up the strings. Immediately Dragonsmouth was animate. His posture became erect and he rattled his handcuffs, which were linked to a chain that looped through eyelets sunken into the concrete floor. His head turned toward Rusk.

"Well?" The voice was now deep and vibrant. It was a voice of command and power. Rusk felt a tremble pass through his body when he heard it.

"Lieutenant Douglas was in Olinda. He's on his way here with all speed."

"Good, that is very good indeed." A wide grin spilt Dragonsmouth's face and his eyes twinkled with mirth. *"See, we all get what we want and then we all get what we want. You can't imagine what a help you've been, Captain. At some point soon, I am going to repay you royally."*

"I don't know what you are talking about, Sir, but you could certainly repay me by answering a few questions, honestly and in detail."

"Oh, Captain, my Captain, you are going to learn far more than you are even bargaining for. You are going to find out a great many things, including things about yourself that you never even dreamed." The voice was so full of dread and menace that Rusk involuntarily stepped back. For a moment he was unsure that he wanted to be anywhere near this man. Then he looked down at the leg shackles and handcuffs and relaxed.

"We'll send Douglas in when he gets here." Rusk gestured for the detective to follow him.

"Y'all come back soon, ya hear." Dragonsmouth's voice and mocking laughter followed them out of the room.

Chapter Twenty-Four

As Whip kissed her lips, he could see flowers forming and dissolving behind his eyelids. He was in love and he knew it. *Funny,* he thought, *everything becomes so fragile when you're in love, yet you feel invulnerable.* It was just how he felt now.

They had made love for the first time that morning, outside in a cloistered setting by the pool with the music of birds and the strong smell of tropical flowers. Even though they had slept together the night before, neither of them wanted to consummate the act. It was as if they could not become any closer no matter what they might have done.

Whip was entranced with everything about Christienne. Her spirit sang to him through the poetry of her body.

"That's one of the nicest things that has ever happened to me," she said. Whip was still inside her and her hips continued to rock as her legs trembled in reflex to the passion that still coursed through her body. All of her defenses were down and her heart hurt with the love that she was feeling. *No matter how close you got to someone, it was never enough. That is the tragedy of love,* she thought. *That and of course, the fact that everyone must part. It was inevitable. People refused to accept it but that didn't change it.*

A single tear had formed in the corner of her right eye and was now about to make its slow and unpredictable journey down her face. One day, like all water, it would find its way to the sea.

"What's wrong?" Whip inquired, arresting the tear with a fingertip and bringing it to his lips. "Are you sad?"

"No, darling, it's more than just sorrow." She looked past him, up into the cerulean sky. Whip could see a cloud float by from one eye into the next. He thought that the essence of all of the world's beauties was trapped in a vast treasure room behind her eyes. He wanted to be something heavier than a cloud and sink into the depths below.

Another tear had come to replace the one Whip had taken. Christienne reached out and pulled Whip's face down upon her own. She kissed him and said, "I feel the way I do because nothing will ever stay the way that it was. Everything eventually ends and all lovers are parted by death, if by nothing else and… and... No matter how close you come, it is never close enough."

"Whatever happened to being in the moment?" Whip asked. He had a wry smile but there was concern etched in his face.

"It's being in the moment that tells me that the moment will pass."

"I can't help you with that, Christienne. I can only love you and hope that it will be enough most of the time."

"Oh, Whip, I love you too. I guess I just know more than I want to… and this has all been so quick." She smiled then, unable to maintain her momentary existential despair. "Maybe that's what laughter is all about."

"What do you mean?"

"Laughter is kind of a way to make music out of sorrow. It's like yeast in a way. It breathes air into sorrow and makes it rise."

Whip laughed. "I've never heard it put like that before. That was beautiful."

"So are you," she said.

Later, they were having lunch on the deck when Christienne told Whip she wanted to go back to her house and get a few things.

"I don't think that's such a good idea, babe. You don't mind if I call you 'Babe', do you?"

"Well," she smiled coyly, "If you're going to treat me like a sex object, I expect you to talk to me like one."

"You sure make it easy." Whip held her with his eyes as he popped the last of his English muffin into his mouth.

"Everywhere I look I see unhappy men and women. They make impossible demands on each other to be something that they're not. The spontaneity gets lost and is replaced by a constant state of uncertainty and calculation. It's a battle where there are no winners. I don't feel like policing the world's language or etiquette. I'm not a behavioral scientist, a humanist psychologist, nor do I have an axe to grind with men. I like men. I got some shabby treatment but that's the breaks. I pity those people. They have no life. Nobody agrees on anything anymore. I just want to live and see what happens."

"So do I." Whip squinted at her through a stream of smoke. "However… and not to change the subject, but the question of you going to your house, I'm more than a little concerned. We don't want to create any opportunities for those assholes before Alan puts them away."

"You really think he will?"

"Babe, can I call you babe?"

She punched him hard in the arm.

"Ow!" Whip cried, rubbing his bicep. "That hurt! Alan has this way, some kind of guidance system. I've asked him how it happens, how he's feeling in the moment he knows. He says for a moment he's somebody else, someone who knows just where to go and just what to do. So, I'd put my money on Alan getting it done."

"Billy Joe could get him."

"That's not an option." Whip stubbed out his cigarette. He was feeling nervous, more so than usual, jumpy too. He wished he had the confidence that his words professed. He'd turned several times to look out the window. "I'm getting bad vibes, Christienne, about going over to your place. We could just buy what you need."

"It's not just clothes. I've got to get my Day Runner and other things. I've got to check my messages. I've forgotten how to access it remotely. My mother calls and if she doesn't hear right back from me, she starts going off. Besides, it's broad daylight. Don't these kinds of goblins only hunt at night?"

"I don't know what their rituals are. I just want to avoid them. But if you've got to go, you've got to go." Whip got to his feet and stretched. He still felt tense. "We don't have to stay very long, do we?"

"No, we don't."

Dr. Abadon entered the interrogation room and seated himself across the table from Dragonsmouth. The Dragonsmouth entity had a big smile on his face. Abadon matched it.

"Good afternoon, I'm Doctor Abadon."

Dragonsmouth sneered, *"How come you dress like a gynecologist?"*

Abadon's face remained unchanged. "Do you need a gynecologist?"

The men in the observation room cracked up, Rusk especially. "Round one to the doctor," he quipped.

Dragonsmouth's face contorted into a frozen mask. "*You're a funny man, Doctor. How funny would it be if I got up and snapped your neck?*"

Doctor Abadon pulled at his ear and shook his head up and down. "You've probably forgotten, but you're pretty well restrained at the moment."

Dragonsmouth rattled his chains and smirked, *"Pretty observant there, Doc."*

"It's what they pay me for. Would you like a cigarette? I know the fellow you used to be didn't smoke but I have a feeling you do."

"Sure, Doc, let me have a cigarette."

Abadon lit two cigarettes and slid one across the table toward the killer. His hands would not reach to his face so he was forced to lean down to get the cigarette to his lips.

"Your present name is quite a mouthful. Is there something else I can call you?" Abadon's eyes studied the man while he spoke.

"I am the Mouth of the Dragon." As he said this his entire body tensed and the cords in his neck stood out like cables. *"I have no other name. I need no other name."*

A detective entered the room and placed an ashtray in front of the doctor, probably at the behest of Rusk.

"What about me?" Dragonsmouth said in the simpering New Orleans faggot voice.

"Use your mouth. It's definitely an ashtray or something worse." The detective laughed.

"Motherfucker!" He jerked against his chains in the detective's direction.

"Please!" Abadon commanded. The detective left and he turned to Dragonsmouth. "Tell me about this Dragon. What's he like?"

"Ha!" Dragonsmouth laughed. It was a bitter dry laugh. *"He is the Dragon. He is the King of the Fire Pits. He coils in the coals. His breath burns the soul and he... hates... every... living... thing..."* The words came out clipped and precise. The voice was that of an English schoolmaster elucidating on a topic.

"Okay." Abadon brought his hands together, the fingers at the tip of his nose and his chin resting on the thumbs. "I haven't spoken with the Dragon yet, but what about the other people who are in there with you? Who are they?"

Dragonsmouth rolled his shoulders and hummed through his nose. *"There are a number of others here. They arrived here by different means. Some were victims of the Dragon for no particular reason. Some had offended the Dragon. Your dead wife, do you think she suffered much at the end?"* His eyes seemed to grow larger and more luminous as he said this.

If Abadon was affected, he betrayed nothing. His voice remained warm and interested. "Do I think she suffered? I think everyone suffers. Pain is a uniquely personal thing. It's different for everyone. I know she's not suffering now."

"You do, huh?" Suddenly a terrible scream filled the air.

"Philip, Philip, help me. I'm being torn to pieces!" It was a woman's voice in the throes of extreme agony.

Abadon remained as he had been. He even smiled briefly. "I haven't heard her voice in so long. It's almost a pleasure, regardless of the circumstances."

The Dragonsmouth threw back his head and roared like a lion. Several detectives jumped behind the glass at the unexpected sound and its tremendous volume. He immediately turned his head and roared at them, his teeth bared.

"That is really impressive," Abadon said.

"Yeah, that and a dollar will get me a cup of coffee." It was the voice from the cavern. It was the ruling voice that spoke now.

Abadon leaned forward. His eyes flickered with interest. It was apparent that he could tell this. "Am I speaking to the Dragon now?"

"How astute, my good doctor."

"What sort of a dragon are you?"

"There is only one Dragon. A dog is a dog, a deer is a deer and a diamond is a diamond. It is the shape that the energy takes. Form is function." As he was saying this, the shape of his face began to shift. Rusk shook his head. For a moment he thought that he had seen something terrible. Probably he had not been getting enough sleep. It was like that. You missed a few hours here and there. You had too many cups of coffee and suddenly you were seeing the Pink Panther out of the corner of your eye.

Abadon did not appear to notice anything peculiar. "What does the Dragon have to say?"

The Dragonsmouth yawned and snaked his tongue in and out of his mouth in a parody of oral sex. From where Rusk was sitting it appeared that he had unhinged his jaw. The opening of the mouth was impossibly large and a burst of flame traveled out of it and washed across the ceiling. Rusk spewed a mouthful of coffee on to the glass and had a coughing fit which did not stop until Klein pounded on his back.

"Did you see that?" he exclaimed after he had gotten his breath back.

"See what?" Klein asked.

"Haven't you been watching?" Rusk's voice was filled with accusation.

"I was watching very closely, Sir, until you started coughing."

Rusk was worried now. The other men were looking at him but no one said anything. He thought maybe he should leave now, leave before something actually happened, but he couldn't go anywhere until he'd found out more about Douglas.

"I speak to any number of subjects, Doctor. Which ones interest you?"

"For the moment there are only two."

"And they are?" The Dragonsmouth pulled at the side of his face as waited for the Doctor's reply.

Here's what Rusk saw: The Dragonsmouth reached up to the side of his face, grabbed the flesh and pulled it like taffy all the way down to the table. Rusk was frozen, holding himself in check. He glanced over at Klein, but Klein gave no indication he was seeing anything out of the ordinary. Then Dragonsmouth released the flesh and it snapped back into place with an audible pop. Then he looked up at where Rusk was seated and winked. Rusk was trembling now.

"You all right, Captain?" Klein asked.

Rusk willed himself to be still. "I'm fine. It's just the caffeine."

"Principally this," Abadon continued. "Why did you kill all of those people and what has Alan Douglas got to do with any of it?"

The Dragonsmouth's eyes narrowed. *"If you were Chinese, Doctor, you wouldn't have any trouble understanding why I killed those people. That's what dragons do. They kill people. They kill them with earthquakes and storms and lightening and floods. It's the nature of the beast. It's his occupation. At this time, this dragon is just diversifying. He's getting into guns now, too. But that's not such a leap. They're always letting off with fireworks when they do the Dragon Dance. Explosions and gunpowder obviously have to do with dragons. Point two, Alan Douglas is a homicidal maniac."*

Rusk sat bolt upright in his chair. His head shot forward straining to hear, although the volume was perfectly audible.

"Mr. Douglas just played the game too long. Surely you are acquainted with the phrase that those who pursue monsters should be careful that they don't become one. Perhaps the death of his wife had something to do with it. In any case, he has killed and mutilated a number of people in the last month."

There was a buzz of conversation in the observation room now. Rusk was quiet. Because, looking into the room, what Rusk saw was a man-sized fire-breathing dragon with a cigarette dangling from his prodigious mouth. It looked like a cartoon. No cigarette could have generated the volume of smoke pouring forth.

"Do you really expect us to believe such an outrageous statement?" Abadon asked.

"I don't personally care what you believe, Doctor. The proof is in the pudding. Whether I am lying or telling the truth does not affect the reality of the situation. You've got the fox watching the hen house. Soon you'll see for yourself."

The Dragonsmouth had now turned into one of the most beautiful young women Rusk had ever seen, a young Brigitte Bardot. She was naked and slowly rubbing her breasts with her hands. In his mind Rusk could hear her asking him if he would like to fuck her. She turned to smile at him and he could see her legs part beneath the table. Captain Rusk was getting an erection and a part of his mind was telling him he was going crazy. Another part of his mind was telling him he should go down into the interrogation room and fuck her. Right now!

"You care to share any of the details with us?" Abadon asked.

"I know so many things you would like to know Doctor, but knowledge has its price and you don't have anything to offer me in exchange. I've been gracious enough to sit here and let you and the morons play tag with me. I'd love to stay and chat but I really have to be going."

Abadon smiled, "Where do you think you're going to go? Are you going to just stand up and walk out of here?"

"Watch me, Herr Doktor." A burst of flame issued from his mouth and seemed to fan out around the doctor's head when it reached it. Abadon sat there as if nothing had occurred. It must not have, Rusk thought, or the doctor's head would be roasting right now. It was just one more impossible phenomenon in an impossible day. A large thick shadow was now rising up over The Dragonsmouth's body. Rusk could see hundreds of eyes staring out of it. It looked like the eyes in the woods that one saw in the funny papers.

"I tell ya, I don't get no respect, no respect at all." It was now the voice of Rodney Dangerfield. *"Hoo boy. I'm out of here!"* There was a wrenching sound and before Rusk's mind could even process the information, the door to the observation room blew open and there stood The Dragonsmouth. He flew up the short steps to the seating level and dispatched both Klein and Santos with lightning blows. Then he proceeded to disable every other officer in the room. It was over in seconds.

Rusk had made to rise out of his chair but he felt like he was under water. From far away his mind was telling him he had to pull his gun, fire it at the lunatic, but it never happened. The Dragonsmouth stood over him and the smell of death filled the room.

"I can't wait around, Captain. I've got places to go and people to see. But if you want Alan Douglas, I suggest you drop by his house tomorrow afternoon. He'll be all wrapped up with a Christmas ribbon just for you." The Dragonsmouth reached down and removed the Captain's Beretta from his holster. *"I'll be taking this with me. I probably don't need it but they're so much fun. I'll try not to kill too many of your men. You can always get more though."* He was leaning close to the Captain's face and the smell of a dead body was overpowering. His stomach was lurching in an attempt to climb out of his throat and run away.

The Dragonsmouth leaned down and kissed him on the cheek. *"You liked the lady, huh? Maybe I'll send her around to see you later. Meanwhile you might want to attend to your men. They aren't dead, just fucked up."*

When Dragonsmouth stepped to the side of Rusk, the vomit roared out of his throat all over the observation window.

"Check it out man. Good one." It was Cheech Marin this time. *"Bye, bye, take care of your men. Don't go screaming through the halls now. I'll just have to kill more cops if you do. Aloha."* And he was gone.

Rusk was on his knees now. Everything that could come up was coming up. Suddenly Doctor Abadon was by his side.

"Captain, are you all right?"

"I'm fine," he sputtered. "Please, help the men." Then he forced himself to his feet. Klein and Santos lay where they had been tossed, tangled up in one another. Blood was running down Klein's face. Rusk couldn't see Santos yet. He picked up the phone and punched in the extension he wanted. "This is Captain Rusk. The prisoner has escaped from interrogation. He's armed and very dangerous. Use extreme caution, repeat that's *extreme caution* and send a medical team up here. We've got injured policemen!" He set down the phone and buried his face in his hands.

"How did he get out of the restraints?" he heard Dr. Abadon ask.

Alan and Ben were half a mile from the police station when they heard the news. Moments later they could hear sirens squealing like deranged bagpipes from several directions.

"Incredible," Alan said. "How the hell could he get away?"

"We'll soon find out," Ben replied. He whipped the car into the Police Station turnaround and parked behind an ambulance. As they went in the front door, they saw three stretchers coming down the hall. Alan recognized Detective Santos on one of them.

They found Captain Rusk in the Command Room amidst a flurry of activity. "The fuck have you two been?" he screamed when he saw them.

Surprised by the virulence of his outburst, neither of them said a word.

"Does 'get down here right away' mean whenever you fucking feel like it?"

"Captain..." Ben began in a conciliatory tone.

"Don't 'Captain' me, you treacherous bastard!"

Now everyone in the room was looking at Captain Rusk, even for him, this was a surprise.

"We came as quickly as we could, Sir. Still, I don't see what we have to do with this." Ben gestured vaguely. "I don't know what you mean by treacherous. I'm as loyal to The Department as any man here."

"We'll see about that, Lieutenant."

"What happened?" Alan asked.

Rusk got a crafty look on his face as he turned toward Douglas. "I would think you'd know 'what happened,' Mr. Douglas — you glad-handing carpet-bagging son-of-a-bitch."

"You got a lot of wind in you Captain. It's a wonder you're not banging off the ceiling like some blimp in a parade."

Rusk lost it and went lunging across the room at Douglas. Several of his men caught him before there was any contact. He struggled for a moment and then relaxed. "Your day is coming Douglas. I don't have to worry about you anymore."

"Well Captain, in the meantime, we're very busy with the case we were assigned to. So, if you don't mind, we'll be getting back to it." Alan said. He and Ben turned to leave.

"Here it is shit-head. Aaron Wilson is not on the island at present. That leaves Richard Finch in charge of you." For the first time, Alan saw Finch standing in the back, outside of the circle of action. "But that is not the point. Lieutenant Kamamoto does work for me and he is detached back to The Department as of right now. Unless he wants an immediate suspension, that is. He's going out with the search party and he is going to report in every half an hour with a progress report and location. I don't care what you do, Douglas." Rusk paused for a moment as if he were thinking the situation over, then he continued, "Maybe you'd like to accompany Lieutenant Kamamoto in the pursuit of his duties? That okay with you, Richard?" Finch said nothing, just gave a barely perceptible nod of his head while his eyes bored into Alan.

Nobody in the room seemed to understand why Captain Rusk was allowing Alan in on a Maui Police Department operation. Alan and Ben were just as confused by this turn of events.

"You want to do that, Douglas?"

"I'm willing to help any way that I can, Captain, but when you called us, we were at a location we believed to be the residence of the kidnappers we are pursuing. Surely your dislike for me cannot be so important that you would stop us from trying to catch them?" Alan's breathing had steadied out. He was angry with himself for losing control of his tongue. He didn't know what had come over him.

"Once again, Douglas, fuck that noise. I've got reason to believe that you're wrong about that, wasting your time and right now, my time. I trust my source a lot more than I do you."

"What source is that, Captain?" Alan couldn't believe what he was hearing. Captain Rusk was impeding a major investigation *and* in front of witnesses.

"I'm not at liberty to discuss that with you right now, you going to go with the program or what, Douglas?" Rusk's mouth was set in a grim line as he waited for Alan's reply.

"I'll help however I can," Alan answered.

"Well then, be about it," Rusk said dismissively and turned back to the officers behind him.

Ben headed for the duty desk with Alan beside him. Neither of them spoke until after Ben had picked up his instructions.

"You get the feeling that someone is trying to stay us from our appointed rounds?" Alan asked Ben once they were in the car.

"Even more corroborative of that was his allowing you to accompany me. It is very eerie, Alan. And where is Aaron? You hear anything about that?"

"I think he had to go to Oahu about something. Seems I heard him say something to his secretary the last time I met with him. He didn't mention it to me. I've got his pager number if we need him though."

Ben steered the car toward Waiehu, which was the area that had been assigned to him. They were on Lower Beach Road. A huge cruise ship sat at anchor across the harbor. On the near side, the flat brown land that stretched to the water was dotted with the pick-ups of local men fishing for dinner.

"You want to call him? Tell him about this?" Ben asked.

"Right now, I don't know what to do," Alan replied. "I do know that later on, when it's dark, I'm going to pay another visit to Olinda."

Whip wove the dune buggy around the turns of the dirt road. It had rained hard recently and the going was slick. Mud was slapping up against the undercarriage as they went. Christienne jounced in the seat alongside him. She was intoxicated by the fresh scent of the rain and the newness of their love. They came around the last turn and Whip slid the car up before the gate. She jumped out and opened it, bowing and waving him through. He pulled onto the property and parked alongside the Rover.

Whip stepped from the car and scanned the grounds. Everything looked normal but the sensation of danger would not leave. If anything it was stronger now than it had been before. Christienne seemed unconscious of Whip's state of mind. She went dancing across the lawn and up the steps to the front door. Whip followed her, somewhat distracted by the outline of her bottom through the tight jeans that she wore. He came through the door and locked it behind them.

Christienne checked the answering machine. One of the messages was from someone named Paul who was going to be on the island next week. He was looking forward to getting together with her. Whip arched an eyebrow and she gave him a mysterious smile. Then she made a note about an upcoming dental appointment and wrote down several numbers for some furniture she had advertised for sale. Her mother had not called. When she was done, Whip handed her a glass of wine that he had poured.

"Thanks," she said. She leaned against him and murmured, "I wish we could just stay here for a while. I love my house. I miss it when I'm not here."

"There'll be plenty of time for that," he replied. "I don't think you realize what kind of a situation we have here."

"Whip," she paused for a moment, took a sip from the wine and looked out the window at the jungle that stretched away below. "I realize there's some danger, but we haven't seen any have we? Now don't get all serious on me," she added when she caught his look. "It's just hard to take this seriously when nothing has happened. Nobody is shooting at us. There aren't any exploding cars like you see on TV. Let's be positive."

Whip's demeanor remained the same, "I'll be positive when we're out of here."

"Oh, honey," she set down her glass and put her arms around him, running her hands down his front until she could feel his cock under her hand. She leaned up and kissed him. The energy between them was so strong that they were both immediately aroused. Whip forgot about his paranoia as he gave in to the liquid sensation of the beautiful woman in his arms. Christienne dropped to her knees and pulled him free from his jeans.

Whip could not get over how perfectly each movement would develop between them. There were no bumped noses or awkward moments. When finally they came together it reminded him of water ballet.

Afterwards, they lay spent and trembling. Christienne looked like an angel to Whip with her tumbling black hair framing the perfect symmetry of her face.

Whip stroked her cheek. "I don't want to seem indelicate, but can we get on our way?"

She smiled and bit at his hand. "I'm easy. Let me grab a few things and we'll be gone."

"All set," she said a few minutes later. A backpack was swinging from her shoulder as she walked up to Whip, who had been standing by the window. The sun was shining through it and its rays were dancing off of the hardwood floor. Whip passed his hand through one and set the dust vibrating in all directions.

"I used to do that all the time when I was a kid," she said.

"Funny how we all discover the same things. It used to remind me of the planets, the atoms spinning around their nucleus. It was hypnotic."

"So are you. Let's go." She grabbed him by the arm and led him out of the door.

Malcolm struck while she was locking the door. He slammed into Whip, who had his back turned, and sent him flying over the railing twelve feet to the ground. Whip was fortunate in several respects. He landed mostly on his feet, going into a roll and barely missed a stack of cinder blocks by inches.

Christienne screamed as she was grabbed and turned, a large hunting knife pressed against her throat.

"How's it going, Sugar?" Malcolm growled in her ear. As she struggled he pressed the knife harder against her throat and a thin trickle of blood began to run down into her blouse. "You want to be very careful right now. This knife is super sharp. Also, nothing says I can't just cut your head off any time I feel like it."

Christienne became still and Malcolm walked her over to the rail. His eyes widened as he surveyed the ground below. Whip was gone.

"Okay, boyfriend, I got your squeeze up here. Either you're going to show up real soon or I'm going to start cutting pieces off her and throwing them overboard." Stuck in a holster at the small of his back was a Smith & Wesson .38 Special. Billy Joe had told Malcolm to use the spray to disable Whip, but something told Malcolm he wouldn't need it. He wasn't supposed to kill Whip. Billy Joe wanted him alive. The fall should have fucked him up. Malcolm was sure it had fucked him up and he was hiding somewhere under the deck

Christienne was in shock. *Whip had been right!* It would be her fault, whatever happened now. She felt the imminence of death. Time had stopped or slowed down to almost nothing. She felt the pressure of a dark fatality about to swallow her.

The man who held her was very strong. She could feel the hard lines of his body and she could feel the pressure of his sex pressing against her. She could feel the evil. She could smell it. There was a raw heat coming off of him that passed right through her clothing. His fetid breath blew past her ear and his rough beard tore at the skin on the nape of her neck.

"I'm waiting asshole and I'm not going to wait much longer!" Malcolm slammed her into the railing so that the top part of her body jack-knifed over it. It knocked the breath out of her. He reached over and handcuffed her right hand to her right leg through the rail posts. Then he stepped back and pulled out the gun. Looking around, he could see no one. Christienne's struggles had given him a major hard-on. Her ass was reared up in front of him and filled him with thoughts that involved a whole lot of sex and a lot more of pain and death. *This bitch is mine*, he thought. It wasn't all that hard to believe that Loverboy had run off and left his girlfriend. Otherwise he could be licking his wounds somewhere. *Nobody had any sand anymore.* He'd recalled how Whip had reminded him of a pussy when he'd first seen him, with his pretty face and slender build. He'd been around the back when they first came in. He'd heard them laughing and talking. Once they were inside, he had slipped up on to the deck. He'd been waiting on the other side of a storage locker that had been fortuitously built into the wall right next to the door.

"I'm waiting, Loverboy. You got one minute!" He probably should go down and look for him but first he thought he might just cut the clothes off the chick's body.

After he hit the ground and rolled, Whip immediately went under the deck. There was never a question in his mind about what kind of an animal they were dealing with. Delay was possible. Negotiation was out of the question. While Malcolm was talking to him, he'd found a small kindling hatchet. It was the only thing around that looked like a weapon. He wished he'd asked Christienne where she had hidden that shotgun. Whip didn't know how many men were here. It seemed strange that only one of them would be sent, but so far, he hadn't seen or heard anyone else. As quietly as he was able, he made his way to the back steps. Under the cover of Malcolm's threats, he slowly came up on to the deck.

Malcolm laughed as he cut Christienne's blouse away. He ran a rough hand over her breasts.

"Leave me alone!" she cried. At this, Malcolm gave her head a sharp backhand.

"Shut up you cunt," he said as he continued to knead her breasts. "These puppies would make damn fine tobacco pouches." He cut her belt and the back of her jeans and then ripped them to the floor. "Gonna go to work now, Loverboy. I ain't seen you, so I expect you don't mind."

Whip took a quick look around the corner, hoping with all of his heart that Malcolm would not see him. He didn't, but Whip saw the gun at his back and the big hunting knife in his left hand. Rage filled his heart when he saw Christienne bent naked over the rail. He drew back and quieted his breath. Anger would serve no purpose here. He concentrated his mind on Ming and the one chance he had. There was no chance of rushing him. Even if Whip got there in time to close, Malcolm could still stick her with his knife before he turned to face-off, gun in hand. There was only one chance. He had done some weapons training but could he do it now, with everything on the line, when any mistake would cost them everything? If he missed it was all over.

"Please, Ming, guide my hand," he prayed. Then quickly, he jumped forward on the deck and whipped the axe through the air at Malcolm. Malcolm was quick. He turned the instant that Whip appeared and he might well have blocked the axe with his hand, but one hand held the knife and the other held his dick. The axe flew past his knife hand and the blunt end caught Malcolm in the mouth. Blood and teeth followed the axe and the knife to the deck. With tremendous presence of mind Malcolm had the gun out of the holster and was raising it toward Whip when Whip, who had been moving with the throw, lashed out with his right foot and sent it ricocheting off of the wall. Reversing his feet, Whip smashed his left foot into Malcolm's gut and sent him tumbling down the stairs to the ground. Then he advanced down the stairs after him, but Malcolm was made out of sterner stuff, the survivor of a hundred brawls and hardened by a lifetime of violent contact. Malcolm was already on his feet, spitting out blood and fragments of teeth.

"I'm going to break every bone in your body," he snarled as he squared off in what Whip immediately identified as a *tae kwon do* stance. Malcolm looked like he knew what he was doing.

Whip came toward him. "You should never have come here," he said. "You should never have come alone and you should never have put your hands on the lady." Whip's face was flushed with a controlled rage. In his entire life he had not ever been this angry and he kept reminding himself that he could not afford to be angry. Anger created another foe along with the one he faced.

"Tough talk, pretty boy, but can you dance?" Malcolm said as he feinted with his right hand and then, quicker than Whip thought possible, brought his left foot up into Whip's ribs. Whip bore the pain, which was considerable, and trapped Malcolm's foot with a Praying Mantis hand lock. He then swiftly drove his left foot into Malcolm's exposed groin. Malcolm screamed and fell to the ground, rolling rapidly away from Whip as he clutched at his privates. Then, to Whip's amazement, he got back on his feet to face him again.

"Must be you don't have anything down there to hurt," Whip said.

"I'm going to kill you," Malcolm managed through gritted teeth, "And then I'm going to fuck you both."

"I think not," Whip replied, closing in. Malcolm lashed out with his left foot at Whip's knee, but Whip hopped left and spun around, stepping in and backhanding Malcolm in the face with his left fist. This turned Malcolm to his right. Now Whip was behind him. He raised his left foot and brought it down with all of his force on Malcolm's left calf. Malcolm screamed and fell to the ground. Whip danced over him and brought the heel of his right foot down into Malcolm's exposed ribcage, breaking three of them. Malcolm howled in pain. Then Whip reached down and grabbed Malcolm's right wrist, stepping over his body he pulled the arm straight up and with a vicious twist dislocated his shoulder. Malcolm was now screaming in continuous bursts. With finality, Whip then drove his heel into Malcolm's nose smashing it flat against his face.

"Sorry about all the pain bubba, but I'm afraid we're not quite done." Whip grabbed his left wrist, reversing the procedure and then dislocated the other shoulder. He could hear Christienne screaming at him to stop, but Whip was not through. He kneeled beside Malcolm and began to break each of the fingers of his right hand. "I know it hurts right now and you'll have a little trouble sleeping for a couple of months, but then you'll be all right. That's Mother Nature for you." Whip went through his pockets and extracted the handcuff key.

Christienne continued screaming at Whip to stop.

"I'll be right there, honey," he said. Malcolm was in such great pain that he had become inarticulate except for a gasping, "Motherfucker!" Whip flipped him over on his stomach and then delivered a powerful, surgically precise, kidney punch. Finally, for the first time in his life, the "Great Kahn" was broken. Sobs of terror and pain were pouring from his throat and he was begging Whip to stop.

"You have no patience," Whip said. "I'm done now, don't you go anywhere."

Christienne was weeping, her head turned away because she could no longer look at Whip and what he was doing. Whip got to his feet and went to her, gently unlocking her hand and foot and pulling her into his arms. She struggled briefly and then collapsed, overwhelmed and unable to fight at all.

She lay there shaking in Whip's arms, disbelief etched in her face. She felt like her whole life had been torn asunder and here was Whip smiling patiently, brushing her hair away from her face as if nothing had happened.

"What did you do?" she cried. "Are you crazy? You're as bad as he is!" She screamed, suddenly pushing him away and just as suddenly reaching out for him again.

"Let's go inside for a moment, Christienne, please, everything's okay. Everything is going to be okay. I promise you. I'll explain everything and you will understand. I know how it must look to you at the moment." Whip held her face, gazing intensely into her eyes, trying to reassure her that he was okay, that whatever possessed him was gone, but it wasn't gone. Whip knew that he would do it all over again with no hesitation or remorse.

When he had gotten her seated, he went to the icebox and poured out a large glass of white wine. Returning, he put it in her hands and she took a large swallow.

"I'm going to try to explain to you what that was all about." Whip was sitting on the floor in front of her, his hands stroking her feet. "First, I had to beat him badly. I had to make him totally helpless. He's a very bad man and anything short of helpless, he could still do us harm. I had to make him helpless enough to get the keys from his pocket."

"Whip! You beat him within an inch of his life!" Christienne took another large pull from the wine. She had nearly emptied the glass. Her face was flushed and some of the hysteria and shock had left her features.

"I know sweetheart but that man was a weapon sent here to torture and kill us. He won't be doing anything like that now. That man, if you can call him a man — Alan told me this — raped and tortured young girls, killed them, lots of them. He's also tortured and killed others of all sexes and ages. You can't begin to imagine what he probably had in mind for you only minutes ago. I punished him Christienne. I don't expect you to understand it. I did not know it was going to happen until it did but you have to know, I don't feel bad about it. I'm not sure why that is. When I thought about what he was doing to you on the deck, when I thought about what he had planned, for all of us... He's not going to hurt anyone else again. He's not going to suddenly get away. He's not going to break out of jail."

"It sounds like you're playing God, Whip."

"Maybe I am, but he's alive. I know this was a terrible shock. I hope you can get over it, forgive me, that it won't damage what we have between us. When

I saw him with the knife, when I thought I was going to lose you to the same malevolent animals that murdered my sister, something happened inside of me."

"Oh, Whip." Christienne threw her arms around his neck. "I was so terrified when he had that knife at my throat. I knew I was going to die. He was pressing his filthy erection against me. Then you were there and suddenly he was off of me and I couldn't even speak, but inside I was screaming for you to take the knife and shove it down his throat, stab him in the eyes, cut his dick off and make him eat it, not go after him unarmed, leaving the knife and the gun behind. For a moment I wanted to kill you for placing me in danger of it all happening again and worse. Then you did what you did. I thought the whole world had gone crazy. You were doing the kinds of things I wished for him but they were actually happening and it was horrible to watch... horrible to watch that happen to anyone." She got up quickly and went to the icebox to refill her glass.

Whip followed her into the kitchen and got a damp cloth. He wiped at the blood on her neck that had already clotted. "Not hurt too badly, babe?"

"Thanks to you," she said and then she smiled. It was a miracle for Whip. He knew it was going to be okay then.

"I've got something unpleasant to do now, and I think you'd better stay inside."

Her eyes went wide with alarm. "What, Whip?"

"Relax, I've got to put him in the Rover for the ride to town. It's going to hurt him a lot. It's okay if I put him in your car? He won't fit in the buggy."

Relief flooded her countenance, air escaped audibly from her lips, "Yes, of course. I'll shower and get dressed while you do it."

"Okay." Whip headed for the door.

"Whip?"

He turned toward her. "Yeah?" Watching him standing there, he looked just like a little boy. It was hard now to connect him with she had seen when the violence was taking place.

"Well, spit it out," he grinned.

"I love you."

"I love you, too."

Chapter Twenty-Five

The phone rang five times before Balfire was able to pick it up. He had to wipe the crap off of his hands first. "Hello."

"We've got an emergency," Billy Joe said. "The cops were there today."

"Yeah, but I told them to come back on Monday. They won't be back, I don't think."

"I don't pay you to think, Balfire. Douglas thinks he's got the house and he has. I've managed to tie him up for a while but he'll be there tonight. You've got to be gone by then, gone with the goods, over to the other house. Two trips should do it easy. It's only a few miles away."

"I'm not done. I can't leave now." Balfire was whining. He didn't want to break it all down. Something could happen. Something could get ruined.

"Listen to me. The other place is just as equipped as that one. You've got everything you need to secure and protect the work for transport. The final result is even more important to me than it will ever be to you. Do it!" The menace in Billy Joe's voice came clearly across the phone, so clearly that Balfire lost all interest in argument. "Before the last trip, hit the switch on the charge then watch them from the lookout, ignition upon arrival. You know what to do. Got it?"

"Yes."

Billy Joe switched off the cellular and slipped it back into the car holster. He seethed as he thought of recent events. This had to stop. He knew about Malcolm. He knew some of what had happened to him, but he couldn't retrieve all the data. Someone or something was blocking the access, just like a CB Radio cut into a TV transmission, or when you went into a tunnel with the radio on. He'd gotten brief images of the girl, at one point a very clear one of Malcolm with a knife at her throat and then nothing but confusion and scalding pain from Malcolm.

Billy Joe felt a searing rage building in him. The need to hurt something was becoming an ache. He could not fucking put up with it anymore. He put the car into gear and went looking for a playground.

The literature was specific. In order to gain a clear insight into a hidden matter, one must procure a virgin child and sacrifice it under very precise conditions. All of the necessary paraphernalia was in a black bag in the trunk. He'd done it before on numerous occasions. It didn't matter at his current stage of evolution in the arts, he had a photographic memory for ritual. He was at the point where evil remembered the nature of itself in every act. Still, there was always great risk in these operations because it was the nature of evil to devour itself. In this relative world, it was understood that every hand was set against its brother.

Treachery was the sweet meat of its existence. Every operation that involved blood had to be approached as carefully as the male black widow approached its mate. There were no second chances. The mental institutions, the graveyards and Hell were full of those who had miscalculated.

He knew there was a fundamentalist Christian school in Kahului. In these days, you had to be very careful. Kids in elementary schools were having sex. One way to be fucked right off the bat was to sacrifice an impure vessel. The demon could use the sexual fluid, saliva or blood as a highway right up your ass. The best you could expect from such an encounter was to spend eternity waiting to exercise a single appetite. That was the thing about Christian schools. The odds were a lot better. "That is," Billy Joe said aloud with a laugh, "unless it's a Catholic school."

His timing was good. Although school had been out for a while, there were still kids milling about. Some were coming from after school activities. Some just hadn't gone home yet. He parked the car across the street in the shopping center parking lot facing the school, rolled down his window and lit a cigarette.

Gradually he sank into a trance state, deep into the realm of images and ideas he descended. Soon he was ready to lay the bait. As with hypnosis, where it was said you could not compel someone to do something that went against their nature, it could be very difficult to draw a child into an activity he or she was not predisposed toward. However, you could attract them into doing something that was presented as something else.

He let his mind expand outward, past the parking lot to the school. Into a circle several hundred yards wide he projected his images, little clusters of pictured thoughts, of candy and sweet kisses wrapped together with two of the cutest puppies, a tall glass of fresh squeezed orange juice with condensation beading on the glass. There was the valentine outline of a beautiful teenage boy, smiling with a kitten in his arms. There were cartoon kisses that floated as lips in the air around him, another boy with a surfboard, the waves pounding on the shore behind him. He sent out Christmas thoughts with the baby Jesus and presents under the tree, a table laden with food and the air filled with the smells of Christmas. There were colored lights winking in a safe backdrop of darkness.

Billy Joe's lip curled in distaste at this last image, but it didn't affect his work. He was a pro.

He didn't have long to wait. Two girls around the age of twelve came out of one of the buildings across the street and, after looking both ways, crossed into the parking lot. They were talking and giggling to one another. As soon as he felt the contact he closed off the images to everyone but them. One was a blonde with freckles and a corn-fed mid-western look, a bit chubby as they often were at that age. The other was a local girl, an Asian mix with an ocean of black hair flowing down her back. Billy Joe decided on her for several practical reasons. She was actively pubescent. He could tell by the smell of her. Also, by being local, he could punch into the demon he sought that much easier because her heritage was here. Also she was, by far, the most beautiful and that was of high account with Zantecxa. She would definitely be the more prized because Zantecxa was a Mayan demon. She was dark and would appear Indian to him.

They were walking on the scent of dreams that had formed in their minds. There was excitement in the air. They did not know or question its source. There was a tingling in the groin area and a fuzzy warmth under the armpits, under the chin, at the base of the spine and on the cheeks just below the eyes. They came up to the driver's side window and paused.

"Little girls, where are you going?" he inquired. He had a warm smile on his face and his eyes were soft and magnetic. His voice had the smooth undulations of the wind blowing through green sugar cane. It was all familiar and safe.

They looked at Billy Joe, both of them swaying with slight hip rotations as if they were hearing music. They did not see Billy Joe as he really appeared. They saw a kind handsome man, a man that they knew.

"Are you Ricky Martin?" the blonde asked.

"No," Billy Joe replied. It always amused him when they reached this altered state, he would often remind them of someone they had seen on TV or in the movies, rather than a family member or adult acquaintance. This was not the first time he had reminded someone of a rock star. "What is your name?" he asked the blonde.

"Kelsey," she replied, reaching up to brush a hand through her curly hair.

"It is a pleasure to meet you." He reached out for her hand and she put it in his. "Kelsey, I want you to go into the mall. What you are looking for is there. We will join you later."

"Okay," she answered and wandered off toward the mall entrance a hundred yards away with visions dancing in her head.

"Now, what is your name?" he asked the other.

"Lei." She smiled shyly and turned quickly from one side to the other, causing her skirt to swirl around her legs.

"What a beautiful name," Billy Joe purred. "I want you to come to the other side of the car and get in. We have somewhere wonderful to go." His eyes were as luminous as the moon and in them Lei could see fantastic shapes dancing in a fairy tale landscape. She wanted to go there. She got into the car.

Billy Joe drove out of the parking lot and was soon on Lower Beach Road, headed through Waiehu, Waihee and further to the remote western tip of the island. When he had driven far enough so traffic was reduced to almost nothing, he reached across and began to unbutton the girl's blouse. Startled, she looked up at him and once again saw the fairy tale shapes moving in the silvered backdrops of his eyes. She smiled softly and watched him as he removed her blouse and her bra. He had the skilled controlled touch of a surgeon. It was the simplest thing for him.

It was funny, he thought. *She doesn't need a bra, hardly any tits at all, those Christians with their repressive anti-sexual mores.* Well, he would spare her a lifetime of guilt and regret, both real and imagined. *She would probably be thankful if she knew.* Pity that he couldn't give her to Malcolm but that would defeat the purpose. Malcolm would not be having any more little girls any time soon it appeared. Billy Joe had finally located him in the Land Rover on the Hana Highway, in terrible pain, the living shit having been beaten out of him. At the thought of it, a frightful anger grew in him and he had to bottle it quickly before it took its toll on his captive.

Once he'd removed her upper clothing, he pushed her forward and pulled at the skin on her back, feeling its texture, rubbing it between his fingers to bring out the natural oils.

Yes, he thought. *This would do very nicely.*

SAND HILL, WAILUKU, HAWAII, AT THE SAME TIME.

"Apparently he threw up in the viewing area, no real reason given. Greely said that he must have gotten scared... It's beautiful up here this time of day!" Ben gestured expansively at the horizon, which included the harbor, the town of Kahului and the brooding heights of Haleakalā crowned with clouds turning orange and red from the descending sun.

"You know what I think when I see clouds like that?"

"Haven't the faintest, Alan."

"Especially in the late afternoon and when they're brawny and full, sometimes it feels as if just behind the clouds is a band of celestial musicians playing the instruments that only they have and the colors in the clouds are the sounds that they make, sounds far more intense and real than anything we can hear down here. The sort of thing Beethoven and Mozart probably heard. Even though I can't physically hear it, sometimes it is as if my heart can and it leaps in my chest and I feel like I'm not really Alan Douglas, homicide cop, but some mystic traveler who dances in the air, unconfined by the boundaries of time and space."

"You've been smoking pot?" Ben said with a grin.

"Uh-huh, thanks. It's nice to know I can share my personal thoughts with you, gives me confidence to be myself, that's what friends are for."

Ben chuckled, "One thing though."

"What's that?"

"I wouldn't mention it to Captain Rusk if I were you."

Alan watched the stream of traffic moving along Lower Beach Rd. In the stream of cars, a black Mercedes moved across their sight line and then disappeared.

"I wonder what really happened in there," Ben mused. "It's incredible how he could pop those chains and then waste all those cops without a weapon. He must have been moving awfully fast, faster than any human I've ever seen."

"He's not human at the moment, Ben. He's more like one of those radio-controlled cars."

"Hard to imagine," Ben popped a piece of gum in his mouth and tapped his forefinger on the steering wheel. "I'd sure like to talk to Klein. He might be conscious. We're not even going to catch a cold up here. Why the hell would he come up here anyway? There's hardly any cover."

"You're right. We're up here to keep us away from whatever is really happening. I'd love to talk to Klein too, but I get the feeling that the Captain wouldn't like it."

Ben snapped his gum, "All the more reason, don't you think?"

Alan scratched his nose and raised his eyebrows, watching Ben. "That is one hell of a motivation, isn't it?"

"Attention, Unit 32, proceed immediately to Maui Memorial Hospital." The radio coming on made both of them jump.

Ben and Alan looked at each other and then laughed.

"Beethoven," Ben said.

"Mozart," Alan replied.

MAUI MEMORIAL HOSPITAL, WAILUKU, HAWAII, 5:08 PM

It had been a brutal ride for Malcolm and Christienne as well. There were times when she was afraid she would lose it and have to make Whip pull over so that she could be sick on the side of the highway.

Whip felt nothing except the determination to take care of business. Though it wasn't his call, he felt that the whole human race would be better off when Malcolm left this planet and was on his way to wherever people like that go. Despite all of the harm Whip had inflicted on him, when he went out to collect him and put him in the Rover, Malcolm had managed to actually crawl part way into the bushes. Lying on his back he had used his feet to propel himself across the lawn.

"You're going to die, you motherfucker!" Malcolm had screamed when Whip dragged him to the vehicle. "You're going to beg for death when we're done with you."

"You, my friend, *are* done with me. I wonder if your attitude might have to do with lying on the wrong side." Malcolm shrieked like a woman when Whip turned him over.

"No more, please, no more!" he cried.

Whip glanced at the house and then turned his attention back to Malcolm.

"What you've got to understand, pal, even though I know you don't like it, is that I'm in charge here. I'm like God as far as you are concerned right now. If you piss me off, I can really hurt you. I can give you a deep tissue massage, with special emphasis on the ribs and the rotator cuff. So you don't want to be anything but polite to me. You just want to stay as quiet as possible until I get you to the hospital. Bad as you hurt right now, it could be worse."

It had taken a lot of effort of will for Whip not to just give Malcolm another really good dose of it. In his mind, he realized that the motivation for this must have been coming from somewhere else. Something wanted him to become like Malcolm. Whip loaded him as gently and efficiently into the Rover as he could manage and then walked away shaking his head. *How careful we must be*, he thought. *It doesn't take very long to go off the side of the road and into the ditch and it doesn't matter how well you drove up until that point. It doesn't count.*

The admitting nurse was a huge black man who looked like he might have played for the Chicago Bears in '85. He had a shaved head and lots of gold in his white teeth. There was a deep scar across his forehead. *He might have gotten that head-butting a pick-up*, Whip thought. He looked mean but that all changed when he smiled.

"Help you?" he asked.

"I've got a guy outside who's pretty badly hurt. He's not going to die but he's in a lot of pain. You're going to want to call the police, especially Special Investigator Alan Douglas and Lieutenant Ben Kamamoto. This man is wanted for questioning." Whip didn't know what else to add.

"You a cop?"

Whip shook his head.

"How bad's he hurt?" The nurse's name tag said "Gene." He didn't seem very excited about Whip's news.

"Dislocated shoulders, broken ribs, broken nose, broken fingers, might have a fractured jaw and injuries to the groin."

"You do this?" he asked and his eyes narrowed as he sized Whip up.

Whip nodded again.

Gene called for a stretcher and then notified the police. "How'd it happen?"

"He was trying to kill me and my girlfriend. In the process he got banged up."

Gene laughed and shook his head. "Got banged up did he? You don't look like what passes for a bad ass around here. What did you use, a baseball bat?"

Whip shook his head "no" and said, "My hands and feet, the martial arts."

Gene's eyes went wide in a parody of surprise, "Oh, Karate Boy."

"Kung Fu actually and I'm not a bad ass."

Gene got up from the desk. He was even bigger than Whip thought. "It's a slow day, let me take a look at this dude and don't ask me who I played ball for. I didn't."

Whip laughed, "I guess you get asked that a lot."

"I do."

Whip lifted the tailgate and Gene looked in at Malcolm. "Shit!" he said. "What did he do, the police want him for?"

"He likes to kill and rape little girls and everything else that gets in his way."

"Damn, Sam, too bad you had to bring him in breathing." Gene looked at Malcolm with distaste.

"Didn't you know?" Whip asked.

"Know what?"

"It hurts more to be alive."

"There is that."

After the stretcher had gone a police unit arrived and Whip was suddenly very busy. He was being questioned when Alan and Ben came double-time into the lobby. They were stunned to see Whip and Christienne standing there with two detectives.

Ben walked up to them and asked, "What happened, Irish?" He was addressing a man named Kelly, in his early thirties. He'd been a detective for seven years. He had cold blue eyes and red hair with a mass of freckles surrounding his pugged nose. Standing next to him was his partner, Amalia Keoho. She looked like the Pillsbury Doughboy, Hawaiian style, 5'4" tall and probably around 160 pounds. Neither she nor her partner were smiling. Kelly snapped his notebook shut and turned to Ben.

"Afternoon, Lieutenant. This fellow here says he knows you two. He brought someone in here pretty badly beaten, says he tried to kill him and his girlfriend, says you're looking for this guy."

Alan looked at Whip. "Who?"

"Malcolm," Whip said.

"No shit!" Ben exclaimed and then turned to Kelly. "We'll take over from here Irish, Amalia." Here he acknowledged Kelly's partner. It wasn't sexism that had made Ben speak to Kelly first. He was the senior partner and everyone knew you didn't talk much to Amalia because she always deferred to Kelly. She was great at interrogation however, and Ben was sure that Whip had been having his hands full with her. "This is part of our current investigation. Thanks for coming down."

"It's not that simple, Lieutenant." Kelly was standing firm, his expression serious.

"How's that?" Ben asked.

"There's some question of whether reasonable force was used here."

Ben looked at the ceiling for a moment. "You want to expand on that?"

Christienne shifted on her feet and her eyes met Alan's. *She's been through it,* he thought. She gave Alan a hollow smile, the corners of her mouth twitching nervously. He winked at her and turned back to the conversation.

"The law says you can use reasonable force to protect yourself, to subdue an assailant. It says you can use deadly force to protect your life. It doesn't say you can torture. It would be better if the guy was dead, but right now he only wishes he were."

"Whip wouldn't torture anybody," Alan said.

Ben put his hand on Kelly's shoulder and said, "Can we talk over here by the chairs?"

"Yeah, sure," he replied, not liking his situation at all. They walked across the room to a lounge waiting area that thankfully was empty. Everybody sat down. Whip and Christienne remained where they were.

"Tell me about it," Ben asked after everyone had gotten comfortable. Kelly related the details he had about Malcolm's condition and what Whip and Christienne had told them so far.

Ben shifted in his chair and leaned forward, closer to Kelly. "This man's name is Malcolm Kahn. He just finished doing almost twenty years in San Quentin for the rape-murders of little girls. Since then, he and his partner have been on a rampage in California and Arizona and now here. They've been in Hawaii about a month we think, and they're the principal suspects in all of the kidnapping-murders we've been having. He's a dangerous animal and whatever Whip had to do to pacify him was completely necessary!"

"No shit!" Kelly exclaimed, "The hearts in Olowalu. I saw the sketches that went around but I didn't recognize him. If he is who you say, there's probably not going to be a lot of concern about his civil rights, but then there's the Captain. We're all aware of the Captain's state of mind lately. He'll see the reports."

Ben looked at Alan. "That's what we want to talk to you about. There's a lot of creative lee..."

"I'm going to wait somewhere else," Detective Keoho interjected and then quickly rose to her feet without any seeming effort. "This way I don't have to hear anything I don't want to hear." She was gone without further comment.

"Welcome to the age of paranoia," Kelly quipped. "I've been on the force for thirteen years, and I've never seen it as intense as this. There's some very spooky shit going down. You need to know that I've got to play this one by the book, well, pretty much by the book that is. I can't get my ass into a sling over this. I might miss a few things but there's not going to be anything to come back and haunt me. You can understand this, I hope." They all looked at each other and Ben moved his head up and down.

"Whatever you can do," Ben murmured.

"That guy is awfully fucked up. Of course it could have happened in the course of normal defense. He might have fallen out of a window and landed on some rocks I guess. It doesn't help that your boy hasn't got anything more wrong with him than some bruised ribs. You know I've got nothing but the greatest respect for you Lieutenant and I've got no reason to share the Captain's concerns about Mr. Douglas here." He nodded briefly at Alan in a non-committal way. "But things being the way they are, I've got to keep my head down!"

"We understand, Kelly. You're a good man. No one's going to blame you for doing your job. I doubt anything will come of this anyway."

"I hope you're right, Lieutenant."

"Please, call me Ben."

"Okay, Ben."

Kelly got to his feet and gestured Whip over. "You're free to go for the moment. No doubt someone will want to talk to you again. Don't leave town," he said with a smile and then walked in the direction his partner had taken.

Christienne followed Whip over and took a seat next to Ben. Whip sat next to Alan and quickly filled them in on the details. Ben asked him why he had hurt Malcolm so much. Whip told him there were a lot of factors at work. Mostly he was making sure Malcolm could do them no further harm. Then he told them about Malcolm crawling away afterwards even with all of his injuries. "One less dislocation and he might have been gone." Whip looked into Ben's eyes and held them.

Alan patted Whip on the back. There was nothing he felt like saying at the moment. He was just glad they were safe. He got up and went to Christienne, pulled her to her feet and embraced her tightly.

5:23 PM, OLD YMCA GROUNDS, MAUI, HAWAII

Billy Joe had undressed the girl and filled her head with music while he prepared for the ritual. She stood there swaying to the beat. In her mind, she was at a school dance. Not like any real dance that she had been allowed to attend in her young life, but the kind of dance she wished to attend, that she hoped to attend. The setting was one of her own imagination, in a school gym somewhere, and she was dancing with the boy who had been holding the kitten. The budding sexuality of her being brought out flashes of the woman she would be some day. The woman she might have become. Her bare feet moved through the grass. Billy Joe took in her slender hips and the suggestion of ripening curves, the smooth tracings of pubic hair on and around her sex, more like fine head hair than pubic hair. He noted clinically that the closer you got to the Orient, the straighter and sparser it was, while the closer you got to the Middle East the coarser and bushier it became.

For many of his rituals, the death of a specific type of person was necessary to appease the dark entity from which he sought a service. It was a given that knowledge of the dark side came only with the spilling of blood. *Lives had to be sacrificed so that certain doors might be opened.* Such was true in most arenas of inquiry. Explorers died so that hitherto unknown lands might be charted.

People died from diseases and the medical experiments practiced on them so that knowledge of medicine might increase. People died because they believed a multitude of different absurdities so that the folly of their beliefs might be known.

People died in Billy Joe's rituals because the beings that guarded the doors, and sometimes *were* the doors that led to the information he sought, required that price. Sometimes, often, their price was worse than death. There were several ways to approach the goal. You could trick the guardians, but this was not advisable. You could only trick them once anyway and you might need them again, not that any effort at fair play had an effect on these creatures. They didn't give a shit about that, but they did remember you.

You could agree to a term of service, or promise a part of yourself. This method he had also rejected, not because he held anything sacred, but because there was no guarantee that you would be released from this service once the terms of your contract had been fulfilled. *After all,* Billy Joe reasoned, *you were dealing with demons, not the most trustworthy sort.* Once you gave any entity access to your being, they knew the way in. You needed specialized information to bar them afterwards. This was true even of devic entities whose interest could often be of the positive sort. The idea that you could sell your soul to the devil for personal gain was a trap that had claimed many with no return given. Anyone who considered selling their soul to the devil had already given up its value, based on their willingness to trade in it as a commodity.

The last option was that you paid for what you desired with the blood of another. Depending on what you were seeking and whom you were dealing with, the circumstances and choices of victim differed profoundly. Some asked for young boys. Some asked for people of a certain color or religious persuasion. One entity that Billy Joe had dealt with asked only for old women. One required a Jewish male baby with a clubbed foot. This explained the huge varieties of victims chosen by the serial killers at work in the modern day. Billy Joe knew it was the influence of various entities that possessed the minds of the killers and worked through them. Too bad for the modern police that they did not know this, but fat lot of good it would do them. It certainly explained how the killers could evade the police and remain successful for so long. They have help and... it isn't them to begin with. Not that they were not partially responsible. The tools used by evil were already predisposed to the function to which they were applied.

From the trunk of his car, he extracted a large black canvas satchel and drew forth a roll of chamois-like leather. With a quick movement of his wrists, he snapped it open and a human skin, all in one piece, rolled out. This he laid carefully upon the ground. He next extracted a burgundy cloth from the bag. Kneeling, he laid this to his side and carefully began to set objects upon it. There was a piece of hawthorn root, a turkey baster with a custom tip, a small container of henbane, an ornate dagger with archaic sigils embossed on its side. The handle was a naked woman's body with the head of a serpent. Then he carefully removed six candles, two red, two black and two white, all of them made from human fat.

There was also a small vial of powdered mushrooms from the Amazon Basin. It took a whole day to die from them, but only ten minutes for them to activate the nervous system with their psychotropic action. He would only need a window of just under a half an hour for the ritual. Since she was being offered to a creature who loved nothing as much as a gift like this, it would be icing on the cake if she could see him when he appeared. The mushrooms would make this possible.

He went to her and said, "Open your mouth darling, Daddy has something sweet for you to eat, just as sweet as sugar." He poured a measured amount on her tongue and told her to chew it slowly and then swallow it. He then placed several more items upon the cloth, dried flowers, a piece of bark, and a vial of ointment. Last he removed a hypodermic needle and a large blue bottle filled with liquid. He set the bottle down and approached the girl with the hypodermic.

"I want you to be still now, darling. You are standing by an ocean watching the waves come to the shore. It is very peaceful." She stood quite still as he drew some blood from her arm. When he was done he told her to go back to dancing. It amused him. It reminded him of something from the Brothers Grimm.

He unscrewed the cap of the bottle and injected the blood into it. The liquid turned instantly into a neon scarlet. It glowed and bathed Billy Joe's hand with its light. He resealed the bottle and set it on the cloth. Next he picked up the vial of ointment and walked to the girl. He poured it liberally into his hand and began to rub her body with it. Her nose wrinkled at the smell.

"Perfume for your lover," he said.

Effortlessly, he picked her up and set her down upon the human skin, telling her she was to remain there. Then he filled the turkey baster with the glowing liquid and drew a circle around her on the ground. Once he had completed this, he drew another circle outside the first, creating a space approximately six inches across. He walked counterclockwise around the circle crushing the dried flowers in his hands and letting the powder fall inside the boundary of the two lines. The candles were then placed at symmetrical locations around the circle inside the boundary lines. He lit each candle by snapping his fingers over the wick and speaking a Word of Power. This done, he removed an ancient quill pen and a stoppered bottle of gold liquid from the bag. He dipped the pen into the liquid and began drawing letters inside the boundary lines just above the ground, chanting one phrase over and over again. As soon as he started, the girl began to rhythmically rotate her hips as if she were using a hula-hoop.

Billy Joe was now at the end of his preparations. Everything he had done so far was designed to keep the demon inside the circle. Should the unthinkable occur, he still had the magical dagger. Now he went to the satchel and removed a very thin cape. Wrapped in the cape was a twisted wand made of a dark heavy wood. He put the cape about his neck and walked purposefully toward the northern end of the circle.

"Turn and face me," he said to the girl. The girl did as he asked. The shadows had grown long. The sun was behind the hills and there was about one half hour until dark. Billy Joe stood motionless for several minutes, waiting for the appropriate moment when he might proceed. When that moment came, he extended the wand in his right hand and drew a series of signs in the air. There was a look of cold power upon his face, concentrated malevolence shone out from his eyes. A haughty majesty sat upon his chiseled features. It was the appearance of a man born to command the elements. There was no fear.

"Oh, Zantecxa, consort of Azaziel, gateway into the darkness, mighty hunting beast of Ashtaroth, I summon thee to the high feast of thy nature. I bring thee the gift for which thy hunger screams across a desolate land." The girl was now tilting her pelvis slightly back and forth. Her eyes stared unseeingly in front of her.

"Come, Zantecxa, *invitunamus svernaum serpentorah bendaunam grelo vandunum.*" The air crackled with electricity as Billy Joe spoke the language of invocation. The girl's form stiffened.

"*Azeziel scorpintimas dredinabam licivintatos augulemas venianimus*!" The air shook with the power of Billy Joe's voice. As he spoke, he continued to draw figures in the air. "I seek a boon to see the face of my enemy and all that passes in his mind concerning me. Come and receive your payment for the service that I demand! Come now! Come now or face the penalty that awaits!"

A thin funnel of smoke began to spin in the center of the circle in front of the girl. It grew in size until it stood twice as high as the girl. A voice spoke out of it. "Who troubles me? I am here. Who has called me to this place? Speak!" The voice was full of anger and menace. The very sound of it would have broken the will of lesser men, but Billy Joe had faced many a demon in his day.

"Show yourself to me first, that I may know you are no impostor. Show me that you are Zantecxa, whom I have commanded into the circle!"

The funnel began to break up and a form emerged, a form out of nightmare. Its bottom half were the hindquarters of a dog and from between its legs an erect red penis jutted forth. The chest was covered with thickly matted, wiry black hair. From the sides hung disproportionately long arms that were scaled in alligator hide, the ends of which were terrible rending claws. The head was the most horrible feature of all. It sat on a slender neck, incredibly elongated, every feature was a gross caricature of the human form. The nose was over a foot long and stuck straight out from the face, above it were two flaming red eyes whose murderous glare bespoke an unquenchable desire to tear and to rend. The forehead rose up and curved outward like a scimitar but the mouth was the centerpiece. It was so wide that it curved around the face and ended just under the ears, which rose to points that stuck six inches out from the head. Its mouth was filled with three rows of razor sharp teeth. Large bat's wings extended to either side from their anchor in the back.

"Who are you and by what right have you called me hither from my torment, foolish mortal?" The demon's eyes bored into Billy Joe's probing for any sign of weakness that would provide him with an access way.

"I am not required to give my name, only to pay the fee, and I am here by the right and power of accepted ritual and in the name of your Master, Ashtaroth. I do also bring you the gift which your services require." Billy Joe brought down the wand, which he had held forth until this time and began slapping it against his thigh like he was an English military officer holding a swagger stick.

"Where is my gift?" asked the demon, seeming to forget his question about Billy Joe's name. A hideous green drool formed at the corners of his mouth as he asked this, and his eyes were hungrily searching from side to side.

"Your gift awaits you when you have fulfilled my request."

"Where is the gift?" he persisted. "I can smell it." There was a snuffling noise like that of a pig rooting in the earth.

"When I have my request," Billy Joe continued, his entire attention focused on the proceedings.

"You seem unaffected by my power." The demon was referring to the mental effort being made to unseat Billy Joe's concentration.

"I am aware of nothing," Billy Joe replied, which was the correct response, as referencing the demon's power would have meant acknowledging it.

"What is your request?" The demon shifted his feet, which made his erection bob from side to side. Billy Joe did not notice.

"As I have told you and you have not forgotten, I wish to see the face of my enemy and to know all that passes in his mind concerning me."

"You have many enemies, too many for me to show all to you. Where is my gift?"

"I wish to see the enemy who blocks my way and hinders me in my destruction of Alan Douglas."

The demon's head moved up and down. "Granted," he said.

At his words, a space opened up in front of Billy Joe as the fabric of existence was rent, and before him stood a form in green and yellow robes.

"What trick is this!?" Billy Joe screamed, "He has no face!" In the place where the face would have been was a cartoon smiley face.

The demon laughed, "This is no trick. I am bound by the law to answer true. This is the face of the enemy as it appears in your contact with him."

"My enemy must have a face! Show me his face or you will not receive your gift."

"Stupid one, this is the only face that it is within my power to show you. Yet even this would tell you something, were you not so dull. You must also know that if you do not provide me with my gift, the agreed upon price of my coming, that I will take both you and the gift."

Billy Joe submerged his growing rage. "I have your gift. Reveal to me the other portion of the request. Show me what passes in my enemy's mind as it concerns me and Alan Douglas."

"As you wish," the demon replied. Instantly, there was the sound of a child's voice singing, "*Tiptoe through the tulips, through the garden, to the windowpane, oh, tip toe through the tulips with me.*"

Rage flared again. "You are cheating me and I have brought you a most splendid gift. Answer me truly!" he cried.

At the mention of the gift, which he knew was fast approaching, the creature had begun to salivate again. Drops of it were falling to the ground where they hissed like steam. "Hear me, ignorant one. You know the rules, as do I. You know that I have shown you what there is, as perfectly as your words required it of me. It is not my fault that this is the appearance of your enemy as he appears in regard to you. It is not my fault that this is what passes through his mind when he considers you, although I find it very amusing. It is almost worth my coming here to experience this, almost. To the point, I have fulfilled my part of the bargain, now you must fulfill yours. Where is my gift, or do you wish to come with me?" The creature brought his claws forward, hopeful still that Billy Joe might make some error here, hopeful that his anger might undo him.

It did not happen. "Your gift is waiting behind you, take it and go."

"Ah ha!" The demon spun around and looked down at little Lei. "Oh, this is very nice. What a fine gift, a very fine gift. I would thank you but there is no gratitude in me. Awaken, my darling." The creature tickled her under the chin and her eyes opened. For a moment she could not comprehend what was before her. Her mind would not register the image. Then it did and a piercing scream escaped her lips. The demon laughed.

Billy Joe didn't stay to watch. He knew what was going to happen. He had seen it before. Angry and disgusted, he gathered up his goods and put them in the car. There was no need to concern himself with what remained in the circle. It would all be reduced to cinders at the demon's departure. The sounds of madness were already diminishing as he got into the car. It was amazing that the fiend could make it last as long as he did, considering his appetite.

The first time he had called it up, he had watched the entire sequence with fascination. It was like watching something from the insect kingdom. There had been no attraction to pay such attention the second time.

Billy Joe knew that this was what separated him from lesser practitioners who would eventually wind up food because of their curiosity. His personal control made him part of a select few. No one who lacked refinement and great discipline could hope to survive on that dark road.

As Billy Joe drove away, he saw the creature snaking its long scabrous tongue around a large hooked talon. He heard hooting laughter as he left and the demon was singing, "*Tip toe through the tulips*" after him. A cold fire of hate and rage burned in him. He could have had the answers that he wanted. The demon knew who it was and what it was that Billy Joe wanted, but the demon was under no obligation to help him. He was bound to answer precisely as he had been asked. The letter, not the spirit of the law, bound him. In the manifest realm, the same is too often true. It was this very thing that gave such a bad taste to the operations of human justice and the reputations of lawyers.

He realized he would have been better served if he had asked to see the *real face* of Douglas's protector. Billy Joe should have asked to see what passed through the mind of the protector in respect to Douglas. There might have been a different outcome. It was too late now to go through the whole routine again, the wrong time of the day and he needed more supplies. It would be another day at least and by that time, the situation would be settled.

Some miles down the road Billy Joe drove into a macadamia nut orchard and stopped the car. He waited there for several minutes until a figure exited from the trees several yards away. He walked toward the car and got in. Billy Joe backed out and continued on his way.

Kimo Nakamura sat with his hands in his lap. The handcuffs were still on his wrists as were portions of chains attached to them. With Malcolm out of commission, Billy Joe needed another pair of hands. He also needed Kimo for a very specific task.

Chapter Twenty-Six

They spoke briefly with the doctor who had treated Malcolm Kahn. Ben had mentioned that it was good politics. "Doctors think they're God," Ben had said. "They're raised that way and the fact that they are not God is a terrible burden for them to bear. The general public does not know how little real information they possess. You're usually worse off after you see them. They get paid a lot of money and they usually marry unpleasant women who like to spend it. Put that all together and you've got a real 'kid gloves' situation."

"Sounds like you don't like the medical profession," Alan had replied.

"I don't like the western allopathic tradition. It's all invasive procedures and toxic pharmaceuticals. Oriental medicine is much more in line with the body's needs."

"I tend to agree with you, Ben, but the real problem is not with the doctors as much as it is with contemporary lifestyles and diet."

The conversation had come about after leaving the doctor's office and the curt unfriendly exchange that had taken place there. Doctor Friedman, a crusty old Kennedy era liberal, had made his feelings about police brutality clearly known. Ben's informing him that the police hadn't done it did not affect his rant much, but it had made the difference in his cooperating with their request to spend a few minutes alone with Malcolm.

Malcolm Kahn lay wrapped in tape and bandages. His hands were folded across his stomach, one of them in a cast. There was a large purple bruise on his right cheek and his lips were torn and swollen, the black tracery of careful stitches painfully evident. The lips had been painted with some kind of clear medication that made them glisten under the fluorescent lights.

They stood in silence at the foot of the bed, taking in the setting, until Malcolm said, "The fuck you looking at?"

His eyes had the glazed over appearance of one who had not too long ago received a serving of high performance pain medication. Still, the meanness and antipathy that was his natural state was unaffected by the drugs.

"Looking at evidence of an efficient crime stopping effort by a respectable taxpaying member of society, who should probably be receiving the keys to the city for it, you shit bag," Ben said. It was clear to both men that no show of sympathy or threats would have any impact on Malcolm. They could only attempt to put him off balance and maybe get lucky. "I'm Lieutenant Kamamoto,

Homicide, and this is Special Investigator Douglas from the DA's Office."

"Ain't nobody dead. What's Homicide doing here?" Malcolm asked.

"We're not here about your little rumble in the jungle, Mr. Kahn. We're here about outstanding warrants from California plus a number of recent kidnappings and murders in the local area. You want to help us out with your feelings on the matter?"

"I don't know what you're talking about," Malcolm replied. It was evident in his eyes that he did know and was amused by their efforts to obtain information.

"You can cut the shit, bro. You've been identified and we know. You know we know, too. We'll have your big buddy in here soon."

"You want to tell us about the guy you're working for... Billy Joe?" Alan interjected.

Malcolm's eyes widened. He had not thought that the police knew anything about Billy Joe. "I see you are not unfamiliar with the name."

"You'll be finding out everything you want to know soon enough and there ain't a goddamn thing you can do about it." Malcolm laughed and then winced in pain. "Motherfucker," he hissed through his teeth. "That faggot son-of-a-bitch is going to pay for this."

Alan smiled, "Looks like you would probably be better advised to stay away from that 'faggot son-of-a-bitch.' But you won't be seeing him again. You'll be going back to California and the little green room with the needle."

"Fuck you. You'll be dead long before I am."

"What's that supposed to mean?" Alan asked, but Malcolm did not respond. He just lay there with a crooked smile full of broken teeth.

Ben brought a chair to the bed and sat down. "Have you considered that you have become a liability to your former employer? You're low man on the scrotum pole now," he said.

Suddenly all of the arrogance and bravado drained from Malcolm's face. It was clear that he had not yet considered this possibility. "You don't know shit. You think you know some things but you don't know shit. All you've got is a name but you don't know who he is. You don't know where he is and you definitely don't know what he is. I'm looking at a dead man, Douglas. I feel like I ought to be waving good-bye or something."

"Doesn't look like you'll be doing much waving or jerking off for a while, my man," Ben said, followed by an abrasive chortle. "In fact, from what we hear, you may never jerk off again." When he said this his eyes were dead serious.

"What are you talking about?" Malcolm stared at Ben.

"The doctor didn't tell you?" Ben looked alarmed.

"What is this bullshit!?" Malcolm exclaimed, annoyance and concern warred with the pain in his face. His crying out had set off the damaged nerve endings in his ribs.

"You've suffered major damage in the groin area. The doctor said it would be a miracle if your dick ever worked again. A lot of little girls will sleep better knowing that. Anyway, the doctor says you're the worst case he's ever seen."

"You're lying!" Malcolm screamed. His face contorted with pain. There was real fear in his eyes now.

Ben shrugged and got up from the chair. "Doesn't matter if you believe me or not, doesn't change the circumstances. Tissue in the testicles often cannot repair itself after that kind of trauma. Best case scenario, you'll have a lot of pain and never get another hard-on, worst case, gangrene sets in and it all has to come off."

"Fuck you! Fuck you! You're lying!" Malcolm was in agony but too enraged to control himself.

"I almost wish we were." Ben added. "No matter what a low life you are, it's still a terrible thing to happen to anyone. I saw it happen in 'Nam. The guy went crazy afterwards. I imagine life's going to be a bitch for you in the joint, no pun intended."

Malcolm's eyes were darting back and forth between the two, looking for some sign that this was all a joke. Alan figured there wouldn't be a better time.

"Oh yeah, we know where your buddies are. We'll be paying them a major visit up there at that Olinda house, the one with the electric gate." *Bingo!* No question about it, his alarmed expression immediately confirmed their suspicions. Malcolm wasn't much of a poker player. "Thanks," Alan concluded. "Let's go Ben."

They left the room with a string of *"Motherfuckers!"* following them out.

"Absolutely nobody goes into that room until you hear from me," Ben said to the guard. "And that includes phone access."

"Billy Joe doesn't need a phone," Alan said as they hurried down the hall. Adrenaline coursed through him. He felt the terrible urgency of the pursuit. Somehow, he believed that if he could get to the house in time, he could head off whatever terrible activity had been planned for him and those that he loved.

His recent moments had been difficult. He was changing. Senses that he didn't know he possessed were sending him information that often conflicted with the information he received from his physical senses. His mental and emotional bodies had become a mystery. He saw and felt things that had not previously existed for him. This did not make the act of living easier because of the new adjustments that constantly needed to be made. Everything felt perilous. He was unsure of the certain course.

Ming had said he would help him. That thought continually came to mind as he struggled with his resistance. It felt as if a herd of horses were thundering deep inside of him, galloping up from some subterranean kingdom, bearing riders who were each another unknown part of his being and it thrilled and alarmed him at the same time. Ming must be helping him, because he never could have endured these transformations so quietly alone. He'd never before wanted so much to run and hide at the same time as he was compelled to pursue things to the end.

"I knew there was something fishy about the timing of that call this morning," Ben said. "I hope we're not too late. We'll have to start looking all over again. Goddammit!" He hit the steering wheel with his fist.

Alan just nodded, his attention on the road and the possibilities ahead. With the help of the siren they were making good time on the Hana Highway. Ben picked up the radio and requested back up and a crime analysis van at the location.

"Let's hope we're in time," Ben said, "I think we've been had. If so, you can be sure that I will ignore every order that comes through at any time that I judge to be questionable."

"Ditto." Alan agreed.

After they arrived it took five minutes to defeat the lock. They had made several attempts at contact via the intercom without any response. Alan had a blank search warrant in his pocket, signed by a friendly judge and courtesy of Aaron Wilson, who had previously foreseen the need. Two patrol cars had followed them. Ben placed an officer at the entrance and three others accompanied them up the driveway.

They fanned out as they approached the house, guns drawn, eyes searching the shadows for movement. Alan slipped under the front side window. He looked in, seeing nothing but shadowy outlines. The light was on over the garage and the glare it threw made further recognition impossible. He silently signaled Ben to go.

Ben leaped quickly up the front steps and crouched with his back against the wall, his right hand on the doorknob. He turned it and the door swung silently inward. From a crouch, Ben reached his hand inside the doorway. The light went on. There was no one home

Alan had already sensed the emptiness as he followed Ben into the house. Most of the house had been unlived in except for a few rooms. The living room had been trashed and was cluttered with wreckage and rubbish. The kitchen was even worse. Two fifty-gallon garbage containers were overflowing with beer cans, fast food packaging and other trash, seasoned with ashes and hundreds of cigarette butts. There were overflowing ashtrays and a number of cigarettes had been put out on the table and the floor. Dishes were piled in the sink along with the congealed matter of uneaten food. There was a rank feral smell in the air. There was also another smell on the air that spoke to Alan of torment, death and unbridled evil.

Pornographic magazines were scattered on the floor and there was a large mirror placed on the backs of two chairs that had white powder smudges across its surface.

"Looks like Peruvian Marching Powder," Ben said. He turned to one of the officers and said, "See if the crime scene unit is here yet and send them up."

They walked carefully through the rest of the house. In one adjacent room there was a mattress against the wall. The mattress was covered with dark stains and small chunks of matter that were covered with flies and ants. Alan staggered backward as his mind reeled from the images of violence that had taken place there.

"Alan, are you all right?" Ben grabbed his elbow to steady him, but Alan went down on one knee, his hands holding his head. Then he got back to his feet and left the room as quickly as he could manage. Ben was right behind him. "What's happening Alan?"

Alan gasped, "I saw it all, too quickly. I saw what they did in there." Alan sat down, took several deep breaths and shook his head, hoping to free it of the high-speed onslaught of images he'd just encountered. "I'll be all right now." He slowly returned to his feet and they continued the search. Nothing remarkable surfaced. Someone had slept in a couple of rooms, which now looked like cheap motel rooms without maid service. It was the kitchen all over again. Alan felt terrible energies swirling around him, but at his center he was calm. Still, he wanted to be out of the house. "Let's check out the garage, Ben."

They set out across the driveway toward the garage with the two patrolmen. Suddenly Alan stopped and put out his hand. "What? What?" he exclaimed.

"Alan?" Ben said, looking at his friend with concern.

Alan stared unseeing into the space in front of him. Then his eyes focused and he cried out, "Run!" He grabbed Ben's arm and pulled at him. The officers were already in flight. They were some fifty feet from the house when there was an enormous explosion. The force of it slammed them into the earth. The blast shattered all of the facing windows in the house and some large object took out a portion of the wall as the garage disintegrated. Wood and glass rained down on them.

Alan woke up to a hand shaking his shoulder. He couldn't hear. There was a huge roar in his head. He rolled over on to his back and looked up into the face of one of the uniformed officers. The man's mouth was moving but Alan couldn't hear him. He wriggled his fingers and toes. He could feel everything. He pointed to his ear and said, "I can't hear anything."

Then he remembered, "Ben!" he shouted and struggled to his feet. Ben had been right beside him, but he was not there now. The policeman tried to pull Alan back down, but Alan brushed him off and went running about, looking in all directions. He found Ben laying face up, motionless, a dozen yards away. Quickly he felt for a pulse at the carotid artery. It was there. Not as strong as Alan thought it should be but there was a pulse. He rubbed his cheeks, then reached down for a wrist, which he alternatively kneaded and slapped. There was no response.

"Get an ambulance!" he cried.

"On its way, Sir," said the officer who had found him.

Alan heard a portion of this reply. His hearing was slowly returning but felt like he had been in the bell tower at Notre Dame. Flaming wreckage was everywhere around him. Parts of the main house were burning and officers were using the garden hose on it, and very little remained of the garage. He thought he could hear sirens in the distance, but that could have been another aftereffect of the explosion. He tore off part of his shirt and soaked it in water, then wiped at Ben's face with it.

"Ben, Ben," he said softly. "Wake up, buddy." This is how the medical technicians found him. Gently they pulled him aside and loaded Ben on to the stretcher. He watched the motionless form of his friend as the gurney was transferred into the ambulance. Then he got to his feet and walked toward the house. He was sitting on the porch when one of the officers came and told him what they had learned about Ben's condition. He had a slashing cut above his right temple. There was no word on a prognosis.

Alan had brushed away the attentions of the medics. He knew he was okay, except for a terrible gloom that now surrounded his thoughts. The other officers and crime scene personnel, attuned to his state, left him alone. He'd been sitting there for some time when one of the officers told him that Captain Rusk was on his way. Then he thought of Whip and Christienne. Where had he been? There was nothing more he could do here. He walked down to the car. At the gate an officer stopped him. "How are you doing Sir?"

"I'm fine," Alan looked at his nametag. "Officer Nobu, would you do me a favor?"

"What is it?"

"Tell Captain Rusk that I went home."

"That's it?"

"That's it." Alan walked away towards the car.

Fifteen minutes after the detectives had left, Malcolm was waiting in dreadful anticipation of any information he might get about his condition. He was sure they had been fucking with him. Then again he wasn't sure and he couldn't ring for the nurse because he couldn't reach the button. He'd called out once, but the cop outside the door had told him to "shut the fuck up." He would have yelled out a lot more at that point, knowing how much it would have upset the prick, but it also hurt Malcolm a great deal to make any degree of noise. The painkillers only worked if he lay still.

A gray mist began to form at the window side of the room. Malcolm didn't see it until it was six feet high and three feet across. He hadn't been paying attention to much of anything outside the arena of his thoughts. When he did see it, it paralyzed him with fear.

"What?" he croaked.

Two eyes appeared in the fog, gleaming like red rubies, and out of the fog came a voice. "Malcolm, my son, you've done well."

Malcolm's eyes were wide with fear. "Billy Joe?" he asked.

"The very same," said the voice. It moved closer to the bed. Some of it dappled over the foot of the bed.

"What's happening?" Malcolm asked. His heart was filled with dread. *Why would Billy Joe be here? Billy Joe showing up could not be good news, could it…? Unless he was here to help him escape, maybe he had come to take him away.* Malcolm held to that thought.

"I've come to take you away," Billy Joe purred. "What kind of a master would

I be if I left you in the hands of the infidels? Could anyone ever trust me if I abandoned my associates?"

Relief momentarily washed over Malcolm but he was still feeling uneasy. *How did Billy Joe propose to take him out of here? Was he going to disappear into the fog and reappear somewhere else?*

"Very close to the truth," Billy Joe said, answering Malcolm's thoughts. The fog was now washing forward across the bed until its edges lapped over Malcolm's chest.

Malcolm was becoming frightened again. "What's going to happen, Billy Joe? I did the best I could." The fear made his voice quaver.

"There's no question of that, Malcolm. And I need you to serve me yet again, in an entirely different way. This will be the last thing I need from you. After this, you can just hang out and wait for me."

The fog was now covering half of Malcolm's face. His face was white with dread and apprehension. "What do you need me for?" he asked.

"I need you to be evidence."

"Evidence, evidence for what? Where am I going to wait for you?" Malcolm's cry was muffled as the fog obscured his features.

"Well Malcolm that's not really anything you have to be concerned with anymore. As to the last question..." Billy Joe paused and Malcolm's body began to buck up and down. "Why, Hell of course."

There was a crunching sound, followed by one that sounded like a straw drawing at the last liquid in a cup and then Malcolm's body began flopping and jerking on the bed. It took almost a minute for the convulsive actions to diminish and stop. When his body finally lay still, the fog rose up toward the ceiling and disappeared into the light fixture.

The black Mercedes turned into the driveway of 154 Kokomo Road in Haiku. It rumbled over a wooden bridge that spanned a dry creek bed and wound up through a series of turns to the large cane house that sat in a copse of eucalyptus and pine trees. Billy Joe and Kimo emerged from the car and walked into the house.

Balfire was sitting in an armchair eating a sandwich. He looked up as they came in. "Where's Malcolm?" He asked.

"Malcolm had an accident," Billy Joe replied. "Kimo here is going to be taking his place."

Balfire stared at the squat hulking weight lifter. "What happened to Malcolm?" His eyes filled with curiosity. It hadn't been part of Balfire's plans that anything was ever going to happen to Malcolm. *Malcolm happened to other people, not the other way around.*

"Balfire, you're not the sort of man to whom details would be of any value. Malcolm is gone, you will not be seeing him again. I have a more pressing matter to discuss with you."

"But where's the baby? You were going to bring a baby." Balfire was getting excited now.

"We're going to have to forget about the baby now," Billy Joe replied. There was a growing sense of menace in his voice.

"But the display won't be complete!" Balfire looked crestfallen.

Billy Joe's eyes narrowed. "Shut the fuck up, Balfire. Right now, I'm a little more concerned with what happened at the house. You were supposed to blow the garage while they were coming up to the house."

"I didn't see them until they were inside. Then I had to make sure it was them. Then I had to wait for them to come out. Then I set it off." Balfire was defensive now, not understanding why Billy Joe was mad.

Billy Joe pulled a chair away from the dining table and sat down a foot away from Balfire. He brought his left foot up and placed the ankle on his right knee and leaned forward. Billy Joe's ears fascinated Balfire. The tops came to a point. They looked like the ears on a Doberman that one of Balfire's biker buddies used to own.

Billy Joe's right palm flashed out too fast for the eye to register and caught Balfire across the cheek.

"Ow! What did you do that for?" Balfire's hand came to his face, shock and confusion in his features.

"I didn't hire you to be an independent consultant, asshole!" Billy Joe had a wide deep grin on his face, a sure indication to Balfire that he was very angry. His eyes were burning and it was painful for Balfire to look at them but he could not turn away. "What happened? You very nearly wasted Douglas. That would have defeated the entire purpose of everything that I have set out to do. Now I have just one question for you. Why?" Billy Joe probed Balfire's mind. *There was nothing there.* Yet, once again, he could sense another hand at work.

"It just seemed like I should do it then. I got confused? I'm sorry!"

Billy Joe shook his head. "It doesn't work like that." He got to his feet and walked across the room to the window. Balfire set his sandwich down beside the chair. His appetite was gone.

Billy Joe could not understand why someone who was protecting Douglas would attempt to kill him. There was more confusion than he wanted. He pulled a thin glass vial from his jacket pocket. Unstopping it, he quickly drank the contents, and all hesitation and concern instantly left his mind. *Nothing was changed. It was testimony in itself that Douglas was okay and now his partner was in the hospital. They were gone from the old house and set up in the new. Everything else was where it was supposed to be except the baby. The baby didn't matter.*

Much as mystics used fasting and prayer to achieve higher states of consciousness, Billy Joe needed his elixirs to assist in communion with the infernal energies. All by himself, he was not complete. He needed contact with the entities, whose powers made Billy Joe more than human. There were powers that he possessed, and most of the time they were enough to gain him whatever he wanted or required. But for the most part, he was, like all of his predecessors and contemporaries, no more than a channel for the servants of the dark side. When he needed certain things done, he had to invoke the one whose abilities made it possible.

It was this that confused the authorities when they had finally arrested Charlie Manson. To them, he was no more than a small-time felon. They did not understand where he got the power to manipulate the minds of others, to compel them to perform such horrendous acts. The fact was that Manson had been only the medium. The evil forces that had used him abandoned him when they had accomplished their goals, which had a lot more to do with the people who were killed than it had to do with Charlie Manson. Of course, Billy Joe was much further along the road than Charlie.

This particular elixir was a powerful catalyst for Billy Joe. It served several purposes. It opened the door immediately to the realms below and provided a bridge. It gave him a sense of exhilaration and control that made it possible for him to direct the raw and savage forces he invoked. It also drew in protective beings that fed on the energies that came off of him when he was suffused with it, as it had served others before him for thousands of years. Just to drink it was to be damned. There was nowhere you could buy it, but it could be made if you had the knowledge and the means. If you looked hard enough, these could be discovered. In most cases, it soon caused a horrible insanity followed by death and terrible swift descent into darkness. In some few cases, it made you stronger. So it was with Billy Joe.

Right now he had to diffuse some part of his anger, so he turned to Balfire with a predatory gleam in his eye. "By some unbelievable luck, you managed to injure his partner and not him. Because of this, I am not going to turn your mind into JELL-O Pudding and let you dispense blowjobs in the medical ward of the joint for the rest of your days. I also need your help in a certain critical area. But if you fail to heed a single directive..."

"What's a directive?" Balfire interrupted. He was frightened that he might fuck up if he did not understand everything that Billy Joe was saying.

"An order, Pinhead!" he roared. "And if you fail to follow my orders at any time in the future, if you fail to follow my instructions to the letter, you will spend eternity screaming in Hell. Is that clear?" While he had been delivering his statement, Billy Joe had altered his form so that in Balfire's mind he appeared with the body of a tarantula and the head of a polar bear. This was apparently the sum of all his fears. Balfire sat quaking in his chair. Too late, Billy Joe realized the effect this image would have on Balfire's nervous system and stopped his projections. Balfire was sent to the kitchen for something to swab out the chair and then to the bathroom to clean himself.

"It wasn't my fault," he was whimpering as he scrubbed the chair.

Billy Joe grinned and lit a cigarette. "That doesn't make any difference does it?"

Chapter Twenty-Seven

Billy Joe walked out on the rear deck and stared up at the growing moon. The moon had been a focus of power for dark rites through the ages, not that the moon itself was evil. But there were aspects of the moon that could be used to great advantage by those who sought to fulfill the ends of the personal will.

In a few days he would again prepare for the ritual that had been denied him decades ago. Soon he would be transformed. He would effectively no longer be a man at all but something else. Certain human characteristics would remain. There would remain the human appearance, for when it was needed. There would be much added though, much that existed beyond the range of ordinary human understanding. He felt a tingling over his body. The anticipation was growing. The excitement was growing. *Soon, very soon now.*

He thought again of the one who guarded Douglas. He had been unable so far to learn anything about him. It was perplexing. Billy Joe was certain that it would not affect the outcome, but it did trouble him that such a shield was in effect. He remembered suddenly the girl in Arizona. She had seen him and she had gotten away. *How had that happened?* She had no connection to Douglas. Certain events made no sense. They weren't supposed to happen and yet they did. In the main, everything had worked perfectly. *But the girl was still out there somewhere.* She would not be seeing her mother again.

All of the killings had been necessary. Billy Joe never left any footprints to be followed. He had identities that he preferred to keep safe. It hadn't seemed important until Douglas had disappeared from New York. That had changed everything. Right in the midst of his depression and alcoholic despair, Douglas had walked away. He'd picked up and gone, just missing the descent of an elaborate trap, before the final piece had fallen into place. He had been forced to begin again from his Los Angeles base. This had made the murders all the more necessary.

Billy Joe had spent a great deal of time and energy in preparation for the *coup de grâce*, only to discover that Douglas was missing. Because of the nature of the plan, Douglas had to be present for the plan to work. He could have worked it differently, but it never occurred to him that Douglas wouldn't be there. Douglas had been so far gone…

He'd been out of town when Douglas had gotten hurt. When he had returned, Douglas was home again. When Billy Joe last checked in on him, his condition was just as it had been before he left town. But it hadn't been the same. It had only looked that way. Someone had interposed reruns in the place of Douglas's actual condition. *Reruns!* How was he to know? The behavior patterns of an alcoholic don't look that different from day-to-day, only by degree.

Until this happened, Billy Joe had experienced no difficulty tracking Douglas's every movement, reading his inmost thoughts. He had been able to enjoy at his leisure the pain, the remorse and the suicidal despair. Then, on the day of reckoning, with everything set perfectly in place, Douglas was gone. He had scanned him in his apartment. but when the phone rang Douglas never picked it up. Billy Joe had watched, not comprehending, until it had dawned on him that the phone was not ringing in the scene that he was watching. He had gone ballistic, especially when the operator came on the line to tell him the number was disconnected. The phone call was supposed to summon Douglas to an emergency that involved Whip. The voice would have sounded exactly like Whip's. He would have been directed to the scene of a massacre at a nearby townhouse. There, drunk and disoriented, he would have been found, passed out with the murder weapon, an axe in his hand, blood on his clothes, perfectly framed. Then there would have been the trial, then transfer to the maximum-security ward at a state facility. There his real torments were scheduled to begin. What Billy Joe had planned for Douglas made all other acts of revenge seem like kindnesses by comparison.

Who was behind this interference? There had been no indication of a new equation entering the mix. Still, Billy Joe had moved on into his carefully crafted Los Angeles identity of "Mr. Poole." Then he eliminated Bettencourt and Morales, through whom he had constructed his very successful drug business. It was mere coincidence that they were changing their supplier. Maybe it had been unnecessary, maybe not. *What did it matter?* Very soon his power would be logarithmically increased. Whatever answers he needed, he could get from Douglas after he stripped him bare, after he did an autopsy on his soul. Every cell in Douglas's body would scream to give up whatever secrets were concealed. Douglas would suffer in a Promethean manner.

Billy Joe had spent a great deal of time watching a parade of horrors. When he had first mastered the secret of accessing the Akashic Records, he had spent months there. He'd watched the day-to-day operation of the Soviet and Cambodian prison camps, the antics of Nero and Domitian, Valens and Valentinus and the pirates of the Barbary Coast. He had enjoyed the exotic cruelties of the Chinese, the Japanese and the Koreans, as they visited them upon each other. He was especially fond of the Turks. He had watched Vlad the Impaler at work, listening to the screams of thousands in their slow, agonizing progression toward death. He'd separated their individual cries from the many and then woven them together like a concert piece for his listening enjoyment. He'd been with Gilles de Rais and he knew the true identity of Jack the Ripper. He traveled with Carl Panzram on his dark journey to the gallows. He watched the execution and had agreed with Panzram's final words, "I wish all mankind had one neck so I could choke it!"

He had seen other terrors too. He had looked into alien landscapes that had never known a human presence. He had looked into the astral hells where the prisoners were given over to the creations of their own imagination. Because he knew the location of every bad thing inside himself, and every good thing too, which he had systematically killed upon discovery, he knew their location in others. He could immediately find the thing that anyone most feared. It was one of his greatest powers that he could assume the shape or manifest the thing they most feared before their eyes. There was a percentage of the world over which he had no power, but it was very small. Anyone who sought to fight him on his own terms always lost.

The only way to counteract him was to deny him. But then, who, when faced with the presence of the thing they most feared, would have enough reason or strength remaining to deny the substance of what they saw? Shadows occurred when something blocked the passage of light. All mortals blocked the passage of light through them to a certain degree, therefore all created a shadow land through which Billy Joe could approach and, through his skillful application of promises and threats, would eventually seduce them into his power.

It was for the protection of humanity from such as Billy Joe that the Guardian Angel was created. But who believed in him today? And if you called upon the agent of deity and had not the faith or grace to compel his presence, then you were doubly damned to do the will of Billy Joe.

Oh, he had been hindered and denied at times in the past. He had in lifetimes previous been soundly thrashed and driven back to his dark hole to lick his wounds. But he was never deterred from his course and that alone always made him stronger. Each time he had learned a greater tactic for future use. He became so skilled at picking his prey that there was seldom any resistance. He was only vulnerable when he was driven by revenge. This passion clouded his judgment more than any other and that is what Billy Joe was all about, settling scores. And of everyone that he would be revenged upon, there was no one like

Alan Douglas. Douglas had stopped him just short of his greatest triumph. His execution had driven the formula of the ritual from his mind. He'd had to pay a terrible price to get it back. Douglas would pay all the more in exchange.

Is it the acts of others that lead us eventually to destruction? *Are we herded into trucks to be driven to Samarra at dawn?* We walk every step of the way to the place where that which we search for resides. If a man wants to go to Kansas City, he proceeds in a certain direction, along certain routes that will eventually take him there. If he is uncertain of the way, there are maps. If he is in a hurry, there are modes of transportation that will more quickly bring him there. He might take a train. He might take a plane. Or he can walk, but he will get there just the same. In the same manner a man can arrive in Los Angeles or Beirut, Bangkok or Timbuktu. You arrive at the place you have set out for. You should not be surprised when you get there. Such is the case with more esoteric destinations. *The intention of one's heart is one's destiny. One carves out every step of one's life with the heart's secret fire in the direction of one's intention.* Some places are reached only with the greatest difficulty. Some places are easy to reach. Billy Joe saw what he wanted to see. He did not care to see anything else.

He reached out into Kimo's mind and created for him a personality that would serve and entertain him. Since he had stopped using him as a channel for his thoughts he had been operating from simple motor controls. He had him in "safe mode" with a minimum of drivers loaded. It was time to program him into something else and certainly someone more entertaining than Kimo had been. Billy Joe didn't give a shit about the Hawaiian culture and he certainly didn't want to hear about it. He outlined the parameters of the new being and then invested it with memories gleaned from the storehouse of souls that he had imprisoned. A specific personality from the past was needed for the coming work and it would be pleasant to be reminded again of victims long dead by his hand. He didn't get elaborate. He wouldn't need him that long.

In the kitchen, the mind of a man once known as Kimo Nakamura and later as "The Dragonsmouth" woke up to find himself eating a sandwich. The transition was so seamless that he didn't remember the little bump that had just passed. He remembered himself as the collection of thoughts, emotions and memories that Billy Joe had just returned to him. He turned to Balfire and said, "Hi, I'm Joe."

Balfire regarded him with raised eyebrows. His surprise passed quickly. The unusual was the usual around Billy Joe. "I'm Balfire," he said. "You like baseball?"

"I've been a fan all my life. Always ready to watch a game."

"Way to go!" Balfire said with real enthusiasm. Even Billy Joe did something nice now and then, though it was assuredly by accident when it happened.

Billy Joe walked into the kitchen and pulled a bottle of Armagnac from a shelf along with a snifter and took it into the living room. Setting it on the table he extracted a bottle of cocaine. He inserted a silver tube into it and took two prodigious snorts. Then he set the bottle on the table and told Balfire to help himself. Billy Joe was feeling expansive. His plans were all very rapidly coming to fruition.

Alan made his way slowly up the walk to his house. Nearly there, his foot found the loose flagstone and it wobbled under his feet, nearly pitching him down the slope into the gully. His disciplined instincts caught him as he spun away, avoiding mishap. "Shit!" he cried out and then laughed. "I've got to get that fixed." *If only everything would conclude so well,* he thought. He was just wondering why the concrete company had yet to arrive, two weeks overdue, when the door opened and Whip stepped on to the deck.

As Alan came closer, Whip saw the state of his clothes and the marks on his face. "Alan, what happened?" he asked.

"Let me get inside and we'll talk."

Whip swallowed any further questions he might have had and held the door open for Alan. Christienne came up behind him and gave a sharp intake of breath. Wordlessly she took him by the arm and led him into the living room. By the time he was seated, Whip had returned with a cold fruit soda that he placed in Alan's hand. Alan took a long swallow of the liquid and then blew air through pursed lips.

"I've had a bad day," he said with a grin. "Ben's day was even worse." He held up his hand as they clamored for an explanation. "Ben's going to be fine, they're keeping him overnight just in case." Alan described everything that had happened since they parted at the hospital, including the death of Malcolm, which Alan had heard about when he last checked in on Ben.

Whip asked, "You want something more to drink or eat?"

Alan shook his head. "I'm too tired."

"I don't know what it is," Whip looked up at Alan, "But whenever I'm in a dangerous situation, I have this overwhelming urge to do stupid shit and laugh like a maniac."

"It's how people process stress, Whip. I hate to be a party pooper, but I'm going to secure the place and get some sleep. We'll talk in the morning." Alan wandered around the house locking up and then disappeared into his bedroom. He made a brief call to the hospital to check on Ben again and was told that he was sleeping peacefully.

He put on his pajamas and went into the bathroom to brush his teeth. When he saw the condition of his face, it startled him. There were scratches and smudges everywhere and a long gash on the side of his neck that had already begun to scab over. No wonder they had wanted to treat him at the hospital. He washed up and then poured peroxide on the cut, wincing at the burn. After he was done, he checked his reflection. Now he no longer looked like one of the winos he used to see bouncing off building walls and parked cars. Thank God he hadn't become one. He climbed gingerly into bed and lay back, closing his eyes.

Very slowly he let his mind go, gently pushing aside every image that leapt forth to dominate his thoughts. Tonight there were many. He could see clearly the scenes of the day. These too had to be gently pushed aside. *Gentle was the only way.* If you fought or struggled against mental images, they became stronger. When his breathing had become deep and rhythmic, he let the visualization flow forth into his mind. He'd been using it for years and it had become easy and like an old friend to him. A golden Star of David came forth.

In its center was a white cross, much brighter than the outline of the star. There were flashes of rose overtones in the light that streamed from the cross. Finally blood red roses began to bloom on the horizontal bar, and underneath and around them sprouted emerald leaves. Alan could see crystalline dew beading on the rose petals and leaves. As he breathed in, he felt himself inhaling the wisdom and intelligence of the divine light. As he breathed out, he filled the manifest world with love. He stayed with this for some time and then dissolved the image. He then imagined his mind merging with the great brotherhood of invisible teachers who labored on the inner planes for the enlightenment of the world.

Ming appeared before him. His face was radiant with an aura of golden light. He was seated cross-legged in the air and dressed in a deep burgundy robe. "Greetings, Alan."

"Hello, Ming. I was wondering when I would see you again."

"I am always around you, Alan, especially now. I gave you that meditation years ago. The power of your thought does not yet vibrate at a level high enough for you to perceive my presence most of the time. I've come to share some things with you tonight. You're going to need to be at your best from here on out."

Alan laughed. It was hard not to in the presence of Ming. He felt that danger and the relative world in which it lived had no meaning, no power. *Nothing besides this moment could ever be real.* "It's getting to zero hour?"

"Yes, Alan. The time is soon at hand. I first want to assure you that no real and lasting harm will come to Whip and Christienne. It is important that you know that and that you believe it, no matter what you may think or be told. Do you understand?" Ming's face had grown serious as he said this and Alan felt an ephemeral disquietude pass through him.

"I think so," he replied. "You mean to say that I may become separated from them and not know where they are, not know what is happening to them and be unable to reach them?"

"Exactly, you must guard your mind and heart against the power of lies. The intrinsic power of a lie is that one might, because of superficial appearances, become inclined to believe in it. This belief is the power upon which lies feed. Nothing can really harm you or your loved ones. Nothing can harm you either, but it is possible to be drawn outside of the circle of protection. The mouse would be safe if he stayed in his hiding place, but the awesome fear of the cat causes him to dash for the safety of a location he cannot find. He is already there. Two things can make you act like this mouse, belief in what is not real, and fear — one generates the other. Love displaces them both. Personal power is useless to you in this situation. In the relative world, Billy Joe is so very much stronger.

"You cannot rely on personal power. It is a trick of the mind that imagines itself a separate entity. To believe that you are a separate entity is to put yourself in harm's way. Sadly, Alan, even when you want to, with all of your heart, to have faith in ideas such as the ones I have just presented, it is not always possible. Even though you believe them in the day-to-day, it is another thing to believe when there is not a single reference point to guide you, another thing entirely to believe in them when they are truly challenged. Therefore," and as he said this, Ming grew in size, becoming much brighter and warmer. The love Alan had felt upon first seeing him increased yet again. "You must not think tonight, you must absorb, swallow whole and let it become part of your very nature. Let it arrive without having to be filtered and judged for its efficacy by your surface mind. You need to fill your tank, Alan. You are in the jungle being tracked by a tiger and you are out of petrol."

Alan saw a flood of images pour across his mind screen. Many critical moments of this and other lives were outlined for him. Suddenly he saw what Ming meant. He saw himself react instinctively and correctly toward the situation's resolution. He saw himself hesitate, weigh relative values or wrestle with doubt or fear and be lost. He saw that the only way to be with divinity, to be with anything that would work for anyone was to "be there all the way." Michael Jordan's face appeared for an instant before him. The faces of many others followed, from all races and sexes. A lot of them Alan recognized from history. In each case, he saw them when they were facing the most difficult moments of their lives. These were not the same moments that history would call their most difficult, but they were the moments that *they* would have called their most difficult. Alan was in awe as he felt himself being changed. He had no idea of what was right or wrong any longer and no idea of who he was at all.

He felt his small and insignificant self caught up in a torrent so great that it seemed he might disappear entirely. He let himself go upon that ocean of immeasurable consciousness, gave himself up for the dissolution and then found that, somehow, he still remained.

"You see it, don't you, Alan? This is one of the greatest of mysteries, you give yourself away, yet you still remain."

"I accept what you say," Alan replied, "If you say it is so, Ming, it must be so."

"Remember that you must not *contend* with Billy Joe. The chance is far too desperate. Accepting the confrontation, he would destroy you, or worse, he would own you. If he destroyed you, you would be beyond his power to injure you further but if he *owned* you, he could keep you in torment for ages. He could put you away like some predator does its meat and then come back for you later, and I could do nothing to aid because you had accepted the conflict.

"Listen further, swallow these truths whole. You will know how to apply them in your hour of need. *This world is a world of darkness.* The light that lights it is a false light. It too is darkness. There are many powers in the darkness and their theatre of operation is the human mind. It is here that the pentagram is drawn and whether a man is upside down or right side up determines how the pentagram is displayed. The mortal consciousness is trapped in the darkness because it cannot experience the light without ceasing to be what it is, without walking away from everything that is familiar into a land that it does not know. It is this fear of change that keeps the human consciousness in bondage to the illusion of death. Here again, lies and fear.

"The divine is perpetual, unending and comprehensible only to itself, none other. It is the power of this self-knowing that causes everything, maintains everything, and reabsorbs everything back into itself. Everything is composed of divine being. In every living thing, there is that animating principle and in every human being there is something more. *Humanity is the Crown of Creation.* The light in us is divine but, because the human mind is given over to darkness, it is only aware of the false light in the darkness. This is what makes it possible to view the objects and images of this world. The human personality has faith in the dark light, not in the true light. Because they do not have faith in the true light, how can they call upon it for aid? Faith in the true light confers upon you the power of the true light. This true light is divine. There is no darkness in it."

Alan looked in awe upon the majesty of Ming. He seemed so many things at once, holy man, saint and now, like a king. Alan was beyond objective thought, though he could register these things, there was no reaction in him.

"This light is in you, Alan, and your faith in it will summon it. You must become a transparency through which this light shines. *It is one light in everyone.* Billy Joe has no power before this light. If it were to touch him it would strip him naked, and all that he has created of himself by manipulation of the darkness would be undone. No matter what may come before you, Alan, no matter how circumstances may appear, believe in nothing so much as the power of this light within you to overcome every condition, every manifestation, no matter how powerful they may seem. Know the difference between substance and appearance. This is the most that you can do. The light does all else. The light is pure consciousness and pure consciousness is Wisdom and Love blended to an indistinguishable One.

"Your mind, though better trained than most, is reactive. It has its automatic patterns. At every point where the mind reacts, seeks to separate itself from the One, the only mind, you must bring it back, as you did in your meditation tonight. You must bring it back ten times, a thousand times, ten thousand times, again and again, until this becomes automatic.

"If you do this, the light will grow very quickly in you. You must remember this when Billy Joe comes for you. Billy Joe is more vulnerable than he thinks, more vulnerable than he appears. He cannot both attack and protect himself at the same time. This is a universal law that applies to us all. It is the nature of the false self to believe in the arrogance of its own powers. You cannot fight Billy Joe on his terms, but you can be the medium for the one he fears and does not expect to see." Ming stopped speaking at this point and gazed at Alan. Alan felt effervescent, as if electric champagne bubbles were bursting in every cell of his body. He felt like he was being laundered from the inside out. He ceased to see Ming's form as a separate entity, there was only pulsing light. The four dimensions he was so used to operating in were gone. All of his senses had blended into one.

When he returned to himself again, he was astonished at how little time had passed. *It was impossible! Time truly was relative.* He was vibrating with electricity. It took a tremendous effort of will not to race again into his garden as he had done the first time. There was no weariness left in him. The door opened slightly and Whip peered into the room. Seeing the light reflected in Alan's open eyes, he said, "He was here, wasn't he?"

Alan grinned like a fool. "How did you know?"

"Jesus, Alan, the whole house was humming like a generator. Christienne thought the place was undergoing a demonic invasion, but I knew the vibes were too good. I finally had to check on you. I hope you don't mind. I knocked earlier but there was no answer." Whip stood there awkwardly.

"I'm fine, Whip, you should never hesitate to check. The positive occurrences have been the rarity lately." He watched Whip shifting from one foot to the other. "No," he continued, "I can't talk about it. It's too new and if I did talk about it, I would lose it. I know you understand that."

"I do," Whip answered. "Just tell me if it was as good as it felt? Is this all going to end soon?"

Alan considered for a moment, his mind surfing back over all that he had just heard. "It was positive, Whip, very positive. As for what's coming, I don't know, maybe everything."

Whip nodded. "Sleep well, Alan."

"Good night, Whip," Alan replied.

Chapter Twenty-Eight

12:00 MIDNIGHT, PAIA, HAWAII

CarryAnn finished weighing out a quarter pound of coke and was about to seal the plastic baggie when she heard the knock on her door. "Who is it?"

"It's Grigo, baby."

"You alone?"

"Yeah," was the muffled reply from behind the door.

CarryAnn got to her feet and opened the lock. He came in and his eyes fell on the small table in front of the futon. CarryAnn closed the door behind him and locked it.

"I thought you'd have had that together a long time ago. We got to meet the dude in half an hour." Grigo was dressed in deck shoes, white duck shorts and an *aloha* shirt. His freshly washed hair fell in waves around his shoulders, perfectly framing his Mediterranean good looks. Willowy and youthful, he looked more like eighteen than twenty-eight. It was in his eyes that you could read his real age.

CarryAnn reached behind her neck and pulled out the thin dagger that hung there in the sheath at her back. She'd realized that she had to appear dangerous if she wanted to be safe alone. A near rape had taught her that Hawaii had all of the elements of anywhere else.

It had been a rough go, getting herself set up here. She'd been hit on constantly, and had to leave two places before she found this one at Grigo's house. She'd wound up hitchhiking on occasion and that had been the worst of it. She'd once run for thirty minutes through a cane field to get away from some local thugs who'd driven her there.

She first met Grigo in a surfer bar down the street. It was early in the day and she had been enjoying the street traffic that passed by the window. Grigo had brought over two drinks and sat at her table. *Here we go again*, she had thought. Then she got a look at him and her interest level grew.

Meeting Grigo had actually worked out very well for her. He was in the drug business, which she'd learned later that evening. He had a nice house, with an extra room and a car. CarryAnn had the money to buy a car, but she would have had to register it. As it worked out, Grigo got what he wanted, up to a point, and CarryAnn got what she needed. At this juncture, she didn't particularly like him, she didn't particularly trust him, but besides that everything was fine.

Now CarryAnn affected a hard exterior and she was prepared to back it up. She'd found that most aggressors were put off by an immediate and determined defense. She had stuck one of her attackers in the cane field with her knife and it was enough of a distraction to gain the advantage. CarryAnn could run very fast. A frightened CarryAnn was very, very fast. The knife was good psychology now. She scraped some coke on to the knife's edge and then licked it with her tongue.

"Some of the guys are starting to call you CarryAnn Bobbitt, with all that knife shit." Grigo had his usual predator smile on his face. CarryAnn thought it was impossible for him to look at a female without conveying the impression that he was either fucking her or about to.

"Good, that's the right impression for them to have. If they think I'm going to cut their dicks off if they touch me, I'll sleep that much better at night."

Grigo sat down on the floor across from her and ran a slender finger across the mirror, coming up with a thick swath of coke. This he rubbed on his gums. "Too bad you have to sell this shit. I've never seen or had anything like it. It would be a lot better if we could just snort it all."

"You get to snort plenty of it and you're doing well money-wise, too. You've got no complaints." CarryAnn gestured toward the coke. "This shit is starting to make me very nervous. I can't relax with it around me. I'm always thinking that someone is planning to rip me off and they probably are. I'm worried about the police too, with you pulling every teenybopper you meet out to the car for some coke and a blowjob. I'm doing too much of it and it's fucking up my head. I'll be glad when it's gone. If we can do another sale like this one, it will be." CarryAnn had never told Grigo how much she had. She hadn't let him know where she kept it either. She had no doubt he'd been in her room while she was gone. He wouldn't find it here.

Grigo rubbed some more coke on his lips and let his eyes roam over CarryAnn's body. Her breasts strained against the brief halter-top and the tight denims fit her like a second skin. He thought about their one night together. *It hadn't been enough.* He didn't think he could get enough of her. "You want to get together later and have some fun?"

"I had sex with you once, Grigo."

"Actually, it was four times," he interrupted, getting the idea of his prowess across.

"One night then, and I don't want to do it again. No offense, but I'm not in the mood for sex with anyone right now. I'm taking a vacation from sex. It seems like that's the only activity anyone in interested in. There's got to be more to life."

"That what you were thinking when you fucked that local boy?"

CarryAnn's face flushed and her eyes narrowed as she turned her gaze toward Grigo. "I did that to wipe the taste of you from my mouth, after you told me a lot of beautiful lies and then bummed my coke so you could go fuck some useless brain dead piece of euro-trash the very next day. And when I walked in on you, you had the nerve to ask me to join you!"

"I am a man, CarryAnn," Grigo answered, all suave insolence and projected magnetism, still hopeful and undeterred.

"As in, *real men don't care*?" CarryAnn, regardless of what she told herself, was hurt by what Grigo had done. She had needed someone to sing in her ear, and Grigo had. She hadn't known at the time that the song was for everyone.

"CarryAnn, Mother Nature has been very generous to you, very generous. The reason she did that is as old as time. If she hadn't wanted everyone to want to fuck you, she would not have built you into a one hundred percent pure fucking machine."

CarryAnn laughed in spite of herself. "Grigo, if I didn't already know that you are full of shit, that you're out for yourself and no one else and that you will use anyone, anywhere, any place, I might possibly find you charming."

Grigo shrugged, "Hey, at least you know what you're getting into."

Carry Ann snorted two lines and tossed Grigo the tooter. "Do I, Grigo? You say you know this guy. I get really bad vibes from him. If I didn't want to get rid of the coke, this would not be happening." She wasn't letting anyone know how much she had stashed. As soon as this coke was gone, she was moving to her own place and a different class of friends.

Grigo snorted up his lines. "Look, this guy has been around here for two years that I know of. If he were a cop, he'd have busted me a long time ago. I've sold him at least five pounds of pot in the last five months."

"And the others?"

"What others?"

"Grigo, you cannot be that stupid, so you have to be fucking with me! The guy he was with when I met him, the people he is going to be selling the coke to, and the people he will be snorting the coke with, those *other people*."

Grigo looked at her with that supercilious glance that she had come to know. He immediately followed it with the patronizing tone she received at all times. "CarryAnn…" he dragged out her name as if he was speaking to an uninformed child. "Vaughn is Tony's lover. Jesus, CarryAnn, didn't you see the way they were hanging on each other? I've seen this guy doing things that no cop would ever do."

"I hope you're right." CarryAnn got up and pulled her windbreaker from the closet and slid the baggie into a pocket. "But there is something I want to know. What makes a cop different from anybody else?" CarryAnn zipped her jacket and tossed her bag over her shoulder.

Grigo followed her out to the car, locking up the house on his way. "You sure you're a California girl?"

"California's a big state."

They entered the Maui Mall at exactly 1:15 a.m. and Grigo parked the car in the back lot by Woolworth's. Even though they were meeting on the other side, CarryAnn had insisted on this. Her bad feeling was getting worse. Several times already she had been on the verge of aborting the meeting but she desperately wanted to get rid of the coke. It was driving her crazy. She couldn't give it away. You couldn't throw it away… Well, you could, but she wasn't going to. She'd sold, traded or used up all but ten ounces after the deal tonight.

"Where's the beer, Grigo?"

He reached into the back seat and came up with a frosty bottle of Oranjeboom. "You never drink ordinary beer do you?"

CarryAnn looked at him with contempt. "American beer sucks and the commercials make me want to hunt down the people responsible and kill them, particularly Budweiser. Dockers and Budweiser must be made by the same people out of the same stuff."

Grigo looked at her in mock injury. "Hey, I wear Dockers."

CarryAnn nodded, "Uh-huh."

He reached into his jacket, pulled out a pocket watch and popped the lid. There was no watch, only coke. "You want some?" he asked.

A few minutes later they got out of the car and walked around the mall until they were looking into the front lot. The mall had been closed for three hours but the supermarket was open all night, so there were still about fifty cars in the lot.

This was one of the things that CarryAnn had not liked. There were a lot of places that would have been safer from her point of view. Tony had argued that there was too much money involved. He was afraid of a rip-off. CarryAnn had pointed out that he and Grigo were "friends." *Who would be ripping off whom?* Tony had replied that he had no friends. CarryAnn had wondered about that too. Against her better wishes, she had finally agreed and now they stood scanning the lot, looking for the dark blue Buick Park Avenue that Tony said they would be driving.

"There it is," Grigo said, pointing to a far corner of the lot where an abandoned hardware store stood. They walked across the lot and as they reached the car, the passenger side window rolled down.

Tony's face appeared in the street lamp's glow. "Get in back," he said.

Grigo opened the door and CarryAnn slipped in. Grigo followed her and shut the door. There was a pungent aroma of marijuana in the car and this relaxed CarryAnn. Her paranoid fantasies seemed less likely with this particular smell wafting through the air.

Tony turned around. "Everything okay?"

"All systems are go," Grigo replied.

"How about you?" Tony turned his attention to CarryAnn.

CarryAnn waved a hand back and forth in front of her. "I'm fine. Let's get it over with."

"Sure," he replied. Tony had a syrupy voice that made CarryAnn's skin crawl. "Grigo told me you were getting all antsy. You should relax… everything's on the up and up. It will all be over soon, right Vaughn baby?"

"You want to do this or not?" she asked.

"Show me the coke."

"You mind showing me the money?" CarryAnn was reaching into her windbreaker as she said this. She was getting uncomfortable again but that could have been for a lot of reasons.

"Look girl, just show me the coke." Tony was smiling now. "Just hold up the baggie. It's in a baggie right? I need to make sure you have it."

CarryAnn held it up and the brilliant white of the pure cocaine was luminescent from the reflected light of the mercury vapor street lamps. "Good, good," he said. Tony reached across the car again and tapped Vaughn on the shoulder. "Okay, sweetie, go get the money so you and Daddy can go party."

CarryAnn could not believe she was sitting here. "What the fuck is going on?" she hissed.

"Look, girl," Tony was giving her the Gleem smile again. "The money's in the trunk, you could have come into this car with a gun and no coke. I've been there before, no offense. We just wanted to be safe."

"Cool out, CarryAnn." Grigo touched her on the arm. "I know this dude. Don't be so tense."

Vaughn got out of the car and went around to the back. Tony hit the trunk latch and it rose behind them. CarryAnn heard Vaughn rummaging in the trunk. Tony was leaning on the backrest, still smiling at CarryAnn, who was looking past him into the parking lot.

All at once she heard the pounding of footsteps on the asphalt and felt an icy cold wave of apprehension rising from her groin and coiling toward her heart. Both passenger doors were suddenly ripped open and the voice on her side said, "Police! Come out of the car with your hands in front of you. Now! Now!" When she didn't move, a large hand reached in and jerked her from the car, spinning her around and slamming her against the car. She could hear Grigo being rousted in the same fashion. There was now noise and lights everywhere as cars pulled up from their locations and orders were being shouted. She looked behind her and saw a burly blonde man with a beard and a handgun trained on her. Tony came around the other side of the car, still smiling. He held out a police badge and said, "Hey, sweetie, you're busted."

7:00 AM, ALAN'S HOUSE, HAIKU, HAWAII

Alan came slowly awake out of one of the most beautiful dreams of his life. He'd been dancing with a woman in a palace that had been carved out of living crystal. A sun had hovered overhead and its rays filtering through the crystal created a prismatic effect that sent rainbows of color washing over them. As is the case with dreams, he knew the woman as well as he knew himself but upon awakening he had no idea of who she was. It was only in the dream and the context of the dream that she had identity. Once he had awakened, all that remained was the sweetness of her presence. *It was haunting.* The aftertaste lingered in his mind, threatening to expose its meaning, but never doing so. He replayed what he could remember over and over again, hoping the memory would not fade, as it always did, once the conscious mind took over.

Climbing out of bed, he padded into the kitchen and made water for tea. Afterwards he went out into the garden. He stretched for a few minutes and then did the "Sun Worship" *asana.* This time, as he did it, the actual meaning of each movement became a reality in his mind. His face creased in amused wonder as he understood the cosmic integrity hidden in each position. Now he understood why he had done it for so long. It was magical. From this he segued into the "Sitting Horse." Alan felt the awesome power of unbridled nature flowing unhindered through him. All these years of practice and so many things he had not understood. *How had he come so far?* That was the marvel. Next he went into an intricate string of different forms woven from memory. For the first time, his instinctive nature was free and the results were tremendous. It was beyond any explanation but the beauty of the event. It was pure rapture. As Alan moved he felt the personalities of those great masters of the East who had been there before. *It was so simple. It was child's play.* Why had he worked so hard, used so much effort, when it never had anything to do with him? *It was there, always, doing itself perfectly. One had only to get out of the way.*

Alan fell back on the lawn, trembling, electrical firestorms moving through his body. Alan felt all of his personal complexities pouring out of him and everything was as simple as a child dancing down a country lane. He wept and laughed.

"Alan?"

Alan opened his eyes and saw Whip. He smiled at and through him, smiled at the sun behind him. "Hey, Whip." He reached out and Whip pulled him to his feet. "And?" Alan asked. His eyes glistened.

Whip looked at him and laughed. "And, I woke up and smelled the coffee."

They walked together back into the house. Neither of them spoke. What could they say? Christienne was in the kitchen making breakfast. It had rained hard the night before and the trees and flowers had drunk their fill. The air was full of scents that permeated the house. Christienne was smiling as Alan walked in and he felt as if a doorway to the heavens had opened.

"Good morning," she said, handing Alan a cup of Ceylonese tea.

"Good morning, Princess." Alan's smile was like that of a little boy.

"Are you okay, Alan?" she asked, but there was no concern in her voice. Something about the way Alan felt and looked was too good, too positive to be alarming by any measure.

"Never better," he said, taking the tea.

They sat on the deck sipping their drinks and eating fruits. Not a word was said by anyone for some time. Occasionally there was laughter and one or another of them would mumble something incomprehensible and then stop, perfectly comfortable to fall back again into the quiet.

After a long while, Alan said softly, "Thank you. Thank you both very much."

8:30 AM, 154 KOKOMO RD., HAIKU, HAWAII

Billy Joe looked out of the window of the upstairs bedroom, staring down the hill across the gulch at Alan's house. The driveway from his house to the road was clearly visible. He raised the Armagnac to his lips and then took a deep draw from his cigarette. An empty bottle of Armagnac and a mirror mounded with cocaine sat on the table behind him, clear evidence of where he had spent the night. Alcohol, like every other mind-altering substance, did not affect Billy Joe as it did other people. Instead of creating a lack of motor skills or delusional thinking, it acted like a whetstone on a knife. It merely amplified whatever else he might have taken. Great already in his mind, he became even greater. It was a bellows effect.

All intoxicants, everything that altered the mind, were food for the entities that used humanity as their cups. Except that one was a realized aspirant, it was always the same. What happened was a matter of degree. This explained the terrible things that people sometimes did to others and to themselves while the influence was upon them. Later they would awaken with a sense of dread, if they awoke at all, knowing that something terrible had occurred but not knowing what. The truth was, when it had happened, they were no longer there or in control.

For Billy Joe this was a *desired result.* He had a position in the hierarchy of evil. Certain intelligences were below him and some were in another relation to him, but they were all evil and, as evil was his basic nature, they never harmed him. They only harmed others. Those who might be manipulated by evil but did not have a reciprocating relationship with the dark powers were merely psychopaths. Intoxicants turned them into cars driven by bad drivers who might get lucky for a while. The disciplines necessary for the practice of real evil made addiction no more than a mosquito bite for the devout practitioner. *The practice of real evil was every bit as strenuous as the practice of real good.* Every time one mastered a particular realm of existence, everything within that realm fell under their control. Video and computer games were a metaphor for this.

The difference between good and evil is, and has always been, very simple. *Evil* is what is practiced out of a motivation for the separate, individualized self, at the expense of anything that opposes it. Its premise comes out of the belief that there really is a self that is separate and apart from others. The needs of that self always take precedence over the needs and wellbeing of anyone else. *Good* is practiced without thought of self, something done for the benefit of another without thought of personal gain, often without the thought that it is being practiced at all. Good is often practiced in opposition to conventional wisdom.

Billy Joe did what he did because he liked it. With Billy Joe, regret never reared its head. If it had, Billy Joe would have kicked its teeth in. For him there was no law but the law of Billy Joe, no rules but his own rules, no cause but his own cause. For him this was the natural order of things. The strong ate the weak.

He had once seen a T-shirt that read, "*New York City, Where the Weak are Killed and Eaten.*" He bought the shirt.

The key for Billy Joe was best exemplified in the famous last words of Hassan-i Sabbah, the old man of the mountain, "Nothing is True, Everything is Permitted." Billy Joe believed in a deity just as certainly as the practitioner of any religion and with an even greater degree of certainty than most. The only difference was that Billy Joe's divinity was just a bigger, stronger, meaner Billy Joe. This is also the case with many who believe that they worship a benevolent and orderly God. Their self-interest is merely hidden from them. They might suspect it but they would never admit it. Many who professed to do *good* often visited far worse horrors upon the earth than Billy Joe would ever do. Billy Joe's evil was more selective. He would hurt you if he could, but if you had not crossed him or crossed his path, if he did not specifically need you, you "might" not concern him. He did not care who ruled the land. He didn't care about fame or its trappings and he already had power and it wasn't just in his mind. This Billy Joe knew. Money was his for the taking. Almost everything was his for the taking except entrance to the True Kingdom, because the one thing that it cost was the one thing he would not give, *surrender of the personal self.* This is where his anger came from. He was angry because the price that a little child thought nothing of was too great a price for him to pay. *It was too much to ask.*

Except for this little flaw, Billy Joe could have been anyone, could have found his way home to the heart of Love. If he had been anyone else, perhaps circumstance and time would have worn down his resistance. But he was not just anyone else. He was Billy Joe. He stood now before the window, full of Armagnac and enough cocaine to kill ten men and he was as cool as a snake in the morning grass. *Redemption was not an option.*

Alan's Jeep came out of his driveway and disappeared down the road. Now, if he wished, he could sweep down upon the house and wreak unholy vengeance upon the remaining occupants. If he would have known more right then, he would have. He might have added them to the presentation to come, but there was that which he did not know and that held him there before the window, waiting. Because of this, he would remain with his primary objective. Later, he would dispose of the peripheral in any way that he might wish. *The torment for Alan would be greater this way.* He raised the bottle to his lips and finished it. He set it on the table and went downstairs.

Balfire and Joe were in the kitchen finishing their breakfast, a gargantuan affair of steak and eggs, pancakes with syrup and fruit, bacon, potatoes and beer.

He'd programmed Joe with the ability to cook, an incidental service thrown to his hounds. It was a consideration of efficiency more than kindness or concern.

"Come into the living room when you are done and we'll go over your tasks." This meant right away and they knew it, rising from their chairs and following him much like the dogs he considered them to be. "In one hour, you will both go down to the house. It's going to take two trips at least. Balfire's in charge. He knows what needs to be done and he will tell you what he needs, Joe."

Joe nodded his head. This was perfectly reasonable to him. It was what he was programmed for. The irony was that who Joe had been previously would never have willingly agreed to anything Billy Joe asked. Now he did.

"Everything has to be in place by 1:00 p.m. The Captain will be coming by soon after that. I don't think we need to go over anything else or how important this is, do we, Balfire? You do understand?"

"Absolutely, it's as clear as daylight." Balfire was listening and grinning. He was into it anyway.

"It had better be clear, Balfire, or you will never see daylight again!" Billy Joe started out as soft as summer rain. He closed with the sound of express trains colliding inside Balfire's mind.

"Yes, Billy Joe." Balfire was not grinning now.

"See that it remains so. This is the most important task of your entire life. There is considerable reward waiting at the end. You too, Joe." Billy Joe turned his attention upon him and suddenly Joe's eyes opened. Implicit in what Billy Joe had just said was the promise of a freedom that Joe, as he was now being called, had given up on long ago.

"I will do whatever you require," Joe said, an actual human intensity burning in his eyes.

"I'm leaving you this bottle of coke. You'll be able to fly through your tasks. Use every precaution that we discussed. When you are done, wait here for me."

They nodded, both of them looking upward at their liege lord.

He turned around and went back upstairs.

9:30 AM, RIGHT DOWN THE STREET AT ALAN'S HOUSE, HAIKU, HAWAII

Whip locked the door and stood on the stairs with Christienne at his side. He looked around him, then above him and said, "What could go wrong on a day like this?" His hands extended in an expansive manner. A soft breeze caressed their faces.

Christienne smiled knowingly at Whip. They danced down the steps and once upon the path, she turned suddenly and threw her arms around his neck.

As she did this, her foot found the loose flagstone and the two of them nearly plunged into the ditch. Once again, the speed of Whip's reflexes saved them from a rough tumble. He spun, grabbing her arm and pulled her against him.

"God, Christienne. I'm willing to die for love but let me accomplish some of it first!"

She smiled, her cheeks flushed and her eyes sparkling with the power of those who know just how much love can protect, or at least believe beyond what can be known.

"Whip, let me finish what I had in mind." She kissed him hard, their mouths the medium of a speech no poet had yet found the words to articulate.

Finally, Whip broke away and said, "I've got to fix that, someone's going to get hurt sooner or later!" He walked off toward the shed.

Christienne stamped her foot. "Not now, Whip! You can do it later, when we get back."

Whip turned around and said, "Babe, we got all the time in the world, you in a hurry or something?"

"No, Whip, but do you really have to do it right now?" She wasn't really pushing him. She just didn't want to stand around in the yard. She had a Queen CD she had never heard before in her hand. It had a clown on the cover and as a devoted fan, she was dying to hear it. If he wanted to fix the path though, she would wait.

Whip felt his heart tug in his chest as he looked back at her. She tapped the side of her head with the CD cover, her eyes resonant with the sweetness and trust that had been passing between them. "What the hell," he said. "Anyway, just remember to watch your step later, okay?"

"Okay," she said with a impish grin.

Chapter Twenty-Nine

9:42 AM, MAUI MEMORIAL HOSPITAL, WAILUKU, HAWAII

Alan walked into Ben's room with a bag in his hand and a smile on his face. "Welcome to the land of the living."

Ben was sitting up in bed with the morning paper. There was a large bandage on his head and he had two swollen black eyes. "Well, I am a little miffed that you didn't sit by my bed through the night reading from *The Tibetan Book of the Dead*." His eyes twinkled as he reached to the bedside table for his cup of coffee.

"I'd have done that, Ben. You know I would have, but Captain Rusk has my only copy. How are you feeling?"

Ben sighed and his eyes grew serious for a moment. "Better than I have a right to, I can thank you for that. I don't know how you knew the garage was wired, but I would be rehashing my life with St. Peter right now if you hadn't stopped me."

"It was my life, too, Ben. The only thing I can tell you is that I actually heard alarm bells ringing, louder and louder. I just knew. I went by the station on my way here. There was a load of dynamite packed in cinder block and a gasoline can, a remote set it off." Alan smiled and dropped a large bag on the bed. "I brought you some food. I'm sure you're hungry. And some of your favorite reading matter, *American Equestrian*, *Hustler*, *Guns and Ammo* and *Tiger Beat*."

"Dammit, Alan," Ben was pulling items from the bag. "You know I don't read *Guns and Ammo.*"

Alan laughed. "So I missed one."

"Anyway," Ben continued. "I'm getting out of here in an hour, doctor's orders or no doctor's orders."

Alan patted Ben's knee. He'd seen officers in worse shape than Ben climb out of a hospital bed and go back to what they were doing, certain no one cared as much about what they were doing as they did, that no one could finish it with the same relentless intensity. Ben was not that badly hurt. The gash in his head was bad, but Alan knew there was nothing he could say that would keep Ben there. The food alone would drive him nuts. He'd been there and Ben was easily as meticulous as Alan was about what he ate. "You're getting out, huh?"

Without resistance, it made it harder for Ben to be insistent. He was stiff and sore.

"Look, Ben, why don't you just give it a few more hours? I've got things to check out that don't involve any danger. I can come back later and get you."

Now there was anger in Ben's eyes. "Excuse me, Alan, but how are you supposed to know if there's danger around or not?" He quickly caught himself. "Okay, you were right about the bomb, but next time it could be me that sees what's coming. Besides all that," Ben was exploring the food now, finding the sushi from his favorite mom and pop operation in Wailuku. "Alan, you shouldn't have!" Ben smiled but the force was still in his eyes. "Okay, I'll wait around here while you do a few things."

Alan could hardly understand him now. Ben swallowed and then continued, "One thing you have to keep in mind, without me around, Rusk could pull almost anything." Ben waved his hand as he pulled a salmon sushi out of the pack. "I know, Aaron is there but Aaron is not moment to moment on this. You need me around just to be around." Half the sushi disappeared in a single bite.

"I have a feeling I can handle Rusk."

Ben stuck the rest of the sushi in his mouth and grabbed his crotch. "Handle this! Rusk is a candidate for retroactive abortion." Ben pulled up an octopus sushi and took a prodigious bite. Alan watched him chew for a while. Ben's eyes looked demented. Then he swallowed and belched. "This is good, Alan."

He pointed at the coffee. "Open this for me will you sweetie?"

Alan removed the plastic lid and handed Ben his coffee. "So what do we do?" Alan asked.

"Okay, you come back for me in a few hours. I've got to check out these magazines and finish the food."

Lately, the hardest thing for Alan was reining in the need to put the feelings that roared through him into words. Ben was one more example of why Alan should trust Ming, why he should trust life, why he should trust period. It amazed him that he could lapse into lingo and camaraderie as if he wasn't seeing as he was. "We'll be in touch, Ben. Speaking of which," he looked pointedly at the magazines that were actually, *Scientific Journal*, *Spy Magazine* and *Vanity Fair*. (Ben had an intense fascination with all things New York.) "Try not to get too excited."

10:36 AM, 154 KOKOMO ROAD, HAIKU, HAWAII

Billy Joe opened his eyes and stared up at the rim of Haleakalā. He pondered what he had just heard of the exchange between Alan and Ben. There'd been no shielding on the transmission. There had also been nothing of useful substance in it. He was surprised that there had been no mention of Malcolm and his passing. Trying to read something useful, he had found nothing. From his vest pocket he removed an opal vial. This one came from the Amazon Basin. He had a standing order that came in once a month. It contained opiates, herbs, animal cortex fluids and certain ingredients that were for the most part unknown to science. Billy Joe took a sip.

In minutes, the world around him was changed. He could now see the invisible ones that followed him about the way hyena follow the track of a lion. Many of them had been with him for years. He used them on occasion, to strike fear at a distance or to initiate an uncontrollable hunger in someone he wished to destroy. Some of them were good for reckless action, providing just enough impetus to drive one beyond the normal controls, across the double yellow line and beyond into the dangerous dark unknown. In parks, restaurants and bars, any location where circumstance, state of mind and the vulnerability of his target combined to create the right chemistry, he might set one or more of them loose. Later he would relive the injury, ignominy, terror or despair that had resulted.

Through the window he could also see the tattered wraiths of those that had died badly and been unable to move on. The powerful magnet of his evil drew them. They shifted and danced like actors in an MTV video. He blew a powerful breath of air at them and several went tumbling and spinning hundreds of feet into the air. He raised the bottle of Armagnac to his lips and felt it pour down his throat. The sensation was orgasmic. With his eyes closed, he could hear the screaming of the damned in Hell. He saw razors and axes, other terrible metal devices, slashing and cleaving and butchering flesh. Bloody chains hung from dark cement walls. Tunnels ran deep under the ground like diseased arteries burning with a dirty red light. Billy Joe was at home.

This was the environment of the elixir. It served the same purpose for Billy Joe that meditation served for a yogi. He trained his mind on Alan Douglas. *If Douglas did have any idea of what was taking place today, he would have never left his house.* Billy Joe could clearly see him driving away from the hospital.

He took another draught of the Armagnac. He felt good, soaring, his mind crystalline clear. It had been a nice touch, the interplay between Rusk and The Dragonsmouth. After that he had only to add a little water and darkness…

The drug was moving full tilt now. Billy Joe had all the time in the world. His minions were handling the details. He let the black subway train with red eyes come ripping up into his vision until he could see nothing else. Billy Joe was at the helm, fear went before him and destruction followed in his wake.

11:05 AM, KANAHA BEACH PARK, KAHULUI, HAWAII

"So, it's clear then? You don't have any questions?" The man sitting next to Captain Rusk would have pleased the architects of the Third Reich. He had the square Teutonic countenance of a Prussian fencing master, complete with dueling scar running down the side of his left check. A knife had actually put it there. The knife had caught the eye as well, leaving a milky white ball. His hair was almost white, cropped uniformly short. The one good eye was blue and had a merry cast to it, but it was not merry. The mouth told the real story about the man behind the mask. It pulled to the right in a thin line, a perpetual sneer. It was a cruel mouth.

Roland "Rollie" Burns was a career criminal. His specialty was arson but he dabbled in whatever was paying the freight. He'd come to Maui from Detroit where he'd made a very good living doing freelance work for both the mob as well as financially stressed landlords and merchants. He'd left there three years ago after doing a straight five in Jackson. The evidence had been there but it was weak. They'd plea-bargained it down to almost nothing. If they had gotten him for the initial charge, he would have done life without parole. People had died.

Six months ago, the Maui vacation estate of a Chicago lawyer had burned to the ground. Arson was suspected. Investigation had shown that the property was over-insured and that the lawyer had large gambling debts. Rollie's name had surfaced. Recently a hardware store owner and a sales clerk at Radio Shack had identified him as purchasing certain items whose purpose, combined, served to equal the components of the device used in the torching. The case was starting to build.

"We went over this last night. I'm a pro, Captain. I know my business."

"You were sloppy last time."

Rollie shrugged, "I was overconfident. I never imagined you had any kind of a police force over here. Tell me again, what I get?" His bad eye was to the Captain's side, and that coupled with the sneer was hard on the Captain's stomach.

"Your case won't go to trial, evidence will disappear and a witness has surfaced who was with you that night, a credible witness. I've got a handle on her. I can also assure you that, provided you are discreet, you won't get arrested again."

"And I'm supposed to trust you on this?" The eye was definitely doing a number on the fish sandwich the Captain had finished earlier.

"I've got a lot more at stake, and a lot more to lose than you do. My dislike for Douglas is well known. If I were connected to this, I would face a departmental hearing with much worse to follow. Anyway, it's not going to come up. It will be overlooked on the discovery of a much greater crime."

Rollie rubbed his hands together. "All right, I need a break. I especially need that asshole Ortega off of my ass."

"As of today, Sergeant Ortega is off the case."

"Good, good, it's a pleasure doing business with you, Captain." Rollie stuck out his hand but Rusk ignored it. "It's good to have a friend in the department." Rollie got up. "I'd better get gone, you want this done today."

"You watch your ass, Burns, don't turn into some kind of a smart ass or you will have a very indirect line to me. I'm not your friend, don't get that impression."

Rollie nodded. "Solid," he said and walked away.

11:55 AM, MAUI MEMORIAL HOSPITAL, WAILUKU, HAWAII

Alan opened the passenger door and helped Ben into the seat.

"Alan, take your hands off of me. You're starting to piss me off. I can get along without you interfering with my natural rhythm."

"Sorry, bro, it's a natural human reaction to help those weaker than ourselves."

"You're a real creep, Alan." Ben was cranky. His body hurt but none of the verbal interplay had any force behind it. Alan smiled and ignored him.

"Speaking of creeps, what's this about Rusk again?"

"Hearing loss, too, huh, or is it the memory this time?" Alan smiled to show that he was kidding. "Rusk wants us in his office. After that it's a late lunch with the Honorable Aaron Wilson at The Charthouse."

"He called you?" Ben winced as he struggled to get comfortable in his seat.

"Matter of fact, no, I called him. I gave him an update on things. He wants to talk about Malcolm." Alan parked the car and they walked into the police station.

Rusk's secretary told them to have a seat while she let the Captain know they were there. After a few moments she ushered them into his office.

"Take a seat, gentlemen." Rusk walked around them and then sat behind his desk. He shuffled some papers around and then leaned back and threw a pencil on top of them. "Either of you have an opinion on what happened to Malcolm Kahn?"

Alan could not get a fix on Rusk's state of mind. It was the first time he had seen him behave in a rational or efficient manner. It was disturbing.

"Not a clue," Alan replied.

Ben gave a negative shake of his head. "We're looking into it."

Rusk studied them both. "Thing is, there was a policeman right outside his door all the while, never heard a thing. When the doctor came to check on him, he looked like he'd been squeezed dry. That's the way the doctor put it. He said it looked like a major struggle had taken place. Kahn sweated several quarts of liquid. He must have sweated blood too, because the doctor said there was very little in his body, none on the sheets. No one knows where it went. You get any of this?"

"First I've heard," Alan remarked. "I guess the autopsy will tell them something?"

"Already under way," Rusk responded.

Alan and Ben looked at each other and then back at the Captain. No one said anything for the moment. The Captain kept smiling. Then he got up from his chair and said, "All right gentlemen, I was hoping for some insights. I know you both have been deep into this case. I'm mostly concerned with all the missing people, sure would like to put an end to it all." He stuck his hand out to Alan and when Alan responded, he shook it. Ben was next. "Thanks for coming down. I know we haven't always seen eye-to-eye but I'm going to do my part to change that in the future. Carry on."

They got up and left. Ben was noticeably shaking his head as they walked down the hall. "What the fuck do you make of that?"

Alan laughed. "Like I told the Captain, I haven't got a clue."

"That was a little more than just strange, Alan. I'm seriously looking over my shoulder now. He acts like he's about to play his hole card."

"He is acting weird, isn't he? Maybe it's a Jekyll and Hyde sort of thing. He's a lot scarier when he's being nice. It would be a real comfort to know what he's up to. Something is rotten in the state of Denmark."

Ben grimaced, "Something is rotten in the town of Wailuku. So, what do you think it is?" Ben stuck a pill in his mouth and washed it down at the water cooler.

"Elementary, Ben, he's about to do something very bad."

12:41 PM, 154 KOKOMO ROAD, HAIKU, HAWAII

Balfire and Joe walked into the house and headed for the kitchen. Balfire pulled a six pack of beer from the icebox and set it on the kitchen table. "We might as well have a few right now. I'm so hot that three of these are going to be gone in about five minutes."

"I hear that," Joe replied, cracking the top of one and nearly draining it in a single quaff. He grabbed another and walked into the living room, followed by Balfire. They both dropped like stones into their chairs. The combination caused the house to shake and a lamp to nearly pitch to the floor from a nearby table.

Billy Joe came down the stairs and sat down across from them in a high backed armchair. He set the bottle of Armagnac next to the still trembling lamp and lit a cigarette. "Good work, gentlemen. You have finished ahead of schedule and from what I can see, everything is just the way it's supposed to be. Is that correct?" He looked to Balfire for confirmation.

"Just the way we planned it, boss. I got a real rush when it was all set up. I'd seen it in my head but the real thing is something else. It's a work of art. My daddy would be real proud."

"Good work, my son. The hard stuff is out of the way. Now comes finesse time."

Neither one of them replied to this as neither one of them knew what "finesse" meant.

"Boss?" Balfire was fidgeting with his beer can.

"Yes, Balfire?" Billy Joe inclined his head like a paternal uncle.

Balfire was acting like he had to go to the bathroom. Billy Joe knew what it was all about, as he usually knew what was going on before it happened, but it was appropriate to play out the string. "Me and Joe were talking and we sure could use some pussy if we got the chance."

"Let's see how the day goes. You certainly deserve a reward for all of your fine work. There are a couple of women just down the road, good-looking women that could use a visit. Neither of them has had a man in a while."

1:16 PM, CAPTAIN RUSK'S OFFICE, MAUI P.D., KAHULUI, HAWAII

Rusk sat at his desk and drummed thoughtfully on his knee. If you had asked him, he would not have been able to explain why he felt so certain that there was something to find at Alan's house. Simple common sense argued against that. It was not a reasonable assumption but then Captain Rusk was no longer a reasonable man. His dislike for Alan Douglas had made him irrational. Billy Joe had slowly but systematically fed this condition via the avenue of telepathic invasion. Like most people, Rusk believed that the thoughts inside his head were his own. *Where else would they have come from?* In fact, the majority of the thoughts in anyone's mind do not originate there. The mind functions like an airport. But the concept of an individual mind is only that. *There is but One Mind shared by all.* Personal consciousness is merely one point in an awareness that cannot be measured.

Each personality has its own predispositions. Some of these are known to the personality and some of them are submerged beyond its reach. All it takes to manipulate anyone is to work within the parameters of what they are sympathetic to. This is yet another explanation for the ones who wake up after the fact and cannot comprehend how they are responsible for the acts they committed. The potential was there. *The motivation was supplied.* A great deal of the world's evil and good is accomplished in this manner.

"Cora, you want to come in here?" Rusk let go of the intercom button and ran his hands through his hair. He'd learned a long time ago that you cover your bases whether you thought you had to or not. Nothing serves one's purposes better than hard data for protection before the fact.

"Yes, Captain?" Rusk's secretary was a pretty Filipino woman in her mid-twenties. No matter what went on around Rusk, she maintained an even disposition that made dealing with the Captain a lot easier than it might have been.

"I'll be looking at some property over around Peahi this afternoon. As you know, there's a lot going on around here lately and I need you to keep me updated if anything happens needing my attention. I'll check in on a regular basis and Lieutenant Nigaro will be handling everything in my absence, but call me on my cell phone if *anything* comes up. Especially anything that might have *anything* to do with the cases we're working on."

"All right, Captain," she said. Cora was a woman of few words. It was what made her such an asset to him. She had heard things in the process of her job that might have compromised any number of issues, but they would never pass her lips. She smiled and left the way she came.

Rusk was thinking that if he told her the world would end in fifteen minutes that she would have acted exactly the same way. He'd made an appointment the day before to look at a two-acre parcel in upper Peahi on the border of Haiku. It was well known that he speculated in real estate. In fact the Captain had made some serious money over the years. He'd have plenty of time to be onsite when the call came in. Hell, he'd probably hear the fire engines. He picked up his hat and went out the door.

1:30 PM, CHARTHOUSE RESTAURANT, KAHULUI, HAWAII

Alan spotted Aaron at one of the window tables with his deputy, Richard Finch. Aaron got out of his chair when he saw them coming, his hand extended.

"Good afternoon, gentlemen." Though he was smiling, there was grave concern in his eyes.

"How was your trip, Mr. Prosecutor?" Alan asked as he shook his hand. Ben followed him and did the same. Finch waved at them both from the table. Apparently certain human courtesies were not as much a priority for him as for his boss.

"I'm afraid it was mostly business and the feeling of being in L.A. You both know Richard?" he said after everyone was seated. Greetings were exchanged and everyone ordered something to drink. Aaron asked them to fill him in on the weekend's events.

Alan looked at Ben to take the lead, and Ben answered, "You do it, Alan."

For the next ten minutes Alan explained events as well as he could considering Richard Finch's presence. When he came to the part where Ben was injured, Aaron expressed his commiseration.

The waitress came and they ordered their food. Once she had gone, Aaron turned to Alan and said, "This is some bad business and we seem no closer than we were before. I'll want to see you both at the office later." It was one of the strangest situations that Aaron Wilson had ever been in. He knew about the interference of Finch and Rusk in the investigation. At the same time it was hard to argue against the logic of all their forces being deployed to apprehend The Dragonsmouth. Now, because of the information he had gained from Alan and Ben previously, he could not openly discuss the case, as he had intended to when he'd first arranged this meeting. He wondered why he had brought Finch along in the first place. Looking back, it made no sense at all. *Maybe there really was some dark occult force at work.* Though he had been understanding about Whip's story, in his gut he had always thought that when the situation finally resolved itself, there would be a logical explanation. For the first time, he was less sure about that than he had been before.

2:04 PM, ALAN'S HOUSE, HAIKU, HAWAII

Rollie slid off the embankment from the highway, grabbing branches and tree trunks on the way down the steeply pitched rise. Once at the bottom, he pushed aside the leaves of a banana tree and looked out over the driveway and parking area of the house. There were no signs of occupation, but Rollie wasn't taking anything for granted, even if Rusk had guaranteed it would be empty and that he could work undisturbed. Rollie stepped into the open and purposely walked to the front door where he rang the bell. He rang it three times and knocked on the door as well but no one ever came. After a turn around the house he went to work.

2:10 PM, POOLSIDE, THE RITZ-CARLTON, KAPALUA, HAWAII

Whip leaned across the deck chair and kissed Christienne on the mouth. "You taste like pineapples," she said.

"Courtesy of that outstanding brunch… I just can't get over our being here, not with everything that's happening."

Christienne stroked his face. "You understood pretty well this morning when we agreed."

Whip's head went from side to side. "That was then and this is now. I can't believe a story about a dead magician has gotten us thirty miles away from any help we might provide."

In convincing them to do this, Alan had told them a story about Aleister Crowley. At one point in his career, Crowley was involved in a magical war and a malicious spell was directed at him. The way he counteracted it was to go to a Charlie Chaplin double feature. Since his mind was occupied with the comedy on the screen, the spell was unable to reach him. Alan then went on to explain that evil which was sent out and did not achieve its objective, invariably returned to its author.

Christienne arched an eyebrow and smiled at Whip. "I think the whole point of a cosmic plan is that it doesn't rely on our input. Am I right?"

"Huh?" Whip thought about what she had just said. "Where did you get that from?"

"I don't know really. It just popped into my head."

Whip smiled to himself. "I'll be right back." He got up and walked into the hotel lobby to the men's room. As he walked back toward the pool, a chill passed through his body and he spun around, scanning the lobby for anyone who looked as if they didn't belong there. He saw nothing out of the ordinary, but Whip knew that didn't mean anything. All day he had felt spooked. Intermittently he would sense Ming's presence, but there was no communication.

2:16 PM, ALAN'S HOUSE, HAIKU, HAWAII

Rollie finished up quickly. He hated working in daylight. It went against a lifetime of habit and instinct. Along with that, he had never before been asked to leave evidence of a crime. If this hadn't been so damned important he would never have risked the exposure, but he was getting too old to go back to prison.

Another important point, if he went to prison over here he'd be in the shit. He wasn't connected in Hawaii. This definitely qualified as the spot between a rock and a hard place. He gave a final check to his circuits and then set the fuse. Quickly, he disappeared back the way he had come.

2:21 PM, PEAHI, HAWAII

Captain Rusk got out of his Toyota Land Cruiser and walked toward the man standing in the field. It was 2.6 acres of rolling meadow that had once been used for growing pineapples. The surrounding land was jungle and the nearest house was two hundred yards up the road. It was a nice piece and Rusk really was interested in it.

He wandered around the land kicking at outcroppings in the ground. The agent trailed along behind him providing a running commentary about the view, the privacy and the resale value. Rusk grunted appreciatively at these remarks. The asking price was a little higher than he wanted to go. This meant it was cheap by any other estimation. The asking price was two hundred thousand, comparable pieces, some not as nice, were at least fifty thousand more. Rusk wanted a better deal and they talked about that possibility until his beeper went off.

Rusk quickly excused himself and went back to his car. He called his secretary on the cell phone. "What's up, Cora?"

"Good afternoon, Captain. You said you wanted to be informed on anything that might relate to the ongoing cases. I don't know if this is relevant but a call came in a few minutes ago about a fire in Haiku. The property belongs to Alan Douglas."

"What!" Rusk exclaimed, feigning surprise. "Do you have any details?"

"Only that fire engines are on their way. Nothing about how bad it is. Some neighbor saw smoke coming from the yard."

"Thanks, Cora. I'm in the area, I'll check it out. Contact Ben and see that Douglas gets the news." Rusk hung up the phone and waved the agent over. *Here goes*, he thought. Rusk explained to the agent that there was an emergency and he had to go. They made plans to conference later that day, after the owner had heard Rusk's offer.

He drove away, excitement and apprehension warring in his gut. *What if this was all bullshit?* How would he look? *What if it wasn't bullshit?* How would he look? Rollie's girlfriend had made the call. He hoped the evidence wouldn't be destroyed and that the Fire Department would arrive in time.

When Rusk arrived, he saw a large fire engine parked on the road. Further down was a fire truck next to the house and two firemen hosing down scorched surfaces of the house and a shed. The attached garage was also smoking and had already partially burned through. A portion of the deck had burned as well as some fascia on the front of the house. A number of roofing tiles were curled and smoking.

Rusk parked next to a police car and got out. Both of the officers approached him. One of them told Rusk that they had just arrived on the scene. They'd been in the living room calling out for any occupants. The front door appeared to have been forced.

"Forced," Rusk replied.

Both officers were of Asian-Hawaiian mix. One of them, Rickie Ogura was well known to the Captain as a very bright, straight arrow officer who had been decorated earlier in the year for bravery. Rusk did not know the other officer, whose name was Ho.

"Anything else out of the ordinary?" Rusk asked.

"The smell, Sir," Ogura replied.

"What smell?" Rusk was walking toward the garage and now he could smell it too.

"A bad one Sir. It's partly chemical and partly something else. Here and in the house."

"In the house?" Rusk continued walking. His pulse was thumping in his head. *This was very good news.* Rusk did not know why it was good news. He did not question it.

"Yes, Sir. It smells like the morgue," Ogura answered.

"In your opinion, Officer Ogura, do you feel that the fire and the forced door constitute the appearance of criminal activity?"

"There is a reasonable indication of that." Ogura did not know where the Captain was going with this and he was choosing his words carefully.

"It seems so to me, too. And there's no evidence of the occupants around?" Rusk was setting out his procedural chain.

"As I said Sir, we called out into the house. We've checked the surroundings. There doesn't appear to be anyone here. We were… I called for an investigation unit first thing, Captain."

"Very good." Rusk was at the garage now and he removed the lock that was open and hanging from the hasp. There were double doors and Rusk pulled them open wide. The smell of formaldehyde mixed with other scents poured out through the opening. Rusk and the officers stood for several moments making sense of what they saw. A large autopsy table was standing near the left wall. The walls of the shed were covered with extended shelves, perches and plaques on which were mounted animals in simulated life, birds with spread wings and the heads of jungle creatures. There were several mature wild pigs with large tusks, mongoose, white owls and pheasants along with two pit bulls and some cats.

"What the hell?" Rusk added, shocked. He hadn't been prepared for anything like this.

Officers Ogura and Ho walked inside the shed and began rummaging about. Unable to make out the contents of the shed clearly, Officer Ho turned on his flashlight. Moments later he backed hurriedly out.

"What is it?" Rusk called. He moved to where Ho had been standing and pulled up an object that he carried out of the shed. Ogura gasped when he saw the Captain holding a human head by the hair.

"Holy shit!" Ogura cried, backing up. It was the face of a young woman. It was a ghastly color. The head looked like it had been torn from the neck, tendons, arteries, veins and muscles hung in a ragged formation.

Rusk grimaced as he studied it. "It's fake."

Ogura came closer. "Are you sure?"

"Very," Rusk replied. "Well done but a fake. There's other stuff back there too, limbs and torsos. What do you think a Homicide detective would be doing with something like this?"

Ogura shook his head. "Hobby of some kind I guess. He isn't very clean though and the stuffed dogs and cats, that could be criminal."

He pointed his flashlight at the autopsy table. There were wet stains on the surface. They looked black and were swarming with flies.

"Jesus Christ," Rusk said. "Blood all over the table and on the floor, too!" He stepped back now from what he had originally thought were oil stains.

"He could have been finishing up a project," Ogura ventured, "But it doesn't explain why he wouldn't have cleaned up afterwards."

Rusk turned on his heel and said, "Let's check the house."

"We don't have a warrant, Captain."

"I know that, Ogura but we do have suspicion of criminal entry. We have a suspicious fire. We've got blood on an autopsy table. I'd say we've got plenty of cause." He waved to Ho, who was standing sheepishly to one side. Rusk wanted as many witnesses as he could get. His palms were itching and sweaty. His forehead was hot. *He knew there was something in the house.* He drew his gun and walked in.

He could smell the formaldehyde again. Rusk looked around the large entryway and went into the living room. The afternoon sun was spilling in through the French windows, washing the furniture and carpet. Everything looked orderly and peaceful. He turned to Ogura and said, "This house appears to have several levels, go downstairs and start there. Ho, you take that corridor by the kitchen, check out the rooms."

Rusk walked around the living room. He was impressed. The white leather sectional was over twenty feet long. There were carved hardwood tables, a deep pile Berber style carpet, a Tiffany ceiling light and *shōji* screens. It was an eclectic mix of East and West. He walked across the room to a doorway that opened on the right side of the lava rock fireplace. Looking in, he saw a combination library and game room with pool table and several old time pinball machines. There was a handsome bar built into the far left corner of the room. Rusk whistled. 'Very nice," he said.

Rusk was walking toward the entrance when he heard a cry followed by choking sounds. Ho came running past him and through the door, his hand over his mouth. Rusk chased him and found him on his knees vomiting to the side of a section of flagstone, trying to wipe his hands at the same time on the ground cover.

"What's wrong, Ho?" Rusk bent beside him.

Ho could not seem to get his breath. Finally he said, "Back there."

Rusk ran back inside nearly colliding with Ogura. "What is it Captain?"

"Ho ran across something that made him sick. Let's check it out." Rusk carefully led the way down the corridor. The first door, on the left, turned out to be a bedroom that looked out over the parking lot. It was neatly made up. The next door, this time on the right, was ajar. Rusk pushed it open all the way.

"Holy Mother of God!" he cried.

Ogura came up beside him and stared dumbfounded into the room. There was an underlying smell of formaldehyde but someone had obviously sprayed a floral deodorizing agent heavily about. It warred with the scent of the embalming agent. The scene before them was so unexpected and bizarre that neither man could say a thing. Neither of them believed that what they were looking at could be real, especially after the garage, but Rusk certainly hoped it was real. Rusk was hoping with all of his might that what he saw was real. Shivers were moving up and down his back. Nothing in his imagination had prepared him for this.

There was a spotlight with a red filter cap shining down from the ceiling. The room and its contents were washed in a blood-colored light. Five human figures sat in rigid formal positions around the back half of a circular dining table. Each figure had its right hand extended toward the table's centerpiece. The middle and index figures were joined together as were the other two and separated from each other to form a V. In the center of the table was a large silver-serving tray. On it sat a naked boy and girl joined in the appearance of sexual union.

"*Are they doing it?*" flashed through Rusk's mind, his gorge began to rise as he pushed the thought away.

The girl's sightless eyes stared over the boy's shoulder right into Rusk's. Her arms were around his back and her ankles were locked behind his buttocks. The mouths of everyone at the table were open and pulled back into maniacal grins that would not have been possible in life. *It was a nightmare scene from Hell.* Rusk felt terror sucking at his gut for the mind that could even conceive of such a horrific display.

Ogura walked into the room, lightly touching the bodies at the table and saying, "Oh, my God, oh, my God."

Rusk walked around the other side, and that was when he saw Wendy at the table's head. The former deputy prosecutor, smiling at the dead lovers in front of her while the light filled her eye sockets with blood. Rusk had seen enough. He turned on his heel and trotted back into the living room. Picking up the phone, he dialed the station. Rusk had to wait a minute to speak with his second-in-command. In the meantime, his imagination raced at the implications of what he had found. Not once did he consider that Alan might have nothing to do with what he had just discovered. It was full vindication for everything that he had felt and thought since day one. *Nothing could help Douglas now.*

"Jack? Listen up." Rusk told Lt. Jack Nigaro what he had seen and the circumstances of his presence at the scene. "I want you to get everyone up here quietly. Do not use the radio, use the telephone. Call the District Attorney and tell him what we found. Find out where Ben is and have him and Douglas come into the station. Keep them there when they arrive. Be polite, but don't let Douglas leave. Arrest him if you have to. We'll seal off the area until everyone shows up." Rusk put down the phone. A big grin broke open on his face. *This was too much!*

Chapter Thirty

3:20 PM, 154 KOKOMO ROAD, HAIKU, HAWAII

Billy Joe turned away from the window and went into the kitchen. He took a bottle of Calvados brandy off the shelf and continued into the living room. Balfire and Joe were playing rummy for a dollar a point. Billy Joe had given them each two thousand dollars of "walking around" money. With nowhere to spend it, they had to be creative.

Billy Joe opened the bottle and held it in the air. "To the sweet, sweet taste of revenge," he cried, holding the bottle victoriously aloft. Balfire and Joe both raised their beer cans to share in the toast. There was a sense of completion in the air.

Balfire was thinking how much Billy Joe's head looked like that of a skull. It was an image that would frequently appear and then be quickly gone, like the shadow of a bird passing overhead.

"Balfire?"

"Yes, boss?"

Billy Joe brought the Calvados to his mouth and took a prodigious swallow. His eyes gleamed with a dark inner light. "Balfire, right now, your work is being admired by a small group of police officers. Others will soon join them, a much larger group of law enforcement professionals. You should be feeling very proud."

Balfire glowed with pride. "Thanks, Billy Joe. I wish there had been more time. Some of the bodies didn't get to cure proper. They weren't really ready for display."

Billy Joe laughed, a harsh cutting sound, and drank again from the bottle. "Balfire, when the world is ready to see them they'll be ready. I have a feeling they will cure just fine in the morgue, or the police property room, seeing as they're stuffed. They've got year-round climate control in there, couldn't be better." Balfire and Joe both laughed loudly at the image of the bodies drying and setting in the police station.

"You should have made them zombies, Billy Joe. Then they could party down at night, do all the drugs and fuck on the tables." Balfire was feeling very loose right now.

"My, my." Billy Joe extracted a thin black cigar from his suit coat pocket and placed it between his lips. He set the bottle down and lit it.

Jesus! It makes him look like Clint Eastwood possessed by the devil, Balfire thought.

"Sometimes you have very good ideas, Balfire, a bunch of zombies in the police property room. So many good ideas, so little time." Billy Joe laughed again and smoke burst from his mouth and wreathed about his head. Balfire and Joe were laughing, too. Their faces were lit up with happiness. They shared in Billy Joe's enjoyment the same way that dogs sense and respond to it in their masters.

"Yes, boys, the early reviews are in – 'A bold new approach by an unknown body sculptor rivets the art world,' 'cadaver artist silences critics,' literally. Let's see, 'Amazingly lifelike,' 'New York art scene embraces serial artist,' 'New York art scene becomes smaller.'" Billy Joe snorted from a Swiss pharmaceutical bottle. Then he tossed it to Balfire who caught it easily. "Yes, Balfire, your work is going to make a powerful declaration to the world. You'll be the darling of the video tabloids and the sewer press. Your work will be thought to be the work of another. An impostor will gather the laurels that were meant to be for you. You must bear with this temporary insult. Your day will come." Billy Joe gave him an evil smile.

Balfire was mostly pleased but a little unsettled. "Your day will come" did not sound as happy as it should have.

"And you Joe, Kimo Joe, are another artist of unparalleled vision. You painted a landscape in the halls of the Kaiser Clinic that rivaled Michelangelo's work in the Sistine Chapel. Your acting skills, with some small help from me throughout your stay as a guest of the state, were the equal of Olivier playing King Lear."

Joe nodded dumbly, glad for the attention, but witless of Billy Joe's meaning. When Joe had last been alive, he was an Army officer who'd had the bad luck to get between Billy Joe and something Billy Joe wanted. In the end, Billy Joe got what he wanted and Joe got dead, but Billy Joe had saved him because of a particular skill that Joe possessed. It was why he was here now.

"I am most grateful to both of you," Billy Joe continued. The coke and Calvados had put him in an excellent frame of mind. The vision of the impending arrest and inquisition of Alan Douglas put him in an even more excellent frame of mind. "You will both be suitably rewarded when your tasks are complete, in the near future, depend on it." Billy Joe sipped from the bottle and his eyes gleamed with the pleasure that only hateful action could bring.

3:11 PM, MAUI POLICE DEPARTMENT, WAILUKU, HAWAII

Ben handed Alan a new list of secluded rentals. They were looking for the backup location. There was a knock on the door. "Come in," Ben said. The door opened and Sgt. Klein came through the door followed by two uniformed officers. He had a black eye that his sunglasses did not conceal very well and was favoring his right side as he walked, courtesy of his scrimmage with The Dragonsmouth.

"Alan Douglas?" he said.

"Yes?" Alan replied. There was tension in the air. *What bad news is it this time?* He wondered.

"Captain Rusk has just given orders that you are to remain here until he returns. These officers will stay with you until that time."

"What the fuck is going on?" Ben exclaimed, rising out of his chair.

"You also need to surrender your firearm. That will be returned to you later." Klein continued as if Ben had said nothing.

"We'll need an explanation before Alan gives you anything," Ben said. He was coming around the desk when Klein held up his hand.

"Lieutenant, there's no reason for alarm. Captain Rusk is in charge and I am following orders. I have no details. Please..."

Alan had already pulled his gun from his holster and handed it butt first to the detective. "It's okay, Ben. If Rusk is going nuts it will all come out sooner or later."

"I don't really give a shit about sooner or later," Ben said. His eyes were slits and he was crowding Klein who took a step back. "You know more than what you are saying. We haven't always seen eye-to-eye, but I always thought you respected me, respected my judgment."

"This isn't about you and me, Ben. This is about following orders. Douglas isn't under arrest."

"Uh-huh," Ben replied. "He's not under arrest unless he tries to leave the building, or am I wrong?"

"You're not wrong, Ben. Something happened up at his house. We've got to wait for Captain Rusk." Klein was adamant and the supporting officers had their hands on their guns. *This was serious business.*

"Ben, whatever is going on, we should expect it in light of what we know. Sergeant Klein is just doing his job. C'mon." Alan came forward as he was speaking and laid his hand on his friend's shoulder. "This isn't about fair play or reasonable action. We hold the winning hand."

"Okay, okay." He held his hands up and shook his head. "I have always hated opportunists and pricks that follow the droppings of whatever animal leaves some flesh on the carcass. So, you do your worst, Klein."

"Hey, that's not fair." Klein was outraged at Ben's short speech. Obviously the arrow had found its mark.

"It may not be fair, buddy, but it's as accurate as it gets. You want Alan Douglas in the house! You get me in the house. Wherever he goes, I go too. You can arrest us both if it comes to that. I've known you as an ass-kisser since day one. You've always been a good cop though, so I've forgiven that ugly brown stain on your nose, but if you haven't learned anything in the last week, then you are out of touch, really out of touch." Ben got up and went to the coffee machine.

"I'm going to let that go for now, Lieutenant. I've got eyes in my head. You got a personal beef with me, we'll settle it some other time. There is some serious shit on the table right now and you shouldn't hold me responsible. If I had refused this, which by the way, I did offer my objections…" Klein stopped at this point. His voice was breaking and he didn't trust himself to be able to continue. He took several deep breaths and then said, "If I had refused, someone else would be here in my place." Once again he stopped, unable to speak. He coughed lightly and both Alan and Ben could see his Adam's apple bob up and down in his throat. "I never knew you saw me as an ass-kisser. I'm ambitious, yes. I think I'm a damn good cop and I want more. I know I'm working for an irrational shit that abuses his men and brings shame on the department, but if you can show me another way, I'm willing to listen. In the meantime, I don't think I deserve this abuse, so fuck you!" Having said this, Klein turned and headed for the door.

"Wait!" Ben called, "I'm sorry. We've been through a lot lately. I know it's not your fault. I'm sorry for what I said." Ben moved with incredible quickness and caught Sgt. Klein's arm before he could leave. "I didn't mean what I said. Okay?"

Klein turned and looked at Ben. "You know, I'm not even supposed to be on duty. My side hurts like a motherfucker. I'm living on painkillers but I'm here and it's not because I'm trying to make rank. I care about this job. I thought you knew that."

Ben grabbed him and pulled him closer. Klein fought him but no one could escape that grip. "We accept the conditions. You and I will talk later. I overreacted. I'm terribly sorry. I don't know what got into me."

Klein freed himself and said, "It's okay, Ben. I don't think I could have worked with you this long with you being able to hide your feelings from me. We all say shit. I don't think he did it either."

"Did what?" Ben asked.

"Ben, I can't say anything and now I've got to go. Hang in there." Klein turned and left.

Ben backed away from the door, made eye contact with the uniforms and then took his seat. "What do you think Alan?"

"I haven't the faintest idea Ben, but I don't think any of it matters. We're just in the movie." Alan looked at the patrolmen who stood quietly by the door. "You guys want some coffee?"

3:45 PM, DISTRICT ATTORNEY'S OFFICE, WAILUKU, HAWAII

Aaron Wilson put down the phone and then put his face in his hands. What he had just heard was unbelievable. It could not be, even if it was, it still could not be.

"What's wrong, Aaron?" Finch had only heard Aaron's side of the conversation, which hadn't told him much.

Aaron explained what Captain Rusk had just told him. Finch's eyes grew wide with astonishment. "What are you going to do?"

"I'm driving up there right now. I have to see this for myself. Alan is being detained at the police station. You want to come along?"

"Assuredly," Finch answered.

3:50 PM, 154 KOKOMO ROAD, HAIKU, HAWAII

Billy Joe told the boys to put the cards away and join him at the kitchen table. He poured a big rock of cocaine and some powder on to a slab of onyx and crushed it with the bottom of a teaspoon. Then he opened a gold-plated straight razor and cut the coke into lines.

"That's a beautiful piece Boss," Balfire said, greatly admiring the gleaming instrument.

"I've had this for a long time." Billy Joe had a wistful look in his eyes. "It's seen a lot of work. You may have even read or heard about it here and there, only I didn't get the credit. I often don't." He shrugged. "I'm an artist like you, gentlemen and although we enjoy the credit for a well-executed piece of work, being artists, it is enough to have been creative, to have given shape to our inspirations.

"Help yourselves, gentlemen. We need to talk about the next thing you have to do." Billy Joe slid the stone over to Balfire along with a rolled up hundred-dollar bill. He watched as they snorted their several lines apiece. Of course, he had control of them at all times. The coke would merely lubricate his access. For his next task he needed a jeweler's precision. He would control them the same way that a car was controlled by the steering mechanism.

"Joe, I want you to go into my bedroom and get the gun case that's in there and bring it back." Joe hurried out and was back before Billy Joe had finished inhaling his own lines. "Open it and give me the gun."

Joe did what he was asked. Billy Joe took the rifle in his hands. "This is a .30-06 Springfield, a fine deer rifle, but also excellent for other large game like bears, mountain lion and of course, human beings. The scope cost twice as much as the gun." Billy Joe jacked open the mechanism. "Half a mile down the highway past Douglas's house is a long ridge with a direct line of sight to Haiku Road. There is a cluster of mango trees there that will provide good cover. A dirt road runs up there on its way to an abandoned house. You can't miss it. It's the second turn to the right after you make a left out of the driveway. Sometimes kids play up there or pot growers pass by on their way to more remote destinations, but no one's going to be there today except you two."

Billy Joe played with the gun some more, whipping it up to his shoulder and sighting on objects in the room, occasionally turning it on Balfire and Joe and going, "Boom! Boom!" and then snickering. Neither Balfire nor Joe appreciated it but neither of them failed to connect it with the importance of today's mission, whatever that was. "Joe is going to do the shooting. Joe used to be a fantastic shot back when he was in uniform. Isn't that right?"

Joe stirred uneasily as if he were having a bad dream. A flash of memory shot through his mind, too briefly for him to capture. "I don't know, Billy Joe."

"No you don't, Joe, but when you get up on that ridge, you will remember all that you need to know. Balfire," he shifted his attention now to the big Viking, clean-shaven for the first time in years.

Balfire's eyes were trained on his master. Where Billy Joe compelled, he would go. "You'll drive the van up and back. In approximately twenty-five minutes, a black Lincoln is going to be coming up that road towards Douglas's house. Joe, you will put one round through the skull of the driver. You will not shoot the other passenger. Then you will drop the rifle and come directly back here. Is that clear?"

They both agreed that it was. Balfire was disappointed that he had not been asked to do the shooting. He was proud of his ability with a rifle. Billy Joe saw this and approved. *They should always be anxious to kill, desiring to do harm, competing for the opportunity.* As extensions of his will, they should mirror both his feelings and his intentions.

"I am proud of both of you, and we're going to party down soon and let the beast out for a little midnight run." Billy Joe's eyes smoldered like red coals with the promise of evil pleasures. Balfire and Joe felt a fire build in their loins as the thought of sex and carnage was transmitted to them. Billy Joe was especially pleased to see it build in Joe. *Joe had been a good man, a decorated war veteran.* Now he was just a killing machine devoid of principles or even identity.

"Balfire?"

"Yes, boss?"

"When Joe throws down the gun, I want you to wipe it down and put your own prints on it." Billy Joe watched Balfire's eyes light up when he realized that he was going to get credit for the job. Balfire glanced at Joe who seemed oblivious to the implications. He was definitely smarter than Joe, even if he was good at cards.

Billy Joe inserted a cartridge into the chamber, slammed the bolt home and then tossed it across the table at Joe, who caught it easily. "All right, gentlemen, on your way."

4:00 PM, THE RITZ-CARLTON HOTEL, KAHANA, HAWAII

Whip kept thinking of calling Alan, but Alan had said he would call them if anything happened. He had given Whip a cell phone for that purpose. "I think I've seen enough of this hotel for today."

They were standing in the manicured landscape by the pool, staring out at the ocean. Christienne put her arm around his waist. "You want to go to Lahaina? Maybe I can find myself a slinky black dress for dinner."

"You look slinky enough right now to be a commercial for slink," Whip said.

Christienne smiled. "I think you're engaging in 'Lookism,' Whip. I may have to demand a hearing in front of some upcountry feminists."

"Huh?" Whip put on his dumb look, "I thought 'No' meant 'Yes.' Let's go?"

They found a place to park in Lahaina beside an enormous Banyan tree. Whip had seen Banyans before but nothing like this. "You mean that's all one tree?" he wondered. It covered an area the size of a square block.

Christienne put on her sunglasses and pulled Whip over to it. "It would be a lot bigger than it is except they cut back the new roots that would allow it to grow outward. I thought it might be the biggest one in the world but then someone told me there was one a lot bigger in Australia. I'd really like to go there."

Whip laughed, "No shit. That is my next stop."

"Really?" Christienne's eyes lit up.

"Really," Whip replied. As he said this, he put his arms around her and Christienne leaned back and lifted her leg behind her. Two passing sailors whistled, which caused Whip to blush.

"What are you ashamed of?" Christienne teased. "I thought you were in love. Come on." She pulled him through the park, giving Whip little time to see the tree. "I want to get our pictures taken with the parrots."

She led him up Front Street to a bird stand at the corner of the Pioneer Inn, where ten beautiful parrots stood on perches and gave off deafening shrieks, fighting and preening themselves. A wild-eyed character in a safari suit and pith helmet was working the large crowd in front of the stand. Seeing them, he turned and said, "Have you held the birds?" His expression was so comical that Christienne and Whip both laughed out loud. Very quickly he snatched a bird off the perch and placed it on Christienne's head. She screamed and raised her hands to her head but then just as quickly dropped them, uncertain of what to do.

"So, you want your picture taken, taken with this handsome man?" He grasped Whip's wrist and suddenly a bird was there on his arm.

"You're fast," Whip said.

"Fast? I haven't even started hitting on your girlfriend yet. Then you'll see fast." He mugged outrageously. His cherubic face flushed with amusement and his deep-set dark eyes twinkled with intelligence and laughter. He led Christienne to an area next to the wooden perches and stood her under some large colored umbrellas. Then, with blazing speed, he began whipping birds off the perches and placing them everywhere on her arms, shoulders and head.

"Wait!" she screamed, delighted. "I want him in the picture with me."

"Him?" the Birdman said with mock surprise. "You are with him?" He shook his head, his face full of feigned sorrow. "What can this man give you? Can he cover your body with birds like I can?" He reached up and grabbed the bird on her head and began pulling it up and down. The bird's feet were tangled in her hair and Christienne was screaming. Whip, too, was laughing, feeling better than he had in a long time.

So we found Chaplin, he thought.

"No! He can't have you!" The Birdman was yelling. "Think about tonight when your heart is crying out desperately for someone to put birds on you. There will be no one to do it. You will remember me then and your heart will be sad." All the while as he said this, he kept pulling up and down on the bird on her head. The large surrounding crowd was going wild. "And then…" he jutted his chin forward at her and cocked his head to one side, looking just like an owl, "And then you will miss me."

Suddenly he turned to Whip, "Okay, you get over here." He pulled Whip over and placed him next to Christienne. Immediately there were birds all over Whip. Whip eyed the large parrots apprehensively.

"Don't worry," the Birdman said, "They won't hurt you. That is, unless I tell them to." The Birdman kept up a comic patter throughout the photo shoot. Very quickly it was over. Just as quickly the birds were gone.

They paid him and went their way. "Very funny guy," Christienne remarked. "Let's go over here and sit on the grass. We can look at the ocean." She led him to an expanse of green grass that fronted the library. There was an ancient whaling ship lying at anchor in the harbor, its triple masts pitching to and fro.

"What about that little black dress?" Whip asked.

"We'll get to that." She pulled him down beside her and kissed him. If it weren't for the hellish events that surrounded them, Whip would have sworn that he truly was in Paradise.

4:20 PM, ALAN'S HOUSE, HAIKU, HAWAII

The house was humming with activity, as professionals from related industries that relied on carnage and death for their continued existence scurried about like ants in a rigid cast system of divided responsibilities. Medical technicians were milling by their vehicles, waiting for the crime scene personnel to finish with their duties so that they could get on with the business of transporting the dead. *There were no lives to be saved here.* Uniformed officers were unrolling yellow tape. There were officers standing by the road to deny the curious admittance. There were always vultures and other carrion feeders that showed up, as if in response to some unknown chemical stimulus wherever there was tragedy.

Captain Rusk moved about radiating authority on one and all and generally making everyone uncomfortable, giving out unnecessary orders and asking stupid questions. This was not because he was stupid, but because he had run out of intelligent questions and he still felt the need to impress himself on the situation. He was filled with a bombastic sense of self-importance and personal vindication at having been proven right about Douglas. At one point he heard someone say, "Douglas should have stuffed the Captain, too." However, when he whirled around he was unable to locate the source. *Not too worry*, Captain

Rusk felt good. *Douglas was a deranged homicidal maniac!* It was better than he hoped for, much better.

4:10 PM, HANA HIGHWAY NEAR HO'OKIPA PARK, HAWAII

The big Lincoln slipped effortlessly around the winding curves that followed the shoreline. Aaron Wilson was busy with a continuing effort to empty his mind. Myriads of thoughts, many in violent contradiction with each other, were turning his mind into a battlefield. It was impossible for him to imagine that Alan could have had anything to do with whatever had taken place at his house. *It smelled contrived. How could something of this magnitude have taken place under everyone's nose?* He had just been there for dinner! *How did Whip fit in – and Christienne? Ben? Had Alan been insane all along?* That was preposterous, Ben would have seen something. *What about Rusk? How had Rusk come to be on the scene so quickly? What about this mysterious fire and the open front door?* It was all very damned convenient. Well, he would get to the bottom of it. If it was a setup, no one was going to hide their handiwork from him for very long.

"You're not saying much, Aaron." He glanced over to find Finch closely scrutinizing him. Finch always appeared to be "scrutinizing" something. There was no question of his brilliance but he seemed to lack something human, as if a vital part of his makeup were missing. He didn't seem to feel things as others did. Aaron thought that that might not be such a bad thing in this profession. *You send a sociopath to catch a sociopath. Only a sociopath knows what's going on with another one.* Of course, this could have terrible effects when Finch was dealing with the occasional innocently accused. This possibility did not exist in Finch's mind. Then again, it wasn't *supposed* to exist in any prosecutor's mind. It wasn't their job to determine innocence, judges and juries did that. They did it from weighing the evidence, or so it was supposed to be. Too often they did it because they were more swayed by the theatrics of one legal practitioner over another.

Finch always explained his position by saying that you had to believe in the guilt of the defendant to succeed. You could not allow doubt to enter your mind. If a case got far enough to require Finch's attention, then you did everything you could to find the defendant guilty. In principle, Aaron agreed with this. In practice, he sometimes made other decisions.

"I really don't know what to say, Richard. We'll see when we get there."

"Well," Finch shifted in his seat, "You know what they say, where there's smoke, there's fire." Aaron had given Finch the details of his conversation with Rusk.

"Richard, I understand how you go about things, but I don't see how Alan Douglas could have had anything to do with this. I know something about the man and I'm not speaking from any sense of fellowship I might feel. I have no fellowship when it comes to crime. My job precludes that. I think we are going to find that there is something else going on."

Aaron made the turn on to Haiku Road, which was composed of a series of winding turns through lush tropical vegetation. "God, it's beautiful! I've been seriously thinking of making the move up here."

"It rains a lot here in the winter, Aaron, all the time on occasion, for weeks and weeks."

"It's not that bad. Besides, I like the rain and if I want it all dry and sunny all I have to do is get into my car and drive back there." He gestured in the direction from which they had come. "That's the beauty of Maui and besides, I have to come down every day anyway." The Lincoln came out of the last curve before the straightaway. Aaron had rolled down his window a few moments earlier in anticipation of the sweet smells that abounded here. "Mangoes will be ready soon, Richard. You like mangoes?"

"Not really, they give me sores in my mouth."

Aaron reflected how that was just like Finch to have this kind of a reaction to one of Nature's greatest creations. "I love them. Sometimes I can eat half a dozen at one time. I compare eating a mango favorably with having sex. Don't tell my wife I said that." Aaron grinned but Finch did not respond. Finch did not see the humor. Aaron pointed with his left index finger to the approaching hill on the left. "There's a couple of great big Mango trees up on that ridge."

4:08 PM, THE RIDGE ABOVE HAIKU ROAD, HAIKU, HAWAII

They'd found the dirt road easily enough. Balfire was giving Joe some of his favorite shooting tips and Joe listened without comment. His mind kept trying to find itself back in the place it had been when Billy Joe was talking to him at the house, but he couldn't find it.

"Just like in the movies," Balfire said as they climbed out of the van.

"How's that?" Joe asked. He shucked the gun from its protective casing and tossed it back over the seat into the van's cargo area.

"You know, everything works out. Everything you need is there when you need it. I like that, except for one thing." The mango trees appeared directly in front of them after a short trek through some jungle. There was an easy, well-worn path for them to follow. They slipped into the trees and were enveloped in a cool twilight.

"What's that?"

"In the movies the bad guys always get killed or sent away. I guess we'd be the bad guys. We work for Billy Joe and he is definitely not a *good guy*. Anyway, in the movies, you get killed or go to the joint. In real life, the bad guys only get caught now and then, sometimes never." Balfire's brain was buzzing from the coke and he was waxing philosophical.

"I guess you're right," Joe answered as he found a good line-of-sight to the highway. "I don't remember being in jail and I'm not dead, I don't think." Joe started kicking leaves into a pile to form a little hummock on the ground. He handed Balfire the rifle and got down on his knees, working to form up a comfortable lean for the shoot. After he tested it several times he pronounced himself satisfied. He took the gun back from Balfire and then got into position.

Balfire dropped to one knee and watched the approach for the Lincoln, ready to cue Joe when it came into sight. All conversation ceased as a deadly calm settled over them.

Several minutes passed, then Balfire touched his shoulder. "Here it comes." Joe shifted his body and twitched his left hand. Something had just been trying to crawl on it, but there was no time to deal with that now. He set the scope on the Lincoln's windshield and Aaron Wilson's face jumped into view. There was a glare on the glass. Very soon the driver's side window would be there for him. *This was very good.* Whoever was sitting in the passenger seat was going to be wearing a lot of brain salad in a few seconds.

Whatever was crawling on his hands was now trying to make its way into the sleeve of his jacket. He crimped his arm against the cuff as best he could to discourage it. Aaron's head was now there, framed in the window. Joe breathed in and tightened his finger on the trigger. Slowly he let the air escape out of his mouth. It was at that moment that the six-inch centipede, finally annoyed by Joe's movements, chose to bite. Fire raced into his hand as he was pulling the trigger. His hand jerked just as the gun went off. The bullet hit Wilson anyway.

"Goddamn, son-of-a-bitching, motherfucker!" Joe screamed, simultaneously with a terrible roar that flooded his mind. Hatred and anger beyond his understanding rushed through him from Billy Joe, who had been sitting there in Joe's mind. The reflex from the bite had been too quick for Billy Joe, catching him completely off guard.

Joe jumped to his feet slapping the centipede to the ground. He stomped it over and over until it was no more than a part of his boot's ribbed impression in the earth. Joe held his hand. The pain was intense.

Balfire grabbed him by the arm. "C'mon Joe, we got to split, there's a lot of cops around!" He picked up the gun and wiped its surfaces, then raised it to his shoulder, pulled the trigger and tossed the rifle aside.

4:18 PM, HAIKU ROAD, HAIKU, HAWAII

"Where's the house?" Finch asked.

"About half a mile from here," Aaron replied. He inhaled the sweet fragrance of the air, thinking that even in the midst of uncertainty and grief, life was still full of wonderful moments.

In that instant, the bullet hit him above the left temple. Aaron was knocked over into Finch, and then back until he finally fell forward, slumped over the steering wheel. The car began to drift toward the right embankment. Finch grabbed at wheel, pushing on Aaron's shoulder in an effort to dislodge him. The car continued inexorably to the right. There was a small shoulder and then an inclined slope that ran a hundred feet down the meadow into thick jungle. Finch was screaming wildly and pushing at Aaron. He finally managed to turn the wheel when they were just inches from the embankment's edge. He kicked at Aaron's foot and managed to free it from the accelerator, getting his own foot in place and stomping on the brake. This sent the car's rear end skidding around toward the embankment and against his best efforts, the car began sliding backwards down the steep embankment.

Finch pissed himself as he felt the bottom drop out of his stomach. He saw the car's nose point upward as the meadow appeared in the rear-view mirror. He fought against the panic that threatened to engulf him and render him useless. He held the wheel as straight as he could and pumped gently at the brakes. There was no telling what kind of a drop-off occurred where the jungle began. Finch watched it approach in the rear-view mirror. Hitting the brakes was not helping, as the car was sliding over the slick grass. The car was slowing down but not enough. *Not nearly enough*, he thought. *I'm going to get hurt. I'm not going to die. I'm just going to get hurt really bad.*

The car continued through the grass and the terrain was becoming uneven. Then, five feet from the edge of the jungle, the car hit a large boulder. First the bumper hit it with a bone-jarring crash, then the car went up into the air and over it, coming down and driving the rock's pointed head into the muffler and then further on into the undercarriage. The front end whipped around and came to a stop, throwing Finch into Aaron.

Finch sat, frozen, staring out of the windshield at the drop-off just a few feet away. His neck hurt from the collision with the rock. At the moment, it was a distant pain. His breath, which had been held tight in his chest throughout the descent, came shuddering out of his lungs. For a few seconds he did nothing but breathe and tremble. Then he remembered Aaron, shot and bleeding in the seat next to him. He checked his pulse, surprised to find that he was still alive. Aaron looked bad, his face white from shock. Finch climbed around to get a better look at the wound, but he couldn't see much for all the blood. He pushed his way out of the passenger door and climbed back up the hill to the road.

4:27 PM, MAUI POLICE DEPARTMENT, WAILUKU, HAWAII

Alan and Ben sat in the office. The officers stood by the door. They'd been talking about what might have happened. Alan was feeling preternaturally calm. It was almost as if some kind of distance had suddenly opened up between him and whatever events were taking place.

Ben said, "It's plain, even if we don't know the details, that some kind of a frame is in place. It's also clear that there have got to be bodies up there. Why would there be all this uproar without them?" Ben studied the backs of his hands. Looking at Alan was disturbing him for some reason so he was concentrating his attention elsewhere.

"Whatever it is Ben, because it's an illusion, is going to prove out to be just that. Nothing we do will change the progress of events to come. The one thing I know is that the less said and done the better. Let them dance all over the gym. The odds are that they will slip and fall down a lot sooner than we will." Alan was staring into some kind of middle distance.

"Whatever it takes, Alan. If you think you'll be okay here, I'm going to head up there and see what's going on."

"That might be good, Ben. I'll be okay."

Ben nodded and got up, parting the officers in front of him. Then he was gone.

4:27 PM, HAIKU ROAD, HAIKU, HAWAII

Finch made it to the top of the bank, wild-eyed and bedraggled. His eyes were searching for the bullet that might find him, which he had not thought of until just now. At that moment an ambulance came up the road, headed for Alan's house. Finch moved into the roadway and frantically waved it down. He ran to the driver's side where a young white man with regular features and thinning sandy hair rolled down the window and asked him what was wrong.

Finch identified himself and explained in rapid bursts about what had happened and about Aaron lying injured in the car down below. Immediately the driver pulled the ambulance on to the shoulder. Very quickly he had a stretcher out of the back, assisted by the other EMT, a wide Asian woman in her mid-thirties.

"Can you set me up with the radio? I need to call the house." The woman ran to the cab and helped Finch with the radio. He was patched in to Captain Rusk, who told him he would be right there. Finch replaced the radio and then slumped back in the seat with his eyes closed.

Ten minutes later Rusk arrived, just as the two EMTs had muscled Aaron Wilson to the top of the hill. Finch saw them plastered with sweat, their uniforms filthy and then it occurred to him how much help he could have been if he had not lost his presence of mind. Shame flooded through him. The help he did not offer could eventually cost Aaron his life. Then another part of him pushed it all aside. He had not shot Aaron. He had done everything to control the car and had run for help immediately. He had done all that he could. This was instantly followed by the thought that he was now the acting District Attorney. Fate had put him right where he had wanted to be for a long time. *Now we will see how things go, with Richard Finch at the helm.*

Rusk trotted over to the ambulance. "How is he?" he asked the male EMT.

"Hard to say," the man replied. "His signs are weak. We don't know what the bullet did." As they loaded him into the ambulance, Rusk looked at Wilson. He did not look good. Rusk thought of how this changed everything. He didn't like Aaron Wilson and it didn't matter to Rusk whether he made it or not. His mind was racing ahead as the playing field rearranged itself right before his eyes.

At that moment, a car whipped around the corner from the direction of Alan's house and slid in behind Rusk's car. A middle aged Oriental man emerged from the driver's side and came running to the ambulance. It was Dr. Hung, the medical examiner. "Why the fuck didn't you tell me what happened?" he screamed at Rusk as he blew past him to the back of the ambulance. Rusk was unable to say a thing. "Let's get out of here," Dr. Hung screamed at the attendants and in seconds, Finch was out of the door and the ambulance was screaming down the road.

Finch and Rusk stood in the road and watched it disappear. "What's his fucking problem?" Rusk asked. "I didn't even know where he was when I got the call. I thought I should come immediately. There was an ambulance here. Ah, fuck him."

"Passions are running high right now," Finch replied. "Where is Alan Douglas?"

"He's at the station. I've got a couple of officers watching him."

"Has he been charged?"

"No, but if he attempts to leave he will be arrested." Rusk watched the police cars arrive. He turned back to Finch. "You're going to have to explain to the detectives what happened. Then I guess you'll want to come up to the house." Finch turned toward the car.

"I'd rather not, Captain. I had an accident while the car was going out of control. It's embarrassing."

Rusk picked right up on it. "Here." He guided Finch around his vehicle. "Get in my car. I'll arrange for you to talk to them through the window. Then what, you just want to go back?"

"I've got a change of clothes in my office. After that, I guess the thing to do is have Douglas formally charged."

Rusk nodded, "You're the Boss now," he said.

Shortly after that they were at the bottom of Haiku Road waiting to pull out on the Hana Highway. Finch looked at Rusk and said, "You knew all the time, knew something was rotten with Douglas. Did you ever expect anything like this?"

"I'm not a psychiatrist Richard, but it doesn't seem that strange that a man could turn into the thing that he chases. But no, I didn't expect anything like what I saw today. You have no idea."

"Well you're going to need to tell me everything and it's probably a good idea that I know as much as possible before we get there."

Rusk pulled out on the highway and headed back to Wailuku. Neither he nor Finch saw Ben's car go past and make the turn up the hill.

Chapter Thirty-One

As Ben pulled into Alan's driveway he thought of how quickly everything had happened. *And what's next?* He wondered. The escalation of events was incredible. He got out of his car, nodding at the people he knew, and went looking for Dr. Hung.

On his way in the door, Willie Hoko, a twenty-year veteran who had obviously been placed there to restrict access into the house, stopped him.

"Ben, what you doing here?" Hoko was a very big man and could have easily replaced the door in terms of denying entrance. Like many big men however, he had a jovial nature even when he was acting as a policeman, though there was always a sense of menace behind everything he said and did. Ben never knew if Willie was seriously playing bad or badly playing serious. It didn't seem to matter, as far as Ben was concerned. He just played along.

"I'm looking for Dr. Hung, Willie."

Willie shrugged. "He gone, l'dat. DA got shot, Hung goes running, hospital now, prolly. Captain Rusk knows you come?"

Ben stared in shock. He felt as if he had been punched in the stomach. "How…? When…?"

"No stay knowing, Lieutenant. Come over radio, Hung go flyin."

All Hell is breaking loose…! Ben shook his head and put the clamoring of his thoughts aside. There was nothing he could do about it now.

Willie showed no sign of moving so Ben asked, "Rusk say I cannot come?"

"No tell me dat." Willie spoke only pidgin, even though he could speak and comprehend otherwise. It was also in his nature to act dumb.

"Well, if he didn't tell you not to let me in, do you mind getting that Haleakalā -sized body of yours out of the way?"

Willie laughed, "No problem, Lieutenant, but what you want now Dr. Hung gone?"

"Cherie here?" Ben was asking for Hung's assistant.

"Cherie in da house," Willie said.

"Then, Willie, if you don't mind I'm going in da house to see her. Okay?"

Willie spread his catcher's mitt hands wide and stepped aside. "Can go, Lieutenant."

Ben thought that one of these days he was going to see just what Willie had on the "plate lunch special" by giving him a serious poke in the gut. He stepped by him and went in search of Cherie Provenzano, a transplanted Texas pathologist who had found a home in the Valley Isle. Cherie was in her early thirties with long black hair and a round face with dark magnetic eyes. She was tall and lush and Hung usually had his hands full telling police officers and others to "shut the fuck up" when she accompanied him to a crime scene. Invariably, a number of individuals would feel impelled to make a colorful comment to get her attention. It didn't matter what tragedy might be the scene of their horseplay.

Ben finally found her. He came around the corner and saw the entire tableau at once. It rocked him back on his heels. *Here was the manifest result of a deep and abiding evil.* His mind reflexively clutched at his gut to hold still. He had never imagined anything like this. Halogen lamps had been set up and the entire room was lit as if by the noonday sun. It looked like a set for a horror movie. When he saw the children on the platter, he felt his heart freeze. Then he saw Wendy. It was overwhelming. Everything until this moment had been either a condition of implied danger or something he'd seen before. This was like walking into a different world. All the rules of engagement had suddenly changed.

"Hi, Ben." Cherie came around the table and put her hand on his shoulder. Ben did not react. He was still frozen, trying to gain some understanding of what was before him. It wasn't going to happen. "Ben?"

Ben turned around and walked quickly out of the room. Cherie followed him. Ben went out on the deck. "I've never seen anything like that..." He shook his head and stared out at the fruit trees and flowers in Alan's back yard. The scene was so pastoral. There was no hint of the gruesome insanity in the beauty that stretched before him. *What a terrible darkness is the human mind?*

"It's worse than it looks," Cherie said. She'd tied her hair in a bun and was wearing a long white coat. "Whoever did this gave a lot of thought to the details. All of the males have rods in their penises. The skin was stretched and a spine implanted to give them enormous erections. You don't see it until you pull them away from the table. The women were spread wide, honey, butter and few other things we won't know until after the lab work. It poured out of them, off of them, on to their chairs and on to the floor. There are *many* ants and dead bees, obviously imported. The boy and girl are sewn together and I mean really sewn together." She sighed.

"I've been looking around. There's an effort that's been made to give the impression that the work happened here, though it's highly unlikely. I'm not a detective, but I do work with the same principles. This was very quickly set up.

Some of the bodies aren't completely ready for display according to the taxidermist's art. Otherwise, the guy who did the work is a pro. There's a lot of animals in the shed outside, also stuffed. I'm pretty sure he only did the humans, not the other creatures. Some of them are much older and the workmanship is different and less precise. I pointed some of these things out to Captain Rusk, so did Dr. Hung. He was breathing down our necks. He said, 'insane acts do not follow rational guidelines' and that, of course, Alan had help. How's the DA?"

"Don't know. I've got to get back down there. They'll be sticking it to Alan." Ben turned around to leave.

"Alan's been arrested." Cherie pushed a wisp of stray hair back out of her face.

"What?" Ben asked, surprised but not really surprised. *They were on a runaway train!*

Cherie walked back into the house with him. "I heard it over the radio just before you came in. Rusk called it into the station from his car. He and the assistant DA are driving back there."

"Doctor, you done in here?" A detective called to her from the hallway.

"Not at all," she replied. "We'll talk later, Ben?" Her eyes were filled with concern as she said this. She knew Ben and Alan were close. She liked Ben a lot. So far though, Ben had not gotten the message. She watched him walk away and then went back to her work.

5:10 PM, MAUI POLICE DEPARTMENT, WAILUKU, HAWAII

Alan sat in the lock-up cell, a bunk, four walls, a toilet and a sink — nothing else. It had all happened quickly. An officer Alan had never seen before came in and read him his rights. Very swiftly he was charged and booked and then put in the cell. That had been just fifteen minutes ago. He sat with his eyes closed, breathing evenly. He let the random thoughts come and go, watching them, detached. He was feeling the absurdity of his situation, marveling at the progression of events.

Ming appeared. His brocaded robe shimmered with the colors of the spectrum as it fluttered in the tug of an unseen wind. Then the air became still and the robe settled and became a dazzling white. Ming raised his hand in greeting and the folds of the robe disturbed by his movement burst into color again. "You like the effect?" Ming asked. There was a wide smile on his face.

"It's very impressive, Ming. I'm sure everyone on the inner planes will be wearing one by this afternoon."

"I doubt it. You don't go to Barneys for one of these." Ming's smile remained constant. "The situation has changed, therefore my appearance has changed. A necessary progression, is the best way to put it. How are you feeling?"

"I feel okay."

Ming nodded, his eyes were warm and benevolent. "Do you feel strong?"

"Does it matter if I am as long as you are?"

"Well said," Ming replied. "But there is *believing* and there is *doing*. I'm not *going* to be here, Alan. *I am here*." Ming laid emphasis on every word. "But now, just like Saint John of the Cross and the dark night of the soul, even if I am *here*, you may not be able to see me. You'll be in uncharted waters." Ming had such a serious look on his face that Alan was taken aback. "Whatever you begin to feel, don't react. It would be like trying to pull Leviathan from the sea."

Alan felt very troubled. Somehow he had thought that if he surrendered, then that was all his mind needed to focus on. Now it seemed that there was more and he did not know what. "I'm confused, Ming. I thought I was supposed to surrender and observe."

"This is true Alan, but there is no *you*. So who is doing the surrendering? If you have to shit, do you just shit, or do you find a place to shit first? Do you pull your pants down before you shit, or do you just shit in your pants? There is a *dynamic tension* to everything, even surrender. There is sequence. There are poles of opposition that resolve to a single pole that is in opposition to another pole. They resolve into yet another pole and so on and so forth. Perhaps you must fight and not fight and fight and *then* you surrender." On this enigmatic note Ming smiled and left.

Alan opened his eyes. Ming's visit left him feeling uneasy. It was not the way he wanted to feel.

5:30 PM, MAUI COUNTY CORRECTIONAL FACILITY, MAUI, HAWAII

CarryAnn awoke from a terrifying dream in which the man from Arizona had found her. He had been cutting away little pieces of her body with scissors. There had been horrible laughter and CarryAnn had been screaming.

She was bathed in sweat. The right side of her face ached where Tony had punched her. She had kicked him in the balls while handcuffed in the parking lot. Tony had been telling her what was going to happen to her after the big *titas* in jail got their hands on her. She had kicked him good.

Now her body was racked with chills and a sense of nervous dread as the cocaine leached itself from her system. She'd been doing pure coke for weeks, and now she couldn't focus or concentrate, hallucinations were appearing in the air. She felt herself breaking down and was scared shitless at what might happen.

She couldn't eat. They'd been served something called *Pork Hekka* for dinner. It looked and tasted like bad *chop suey* that the cook had shit in. She was shaking like a leaf.

The jail was the way she had imagined it, but then she'd never been in jail and really had no idea of what to expect. The female guards had been brutal. The other prisoners, both male and female, had yelled taunts and racial slurs at her and the guards had laughed. One of them said, "Don't worry little *haole*, it gets worse." Still there seemed to be little real danger at the moment. As a new inmate, she was in quarantine until she'd been processed. That might take several days. She had to go to court first.

She'd seen a doctor earlier and he said he would give her something for her nerves and to help her sleep, but nothing had arrived. She was trembling from fear and anxiety and she stank.

Would they find her now? Would that freak find her here? CarryAnn wondered about the voice she had heard at Tommy's house, the man who had made her so small that the vampire could not see her. That is how she thought of him, as a vampire. She remembered the sharp little teeth and the oh-so-red lips. *Where was the one who had helped her?*

CarryAnn was in big trouble, but she knew the legal trouble was not as big as they were making it seem, because she was not as old as they thought she was. The detectives who had interrogated her had wanted to know where she got the coke. They'd told her that she would be getting a mandatory twenty-year sentence for sale of cocaine. Maybe that was true for adults but not for her. She was not an adult, not chronologically, and not legally.

She had known that something was wrong. She'd felt it in her gut, but like most people, she had ignored her intuition. Last night she'd found out what Grigo meant when he said that Tony had done things no cop would do. Grigo had slept with Tony. She was completely baffled.

A policeman had told her she would have a hearing for bail in the morning. She'd wait and see what happened. At any time, she could tell them she was a juvenile and they'd send her back to California. Once there, in the hands of the authorities, she could tell them about Royce. After that she was sure she would not have to go to jail. But jail was not her immediate danger. Jail was a remote and distant concern against the backdrop of the vampire and his friends. Jail, in fact, might be a good thing. *It wasn't likely that they could get to her in here, or could they?*

Her thoughts scattered again as a spasm racked her body. Fear rode into her mind on a black horse. Fear was raising his helmet and under the helmet were a million things that crawled into the openings of the human body and ate the soul. *The bad man from Arizona was going to kill her.* A part of her mind knew that this was unavoidable and that part of her mind was now becoming the strongest part. Every fear that could be illustrated was making cartoon scenarios in her mind. There were twisted explosions of color, muddy reds, slimy puke greens and shades of black. In most of them, the bad man from Arizona was the prominent character. Her mother was being raped by South American drug dealers and assorted animal life that did not exist on Planet Earth. Royce was having his eyes burned out. Tommy was hanging from hooks like a pig in a slaughterhouse full of industrial sounds. *There was nowhere to go.* She prayed to God but God appeared as a demented Elmer Fudd with a huge throbbing penis and he wanted her to suck it. Behind him were other creatures waiting in line. The bad man from Arizona was also in line. He held a razor.

Her teeth were gritted tightly together, both hands clamped between her knees. Little whimpers were escaping through her lips and there were bugs crawling under her skin. The most terrible thing was that she needed more coke and she couldn't get to it.

She heard the sound of keys at her door and then it opened. A guard was standing there. She had two pills in a paper cup. "How'zit?" she asked. The woman was big but she had a pleasant smile. "Not so good, eh? The doctor give this prescription for you but the last shift forgets." She smiled and extended the cup.

CarryAnn jumped up from the bed and pitched to the far wall, catching her balance before she tumbled to the floor. She righted herself and extended her hand. It was trembling.

The guard put her arm around her and walked her back to the sink. When they were standing over it she said, "Open you mouth, little *wahine*."

CarryAnn did as she was asked and the guard put the pills in her mouth. She filled the paper cup from the sink. Gently, she poured the water into CarryAnn's mouth. Then she held her for a moment while CarryAnn swallowed.

"Little girl, you need find help," the guard murmured. "Maybe you don't want do drugs no more. Maybe you can live and make you life." She walked CarryAnn over to her bunk and helped her on to it. Then she stroked her brow for a time as CarryAnn lay there trembling. Her eyes were clenched shut and tears were burbling at the corners. "You be okay, not do the drugs no mo, heh?"

The guard squeezed her shoulder and then left.

A river of tears broke forth from CarryAnn's eyes as she heard the door close. Her body was racked with sobs that came from deep in the well above her hips. She turned over on her knees and beat her mattress with her fists, a terrible fury purging itself from her heart, her denial broken. No one had ever been as kind to her as that guard, no one. She had not seen such tenderness since she was small and that was from her mother. It seemed a lifetime away since anyone had shown her anything like what she had just received and she needed it more right now than at any time before in her life. She cried until she had no tears left, then mercifully, the pills took effect and she fell asleep.

6:00 PM, AVALON RESTAURANT, LAHAINA, HAWAII

Whip and Christienne sat under a large umbrella on the deck overlooking the ocean. The sun was low in the sky. A glorious sunset was slowly weaving itself together through the fulsome clouds. A radiant splatter of mauve stretched across the skies, now and again there were green flashes that came and went in the blink of an eye. Whip and Christienne had pulled their seats close together. Their backs were to the other patrons as they watched the sky. Christienne had her legs splayed as she leaned back into her chair, a glass of Chardonnay in her hand. Whip's hand rested comfortably on her thigh, his fingers lightly brushing her skin through the fabric of her dress. It was an island moment filled with magic. Ben E. King's "Gypsy" was playing over the sound system.

Whip frowned and Christienne instantly turned toward him, such was the nature of the rapport developing between them. "What's wrong, Honey?"

Whip shifted minimally in his seat. "I really don't know. I've been getting funny flashes all day long. I used to know Ben's cell phone number and all day I can't remember it. I'm sure I had his card, now I can't find it. I could have sworn I brought the phone with me, but apparently not. Maybe it's in the car." He took a sip of his Guinness and then set it on the table in front of him. "I feel like I'm in a dream. You know, like when you're staring into a fire, it's incredibly hypnotic and although you're lulled, the fire will still burn you. I feel like bad shit is happening, but in the meantime, it's miles away from me and I feel great. I'm with the woman I love. I'm about to have dinner and then stroll through town but underneath there's this unsettling noise." He reached over and stroked Christienne's cheek with the back of his hand.

"Babe, can I call you babe?" Christienne said impishly. "Once again, no matter what you're feeling, it doesn't change anything. We've discussed this. I don't mind you being concerned but worry is only useful if it helps the result. I've never seen it do that. I've never seen it change anything for the better. You tell me how good Alan is. Let him wail against the rock. If he breaks, we'll pick up the pieces and glue him back together."

"Jesus, sometimes you are so… so matter-of-fact."

"Whatever. If I can't do something about something then it gets no tears from me. Any of the things I say would be perfectly okay coming from a man, coming from me it gives the impression of being hard, cold or indifferent. I am none of those things as you well know." She emphasized this point by running her hand up Whips thigh.

Whip jumped and nearly spilled his beer in his lap. "Damn!" he exclaimed, looking quickly around to see if anyone had seen Christienne in action. "You are something else."

"I am indeed," she replied impishly and then kissed him on the mouth.

"Let's go and get you that little black dress."

6:00 PM, 154 KOKOMO ROAD, HAIKU, HAWAII

Balfire and Kimo-Joe came through the door of the house. Joe had no expression on his face. Balfire, on the other hand, was apprehensive. He didn't know if the target was dead or not. He certainly hoped so.

Billy Joe sat slouched in an armchair looking like a character in one of those high-powered stereo speaker ads. He raised one hand and pointed to the couch. "Sit down," he said.

The two men went directly to the couch and sat.

"You fucked up," Billy Joe said simply. "The man is not dead and he should be. Gratefully, he is in a coma and that serves my purposes for now. It's possible I will have things where I want them by the time he is in any shape to oppose me."

"However," Billy Joe suddenly slithered like an eel into an upright position. This scared the hell out of Balfire who was watching him. He never saw him use his feet or hands at all for the effort. "Now we need to make adjustments. We need to add a new ingredient to the mix." Billy Joe looked pointedly at Balfire.

"In any major conflict, as history shows, sacrifices have to be made. Men have very often laid down their lives for a cause they believed in. Tremendous acts of heroism have been recorded. These acts have gone on to inspire the other combatants and perhaps to change the momentum, the very course of the war."

Billy Joe got up and spun around theatrically in the middle of the room. "Such a sacrifice is called for now and who better to make this effort than our own Viking Prince, the redoubtable Balfire Tweeds." Billy Joe was now looming over Balfire who had scrunched into the couch as if to diminish himself. It was an ineffective action.

"Boss, it's not fair," he whined. "It wasn't my fault."

"And what possible difference could that make?" Billy Joe said with a sarcastic smile. "In the old days they would kill the messenger just because he brought bad news. Only a fool expects life to be fair and only a total fool would expect *me* to be fair."

"A bug bit Joe. I wasn't even the shooter!" Balfire cried.

"Balfire," Billy Joe leaned in and put his hand on Balfire's shoulder. "It isn't about anything you've done wrong. You don't even know what's required of you and you're already acting *like a bitch*." Billy Joe clipped off the last three words sharply. "Let me make this brief. You're going to do what I ask for the greater glory of the cause. There isn't any room for argument." A power began to transmit through Billy Joe's hand. Balfire's expression changed from one of concern to relaxed immobility. "You are going to drive the van down to the police station and turn yourself in. Then you're going to tell them a tale. They'll lock you up for a while but you know that Billy Joe will get you out again, don't you?"

Balfire nodded his head. "Yes, boss." Balfire immediately saw that Billy Joe would handle everything and that once he was done, Billy Joe would free him. He laughed at his previous dismay. Billy Joe was all-powerful. It was as certain and true as the wind and the rain.

Balfire got up from the couch and headed for the door.

"Balfire?"

He turned at the sound of Billy Joe's voice. "Yes, boss?"

"You done good son. Bye-bye." Billy Joe waved and Balfire went out the door.

6:30 PM, MAUI POLICE DEPARTMENT, WAILUKU, HAWAII

The cell door opened and Ben walked in carrying two take-out containers and a paper bag. He smiled at Alan and set everything down on the cot beside him. "I knew you were going to wind up in jail one of these days."

Alan leaned back against the wall with his hands behind his head. "I know, Ben, I should have listened to my saintly old ma when she warned me not to go out a drinkin' and a gamblin.'"

"How you doing, Bubba…? I see they didn't confiscate your sense of humor." Ben studied him looking for any signs of the effect his arrest might have had on him, but Alan seemed fine.

Alan patted the bunk and said, "Have a seat. I'm doing okay. At least I know what I'm up against. Sooner or later comes the duel in the desert."

Ben sat down on the bunk and opened one of the take-out containers. "You want the details before dinner or after dinner?"

"During is fine. Rusk knows you're here?"

"Captain Rusk and acting DA Richard Finch are most likely busy with the construction of the scaffold from which they are planning to hang you at dawn." Ben's face had turned serious as he said this.

Alan felt trepidation in his heart. "Where's Aaron?"

"Aaron met with an accident, Alan."

"What!" Alan exclaimed.

"Be at peace, little brother. You eat and I'll talk." Ben went on to describe the events that had taken place during his absence and what he had seen at the house.

Alan's face showed a wide range of expressions as he listened to Ben's account. He stared in disbelief when he heard what had been found at his house. "You've got to be kidding!"

"I wish I were, certainly the people seated at that table wish I was joking." Ben told him about Aaron and what he had learned just minutes before.

"So he's going to be okay then. He's going to live."

"Right now, nobody is saying anything, Alan. We'll know more tomorrow."

"Damn, I never expected anything like this. Aaron's in real danger!"

"I've covered that. There are two policemen inside the room. Whether even that is going to work, I don't know. I've got another list of houses. I'll be checking them tonight. There's one location right near your house. I'm going there first. If I can find this fuck, it's going to be all over, termination with extreme prejudice." Ben filled his mouth with crispy noodles.

"We've not going to get Billy Joe that way Ben."

"And what the fuck am I supposed to do with information like that, lay down and play dead? I've got to keep at it, Alan. If everything is part of everything, then what I am doing has got to be part of something. Maybe I won't get him through ordinary police work, but I might get his elves."

Alan set his food down and took a sip of coffee. "Just be careful, Ben. There's no question he's got something in mind for you too."

"Maybe, but I have a feeling that the closer he gets to his goal, the less attention he's paying to anyone but you."

The cell door opened and a guard stepped in. "You're going to have to leave Lieutenant, Captain Rusk's orders."

"We were expecting that," Ben said. He got up and shook Alan's hand. "You got a lawyer?"

"Haven't thought about it, Ben."

"I'll look into it." Ben stood for a moment as if there might be something further to say but nothing came.

"Get in touch with Whip, tell them to stay where they are. Tell him to stay away from here, no questions."

"I'll do that." Ben left. On his way out the door, the officer told him that Captain Rusk wanted to see him in his office, so Ben went directly there. Once he arrived, Cora sent him right in. Rusk and Finch were having coffee when Ben entered the room.

"Lieutenant Kamamoto, maybe you can answer a couple of questions for me." Rusk's mouth was set in a thin line. There was a red cast to his eyes that told Ben he'd been visiting his desk bottle. "Why were you up at the crime scene and why were you visiting with the prisoner?"

Ben was surprised at the questions. They didn't seem to have any purpose. "I was at the scene as a member of the task force assigned to this case and I was visiting Alan Douglas because he happens to be a friend of mine."

Rusk looked at Finch and nodded curtly at Ben. "You're not on the case anymore and you have no permission to visit the prisoner, which must come from me. Douglas is being held in isolation until we interrogate him."

Ben felt the anger begin to coil in his stomach. "What do you mean, I'm not on the case? Unless you've forgotten, I am attached to the District Attorney's Office."

"Uh-huh," Rusk said. "Technically that is true. However, Richard Finch is now the acting DA and Mr. Finch has decided your relationship with the prisoner might compromise the investigation. Klein and Santos are now handling the case. You're on desk duty until a decision can be made regarding your position with the department."

Ben looked at Rusk as if he were a wino who had just soiled himself. He turned his attention to Finch who gazed directly back at him out of eyes that revealed nothing. "So that's how it is. Aaron Wilson isn't dead the last I heard, and when he finds out what the two of you have cooked up, neither one of you will have a job."

Rusk got up from his chair, his face flushed to the roots of his hair. "You're going to want to shut your fucking mouth Kamamoto. You are a hair away from being in jail yourself and that may come sooner than you think. Mr. Finch will be investigating your relationship to the crimes for which Douglas is presently charged."

Finch interjected. "I expect you to be available for questioning in the near future, Lieutenant. You may want to consider retaining a lawyer at this point."

"Understood," Ben replied. It was imperative now for him to not alienate either of these men any further. The thought had come into his mind to get out of the office as quickly as he could. "Can I please go now?"

Rusk squinted at Ben. He and Finch had a great deal to take care of and could deal with Ben later. "Dismissed," he said.

Ben turned and left quickly. Once on his way, he realized he still had his badge and his gun. He wasn't out of the game yet by a long shot.

Finch watched Ben walk out of the office. In a short time he expected to have enough evidence to put him away, too. There was no way Kamamoto could have been as close as he was to Douglas and not known something. His mind was moving at a high rate of speed over the day's events and their implications for his future.

It had been easy for Billy Joe to gain control of Finch's mind. Finch's vanity and arrogance were superhighways of access. Finch had already accepted that Alan was responsible for the murders. With his superior in the hospital for an indefinite period, he was in the driver's seat. It was his case. The prosecution of a celebrated New York City Homicide detective as a serial murderer would win him international attention. The video and print tabloids would be slathering at his heels. His success would be assured, book deals, higher elected office, all of these things would be readily within his grasp. He would be symbolically revenged on his father. Not a bit of this registered itself on Richard Finch's face. If anything, he looked bored.

Billy Joe moved between the two men. Some time ago he had become a presence in their thoughts, though they knew nothing of it. Their thoughts and actions seemed no different to them than they had ever been. They had been changed though, not essentially but by degree. They were more of what they were. They were changed in the way someone might be after drinking several glasses of wine. There was a greater potential for reckless thought and action. Billy Joe's urgings had the same effect on them that a beautiful woman might have. *A beautiful woman often brought out the fool in a man. If the man were a fool to begin with there was hardly any effort required.*

"I want Doctor Abadon to interview him," Rusk said suddenly.

"What?" Finch came back into himself. Even if he had been paying attention, he would not have understood Rusk's statement.

"Doctor Abadon, he's a psychiatrist, a specialist in serial murders. He's also a law and order man."

"I know who he is, Millard. Aaron and I have talked about him. I've also read one of his books. I just don't understand why you want to bring him in on this." Finch shook his head. The idea of a psychiatrist intruding on the scene had a disagreeable flavor to it.

"Richard, bear with me a moment," Rusk said patiently as he reached into his desk drawer and pulled out the bottle of bourbon. He set two glasses on his desk and poured out drinks for the two of them. He handed Finch his drink and then continued. "You and I both know, right down to the soles of our shoes, that that son-of-a-bitch Douglas is guilty. However, Douglas has powerful friends and I can see how an entirely different case might be made from the evidence and the perception of Douglas's character in the eyes of others. Aaron is well disposed to him, as are others. They constitute a factor we need to be aware of."

Finch's head bobbed up and down. All of what Rusk was saying made perfect sense. He'd considered all of this previously.

"If Dr. Abadon were to interview him, just consider the evidence, Richard. He would have to at least make the recommendation for a period of observation at the state institution at Kaneohe. That's all the way over on Oahu. Once there, isolated from his support structure, he'd be far more vulnerable to interrogation. He might even require medication."

Finch interrupted him. "Some of what you're saying has merit. Once he's been sent off for observation, there he sits for ninety days, no matter what. But I think you're going a little far afield when you mention medication and all that. He'll have a lawyer by then. Kamamoto is probably working on that right now."

"Whatever." Rusk took a serious belt from his drink and then let out a slow breath of air. "Once he's been sent off, any efforts by misguided associates would be derailed. If Abadon becomes convinced of Douglas's guilt, he'll be a powerful ally in putting him away for good. He doesn't believe in the insanity defense."

"He knows Douglas. He's spent time with him. For all we know, he respects Douglas. It could work the other way." Finch held up his had to cut off Rusk's protest. "Look, I'm just playing the devil's advocate here. I just want to do this right. You think there's going to be some kind of a movement afoot to get Douglas released pending further investigation? The right people could do that. Aaron could do that, but Aaron can't countermand a judge's order. It certainly has a nice cast to it. You think that if Abadon finds, or if we can convince Abadon that Alan is psychotic, we can bypass a lot of potential bullshit? It's a nice touch. Alan is a danger to others and himself. He needs to be in a hospital. Meanwhile, we build a solid case. The press paints him as Jack the Ripper. It could work, but what makes you think Abadon will play along *and* who's the judge?"

Rusk poured himself another drink. Finch put his hand over his glass. "I spoke with Doctor Abadon shortly before you came back from your office. He'll come by this evening. If he comes in this evening, we could have him in front of Hirano tomorrow. Hirano is sitting tomorrow and as I remember, he'll do anything you say, Richard."

Finch smiled. What Rusk said was true. A defense attorney had once referred to Judge Hirano as "Finch's buttboy." He played it over in his mind. It had a lovely feel to it. Perhaps Finch would have been more objective in another circumstance. Perhaps Rusk would have been too, but they were sailing a course set by a navigator unknown to them. *The mind of a particular navigator currently nestled down inside of Richard Finch. It stretched and extended its arms and legs in a feel good, getting-to-know-you fashion. It tasted the environment, sipping it in and breathing it back out.* Billy Joe simply imagined the sequence of events necessary to place Douglas where he wanted him and instantly they became Richard Finch's personal priorities.

"Set it up," Finch said. "Has the press been informed?"

"Well, we've had the lid down on the details, but they know something was up at the house. I expect that very soon now they will know about the bodies and about the arrest of Douglas." Rusk smiled conspiratorially. *In the back of his mind, the evil presence coiled and snuggled up inside the alcoholic mist, making itself warm and comfortable.*

Chapter Thirty-Two

8:05 PM, PACIFIC'O RESTAURANT, LAHAINA, HAWAII

They had just finished a remarkable meal and two bottles of wine that cost several times more than the dinner. For the last hour, Whip had forgotten all about the troubles. He was adrift on a sea of love. Whenever he looked into Christienne's eyes he felt a euphoric expansion in his chest. A great delight spread throughout his being.

As lovers are, Christienne was very aware of this. It was a mirror of her emotions. Anything was possible with such a love. She felt she had known him forever.

Whip could still not remember Ben's cell phone number. When he called the police station he had been told that both Alan and Ben were unavailable. It was time to try again. This time he would try the house. Alan was definitely home by now. As he was getting ready to excuse himself the chef/owner of the restaurant came over to inquire about their meal. He was a pleasant man with a moon-shaped face and a long black braid running down his back. Whip told him it was one of the finest meals he could ever remember. He then excused himself and left Christienne to continue the conversation.

He dialed Alan's house and a stranger answered the phone. Whip asked for Alan and was told he wasn't in.

"Who is calling?" the man asked.

"I'm the Emperor of Ice Cream." Whip replied and then hung up. Something had happened. Suddenly, Ben number popped clearly into his mind. He called it immediately.

"Ben, it's Whip."

"Whip! I've been calling you for hours! What happened to the phone?"

Whip kicked his foot at the wall in anger at himself. "I lost it somewhere Ben. What's going on? I called the house…"

"I'm afraid the shit has hit the fan." Ben quickly related the events of the day.

"We'll be there as soon as we can."

"No!" Ben said emphatically. "Under no circumstances are you to come here. Alan insists. The danger is now very real and it's not just Billy Joe you have to worry about. It's Captain Rusk and Richard Finch as well. There's no telling what they might pull with Aaron out of the way. You could be rearrested for the episode with Malcolm. You could be charged with Malcolm's death."

"I don't much care about what could happen to me, Ben. Alan needs my help and I'm coming back."

Ben sighed. "Listen, Whip, if you've got to come back, then meet me somewhere else. You can stay at my house tonight. You can come out with me if you want. I'm looking at some locations. I could use the help. Rusk pulled me off the case. Anyway, you can't get in to see Alan. No one can. At least do it this way?" He was pleading with Whip now.

Whip was quiet for a moment, thinking it all through. *Ben was right.* He probably would not get to see Alan. He would run into trouble. "Okay, Ben. Where do you want to meet?"

Ben gave him directions to a coffee shop in one of the malls. "Just give Christienne the name. She'll know where it is."

"See you in an hour, Ben."

When he got back to the table the owner had moved on. Christienne was sipping her wine and smoking a cigarette. As soon as she saw his face, she knew there had been trouble.

"What is it, Whip?"

He told her and very quickly they were out of the restaurant and headed for the car.

Whip had seen the three men in the distance, but they were only twenty feet away when he tumbled to what was happening. The parking lot was little more than a block off of Front Street but it was dark and secluded. Their proximity to the car was too much of a coincidence, coupled with the vibrations of menace that Whip was receiving.

"Christienne, I want you to do what I say immediately, *no questions.* Go now and bring a cop back with you."

"Whip?"

"Do it now." His voice was cold and commanding.

"Damn, Whip!" Christienne stopped in her tracks. "I forgot my cigarettes, honey. I've got to go back." She said it in a voice loud enough to carry, then turned on her heel and went back the way they had just come.

One of them pushed himself off the hood of a car and came immediately after them. "Wait up lady, hey, you got a light?" He was moving fast.

They knew what they were doing. As the one continued toward Christienne, the other two detached themselves from their perches and came toward Whip, fanning out to either side.

Christienne looked back and saw the one gaining quickly on her and began to run. As he came by to pass Whip, Whip sidestepped into the air, coming down on his right foot. He spun to his right and brought his left foot down hard into the man's right knee. The knee gave inwardly and the man cried out and fell to the ground. Christienne was now out of reach.

Whip turned to face the other two. They were close now, and Whip could see their features, brutal men with hard malicious eyes.

They were advancing in the grappling mode that Whip had seen practiced by exponents of Gracie Jiu-Jitsu and professional wrestlers. This was the most difficult form for him to defend against. His safety would lie in his ability to stay out of their grasp and they were making sure that this would be hard for him. Backing up and moving laterally further into the lot, he now had nowhere to go except over the chain link fence that was coming up behind him.

"What do you want?" he asked.

"Fuckin' *haole*, we gone beef you up," said the one on the left, continuing to advance.

"You inna wrong island, muthafucka," the other added.

It was the moment of decision. Whip leaped toward the one on his left. He went into the air and threw a scissor kick, leading with his right foot. As he expected, the man grabbed for it with both hands. Whip turned in the air, following through with his left foot, which smacked into the bridge of the man's nose. The other man was just about on top of him, coming fast to slam Whip into the fence and pin him there. Whip landed and turned. When the thug was almost on him, he dropped into a crouch and thrust his right hand forward and up, catching him hard in the crotch with the curve of his hand.

The man groaned and bent forward involuntarily. Whip came straight up, headbutting him. In the same moment, the man crashed his fist into the side of Whip's head. He saw stars. But the punch also sent him just out of reach as he scrabbled away.

"I gone break your head, *haole*," said the other man who had now recovered from the kick and was coming again, with more caution this time.

Whip danced away, trying to keep an equal distance between his antagonists. He was going to have to hit a lot harder if he was going to stop these guys. He was moving away from the fence toward parked cars. The first man he had kicked was struggling to his feet and the second was approaching fast, putting him in a vise with the third man. *I need help*, he thought. He jumped quickly at the third man, who was the closest. The man swung his right fist at Whip's head. Whip brought his left hand up and caught the back of the man's wrist, pushing the blow past him. Very quickly he stepped up close and raked his left foot down the man's shin and hard onto the top of his foot. He could feel the bones break. The man screamed and dropped.

Whip turned to the second man who was now back on top of him. Before Whip could react, he was slammed into the side of a car, which knocked the breath out of his body. The man grabbed his throat and drew his fist back to smash Whip's face. But the punch never arrived. Suddenly the man was gone, spinning away toward the fence. Whip fought to get his breath back. He saw someone dispatching his assailant with a series of hand blows to the head and the body. Then he was occupied with the first man again, who limped toward him with a crowbar. Whip quickly broke his arm.

Suddenly, Christienne was holding him. "You okay?" She touched the swelling abrasion on his head. Whip winced and caught her hand.

"I'm okay. Where are the police?"

"There were no police."

"You want to watch these dark alleys." Whip looked up and saw it was the Birdman that had come to his rescue. His eyes crinkled with amusement as he looked at Whip. "It probably wasn't an accident, was it?" He gestured at the fallen men. "Your evening's entertainment..."

"What do you mean?" Whip was startled by the question.

"Not much," the bird wrangler answered. "You might want to think about being more careful in these dark locations. I'd think about running in the future. Those are some bad boys and even a good martial artist can wind up in big trouble against determined opponents in a confined area. Here's your phone by the way." He handed it to Whip.

"Thanks. You're right," Whip replied. "I would have been toast if you hadn't shown up."

The Birdman laughed. "Oh, you pretty much had it wrapped, but," he winked, "we'll never know now. I've got to go and you should too. The police might actually show up, now that there is nothing they can do. Your girlfriend was yelling on the street there. I don't think you want to spend the rest of the evening tied up at the police station."

"No, no, we don't. Look, thanks again." Whip extended his hand but the man had already turned around and headed back toward the street.

"*Para Gate*," he said over his shoulder.

"Jesus," Whip commented.

"What was that he said?" Christienne asked as they drove out of the lot.

"Very strange, it's part of a chant, '*Gate, Gate, Para Gate.*' It means, 'Gone, gone, gone beyond.' Ming would occasionally say the last part when something amused him. It was his way of saying 'far-out.'"

8:22 PM, MAUI POLICE DEPARTMENT, WAILUKU, HAWAII

Captain Rusk and Richard Finch were sitting in Rusk's office waiting for Dr. Abadon to show up when the phone rang. Rusk picked it up. He listened for a few moments and then said, "No way! No fucking way! We'll be right down." Rusk's face broke into a huge smile. He listened some more and then set the phone back in its cradle, grinning at Finch as if he had just won the lottery. "You're not going to believe this!"

Finch moved forward in his chair, his eyes cold and focused behind his rimless glasses. "Try me."

Rusk reached into his desk drawer and retrieved his bottle again. Like most alcoholics, he was subconsciously programmed not to display the evidence of his passion. A controlled drinker wouldn't have cared if it were left in sight. Perhaps Rusk felt he was showing mastery by returning it to its place each time. He poured his drink out slowly, milking the moment, grinning at Finch.

Finch was getting pissed off but he showed nothing. He wasn't going to play Rusk's game. He would wait as long as he had to.

Rusk took a long sip of his drink and smirked. Finally he said, "The desk just called to tell me that a Balfire Tweeds, wanted throughout California and Arizona for murder and other crimes and wanted here for suspected kidnappings and murder, has just turned himself in. He wants to turn state's evidence and tell us all about Alan Douglas and the role he played masterminding the whole ball game." Rusk laughed and drained the glass.

Finch stared at him incredulously. If what Rusk was telling him was true, Alan Douglas was history. *Nothing and no one could help him now.* "Why would he do that? Why wouldn't he cut and run?"

Rusk smirked again. "Check this out. He said he was afraid."

8:37 PM, 154 KOKOMO ROAD, HAIKU, HAWAII

Billy Joe laughed and ruffled Kimo-Joe's hair. "Everything is going so well. I just love unhappy endings." He poured a quarter of a bottle of Armagnac down his throat in a single swallow. The fire burned in his belly and he imagined he could see it rushing up through his esophagus and blasting forth from his mouth in flames. Kimo-Joe jumped in his seat when he saw them shoot across the room. Billy Joe had a very powerful imagination.

"I want you to stay here and entertain yourself, watch TV, drink beer and look after the house. There's a sawed-off shotgun by the door. You have those great instincts and that mighty rage. It would take an awful lot to bring you down." As Billy Joe was saying this, all of it became active in Kimo-Joe. Suddenly, he was far more alert than he had been and a great deal angrier.

Billy Joe made a few more adjustments in Kimo-Joe's mind and then, without another word, he walked out of the door.

Kimo-Joe got up and went to the door. He picked up the shotgun and on his way back pulled a six-pack of beer from the refrigerator, turned on the TV and sat back down.

8:41 PM, MAUI POLICE DEPARTMENT, WAILUKU, HAWAII

"We'll be in the interrogation room," Rusk told the officer at the desk. "When he's done being processed, have him brought in. Also send Doctor Abadon in there as soon as he arrives. Make sure he has a cup of coffee." Rusk didn't wait for a reply. He and Richard Finch continued down the hall to their destination.

They were waiting at the table when the detectives arrived with Balfire Tweeds. One of the detectives set up the video camera. Once it was in operation, Finch began his interrogation.

"Now," Finch shot his cuffs and folded his hands on the table. "You wanted to make a statement?"

Balfire picked his nose and looked at Finch. Then he ran the offending hand through his shaggy red hair.

Rusk wrinkled his nose in disgust, but Finch remained implacable, waiting.

"I know what I'm going to tell you will sound unbelievable, but it's true. If poor Malcolm were here he'd tell you the same thing. We would have never done the things we did except that Alan Douglas made us do them."

Finch nodded, "So you must have known him on the mainland then."

"I didn't say that."

"Well, you're wanted for a lot of crimes on the mainland. If you didn't know Douglas at the time, then he wouldn't figure into any of them, would he?" Finch probed Balfire with his eyes.

Balfire leaned forward in his seat and said, "I don't want to talk about that other shit right now except to say that Douglas *might* have been responsible for everything that happened to me and Malcolm ever since we got out of Q. He's got magical powers. He can do shit you wouldn't believe. I've seen it!" Balfire's eyes grew wide at this last statement. There was fear apparent in them.

"What kind of things can he do?" Rusk asked.

"I don't want to talk about that now!" Balfire was becoming agitated. "You've got to promise he won't be able to get near me!" His hands were shaking where they rested on the table.

Finch looked at Rusk. Neither of them could make sense of this hulking beast being afraid of Douglas or anyone else for that matter.

"Why don't you tell us how you met him and what happened afterwards," Finch said in a soft voice.

"We were in a local bar in Waiehu, me and Malcolm. We was having beers and looking for a little action. There was some native chicks we were getting friendly with. This guy was at the bar and every time I looked up I could see him watching me, so finally I go up to him and I tell him that I'm going to kick his faggot ass into another world less he turns the fuck around. He flashed a badge on me, said he wanted to talk to me and Malcolm. He used Malcolm's name. We'd neither of us seen him before.

"There was nothing to do but talk to him. No way to tell if he had backup in the place, so we sent the girls away and he bought us drinks. He would make funny signs with his hands. I thought he was signaling to someone in the place. Malcolm wanted to stick him. Nothing like that happened though. He said he knew what kind of guys we were and he had a way for us to make a lot of money. He handed us ten grand right there that night. He called it a 'good will offering.' Can I have a cigarette?" Balfire's hands were still trembling. Finch and Rusk were engrossed. *It was too good to be true, but there was no indication the man was lying.*

Finch asked a detective to get Balfire a pack of cigarettes. When Balfire had his cigarette, Finch asked him to continue.

"He knew we were wanted in California. He knew things nobody could have known about, places we'd been, things we'd said driving on the highway. It scared the shit out of us. Then he asked us if we believed in the devil. Malcolm said 'Yeah.' Malcolm was always into that kinda shit. Me, I don't know anything about it and I don't want to know." Balfire lit another cigarette off of the first.

"This cop, Douglas, said he knew the devil personally and that he had a way to gain unlimited power and wealth. That's how he said it, 'unlimited power and wealth.' Malcolm was hooked. Malcolm always thought he'd meet the devil someday. Douglas promised him this would happen. Douglas told us he needed some people kidnapped and brought to his house. He had to perform a ceremony and create a display. That was all it took. We didn't know, me and Malcolm, what all was involved, not then anyway."

"He told you he needed these people for a satanic ritual?" Rusk asked. He had begun smiling earlier and now seemed unable to stop.

"Yeah, he said he'd give us ten grand just like he'd done, for each one we brought. They had to be a certain age and sex. Malcolm told him that was no problem. I didn't like the idea." Rusk looked over at Finch and rolled his eyes. Finch pretended not to notice. "Then Douglas said I could just go to jail and Malcolm told me to shut up. Malcolm was acting pretty strange. Usually he didn't buy into shit. He'd take what he wanted and then fuck you up. I thought we were just going to catch this guy in the parking lot and take every cent the crazy son of a bitch had, fuck him up in the bargain. Not this time." Balfire shuddered and looked rapidly all around the room.

"You okay?" Finch asked.

"I'm afraid he's going to get in here and do me," Balfire replied.

"That's not going to happen," Rusk assured him. "He's locked up in a special security cell with an armed guard outside the door, no way is he going to get near you."

"You don't know him at all," Balfire replied as a shadow of remembered pain passed across his face. "You didn't protect Malcolm very well."

"What about Malcolm, did Douglas have anything to do with that?" Rusk's smile had still not changed. Finch couldn't even look at him anymore.

"He told me he took care of him."

Finch shifted in his chair and waved his hand in the air. The smoke from Balfire's continued cigarettes was getting to him. "Alan Douglas told you that he had killed Malcolm?"

"Said he would do the same to me, but now he's locked up. That's why I come in. It's not safe out there. He knows other people. He would have me killed."

"Uh-huh," Finch murmured, "Tell us about the kidnappings, what happened to those people?"

"Douglas killed them and he made me stuff them. I'm a taxidermist. He knew that. That's another reason he came after us."

"You saw him kill them?" Finch asked.

Just then a policeman walked into the room and spoke quietly to Captain Rusk.

"Excuse me for a minute." Rusk got up from his chair and left the room. While he was gone, Balfire went back to picking his nose and staring nervously into the camera and occasionally at Finch. Finch sat quietly in his chair studying Balfire as if he were an alien from another planet.

Rusk came back into the room. "Doctor Abadon's here, I put him in the box." This was Rusk's way of letting Finch know that the doctor would be viewing the rest of the interrogation from behind the two-way mirror.

Balfire seemed not to notice. His eyes still darted about the room as if he expected Alan Douglas to show up at any moment and rip his still beating heart from his chest.

"Getting back to your story," Finch said. "You saw Alan Douglas kill these people, the people that you and Malcolm Kahn kidnapped for him, at his request?"

"Yeah and not only that, he fucked some of them first, especially the boy and girl that he had me put on the platter. Then he gave them to Malcolm. Malcolm liked that kind of shit."

"You, of course, didn't participate in any of that," Rusk stated.

''No fucking way man!" Balfire was vehement. "I don't play that shit. I waited in the kitchen. The two of them were doing all kinds of evil shit."

"Uh-huh..." Finch removed his glasses and polished them with a cloth from his pocket. "Let me ask you about the attack on his brother-in-law. What was that all about?"

"He was going to kill them too. The brother-in-law was getting hip and then he met that girl. He sent Malcolm to do them." Balfire shivered and then lit another cigarette.

"And the shooting of the District Attorney, who shot the DA?"

Balfire nodded. "Douglas called us early this afternoon. He told me and Kimo-Joe to do it."

Rusk jumped out of his seat. "Who's Kimo-Joe?"

Balfire lit another cigarette. "Some short little local guy that just showed up last night, Douglas said he was a performance artist who had a show at the Kaiser Gallery. I don't know anything about it."

"Where's this Kimo-Joe now? Finch asked.

Balfire shook his head. "I don't know."

"Okay, I think we have enough for the moment." Finch rubbed his eyes before placing his glasses back on his nose. "I just want to ask you one more thing. You said earlier that Douglas might have had something to do with events in California. I still don't understand what you mean by that. Alan Douglas was living over here. As far as we know, he didn't leave the island during that period. What did you mean?"

Smoke wreathed Balfire's head, twisting sinuously around his face. "He told us that he had done it. He told us he controlled our minds and I believe him. He was two different people and you never knew which one you were dealing with. You never saw how he changed Malcolm. He was like a dog. I knew Malcolm for years. I never saw him like that before."

Finch motioned to the detectives. "We'll be talking with you again later. There'll be a statement for you to sign. Thank you for coming forward."

As Balfire was being led from the room Rusk asked, "How come you didn't ask for a deal?"

Balfire turned and looked at him with the eyes of the damned. "I'm fucked. It doesn't matter. I'm fucked."

Chapter Thirty-Three

8:53 PM, MAUI COUNTY CORRECTIONAL FACILITY, MAUI, HAWAII

CarryAnn woke up feeling much better than the time before. Whatever the doctor had prescribed for her had pushed the panic and fear to the back burner. The walls and ceiling of her cell were white and now everywhere she looked there were rainbows that formed and then disappeared. She hoped that there was another dose coming before the lights went out. She didn't want to be alone in the darkness when the pills wore off.

She sat up and went to the sink where she drank some water. She looked around her cell. There really wasn't much for her to do except go back and sit on her bed. Images from her recent past entered her mind and she winced as she thought of some of the things she had done and done easily. It seemed as if the events had been happening to someone else. She knew better though. They had all happened to her.

She wondered how she was going to look at twenty-one, if things kept on the way they were going. She'd look like a whore with a lot of evil little lines in her face, having slept with too many men whose names and faces she could no longer remember. She wished now with all of her heart that she hadn't ever had sex with anyone. Something precious was gone and it probably would never come back.

Tears rolled down her face as she thought of her mother. She was sure that she must be dead. She had called the house for two weeks and there was no answer. Then a stranger answered the phone. She had hung up. She was worried about her mother but she had not looked at a newspaper or the television since arriving in Hawaii. She had been afraid to.

She thought of what Royce had told her, that she had been created for no other purpose but for sex. Grigo had told her pretty much the same thing. Was that really her destiny? Was she supposed to spend her life rotating underneath someone whose enjoyment came from fucking her? She wondered briefly if plastic surgery had ever been used in reverse. She laughed bitterly. Maybe getting arrested was the best thing that could have happened to her. Maybe she could find another life, if she lived through this, if the vampire didn't get her first. Her mother had told her that people were ruled by fate, "But," she had added, "We make our own fate."

She'd see what happened in the morning when she got to court. If she told them the truth then she'd be sent back to California. Once she'd told her story, they wouldn't put her in jail. They'd send her to Italy to live with her dad. It could be like *The Birdcage* and she could pretend her father was Robin Williams. Not really a stretch when you thought about it. She laughed briefly. The image was such a cartoon.

Her cell door opened and the same female guard entered with another cup of the medication. "You looking betta."

"I feel a lot better, thanks." CarryAnn got up off of the bed and took the cup.

The woman smiled at her. CarryAnn looked into her eyes for a moment. There was something very familiar in those eyes, as if she had looked into them before in another place and time, even though she knew this could not be true. She took the pills and swallowed them gratefully.

9:00 PM, MOM'S COFFEE SHOP, KAHULUI INDUSTRIAL PARK,KAHULUI, HAWAII

Ben sat at the counter nursing a cappuccino. His mind was moving over what he knew of the day's events. In front of him were the addresses of the new locations. One of them was on the ridge that overlooked Alan's house. He would go there first. If he saw Billy Joe, he would shoot him and then interrogate him later. He shook his head. He didn't even know what he looked like.

It was getting harder for Ben to maintain his purpose. There was a leaden weight on his heart. He felt like a swimmer caught in a powerful current, someone who had been swimming in sight of the shoreline for hours and had come no closer in all of that time.

He rubbed the bridge of his nose with his thumb and forefinger and let his thoughts sink to the pit of his stomach where the radiant energy lived. He pressed on the thoughts that danced in his mind, pressed them downward. Down into a single thought, the thought of harmony with his deeper nature, a place where there could be no conflict, only certainty.

Whip and Christienne found him sitting there, his hands clasped around his coffee cup. "Hi Ben..." Whip laid an arm around him and gave a quick squeeze.

Ben turned around on his stool and gave them a short smile. "Glad you made it. You want some coffee before we go?"

Whip and Christienne both shook their heads no.

"Well, then." Ben got up from his seat and they followed him out of the door.

AT THE SAME TIME IN HAIKU, HAWAII

Billy Joe drove into the night, his thoughts upon the future. In a few days' time he would be at the location he had prepared. The Ritual of the Black Moon would take place, as it should have decades ago. Billy Joe felt his chest swell with power as he thought of the doorway that would open, a doorway through which he would pass into a new realm of knowledge and power. With it would come the abilities he had desired for such a long time. Nothing on this earth would ever be able to hinder him again. He would become a select member in a fellowship of evil, a God on Earth.

A slight apprehension nagged at him as he studied everything in his mind, moving precisely over each facet of his plan. He probed for answers to the disquiet as he drove through the darkness. *There was nothing there.*

9:45 PM, WAILUKU POLICE STATION, WAILUKU, HAWAII

The three of them were sitting in Rusk's office. They had just watched the complete videotape of Balfire's confession. Dr. Abadon pulled a cigarette from a silver case and put it in his mouth. He stared at Rusk and Finch as he lit it. He inhaled and let the smoke filter out through his nostrils. "Extraordinary. What a story, and he appears to be telling the truth. This does not jibe with my impression of Alan Douglas. I can't believe I could have missed seeing at least some indication." Dr. Abadon shook his head. He looked at Finch and said, "I heard about Aaron Wilson. How is he?"

"No change as yet, he's still in a coma," Finch replied.

"I'm very sorry to hear that."

"We all are Doctor," Finch replied. "It's another reason that we've got to lock Douglas down tight. Aaron and he were," Finch pulled at his right earlobe, "well, if not friends, certainly warm to each other."

Rusk sipped at his coffee, which he had enhanced with bourbon. Rusk was feeling very strange and it wasn't the liquor. He'd been drinking this way for twenty years and it had never made him feel like this. There was this crawling feeling at the top of his scalp. Every now and then it would scudder down his neck and back up again. It wasn't unpleasant, quite the opposite in fact. The one thing that was really disturbing was that it had just given him another erection. He was glad he was sitting behind his desk, closer now than he had been initially. His cock was actually jumping like a fish in his pants, rubbing against the fabric of his underwear. He was afraid he might come if it didn't stop. *Maybe it's the idea of finally getting to fuck Douglas*, he thought. This did not sound crazy to him. It made perfect sense. "So, what should we do?" he asked Dr. Abadon.

Dr. Abadon looked immaculate in a cream suit, white shirt and a burgundy tie. His black hair was combed back and glistened under the overhead light. He moved with a languorous ease as he tapped his cigarette into the ashtray on the desk. "Well now, you have this videotape. It is a damning piece. Then again, it is the confession of a psychopath. Now, psychopaths are not always lying, just as non-psychopaths do not always tell the truth. Still, he is a psychopath, a convicted felon and a wanted killer. Alan Douglas is a police officer with many commendations and no history of previous offense."

Finch and Rusk both interrupted at the same time. Finch held his hand up to ward off Captain Rusk and said, "There's a preponderance of evidence here, Doctor."

"The fucker did it!" Rusk expostulated. He was giving the doctor a murderous look, his face flushed and his eyes wild. There was a vein throbbing at his right temple. *This was too much, the law and order doctor suddenly showing his liberal underbelly!*

"Wait!" Dr. Abadon held up his hand and silenced Rusk with his eyes. "Hold your horses, Captain. Let's maintain an air of professionalism here. I'm merely outlining certain things which we have to take into consideration."

Rusk was bristling. There was this terrible uncomfortable heat in his head and he struggled to control the matching rage that was boiling in his gut.

Abadon waited for a moment then continued, "Balfire Tweeds has devoted his life to the injury of others. He has acted without conscience or regard for the suffering of his victims. I don't think we can eliminate the possibility that he would lie. Then again, what possible good does it do him to implicate Douglas when he also implicates himself? And he did this without seeking future latitude."

Dr. Abadon pulled at his jaw with the knuckles of his thumb and forefinger. His eyes moved about the room. Then he looked suddenly at Finch and then back at Rusk. "I am going to need an interview with Alan Douglas. If I find that there is any reason, any reason at all to suspect him of complicity in these crimes, I give you my word that I will do everything in my power to see that he never walks as a free man in this world again. At the same time, we must be very certain we have all of our ducks in a row. This would not be the first time that some elaborate *façade* was created with the intention of framing an innocent man. And, if I feel that he is innocent, I will do everything to free him. Just so we know where we stand.

"Let me also be very clear here. I am not implying in any way that a member of the District Attorney's Office or the police department would act in collusion against a suspect. I know you want to see justice done. It's your business. It's my business, too." He looked at them both with emphasis. "I've made it my business to free the streets of dangerous elements. Because of my perspective, I may have given the impression that is the only motivation I have. This is not the case. I believe deeply in justice and I will not work contrary to its triumph." There was no mistaking the look that Abadon gave both of the room's other occupants.

Finch said, "Of course, Doctor Abadon. We want everything on the up and up. It's my responsibility that every precaution is taken. Still, you weren't at the scene." He shook his head.

"That's true." Dr. Abadon rose to his feet. "Let's go see Mr. Douglas."

ON THE WAY UPCOUNTRY, HANA HIGHWAY, MAUI, HAWAII

They were arguing heatedly in the car, Christienne on the one side and Ben and Whip on the other.

"You're not going in." Whip said this with his jaw set.

"You don't tell me what the fuck to do. I can shoot as well as anyone."

"It doesn't matter here if you're Annie Oakley, Christienne. It's got to do with preparation and training. We've got no game plan and, I hate to be a chauvinist, but look at the way you're dressed!" Ben said with exasperation.

Christienne still had on her black evening dress.

Whip tried to put his arm around her but she brushed him off.

"Leave me alone," she said. "And what am I supposed to do if something happens to you, something I might have kept from happening?" There was resignation in her voice now. She knew she wasn't going to get her way this time. It was true the way she was dressed was very inappropriate unless she was planning on romancing them to death. She chuckled.

"What's so funny?" Ben asked.

She told them and both men laughed appreciatively, most grateful for the sudden shift in her mood. Neither of them doubted her competency but in an uncertain environment, with no clear plan, the greater number of people involved the more things that could go wrong. Ben planned to stash her in the one place nobody would be looking for her. From there they would have to do the best they could.

It had been bothering Ben all day, teasing at him. *How had they managed to set up the scene so quickly?* They'd only had a few hours to arrange everything. It must have taken a considerable amount of energy and movement, both inside the house and in the workshop. They hadn't brought everything there in one truckload. When he'd seen how close the location on Kokomo Road was, he knew how they had done it. *They had been right around the corner.*

Ben pulled the car into Alan's driveway. There was one patrol car with two uniforms on guard duty. He had expected that Rusk would put the house under twenty-four hour guard and he was right. One of the officers informed him that they would be there until eleven when their relief came on. Ben explained the situation creatively. Neither of the officers were aware of his change in status with the department. He asked them to let Christienne sit on the deck until he returned and told them she was a material witness in the case.

Christienne hugged and kissed Whip, begging him to be careful. He told her that he would. There was no way he wasn't coming back for her. He turned and watched her wave to him as the car pulled back out on to the highway.

10:00 PM, MAUI POLICE DEPARTMENT, WAILUKU, HAWAII

The steel door opened and Detective Klein entered the cell. Alan was lying on his back staring at the ceiling. He'd been like that for an hour. After fifteen minutes he had entered a world that had dissolved the walls around him. He had been rafting through the realm of memory, seeing Elizabeth again. Of course, she wasn't actually there and he knew that. It was enough to relive those special moments that had no extraordinary features other than the heart's perception of them. There was a day in Central Park when they'd first met, an evening at Lincoln Center, a morning in the Bahamas. He was in the Bahamas when Klein walked in. Klein had to call his name several times before Alan slowly opened his eyes.

"Are you all right?" Two officers accompanied Klein. Even so he looked ready to jump back out the way he had come. He'd visited the crime scene and watched Balfire's confession on video. Alan Douglas was now a new life form for Klein. He could not have been more alien if Klein had seen him emerge from a spaceship.

Alan sat up on the bunk. He looked at Klein as if he did not recognize him. It was very much the way that Klein was looking at him, except for the apprehension. With his new empathetic powers, he immediately perceived the state of the detective's mind. He smiled. There was not much he could say and he knew it.

"You're wanted for interrogation." Klein moved nervously on the balls of his feet, his eyes fixed on Alan.

"That wouldn't be Room 101, would it?"

Klein just looked at him, not comprehending.

They brought him into a modern rose-hued room with muted lighting. It was part of a new dynamic that was making its presence felt in prisons and police stations throughout the country. Color and lighting affected the state of a person's mind and it was thought that certain environments made the subject more agreeable to disclosure.

Dr. Abadon was alone in the room except for an officer who was preparing the video camera. Of course, they would not really be alone. A number of law enforcement personnel were behind another two-way mirror. Included among them were Rusk and Finch.

Alan's eyes opened wide when he saw Dr. Abadon. This was a total surprise. He sat down at the table across from him. "Hello, Doctor."

Abadon's eyes twinkled with warmth. He smiled and said, "Please, Alan, do call me Philip. I'm sorry we have to meet again under such grim circumstances."

Alan folded his hands on the table and looked at the doctor. "It is a difficult situation, Doctor, especially if you're sitting where I am." Alan looked up at the two-way mirror and said, "How are you doing Captain Rusk, Counselor Finch?"

"What makes you think they're here, Alan?"

"Anything that's happening to me here has their efforts behind it, Doctor. You may be sure of that and since you know they are watching as well as I, your question is moot."

Dr. Abadon smiled, "Captain Rusk and Richard Finch have an adversarial relationship toward you. They want to do you harm. Is that what you are telling me? I want to separate this thought from any effort they might be making toward you in the pursuit of their duties, however zealous they may appear. You believe it is personal?"

"Doctor, Philip, I think you ought to talk to Ben Kamamoto, to my brother-in-law and his girlfriend. Aaron Wilson would also corroborate my assertion."

"Aaron Wilson is in a coma, Alan. He can't corroborate anything right now. I don't have access to the other individuals and I'm not here for that anyway. That's police work, Alan. I'm here to talk to you."

"I understand that Philip, but if the truth is your game you need to find it where it lies, pun intended. If you want the whole picture, you have to look at the whole picture, otherwise you're looking through a glass darkly. I don't want to tell you your business. You know it far better than I do, but I can hear a train when it's running and I know the sound of a railroad."

"You seem very calm, Alan, not distressed or anxious as I imagine a man in your position might feel. Why is that?"

"I have the satisfaction of knowing I'm innocent." He stared back into Dr. Abadon's piercing gaze. All of a sudden he *was* beginning to feel uncomfortable.

It felt like the temperature in the room had risen ten degrees or more. He felt a light patina of sweat on his brow. There was an irritating itch in the middle of his back now. He couldn't scratch it. He was aware that Dr. Abadon was scrutinizing him closely. Dr. Abadon might find it strange. *Why did he care about that?*

"Are you all right Alan?" Dr. Abadon was looking at him with concern.

"I'm fine, Doctor except for this itch in the middle of my back." Alan now felt free to deal with it. "It's also a lot hotter in here than when I first arrived. Are they playing some kind of a game with the thermostat?"

"I don't feel any change at all, Alan." It was true. He was in a suit and he didn't appear to be affected. Sweat was beading on Alan's forehead now and starting to stain his shirt under the arms.

"Can we get some water in here?" Dr. Abadon said. He turned his attention back to Alan. "Are you aware of what was discovered at your house, also that a Mr. Balfire Tweeds has implicated you in the murders? Indeed, he says that you actually masterminded them."

This startled Alan and really got his attention. "They caught Balfire Tweeds?"

"Yes, they did."

"That's good news. Look, Doctor Abadon, I don't know the entire why and wherefore of this situation. What I do know is that Tweeds is lying. What I do know is that I had nothing to do with any kidnappings or killings." Alan squirmed in his seat. The sweat was pouring off his brow now. "I don't get it. I'm really hot now. It feels like a hundred and twenty in here." *What's going on Ming?*

The itching was getting worse now in several locations around his body and it was with great effort that he controlled his desire to scratch. It was ridiculous but he didn't want to start looking like a junkie in need of a fix. His eyes were starting to blur as well. He started blinking and wiping at his eyes.

Dr. Abadon had asked him again if he was all right. It was getting harder to hear him. Alan had begun to scratch himself. Tears were running freely down his cheeks now. Through the haze in front of his eyes he was beginning to see things.

He struggled for control. He was beginning to hyperventilate. With an intense effort of will, he gained control of his emotions. He knew now that Billy Joe was at work. *He was moving in for the kill.* Knowing this was happening and gaining the proper detachment from his increasing physical unrest were two very different things. Consciously he breathed in and out as slowly as he could manage considering the phenomenon impacting on him in the moment.

"Think you'll make it, pardner?" This was a new voice. No, it was not a new voice. It was a voice Alan had heard before. *"I'm a long tall Texan. I ride a big*

black horse." It was singing now and it sounded like Johnny Cash.

"You ever hear of Remote Viewing, Douglas? This is remote audio. I'm using the doctor and the men in the viewing room as speakers. It's a relay effect. How's the signal, STRONG AND CLEAR?"

Alan's hands went over his ears and he screamed. He could now clearly see on the table in front of him twelve-inch representations of The Village People and The Bee Gees. They were singing a weird cacophonous duet of "Macho Man" and "Staying Alive." The Indian guy was thrusting his hips at Alan and winking. *"Think you can stay alive, Douglas?"*

Alan concentrated with all of his might. He let go completely. He breathed deeply in and out, but there was no appreciable effect. The tiny rock groups were still gyrating in front of him. Robin Gibb still had his hand to his ear.

Now there were changes. The singers no longer had human bodies. Now they had the bodies of centipedes, scorpions and spiders. The heads remained the same save for one difference. There were now caliper-like stingers extending from their jaws. They began to slowly march toward Alan. From somewhere over a great distance, he could hear Dr. Abadon asking him what was wrong. His heart was racing. He could feel it thumping in his chest. Now Stanley Clarke was plunking in time to the scene on his six-string bass. He had joined The Village People. He had calipers coming out of his mouth too.

Alan knew that this could not be real, but his mind refused to accept his judgment. He told it to stop, stop freaking out, but it was like trying to tell your bowels that you didn't have to shit twenty minutes after eating that bad Mexican dinner. It was like trying to tell your bladder that you didn't have to pee when you couldn't get your key into the door after one too many beers at the bistro ten blocks from home. *It was like trying to tell yourself that you didn't need another drink, after you saw the pictures of your dead wife one more time in your mind.* Alan swam and the current pushed. Alan swam harder and the current pushed harder.

He focused beyond the carnival of madness taking place on the table, looking at Dr. Abadon but Abadon no longer looked the same. His face was now that of a gargoyle's. The eyes were slits from which a venomous green light shone forth. The head rotated completely around the neck several times and then came to a stop.

The officer at the video camera had lost his pants and was now jerking off as he looked through the camera at Alan. None of this was *really* happening. It was a movie being projected into Alan's mind. If he did not resist, if he held to the idea that it was an illusion, then it must shortly disappear. As he focused all of his thought on this idea, the construction worker from The Village People danced over and stung him on his hand.

Alan screamed in pain and shook his hand. The construction worker/centipede would not let go. Alan grabbed him around the neck with his other hand and squeezed and pulled until the head popped free from its body. Blood shot out of the torn neck opening. Once released, the body spun and danced, moonwalking across the table to its center. Then it dropped into a crouch with its arms folded across its chest and began kicking out its feet and then whipping them back and forth like a Russian dancer.

His hand was on fire and he could not free it from the centipede's head. The other musicians and singers were still marching towards him. Barry Gibb sprang from the table and buried his pincers into Alan's chest. Robin Gibb followed and landed in his hair. In a heartbeat they had all fastened on some part of Alan's anatomy. The Indian landed in his crotch.

Alan went berserk from fear and the burning pain of the bites. He leapt to his feet, twisting about the room, knocking over his chair and then the camera in a frenzied effort to leave the room. He screamed for help as he tore at his attackers, but help did not come.

It took several minutes for the police to subdue Alan long enough for Dr. Abadon to get his bag and administer an injection. Alan fought like a madman. At the end, eight police officers were involved in holding him down.

"I am as shocked as I have ever been in my life." Dr. Abadon's hands were trembling as he replaced items in his bag. Alan had caught it with one of his feet and sent it crashing into the wall. "I would never have expected this. I fully expected to discover nothing, gentlemen."

"So what do you think now?" Rusk asked. He was euphoric. *Fuckin' Douglas was going DOWN, Dude!*

"For the moment, my recommendation is that Mr. Douglas be taken to a secure facility at the hospital and kept under sedation and close observation until tomorrow morning."

Finch stood close by, once again betraying nothing in his movements or his features. Inside his thoughts were roiling. *Alan Douglas killed all of those people. By tomorrow afternoon it will be national news and it will be my case!* "I expect we'd better get all of the legal work in order. I'll call the judge right now."

"You can do that from my office," Rusk said, "I've got some single malt scotch in my cabinet. I think the doctor could use a drink."

Dr. Abadon nodded his head. "Whatever I can do," he replied.

Once again they were sitting in Rusk's office. Dr. Abadon and Richard Finch had a glass of Glenlivet in their hand. Abadon was smoking a cigarette.

"What happened to him?" Rusk asked.

"It's apparent that he suffered a major psychotic episode. It can be brought on by the denial of one part of the mind to the existence of another. Sometimes it is so severe that a permanent state of catatonia is the result. In others, the different personalities split off and you get someone like the girl in *The Exorcist*. There's really no telling who or what we'll find in the morning.

"For your purposes, there is no question that he needs to be moved to a locked facility. I would assume Kaneohe." Dr. Abadon was referring to the state mental hospital on the windward side of Oahu. "At this time he clearly appears to present a danger to himself and others. I am willing to provide that diagnosis to a judge at whatever point that might become necessary."

Richard Finch placed his glass on the desk and said, "Judge Hirono is sitting in for Prelim's and Bail tomorrow. I'll process all of the paperwork. If you wouldn't mind being in court at 8:30, we'll take it all from there." Finch had been as disturbed as the doctor by what he had just seen. He was utterly convinced that Douglas was guilty. *Now there was no question.*

"More scotch, Doctor?" Rusk then poured a generous portion into the glass.

Dr. Abadon sipped at his drink, enjoying the warm glow that spread through his body. "You know, Captain, as long as I have been in this business I never stop being surprised. But you knew all along."

Rusk's arrogance, never very far away at the best of times, was asserting itself with the addition of alcohol as fuel. "I knew he was a crazy fuck from the beginning. I don't know if it's an instinct thing, he just smelled bad." Rusk's eyes gleamed. He had no awareness of the darkness coiling in his soul. He was adrift on his own sea of vengeance. "I feel vindicated now. I'm sure there was a lot of talk around this department about my state of mind. This changes everything." Rusk poured himself another four fingers of scotch.

Dr. Abadon replied, "I've dealt with a lot of murderous intelligences over the years Captain. Invariably they turn out to be a mixed bag of contradictions. Tracking backwards to the cause can take years and we often never find out why they did what they did."

Rusk snorted. "What does that mean, Doctor? Alan Douglas is now a victim of causes separate from himself, another victim of an unfeeling society that doesn't understand him? You're not saying that are you?"

Dr. Abadon laughed. "No, Captain, I'm not saying that. I'll need to spend more time with Douglas before I know precisely what is wrong."

"I'm just afraid of some kind of a miracle recovery, some overnight cure. They seem to happen these days. Douglas could have faked all that to throw his competency into doubt. He knows what he's facing. It makes some sense." Rusk was paranoid. He liked the idea of Douglas being sentenced for his crime. He wanted him sent for observation but he feared one possible result. He did not want Douglas found insane and then back on the street in five years.

Dr. Abadon set his glass on the desk. "There's no way he can maintain any kind of a *façade* under the scrutiny he'll be receiving. Trust me on that, it's my field. It's up to you now, Richard. If you want me on the case for the prosecution, you'll have to appoint me. I'm available." Dr. Abadon got to his feet and said good-bye, assuring them that he would be there in the morning.

"Everything will be ready when you get to court," Finch said and walked him to the door.

Ben and Whip slowly made their way to a vantage point from which they could observe the house. Ben had night vision glasses. It took them fifteen minutes of slow going to find a place from which to view the interior of the house through a large bay window. The Hawaiian landscape could be very treacherous even in domesticated areas. They picked their way with caution. Ben held the glasses to his eyes for some time. Whip waited patiently until Ben brought the glasses down.

"I want you to take a look and tell me if you see what I do. It looks like Kimo, The Dragonsmouth, sitting on a couch. It also looks like he's got a rifle of some kind across his lap."

"I've never seen the guy, Ben."

"Take a look anyway, a second opinion never hurts." Ben handed him the glasses. Whip brought them to his eyes and looked into the interior of the house. There was a single light burning somewhere inside. In the room directly ahead, Whip could see a figure sitting in a chair. Flashes of light passed across his face and Whip assumed he was watching television. He could tell that it was a local male. It wasn't anyone he had ever seen before. There was definitely a gun lying across his lap. Whip thought it might be a shotgun.

"Nice glasses," Whip said, handing them back.

"We didn't get these at K-Mart, Whip. What do you think?"

"It's a local, young male, gun in his lap. No sign of anyone else around but then you've already got the other two. There's only Billy Joe left now, right?"

"Billy Joe could have a lot of help we don't know about. If you're going to help, here is what I want you to do." Ben outlined a plan, which had Whip slipping on to the deck, while Ben went to the front door. When Ben came through the front door, Whip would have a clear line of sight to the house's occupant should he attempt to flee or open fire on Ben. They waited in the shadows for another fifteen minutes to see if there might be any other occupants. In all that time the man on the couch never moved, nor did anyone else show up.

"Let's go," Ben patted Whip on the shoulder.

With the gun Ben had given him stuck in his waistband, Whip quickly pulled himself up on the deck at a point about twenty feet away from the window.

Ben came to the front door and tried the doorknob. It opened easily. He slipped inside and quietly made his way to the room where the man was sitting. Soon he was standing beside the doorway into the living room. There was a movie playing and Ben recognized Humphrey Bogart on the screen.

"Good evening, Lieutenant," the man said.

"I want you to set the gun on the floor and stand up facing the television." Ben had gone into a crouch and his gun was pointed at the back of the man's head.

"Don't I get to hear about my rights? Aren't you supposed to say something about a warrant? Did you just walk in here without announcing yourself? I think you may have committed some procedural errors, Lieutenant. Not to worry, it's too late for any of that now. Watch this and don't come any closer, Lieutenant!" Very quickly, Kimo pulled the gun barrel up and set it under his chin. "If you come too close I will have to finish this business and you will never hear what I have to say. Come around and have a seat across from me." He gestured at a chair by the television about ten feet from where Kimo-Joe was sitting.

Ben kept his weapon trained on him as he made the turn and came up with his back against the window.

"You can tell young Whip it's okay to come in off the porch. I'm the only one here and there is a reason for that. You might even say that your being here is very important."

"Put the gun down," Ben said.

Kimo looked up at Ben. "Let's establish some ground rules here. I have only to pull this trigger and I will be no more. What are you going to do, shoot me?" Kimo made a harsh laugh. "That's okay, too. My usefulness is at an end now. You will sit down. Bring Whip inside and we will talk for a moment. It's all you're going to get, a stalemate."

Whip had heard the exchange and came in through the front door.

"Stay outside!" Ben screamed.

"It's okay, Lieutenant. Nothing is going to happen to either one of you. Not right now anyway."

Whip stepped into the room and stood against the wall.

"What have you got to say?" Ben asked.

"Not much, Lieutenant. Shit is coming down like a black fucking fire from Hell. Let me first say that I want you both to stay right where you are or I will pull the trigger. Remember too what I did at the police station. Neither of you can stop me right now. You could already be dead meat, but it has been decided you should die in a more fitting manner than I can provide. You are safe for the moment."

Whip felt a terrible shiver run through his body as Kimo said this. Something was terribly wrong but he had no sense of what it might be. He was shaking but he did not know why.

Kimo said something in Hawaiian that Ben did not catch. Then he said, "I do not welcome death. I am a young man. The man speaking to you now is me as I would have been if young Kimo had lived. I got caught. I was a fool and I didn't know. Now it is too late. It is too late for you, too. Had I known, I would have done so many things differently." Kimo had a rueful smile on his face. Ben felt a tug at his heart in that moment. Kimo no longer looked threatening at all. There was a sense of utter desolation upon his face.

Ben leaned forward. "Look, whatever has happened. It's not the end. A lot of people make it through prison and out the other side. Time makes a lot of transformation possible."

Kimo interrupted, "You don't think I know that? You don't think I've seen my whole life, the way it could have been if this shit hadn't happened!" Tears were flowing down Kimo's cheeks now. There was anguish there that tore at both Ben's and Whip's hearts. "Nothing can be done now. You are dealing with a force beyond your power to understand. You know it's there and you still think you can do something about it. You are both fools." There was a sorrow in Kimo's face now that was difficult for both of them to see.

Whip had great difficulty controlling the disturbance inside of him. He was supposed to be somewhere else, but where? He thought something might be happening to Alan. He remembered Ming saying that it would be "okay" but what did Ming mean? *Eventually everything was okay, but it might take a thousand years.*

"Nothing is over until it's over," Ben said. "Why don't you at least hang on and see. You could always hang yourself in your cell if it's as bad as you say." Ben was extremely troubled now. He had come in the door expecting anything but this. Now his most overpowering thought was to put down his gun and give Kimo a hug. *It was absurd.*

"Not that strange really," Kimo said in answer to Ben's thoughts. "It is the feeling of empathy that will eventually undo you. Billy Joe is constrained by no such thing. You will be eaten alive. You will pray for death but there will be no help, no one you can call. I am the lucky one. Hell does not even seem that bad right now."

"This is an illusion, man." Whip moved across the room into Kimo's line of sight. "There is help. There is one who will help you. You just have to hold on. Put down the gun and go with us." Whip felt his hair brushed by an invisible wind. The air was charged with electricity.

"Really?" Kimo asked. His eyes were vulnerable with hope. Both of them saw then that he might put down his weapon if he thought there might be some way out.

Whip opened his mouth to tell Kimo about Ming. Instantly he was frozen, no words passed his lips.

"Yes?" Kimo was leaning forward now looking at Whip. In that moment there was a thought that transmitted to Whip all that he needed to know. Billy Joe was at work and he had almost made a terrible error.

"Be gone, demon!" Whip cried, having no idea where his words had come from.

Kimo sighed and then a terrible malevolence came into his eyes. "*Okay, motherfuckers.*" His voice was different now, hard and cold as an arctic landscape. *"Well, my friends, where is your beautiful Christienne, eh?"* Kimo's head was cocked to one side. *"Your shit has just begun..."*

The voice switched back to Kimo's, "And now mine is over."

"No!" Ben screamed.

"Too late," Kimo replied and pulled the trigger. There was a thunderous explosion and Kimo's head disappeared in a mist of blood.

"Fuck!" Whip cried. "I knew something was wrong!" He went racing for the door with Ben following after. There was nothing more for them to do there. Neither of them was a priest.

When they arrived at Alan's minutes later, everything looked the same as it had been. Both police officers were standing outside the house.

Whip jumped from the car. "We've come for the lady?" he said, walking purposefully toward the house.

One of the officers raised his hand, "Stop right there." Then he saw Ben. "What's up, Lieutenant?"

Ben walked toward them. "Where's the woman we left here?"

"What woman?" the officer asked.

Both Whip and Ben stood there. Neither of them could say anything. It was already apparent. *Christienne was gone.*

"Oh, by the way," the officer said. "I got a message for you but I forgot." Both officers started laughing. One of them slapped his knees. "He said to tell you he would fuck her before and after she was dead."

Whip rushed at the officer but Ben caught him and lifted him up in the air. "It's no use Whip. It's not their fault."

Whip let go, an awful sorrow filling his heart. He went limp in Ben's arms.

"Hold on, brother. We'll find her." Ben held him close trying to convey through his touch the confidence that he knew Whip required now. The road ahead was darker than it had ever been.

As they got into the car they could see the officers dancing a waltz in the parking area, spinning one another about. It was graceful and terrible all at once. Ben gunned the car and they fishtailed all the way out of the driveway. It wasn't until they came to the road that they fully realized how many possible directions lay in front of them.

Chapter Thirty-Four

Billy Joe cruised through the town of Paia, chuckling to himself. This was too easy. It was like playing pool with two year olds. They couldn't even reach the table. How were they going to get a shot?

The coming ritual had been performed many times over the centuries. Certainly many had sought for the means to attempt it or had attempted it. It was the only doorway into the next state of being. It was an exponential increase in consciousness, evil and power. Most had failed the test, certainly far more than had succeeded. Most were simply unprepared for the results. Some had made errors in their preparations. There were many reasons why the ritual might fail. To Billy Joe this particular ritual was easier than most. The most difficult parts of this ritual were the things the practitioner had to go through to get there. The man you had to become before you could even recognize the energies to which you would be introduced. Unless the evil in you had become supremely predominant, you would not have the sand. *Beyond was the Ring Pass Not.*

The light of the divine does not ever reach there. *This is the single thing that made it so very attractive.* Men such as Billy Joe were propelled by a hatred for the divine. It was the driving impetus that made all of their personal atrocities possible. The love of the ineffable light is so great that it does not allow the thought that anyone or anything could not be loved, but it was possible for human beings to change themselves into something that was no longer human. They would no longer be human, but what did that matter?

To say that the divine consciousness might be unaware of them was not so. *There is nothing of which the supreme is unaware.* But the mind of the supreme is not like the human mind, even though they occupy the same space, even though they are part of the same mind. It knows everything as it knows itself within the integrity of its being. Those who have passed over through the ritual become something outside of the divine registry. They become something *other*, a closed elemental force. This was what Jinns and Demons were, the furthest reach of the personal self. It was the reverse of the impersonal kingdom of Heaven. The state of impersonality appeared to the unrealized as the loss of their precious individuality, somehow absorbed into an anonymous group consciousness. Although in one regard, this was true, those who achieved to this higher state knew their individuality in a way they never had before.

The citizens of the light were the blueprints for an immortal progression into a greater and greater sense of self. For those who sought out the darkness for its own sake, there was the *appearance* of a greater sense of self. There was the illusion that one acted out of one's own impulses and by degrees, gained a greater and greater freedom to do what they willed. *Such is not, nor ever was, the case.* Eventually, they were swallowed up in something that had existed before identity, something similar to the primordial ooze. Something similar to the chaos of darkness that had existed before, "let there be light." It is not a place that reason bids us enter. *It carries within itself, as does every word, every thought, and every action, the reward attendant to its nature.*

Billy Joe wanted to go there. At this next stage he could act with impunity on a grand scale. He could have the impact of a typhoon, a hurricane, an earthquake. He could achieve to a personal evil that would match the impersonal good. He knew the essence of Adolph Hitler and Joseph Stalin and all who had preceded them. He had felt their mastery of total power over life. He had lived inside the moment where a man knows himself to be a God on Earth. He had known what it was to be Pol Pot and a thousand other known and unknown butchers of the human body, destroyers of the heart and mind. He would surpass them all. Once the ritual was complete, he was going to the Middle East.

He laughed a murderous laugh. "Armageddon, here I come," he said.

There was a whimper from the back seat.

"Shut up, you worthless fucking cunt." Billy Joe's speech was as even as if he were saying, "excuse me" to someone he had bumped into on the subway. A fierce joy filled his heart. *The wheels were greased, the condiments at hand. They sat upon the table of the black featureless night, upon which were to be served the dreams of appetite.* One of the peculiarities of the ritual was that it did not require virgin blood. In fact, virgin blood would not work. It was only important that the sacrifice given was a soul much loved by another. The archdemon that watched the gate fed from the milk of human sorrow. To appease and distract him it was only necessary to give him the specific broth whose main ingredient was an overwhelming sense of loss. This Billy Joe had in hand. Besides that, it was only important who you were when you showed up, not what you knew (though they were the same)… that and an iron will and complete absence of fear. Billy Joe had no concern that all would not be as it should. He could not imagine that anyone, not even his unknown adversary, would be able to do much now.

It had been very close. When he was monitoring Kimo, there was a moment when he was sure Whip would divulge the name of his adversary. He had tasted a hundred things in the short space where Whip had stood on that precipice. He had seen colors and smelled things. He had heard sounds. Now he knew that his opponent came from the East. As he drove through the night and prepared himself for the next day, another part of his mind worked tirelessly on the images he had received. Somewhere in that flood of unspoken information lay the key to identifying his enemy. Once he knew who it was, once he could affix an identity, someone was in deep shit. In two days, this one who chose to fuck with him would have his eyes sucked from his head and be forced to crawl through sewer pipes and garbage dumps until there were no longer stars in the skies.

MAUI POLICE DEPARTMENT, WAILUKU, HAWAII

Alan was scared, very, very scared. He kept telling himself that there was no reason to be scared. Well, that was bullshit. There were plenty of reasons to be scared. He had just had the shit chewed out of him by The Village People and The Bee Gees. The wounds still hurt but you couldn't see them! Okay, nothing was happening now, but he was completely on his own. If he had ever needed Ming, he had needed him then. *Maybe Ming couldn't intrude.* Okay, but Ming damn well could have been in his head giving him some cheerleader advice or pouring another romantic religious fantasy into his head. He was fucked and he knew it. It was possible that the whole idea of Ming, everything Alan had experienced in connection with him, had been a hallucination orchestrated by Billy Joe to increase his torment. *It was one thing to have no hope. It was another thing to have had hope and faith and then find that there had been no basis for them.*

The terror Alan felt had a familiar quality to it. It reminded him of the way he had felt on a particular morning when he had managed to consume all of the alcohol in the house. After searching for a hidden bottle and finding none, he was compelled to go out. Once he did and there was no question that he would, every nerve felt stripped, every face he saw glowered at him. Inside he was as weak as a puppy. It would have been rough anywhere but in New York City it had been pure Hell. Negotiating the streets for the few blocks to the store had been as harrowing as anything he had ever done. Coming to the checkout counter he saw that he had left his wallet at home and had only two crumpled dollar bills and some change in his pocket.

He was forced to put the Wild Turkey back on the shelf and buy a pint of cheap Port wine. The humiliation had been suffocating. He'd had to drink the wine on the street in order to make it back and his hands had been trembling so badly that he'd had to hold one wrist with the other in order to get the bottle up to his mouth. He drank it too fast and threw up on the sidewalk one block from home. Then he had to go out again. All this because he could not wait the hour it would have taken for the deliveryman to come on duty.

It was like that now. The worst of it was the dreadful fear that the demented musical groups would show up again. He could smell the rank aroma of his body. There were spots of light in his vision. He began to cry. He had less control over himself that he had ever imagined. He was weak, insignificant and very possibly doomed.

Into this moment came a rushing warmth. As the sobs escaped his throat, Alan felt the power of limitless love wash over him. He brought his hands away from his face and saw a form materializing in the cell. Ming appeared before him, his right hand extended in blessing, "Greetings, my son. So now you have had a taste of what Billy Joe can do to the untrained mind."

Ming was dressed in a brilliant yellow Manchu gown with green cuffs and borders. The high-necked collar was also green and there was a white rose at his throat. Ming's eyes were cheerful and fresh, but there was remoteness about them as if everything that could have ever happened to him already had. Alan had the briefest image of Ming crawling across a tortured landscape of garbage and mud. There was twisted machinery with its stark arthritic hands stretched into a cold, unforgiving gray sky. Black smoke was billowing from underground fires. Ming was filthy as he crawled. His clothes were torn and there was blood leaking from his body into the wet muck through which he moved. There seemed to be no purpose or direction to Ming's movement except to avoid the whip that kept falling relentlessly upon his back. Alan could not tell from whom the blows were coming.

"We all have a price to pay," Ming said. Nothing registered in his eyes. "You have had a small taste of what Billy Joe can do. You thought your mind was trained, Alan, just as so many of us who are given to discipline believe that we will be worthy when the time comes. It is one thing to shoot free throws into the hoop over the garage door, quite another to sink them in the seventh game of the NBA Finals."

Alan's breathing had returned to normal. He looked at Ming. He wondered if this too was not a hallucination. He was afraid to ask. Even the comfort he was feeling now seemed suspect in light of what had happened. "Where were you, Ming?"

"I was crawling through the mud inside your thoughts, Alan."

Alan felt an electric current run through him when Ming said this. The image of Ming crawling leapt once more into his mind and now he could see who it was that was wielding the lash. It was Alan, his face filled with fury and fear, lashing Ming again and again with the black whip.

"It happens all the time and no one is aware that they are doing it. Christ even had some very special comments he made concerning this phenomena. It's not about my pain. I don't really feel it the same way you would. At a certain point everything turns into Love."

Alan could not contain himself. Tears flowed down his face.

"I am not of Billy Joe, Alan. That is his suggestion. In every human heart there is a world of injury, waiting to be born into the mind of the one who feels he has no choice but to inflict punishment on others, or himself. It's all bad parenting, Alan, the endless inheritance of lies and bad advice. Our only true parent is within. Each of us who carry the burden of earth, the cloak that makes us visible in this realm, must suffer from the thoughts and actions of those who brought us into this world, those who surround us in this world and our own desire to be in this world until the last farthing is paid. Through suffering, we are made magnificent. Through suffering, all of the veils fall away."

Alan's heart soared at Ming's words. He could feel veritable wings beating against the cage of his chest. He wanted nothing now so much as to be where Ming was, where it is. "I know absolutely nothing," he said.

"No one does, but it's a good place to start. This is what testing is all about. Here I am before you. You see and feel me. You think I am real, but there is a part of your mind that rejects this belief because I seem to be a thing apart. We must be shown over and over again until we really do *believe*. Until we become what we believe in, there is always some sense of separation where doubt may live. I cannot work through you unless you trust me absolutely, and you will not succeed unless you can. Even though you know that you are helpless against Billy Joe, another part of your mind insists on driving. It is like Krishna and Arjuna in the *Baghavad Gita*. The charioteer is not the charioteer. You were never in danger, Alan, you just thought you were. It was necessary for you to go through this ordeal in order that you might come to understand. It will happen again until you do. Do you think you understand, Alan?"

Alan shrugged and said, "I don't know." He sat watching Ming, waiting for him to disappear again but Ming was solidly in front of him.

His brow had furrowed as he studied Alan. He did not look unkind but rather more remote again. "Alan, divinity does everything but can only accomplish within us what we allow. These accomplishments are measured by humanity's ability to get out of the way. Do you remember your father?" As Ming said this Alan saw his father when he was sixteen years old in Hong Kong. He saw his father pushing him to excellence, screaming at him, telling him that failure was unacceptable. Then he saw himself pushing, pushing toward results, failing and then pushing again until he had achieved them. At no point did he see or remember anything positive that his father might have said. He had been impossible to please, yet he had not been a cruel man. He wanted his son to be a man. In his mind, men were composed of certain elements that were equal to whatever challenges life might throw at them. To be unable to meet and survive a challenge, to be unable to resolve the challenge into a greater state of strength, was unacceptable to his father.

Now Alan saw that because he had not perceived his father's love, he had never been sure of its presence. His father loved him but his father was of that generation of men who viewed open expressions of love as a sign of weakness.

"Love is everything, Alan. It takes many forms but it is still love in expression through that medium. Wisdom is a form of love. One might say that Wisdom is a conscious awareness of the power of love and its effects. The highest form of love is sacrifice. Sacrifice implies the willing acceptance of one's own diminishment, even the seeming end of one's own being. If you are forever giving yourself away, of which the Sun is a perfect example, there will be no end to you, relatively speaking. It is this mindset that you want to cultivate. Billy Joe has no power over such a state of mind. In fact, he would flee it in terror. It would act like Kryptonite on Superman.

"Do you remember the vision you had with Michael Jordan in it? Some would call Michael a ball hog, an overachiever. Many resented him. What makes a man like Michael Jordan great is that he *knows* he can do what he does. He was made as an example of this. Michael, through his own evolution, devoted himself to this achievement. It was a cooperative thing. If Michael was what his critics accused him of being, he would not have been able to do what he did. He understood the nature of teamwork on a very fundamental level. He understood sacrifice and, even though he was just a basketball player, as a result of his awareness of this power he was much more than a basketball player, just as Martin Luther King was a lot more than a preacher and Muhammad Ali was a lot more than just a boxer. True heroes are all in the image of the divine. They have their personal woes to bear and they fall short of the ideal in many small ways, but overall, they embody the magnificence of divinely directed energy. Otherwise, quite simply, they could never do what they do."

Alan could not help but be amused by Ming's use of Michael Jordan as an analogy for the point he was making. *Ming just used whatever was available to make his point.* He could imagine him talking to a Brazilian in terms of soccer.

"You are a lot more than a Homicide detective, Alan. It was a logical progression for you to come up against a Billy Joe. The variation in him is the difference in the playing field. Billy Joe does not operate with the same limitations as others. He cannot be brought to ground by smart police work or by any of the tools that you possess. Your discipline will not help you now. Only love will win the day.

"One of the things that makes love what it is, it's always greater than the one who feels and practices it. Love effects change on its own terms and by the power of its intrinsic nature. An alchemist would refer to it as the 'cosmic vitriol' in that it reduces everything it touches to the same thing. It acts of its own accord. It does not require our direction or supervision to accomplish its intentions. Any attempt to manipulate it and it is no longer love.

"You are a medium only. Within your studies of the martial arts lie all of the awareness that you need to achieve victory. Aikido, the Japanese way of unifying with life energy, personifies the position you must occupy. Billy Joe can only be destroyed by himself. You will simply assist him in his effort to accomplish the destiny that is attendant with his intention."

Alan felt as if Ming had said this to him many times before. This time it sank down deep within him. He understood now the difference between an intellectual understanding of reality and the visceral experience of it. It wasn't anything that Ming was saying as much as it was the energy behind the words. *The words were nothing but the paint and the forms that gave appearance to the idea. It was the power that held it all in place, that was the truth of the thought from which it emerged.* Suddenly, he knew the difference between shadow and substance but he could not have explained it. *It was and would forever remain a mystery.*

"I feel like a fool," Alan said.

"It is no wonder that the major trump card of all is numbered zero. The spirit, in search of experience, always completes a circle in the achievement of wisdom." Ming's eyes were merry now. There was no remoteness in them. Alan understood that the remoteness was just the manifestation of his own separation from the truth. Ming's idea of The Fool card from the Tarot communicated more understanding than all of the years of Alan's studies. The Hermit then appeared before his eyes. He could almost see Ming holding out the lantern from beneath his robe, the six pointed star gleaming with brilliance brighter than any light Alan had ever seen.

"You are close now to something you have been approaching for lifetimes. Certain necessary experiences stand between you and this goal and they will not all be resolved by your present conflict. In the end, you will owe as much to Billy Joe as to anyone."

Ming looked wonderful to Alan. Here stood his salvation and the sum of his hopes, capsulated in a tiny man with a kindly smile. "A wise man throws nothing away," Ming continued, "He uses everything for a higher purpose. The ability to know Truth, to become a conscious embodiment of the divine, resides in each human heart. Most reject this opportunity in favor of suffering and mortality. This is the most irrational of all perspectives, yet it is the most common and accepted thing in the world.

"The divine consciousness, like a mother, must allow the child to run away and experience what is outside. The child does not know what is out there but insists on being allowed to go. The child bangs and stumbles through its world, becomes muddied and injured, tired, frightened and confused. The mother loves the child so much that the child is not compelled to do otherwise. The mother knows that the child must one day return of its own volition and waits against that day, guiding and assisting as is possible. The love that is borne for the child is incomprehensible. The child knows only its own thoughts and feelings, it acts irrationally and thinks it is rational. It demands what it already has. It weeps for what it cannot lose. It fears what cannot harm it and rushes toward what can. In the end, it all comes down to trust, and trust comes from understanding." Ming paused in his speech. The entire room was bathed in a wash of light. The air was perfumed and there was the sound of voices singing faintly in the unseen distance.

"What's that all about?" Alan asked.

"Special effects," Ming replied laughing. "You get to a certain place and these kind of things start following you around. It's all very embarrassing."

Alan laughed. It didn't even seem to matter right now what lay ahead.

"You are learning what it is like to become impersonal. All of humanity's anguish is caused by the false sense of a personal self, yet they fight to the last breath to protect what enslaves and torments them. In the end, there is no protection for the personal self. This is why men like Billy Joe carry the seeds of their own destruction with them every step of the way. Separation cannot be maintained indefinitely. *Evil always defeats itself.* These men are always under a sentence of death, even when they have mastered the dark arts and learned how to preserve their identities and bodies far beyond the normal span. This is the case with Billy Joe. He has nothing to fear from the common mind. He manipulates, controls and destroys others through their passions and fears.

"To one who has mastered their passions and fears, Billy Joe can do nothing. Indeed he fears such a one as this, though he would never admit it. It is such a man that you are meant to become, once you understand how insubstantial the personal self is and how very real is the watcher behind it. The watcher... the witness who is the true self that all have in common. The personal self is a ghost who lives in a dream world filled with funhouse mirrors."

Alan could feel pieces of himself breaking off and floating away. As this was happening he felt himself being gripped by a fear greater than anything he had ever experienced before. Raw panic tore at him. Ming continued to smile. That smile was all he had to hold on to as he felt everything familiar disappear. He no longer knew who he was. He could not remember who he had been. All of his instincts screamed at him that he was in the greatest danger of his life. Still Ming continued to smile and radiate peace. Alan could see the river of joy flowing in the vastness behind those eyes. It overwhelmed him. He knew that he could not bear this and live. He knew that he must die.

"That is precisely it, Alan. That is just what you must do. You must die, die to everything and everyone you have ever known. Die to what is familiar and which is itself death. Die and be reborn as a conscious immortal, one of the Brotherhood of Light."

Alan could no longer hold together the disparate parts of his previous self. There was an unstoppable force flowing through him. It was powerful beyond his comprehension. Suddenly, all that he knew and remembered was gone, including the room he had been in and Ming as well. An utter and complete darkness surrounded him. He cried out from the base of his being, wept with all of his essence. He knew that he had gone insane. He was alone.

Then, at the central point of his being, he felt a vibration which soon grew into a sound. Every molecule of his being was humming with the sound. Gradually the pitch changed by degrees, becoming higher and higher. As the pitch increased, Alan felt the darkness around him begin to brighten, then it burst into light and he understood. When he returned to awareness of the jail cell again, he saw that everything was composed of light. The rusting bed frame was glowing with a beauty greater than gold. His shoes, the walls, his hands — all were pulsing with a rich bejeweled light.

11:23 PM, MOKULELE HIGHWAY, PU'UNENE, HAWAII

Christienne huddled inside herself. Her hands were pressed against her sex, her knees pulled into her chest. Earlier she had felt something cold and wet attempting to crawl between her legs and inside her.

There was a maniac driving the car. He kept laughing and it sounded like sawing glass. She couldn't bear it but she could not cover her ears or that awful thing might try to crawl inside her again. She knew there was no rational explanation for what had happened. The man had just appeared on the deck and she had gone away with him. There had been no thought of resistance. The police had offered none either.

She knew she was in the presence of real evil, a cold, merciless wickedness. Crystal clear pictures kept appearing before her eyes. It was just as if she were watching a movie, there was no way to shut them out. They were pictures of terrible things happening to her, to Whip, to Alan. They were the bloody violence and depraved acts of a twisted imagination, followed by attacks of bone-chilling fear. Her emotions were as taut as an extended bowstring, yet something made her feel she would endure. She could feel a strength within that was not her own. There was no way it could be her own. It was all that was holding her reason in place.

In the front seat, Billy Joe sensed this intrusion and he probed at it, worried it like a wounded tooth. Nothing for him to find yet again, but this time he laughed. No friends of the crucified God were riding in with the cavalry this time. His master had a kingdom too and his interests were always served. When the time came he would probe more deeply. He would probe until he had stripped away every defense, until her mind was stripped and naked before him. It was a pity there was so much to do, so many preparations to make, otherwise he would devote that time now. Nonetheless, her real service and greater torment would all be served at the ritual.

11:23 PM, HANA HIGHWAY, NEAR HUELO, HAWAII

Ben pulled the car to the side of the road. "I'm sorry Whip, there are so many ways he could have gone. I guess I didn't expect much. We don't even know what kind of vehicle he's in."

Whip was silent. There was nothing he could say. Together they sat in the darkness by the roadside. The sound of the crickets was deafening.

11:30 PM, MAUI MEMORIAL HOSPITAL, WAILUKU, HAWAII

Aaron Wilson opened his eyes to smears of color. He tried to wet his lips with his tongue but there was no moisture on it. He could not remember why he was laying in this strange room. His head throbbed with the mother of all headaches. Slowly, over the next few minutes, pieces of the past began to fit together.

A nurse entered the room. She saw Aaron with his eyes open, searching the ceiling. She ran back into the corridor and returned with the doctor. The doctor flashed his penlight into Aaron's eyes and asked him how he was feeling.

"I feel like shit," he croaked. Aaron struggled to come up off the bed. The blood thundered in his head like a tsunami. "I've got to get up."

The doctor smiled and brought a glass of water to Aaron's mouth. He sipped at it greedily. "You're not going anywhere right now, counselor." After he had emptied the glass, the doctor pressed him back into the bed. He rubbed an alcohol swab on Aaron's arm and then gave him a shot. "We'll talk about your travel plans tomorrow."

In moments, Aaron's eyes had closed and he was fast asleep.

12:15 AM, KAHULUI, HAWAII

Ben had dropped Whip at his car. Whip had insisted that he would stay at Christienne's. Now Ben lay in his bed unable to sleep. His mind turned over the events of the previous twenty-four hours. It was clear that Billy Joe had sacrificed his tools to further his objectives. If he needed new tools he'd just pick them up on the way. *Why had Aaron been shot? Where was Billy Joe going with his orchestration?* Ben played with the ideas in his mind, fitting the elements one way and another. Rusk has always been a hard-nosed, arrogant, small-minded prick and those qualities were even more exaggerated now. Regardless of the personal defects however, Rusk had generally been systematic and rational. Except for the negative serendipity that was taking place, this whole affair could have blown up in Rusk's face. It still might, but Rusk was charging for the finish line without an apprehension in the world. *Those whom the gods would destroy…*

Then there was Finch, in the driver's seat for the moment and certainly no friend of Alan's. Aaron could come back at any time. *He'd need to recover but what would happen to Alan in the meantime?* That must be it. Something was going down *soon*. Anything they could do to Alan would have to go through the courts. Now it was getting very clear for Ben. Alan had told him he didn't want a lawyer, he was going to wait for Aaron to regain consciousness. Alan was confident that Aaron would see the absurdity of the charges. *What did they have, planted evidence, the testimony of a homicidal maniac?*

Ben sat up in bed. *Something was going to happen tomorrow and Alan didn't have a lawyer!* It was late, but for the money they made, that shouldn't make any difference. It didn't matter. All Ben got was an answering machine. *Probably out at one of the hotel discos.*

"Les, this is Lieutenant Ben Kamamoto. I'm calling on behalf of Alan Douglas. He's presently incarcerated in Wailuku. He has requested your representation as soon as possible. Call me at home if you can Les, or meet me at the lock-up early tomorrow. Seven thirty is not too soon." Ben hung up.

Les Moriyama was one of Maui's best criminal lawyers. He'd once had one of Ben's most important cases thrown out on a technicality. Ben had hated him for a while, but he more or less forgave him when he was able to send the felon away for life just two years later. They'd developed a mutual respect for each other over the last several years, but you couldn't really call them friends. Moriyama had even helped Ben out a couple of times on legal points when there had been no danger of conflicting interests. The rest of the department hated him with a passion. They had a reason. *If anyone could ferret out what was happening to Alan and defend against it, it was Les Moriyama.*

1:00 AM, SOMEWHERE ON MAUI, HAWAII

Christienne lay on a purple bed cover. Billy Joe has put her in the shower after she had fouled herself during the torment. He'd looked into her eyes and found her special fears and then he had brought them to life for her. While she thrashed in terror, Billy Joe had sung "Nowhere to Run, Nowhere to Hide" as an accompaniment. Now she lay naked on the bed trembling with fear.

Billy Joe sat down beside her and stroked her forehead, already beaded with sweat again. "Never had a bad dream quite like that one did you, dear?" The brotherly concern in Billy Joe's voice made his comments far more terrible than they would have been if delivered in a menacing tone.

Christienne could not fight him. His will made her limbs feel as if they were made of concrete that had been epoxied to the mattress. Now that she had finally seen him, she understood the quotation that had dealt with the banality of evil. *He looked like an aging British rock star, perfectly coifed, elegantly thin.* There was nothing in his eyes or his features that spoke of evident malice. Christienne thought that this might have been the way Dr. Mengele had been, having the appearance of a kindly country doctor. She was terrified. There was no way that Whip or anyone else was going to find her now.

"I can read your mind, but of course you know that, don't you?" Billy Joe drew his lips into a purse, his eyes filled with polite inquiry. "No need to respond, my dear." He patted her shoulder. "As you know, I can do anything I want to you. You don't even know what *anything* might involve. Your mind can't even conceive of the possibilities of what *anything* might mean. *I can though.*" Billy Joe's face was now lit with an unholy light and his features morphed into a face that would have been at home in every dark alley she had ever walked down alone.

Billy Joe played with the nipple of her right breast, softly at first and then pinching it brutally. Christienne screamed in pain.

"Ah, the music, forgive me, my sweet. Some prefer Mozart, some prefer Jazz, some of course like rock and roll or sundry supplements to the potential for organized melody. I prefer nothing so much as a piercing scream, a moan of agony, a whimper of fear that knows no defense against the inevitable might of the practitioner, myself. You do me such a kind service when you bring a voice to your torment. Even as I hear it, I think of how much deeper the music can go.

"Once, long ago, this music intoxicated me so much that I would hear it through a red haze. My control was not what it is today. I became incontinent, metaphorically speaking. Now, of course, the training pants have long since been removed. Subsequently, my command and invention have brought me to a world of patient experience that someone like you would never understand." As he spoke, he lightly touched different areas of her naked body, and an angry welt would instantly rise. Christienne screamed each time and Billy Joe would raise his head and close his eyes, seeming to sip from an invisible glass, his head tilted back as the unseen nectar flowed down his throat.

"In a sense, you are a very lucky girl, for I would surely prefer sending you to the land of madness this very night. I need you intact however. Soon enough, you will come to the end of your reprieve and you will receive all of the delicate ministrations that have been temporarily denied you. You must be a patient girl." Billy Joe stroked her forehead again. This time the eyes that touched her own were filled with such a cold savagery that Christienne shook with dread. *There was no exit.*

Billy Joe's features changed again into a kindly visage. "I must leave you now. There are those small details of my work that I must attend to, but I will not leave you alone. Tonight, while I am busy elsewhere, I will provide you with a special entertainment." Billy Joe got up from the bed and walked to the door. “On the wall in front of you, you will see what awaits your young lover, Alan Douglas and of course, yourself. Should you wish to close your eyes you will have a more personal viewing screen.”

Billy Joe waved and blew Christienne a kiss as he went through the door. He made his way down the corridor to the sweet refrain of her anguished cries.

Chapter Thirty-Five

2:00 AM, MAUI COUNTY CORRECTIONAL CENTER, MAUI, HAWAII

CarryAnn awoke from a deep sleep. As she rose out of the subconscious, she could hear her mother's voice speaking the words from a poem, something about "heaven in the palm of your hand." That was all and then it washed away, like an ocean wave across a series of footprints. It gave her a warm feeling that remained until she became conscious of the darkness of her cell. It wasn't a cell in the classic sense. There were no bars. The bare room had a steel door with an eye-slit the guards could pull back from their side in order to look in on the prisoner. Still, it was a cell in the respect that you couldn't turn the handle and walk out of it. She felt good until her conscious mind took over and she felt the mind, the probing mind of the man from Arizona.

CarryAnn almost voided her bowels as she felt the consciousness of the one who had pursued her from the day she had first seen him. *There was no mistaking the dark heat of his energy.* She froze. There was a sound like rushing wind, a beckoning cry to recognize. In that instant she felt how very alone she really was. The shadows on the wall were alive with a power being fueled by her imagination. There was a snickering sound. If she wanted, she could really hear it. The voice was begging her to turn up the volume. There was a sense that Klipschorns were available, very possibly Braun's or Voice of the Theater monitors. Somewhere there were Crown amps or some Macintosh inspired power sources that would deafen any sound of protest she could muster.

Not now! She thought, *please not now!* There was a deadly intensity in the room. Just outside of the perception of thought loomed a world of fear that she could not endure if she allowed it entrance.

CarryAnn slipped from her bed and fell to her knees, speaking from a place she had not known since she was four years old and used to recite, "now I lay me down to sleep. I pray the Lord my soul to keep."

Her brow furrowed with concentration, such a horror was upon her that her mute lips could not give witness. She was very frightened indeed. Her stomach boiled from an acid discharge. Her hands trembled as they clasped one another in the empty darkness, made even darker by the clenching of her eyelids.

"Help me. Help me," she cried, suddenly finding voice.

"I am here," is what she heard.

There was a terrible cry in her mind. CarryAnn dropped to the cold floor.

"What the hell!" she screamed in panic. This new voice was even more fearful than the last. It touched her like a natural disaster. It burned her like a fire that could not be escaped. This voice commanded her attention and she wanted to pull the concrete of the floor beneath her up over her head.

"I am not as bad as all of that," the voice said. It had changed its tone now. It no longer thundered to the exception of every other sensation. *"How can I protect you if I cannot drive my foes out before me?"*

"Who are you?" CarryAnn asked. Her body was coiled into a tight bundle on the floor.

"I am your friend, the evil is now gone." The chemical peace she had known before was now replaced by a real peace. There was a relaxed disregard for danger that said to her, on a deep cellular level, *"Nothing can touch you now."*

2:00 AM, SOMEWHERE ON MAUI, HAWAII

Billy Joe took the heavy crystal globe and hurtled in at the wall. It hit the hard oak paneling with tremendous force and rebounded back into the room in a thousand pieces. "Motherfucking, cocksucking, son-of-a-bitching bastard!" He grabbed an ancient pike and stabbed repeatedly into the table before him until it had been reduced to kindling.

"Do you know who I am!" he screamed. "Show yourself, you coward. You hide because you know that I would burn you into cinders!" Billy Joe threw off the black cape that he wore and tore furiously about the room. "Show yourself you shit! You cunt! You filthy cunt! You have nothing! Nothing!" Flecks of white foam were visible at the corners of his mouth. His eyes were red like an enraged beast. He jabbed with the pike into the carpet where the table had once stood. "I will crucify you with burning nails! I will finish the job!"

It was only when he saw the curtains at the windows beginning to smoke that his rage backed off. He could not afford to have his realm burn down around him now. Billy Joe compressed himself and thought of the ocean. He could see it hissing and steaming in his mind. After a few minutes the fury was gone.

"I will fuck you," he said. *This time his voice was very quiet, just above a whisper.* "I will fuck you and I will finish it."

6:00 AM, MAUI MEMORIAL HOSPITAL, WAILUKU, HAWAII

Aaron Wilson was looking through a film of blue gossamer. There was a landscape of cypress trees and clover fading away into infinity. Dancing on the green field before him were two feminine shapes. It was a perfect Maxfield Parrish poster scene. He was watching them dance as he struggled to breathe. He felt as if he were swimming upward through cotton candy. There was a gauzy film in his lungs. He gasped, again and again as his consciousness came slowly to the surface.

The terrible pounding that had been in his head had diminished, but he still felt like he had been dropped on a rocky creek bed. Everything ached. His throat was parched. He shifted in the bed and groaned from the sensation of the many parts of his body answering the movement. As bad as he felt, he was going to be getting up. He had a very strong sensation that all was not well in his world. Certainly he could base that assumption on his own condition. *There was a whirling shit storm loose, ripping up trailer parks and recreation fields.* For a moment he could see Paula Jones and Tanya Harding flying through the air, pit bulls and pickup trucks following them. He laughed at the image and then groaned again. *Getting up and getting around was going to be a real adventure.*

The door opened and someone entered the room. Aaron turned his head and saw an attractive blonde woman with a stethoscope around her neck. "Good morning, Mr. Prosecutor. Welcome back to the land of the living." She smiled and took his pulse.

Aaron returned as much of a smile as he could. "I'm not sure I'm glad to be back," he croaked. "I feel like I got hit by a train."

She nodded. "You're going to need some R & R before you even think about your tennis game," she replied.

"I'm afraid that's not possible. I'm getting out of here this morning." Aaron winced as he lifted himself up on his elbows.

"You're not going anywhere, Counselor. You've got a serious wound and a bad concussion." She pressed him back into the bed.

Aaron wasn't going to argue with her. When the time came, he was going to climb out of the bed and go out the door and woe unto anyone who got between him and the exit. For the moment though, he was going to have to marshal his forces. He knew that you always felt worse on awakening than you did half an hour later. He remembered days in his youth that followed a brutal physical contest. There were moments when it had been an agony to move but once he had begun the process, it got better from there. He'd glanced at the doctor's watch while she was taking his pulse. It was only six in the morning.

7:30 AM, HUELO, HAWAII

Whip had slept very little through the night. Many times he got up and paced about, then returned again to the bed. There was a cold emptiness in his heart.

Anger was impossible for him. He was completely drained. Christienne could be dead or worse and he was responsible. It didn't matter that it had been Ben's idea. He should have known it was a set up. *The first rule in their situation was never to become separated.*

At one point he had tried to still his mind and contact Ming but it had not occurred. In his heart he knew that Christienne was dead. Now there was only the waiting for Billy Joe to come for him. He hoped he would acquit himself well. It didn't matter if he survived the encounter.

When the phone rang, Whip ran across the room for it. "Hello."

"Whip, it's Ben."

"Have you heard anything?" There was a wave of apprehension as he waited for Ben's reply.

"Nothing, Whip, not as far as Christienne is concerned, but I have an idea something's going to happen with Alan."

"What do you mean?" Whip had thought only briefly of Alan in the last hours. Christienne's abduction had driven every other concern from his mind. At this point in the game it seemed clear that Billy Joe's efforts against them would continue to escalate. Whip felt overwhelmed by his ignorance. Instead of a force for good he was nothing more than a pinball at the mercy of random bumper hits. He had no control over events. It was a recipe for total despair.

"I don't *know* anything Whip, but I've got a real strong hunch. Whatever is going to happen is going to happen this morning. I think the key to finding Christienne lies with whatever is going to happen to Alan. I think we need to be there. I'm going to do some snooping around and see what I come up with. You want to get together with this?"

"I'll be there in an hour, Ben." They talked for a little longer about where they would meet and then broke off the connection.

Whip's sorrow across the phone line had been so great Ben hadn't known what to say, better to just stay matter-of-fact rather than lapse into useless commiserations. Years of first-hand experience with human misery had given Ben a certain detachment. *You had to be able to detach yourself or it would bury you.* Ben had seen it happen. You had to recognize the limits of what you could do in any situation. *Bad shit was a given.* There was no limit to the creative applications of terror and injury that man could visit on his fellows. What Ben hadn't seen, he had heard about. He found it to be the hardest thing in the world to be able to put yourself into the mind of the perpetrator as Alan seemed able to do. It was impossible for him to imagine how you got there. People did horrible things to themselves as well. A few years earlier a woman in New York City had emptied her dishwasher, dialed it to its highest setting and then climbed inside and pulled the door shut after her. She had actually killed herself this way.

It impressed him that Whip was not running around like a madman with no sense of purpose, while the woman he loved was in the hands of a merciless fiend. He hoped it would end well, but he knew there was very little chance of that. *Billy Joe possessed no human qualities.* Ben hoped it would end quickly but there was even less chance of that. He pushed it from his mind. Involving himself in Whip's sorrow was not going to help him solve this case.

8:00 AM, MAUI POLICE DEPARTMENT, WAILUKU, HAWAII

The black Lexus slipped into the parking lot and came to a smooth stop next to a new Chevy Blazer jacked up six feet in the air. The driver's door opened and from it emerged a small lithe form in a blue on blue pinstriped suit. Underneath was a brilliant white shirt topped with a cocoa colored tie. Les Moriyama had arrived.

He pulled his briefcase from the back seat, closed the door and set the alarm with the remote switch. This was typical of him, even though he was parked in broad daylight in front of the police station and there was nothing in the car to steal. The remote had also recessed the stereo back into an unremovable burglar-proof safe. Les Moriyama may have defended the scum of the earth but he had no illusions about them. They would steal and/or fuck or kill anything that was not nailed down or defended with guns. He kept everything in his life secured at all times. There were a lot of people who would have taken any chance to bring him down, not to mention the random assholes who lurked in every shadowy corner. Les assumed that every hand was against him and that trouble was a constant. He was therefore always prepared for it.

He had been compared to an eel, a seal and a snake, as well as other less flattering life forms. Although he was only 5'6", he was an imposing man. He possessed the natural charisma that so many short entertainers and politicians had. He could instantly put you at ease if he chose. He was very handsome, the offspring of an Asian father and an Austrian noblewoman. He had a full head of wavy black hair and luminous green eyes, perfect even features and pearly white teeth. He was much admired and a hated man. He evoked strong emotions wherever he went and he used that and everything else to his advantage. He was murder in the courtroom and if he hadn't picked that occupation as his theater of operations, he could have picked any other theater. He was on stage now as he entered the building. He was pumped. Someone he liked had asked him for help. He was there to kick ass and he loved to kick ass. This was his passion, meeting the opponent in the open field and destroying him utterly. It made him sing inside. It made him want to dance and sometimes, it even made him hard. If he had been a criminal and many thought that he was, he would have been legendary. But he never broke the law, not even little laws.

His personal code was written in stone. Whenever anyone asked him how he had come to be the way he was, he always had the same answer, "good genes." He explained that his parents came from the best stock in the world. He had nothing to do with it and no real reaction to it, other than gratitude. Both of his parents had died in a plane crash when he was sixteen years old. If he had a religion besides the law, it was ancestor worship. He had an impressive shrine built to them in his home in Sand Hill, Wailuku. He revered his parents.

Les had never married. In those times when he needed a physical release and he couldn't get it on the handball courts, he would travel to certain nightclubs or discos and pick his partner for the evening. Finding a woman was never difficult. He often went to the clubs with no intention of finding a partner but because he loved to dance. Music and movement were a consuming passion in his life. During the time he was dancing, he could forget there was any other reality but the pumping of the bass and the gyrating bodies surrounding him. He drank only sparkling water with a twist of lime.

Les Moriyama pushed himself up the stairs and into the large entry foyer, heading for the lock-up area. He had never taken LSD but he figured it had to be a lot like the way he felt right now, three hundred and sixty degrees of awareness, turned on, tuned in and ready to take over. *Life was good.*

8:15 AM, WAILUKU POLICE STATION, WAILUKU, HAWAII

Alan sat in his cell waiting. He was a different man than he had been the day before. Nothing was the same. Billy Joe's visit had faded entirely. Ming's presence was now a continuous fact, the way the sound of rushing water was to someone who lived nearby. They might not see the river, and there would be many times when they did not hear the river, but the river was always there. Alan felt encircled by love. It was not a rising ecstatic love, more of a peaceful hum of unity with his surroundings. He understood now that love was the key to unity and that unity was the perfect state of awareness. *To possess the sense and intention of unity with one's surroundings was to be in harmonious accord with all life.*

It was the complete defensible position. You could not be attacked by anything because everything's innate sense of you was one of likeness.

What a profound truth! It was so simple, yet almost universally unknown. The adversary of unity was the perception of difference. Hunger and fear were the two main propellants of disunity. Illusion was another, though differently aspected, but all illusion came out of the sense of separation from the whole.

He could feel the power of the *prana* in the air. The experience of breathing felt sexual. Indeed, breathing was an act of sex. He realized now why so many saints had that particular look on their face. They were all in the same place. He felt like he had died and gone to heaven.

The door opened and two guards entered. One of them had handcuffs and leg irons. "You're going to Court," he said.

Alan stood up and let them apply the chains to his body. They led him shuffling down the hospital corridors until they emerged outside into the back parking lot. They put him in the back seat of a patrol car and drove away.

The scenery from his window was overwhelming. There was an aura over every form. He could see the bodies of plants breathing and absorbing the sunlight. Tears formed at the corners of his eyes at the beauty and wonder of life. How truly sad it was that all did not see as he did now. He looked up and saw the driver watching him in the rear-view mirror. The man's eyes were cold. Alan could feel the suspicion and belief system that drove the man. He was in another world. In that world everything was seen through the lens of the man's sense of self. *It was not a happy place.* Alan stared back at the man, his heart speaking through his eyes. The man quickly looked away.

They arrived at the underground parking garage below the courthouse. Quickly, Alan was trundled into the building and onto an elevator. They got off at the third floor and entered a courtroom. Alan had no idea why he would be in court already. It was too quick for the preliminary and he didn't even have a lawyer. It might be a bail hearing, *"but does it really matter?"*

He was led to a bench at the front and seated next to several people, all shackled as he was. One of them was a strikingly beautiful girl. She seemed sad and old beyond her years. *How ironic that someone so young and beautiful could look so overwrought.* Alan touched her in his thoughts, hoping that what would come for her would be better than what had come so far. The rest were a collection of local males. He could literally smell the outrage and apprehension that filled the air. Here passion had proven too strong for reason. There was a great deal of regret attendant.

Alan was without apprehension. He knew Billy Joe was actively engaged in bringing him along to some certain destiny. The courtroom was just a scene in a movie. He was there to watch and play his part, nothing more. Appearances were one thing and reality was another. Only the real concerned Alan. *All power lay with the real and not the sub-creation that held the world enthralled.* He thought of the irony that conferred power on those who renounced the appearance of power, who renounced the personal for the impersonal.

He looked to the side and saw the girl watching him. She was very beautiful. He could imagine a thousand surfer boys crashing into the rocks in an attempt to get her attention.

There was a loud commotion at the courtroom door. Alan heard yelling but could not decipher the words. Suddenly the door opened and Les Moriyama burst into the room, followed by the bailiff and two sheriff's deputies. Halfway into the room, he stopped and turned toward the officers. "I want a room for my client and myself, now!"

Alan could see the self-assurance pouring off of the diminutive man. There was no question about who was in charge. The officers conferred and then the deputies stood Alan up and led him to a door next to the one marked "Judge's Chambers." Next, they entered a sitting room several yards down a corridor. Moriyama closed the door behind them. He pulled out a chair for Alan and helped him to sit down.

"I'm Les Moriyama," he said. "Ben Kamamoto has retained me for your defense."

Alan shook his hand. "Alan Douglas, sorry I have to meet you looking like Marley's ghost."

"*Da nada.*" Moriyama waved a hand in the air. "We need to talk and we are short of time." Moriyama sat down on the other side of the heavy metal table. He was grinning from ear to ear. "They stuck you in the hospital and sent me to the lockup, while I was looking for you at hospital, they brought you here. Next, they tried to tell me you weren't here, that there was a mistake and you were really still back at the jail. Why do you suppose they are so hot to violate your rights?" Moriyama opened his leather notebook and twisted open a gold Cross pen.

Alan smiled. "The only time anything is not strange in this whole affair is when something normal happens, and I haven't seen anything normal yet."

"You don't seem to be very concerned about things. I've had a little time to get some background. There is some very strange shit going down."

Although he had a masterful grasp of the English language, Moriyama loved to slip in and out of a colloquial persona. It was a very necessary talent in a land where the primary *lingua franca* was a constantly shifting polyglot.

He shot his cuffs and leaned forward with his elbows on the table. "Not the least of which is someone shooting Aaron Wilson. What's going on here, Mr. Douglas?" Moriyama stared directly into his eyes. Alan could tell this was a man from whom it would be very difficult to hide the truth.

"I had nothing to do with the events that put me here. There is a complex effort taking place to frame me with kidnappings, murders and probably other things as well. I can't really tell you who or why. I can only assure you I had nothing to do with it."

Moriyama studied Alan for a few moments and then shook his head up and down. "I haven't seen the confession of this Balfire Tweeds. I have not seen the tapes of your interrogation or the interview with Doctor Abadon, which is directly responsible for your presence here. No one seems to know anything, so I called the clerk. You're scheduled for a competency hearing, the intention of which is your commitment to the state mental hospital for observation. Did you know that?"

Alan shook his head. "It doesn't surprise me."

Moriyama pulled briefly at his bottom lip. "I wouldn't have known anything about the doctor's interview but the clerk was kind enough to tell me that the judge had just finished viewing it. It seems that you threw some kind of a fit, assaulted several officers and became incoherent. What happened?"

Alan sighed and searched the ceiling as if some plausible explanation would descend on him from above. "If I tell you what is really going on, you are going to share the opinion that I am insane."

"Try me," Moriyama said.

Alan looked at Moriyama. There was an inherent decency to the man that he found compelling. Moriyama's aura was huge and pulsed with energy and positive qualities. There was also the sense of a deep and penetrating intelligence. Alan pondered his response. *Sooner or later it was all going to come out.*

"The reality of what is happening is incredible. I wouldn't expect anyone to believe it. I didn't believe it myself at first. As events progressed, it became much easier to believe. If I tell you what has happened, will you still be able to represent me, especially if it then appears to you that I actually am insane?"

"I could represent a pig at a barbecue," Moriyama replied. "Ben Kamamoto has my respect. When he asks a favor of me, I am inclined to believe that he has used his considerable judgment in asking it."

"Ben can confirm all that I will tell you now."

Moriyama arched his right eyebrow. "That would certainly cause me to suspend my disbelief prior to inquiry."

"Not just him, but two other people as well." Alan then gave him an abbreviated version of events. When he was done he gave Moriyama a wide Cheshire cat smile. "Still ready to suspend disbelief?"

Moriyama had not moved throughout the length of Alan's narrative. His hands were clasped on the table in front of him, his attention riveted on Alan. "If true, it is an incredible story," he said softly.

Alan could see Moriyama's mental processes working behind his eyes, weighing the information against his perception of Alan and his knowledge of Ben Kamamoto.

"You realize that a lot of what you have told me could have been orchestrated by normal means. The only thing that doesn't compute is this man's vendetta against you. Then again, it could be coming from another source entirely, since we have no real proof that this man exists. Do we?"

Alan spread his hands, stretching the chain. "Well, meanwhile here I am and once you see the greater body of occurrence, the mysterious death of Malcolm Khan, the madness of Kimo Nakamura, the shooting of Aaron while I was elsewhere… these are just a portion of the events…"

"If I look at it that way, it is not necessary for me to accept the totality of what you have told me." Moriyama smiled, "Here's what we're going to do. I'm going to demand a diagnosis from two other psychiatrists prior to the granting of the state's request for observation. I'm also going to request a delay in the proceedings so that I can get up to speed on your case. There's no precedent for sending a client out of town before he has had reasonable opportunity to confer with his lawyer. That should slow them down a little. You ready to go?"

"Ready as I'll ever be," Alan replied.

"Okay," Moriyama got up from his chair. "Let's get down to the courtroom."

8:30 AM, DISTRICT ATTORNEY'S OFFICE, WAILUKU, HAWAII

Rusk and Finch were sitting in Finch's office when the door opened and a sheriff's deputy walked in. "The Weasel just showed up at the courthouse and demanded to see Alan Douglas, apparently he's retained him."

Rusk's face turned purple, "Son-of-a-motherfuckin' bitch! How the fuck did that happen?" He turned quickly to Finch, his mind in turmoil as he saw his beautiful plan unraveling in front of him.

Finch raised a restraining hand. "Just hold it together, Millard. As unstable as Douglas is, once the doctor testifies and I start questioning him, he'll more than likely flip out again. What's Moriyama going to do then?"

"What do you think he's going to do?" Rusk asked, his hand shaking from the effects of the alcohol he had recently been consuming.

"The only thing I can imagine is that he's going to request a second opinion. I'll request that they get those opinions at the facility. I'll go into great detail about the heinous nature of the crimes and the overwhelming evidence. Hirono hates Moriyama and the defense does not have the latitude here that they would have at trial. This is a judge's decision. I like our odds. Moriyama has had no time to prepare, he doesn't know what's going on, and when he doesn't know what's going on, he goes into his Laurence Olivier mode and Hirono really hates that.

"Doctor Abadon is meeting us outside the courtroom. We should be able to get a few words in with him." Finch said as he got to his feet.

By a stroke of good timing, Dr. Abadon was just getting out of his car as Finch and Rusk drove into the parking lot. They parked in a space marked reserved for "Officers of the Court."

Abadon walked over to meet them. "Good morning, gentlemen." Abadon had a cheerful smile. He looked closely at them. "How is everything?"

Finch told him about Moriyama.

"How did he come into the mix?" Abadon asked.

"Probably it was his fucking buddy Kamamoto," Rusk answered. "He's kind of a loose associate of Moriyama's." Rusk thought about what he was going to do to Kamamoto when this was all over with. Lt. Kamamoto would learn the price to be paid for fucking with him.

Dr. Abadon seemed nonplussed by the information. "So where does that leave us?"

"We've still got the edge," Finch replied. "We'll just play it the way we discussed and, barring something unforeseen, Douglas will be on the afternoon plane to Oahu."

8:45 AM, JUDGE HIRONO'S COURTROOM, WAILUKU, HAWAII

Judge Hirono had once been a robust man but age, chronic alcoholism and some as yet undetermined wasting disease had taken their effect upon the man. A large percentage of the people whose jobs or offenses took them into his courtroom prayed that nature would soon reach in and take him from the bench.

He'd once been in possession of a fine legal mind. Lately he had become a rubber stamp for the prosecutor's office and his vision had narrowed to where all of the accused that appeared before him were relegated to a place near the bottom of the food chain. One did not easily remove a sitting judge, so most of his victims and critics simply prayed. It was their only recourse.

The bailiff stood and read off the first case number. It was for Alan Douglas. Hirono looked over the brief in front of him for a moment and then said, "Proceed."

Before Finch had said a dozen words, Moriyama leaped to his feet with an objection, "Your honor, the prosecution has no right to send my client to Kaneohe on the basis of a single psychiatric opinion or evaluation. We request the opportunity to have my client examined by at least one other psychiatrist."

Judge Hirono looked at Moriyama with distaste and Moriyama was grateful that it was still early in the day. By the time court reconvened after the lunch recess, Hirono was usually bombed and deaf to all reason.

"Mr. Moriyama, I asked the prosecution to present their case. That is what I want to listen to now. I do not want to listen to you until after the prosecution has presented their case and I have asked you to speak. In fact, I know that I do not even want to listen to you then, so sit down and shut up."

Moriyama complied.

Finch continued presenting his argument and then told the judge he wanted to call Dr. Philip Abadon to the stand to testify as to his expert opinion on Alan's mental state.

Hirono nodded and Finch called for Dr. Abadon, who had been sitting in the back of the courtroom.

Alan's eyes wandered around the courtroom. Ben sat just behind him and placed a reassuring hand on his shoulder.

Dr. Abadon walked past Alan and up to the witness box. He sat down and scanned the faces of the people in the courtroom.

Alan heard a sharp gasp to his right. He turned and saw that it had come from the girl. Her eyes were fixed on Abadon. She was trembling in her seat. Alan wondered what was happening.

The doctor's eyes found the girl's and they widened. Alan could feel the crackle of tension in the air. The doctor suddenly looked like a different person. His features were undergoing a subtle change. There was cruel twist to his lips and a hostile look in his eyes.

The girl was starting to rock back and forth in her seat now. She appeared to be mumbling to herself but Alan could not make out what she was saying. He felt the hairs on the back of his neck stand up as he smelled a rank feral odor.

Finch, unaware of what was taking place in the room, asked the doctor to state his name and the nature of his profession.

"My name is Philip Abadon. I am a Doctor of Psychiatry specializing in…"

The girl screamed. It was incredibly loud. Half the people in the courtroom jumped. Alan's attention was fixed on the doctor while everyone else was looking at the girl. The doctor's face had become a mask of concentration. His forehead was drawn into a grove between his brows. His lips were a thin line and his nostrils were flared.

The girl had stopped screaming and was now rocking back and forth in her seat, her arms tightly clenched around her.

Ben leaned forward and asked, "Do you see what I see?"

Alan nodded his head.

Judge Hirono was banging on his gavel. "Quiet! Quiet! What's going on here?" He looked at the girl. "I don't know what's wrong with you young lady, but you're going to be quiet in my courtroom or you're going to be taken out of here. Am I clear?"

"Yes," she replied in a monotone. It reminded Alan of the computerized voices at the supermarket cash registers.

"Continue," Hirono said to Finch.

Finch returned his attention to Dr. Abadon. "You were going to tell us about your area of specialization."

Abadon continued to look at the girl as he spoke. "I specialize in Forensic Psychiatry," he replied.

"Would you please explain to the court what that involves?" Finch asked.

The girl was squirming in her seat again.

"Forensic Psychiatry is the inquiry into pathological states in the human mind. It is often used to create a profile of criminal perpetrators when their identity is still…" Abadon was cut off by another outbreak.

This time the scream was even louder. The girl had risen to her feet and her eyes were blazing as she looked at Dr. Abadon. "You're a murderer!" she screamed. "You killed Royce and the others! You killed my mother!" CarryAnn was shaking from the effort to speak.

Alan stared at Dr. Abadon. When the girl had screamed his head had turned as if it were on a swivel. His face was now a mask of rage. Now he no longer looked anything like Abadon. Alan was not sure who he looked like. He was on his feet as well, his hands grabbing the rail in front of the witness box. Alan could see the force of his will dance across the room like an electric charge and strike the girl. Her body arched and she was slammed backwards into the bench. She collapsed and slid to the floor.

Ben's hand was gripping Alan's shoulder. "It's him," he said. Hirono was banging his gavel again and calling for quiet. Dr. Abadon had stepped out of the witness box and had his hands extended before him. Immediately Alan could feel a heavy lassitude filling the room. It was as if the air had turned into a thick clear pudding. He looked around the room and saw that every head was bowed. The bailiff was walking in slow motion toward the girl. The only thing in the room that seemed to still be able to operate at a normal pace was Dr. Abadon as he made his way to the aisle.

Finch watched him like someone in a dream. He extended a slow motion hand out to catch the doctor by the arm as he walked past. He missed him by several feet.

Alan caught his eyes as he walked past. They seemed to be on fire. Alan was unmoved by their intensity. It was another force beyond his own that lifted him out of his seat and into the aisle. With his cuffed hands in front of him he grabbed the pocket of the doctor's coat as he came abreast. "You're not going anywhere," he said. The doctor's coat tore open as he continued moving toward the entrance. As it came away, the contents of his pockets spilled into Alan's hands.

Dr. Abadon spun about and his eyes met Alan's. He hissed like a snake. Alan looked directly back into them. "I'm not through with you, you son-of-a-bitch. You'll blow me in Hell before I'm done." His words hung in the hypnotized air of the courtroom and though their import had not yet registered on the courtroom's inhabitants, they would. There was no way for him to take the words back. His mind was stunned by the betrayal of his mouth. He slapped away Ben's feeble effort to grab him and with great speed departed the courtroom. As soon as he had gone through the door, the spell was broken.

The bailiff instantly came back up to speed and was bending over the unconscious girl. Ben bolted from his seat and ran after the doctor. Finch was standing in a state of shock. His mouth was moving but no words were coming out. Alan believed that he was mouthing the doctor's departing words. He was right.

Alan looked down at his hands. He was holding the contents of Abadon's pockets. His eyes went wide when he saw what they contained. They were

Polaroid photos of the bodies that were found in Alan's house but they had not been taken in Alan's house. They were single shots of the victims in various states of the taxidermy process. *"Oh, what have we here,"* he said softly to himself.

Hirono, in the most vigorous display of energy anyone had seen out of him in years, had managed to return the courtroom to order. "Mr. Finch, what was that comment about Hell and where has your witness gone?"

Finch looked up at the judge and said, "I don't know Your Honor."

"Well you had damn well better find out. I'm adjourning this court until 1:00 p.m. All prisoners are remanded back into custody. Bailiff!" Hirono screamed, "Stop slapping that girl and get some medical personnel in here. Court adjourned." Judge Hirono got to his feet and disappeared into his chambers, where he would proceed to get drunk. This time he probably deserved it.

No sooner had the door closed behind the judge than the courtroom doors opened and Aaron Wilson came limping though them. He walked directly up to Finch and said, "Come with me, bring Alan Douglas and by all means, please bring Captain Rusk." The look on his face told Finch that no reply was required or smart.

Finch called a sheriff's deputy over and gave him instructions to bring Alan along. He motioned to Rusk, and they followed Aaron Wilson through the door into the judge's chambers.

Through the judge's open door, Aaron could see Judge Hirono upending a water glass. He kept walking until he came to the law library. Then he entered and sat down, waiting for the rest to follow him in. He curtly told everyone to have a seat and then dismissed the sheriff's deputy.

"Do you think that's wise, Aaron?" Rusk asked.

"Shut your fucking mouth and keep it shut. You're here to listen. I'm a heartbeat away from calling the mayor and putting an end to your illustrious career. Whether that comes about at a later date is something to be decided after I find out just what the hell has been going on. I've been on the phone with a few people this morning. I've got some ideas about what's been taking place here and I don't like any of it." Aaron had a huge bandage over the left side of his head and both of his eyes were black. He looked awful but there was strength in his eyes that pushed away all thought of infirmity for the moment.

Rusk did not reply. Something terrible had happened to him since Abadon had left the courtroom. He saw all of his recent actions as rash and unjustifiable. He even felt shame, something he had not felt in many a year. His mind was in confusion. He could no longer understand why he had done the things he had done.

Aaron slammed his hand on the table and looked at Richard Finch. "You and I have not always agreed. However, in the past, you have always been a reliable and competent assistant. I'd like to emphasize the word *assistant.* Why you have acted in this outrageous manner is beyond me. Is there any possible explanation, Richard?"

Finch said nothing. He was in the same state as Rusk. When Dr. Abadon walked out the door he had seen his career plans dissolve in front of his eyes. He could not now comprehend why he had done anything at all.

The door opened and Les Moriyama stuck his head into the room. "Hi Aaron, I'm Mr. Douglas's attorney. Can I come in?"

Aaron studied him for a moment and then said, "Come on in, Les, but I don't want any argument here right now. We're not in a courtroom."

Aaron turned to Alan. "As I was coming across the parking lot I was nearly run over by Doctor Abadon. Very shortly afterwards, Lieutenant Kamamoto went flying past me. Two cars tore away out of the parking lot. What's going on, Alan?"

"The man you know as Doctor Abadon is the mastermind behind all of the kidnappings and murders. He's the brain behind Malcolm Kahn and Balfire Tweeds. Abadon has certain mental powers that make it possible for him to influence the minds and actions of others. He can cloud the minds of good men. He has great powers of confusion and fear. He's a type of Svengali, a Rasputin. I think Mr. Finch understands this now."

Finch looked at Alan and shook his head. Whether this was a kind of assent, Alan did not know. Finch looked completely drained.

"I need to be cut loose now, Aaron. He's got Christienne and I'm sure he's headed back that way. Ben's after him and that means Ben is in danger."

"He's got Christienne?" Aaron's face filled with concern.

"I can't explain anymore, Aaron. You've got to trust me. I'm the only one who can do anything now. You'll want to take a look at these, too. They fell out of Abadon's pocket when he left." Alan handed Aaron the pictures.

Aaron studied them and then tossed them across the table at Finch and Rusk.

Aaron and Alan exchanged a look. Then Aaron called for the deputy sheriff. When he arrived, Aaron ordered the shackles removed.

Les Moriyama stepped forward and pressed his keys into Alan's hands. "The black Lexus, it's got cellular and scanner. There's a registered Beretta in the trunk and the clip is in the glove compartment. Now get out of here!"

Alan thanked him and then he ran out of the door.

Five minutes later, Whip walked into an empty courtroom. He'd been delayed for twenty minutes by road construction and another fifteen minutes at the police department looking for Alan. By the time he got to the courthouse, everyone was gone. He learned enough from the bailiff to get an idea of what had happened. Then he met Aaron, who told him about Abadon and gave him the doctor's address.

"Ben, it's Alan."

"Alan! Where are you?"

"Aaron cut me loose. I'm headed Kihei direction. Where are you bound?"

"Same thing for now, I'm three cars behind the bastard near the middle of the Mokulele. He's doing the speed limit, doesn't seem at all concerned, the cocky bastard."

"Listen, Ben, whatever you do, don't approach him. The guy is very dangerous. Just keep a line of sight. I'm moving and I should catch you on the Pi'ilani, provided he goes that way. Les gave me his car."

"He what?" Ben laughed. "That's a first. Les loves that car. He doesn't even let other people ride in that car. He has it detailed every week. That's five thousand a year to keep a clean car clean. You shouldn't have any trouble making up the distance, not that he's trying to get away."

"Ben, I need you to do this my way. When we get to wherever we're going, you've got to stay back. This isn't going to be won by conventional means. This is a whole different thing. You understand?"

"It's your call Alan, but if you go down all bets are off."

"No, Ben, no matter what it looks like, you can't react. It could be fatal. He can make things seem like they have happened, like they are happening. You must trust me. He'll use you to get what he wants. It could kill us both, or worse. I can't explain it right now but I know what to do. Will you do what I ask?"

There was no answer from Ben for a long time. The old Alan would have asked again, added more argument and been more persuasive. The new Alan didn't have to. He was as much in Ben's mind as he was in his own. He knew what Ben was wrestling with. He also knew that if Ben agreed he would stick by it.

"Okay, I'll play it your way."

Alan signed off and concentrated on his driving. He was whipping around cars at every opportunity. There was no apprehension in him, no sense of risk. He drove like a machine. Everything was a matter of mathematics. He knew where the inches were. He knew how much space he needed to occupy the space he wanted. Very few people had ever driven the Mokulele in this fashion without serious incident. It was a dangerous road. He was halfway through when Billy Joe's voice entered his head.

"Well, Detective, you're doing better than anyone would have thought, better than I imagined. Were you faking it last night? Somehow I don't think so."

"No, Billy Joe, I wasn't faking." Alan whipped around another car and back into the next slot. Now there was a good stretch of road ahead and he stepped on the accelerator.

"Who's helping you, Detective? You could never have come this far without help."

"Surely with your vast resources, you should be able to determine the answer to that."

"Oh, there is an answer, Detective, but so far I have failed at its discovery. The search included a very bloody rite that has never before failed to elicit a revelation."

"There is still time to come out of the darkness, Billy Joe."

Billy Joe laughed like crackling cellophane. Alan was reminded of T.S. Elliot's line from *The Hollow Men*, "like…rat's feet over broken glass…"

"Your mistake, Detective, is in trying to understand me. You cannot comprehend me any more than the one that you serve. Tell me, who is helping you? I would like to know. You can't really endanger him in any way by telling me. What advantage would I gain by just knowing his name?"

Alan shot past two more cars and then beat the light at the intersection of the Pi'ilani Highway. "You are a most persuasive man, Billy Joe." He could feel the probing pincer-like intention of Billy Joe's mind. If he moved in any direction, he would be vulnerable to the other. "I can't imagine that it is pure curiosity that motivates you here, so there must be a reason and, as you know, if you were supposed to know, you would know."

"I'll take your reluctance into account, Detective, when I dispense with you."

"You can't add anything to an equation of fear that does not exist, Billy Joe. In any case, you have never shown any mercy up to this point. I think your bluff is about to be called. You need to think this moment through."

"True enough, Detective. Just tell me who is helping you. Surely you know. I know they all look the same but usually you can tell them apart, no matter how self-effacing they like to appear. They each have their trademark. I've run across a few in my time."

"Not like this one, Billy Joe. What was going on with that girl took you by surprise, didn't it?"

There was another high-pitched brittle laugh. *"Another slick effort on the part of your mentor, whoever that might be. Despite all of that, you will not prevail."* Billy Joe started singing in a high pitched voice, "*I've got a little list, there's none of them be missed...* But Christienne will be missed won't she?"

Alan let the calm equanimity of the impersonal Self wash over him. It was evident what Billy Joe was trying to do. "What are you talking about?"

"I cut her to pieces, Alan, in one of my many splendored bedrooms. I heightened her sensitivity. I stripped the nerve sheath away so that she could really get into it. Then it was just a piece at a time." His voice was intoxicating. Hot red images of bloody death slipped into Alan's mind. He did not resist. He let them flow by as if they were memories of a garden party, which is what he turned them into. The secret was not to oppose, but to transform. Mind stuff was like water. Its shape was easily changed. Resistance strengthened the image through negative reinforcement.

"If she's gone, she's gone, Billy Joe. Nothing we can do about that now. She's at peace."

"Are you very sure of that last part, Detective?" Billy Joe snickered.

"All that I am really sure of, Billy Joe, is that your time is at hand." Alan was roaring past the other cars using the right hand bike lane. Horns were going off. Alan drove with absolute control.

"Would that be so very bad?"

"For someone like you, it would be very bad indeed. Total disintegration, nothingness, starting all over again as a rock, not very pleasant for one whose whole focus is on himself."

"*You're getting fairly knowledgeable, Detective. Has someone been telling you little secrets? Do you think you can take me, Detective? You know that you cannot. I don't know how many tricks are left in that little magic bag of yours, but if you lose, you lose big.*"

"I'm aware of the risks, Billy Joe. What will be, will be."

Billy Joe laughed again, a harsh cawing sound and it made Alan think of crows picking the eyes out of sick sheep. *"I find that statement to be almost frightening, Detective. There is such a certainty in your voice, such a finality of acceptance. Is it real, Detective? Will it be real when it has to be? I'm good at reading these things. I think the smart money is on me."*

Alan saw Ben's car up ahead of him. He honked his horn and saw Ben's arm come out of the window acknowledging him.

"Well, Batman, it looks like you've found Robin. We'll chat again real soon." Then Billy Joe was gone from his mind.

Alan picked up the phone and called Ben. "I think he's going to his place in Maui Meadows. He says that he killed Christienne."

"Oh, God!" Ben cried. "Poor Whip."

Alan did not reply. There was nothing he could say to that. When Billy Joe came to the turnoff for Maui Meadows he passed it by and continued on the highway toward Wailea.

"What the hell?" Ben remarked.

"I don't know," Alan replied. They continued on, past the hotels and headed toward Makena Beach and the ancient lava flows.

"Looks like we're headed into rough country," Ben said.

Chapter Thirty-Six

Whip fought to keep his sense of urgency under control. He wouldn't be much good to Christienne if he wound up dead on the highway. The dune buggy offered poor protection in the event of a wreck and a truck on the Mokulele had nearly creamed him when he passed a car without checking the oncoming lane.

His heart was pounding in his chest. He was in a terrible anxiety over what he would find when he got to Dr. Abadon's house. There was no way that he could bear it if the worst had happened. It was unthinkable and he did not think it. As tortured images rose into his mind he pushed them aside. He had a course of action. It was enough for the moment.

He made the turn into Maui Meadows. It became quickly apparent to him that he was not going to just come across the road he was looking for. There were roads going everywhere. He pulled up next to a jogger and asked him for directions. In less than two minutes he was at the gate of the estate.

The gate was closed. Whip pulled the dune buggy into the entrance and parked it sideways, blocking the gate. He reached under the seat and retrieved the gun. Very quickly, he scaled the gate and dropped down inside the compound.

KING'S HIGHWAY, NEAR MAKENA BEACH, MAUI, HAWAII

Billy Joe's car went past the Makena turnoff and then increased its speed. The road was lined with *kiawe* trees and large *saguaro cacti.* At this point it was little more than a narrow lane, with huge dips that constantly obscured the line of sight, but Billy Joe drove as if he had the road to himself.

Ben cursed and slammed the steering wheel with his hand as he labored to keep up with the big Mercedes that was gradually getting away from him.

Alan heard Billy Joe's maniacal laughter thundering in his head, along with cries of anguish and sobs of heartbreaking regret. He could hear Christienne screaming for mercy and cursing him and Whip for abandoning her, damning them. He let it wash through him. He imagined a brilliant light as thick as syrup pouring through his mind.

"Good work there, Detective! There are a lot of techniques on the market but you've found one that works, for the moment. Do you think I am trying to get away from you? Your partner thinks so. I could have gotten away at any time. I'm tired of fucking around. I think we should just get it done. It won't have all of the subtleties that

I would have liked, and the deaths won't happen in the order that I wanted them to. Still, since you are going to die now and since the souls of your associates will soon all belong to me, it's the results that count. Isn't that right?"

Alan made no reply. Billy Joe's words danced before him like the flora outside his windshield. There was no personal aspect to it. It was just phenomena.

"You disappoint me Alan. I would have thought, after the separation of so many years, that you would have been looking forward to our little chat. And, when you consider how little time remains to you, I would think these last moments would become exceptionally precious."

"No moment of life is more precious than any other Billy Joe, nor does preference make it so."

"Hmmm, nicely put. Now I wonder who it was that said that? It doesn't sound like you Alan. It reminds me of someone. I can't quite place it. Isn't that strange? It can only be fear that keeps your mentor behind his veils. This, of course, improves my confidence, not that I've ever lacked any."

Never before had Alan been able to so clearly feel the line that ran between conflicting choices. There was the certainty of himself and the pull of Billy Joe. One was internal and one external, though that was no way to put it. *There was no way to put it,* he thought. *It's been like this forever.* Every human soul is in a continuous relationship between what is and what seems. Evil is never completely evil, nor good, good. There was just the ongoing spiraling awareness of change. Finally, one is revealed to one's self beyond definition, beyond extremes, as the veritable source and goal of life.

Billy Joe laughed, *"My, my, Douglas, William Blake ain't got nothing on you. Have you considered the possibility that even that line of reasoning may be just a construct too? You might want to consider essential nature — as above, so below. How does that fit in when you try to explain me?"*

Alan felt the ease that only great clarity can bring. There was no personal mission to confuse him, to drive him, to manipulate him into visualizing the image of a specific, realized conclusion. He didn't know where this was headed and it didn't matter. It wasn't about him. This was the planets moving in their courses. This was just the outworking of universal laws. Gravity didn't depend on Alan or Billy Joe to be. Gravity didn't know anything about either one of them in respect of its application. *Gravity just was.* He laughed suddenly as he remembered a line from a film he'd once seen about the Mafia, "Look, this is just business, nothing personal."

He felt a wave of black hate that began to smolder and coil around him.

Immediately, Alan began to weave it into a multitude of bright colors. The black looked nice against a field of ever-changing hue, a constant thread of contrast and deeper backdrop against which the richer living hues were vibrating. He could hear the music that was the result of their interplay.

"We will see about all of that, Douglas. We shall see how long this veneer of dispassion and selfless containment will wear. Soon your puppet master will have to come forth. You'll have nowhere to run when he falls. You're really counting on him, but he and I are the same Douglas. He's just another side of me and in the end, mortal interest is not an issue of concern for either of us. You're alone Douglas, more than you know and it really is very, very personal."

A moment of uncertainty passed through Alan's mind. There was something he didn't quite get from the exchange. He could feel his mind begin to separate in order to define it. Instantly he saw where that led and fell back again into unity. The revelation of what he had just accomplished dwarfed every understanding that had ever come to him before. Instinctively, he realized that this revelation had not been made known to Billy Joe and never would. Suddenly his state was no longer an article of faith. It had become substance itself.

The cars were now moving at over forty miles an hour, double the speed limit. Billy Joe went into a hairpin turn and creased a van that was coming the other way. This sent the van rocking from one side of the road to the other. Ben had nowhere to go and left the road, ramming into a large stand of cacti. Pods flew everywhere.

Alan felt time disappear as the large panel van came at him. Then, like a bullfighter, he swerved to the right precisely as the van went left. He pulled over where Ben had crashed and ran to the car, kicking at the cacti, disintegrating them. Opening the door he pulled Ben from the car. The air was filled with the chemical stink of the exploded air bag.

"I've always wanted to do that." Ben said. He held his left hand against the side of his head.

"You okay?" Alan asked.

"Yea, they ought to do something about smoothing out that airbag fabric. It's like sandpaper." He brought his hand away and Alan could see an angry scrape across his forehead.

They ran back to the Lexus. Now, Alan kept the car at a lower speed. There were a lot of tourists on this road who didn't drive all that well even where they came from. Here on Maui with its lush scenery, they were a constant menace — throw in the inebriated with Andy Granatelli locals in their pickup trucks and you had a state-of-the-art video game in real life. If Billy Joe were running away, he was running in the wrong direction, unless he was going to jump in the water, turn into a fish and swim away.

The road straightened out as they came into the lava fields of La Perouse. An immense lava flow had tumbled down the southeastern side of the mountain long ago and the landscape was a twisted wreckage of tumbled lava rock, almost totally devoid of vegetation. For miles around it looked like the surface of the moon.

They rode in silence, their thoughts centered on the chase. They didn't have long to wait. Coming around a slow bend, they saw the Mercedes pulled over on the left hand side of the road. Alan drew the car up behind it and got out. Ben came out of his side with his gun drawn. Alan closed his door. The sound was loud in the silent emptiness of the lava fields.

Ben advanced on the car and quickly checked inside. "He's gone."

"I know where he is, Ben. He's gone down into the lava. There's a path here that leads to the tide pools by the ocean. I used to come here often, soon after I arrived. It's a great place to be alone with your thoughts. I expect he wants to finish me here."

"What are you going to do?" Ben asked.

"Give him his chance."

"What!?"

"Just trust me, Ben."

Alan led them off the road onto a path worn smooth by countless feet. Soon they were swallowed up in the outcroppings of rock. There were many crevasses, sometimes opening right at their feet. Ben thought that at night this would be a very dangerous place to negotiate.

"It's funny, Alan. I've lived all of my life on Maui and I've never been on this particular path. As small as Maui is, she has a lot of secrets."

Alan didn't reply. He was aware of a foul odor creeping into the air. From the sea, dark clouds were racing in to the shore. It very seldom rained in La Perouse. These were not ordinary clouds.

"Ben, I need you to drop back now and wait for me. Keep me in sight but don't get any closer than that."

Ben started to argue and then remembered their agreement. "Go then."

Alan walked on ahead. The air grew more fetid with every step. As he came over a rise, he saw the landscape below was littered with corpses, as if there had been a great battle. They were strewn about in all positions, men, women and children. Flames licked up out of cracks in the rock, the smell of brimstone intermingled with the smell of rotting flesh. Terrible screams rent the air. He could see some of the bodies crawling about. He caught the eyes of a young man and saw in them a look of utter despair. He felt again the tug that sought to displace his state of mind with that of another, the opportunity to exchange his mindset for the mindset of the young man. Every visual event external to him was a commercial for something. He understood now the intrinsic purpose of commercial advertisement, the process of self-identifying. *The seven chakras of the body were portals into entire worlds.* It was like being in the elevator of an enormous department store. Everything was happening on its own level. People were living their entire lives in one particular location, without realizing how many other locations that were available.

"This is where I am," Billy Joe said. *"And they all work for me. They all belong to me."*

Alan fixed his mind on the light within. He could feel it growing in intensity. Deep within he could feel a great engine turning. Power was rushing up from far away up to the surface of his being. Within it was the sound of blowing horns and other instruments he did not recognize. He felt the immensity of an enormous force that appeared to be everywhere at once.

In his mind, he could hear Billy Joe speaking again, *"Power is power. It has no conscience, conscience is fear. Fear is slavery. Fear hungers for a Master. Self is the only Master. Weakness presents its rear for the penetration of the Master. It is the estrus of mortality seeking its lover, Death!"*

His voice screamed within Alan's mind. Everywhere around him, Alan could feel unity attempting to divide in two, but at each possible breaking point, unity flowed back in to close upon itself. Effortlessly, the unity moved in an automatic response to every mental, emotional and dimensional rift. He saw how any point of view might appear correct. He saw how men would suffer and die for a lie that appeared to be true. He saw the purpose of religions and governments. He saw their seeming need and their utter limitation and failure. The totality of the world from every point of its perception by the senses was a lie. No sense could perceive the entirety. *All perception was flawed.* Every outer thing was an insubstantial and fading picture of an inexpressible idea. And, Billy Joe was right, he was as "right" as anyone else. From where Billy Joe sat, it could only look just as it did. Billy Joe and what Billy Joe saw was the exact same thing.

"Now you see. Do you not?" Billy Joe continued, *"And you will join me? The appearance of conflict between us was merely a gestalt meant to unify us in both mind*

and purpose."

He could see the clouds coming closer. The wind began to tug at his clothing. A few isolated raindrops splattered on the rocks, heralding an incoming flood. Alan saw a flash of lightning in one of the clouds. It was an event apart. It had nothing to do with him. He watched with detachment and answered, "I see that I can live in darkness or that I can live in light. I can drink from the sewer or the mountain stream. They are both water after all, aren't they?"

"The darkness is the light. Pain is pleasure and separation is unity. I smell the flesh of the lamb grilling on the fire. I can taste the succulent corruption of the sustaining life. Will you dine with me, Alan?"

He felt his mouth awash with saliva. His nostrils filled with the essence of hunger and its satisfaction. He felt his cock swell. For a moment there was the sense of wrong and a rift began to open, but the unity washed forth again. Cocks did swell. There was nothing wrong with that.

"Oh we are clever, clever. What a clever boy we are. But this can't be you Alan. You are a corporate self. You are the man who wept for his wife. You are the man who refused to dance with the Village People." Again the rifts came, brief images of the past, images that required the observer and the perceived and the speculating movement of the mind between. Then, once again, unity flowed and everything it touched became one.

As he came among the bodies, he saw creatures the size of house cats tearing at them and eating the flesh. They looked like cartoon caricatures of devils. They had hairless bodies and wide grinning mouths. They were bright red with horns and pointy tails.

Billy Joe's voice now came from outside of him, its tone and tenor changed. "Do you know who these poor unfortunates are, Detective? They are all victims of mine. Look how many of them there are. I have left my mark upon this world and in just two nights hence, I will advance to a power unimaginable to the ordinary mortal.

"Look about you at the garden I have grown. Here they will lay in their torment for as long as I am alive. Soon, you will join them, but not all of their torment put together equals what I have in store for you. You were very foolish to come here, but then I knew you would. This is a power spot for me. Perhaps you've read your Castaneda? It is the foolishness of your kind that believes some personal virtue, some sense of the rightness of things, will prevail over a quality that you describe in such a limited way as evil."

The wind had increased in strength and volume and it tore at him now. The rain was falling in earnest and his clothes were instantly soaked, his hair matted to his head. Still he held to the rising light within him. He was the light. *There was no other self but this light.*

Directly in front of him was a cone of swirling darkness, a twister of black. It was magnetic and it pulled at him, setting a contrast to the wind. He could hear the whispering urgency of it. His emotional body was feeling all the seductive promises that the darkness offered him. There was a sweet annihilation, an end to the troubles of life, a warm, luxurious forgetfulness. It reminded Alan of the morphine they'd given him in the hospital as he was recovering from a gunshot wound. The light inside him grew. He could hear Ming's voice but there were no words in it. It was pure intelligence transmitting without a medium. He knew that Billy Joe must sense this.

The whirling darkness approached and now Alan could see in its center a human form, backlit with a pale white glow, like moonlight. It was Billy Joe. A large cape floated about him, woven from blood and midnight. The face had changed, but it was still Billy Joe, stronger, fiercer and more charismatic. He had the reckless look of a highwayman, wearing silver boots and tight black pants. There was a tunic through which red and blue stars shined. The tornado came quickly forward and engulfed Alan in complete darkness. There was nothing visible anywhere except Billy Joe, who glowed before him.

"Welcome to my world mortal, ignorant fool who would contend with me. I have been since the very foundation stones of the world were set. I have had as many names as there are lifetimes to define me. I rule the house of the dead to which you have come." Billy Joe gestured with his right hand and a window opened into a world of horrors. Alan felt a tiny tremor of doubt, a separating inside himself. There was a thought that he would not suffer if he would only lay down and surrender. Billy Joe was not his enemy, he was in fact his benefactor, a god who would free him from his imprisoned state. Pain was what he already had. *It could all end with Billy Joe.*

"What you know as evil is not really evil, Detective. You have been lied to from the beginning, denied the freedom and the station that are yours by right. You have been the plaything of a sadistic God from whose clutches only I can free you. I can grant you every pleasure that you think is forbidden. You can roll in it like a dog. You can rule as I do."

All of the force of Billy Joe's will was now focused on Alan. He saw himself as a man of power. All eyes gazed upon him with admiration and desire. He had only to gesture for someone to live or to die. Inside the window, the scenery had changed from a bacchanalian slaughterhouse to a series of tableaus in which Alan commanded the world. He could feel the thrill that came with such absolute power, but he was unmoved. It meant nothing to him.

Why was Billy Joe tempting him? He had promised to destroy him and now he was embracing him as a friend. He felt the impressions from Ming's mind. If Billy Joe could sway him into willing servitude, then Alan would be truly lost.

"I have no desire to be like you, Billy Joe. You would do well to consider the small window of hope that still exists for you."

"Fool!" Billy Joe rose up over him. "I am as far beyond the reach of your imagination as the sun is from a firefly. You can do nothing to me. Even were I offered full redemption, I would immediately kill a small child in response. *I do not care.* I will show you what it is I plan to take from you. Your body is an inconsequential thing. I shall take it but I will also take your soul and every life that it provides for itself. I will hold you through time and beyond time, until time itself has become psychotic in the face of your pain. The suffering of all humanity will be like a toothache in comparison. I am going to hurt you now. You will scream for help, but no help will come. You will scream and scream, but only I will hear you. *Now comes the moment of my great pleasure.* Your friend is in Hell already, as soon will be everyone you care for."

Alan got the reference to Ben but he paid it no mind. The power inside him was all that he knew. He could feel the terrific wave of hate that bore down upon him. No human mind could have withstood it. Alan felt only joy. The rage and force increased. Alan sucked it into the inferno of love within and transformed it into yet more joy. He breathed it out upon Billy Joe.

"Show yourself!" Billy Joe roared. *"Come forth you coward and face me!"* Wave after wave of suffocating evil poured out of him. Alan continued to transform it and pour it back. From out of the shell of Alan Douglas there rose a luminous shape. It grew and grew. Matching it, Billy Joe increased in size, until there were two great shapes facing off against each other. It was Ming as Alan had never seen him, majestic, impossibly brilliant, beautiful beyond description. In Ming's right hand was a mirror.

"You!" Billy Joe howled. "I destroyed you centuries ago!" He pulled a sword from the folds of his cape. Lightning flashed across the blade. Alan could see fiery letters inscribed in the metal.

"You only killed the body, demon. You have offered Alan things that do not belong to him. Your hatred, your rage and the injuries you have visited do not belong to him. He has not accepted them. Therefore they must be returned to you. It is the law."

"There is no law but my will!" Billy Joe cried. He launched himself across space at Ming, the sword arcing through the air.

"Take now that which is yours," Ming said, and turned the mirror upon Billy Joe. Light flashed from it and enveloped him. In it was the reflection of that tiny point of light remaining within Billy Joe. *Every living thing was connected to the divine.* It did not matter what the life form thought. It could have had no existence otherwise. It was this light that came forth to the mirror and then reflected back upon Billy Joe, and all that was "Billy Joe" was also reflected there. The sword vanished in a puff of smoke. Etheric images followed the light out of the mirror and washed over the magician.

As the first of these images touched him, the darkness that surrounded him began to crack. Streams of light entered into the openings, then streams of light poured back out of the cracks. Billy Joe screamed in agony. The tornado that surrounded him began to spin furiously as Billy Joe sought to escape from the impact of his own returning evil and the liberating light. It was to no avail. The terrible forces that he had unleashed were already at work inside him. His form was breaking up. The energies that tore at him were his own children, born of his thoughts. Pieces of Billy Joe broke away and were sucked up into the funnel of black wind. Soon there was nothing left but a fading scream that was swallowed up in the wind. The tornado danced away across the lava and then out upon the sea, where it fell apart and disappeared over the waves. *Billy Joe was no more…*

Now from the sky came forms of shimmering light who picked up the bodies from the rocks and bore them away. Very soon, all traces of Billy Joe and his evil were completely gone.

Ming shrank back to his normal form and stood before Alan. "Well done," he said. "There was no other way to defeat him. He had to be the instrument of his own destruction."

They stood there in the lava field communing without words.

Finally Ming said, "You have your work to finish." He extended his hand in benediction and then dissolved. There had been no words of farewell. They were unnecessary and did not apply.

Alan quickly made his way back to Ben who was sitting on a rock. "It's finished," he said.

"I know. I saw the whole thing. Nothing will ever be the same again. It's one thing to suspect that there are things like that, it's another to actually see them."

“We’d better get up to the house and see about Christienne.” Alan looked back at the sea, swallowing whatever else he had been about to say.

10:00 AM, DR. ABADON’S HOUSE, NEAR WAILEA, HAWAII

Whip ran in a crouch to the front door. He tried the handle but the door was locked. He ran around the building into the garden. The house was unbelievably large. He tried more doors but all of them were locked. In desperation, he picked up a rock and smashed it through a French door. Reaching through, he unlocked the door and went into the house.

“Christienne!” he called. The house was silent. He ran down a hallway, pulling open doors. He did not find her. There were so many rooms to look in and each one seemed as if it belonged in a different house. Several of the rooms he entered had such a raw smell of fear within that Whip found himself turning in all directions looking for an aggressor. There was nothing but the fear. *Bad things have happened in these rooms*, he thought.

In one of the bedrooms, Whip found her purse. Hope roared in his heart. Until now he had no proof that she had ever been in this house. Billy Joe could have taken her anywhere. He ran through the house screaming her name. He came to a spiral stairway that went down to a floor below ground level. It contained another labyrinth of rooms and passages. He went along one corridor that ended in a circular sitting room. Three more passages ran off of it like the points of a compass. The room was in shadow, and Whip could not see from it into the other corridors. *There was someone close by.* Whip could feel a presence. All of his antennae were up. He scanned about him on all sides but could detect nothing.

He searched the wall for a light switch. When he flipped it on the room was bathed in light. Almost more quickly than his eye could register, a form appeared to move away down the corridor in front of him. Had he actually seen anything or not?

Again he called out Christienne’s name. Then, he cautiously entered the passage where he had seen, or thought he had seen, the movement. He could hear a knocking sound. He continued along the corridor that quickly darkened as he moved away from the light. In haste, he returned to the central sitting room and searched for another light switch. It was just where it should have been, at the entrance. Now he could see clearly to the end of the hallway. Calling Christienne’s name, he moved toward the knocking sound. He stood before a door, all of his senses atremble.

He jumped suddenly, thinking he had seen movement to his left. He was nervous as a cat. He grabbed the door handle and turned it, but the door was locked. Looking to both sides, he jumped back and then launched himself forward, the heel of his left foot aimed at the space just below the handle. There was give, but the lock did not break. On the fourth try, the door crashed inward. Just as he was about to enter, there was a flash of color at his left. He turned and saw a tall figure moving with incredible speed toward him. Whip had only a moment to whirl and fire. It was enough. The person spun around and came to a brief stop. Then, incredibly, it was all of the way back up the corridor. Whip was awestruck.

"Freeze!" he commanded. In the time it had taken him to say the word, the figure was gone.

Above him now he could hear the pounding of feet. *"Hallelujah, the cavalry is here!"* He quickly ran into the room.

She was strapped to a wooden table that was slowly rotating. Like a piano stool, it was moving slowly upward as it turned. Above her was a large cutting tool that looked like a router bit with jagged teeth, but there was no router that large he had ever seen before. It was three feet in diameter and it was going to tear Christienne to bloody shreds when it reached her, which would be very soon. It was now only inches away from her body.

Whip jumped across the room and grabbed the table. With all of his strength he pushed it in reverse. Instantly it slowed, but it did not stop turning. No matter how hard he pushed, it would not stop. Whip was frantic. If he let go of the table to run for help, Christienne might die before he could return, so short was the distance between her and the cruel blade. If he held on to the table there would be more time, but would help find them in time? Whip hung from the board and let it drag him. His eyes searched the room for a switch or a button. He could find nothing. Christienne lay still upon the table, her eyes open, but with no recognition in them.

Whip pulled the gun from his waist and fired two shots into the wall, hoping to attract the men upstairs. Whip was screaming for help. The teeth were now less than four inches from Christienne's body. She moved slightly as he struggled with the table and his heart leapt with hope.

Ben flew into the room followed by two police officers. Quickly they positioned themselves around the table. From their combined efforts it slowed measurably, but it still did not stop. Alan came into the room. He stood there for a moment and then ran out. The table continued to ascend.

Alan returned with a large chef's knife. Quickly he cut through the heavy straps that bound Christienne to the table. Then he pulled her free and down on to the floor. Alan turned her over to Whip. The table, now freed from any restraining hand, continued its upward course.

"Interesting," Alan murmured.

"What's that?" Ben asked.

"Billy Joe's contingency plan, just in case anything did go wrong for him, Christienne would still die. I don't think this was his final plan for her. It seems there was a seed of doubt in his mind all along, whether he knew it as such or not. Evil never trusts its own inventions. It is always covering and plotting from more angles than it will ever be able to stay on top of. Eventually it fails. It always fails. Kim must have known what happened and turned on the machine."

They watched the heavy cutter as it met the table and begin to score the wood. Large peelings drifted slowly to the floor.

"Let's get out of here," Ben said.

Outside the house, an ambulance waited. They transferred Christienne inside and Whip rode away with her to the hospital. Two more squad cars arrived, bearing more police and two detectives. Ben went with them on a room-to-room search. He was looking for Kim. They found no sign of him except for a blood smear on the wall where Whip had shot at him. He met up with Alan in the library.

Alan turned at Ben's approach. "I'm going to leave now, Ben. Maybe you can see that Les gets his Lexus back? I'll take the dune buggy."

"Where are you going, partner?"

"I don't know." They walked down to the gate together, neither of them speaking. Without any words, Alan got in the dune buggy and waved as he drove away. He felt as if he had been emptied out. The best thing for him right now was to just do normal things. He was very high, light as a feather, not in the world at all. He knew it wouldn't last. He would be forever changed, but as time progressed he would be reintegrated back into his life.

He took a deep breath and slowly let it out. Then he laughed. *Maybe that was all there was to it. You just breathed in and out.* He drove to the Hana Highway and then continued until there was only jungle on every side of him. The air was filled with the fresh smell of a recent rain and the clarity that always followed precipitation. The profusion of life was everywhere, all of it struggling for the sun.

Alan pulled into a lookout hundreds of feet above the ocean. There he sat and stared out at the ceaselessly moving waves below.

Epilogue

2:21 PM, CARLENE'S RESTAURANT, WAILUKU, HAWAII

Aaron forked a piece of steak into his mouth and kept right on talking, "Well, the only thing to do is to list him as a fugitive and let it unravel from there. We don't have the body and I sure can't tell anyone what you told me."

Ben had just finished relating the events at La Perouse. Whip and Christienne were at the table as well. She had completely closed down inside, following the relentless assault of images from Billy Joe, most of which she could no longer remember, but she'd been remarkably restored after recognizing Whip. She had absolutely refused to stay at the hospital.

Whip and Christienne told him their portions of the events. Aaron just kept shaking his head, as if the action might shake something loose, something that might help him understand what had happened.

"I don't think it matters, Aaron, as long as we know that Billy Joe is gone, our sense of justice and duty are intact," Ben said.

"It's just the implausibility of it that racks me. How many others like him are out there doing this shit? Society has no way of protecting itself from these guys. Do we start issuing squirt guns with holy water… and amulets? Am I supposed to check and see if a criminal might be under the control of a black magician every time one is arrested? It raises a whole area of legal questions I don't even want to think about!"

Christienne was on her second meal and her third glass of wine. She was alternatively giggling and humming to herself as she polished off her second sandwich and salad. The men eyed her with some concern. She saw their looks and said, "I'm so damn glad to be alive that I can't get enough of everything."

"In that case, things look real good for Whip later on," Ben quipped. Everybody laughed and Christienne started choking so hard that Whip had to get up and pound her on the back. A trickle of wine ran out of her nose.

"How's Alan doing, Ben?" Aaron asked.

"Hard to say, he's changed. It's too soon to tell just what that means, but I'm not worried about him."

"He saved my life," Christienne said, "Him and Whip." She took Whip's hand and kissed it.

"He saved a lot of people's lives," Whip added. "We'll never know how many. Ming would say that nobody did anything. What happened was what was supposed to happen. There's got to be more than that though. Alan's big contribution was standing aside so that Ming could come through. I guess that's a whole lot harder than it sounds. Ming said that was the only thing that could have gone wrong. Then again, how can anything go wrong when it's supposed to be that way? He told me once that was the one thing on which everything depended and you never knew which way it was going to go until it happened."

Ben laughed. "Those guys always talk in circles. First it's fate and then it isn't fate."

"It is and it isn't," Whip replied. "It is a paradox. Everything is certain, nothing is certain. Ming says the only way to understand it in the realm of words is as a contradiction. Above the realm of words it resolves into something else."

"Thank God, Ben and I are in a field that doesn't allow for that kind of speculation. We'd be in straitjackets by now," Aaron added.

"Agreed," Ben replied. "But it wouldn't hurt if people knew more about these kinds of things. That was Billy Joe's greatest asset. No one believed in his existence. It could have gone either way. Good thing it didn't."

"Oh yeah, what about Richard Finch and Captain Rusk?" Ben asked Aaron.

"I haven't made my mind up about Richard yet. It's hard to see justice done if it looks like Billy Joe was manipulating him. Rusk is going to have to retire. That ball is already rolling. He'll be given the choice of retirement or a departmental inquiry that might look a little deeper than he can weather."

"And the girl in the courtroom, what was her story?"

"Ah, now there is a mystery that looks like this Ming might have had a hand in. She was in Arizona with those drug dealers that were killed. She was out of the room when it happened and returned to find the aftermath. Billy Joe nearly got her then, but she managed to get away. They nearly caught her a second time back in L.A., but somehow she managed to escape yet again. Then, she came here to hide from them and this was their destination all along. The kicker is that she had seen Billy Joe's face. She got arrested for selling cocaine and wound up in the courtroom on the same day that Billy Joe was to appear in his disguise as Doctor Abadon. It's like something right out of the Twilight Zone. Turns out she's only fifteen years old."

"What's going to happen to her?" Christienne asked.

"Well, now," Aaron tugged at his ear and looked at Christienne. "What do you think we should do to the person who brought down the whole house of cards?"

"Cut her loose," Christienne replied.

"Well, we can't do that, but if we can find her parents we can let her go then. If not, we'll find some way to take her out of the punishment side of the deal. She must have a daddy somewhere, seems her mother is that famous TV star who went missing recently."

"No shit!" Ben exclaimed.

"I've got to git," Aaron said. "I hope to see you around sometime. It's been a real pleasure." His eyes took in the three of them sitting there. They got up and said their farewells.

7:00 PM, ALAN'S HOUSE, HAIKU, HAWAII

Alan climbed out of the dune buggy and looked up at the lights of his house. He saw Christienne's Land Rover. It made him glad. He'd driven all the way to Hana. On the way, he visited the church where he'd been married years ago. Then he wandered around the town drinking in the flavor of old Hawaii. It had been the best day he had seen in a very long time.

Ben's sedan was parked next to the Jeep. He hadn't thought about whether he wanted to be alone tonight or not, but the thought of his good friends waiting for him inside the house brought a smile to his face. Maybe now he would have the chance to really enjoy them.

He'd come to some definite decisions about his life today. Once he thought it all through, it was amazing how it came together in his mind. He'd wondered how he might put a new life together, considering what he had become. None of the usual goals applied anymore. He was in a sort of no man's land. He didn't know if he should stay here, but he didn't really know where to go. He'd thought about it all day. It was obvious that the decision was being left up to him. When the answer finally surfaced, all of the doubt went away. He felt good about it. He was even excited. No matter where he was, he would still have to chop wood and carry water. It might as well mean something. He looked forward to the evening and the comfort of his friends.

The door opened and Ben appeared at the railing. "Welcome, conquering hero." Ben popped the champagne cork. Whip came out on the deck with Christienne. They had their arms around each other. Alan felt a nostalgic ache for the world he had once known, had fought so hard to protect, perhaps for the very image he saw in front of him now. He felt at peace. Certain things might be gone forever, destroyed by the knowledge that made belief in their permanence impossible, but they would forever be replaced by some new perspective that included the old in another, more perfect light.

He climbed up the flagstone walk, then stopped for a moment to look at the stars in their impossible distances across the black carpet of night. He felt the rush of union with the cosmos that always came when one brought far off things into the central habitation of the self.

When Whip screamed, Alan didn't even jump. He wasn't apprehensive enough anymore. Life was a continuous flow now, not a series of separated incidents. He felt someone coming behind him. Without thinking, he dropped to a crouch and felt the wind of something pass above his head. Now he leaped forward, turning in the air. In front of him was Kim, readying himself for the next stroke. He was dressed completely in black. All that Alan could see of him was the moonlight on his sword and the serenity of his features. He might have been tending to orchids as much as seeking to kill Alan.

Alan danced backwards and Kim glided forward. There was not a lot that Alan could do. He'd removed his gun and put it in the glove compartment. He was up against a master with a sword. Alan was now at the last step before the stairs. He heard Ben departing into the house. He sensed Whip vaulting the deck rail. He could feel him in the air. Alan waited. Kim leapt forward and the blade began its journey. Alan awaited the blow. It was okay, he'd just be going home a little ahead of schedule.

Then Kim made a curious movement. Alan was puzzled. It made no sense, but Kim seemed to be sliding away at the same time as he was moving toward him. The sword was in motion but now it was cutting upward and moving away from Alan. Kim's whole body was at an absurd angle. Then, Alan looked down and saw the loose flagstone giving way, the force of Kim's swing taking him with it. Alan stood perfectly still and watched Kim trying to make an adjustment. There was no purchase and there was no time. Kim tucked his body in for the roll down the hill. He tossed his sword aside so that he would not be cut by it in his fall. *It was the perfect move*, Alan thought. *When control is lost, do that which removes harm from harm intended gone wrong.* A textbook move and, ninety-nine times out of a hundred, it was guaranteed to grant you all that was needed for recovery or escape.

The one thing Kim was unable to defend against or prepare for were the rebar supports that were fixed at the bottom of the incline, awaiting the belated concrete pour. His downhill roll was halted abruptly when one of the bars penetrated his left eye and continued onward into his brain. Kim was dead instantly. *So ended Billy Joe's final effort at revenge.*

In that moment, Ben reappeared on the porch, gun in hand. He saw Alan and screamed, "Where is he?" Then he was down the steps and sliding down the slope, his gun on Kim. He quickly realized that the danger was over. "Thank God for irresponsible homeowners," he pronounced quietly.

Whip stood beside Alan, soon joined by Christienne. They held each other wordlessly, swaying in the silence. Christienne was crying softly. Alan was calm, warm as the sun and remote as the stars he had so recently been watching.

Ben climbed up from the bank. "I'll make the call," he said and then disappeared into the house.

"God, I hope this is the end." Christienne said through her tears, holding tightly on to Whip, afraid of still more danger waiting, there in the undefined darkness, just beyond the small perimeter of light.

"Nothing is ever over," Alan said, "It just improves as you do."

She laughed, loving Alan for his unshakable calm. "So," she said, brushing her hair from her eyes and looking at him, her impish face now mostly returned to its previous state of welcoming grace. "What are you going to do now?"

"Go to India," he replied. "But not tonight." With his arms on their shoulders, he followed them both into the house.

LES VISIBLE is a writer and recording artist. He has had a lifelong love affair with the Hermetic Sciences and the Martial Arts. He is a seasoned traveler in psychedelic realms and prefers the Devic Kingdom over the suffocating confinements of the Sub-Matrix. Along the way he has matriculated from the military to prisons and the maximum security wards for the criminally insane. He has owned a metaphysical bookstore and some restaurants and worked in construction, as a cook, a club bouncer, a newspaper editor, a resort manager, a radio announcer, a standup comedian, as a lead singer in a rock and roll band and whatever else he had to do to get by. He currently lives in Europe with his consort Susanne, his dogs and his memories. A collection of his works in various media can be found on his website and blogs:

smokingmirrors.blogspot.com
zippittydodah.blogspot.com
lesvisible.blogspot.com
profilesinevil.blogspot.com
www.soundclick.com/pro/?BandID=33200&content=music
www.soundclick.com/bands/7/lesvisible2music.htm
www.soundclick.com/bands/8/lesvisibleandthecriticallistmusic.htm

Available through bookstores or purchase direct from
Les Visible™ Creations.
Visit our website at www.lesvisible.com/books.html
les.visible@gmail.com
www.lesvisible.com

Lightning Source UK Ltd.
Milton Keynes UK
UKOW051435160412

190843UK00001B/252/P

9 780615 468921